Spirits in the Wires

Charles de Lint

TOR®

A Tom Doherty Associates Book
New York

SPIRITS IN THE WIRES

A Tor Book
Published by Tom Doherty Associates, LLC
175 Fifth Avenue
New York, NY 10010

www.tor.com

Tor® is a registered trademark of Tom Doherty Associates, LLC.

Library of Congress Cataloging-in-Publication Data

De Lint, Charles, 1951–
    Spirits in the wires / Charles de Lint.
        p. cm.
    "A Tom Doherty Associates book."
    ISBN 0-312-87398-0
    1. Fantasy fiction, Canadian. 2. Technology—Fiction. I. Title.

PR9199.3D357S65 2003
813'.54—dc21
                                                            2003041410

First Edition: August 2003

Printed in the United States of America

0   9   8   7   6   5   4   3   2   1

This one's for my long-time pal

Rodger Turner

Break the bowl—
instead of regret,
fall back into
the potter's hands
and be reborn.

—SASKIA MADDING
"Falling" (*Spirits and Ghosts*, 2000)

Contents

Author's Note

The impetus to write this book, and the title as well, was sparked by some offhand remarks made by my friend Richard Kunz concerning how, with the ever-growing prevalence of technology in the world, some of the spirits of fairy tale and folklore have probably already left the woodlands and other pastoral settings to take up residence in the wires that seem to connect us to everything: telephone, cable, electricity. No doubt they're in the satellite feeds as well.

I'd touched on this in some previous short stories (such as "Saskia," which you can find in my collection *Moonlight and Vines,* and "Pixel Pixies," in the more recent *Tapping the Dream Tree* collection), but the more I thought about it, the more I wanted to explore it at a longer length. So finally I put aside the plans I had for the next novel I was going to write and jumped happily into this one instead, even though it will be the second novel in a row to feature my regular repertory company of Newford characters taking their turn on the main stage, rather than going about their lives in the background of the books as they usually do.

Considering the origins of *Spirits in the Wires,* I should first thank Richard for those conversations, not forgetting his wife, Mardelle, who is not only a friend, but who has also done such a fine job of copyediting on a number of my books—those would be the ones without typos and the like.

I'd also like to thank:

Rodger Turner for great heaps of technical advice (with the usual caveat that any screw-ups are my fault, not his);

my coterie of friends, family and well-wishers (too numerous to name—you know who you are), without whom writing these books would be a far lonelier proposition;

my editors Gordon Van Gelder, Jo Fletcher, Patrick Nielsen Hayden, Sharyn November, and Terri Windling, all of whom are friends more than business associates;

Cat Eldridge, David Tamulevich, and the handful of readers who continue to send such wonderful music my way, as well as all the amazing musicians who, through the years, have kept my brain fertile and my spirits lifted with their music;

and last, but never least, MaryAnn for her love, comfort, and support; for the music in her heart and the poetry in her soul; for her astute reader's eye and red pen, and her sharp negotiating skills. And you know what? She's wilder than me.

If any of you are on the Internet, come visit my home page at www.charlesdelint.com

—Charles de Lint
Ottawa, Autumn 2002

Extract from the journals of Christy Riddell

According to Jung, at around the age of six or seven we separate and then hide away the parts of ourselves that don't seem acceptable, that don't fit in the world around us. Those unacceptable parts that we secret away become our shadows.

I remember reading somewhere that it can be a useful exercise to visualize the person our shadow would be if it could step out into the light. So I tried it. It didn't work immediately. For a long time, I was simply talking to myself. Then, when I did get a response, it was only a spirit voice I heard in my head. It could just as easily have been my own. But over time, my shadow took on more physical attributes, in the way that a story grows clearer and more pertinent as you add and take away words, molding its final shape.

Not surprisingly, my shadow proved to be the opposite of who I am in so many ways. Bolder, wiser, with a better memory and a penchant for dressing up with costumes, masks, or simply formal wear. A cocktail dress in a raspberry patch. A green man mask in a winter field. She's short, where I'm tall. Dark-skinned, where I'm light. Red-haired, where mine's dark. A girl to my boy, and now a woman as I'm a man.

If she has a name, she's never told me it. If she has an existence outside the times we're together, she has yet to divulge it either. Naturally, I'm curious about where she goes, but she doesn't like being asked questions and I've learned not to press her, because when I do, she simply goes away.

Sometimes I worry about her existence. I get anxieties about schizophrenia and carefully study myself for other symptoms. But if she's a delusion, it's singular, and otherwise I seem to be as normal as anyone else, which is to say, confused by the barrage of input and stimuli with which the modern world besets us, and trying to make do. Who was it that said she's always trying to understand the big picture, but the trouble is, the picture just keeps getting bigger? Ani DiFranco. I think.

Mostly I don't get too analytical about it—something I picked up from her, I suppose, since left to my own devices, I can worry the smallest detail to death.

We have long conversations, usually late at night, when the badgering clouds swallow the stars and the darkness is most profound. Most of the time I can't see her, but I can hear her voice. I like to think we're friends; even if we don't agree about details, we can usually find common ground on how we'd like things to be.

First Meeting

*Don't make of us
more than what we are,
she said.
We hold no great secret . . .*
—SASKIA MADDING,
"Arabesque" (*Moths and Wasps,* 1997)

Christiana Tree

"I feel as if I should know you," Saskia Madding says as she approaches my chair.

She's been darting glances in my direction from across the café for about fifteen minutes now and I was wondering when she'd finally come over.

I saw her when I first came in, sitting to the right of the door at a window table, nursing a tall cup of chai tea. She'd been writing in a small, leather-bound book, fountain pen in one hand, the other holding back the spill of blonde hair that would otherwise fall into her eyes. She looked up when I came in and showed no sign of recognition, but since then she's been studying me whenever she thinks I'm not paying attention to her.

"You do know me," I tell her. "I'm pieces of your boyfriend—the ones he didn't want when he was a kid."

She gives me a puzzled look, though I can see a kind of understanding start up in the back of those pretty, sea-blue eyes of hers.

"You—are you the woman in his journals?" she asks. "The one he calls Mystery?"

I smile. "That's me. The shadow of himself."

"I didn't . . ."

"Know I was real?" I finish for her when her voice trails off.

She shakes her head. "No. I just didn't expect to ever see you in a place like this."

"I like coffee."

"I meant someplace so mundane."

"Ah. So you've made note of all those romantic flights of fancy he puts in those journals of his." I close my eyes, shuffling through pages of memory until I find one of them. " 'I can see her standing among the brambles and thorns of some half-forgotten hedgerow in a green bridal dress, her red hair set aflame by the setting sun, her eyes dark with mysteries and stories, a wooden hare's mask dangling from one languid hand. This is how I always see her. In the hidden and secret places, her business there incomprehensible yet obviously perfectly suited to her curious, evasive nature.' "

I get a smile from Saskia, but I don't know if it's from the passage I've quoted, or because I'm mimicking Christy's voice as I repeat the words.

"That's a new one," she says. "He hasn't read it to me yet."

"You wait for him to read them to you?"

"Of course. I would never go prying . . ." She pauses and gives me a considering look. "When do you read them?"

I shrug. "Oh, you know. Whenever. I don't really sleep, so sometimes when I get bored late at night I come by and sit in his study for awhile to read what he's been thinking about lately."

"You're as bad as the crow girls."

"I'll take that as a compliment."

"Mmm." She studies me for a moment before adding, "You don't read my journals do you?"

I muster a properly offended look, though it's not that I wouldn't. I just haven't. Yet.

"I'm sorry," she says. "Of course you wouldn't. We don't have the same connection as you and Christy do."

"Does that connection bother you?"

She shakes her head. "That would be like being bothered by his having Geordie for a brother. You're more like family—albeit the twin sister who only comes creeping by to visit in the middle of the night when we're both asleep."

I shrug, but I don't apologize.

"I'm only his shadow," I say.

She studies me again, those sea-blue eyes of hers looking deep into mine.

"I don't think so," she says. "You're real now."

That makes me smile.

"As real as I am, anyway," she adds.

My smile fades as I see the troubled look that comes over her. I forget that her own exotic origins are no more than a dream to her most of the time—a dream that makes her uncomfortable, uneasy in her skin. I wish I hadn't reminded her of it, but she puts it away and brings the conversation back to me.

"Why won't you tell Christy your name?" she asks.

"Because that would let him put me in a box labeled 'This is Christiana' and I don't want to be locked into who he thinks I am. The way he writes about me is bad enough. If he had a name to go with it he might be able to fix it so that I could never change and grow."

"He does like his routines," she says.

I nod. "His picture's in the dictionary, right beside the word."

We share a moment's silence, then she cocks her a head, just a little.

"So your name's Christiana?" she asks.

"I call myself Christiana Tree."

That brings back a genuine smile.

"So that would make you Miss Tree," she says.

I'm impressed at how quickly she got it as I offer her my hand.

"In the flesh," I tell her. "Pleased to meet you."

"But that's only what you call yourself," she says as she shakes my hand.

"We all have our secrets."

"Or we wouldn't be mysteries."

"That, too."

She's been sitting on her haunches beside the easy chair I commandeered as soon as I'd picked up my coffee and sticky-bun from the counter, leaning her arms on one of the chair's fat arms. There's another chair nearby, occupied by a boy in his late teens with blue hair and razor-thin features. He's been listening to his Walkman loud enough for me to identify the music as rap, though I can't make out any words, and flipping through one of the café's freebie newspapers while he drinks his coffee. He gets up now and I give a vague wave to the vacant chair with my hand.

"Why don't you get more comfortable," I say to Saskia.

She nods. "Just let me get my stuff."

Some office drone in a tailored business suit, tie loose, top shirt button undone, approaches the chair while Saskia collects her things. I put my scuffed brown leather work boots up on its cushions and give him a sugar and icicle smile—you know, it looks sweet, but there's a chill in it. He's like a cat as he casually steers himself off through the tables and takes a hardback chair at one of the small counters that enclose the café's various rustic wooden support beams, making it look like that's what he was aiming for all along.

Saskia returns. She drops her jacket on the back of the chair, puts her knapsack on the floor, and settles down, tea in hand.

"So, what were you writing?" I ask.

She shrugs. "This and that. I just like playing with words. Sometimes they become something—a journal entry, a poem. Sometimes I'm just following words to see where they go."

"And where do they go?"

"Anyplace and everyplace."

She pauses for a moment and has a sip of her tea, sets the cup down on the low table between us. Later I realize she was just deciding whether to go on and tell me what she now does.

"You know, we're like words," she says. "You and me. We're like ghost words."

I have to smile. I'm beginning to understand why Christy cares about her the way he does. She's a sweet, pretty blonde, but she doesn't fit into any sort of a tidy descriptive package. Her thinking's all over the place, from serious to whimsical, or even some combination of the two. I think I just might have a poke through her journals the next time I'm in their apartment and they're both asleep. I'd like to know more about her—not just what she has to say, but what she thinks when there's nobody supposed to be listening.

"Okay," I say. "I'll bite. What are ghost words?"

"They're words that don't really exist. They come about through the mistakes of editors and printers and bad proofreaders, and while they seem like they should mean something, they don't. Like 'cablin' for 'cabin,' say."

I see what she means.

"I like that word," I tell her. "Cablin. Maybe I should appropriate it and give it a meaning."

Saskia gives a slow nod. "You see? That's how we're like ghost words. People can appropriate us and give us meanings, too."

I know she's talking about our anomalous origins—how because of them, we could be victim to that sort of thing—but I don't agree.

"That happens to everybody," I tell her. "It happens whenever someone decides what someone is like instead of finding out for real."

"I suppose."

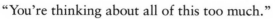

"You're thinking about all of this too much."

"I can't seem to stop thinking about it."

I study her for a long moment. It's worrying her, this whole idea of what's real and what isn't, like how you came into this world is more important than what you do once you're here.

"What's the first thing you remember?" I ask.

How We Were Born

Words are like a corridor;
put enough of them in a line
and who knows where
they will take you.
　　—SASKIA MADDING,
"Corridor" (*Mirrors*, 1995)

Saskia Madding

I remember opening my eyes and—

You know how if you blow up an electronic image too much, you don't have a picture anymore? When you push the image that far, all you really have left is a pixelated fog, a screen full of tiny coloured squares that don't form a recognizable pattern, never mind an image.

That was the first thing I saw.

I opened my eyes and I couldn't focus on anything. A hundred thousand million dots of colour and light filled my vision. I stared hard, trying to make sense of them, and slowly they started to come together, forming recognizable objects. A dresser. A cedar chest. An armchair with clothes draped over the arms and back. A closed wooden door. A poster from the Newford Museum of Art advertising a retrospective of Vincent Rushkin's work. Close by my head on the night table was an unlit candle in a brass holder, and a leather-bound book with a pattern of pussywillows stamped into the leather, a fountain pen lying on top of it.

It was all familiar, but I knew I'd never seen it before. Just as I myself was familiar, but I didn't know who I really was. I knew my name. I knew there was a computer and paper trail tracing my background—where I was born, grew up, went to school—but I couldn't actually recall any of it. The details of the experiences, I mean. The sounds, the smells, the tactile impressions associated with them. All I knew were the bare bones of cold facts.

I studied the explosion of pigeons in the painting they'd used in the poster for the Rushkin show and tried to make sense of how I could be in my own bedroom, but have no sense of where it was or how I got here or anything that had happened to me before I opened my eyes at that moment.

And I was strangely calm.

I knew I shouldn't be. Somewhere a part of me was registering the fact that none of this was right—neither the where and how of where I'd found myself upon waking, nor my reaction to it.

I had the strongest sense of being temporary. A shadow cast by a light that was about to move or be turned off. An image in a film that the camera had lingered up on before moving on.

I held one of my hands up in front of my eyes, then the other. I sat up and looked at the reflection of the woman in the mirror on the back of the dresser.

Me.

A stranger.

But I knew every inch of that face—the blue eyes, the shape of the nose and lips, the way the blonde hair fell in a sleepy tangle on either side of it.

I swung my feet to the floor and stood up. I pulled the flannel nightie I was wearing over my head and faced the mirror again.

I knew this body as well.

Me.

Still a stranger.

I sat down on the edge of the bed. Plucking the nightie from the floor, I hugged it to my chest.

An odd notion came into my head. I had a sudden impression of some other place, a pixelated realm that lay somewhere in cyberspace—that mysterious borderland of electrons and data pulses that exists in between all the computers that make up the World Wide Web. I could almost see this deep forest of sentences and words secreted in a nexus of the Web, and as I did, I sensed some enormous entity swelling up out of it, a leviathan of impossible proportions that had no physical presence, but it did have a vast and incomprehensible soul.

The thought came to me that I was a piece of that entity. That I had been broken off from it, born there in that forest of words and sent away. That I was separate, but also still a part of that other. That it had made me up through some curious technopagan ritual, given me flesh and then set me free to make a life for myself in the world beyond the endless reaches of cyberspace.

I know. It sounds like science fiction. And maybe it was. But it was magic, too. How else can you explain a computer program that was self-aware? Some voodoo spirit, itself made of nothing but ones and zeros, that was able to create a living being out of neurons and electricity and air and send it off into the world to be its own being.

The island of calm I'd sensed before whispered to me through this whirlpool of disquiet and speculation.

In a normal person, it said, *what you are experiencing would be considered madness.*

But I already knew I wasn't normal. I wasn't even sure I was a person.

Finally, I lay back down on the bed and closed my eyes.

Maybe it was all a dream. Maybe when I woke up in the morning I'd remember my life. I'd be myself and just shake my head as I went about my morning, dimly recalling the very strange dream I'd had the night before.

But in the morning, nothing had really changed. Only the force of what I was feeling had.

I could see normally as soon as I opened my eyes. The sensations of dis-association and confusion I'd experienced in the middle of the night were still there, but they weren't as intense.

This time I was able to get up and get as far as the door of the bedroom. I looked down the hallway into familiar/unfamiliar territory. I/my body had to pee—but it was something I only knew from the pressure in my bladder. I knew the mechanics of how I would do it. I knew where to go, to lift the lid, and sit down. But I couldn't seem to call up one memory of the actual experience. The only real, tactile memories I had were of waking last night.

Panic came rolling up through my body, quickening my pulse, making me sweat, creating a worse confusion in me than I was already feeling.

Let it go, that small calm place inside me said. *Stop thinking about it for the moment. Give your body control—it knows what to do.*

What did I have to lose?

I took a deep, steadying breath. Another. I don't even know how I did it, but somehow I managed to step back from the panic and confusion and follow the voice's advice.

I was like a passenger as I made my way to the bathroom, peed and showered. Back in my bedroom, I looked in the closet and was momentarily overwhelmed by the choices. It's not that there were a lot of clothes—because there weren't. But there was still too much choice. I was still confounded by knowing exactly what all the various materials were, but not what it would be like to touch or wear them—their texture, their weight, the feel of how the fabric would hang.

I took another steadying breath and let the decision go. I watched as I chose a cotton T-shirt and a pair of jeans, enjoyed the sensation of the cloth as it covered me. Slipped on a pair of moccasins and wiggled my toes in them.

It wasn't until after I'd made toast and coffee and was still drinking the coffee at the kitchen table that the immensity of my disassociation began to ease. It came and went throughout the rest of the day, like the ebb and flow of some inexplicable tide, but the troughs and crests began to even out and calm.

The oddest thing was how whenever I had a question about something, that calm voice would speak up from the back of my mind in response. Like when I took the coffee from the fridge and I wondered about the beans as I spooned some into the grinder.

Coffee, the voice in my head said. *It's a beverage consisting of a decoction or infusion of the roasted ground or crushed seeds (coffee beans) of the two-seeded fruit (coffee berry) of certain coffee trees. It can also be the seeds or fruit themselves, or any of various tropical trees of the madder family that yield coffee beans, such as* Coffea arabica *and* C. canefora.

It was like I had an encyclopedia sitting in the back of my head. One that knew everything.

I didn't leave the apartment all day. I didn't dare. I explored its four rooms—bedroom, kitchen, bathroom, and the final all-purpose room that looked to be a combination of study, library, office, and living room. I opened the patio door that led out of that last room, but I didn't go onto the balcony. I simply stood in the doorway and studied the street below, the buildings on the other side.

Mostly I poked through the books and magazines I found, studied the contents of my purse and the wallet inside it, turned on the computer and explored its various document files.

It turned out I wrote poetry. A fair amount of it. I'd had three collections published, with enough in these files for at least a couple more, though some of the poems were obviously works-in-progress.

I also did freelance writing for various on-line magazines and wrote some op-ed pieces for *Street Times,* a little paper produced mostly by street people for street people—to give them something to sell in lieu of asking for spare change.

I found a financial program and saw that while I wasn't rich by any means, I had enough money banked to keep me solvent for a few months. When I thought about where that money had come from, my own work history popped up in my head. Dates, places of employment, job descriptions, salary and benefits. But I had no personal, hands-on memories of even one of these places where I was supposed to have worked.

I closed all the files and turned off the computer.

After a supper of asparagus, tomato, feta cheese and shredded basil on a small bed of pasta, I was finally able to go outside and sit on the wicker chair I found out on the balcony. The flavour of my meal still lay on my palate, the food itself a comforting pressure in my stomach. It was dark now, the city lit up with lights, but I was safe and unseen in a pool of shadow since I'd turned out the lights in the room behind me.

I watched the people passing below, each of them a story, each story part of somebody else's, all of it connected to the big story of the world. People weren't islands, so far as I was concerned. How could they be, when their stories kept getting tangled up in everybody else's?

But all the same, I understood loneliness right then. Not the idea of it, but the empty ache of it inside me. How one could live in a city of millions and realize that there was not one person who knew or cared if I lived or died. I searched my mind, but nowhere in amongst the neat and orderly lines of facts and work histories was there the memory of someone I could call a lover, a friend, or even an acquaintance.

That will change, the calm voice in the back of my head assured me.

But I didn't know—not how my life could have come to this, or if it even should change. Either I was so unlikable that I'd been unable to make a single friend in the—I counted out the years from the facts in my head— four years since I had apparently moved here from New Mexico—or I was some kind of freak. Neither, it seemed to me, deserved friends.

I dreamed that night that I was flying, soaring, not over city streets, but over circuit boards, and rivers of electricity. . . .

The next morning—my second that I could truly recall—I felt a little better. I still had a lack of hands-on memories and a calm, quiet voice in the back of my head that was happy to play encyclopedia for me, but the weight of a full day's experience seemed to have steadied me. Even if all I'd done for the whole day was wander around in my apartment and then get terribly depressed as I sat out on the balcony in the evening, that one day still felt as though it had anchored me to the real world.

In the morning light, things didn't seem quite so bleak, so desperately black and white, it had to be this way or that. I was able to consider that I might be different and it didn't cripple me. Last night's loneliness and despair had no real hold on me this morning. I didn't know quite how or where, but I was sure I had to fit in someplace.

Today I meant to go outside.

I finished my coffee and washed my breakfast dishes, then put on a pair of running shoes. I found my purse. After checking it for apartment keys, I stepped out into the hall.

My neighbour across the way opened his door at the same time and smiled at me.

"So there is someone living in that apartment," he said. "I'm Brad." He jerked a thumb over his shoulder. "In 3F, as you can see."

"I'm Saskia," I said and we shook hands.

He was nice looking guy, dark-haired and trim, dressed in casual clothes. I could tell he liked what he saw when he looked at me and that made me feel good. But as we stood there talking for awhile, I saw something change in his eyes. It wasn't like I had a bit of egg stuck between my teeth or something. I was just making him uncomfortable. By the time we'd walked down the two flights of stairs to the streets, I got the sense he couldn't get away from me quickly enough.

He gave me a brusque goodbye when we reached the street and headed off in the direction I'd been planning to go. I stood there by the door of the building, letting some space build between us before I set off myself. While I waited, I went back over our conversation, trying to see what it was I'd said or done to make his initial attraction toward me cool off so quickly. I couldn't think of a thing. Whatever it was seemed to have happened on some purely instinctual level—almost a chemical imbalance between us. The longer he was in my presence, the stronger it had become.

I won't say I wasn't disturbed by it, because I was. But there was nothing I could do about it now. He'd finally reached the end of the block, so I started off myself, aiming for the Chinese grocery store on the other side of the street, across from where he was. By the time I reached the corner, he was long gone.

There was a scruffy little dog tied up outside the grocery store, one of those mixes of a half-dozen breeds, but the terrier seemed strongest. He watched me approach, tongue lolling, a happy dog look in his eyes.

"Hey, pooch," I said, bending down to give him a pat.

He snapped at me and I only just pulled my hand back in time to avoid getting bitten. He was still growling at me as his owner came bustling out from the store.

"Rufy," she said. "Don't do that." She turned to me. "I don't know what's gotten into him," she added. "Rufus is usually so sweet tempered."

But I could see the same instinctive discomfort start up in her eyes as I'd already seen in her dog's, and in my neighbour's eyes earlier. Before it grew too strong, I slipped past her into the store where I picked up some milk, a bag of rice, and some vegetables for a stir fry. I completed the transaction as quickly as I could, not looking at the elderly Chinese man behind the counter. When I was outside the store again, the woman and her dog were already gone.

I stood there for a long moment, just watching the traffic at the intersection and not knowing what to do.

I was ready to retreat to my apartment, to stay there and stubbornly wait for them to show up—the people who had played around in my head and erased most of my memory, or the people who had created me and left me there to fend for myself. I didn't know which, but it had to be one or the other.

For a moment I had a shivering recollection of some invisible voodoo spirit in cyberspace, but that I firmly put out my mind. No, whatever the origins of my present condition, they weren't that improbable.

But maybe I'd been in an accident. Banged my head on something.

I felt through my hair, searching for bumps or a sore spot, but could find neither. That didn't really prove anything. It could have been a while ago. Or it could be some recurring medical problem. Perhaps there was someone coming to check up on me—I just couldn't remember who, or when they'd come.

Or I could be crazy.

I took the long way back to my apartment, circling the block that the grocery store was on. When I saw a homeless man sitting in the doorway of an abandoned store, I dug into my pocket for a dollar. I dropped it in his hat and smiled down at him, ready for a repeat of the reactions I'd already gotten from the other people I'd met so far today.

But he only returned my smile.

"Thanks, lady," he said. "You have a good day."

I couldn't tell his age—it could have been anywhere between thirty and sixty—but he had kind eyes. They were deep blue, clear and alert, which seemed a little at odds with his shabby clothes and weather-beaten skin. They were the eyes of someone at peace with the world, not someone living on the street and barely able to eke out a living.

"I'll try," I told him. "So far it's sucked big-time."

He nodded, eyeing me in a way that put me on edge again.

"Maybe you should try and turn down that shine of yours a watt or two," he said before I could go. "My guess is that's what's making people so uncomfortable around you."

I just stared at him, not really sure what I was hearing.

"What did you say?" I asked.

"Come on," he said. "Don't tell me you don't know. You've been touched by something—call it whatever you want. A mystery, the spirits, some kind of otherness. It's left a shine on you that most people aren't going to see, but they'll feel it and it's going to make them feel edgy and weird. It's like the world's shifting under their feet and no one likes that feeling."

"And it doesn't bother you?"

He shrugged. "I know what it is. I also know it's not going to hurt me. So why would I be bothered?"

"How do you know all this?" I asked.

"Hey," he said. "I wasn't always a bum, you know. I used to run a New Age head shop and while we sold a lot of let's pretend, some of our customers were the real thing and I learned a thing or two from them. Reading auras is pretty basic stuff."

"What happened?"

"I wasn't paying attention. That's the big lesson life teaches you: You always have to pay attention. Your marriage broke up? You weren't paying attention. Your partner cleans out your bank account and sells all your store's assets, leaving you bankrupt?"

He gave me an expectant look.

"You weren't paying attention," I said.

He nodded approvingly. "Exactly. I lost everything when the creditors came calling."

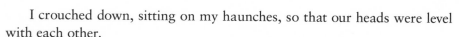

I crouched down, sitting on my haunches, so that our heads were level with each other.

"I'm sorry," I said.

"Yeah, me, too. But it's all water under the bridge now. Life goes on and most of us, we're just along for the ride."

A bus came by, making conversation impossible for a moment.

"So how do I turn down this . . . shine thing?" I asked when it was gone.

"Beats me. But the good news is, the longer you're away from the source of whatever put it on you, the weaker it'll get."

"And if it doesn't go away?"

"Then you'll only be comfortable with people like me who already believe. Who accept that there's something else out there and it's just as much a part of this world as you or me. The only difference is, it's in some hidden part that most people don't get to see. Hell, that most people don't want to see."

"Which is why I make them uncomfortable."

He nodded. "What was it that you experienced?"

"I have no idea," I told him.

I didn't really want to get into how weird my life had become in the past two days—not with a complete stranger, no matter how helpful he might be.

"Can I do anything for you?" I asked instead.

"Hey," he said. "You gave me a dollar and treated me like a human being—that's more that ninety-nine percent of the people I run into would do. So no. I'm good."

"But—"

"Just say hello the next time you see me," he said. "Let me know how you're doing."

"I will. What's your name?"

"Marc—with a 'C.' "

"I'm Saskia," I said, offering him my hand.

He cocked his head as he shook.

"Saskia Madding?" he asked.

I nodded. "How would you know that?"

"I've read some of your pieces in *Street Times*. No wonder you took the time to talk to me."

"Why—" I started, then stopped myself.

He'd already told me how he'd ended up on the street. It was none of my business what kept him there.

"Why do I live like I do?" he finished for me.

I shrugged. "I know it's not like you'd be doing it by choice."

"I suppose. But the truth is, I'm damned if I know. I guess I just gave up. Got tired of trying to find a job. I'm forty-eight and my back's shot. So I can't do heavy work, and nobody wants to hire an old man when he can get some bright-eyed kid with twice the energy and all the office smarts."

"Forty-eight's not old."

"It is in the work force. It's ancient. And it doesn't help that I'm a little too familiar with the bottle."

I paused for a moment, then asked, "Do you have someplace to stay?"

He smiled. "Come on now, Saskia. Don't go all caseworker on me. Let's just be friends."

"I wasn't trying to . . ."

"I know. It's just that your heart's too big. I already got that out of those pieces you wrote. But you don't want to be bringing home strays— not unless you've got a mansion on a hill and more money than you know what to do with. If you're not careful, you could end up with a mob of street people taking advantage of your goodwill and . . ." He gave me a toothy grin. "They wouldn't all be as pretty as me."

"But—"

"It's okay. I'm sharing a room with a guy in a boardinghouse off Palm. I make do. And who knows, one of these days I might actually get it together and try to rebuild my life. Next time I see you, maybe we'll go for a coffee and I'll share all these great plans I've got for fixing the world— starting with yours truly."

"All right," I said. "I'll hold you to that."

"Thanks for stopping by," he said.

I smiled and stood up. "No, thank you for helping me figure out my problems. Maybe you should consider becoming a counselor."

He laughed. "Yeah, I'm just chock-full of good advice, even if I don't put it into practice for myself."

"See you, Marc," I said.

"You know something?" he said as I started to walk away.

I paused to look back at him.

"If it was me, I wouldn't be in such a hurry to get rid of that shine of yours."

"Why not?"

"Well," he said. "It seems to me that everything's got a spirit, a mystery that most of us can't see. But invisible or not, that doesn't stop these secret

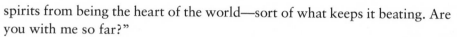

spirits from being the heart of the world—sort of what keeps it beating. Are you with me so far?"

I nodded.

"Then tell me this: Why would you want to hang around people that get uncomfortable, or even scared, about that kind of thing?"

"Maybe just to feel normal," I said.

He laughed. "Normal's not all it's cracked up to be."

"You think?"

"Hell, I know."

I don't know if I could have taken Marc's advice even if I'd wanted to. So far as I could see, whatever was different about me came from inside. How do you avoid yourself?

But he made a good point about normalcy. Except I don't think it was so much that I wanted to be normal. It was more how nobody likes to be the brunt of other people's ill will—especially when you've done nothing to earn it.

I think the bigger question for me was that I needed to know *what* I was, and not even the voice in the back of my head seemed to have an answer to that.

In the weeks that followed I made a point of getting out and seeing people. It was hard. Most of the time I got the same kind of reaction as I had from my neighbour across the hall, or the woman with her dog outside the Chinese grocery store. I'd go to music shows, art openings, poetry readings—any place that a person could go by herself to meet other people. Invariably some guy would start to hit on me—especially in a club—only to back off as though he'd suddenly realized that I had a third eye, or a forked tongue, or who knows what? I'd stay for awhile, but eventually the general level of barbed comments and ill will directed toward me would get to be too much and I'd have to go.

Later, when I got to know Jilly and her crowd, I discovered that I'd been going to the wrong sorts of events—or the right events, only attended by the wrong sorts of people. But at the time, I didn't know and there were a lot of nights that I left hardly able to keep my tears in check until I was safe in my apartment with no one to see my despair.

I didn't have the same problem when people weren't actually in my presence. I was able to submit pieces to *Street Times, In the City, The Crowsea Times,* and some of the daily papers—soliciting commissions over the phone and submitting the finished pieces by e-mail. I developed a number of friendships that way, though I made sure to maintain them at a distance. The one time I didn't was a complete disaster.

Aaran Goldstein was the book editor for *The Daily Journal* at the time—still is, actually. I'd done a few reviews for him and we'd talked on the phone a number of times when he asked me if I wanted to get together for a drink before a book reading that he had to cover that night. Against my better judgment, because, logically, I knew it wouldn't work out—why should this be any different from all those openings and shows I'd attended?—I said yes.

We made plans to meet at Huxley's—not somewhere I'd have chosen on my own. It's that bar on Stanton across from Fitzhenry Park where the young execs on their way up congregate after work. Lots of chrome and leather and black glass. Lots of big exotic plants and various flavours of ambient techno music on the sound system. Lots of people who want nothing to do with mysteries or myths or magic, so you know how they'd react to me.

I started to tell him I was blonde, but he stopped me and assured me we'd have no trouble finding each other.

"Descriptions are for peons," he said. "But you and I . . . fate has already decided that we should meet."

The weird thing is, he was right. Not about fate—at least not so far as I know—but about our not needing descriptions. I stepped in through the front door of Huxley's at a little past seven that evening and immediately saw him standing at the bar. I've no idea why I recognized him. I guess he just looked like his voice.

He lifted his head and turned in my direction, smiled, and came to meet me.

"You see?" he said, taking my arm and steering me back to the bar where a pair of martinis were already waiting for us.

He clinked his glass against mine.

"To radiance," he said. "By which I mean you."

Aaran was a good-looking, confident man in his thirties—very trendy with his goatee, his dark hair cut short on the top and sides, drawn back into a small ponytail at the nape of his neck. One ear lobe sported two earrings, the other was unadorned. Pinky ring on each hand. He was wearing Armani jeans, a white T-shirt, and a tailored sports jacket that night. Shoes of Italian leather.

But the best thing about him—what let me overlook his overly suave mannerisms, what meant more to me than his appearance or his sense of fashion—was that he didn't get the look in his eyes.

Five minutes went by. Ten. Fifteen.

Not once did he seem to get creeped out by me. We just talked—or at least he talked. Mostly I sat on my stool, leaning one arm on the bar top, and listened. But it wasn't hard. He was well-spoken and had a story about anything and everybody: droll, ironic, sometimes serious.

We had two drinks at Huxley's. We went to the reading—Summer Brooks had a new book out, *So I'm a Bitch,* a collection of her weekly columns from *In the City*—and it was just as entertaining as you might imagine, if you follow the columns. We had a lovely dinner at Antonio's, this little Italian place in the Market. We went down the street to the Scene for another drink and danced awhile. Finally we ended up back at my place for a nightcap.

We'd been getting along so well, it seemed inevitable to me that we would end up in bed the way we did. I remember thinking I was glad I'd worn some sexy black lace underwear instead of the cotton panties and bra I'd almost put on when I'd been getting dressed earlier in the evening.

Sex had definitely been one of the things I'd wanted to experience as soon as I could. My own recollections of it seemed to have come out of books, and like everything else in my life, I couldn't find one real tactile memory of it in mind. From what I did know about it, it was supposed to be totally amazing, so it was disappointing to have it all be over as quickly as it was.

Later, I realized it was only because Aaran wasn't a particularly good lover, but at the time I just felt let down. Not so much by him, as by the whole build-up about the act of making love.

"Is that it?" I let slip out as he rolled over onto his back.

I hadn't meant to say it aloud and when I saw the dark look on his face, I really wished I hadn't.

He sat up. "What do you mean?"

"Nothing."

"Wasn't it good for you?"

"Of course. It's just . . . I thought . . ."

I stopped myself before I made it worse, even though what I wanted to say was, no, it was disappointing. I thought it would be more tender, and also more abandoned. That it would last longer. That the world would turn under me. That everything would stretch into this long moment of unbelievable bliss before finally releasing in long, slow waves that would leave me breathless. The way I could make it feel with my own fingers.

Yes, I stopped myself from saying any of that, but it was already too late.

"Jesus, I can't believe you," he said.

He swung his feet to the floor and stood up.

"I mean, it's not like I didn't know there was something weird about you," he added as he put on his briefs. "But I was willing to overlook it—you know, that twitch you put in people that just makes them want to back away?"

I stared at him, speechless. He found his T-shirt and pulled it on over his head, stopping to smooth back his hair.

"It's not like I'm alone in this," he said. "Sure, you look hot, but everybody who's spent any kind of time with you talks about how you've got this thing about you that just rubs them the wrong way."

"You've *talked* to people about me?"

"Well, sure. It's a small world. When a good-looking woman like yourself turns out to be such a cold fish, of course it's going to get around. What did you think? But I thought, 'I'll do her a favour. Show her a good time. Teach her how to loosen up a little and enjoy life.'"

"Get out," I told him.

"Right, like you're the one who should be pissed."

I got out of bed and gave him a shove toward the doorway.

"Now you just wait a—" he started, but I pushed him again.

He was still off-balance from the first push and stumbled backward, out into the main room. I collected the rest of his clothes and followed after him. There was a moment right there when I thought he was going to hit me, or at least try to, but I dumped the clothes and shoes into his arms and he instinctively grabbed hold of them. That gave me time to slip around him and open the front door of the apartment.

"Out," I told him, pointing to the hall.

"Jesus, would you let me put my pants—"

"Out," I repeated.

I grabbed my umbrella from where it was leaning by the door and held it like it was a baseball bat. He took one look at my face and went out into

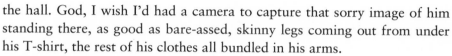

the hall. God, I wish I'd had a camera to capture that sorry image of him standing there, as good as bare-assed, skinny legs coming out from under his T-shirt, the rest of his clothes all bundled in his arms.

"This isn't the end of this," he told me.

"It is for me."

He shook his head, his face flushed with anger.

"Nobody treats me like this," he said. "I'll make you sorry you ever—"

"I already am," I said and shut the door in his face, engaged the lock.

I cried for a long time after he was gone. It wasn't because of what had happened with him—or at least not *only* because of that. Mostly it was because I felt so bereft and alone, abandoned in this unfair world where my only intimate human contact so far had been with such a sorry excuse of a loser. Now that the happy blush of just being accepted for once had been swept away, I realized that he was completely self-centered. He was full of words, but empty of anything meaningful. Our evening together had been for him, not for me, or even to be with me.

If Aaran Goldstein was an example of what it meant to be human, I wasn't so sure that I wanted to be one anymore.

I had my flying dream again that night, soaring over an endless landscape of circuit boards, their vast expanse cut with rivers of cruel electricity. . . .

I had gained some useful experience from my evening with Aaran, but otherwise not a lot had changed. Everything was still new and fresh. I knew what things were—and if I didn't, the voice in my head could give me its history—but not how they tasted, or felt, or sounded. Not how their essence reverberated under my skin.

I didn't stay away from readings or openings or clubs after that—I was too stubborn to give Aaran that small victory—but I didn't look to find acceptance or kindness at them anymore, and didn't find it either. Turns out, what honest friendships I came to make, I made on the street.

There was Marc, of course. I'd see him from time to time, always in some different doorway, panhandling on a street corner, dozing on a park bench. He carried a constant undercurrent of bitterness inside him—

directed at what he saw as his own personal failures, as much as at the uncaring world he was in, a world that had no time or place for those such as himself who, for one reason or another, had fallen through the cracks.

But most of the time, he kept that bitterness locked behind a cheerful front. I think what he liked best about me was that, no matter which face he showed me, I accepted him as he was and made no judgments. I also didn't hand out advice, or try to change him. I'd just buy him a meal or a coffee, and share it with him as though we were simply friends out to enjoy each other's company.

Charity didn't enter into it. He knew I'd give him a place to stay, or money, if he asked. But he didn't. And I didn't offer.

Then there was the woman that everyone called Malicorne whom I met on the edge of the Tombs one day, that part of the city that the citizens have abandoned, leaving I don't know how many blocks of empty lots, rubble-choked streets and fallen-down, deserted buildings. Factories, tenements, stores. The only legally-inhabited building was the old county jail, an imposing stone structure that stood on the western border of the Tombs, overlooking the Kickaha River, just north of the corner of Lee and Mac-Neil, but you couldn't call what the prisoners in there did as living. They were just marking time.

Malicorne was tall and horsy-faced, her eyes so dark they seemed to be all pupil. Her long chestnut hair was thick and matted, hanging past her shoulders like dreadlocks. But the thing about her—the strange thing, I mean—is how she had this white horn curling up into a point coming right out of the middle of her forehead. Now that's unusual enough, but even stranger is how nobody really seems to notice it.

"People don't pay attention to things that don't make sense to them," she said when I asked her about it.

Now I had a maybe strange origin, if my dreams and the voice in my head were anything to go by. She had one for certain. So why didn't people treat her the way they treated me?

She laughed. "Look at me," she said. "I'm living in a squat here in the Tombs, sharing meals and drinks with hobos and bums. Regular citizens don't even see me. I'm just one more street person to them. And if they don't see me—if I don't even register on their radar—how would they ever notice anything strange about me?"

"So why do you stay on the streets?" I asked.

"You mean, why don't I become a citizen?"

"I guess."

"Because the only stories that matter to me are the ones that are told here—on street corners, under an overpass, standing around an oil drum fire. It wouldn't be the same for someone else, but I'm not someone else, and they're not me."

I liked talking to her. She didn't just absorb stories other people told; she had countless ones of her own to tell. Stories about strange places and stranger people, of gods living as mortals, and mortals living with the extravagance of gods. I often wondered what my own story would sound like, coming from her lips. But I supposed first I'd have to figure out what it was for myself.

She left town before I could. One day she just wandered off and out of our lives the way street people do, but before she left, she introduced me to William.

He was living on the street at the time, too. There was a whole family of them that got together at night around the oil drums. Jack, Casey, William, and just before Malicorne left, a slip of a girl named Staley Cross who played a blue fiddle.

William was in his fifties, a genial alcoholic—as opposed to a mean drunk—with weather-beaten features and rheumy eyes. Something about Malicorne's going motivated most of them to get off the street. In William's case, he started attending AA meetings and got a job as a custodian in a Kelly Street tenement, just up from the Harp. He's still there today, surviving on the money he gets from odd jobs and tips.

I go to the AA meetings with him sometimes, to keep him company. He's been off the wagon for a few years now, but he's still addicted to one thing they don't have meetings for: magic. I don't mean that he's a conjuror himself, or has this need to take in magic shows. Or even that he's some kind of groupie of the supernatural and strange. He just knows a lot of what he calls "special people."

"I'm drawn to people like that," he told me one afternoon when we were sitting on the steps of the Crowsea Public Library. "Don't ask me why. I guess thinking about them, listening to them talk, just being with them, makes the world feel like a better place. Like it's not all cement and steel and glass and the kind of people who pretty much only fit into that kind of environment."

"People like Malicorne," I said.

He nodded. "And like you. You've all got this shine. You and Malicorne and Staley with that blue spirit fiddle of hers. There's lots of you, if you look around and pay attention. You remember Paperjack?"

I shook my head.

"He had it, too. Used to give you a glimpse of the future with these Chinese fortune-tellers of his that he made out of folded paper. He was the real thing—like Bones and Cassie are."

"So we've all got this shine," I said, remembering how Marc had told me he could see mine that day I first met him.

William gave me a smile. "I know it makes some people uncomfortable, but not me. I guess maybe I don't have a whole lot else left in my life, but at least I've got that. At least I know there's more to the world than what we see here."

"I suppose," I said. "Still, I wouldn't mind learning how to turn it down a notch or two."

"Why?"

"I don't know, exactly. So that I can fit in better when I want to fit in, I suppose. It's hard walking into a room and after five minutes or so, pretty much everybody's making it clear that it'd all be so much more pleasant if you'd just leave."

"That's important to you?" he asked. "Fitting in?"

"Maybe. Sometimes. I guess it's mostly wanting to do it on my own terms."

"Well, I know a guy who might be able to help you."

We tracked Robert Lonnie down at the Dear Mouse Diner, just around the corner from the library. He was sitting in a back booth, a handsome young black man in a pinstripe suit with wavy hair brushed back from his forehead. There was a cup of coffee on the table in front of him, a small-bodied old Gibson guitar standing up on the bench beside him.

"Hey, Robert," William said as he slid into the other side of the booth. I sat down next to William.

"Hey yourself, Sweet William," Robert said. "You still keeping your devil at bay?"

"I'm trying. I just take it day by day. How about you?"

"I just keep out of his way."

"This is my friend, Saskia," William said.

Robert turned his gaze to me and I realized then that he was another of William's special people. Those eyes of his were dark and old. When they looked at you, his gaze sank right under your skin, all the way down to where your bones held your spirit in place.

"Saskia," he repeated with a smile, then glanced at William. "If this isn't proof positive we're living in the modern world, I don't know what is."

I gave him a puzzled look when his dark gaze returned to me.

"Well, you see," he said. "I know that machines have always had spirits, but I look at you and see that now they're making babies, too."

I suppose that was one way of putting it.

"That's why we're here," William said. "We're looking for some advice on how to turn down her shine."

Robert pulled his guitar down onto his lap and began to pluck a melody on its strings, playing so soft, you'd have to strain to hear it. But the odd thing was, while I couldn't hear them clearly, I could *feel* those notes, resonating deep down inside me.

"Turn down your shine," he said.

I nodded. "It makes it hard to fit in."

"You should try being black," he said.

He improvised softly around a minor chord, waking an eerie feeling in the nape of my neck.

"I know it's not the same thing," I started, but his smile stopped me.

"We all know that," he said. "Don't worry. I'm not about to go all Black Panther on you."

His fingers did a funny little crab-walk up the neck of the guitar that took away the strange feeling the minor chord had called up.

"So can you help her?" William asked.

Robert smiled. "Turn down a shine? Sure." He looked at me. "That's an easy one. You've just got to stop being so aware of it yourself, that's all. Have you got any hard questions?"

"But . . . that's it?"

"Pretty much. Oh, it won't happen overnight, but if you can stop yourself from remembering, or believing, or what it is that you're doing inside that head of yours, soon enough everybody else will be seeing it your way, too. It'll be like you'll all start to agree that this is the way things are. Or should be."

"Making a consensual reality," William said. "Like the professor's always talking about."

Robert nodded. "Of course, you've got to ask yourself," he said to me, "why would you want to turn down a shine?"

Now it was my turn to smile.

"I've already been through that with William," I said. "Like I told him, I want the option of fitting in if I want to."

"Curious, isn't it?" Robert said. "All the magic people want to be normal, and all the normal people want magic. Nobody ever wants what they've already got and that's the story of the world."

He started a twelve-bar blues, humming a soft accompaniment to the aching music his fingers pulled from the guitar.

William and I sat there for a long time, just listening to him play before we finally left the diner.

I don't know if this happens to you, but it's a funny thing. There's this synchronicity with street people. Doesn't matter how unusual they might be, like Tinfoil Annie making her animals with aluminum foil that she then sets free in the gutters, or talented, like Robert Lonnie and the way he can play a guitar. See them once and suddenly you're seeing them all the time and you have to wonder, how was it that you never noticed them before?

After that afternoon in the diner, I started seeing Robert everywhere, playing that old Gibson of his. He was so good that I asked William once why Robert wasn't playing out, doing real gigs instead of sitting in the back of clubs, after-hours, or all the other places you might find him making music: on park benches, in diners, on street corners, in the subway.

"The story is," William said, "that he traded his soul to the devil to be able to make the kind of music he does. But it wasn't a fair trade. Turned out, Robert had that music in him all along—he just hadn't been patient enough to take the long way of getting it out. Anyway, he's supposed to have figured out a way he can live forever—just to spite the devil, he says—but he likes to keep a low profile anyway. Seems the devil will let you get away with a thing or two, just so long as you don't rub him in the face with it."

"Do you believe that?"

William shrugged. "I've seen enough things in this world that I'll keep an open mind about anything. And I like the idea of somebody putting one over on old Nick." Then he smiled. " 'Course there's others say Robert just ages well and has a natural talent."

Not everybody I met on the street actually lived on the street, even when, at first, it seemed as if they did. I guess some people were like I came to be— they just felt more comfortable carrying on their business on the edges of society.

. I thought Geordie was homeless when I first met him—busking with his fiddle for people's spare change instead of panhandling. But once I got to know him, I realized that he just liked playing on the street. He played in clubs, too—had an apartment on Lee Street and all—but busking, he said, kept him honest. He was one of the first street musicians you'd hear in the spring—standing on some corner, all bundled up, fingerless gloves on his hands—and one of the last to give it up in the fall.

Geordie and I hit it off right away. I suppose we could have become more than friends, but I could tell he was carrying a torch for someone else and that kind of thing always gets in the way of developing a meaningful relationship. One or the other of you ends up settling for what's in front of you, but you're always remembering the something you couldn't have.

At first I thought that something was Sam, this old girlfriend of Geordie's who did this mysterious sidestep out of his life, but once I got to know him better, I realized he was really carrying the torch for his friend Jilly. I got the idea that neither of them was aware of it—or at least would admit it to themselves—though everyone else in their crowd seemed to be aware of it.

It's funny, considering how close he and Jilly are, that I must have known Geordie for almost half a year before I ever met Jilly and got pulled into her mad, swirling circle of friends. Geordie often talked about her and Sophie and Wendy and the rest of them, but somehow our paths never crossed. I know it's a big city, but when we finally did meet, it turned out we knew so many people in common, you'd have thought we'd have run into each other a lot sooner than we did.

Something similar happened with Christy, though in his case I'd actually seen him around before. I just hadn't known who he was.

The way we met, I was walking down Lee Street and saw Geordie at a table on the patio of the Rusty Lion with some fellow whose face I couldn't see because his back was to me. By the time I realized who it was, it was too late to retreat because Geordie'd already seen me. I made myself go up to their table to say hello.

You see, I'd already noticed Christy and been attracted to him long before we actually met. The first time was at a poetry reading. I spied him across the room and there was something about him that I liked enough to almost give up my promise of not trying to connect with people at those things. But then I saw that he was with Aaran and a woman—that I didn't get along with either—who worked for another paper. If they were his friends, I didn't want to be one myself.

I noticed him from time to time in the neighbourhood after that, usually on his own, but never put it together that this brother Geordie often talked about was the same person as this attractive stranger with his bad taste in friends.

Turns out I was wrong about the friends. Christy has impeccable taste in them, not least because he dislikes Aaran about as much as I do, though not for all the same reasons.

Once we got that out of the way, one thing led to another and . . . well, that's how I came to be where I am now, living with Christy.

I've learned to turn down my shine enough to get along in a crowd when I want to, but the price I paid for that is losing the voice in my head. And when I lost it, I lost my connection to whatever that big voodoo spirit in cyberspace might have been. I don't dream about flying over circuit boards anymore. I don't dream about pixels and streaming bands of electricity or any of that. Most of the time all those ideas just seem like some crazy notion I once had.

But I don't trust this flesh I'm wearing, either.

I don't trust the experiences that fill my head because they only date back to when I first appeared in this world. Like I said, I can follow a computer and paper trail tracing my background—where I was born, grew up, went to school—but I still can't recall any of it.

So, sometimes I still think that there used to be something else in my head, some vast world of information—or at least a connection to the spirit that people surfing on the Net can access as the Wordwood. Or perhaps it's still there, but I'm cut off from it.

I guess I'm not really sure of anything, except I know I'm in this world now. And I know I can count on Christy to stand by me.

Most days that's enough.

Christiana

It was different for me.

The first time I opened my eyes I knew exactly what I was: all the excess baggage that Christy didn't want. How does he put it in his journal?

> *. . . at around the age of six or seven we separate and then hide away the parts of ourselves that don't seem acceptable, that don't fit in the world around us. Those unacceptable parts that we secret away become our shadow.*

I know. It sounds desperately grim. But it wasn't all bad. Because the things that people think they don't want aren't necessarily negative. Remember, they're just little kids at the time. Their personalities are still only beginning to form. And all of this is happening on an instinctive, almost cellular level. It's not like they're actually thinking any of it through.

Anyway, in my case . . .

Even as a little boy, Christy shut people out. That let me be open.

He was often so bloody serious—because he didn't trust people enough to relax around them, I suppose—and that let me be cheerful.

He didn't make friends easily. I could and did.

But I got his dark baggage, too. A quick temper, because he held his in check. A recklessness, because he didn't take chances—

Well, you get the picture. I was the opposite parts of him. Elsewhere in his journals he describes our physical differences:

She's short, where I'm tall. Dark-skinned, where I'm light. Red-haired, where mine's dark. A girl to my boy, and now a woman as I'm a man.

Basically, I opened my eyes to find that I was this seven-year-old girl who knew everything about being a seven-year-old boy, but nothing about being herself.

I suppose it could have been dangerous for me, trying to make my way through the big bad world all on my own at such a tender age, but it didn't quite work out that way. For one thing, when a shadow is created . . . yes, she's all the unwanted parts of the one who cast her, but she takes an equal amount of . . . I don't know . . . spirit, perhaps, or experience . . . some kind of essence from the borderlands. So right away, I was this unwanted baggage and something more.

What are the borderlands?

Once we started talking to each other, Christy was always asking, "Where do you go when you're not in this world?"

I wouldn't tell him for the longest time—as much because I like to hang on to the "woman of mystery" image he has of me as for any logical reason. But one night when he was going through one of his periodic bouts of self-questioning, I relented.

"To the fields beyond the fields," I finally told him, explaining how they lie all around us and inside us.

What I didn't explain is that they're part of the border countries, the fields that lie between this world he knows so well and the otherworld—Fairyland, the spirit world, the dreamlands, call it what you will. That otherworld is what the mystics and poets are always reaching out for, few of them ever realizing that the borderlands in between are a realm all their own and just as magical. They lie thin as gauze in some places—that's where it's the easiest to slip through from one world into the other—and broad as the largest continent elsewhere.

The beings that inhabit this place are sometimes called the Eadar. Most of them were created out of imagination, existing only so long as someone believed in them, though it's also the place where shadows like me usually go. The Eadar call it Meadhon. The Kickaha call it *àbitawehì-akì*, the halfway world. I just think of it as the middleworld. The borderlands. But I didn't get into any of that with Christy.

What I also didn't explain is what I was just telling you about how a shadow takes as much of her initial substance from something in the borderlands as it does from the one casting her. I don't know what it is. Maybe it's just from the air itself. Maybe something in the borderland casts another shadow and people like me are born where the two shadows meet. What I do know is that I had an immediate connection to that place and when I first slipped over, I met my guide.

I say "my guide," like everybody gets one, but that's not necessarily the case. I just know there was someone waiting for me when I crossed over.

Being new to everything, I simply accepted Mumbo at face value. It was only in the years to follow, as I began to acquire a personal history of experience and values, that I thought, isn't this typical? When other people get spirit guides or totems, they're mysterious power animals, maybe wise old men or women, like the grandparents you maybe never had.

I got Mumbo.

She was basically a mushroom brown sphere the size of a large beach ball with spindly little arms and legs that were folded close to her body when she wasn't using them to roll herself from one place to another. Much like those Balloon Men that Christy wrote about in his first book, *How to Make the Wind Blow,* I suppose. Today I can't imagine anything less mystical or learned, but she had a kind face and I was a newborn seven-year-old when I first met her. No doubt she was an appropriate shape to capture the interest of that child I was, and the immediate affection I had for her carries on to this day, for all that she's just so . . . so silly-looking.

But I'm getting ahead of myself.

The first time I opened my eyes, I was this scruffy little girl in a raggedy black dress, skin the colour of a frappuccino, eyes the blue of cornflowers, red hair falling in a spill of tangles and snarls to my shoulders. I was in the field behind the Riddell house. I sat up and looked at the window that was Christy and Geordie's bedroom. Paddy, their older brother, was already in juvie.

I knew who they were. I knew everything Christy knew up until the moment he cast me off. After that our lives were separate and we had our own experiences, although I still knew a lot more about him than he did of me.

He didn't even remember casting me out. That came years later, when he was reading about shadows in some book and decided to try to call his own back to him.

But I remembered. And I knew him. I'd follow him around sometimes, until I got bored. But I always came back, fascinated by this boy who once was me. Or I was once him. Whatever.

When he started keeping a journal, I pored over the various volumes, sitting at the shabby little desk beside his bed, reading and rereading what he'd written, trying to understand who he was, and how he was so different from me.

He woke once or twice to see me there. I'd look back at him, not saying a word. Closing the book, I'd return it to its drawer, turn off the desk light, and let myself fade back into the borderlands. I'd read later in his journal how he thought he'd only been dreaming.

But that first night I didn't go into the house. I was too mad at him for casting me out of the life we'd had together.

How dare he? How *dare* he just cast me off. Like he was putting out the trash. Like *I* was the trash. I'd show him what trash was.

Little fists clenched, I took a step toward the house, planning I don't know what—throw a rock through his window, maybe—but I accidentally stumbled out of this world and into the borderlands.

Where Mumbo was waiting for me.

Remember how easily distracted you could be as a kid? Oh, sorry. I guess you don't. Well, take my word for it. You can be in a high temper one moment, laughing your head off the next.

So I stood there, blinking in this twilit world that I'd suddenly found myself in, too surprised to be angry anymore. I can't tell you how I knew I'd stepped from one world to another, I just did. The air was different. The light was different. The biggest clue, I guess, was how the Riddell house at the far end of the field that I'd been walking toward wasn't there anymore.

I suppose I might have gotten scared, though I've never scared easily, except that was when Mumbo showed up.

I watched this brown ball come bouncing across the meadow toward me. When she stopped herself with her little spindly limbs and I saw her face, the big kind eyes twinkling, the easy smile so welcoming, I clapped my hands and grinned back.

"Hello, little girl," the brown ball said.

"You can talk."

"Of course I can talk."

"I've never heard a ball talk before."

"There are a thousand things and more that you have yet to experience," she said. "If you spend less time being surprised by them, you'll have more time to appreciate them."

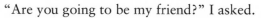

"Are you going to be my friend?" I asked.

"I hope so. And your teacher, too, if you'd like. My name's Mumbo."

"I'm Christy," I said, then realized that wasn't true anymore, so I quickly amended it to "Anna," taking the first name that popped into my head.

Anna was a girl in Christy's class at school that he was sweet on at the time. Actually, Christy was always sweet on some girl or another—a serial romantic, that boy of ours. Or at least he was until he met you. But he'd never do much. Just give them moony looks and write poems that he never gave to them.

"It's nice to meet you, Christiana," Mumbo said.

I almost corrected her, but then I decided I liked the way it sounded. It was a new name, but it still had history.

"What kind of things are you going to teach me?" I asked.

I was a little nervous. Seven years of being part of Christy had taught me not to trust grown-ups. I knew Mumbo was a ball, and all of this was like out of some storybook, but she still had a bit of the sound of a grown-up about her when she spoke.

"Whatever you want to learn," she said. "We could start with my showing you how to move back and forth between the worlds. That's a very handy trick for a shadow."

"What's a shadow?" I asked.

I could tell from the way she said the word that she meant something different from what a light casts. But as soon as she started to explain, I realized I already knew. It was me. Cast out of Christy.

Not everybody has a shadow the way Christy describes it in his journal.

Wait. That's not right. What I meant to say was that while everybody has a shadow, not everyone has access to the person that shadow might be become.

First you have to call the shadow to you.

Some children do this naturally and never recognize these invisible companions and friends as ever having been a part of them. And most of those children put aside their shadows once they grow up so the poor creatures are rejected twice. Those that do remember, or learn about us somehow, are often surprised at who they find. I know Christy was.

At first he thought he might be going mad because I only came to him as a voice. I'm not sure why I did that. I think it was probably nervousness on my part. I wanted him to like me—I was a sort of twin, after all, and I'd long since gotten over being mad at him for casting me out of him—but I wasn't sure he would since, after all, I *was* all those parts of himself that he'd put aside.

Being born from the cast-off bits of someone else's personality isn't necessarily a bad thing. Because just like the people we echo, we go on after the split. We have the same capacity for growth and change as they do. We may begin life as evil, or clumsy, or outgoing, but we can learn to become good, or agile, or shy.

And I shouldn't have worried about Christy's reaction to me when we finally met in the flesh. He proved to be quite taken with me, half in love at first, though I've learned that isn't so surprising in situations such as this. It's also why shadows are drawn to those who cast them off, no matter what the difference is between them: You're meeting your other half, your missing half. In many cases, the changes you go through make you more alike, rather than less. Perhaps we teach each other the best parts of ourselves.

After his initial infatuation, Christy and I settled into more of a sibling relationship. He treats me as the older and wiser of the two of us, the one who understands Mystery because I live in it, because my very origins are so extraordinary. I don't feel that way. I learn as much from him, but I let him keep his misconceptions. Let's face it, a girl likes to be mysterious, doesn't matter if she's human or a shadow.

What's life like for a shadow? I don't need to eat or drink, but I love good food and a fine wine. I don't need to sleep either, but I still enjoy luxuriating under the sheets or spending the whole morning just lying in bed when the rest of the world is up and about its business.

And sometimes when I close my eyes and pretend to sleep, I actually dream.

I'm not doing such a good job of this. I should be explaining things in a more linear fashion—the way you did—but my brain doesn't work that way. Another difference between Christy and me, I guess. He's so logical, working everything through from start to expected finish, while I flit about like a moth attracted to any light with a strong enough flicker.

So where was I?

Right. Growing up as a shadow.

I grew more quickly than Christy. It wasn't just a matter of girls maturing sooner. Shadows can choose their age. We can't change our specific looks—I mean, I can't suddenly appear in front of you as a cat or a dog—but we can appear to be whatever age we want to be and that's a handy thing.

But I did mature mentally and emotionally much more quickly than he did.

That can't be helped when you spend most of your time in the borderlands where there's always something to learn. Not to mention that the spirit world lies just beyond the borderlands, and in the spirit world, anything you can possibly imagine and then some exists in one corner or another.

I also think that—remember I told you how some piece of the borderlands helps give a shadow her substance? I think it also allows you to acquire and understand knowledge more readily. It's not that you're smarter. That connection just allows you to assimilate things more easily. And you have access to more information and experience than the one that casts you off does, because you have three worlds to explore, instead of only one.

Plus, in some parts of the spirit world, time moves differently than it does here. Strictly speaking, I suppose I'm a lot older than Christy anyway because of living in some of the Rip Van Winkle folds of the spirit world, where the passing of a year is no more than the length of a day here.

And I was certainly sexually active a lot earlier than him. Truth to tell, by the time I was in what would have passed for my teens, I was pretty much an incorrigible wanton. I wanted to try everything.

I'm way more choosy about who I sleep with now.

"Why were you waiting for me?" I asked Mumbo one day after we'd known each other for a few years.

She was showing me how to braid sweetgrass into a strong, sweet-smelling rope. I don't know why. She was forever telling me about stuff and teaching me how to do things that seemed to have no relevance at the time, but proved to be useful later. So maybe at some point in the future, knowing how to make a grass rope was going to come in handy.

"You know," I added. "That first time I crossed over."

"It's what I do," was all she said. "I teach shadows."

Like that was all there was to it. But you know me—well, I suppose you don't, or we wouldn't be here talking. But I'll worry at a thing forever until

I figure out what it is or how it works. Someone told me once, "Curiosity may have killed the cat, but I'll bet she had a really interesting life up until then." I'm like that cat. I do have a really interesting life.

Still do, because I'm not dead yet.

There's always something going on in the borderlands. Between storybook characters, faerie, spirits and shadows, there's no time to be bored. Instead, you just appreciate any time you might get on your own.

You'd like the place I have there. I should take you sometime.

It's this little meadow the size of a loft apartment that I plucked out of a summer day—that's a trick Mumbo showed me. You choose it like you'd call up a memory snapshot, except it's got a physical presence that you can store away in a fold of space where the borderlands meet this world. You can visit it whenever you want and it just stays there, hidden away, forever unchanging.

I've got this meadow decked out like an apartment. I have a dresser and a wardrobe at one end where the birch trees lean up against a stand of cedars. Sofa and easy chairs, with a Turkish carpet between them, at the other end, under the apple tree. A coffee table and a floor lamp, though I don't need it because it's always light there—morning light, when the day's still fresh and anything's possible.

There are chests and bookcases all over the place because I'm a serious packrat and collect any and everything. My bed's tucked away in a shaded hollow under the cedars. I hang things from the branches of all the trees— ribbons and pictures and prisms. Whatever catches my fancy.

Christy wonders what my life is like when I'm not with him. He says, "Isn't that what we always wonder about those close to us? What are they doing when we're not together? What are they thinking?"

I know it bothers him that I don't appear to have the same curiosity about him—he doesn't know that I still go walkabout in his journals at night when he's sleeping.

But as you can see, I don't live a life seeped in ancient mystery and wonder the way he thinks I do. I have an adventurous life, a lively one, and I certainly rub elbows with all sorts of amazing people and beings, but I'm just an ordinary girl. Oh, don't smile. I am. An ordinary girl in extraordinary circumstances.

I was at a party once, in Hinterdale—that's this place on the far side of wherever. In the otherworld, you know?

You'd have to see this place to believe it. Imagine one of those old fairy tale castles, up on a mountaintop, deep forests spilling from near the base of its stone walls all the way down into the valley below. It doesn't have a moat, but it has the towers like spires and a grand hall as big as a football field. Or at least it feels that way. But the best thing about it is that there's this enormous tree growing right in the middle of that field-sized hall—an ancient oak that's I don't know how many hundreds of years old.

I guess what I like the most about it is the fact that it's indoors. Like my meadow apartment's outdoors. They're just off-kilter enough to make me feel comfortable.

I can't remember whose party it was—the castle's sort of a communal place with people coming and going all the time—but there must have been at least a thousand people still there after midnight, every kind of person you can imagine. Faeries, shadows, Eadar, ordinary folks who've learned how to stray over into the borderlands. Everybody was in costume.

What was I? A blue-masked highwayman—highwaylady? Whatever. I had the three-cornered hat, the knee-high boots, breeches and ruffled shirt under a riding jacket, a pistol as long as my forearm except it wasn't real.

Anyway, I was sitting with Maxie Rose in a window seat that overlooked the courtyard outside and we got to talking about the meaning of life—which, let me tell you, is an even bigger question in the borderlands than it is here—and all the other sorts of things you find yourself talking about at that time of night.

"What I don't get," Maxie was saying, "is how people keep trying to come up with these theories to unify all the various myths and folk tales you find in the world. I mean, I know there are correlations between the folklore of different cultures, but really. Half the point of mystery and magics is their inconsistent and often contradictory nature. We live in a world of arbitrary satisfactions and mayhem. Why should Faerie be any different?"

"People just need to make sense of things," I said.

"Oh, please. Sense is the last thing most of us need, though I suppose it does keep me pretty and alive."

"What do you mean?" I asked.

She shrugged. "It's how Eadar stay potent. You know *here*. We teach sense to the shadows."

Maxie was an old friend of mine, a green-eyed, pink-haired gamine, not quite as tall as me, with a penchant for bright-coloured clothes, clunky boots and endless conversation. Tonight she was dressed as a punk ballerina. Her tutu was the same shocking pink as her hair and her leggings were fishnets that looked as though they'd lost an argument with a shark, they were so torn and tattered. Big black Doc Martens on her feet. Truth is, her costume wasn't much of a stretch from her usual wear, except normally she didn't wear the Zorro mask—a black scarf with eyeholes cut in it.

She was always full of life, always so *present* that it was easy to forget that she'd been born as a minor character in an obscure chapbook that had been mostly unread in its author's lifetime and forgotten thereafter. Since Eadar—such as she was—depend on their existence by the potency of the belief in their existence, it never made any sense to me that she would continue to be as vibrant and lively as she was. From all I know of them, she should have faded away a long time ago.

"Teaching," I repeated, my mind going back to that day I'd asked Mumbo why she'd been waiting for me the first time I'd crossed over. "Like Mumbo did with me?"

Maxie nodded.

"And doing that makes you stay real?"

Maxie grinned. "I always said you were a quick study."

"Are there a lot of you doing that?"

"Oh, sure. Mumbo and Clarey Wise. Fenritty. Jason Truelad. Me. Whenever you see an Eadar who's *particularly* present, it's either because they were born in a story that was really popular—so lots of people believe in them and keep them real—or they're connecting with shadows."

"So Mumbo wasn't there to help me. She was only there to help herself."

"No, no, no," Maxie said. "It doesn't work like that. You really have to care about your shadows. Lots of Eadar don't even like them. I mean, think about it. You shadows show up in the borderlands, snotty little toddlers full of new life but without a clue, most of you with a chip on your shoulder and the last thing you want is advice from anybody."

"I wasn't snotty," I told her.

She grinned. "Says you. Regardless, it can be so frustrating teaching some of you how to get along. I can't imagine anyone getting into it unless they really, truly loved the work. The fact that it keeps us real is a side-benefit. Or at least it is now. I can't answer for the first Eadar who figured out that the relationship benefits them as much as the shadows under their care."

"I never knew."

"Lots of people don't. Lots of *Eadar* don't, which, when you think about it, is being really dumb. They just piss and moan and fade away. But like I said, if it's not something you feel comfortable doing, it's better that you don't try."

"But why shadows? What makes us so important to you?"

Maxie shrugged. "I don't know. For some reason your belief is really potent. All it takes is one of you to keep us *here*."

Isn't that a kick? One shadow, cast off and all, is equal, at least in this particular case, to all the readers of some bestseller.

The first time I met Christy?

I can't remember the exact when of it, but I remember the where. And the look on his face. He can be so cute, don't you think? You know, when something really catches him off-guard.

So what I did was, when I saw him out on one of those late night rambles of his, I followed along until I got a sense of where he was going then slipped on ahead of him. By the time he stepped onto the Kelly Street Bridge, I was already there, leaning on the stone balustrade and gazing down into the water. It was a lovely night, late summer, the sky clear above and full of stars. There was a bit of a wind and the moon was just coming up over the Tombs.

I listened to his footsteps, timing it so that I looked up just when he was getting close.

He started to give me a nod, the way you do when you meet someone out on a walk like this, but then he stopped and gave me a confused look. You know—he thought he knew me, but he didn't.

"Need some directions?" I asked.

I knew that my voice was just going to add to the off-kilter sense of familiarity he was feeling.

"No," he said. "You . . . I feel like I should know you."

"I'll bet you use that line on all the girls," I said, smiling when it called up a blush.

"No . . . I mean . . ."

I relented. "I know what you meant. You should know me. I'm the voice in the shadows."

I saw understanding dawn in his eyes and he got that look I was talking about, so cute.

"But . . . how can you be real?"

"Who says I'm real?"

Okay, so I was being a little mean. But I guess I still had some issues with him at that time, like how he cast me off when we were only seven years old.

He leaned against the balustrade, looking like he really needed its support.

"Relax," I said. "You're not going crazy."

"Easy for you to say."

I was going to reach out and touch his arm, just to reassure him, but something made me stop, I'm not sure what.

"I just thought we should meet," I said instead. "Rather than you sitting in your reading chair and me talking to you from the shadows. That's starting to get really old."

He was studying my features as I spoke.

"I've seen you before," he said. "How can I have seen you before?"

"Remember when you first started to keep your journals?"

He nodded. "And sometimes I dreamed that I woke and there was this red-haired girl sitting at my desk, reading them."

"That was moi."

"You've been around *that* long?"

"I've been around since you were seven and cast me off."

"I didn't know I was casting you off," he said. "I didn't even know about shadows until a couple of years ago when I came across that reference to them in a book about Jung."

"I know."

A cab went by, slowing as it neared us to see if we might be a fare, then accelerating again when we looked away.

"Did it hurt?" he asked.

"Did what hurt?"

"When you were cast off."

"Not physically."

He gave a slow nod. "Are you okay now?"

"What do you think?"

"I don't know. You seem very self-assured. I got that from our conversations. You don't seem unhappy. Actually, you seem nice."

"I am nice."

"I didn't mean—"

"I know," I said. "You just figured that all the cast-off bits of you would make some dark and evil psycho twin."

"Not exactly that."

"But someone the opposite of who you are."

He nodded.

"But you cast me off when you were only seven," I said. "Lots of what you got rid of were positive traits. And we've both grown since then. We're probably more alike than you'd expect, considering my origins."

"So . . . where do you live? What do you do?"

I smiled. "You know how you like to write about mysterious things?"

He gave another nod.

"Well, I live them," I said.

"And you won't tell me about them because—"

"Then they wouldn't be mysterious, would they?"

We both laughed.

"But seriously," he said.

"Seriously," I told him, "I live in between."

"In between what?"

"Whatever you can be in between of."

He gave a slow nod. "Where magic happens."

"Something like that."

"So why are you here now?" he asked.

"I already told you. The whole speaking from the shadows bit was getting old for me. Besides, I thought you'd be interested in us finally meeting."

"I am. It's just . . . ."

I waited, but I guess for all the words he puts down on paper, he didn't have any to use right now.

"Disconcerting," I said.

"That's putting it mildly."

"Tell you what," I said. "Why don't I just let you deal with this for awhile."

He grabbed my arm as I started to turn away and an odd . . . I don't know . . . something went through me. Bigger than a tingle, not quite a shock. He let go so quickly that I knew he'd felt it, too.

"Do you have to go?" he asked.

I shook my head. "But I'm going to all the same. It's not like we won't meet again."

"When? Where? Here? On this bridge?"

"Wherever," I told him. "Whenever. Don't worry. I can always find you."

"But . . ."

I let myself fade back into the borderlands.

I'd been as interested meeting him as he'd appeared to be meeting me, but I felt a little strange, too, and suddenly felt like I needed some space between us. That strange spark that had leapt between us hadn't been the only indication that there was something going on—just the most apparent.

"It's good to keep some distance between yourself and the one who cast you," Mumbo told me when I asked her about it later.

We were on the roof of an abandoned factory in the Tombs, looking out at the lights of the city across the Kickaha River. Below us on the rubble-strewn streets, the night people who made this lost part of the city their home were going about their business. Junkies were shooting up. Homeless kids and tramps, even whole families, were picking their squats for the night and settling in. Small packs of teenagers from the suburbs and better parts of town were travelling in small packs, avoiding the bikers and such, while looking for weaker prey they could harass. Business as usual for the Tombs.

"I kind of felt that I should," I said. "Except I don't really know why."

Mumbo went into her lecture mode. "The attraction between a shadow and the one who cast her is understandably strong. You were once the same person, so it's no wonder that you'd be drawn to each other. But spend too much time with him, get too close, and you could be drawn back into him again."

"What do you mean back into him?"

"He will absorb you and it will be like you never were. It's happened before. It can happen again."

Sometimes I'd get curious about the Eadar I met, and I'd go haunting libraries and sneaking into bookstores when they were closed to see what I could find. I was probably most curious about Mumbo and Maxie Rose. It took me awhile, but I finally tracked down the books that they'd first appeared in.

Maxie's was particularly hard. There were only fifty made and it was so dreadfully written that their original owners tended to throw them away.

Oddly enough, the copy I eventually found was in Christy's library. It was a thirty-page, saddle-stitched chapbook called *The Jargon Tripper* by Hans Wunschmann and though I managed to read it all the way through twice, I never could figure out what it was supposed to be about. The only character he brought to any semblance of real life in its pages was Maxie and, in the context of the abysmal prose that made up the greater portion of the text, that seemed more by accident.

I never did find out who the "jargon tripper" of the title was, or what it meant.

"Did you ever figure out what Wunschmann was trying to say?" I asked Maxie the next time I saw her. "You know, in that story he wrote that you were in."

Maxie laughed. "Sure. He was saying, 'Look at me. I'm pathetic and I can't write a word, but that's not going to stop me from being published.' Though he didn't say it in so few words." She grinned at me. "He didn't have to. All you had to do was try to read it."

"That's a little harsh."

"You *did* read it, right?"

"Yeah. But I'm sure he must have been trying to do something good. There must have been something in what he was writing that meant a lot to him if he'd spend all that time writing it and then self-publishing it."

"You wish."

"Come on, Maxie. At least allow that he gave it his best shot."

"Did he?" Maxie said. "And don't get me wrong. I've nothing against self-published books, so it's not because of that. I just don't like crap."

"But—"

"And I guess it particularly ticks me off because *that's* the story I got born in. It couldn't be a good book. Oh, no. I had to get born in the literary equivalent of an outhouse."

"But he made you," I said. "You were good in the story. And you're still here, so there must have been something in what he was doing."

Maxie shook her head. "The only reason I'm here is because I'm tenacious and I was damned if I was going to fade away just because I had the bad luck to be born on the pages of some no-talent's story. I don't know what I'd have done if I hadn't discovered I have a gift for teaching shadows. But I would have done something."

Some days I really feel bad for the Eadar. It must be so hard to be at the whim of someone else's muse.

———

I also asked Christy about Wunschmann.

"I still have that?" he said when I showed him the chapbook. "I thought I'd thrown it out years ago."

"Did you know him?"

"Unfortunately. He was this little pissant who was in some of the classes I was taking when I was in Butler U.—always talking, full of big ideas and pronouncements, super critical of everybody. But that little chapbook's all he ever produced. I remember he used to really be down on me and anyone else who was actually getting stories published."

"So you didn't like him."

Christy laughed. "No. Not much."

"And the story?"

"Well, I liked this one character—Mixie, Marsha . . . ?"

"Maxie Rose."

He nodded. "Yeah. She deserved a better writer to tell her story."

"Maybe," I said. "Or maybe she figured out a way to do it herself."

He gave me a funny look, but I didn't elaborate.

Mumbo's was a sweeter story. Or perhaps I should say it was bittersweet. It was certainly better written.

The only edition was a little hardcover children's picture book called *The Midnight Toyroom* that I found in the Crowsea Public Library. The author was a man named Thomas Brigley. The watercolours, done in that turn-of-the-century style of children's book illustrators like Rackham or Dulac, were by Mary Lamb.

The book was published in Newford in the late nineteen-twenties to some local success but never really made much of a mark outside of the city. I looked Brigley up in a biographical dictionary, but he didn't even get a mention. I did find him in *The Butler University Guide to Literature in Newford,* where he got a fairly lengthy entry. He was a life-long bachelor who worked for a printing company, writing and publishing his books in his spare time, which I guess he had a lot of. Of the thirty-seven books that were published under his by-line, only one was for adults—a nonfiction history of the tram system called *Cobblestone Jack,* named after a fictional conductor he had telling the history.

Mary Lamb, his collaborator on all the books, was a librarian who, like Brigley, worked on the books in her spare time. She never married either, which made me figure there was a story in there somewhere, but I couldn't find anything about them ever having been an item—or what might have stopped them from becoming one—in any of the library's reference books. I did find pictures of them, including one of the two of them together. They made an attractive couple in that shot, and there was an obvious attraction between them from the way they were looking at each other, so it didn't make much sense to me.

I tried tracking Cobblestone Jack down, but unlike Mumbo, he'd faded away a long time ago the way most of Brigley's other characters had.

Mumbo only survived because of her connection to shadows like me, but after reading her story, I didn't understand why she'd needed us.

The Midnight Toyroom is about this girl who loves a boy so much that she has the Toy Fairy change her into a ball so that she can be with him. See, he was from this rich family and her parents were servants, so there was no way they could be together. Weren't things weird in those days?

Anyway, he loved the ball and called it Mumbo. Played with it all the time. Only when he got older, he left it out in the woods one day and never thought about it again and there she would have stayed, except the Toy Fairy had allowed her to come alive when no human was watching, so she was able to make her way back to the house. The trouble was, once she got there, she was found by the housekeeper who was packing up all of the boy's old toys to send to an orphanage, and she put Mumbo in with them. The last picture in the book is of Mumbo sitting on the top of a pile of toys in a cart as it slowly draws away from the boy's house.

It was sweet and sad, really well written, and the pictures were beautiful. So I couldn't understand why it hadn't been more of a success. Maybe it was the downbeat ending, but it's not like Hans Christian Andersen didn't write some downers that were still popular. I mean, have you ever read "The Little Match-Girl" or "The Little Mermaid"?

When I found Mumbo's book in the library, it wasn't even on the shelves anymore. I had to dig it out of the stacks because it hadn't been taken out in years. No surprise, I suppose, hidden in the back the way it was. But it was still listed on the card index, so if anybody had wanted it, they could have requested it.

It's just that nobody did.

Have I ever had a meaningful relationship? You mean like what you and Christy have? Not really. Like I said, I had a lot of . . . let's be poetic and call them dalliances, but nothing long-term. Friendships, yes. Lots of them, some I've maintained for years. But to be more intimate . . .

I've never met anyone in the borderlands or beyond that did it for me, and it's way too complicated for me to even think about it in this world. I mean, I'd either end up being this oddball curiosity—after I've told them what I really am—or I'd have to lie and make up a career, where I live, that kind of thing. It just gets too complicated.

Although I just got a cell phone that even works in the borderlands— works better there, actually, than it does here, since Maxie showed me how to rewire it so that we tap into the essence of the borderlands to make our calls, instead of having to worry about satellites and phone companies. So I suppose I could give out a number now if I wanted to and just be all myste- rious about where I live and how I make a living.

Oh, don't smile. So I have this thing about being mysterious. You can blame Christy and his journals for that.

Sure, I can give you the number. But you have to promise not to give it to Christy.

No, it's not just books. Eadar are created out of the imagination, period. It doesn't have to be words on paper. It can be anything from a painting to a passing daydream, but they're not like Isabelle's numena. Eadar depend on belief to exist whereas numena are bound to their painting. The less invested in an Eadar's creation, and therefore the less belief in it, the quicker they fade. It's really sad how ephemeral some of them are, no more than ghosts, barely here and then gone. There are parts of the border- lands—those that are closest to the big cities, usually—where Eadar ghosts are as thick as midges on a summer's day.

But while they can be sad little sorry creatures, that's not always the case. Some have so much belief in them that just glow with energy. For me—probably because of Christy's influence—the really interesting ones come from mythologies.

In the borderlands, faerie are making a big comeback. And so are earth spirits—you know, earth mothers and antlered men. On the down side, so are vampires and other less pleasant creatures. And then there are new ones.

You know why you keep hearing about Elvis sightings? So many people believe he's still alive, that he actually is, except now he exists as a very potent Eadar. As more than one, actually. There's a young, kind of tough one from the early years—though he's still polite as all get-out. But there

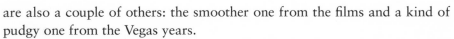

are also a couple of others: the smoother one from the films and a kind of pudgy one from the Vegas years.

You should see it when the three of them get together. You've never heard such arguments. But then you've never heard such music, either.

Anyway, you get the picture. Maybe I started my life as the cast-off bits of somebody else, but I've made my own way ever since. I grew. I changed. I became somebody that no one else is, or can be, because they don't have my life. They don't know the things I know. They don't know what I've felt, what I've experienced.

See, that's what I figure being real means. If you're able to adapt, to mature, to become something other than what it seemed you were supposed to be, then you're real. You've got a soul. Because something that's just a fictional construct, it can't do that. It can only be what its maker says it is. That's what's so sad about the Eadar. They can be as fiercely independent as Maxie Rose, but if Hans Wunschmann decided to write another story about her and changed her personality, or her history, or whatever, those changes would reflect on the Eadar that she's become and all her personal history as an Eadar wouldn't matter.

Continuity's another big topic of discussion in the borderlands and the lack of it's why so many Eadar suffer from various personality disorders. If they don't fade away first. Longevity's not exactly a big part of most of their lives.

But that's not something you or I have to worry about. Our origins might have been outside the norm, but we've grown into the skins and souls of real people. We can't be changed by a few brushstrokes, or bits of new description, or keystrokes.

And I'd like to see someone try to tell me what I'm supposed to be. Anyone does, they'd better have quick reflexes. Why? Because I'd smack 'em so hard they'd be sitting flat on their asses before they ever knew what hit them.

Oh yes. I can be fierce when I need to be. That's one of the first things you have to learn if you want to survive in any world.

And Here We Are

It's not
the words you use;
it's what
they make you see.
—SASKIA MADDING,
"Poems" (*Spirits and Ghosts,* 2000)

Christiana

"So I guess we're both misfits," I say.

It's funny. I can't remember the last time I've talked this much. I guess I'm like Christy in that—I like to sit back and listen, just take things in. Mind you, he's always been quiet. I had to learn to be that way.

Saskia nods. "I suppose we are."

I meant it as a joke, but she seems to take it seriously. I study her for a moment, her gaze going past me, out the window, but she's not looking at anything. She's gone someplace deep inside herself and I'm not here anymore. Not for her. Everything's gone—the café and everybody else in it.

After a moment I get up and get us each another drink—chai tea for her, black coffee for myself. Saskia's back when I return, her gaze focused, tracking me as I approach where we're sitting.

I set her tea on the table in front of her and she smiles her thanks.

"I was reading this science fiction book about A.I.s," Saskia says when I've settled back into my chair. "You know, machines with artificial intelligence?"

"Mmm."

"That's what's got me thinking about all of this. Life's not that much different than that book, really. If they knew what we were, humans really would hate us—just the way they do androids and A.I.s in fiction."

I shake my head. "We're as real as humans."

"But they're flesh and blood."

I lean forward and pinch Saskia's arm.

"So are we," I say.

"Maybe now we are, but—"

"When . . . how—what's the difference? We have spirits. We have souls. How we got them isn't important."

"It is to humans."

I smile. "Screw humans."

But she doesn't smile back.

"And maybe it's important to me, too," she says. "I guess you're okay with what you know about where you came from, but I don't even know that. I start to think back and I've got ahead full of memories, but they only go so far before I hit a wall. Did I come out of nothing? Can I still have a soul?"

"Well, there's an easy way to find out," I say.

She gives me a puzzled look.

"We'll go back to where you came from—you and me. I'll take you back into the Wordwood. The answers might not be here, but they've got to be there."

"I . . . I don't know."

"What are you worried about?"

"What if once I get there, I can't come back? What if I'm only a piece of whatever the Wordwood is and once I get there, it just absorbs me again? What if it absorbs you, too?"

I shrug. "That's just the chance we'll have to take, I guess. I mean, it all depends on how badly you need to know this thing."

Saskia gives me a considering look.

"Are you really this tough?" she asks.

"Don't forget fierce, too," I say, adding a smile.

"I wish I was. Tough and fierce. Sure of myself."

"It takes work," I tell her. "And it doesn't mean you don't get scared anymore. It just means you don't let the fear stop you from doing what you want, or need, to do. That's where the work part comes in."

She gives me a slow nod.

"And how do you plan for us to get there?" she asks.

"I'll take you by way of the borderlands."

"We can get to the Wordwood through these borderlands?"

"You can get anywhere from the borderlands," I tell her. "And if you're right, if there is some great big voodoo spirit running that Wordwood program, he or she probably lives in the otherworld."

"The otherworld . . ."

I nod. "Mind you, I can only bring you across—you'll have to figure out where we're going once we're over there. Depending on how good your homing instincts are, it could take awhile, so we should probably go sooner than later. At least that's what I would do. I mean, why wait?" I have a sip of my coffee and raise my eyebrows. "Hell, we can go right now."

"No, I'd have to talk to Christy first. I couldn't just leave him hanging."

"And he so hates change."

"He's not that bad."

"We could bring him with us," I say, though I know that could be problematic. I can't spend too much time with him or who knows what might happen.

Saskia shakes her head.

"Oh, come on," I say. "He's not that stodgy. He'd jump at the chance to visit the otherworld."

"Probably," she says. "But I think this is something I should be doing on my own. For myself. And because . . ." She hesitates, that far distance filling those blue eyes of hers again for a long moment. "Who knows what I'm going to find."

"Nothing you could find could make him feel any different about you. Those Riddell boys are so true blue loyal they make dogs seem unreliable."

"I know. But still . . ."

I wait to see if she's going to finish her sentence.

"But still," I agree when she doesn't. "I understand. How about if I come by to pick you up midmorning, then? That'll give you a chance to talk to him and get ready."

She gives me a nervous look.

"It's funny," she says. "This is something I've been thinking about for ages. But now that you're offering me this easy way to actually do it, suddenly I don't feel even remotely ready."

"That's okay, too," I say. "Why don't you think about it, talk it over with Christy, and decide in the morning. I'll come by and you can tell me what you've decided."

Now it's her turn to smile. "And you'll knock on the door like a regular visitor?"

"Maybe. We'll have to see how I'm feeling. I do like the look on Christy's face when I just step out of nowhere."

"You're incorrigible, aren't you?"

"I try to be."

We both have some more of our drinks, silence lying easily between us.

"Why do you want to do this?" Saskia asks after a few moments.

"Maybe I'm just the helpful type," I say.

"Okay."

I can tell she doesn't believe that.

"Or maybe I just like the adventure of doing something new," I add. "I've never been inside a computer program before. It's got all the promise of an interesting experience."

"And the danger doesn't worry you?"

"Tough," I remind her. "Fierce."

"Foolhardy," she adds.

"Probably that, too."

The World Wide Web Blues

The puppet thinks:
It's not so much
what they make me do
as their hands inside me.
—SASKIA MADDING,
"Puppet" (*Mirrors*, 1995)

Aaran Goldstein

One week before Christiana and Saskia met in the Beanery Café and shared their life histories with each other, Aaran Goldstein was in Jackson Hart's apartment, having a conversation with the young computer wizard.

"This is really strange," Jackson said, leaning forward to study his monitor more closely.

Aaran nodded. "I already know it's a weird site," he told Jackson, making an effort to keep the irritation he was feeling out of his voice. "The question is, can you hack into it?"

Jackson was one of the paper's programmers and computer trouble-shooters. Younger than *The Daily Journal*'s book editor and probably twice as smart, he was in his early twenties and lived on a diet of soda and junk food, but his coffee-coloured skin remained clear and he never put on any weight—all facts that annoyed Aaran to no end since it had taken him a strict regime of proper diets and exercise to finally get rid of the acne and flab that had plagued him all through his high school years. But while Jackson's metabolism and higher intelligence annoyed Aaran, it didn't stop him from taking advantage of Jackson's expertise. Using people was second nature to Aaran at this point in his life.

They were sitting in Jackson's home office, a room that held more computer equipment than Aaran had ever seen before outside of a computer store's showroom. He didn't know what half of it did, but that didn't matter. All that mattered was that Jackson did.

"I really don't know," Jackson said in response to Aaran's question. "This is a new one on me. Here, take a look at this."

Using his mouse, he brought the arrow on his screen up to the menu bar, clicked on "View," then on "Source."

"See?" he said. "There's no code."

"And that means?"

"I don't know what it means. It's impossible. There's always code. You can't have a Web page without code. Without code, there's no way for your computer's browser to translate what's stored on the site's ISP into something you can see on your computer. What we should have here is HTML text all over the screen."

"Except it's blank," Aaran said.

Jackson wheel his chair back from the desk to look at him. "Exactly. So what's really going on here?"

Aaran shrugged.

"Because I've heard of these ghost sites before," Jackson said. "They're like the big voodoo mystery of the Internet. This is the first time I've run across one of them, but I've heard enough to know that they're trouble."

"What kind of trouble?"

Jackson's gaze returned to the screen. There was a white box in the center of the screen that doubled as a search engine and a kind of message board. Behind the box a video of a forest was displayed—very smooth streaming. You could see the leaves moving in a breeze and there was nothing jerky about their shivering movement. The resolution was crystal clear. The sound of the breeze came out of his speakers—soft and soothing. Occasionally there was movement in a tree branch—little birds and animals, though sometimes they looked like people. Or animals wearing clothes.

"I don't know," he said. "Just trouble."

"But it's interesting, isn't it?"

Jackson regarded him. "I suppose." He waited a beat, then asked, "What exactly is it that you want me to do if I can hack into this site— which, I'm telling you now, I don't see happening."

Aaran leaned back in his own chair.

"It means a lot to someone who fucked me over," he said. "So I want to mess around with it, let her know that it may take awhile, but Aaran Goldstein always pays you back."

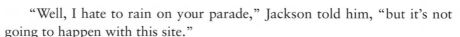

"Well, I hate to rain on your parade," Jackson told him, "but it's not going to happen with this site."

"Okay. New plan, then. Can you shut it down?"

Jackson took another look at the screen. "Probably. If I can get whoever's on the other side of its firewall to open an attachment."

"You're going to use a virus?"

Jackson nodded.

"That works for me," Aaran said. "The site gets shut down and you get to add another notch to your joystick, or however it is you guys keep score." He smiled. "So I guess I'm doing you a favor, really. Now you'll get to brag to your buddies about how you just took down another big bad site."

Jackson gave him a cold look.

"No," he said. "All that's happening here is you're blackmailing me into fucking up somebody's life and destroying a lot of hard work."

"Blackmail's such a harsh word," Aaran said.

"Oh, yeah? Then what would you call it?"

"An exchange of favors."

"You're not doing me a favor. I don't get any kick out of what you're asking me to do."

"That's a good line. Remember to use it when the cops come knocking at your door."

Jackson glared at him, but Aaran only smiled. It was too late for Jackson to get out of this now. If he'd wanted to stay safe, he shouldn't have gotten drunk and spilled all his secrets.

It had happened a few weeks ago. Aaran was returning from a club on Gracie Street where yet another hot babe had shut him down—something that been happening on an increasingly regular basis ever since that night Saskia Madding had thrown him out of her apartment, leaving him standing there in her hallway with his clothes in his arms and anger churning like a hot cauldron in his stomach.

An anomaly, he'd told himself. She was the loser, not him.

But it had brought back all the lonely years of being the fat, pimple-faced reject with glasses he'd been in high school. Brought them back in an instant, just like that, as though they'd never gone away. He went in a flash from the guy with the cool to the loser getting turned down for the school dance by Betty Langford, who was more of a loser herself, but still thought she was too good to go out with the likes of him.

He'd been doing so well at forgetting those days, at reinventing his childhood.

Me? he projected. Hell, I've always been cool.

All he had to do was look in a mirror. That poor fat little kid with the zits and glasses was gone as though he'd never been. People he'd gone to school with weren't able to see the kid he'd been in the man he'd become. Maybe that wasn't such a surprise. That kid hadn't even registered for most of them.

But every so often something came along to remind him. Like tonight. The woman he'd been hitting on had given him such a look of disdain that when he looked away from her, his gaze locked on the mirror behind the bar where, for one painful moment, his own reflection was replaced with that of a sorry-assed little kid with a spray of zits across his face, staring back at him, hurt puppy-dog eyes bewildered behind their glasses.

He didn't know how he knew. He just knew it was Madding's fault. There was something spooky about her, always had been. Not spooky enough for him to forgo taking advantage of her the way he had. But certainly enough so that in retrospect, he realized maybe he should have stayed clear of her. Maybe then she wouldn't have cursed him, or done whatever it was she'd done to put this hex on him.

Because ever since that night it was as though the sorry vapors of his high school days had risen up and were clinging to him once again—a clear warning to any woman with her loser-radar turned on, which these days was every one of them. And the more times he got turned down, the worse it seemed to get.

He left the club, staring at the ground, walking aimlessly down Gracie Street, not ready to give the courting game another try, certainly not ready to go home. Another night shot and no way for him to get back at Madding for bewitching him, or at her little crowd of boho friends for making fun of him every chance they could.

Except fate smiled on him.

Stepping into Lobo's for a last drink before he headed home, tail between his legs, who should he see but Jackson Hart, one of *The Daily Journal*'s computer nerd squad, deep in his cups and obviously bumming, big time.

There was nothing like somebody else's misery to make you feel better about your own sorry little life.

He slid into a stool beside Jackson, ordered a beer from the bartender, then turned to his coworker.

"Having a bad night?" he asked.

Jackson lifted his gaze from where it had been locked on the empty shot glass in front him and turned to Aaran. He seemed to have a moment's trouble focusing. When he did, he gave a slow nod.

"Woman trouble?" Aaran said. "Because let me tell you, I've been there."

"I wish."

This wasn't good, Aaran thought. Come on. I want details. I want something to make me feel better.

"Well, you've got a good job," he said, "and if it's not woman trouble, then I can't think of a single reason for a successful fellow like yourself to be so depressed. Unless it's a health issue?"

"Even that'd be better," Jackson said.

Now Aaran was intrigued. He got the bartender's attention and ordered a refill for Jackson. He was drinking sipping whiskey, but he wasn't sipping it.

"Well, you know," he said. "My grandfather was always full of good advice and one of the best pieces he gave me was this: trouble shared, is trouble halved."

Actually, he'd read that in one of the endless flood of self-help books that came to the paper. This one had annoyed him so much, he'd actually taken the time to trash it in a quarter-page review.

"So if you need a sympathetic listener," he added, "I'm here."

Jackson swallowed his drink in one shot, looked blearily at the glass for a moment, then set it down on the bar top with exaggerated care.

"I screwed up," he said. "Big, big time."

Aaran waited. He had a sip of his beer. The reporters at the paper were always saying that if you kept quiet, people'd feel obliged to fill the hole, saying more, perhaps, than they meant to. And sure enough, patience paid off.

"I just wanted to see if I could get inside," Jackson said finally. He spoke slowly and carefully, a drunk trying to sound sober. "To see if I could, you know? I mean, these banks . . . it's like they think they're doing *us* some big favor by letting us pay them to keep our money, not to mention shelling out a few bucks for every little transaction that comes along. I wasn't really going to do anything once I got inside. Maybe leave a message for the manager—you know, thumb my nose at him. Here's one for the little people.

"I didn't mean to mess everything up."

He fell silent for long enough that Aaran realized he'd better offer some input.

"Nobody ever plans to mess things up," he said.

Jackson nodded. "I guess. But most people's mistakes don't have money machines spitting out twenties all over town until they run out of money."

"That was *you*?"

"It was an accident."

"Hey, I believe you," Aaran assured him. "Who cares anyway? That kind of a loss is no more to the banks than you or me getting short-changed at the grocery store. Screw them."

"I suppose. Though they aren't going to see it that way. And neither are the cops."

"First they'd have to catch you," Aaran said. "Did you leave any kind of a trail?"

Jackson shook his head. "Nothing that'd be of any use to them unless they were already looking in my direction."

"Any chance of that?"

"I guess not. I'm nobody to them."

"So like I said," Aaran told him. "Screw them all."

He ordered another round for them from the bartender. When their drinks came, he tapped the lip of his beer mug against Jackson's shot glass.

"Here's to thumbing our noses at the moneymen," he said.

"I guess," Jackson said and swallowed his shot in one gulp.

And that had been that. Jackson felt better getting the burden of guilt off his chest and Aaran came away with informational leverage that he knew would come in useful at some point in the future. He didn't know where or when—not until he'd found himself logging onto the Wordwood this morning and remembering how Madding had waxed so enthusiastic about the site that one night they'd had together. Before she tossed him out on his ear. Before she put the hex on him that had turned his love life into no life.

"Maybe I *should* tell the cops," Jackson said now, still glaring at Aaran. "Just to get you off my back."

No, that was a bad idea, Aaran thought.

"Hey, come on," he said, turning on the charm. "I was just being an asshole. You do this for me and we're square. I don't want to see you rotting away in a jail cell, turning into some big-ass biker's girlfriend, anymore than you want to be there."

Jackson wouldn't look at him. His gaze rested on his computer screen, his face giving away nothing of what he was thinking.

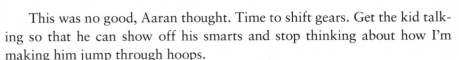

This was no good, Aaran thought. Time to shift gears. Get the kid talking so that he can show off his smarts and stop thinking about how I'm making him jump through hoops.

"So how come you don't hear more about these sites?" Aaran asked. "You know, like in the press?"

For a moment he thought Jackson was going to continue to ignore him, but he finally looked away from the screen and back at Aaran.

"That's just more of their weirdness," he said. "It's like you can't talk about it—at least not publicly. You can send the URL to someone, but you can't seem to write about it."

"I don't understand."

"There's no point in trying to figure it out," Jackson said. "I knew a guy who was doing a piece on another site like this for *Wired* and he just couldn't submit it. When he tried to e-mail it to his editor, it came back as undeliverable. But here's the really weird part: It was also erased from his hard drive. After that, whenever he tried to write about it, the files would disappear from his hard drive—like someone was sitting inside his machine, keeping tabs on what he was doing. Finally he wrote it out by hand, but that doesn't do you much good."

"Why not?"

"Everything's on-line these days. Everything's connected. The same computer a publisher uses to lay out an issue is hooked up to the Internet. And if his isn't, the printer's is. Somewhere along the line these things always just disappear. The only pieces I've ever seen on sites like this are what somebody photocopied."

"So you *can* get the information out."

Jackson shrugged. "I guess. But who reads hardcopy anymore?"

"Hopefully *The Daily Journal*'s readers."

"You know what I mean. Everybody's getting their information off the Net these days. It just makes more sense."

"I can't argue about the convenience."

Hell, he cribbed half the stuff he used in his own pieces from on-line reviews and articles—suitably rephrased and given his own spin, of course.

"Look," he said, figuring Jackson was calmed down enough by now to get back to the business at hand. "We've gotten off on the wrong foot here. I know it seems like an unfriendly thing that I'm asking you to do, but this woman's just been asking for it. I've let it slide for a few years—truth is, she burned me good, but I was willing to let it go if she would. But lately she and her little circle of friends have been making my life hell. Every time there's the smallest mistake in the book section, they're all over it with letters to the editor, badmouthing me to publishers' reps and in the bookstores. It's gotten to the point where my boss is on my case about it."

He took a breath.

"See, it's never anything big," he went on, "but if you get enough people complaining, it looks worse than it is. My boss doesn't know a book from a coaster, but he understands negative feedback and he doesn't like it. Which means it comes down on me and . . ."

He let his voice trail off when he realized that he was beginning to rant. Just thinking about Madding and her friends these days was enough to get him going. But from the look on Jackson's face, Jackson couldn't care less, and he wasn't here to air his own dirty laundry. He was just here to get a service done.

"So I take the site down," Jackson said, "and we're good? You won't be coming around asking for another favor two weeks down the road?"

Aaran shook his head and put his hand up in a Boy Scout's salute.

"Scout's honour," he said.

Which would mean something if he'd ever been a Scout.

Jackson studied him for a long moment, then finally sighed.

"Okay," he said. "I'll get on it."

"Any idea how long it'll take?"

"Two, three days. By the weekend, for sure. Unless . . ."

"Unless what?"

"Whoever put that site up is smarter than me."

Jackson Hart

True to his word, Jackson started working on the problem as soon as Aaran left the apartment. The first thing he did was write a simple virus program—nothing fancy. Simple was as capable of shutting down a computer as complicated. Maybe it wasn't as impressive, but it usually had a better chance of slipping in and getting the job done.

The virus he wrote now would worm into the ISP's computer that housed the Wordwood's site, dig through every file stored on it, and erase any HTML links it found, replacing them with random gibberish. Any site hosted by that ISP would immediately be rendered useless.

It wasn't a permanent meltdown. But it would require anyone using that ISP as the host for their site to send clean files to replace the ones his virus had damaged. That could take anywhere from a few hours to a few days, depending on how much material they had to transfer back onto the site. Considering the size and complexity of the Wordwood site, it should be enough of an inconvenience and take them long enough to satisfy Aaran's need for revenge.

All Jackson had to do was get somebody at the Wordwood end to open an attachment, but he didn't think that would be too hard. Since they seemed to collect texts of books, he'd simply hide the virus as a macro inside a file purporting to be a book with a trigger that would make the macro run as soon as the file was opened. Then the next time the Webmaster updated his site, the virus would piggyback along with whatever he sent and the server would go down.

Piece of cake, really.

He hummed as he worked on the program, then tested it. The programming soothed his anger the way it always did. That was half the reason he'd gotten into computers in the first place. Mostly, he loved the clean logic of programming. Computers were so much better than people. They were straightforward, doing only what they were programmed to do. They didn't lie to you, or make fun of you. Or blackmail you.

He was ready to send the virus by two A.M., only a few hours after Aaran had left.

Now, he thought, we'll see how tight the Wordwood's security is.

Logging back onto the Internet, he established his protocols through a confusing labyrinth of false trails and dummy ISPs that left no way to trace him back to the computer he was actually using. He aimed his browser at the Wordwood's site. When the forest background appeared on his screen, he began to type into the white box floating in the center of the screen.

Love your site. How do I submit a book to add to your library?
An eager reader

He'd barely finished typing when a response appeared, replacing his own text:

Hello eager reader.
Simply send the document file as an attachment addressed to:
webmaster@thewordwood.com

Whatever you say, he thought.

He opened Eudora, typed "a book from an eager reader" as a subject heading, attached his file, and hit "queue." When he closed the e-mail software, he got a prompt telling him he had an unsent message. He chose "send and close" and watched the progress bar until the file had been sent. Eudora closed and he was looking at the Wordwood site once more.

He stretched his arms over his head, then got up and went into the kitchen, returning with a can of soda and a bag of chips. He doubted that anything was going to happen immediately. If the Webmaster at the Wordwood was anything like every other Webmaster Jackson knew, he'd be so overworked that he probably wouldn't get to the e-mail for a few days. And then he'd have to actually update the site before the virus could even start to do its thing.

He had a sip of his soda to wash down a mouthful of chips.

This really was an amazing site. The video and audio of the background alone were enough to mesmerize him. No matter how long he studied it, he couldn't detect a loop in either. Then there was the swiftness of response time to messages and the sheer volume of material on the site itself.

He did another check for code, but there was still none available to view.

Whoever had done this really knew his stuff. How did you make code invisible, but still readable to the viewer's browser?

Magic.

Voodoo.

His mouth went dry, and not because of the chips. He had another sip of his soda, remembering what he'd been telling Aaran.

He wasn't entirely ready to believe that the Internet was spawning A.I.s somewhere out there in its pixelated reaches, but there was no denying that there were some brilliant programmers. If the Webmaster of the Wordwood was as good as he appeared to be, he might just detect the virus before it ever did any damage. Worse, he might be able to track it back to this computer.

You didn't need magic for that. You just needed good hacking skills.

And maybe, once the Webmaster had Jackson's I.D., he might want to deliver some payback. Do a little walkabout through, oh say, Jackson's bank accounts and set all the balances to zero.

Jackson stared at his monitor and began to regret sending the virus. He hadn't wanted to do it in the first place—who got pleasure out of trashing somebody's hard work except for emotional misers like Aaran Goldstein? There was something creepy about this whole business. The site. Aaran's need for revenge. The blackmail.

The forest on his screen was starting to give him the willies just the way a real-world forest did. The few times he'd been out in the country in the past few years, he'd always gotten the feeling that something was hidden in among the trees, watching him.

It hadn't been like that when he was a kid. As a kid, he used to spend all his spare time in the wood lots behind the housing development where he'd grown up. At least he had until a bunch of kids had taken to lying in wait for him, chasing him through the trees and beating him up whenever they could. That was when he'd first started to spend so much time in front of a computer.

Maybe that was why forests still creeped him out. Why he always felt like he was being watched. Logically, he knew it wasn't true anymore. Just like there was nothing hidden in the branches and leaves of the Wordwood's index page, watching him now.

But it *felt* like there was.

He started to reach for his mouse to click himself off-line, when his screen flickered and went blank. A moment later, a familiar message appeared along the left side of his browser window:

This page cannot be displayed.
The page you are looking for is currently unavailable. The Web site might be experiencing technical difficulties, or you may need to adjust your browser settings . . .

Followed by a list of the things he could try to reconnect with the site. Yadda, yadda, yadda.

He watched, unable to move, expecting he didn't know what. But finally, he reached forward again and disconnected his computer from the Internet.

What do you know. His virus had worked. And quickly, too.

He didn't feel any sense of accomplishment—not like when he'd finally gotten past the bank's firewalls and realized he was actually in. He just felt kind of dirty.

I should take a shower, he thought. But first . . .

He picked up his phone and dialed the number that Aaran had left him. He got an answering machine on the first ring. It was going on three A.M. He supposed not everybody was up at this time of the morning.

"I don't know how long it'll last," he said into the receiver, "but the site's down for now. They'll be able to get it back up again, but it'll probably be a few days." He paused, then added, "So we're square now, right?"

He looked across the room, the receiver still at his ear, but he had nothing else to say, so he hung up.

He took his shower and went to bed, but lay in the dark, staring at what he could see of the ceiling above his bed for a long time. He found he could still hear the breeze of the Wordwood's site. When he closed his eyes, the forest was there, as though the streaming video was playing across his eyelids.

———

Neither left him as the rest of the week went slowly by.

He had the breeze in his ears. It was like what you heard after a loud concert—a faint, steady ringing. Because he was always focused on it, it seemed louder than it really was, a constant soundtrack to the routine of his life. Sometimes it was just static.

The forest lived on the inside of his eyelids like a video tattoo. He caught glimpses of it every time he blinked. When he closed his eyes for longer periods of time, the breeze in his ears grew louder and he felt swept away someplace. Then he'd start, look around, check his watch. He'd lost a minute or two. By the end of the week, sometimes the pieces of lost time stretched into half an hour.

He didn't see Aaran again until two days after the Wordwood went down. Walking down a hallway in the offices of *The Daily Journal,* he came around the corner, and there was Aaran. Jackson hadn't been avoiding the paper's book editor, but also hadn't gone out of his way to contact him again after he'd left the phone message the other night.

"Jackson," Aaran said, smiling. "My man. I got your message. Excellent job. Fast service and the sucker's still down."

"I guess."

"You don't look too happy about this."

"I don't see anything to feel happy about."

Aaran shrugged. "Yeah, well, that's because you don't have the personal stake in it like I do. Man, I can't wait to see one of Madding's crew. Drop a little hint. Let them know who they're screwing around with."

Don't, Jackson wanted to say. But what was the point? Sensitivity and discretion weren't exactly among Aaran's personality traits.

"And we're good now?" he asked instead. "You know. About the bank . . . ?"

"What bank?" Aaran said. He gave Jackson a light punch on the shoulder. "Gotta run. Editorial meeting."

Jackson nodded. "Sure."

He closed his eyes for a moment as Aaran turned away. The forest reared up on the backs of his eyelids, something still watching him from within the foliage. When he opened his eyes again, Aaran was long gone and he stood alone in the hallway.

He kept checking the Wordwood site through the rest of the week, but it remained down.

On the night that Saskia and Christiana met at the Beanery Café, Jackson was in his apartment. After heating up a frozen burrito in the microwave, he sat down in the living room to eat it while he watched some TV. He never noticed when he'd dropped off, but when he snapped back into himself, he realized that he'd lost four hours this time.

Four hours.

The half-eaten burrito was sitting cold on a plate on the coffee table. He picked up his can of soda and had a drink. The soda was warm and flat. He looked around the clutter of his living room. There seemed to be a space between himself and everything familiar. The TV caught his eye as whatever show had been on went into a commercial.

He picked up the remote. Pointing it at the TV, he hit the off button.

He remembered . . .

Trees . . . branches . . . leaves . . . an endless forest . . .

But not a real forest, not even a video pretending to be a real forest like at the Wordwood site. Instead it was like someone had gone into a stretch of woods and sprayed a thin sheen of metallic paint onto everything. All around him the leaves and branches, the undergrowth, every blade, every leaf of every plant, was metal and ore. Gold and silver and steel. Copper and iron. Burnished and gleaming, but also rusty and black. When a branch brushed a wafer-thin leaf, sparks flew. Thousands of tiny firework displays were discharged whenever a breeze came sighing through the trees.

Underfoot, when he kicked at the metallic plants and dirt, the ground was made of circuit boards and wires.

And there was the voice.

He remembered hearing a voice, a quiet, murmuring voice, talking to him, but either he was just out of range, or it was speaking in a language he didn't understand, because he hadn't been able to make out a word of what it was saying.

No, that wasn't true. In amongst the gibberish he could distinguish two words, repeated so often they might have been on a loop.

Find . . . can't find . . . can't . . . can't find . . . find . . .

And though the volume of that voice had never risen, he remembered an urgency in it.

What couldn't be found?

He rubbed at his face. His eyes felt gritty, his mouth too dry. He had another drink of the flat soda, then got up and went into the washroom. He

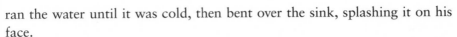

ran the water until it was cold, then bent over the sink, splashing it on his face.

The metal forest flickered on the back of his eyelids every time he closed his eyes or blinked. The breeze remained constant in his ears, like radio static now. The sense of being watched by whatever was in among those trees was stronger than ever, as though the watcher was looking for something.

Can't find . . . can't . . .

He stared at his face in the mirror, wondering, what couldn't be found? Was the thing in the forest looking for him? Or was he just going crazy?

He turned away and went over to his computer work station, turned the computer on.

He knew when all of this had started. When he'd sent that e-mail to the Wordwood site. Maybe he could stop it by sending another. He couldn't think of anything else. He just knew, if he didn't do something soon, he really would go crazy.

The e-mail he composed was short and to the point. He confessed to the virus he'd sent and included instructions on how to remedy the damage it had caused. When he was finished, he queued the e-mail and called up his dial-up window. Once he was on-line, he pressed send.

He knew that it would take hours, if not days, for the Wordwood's Webmaster to be able to fix the damage that his virus had done, but he opened his browser and aimed it at the Wordwood site anyway. The "This page cannot be displayed" message appeared almost immediately.

As he started to close his browser, the page on his screen shivered. He held his hand still on his mouse. The browser page shivered again, then a ripple ran from one side of the screen to the other and a small black dot appeared in the center. When the dot began to expand, Jackson let go of the mouse and pushed back from his computer station.

It reminded him of a pupil. As though his monitor was an eye, and the expanding dot was its dilating pupil. Looking at him. Directly at him.

The static breeze in his ears grew louder. He wanted to shut off the computer—at least go off-line—but the truth was, he was scared to even touch the machine now. It was all just too weird. His hacker's paranoia was operating at full throttle—who's watching me, who knows, what will they do? He remembered all the supernatural voodoo talk about spirits in the Net that got talked about in newsgroups and when he got together with his computer friends.

What if those spirits weren't locked into the Net? What if they *could* get out? What if they were *already* out?

Something was screwing around with his hearing.

Something was making him hallucinate—flashes during the day, dreams of metallic forests.

He didn't want to think about it. Don't articulate your fears, he'd heard once, or you might make them true. But he couldn't help it. How could he help *not* thinking about it?

Something *was* watching him.

He could feel its presence, even if he couldn't see where it was hidden. He didn't know what it was. He couldn't say if it was in his computer, or somewhere in the room with him, but it existed. The animal part of his brain, the part that operated on pure instinct, could sense its interest in him. It woke a pin prickle of warning at the nape of his neck that made the little hairs stand up and sent nervous twinges snaking down his spine.

And something *was* exerting a physical effect upon him.

The static breeze grew louder in his ears. Every time he blinked, the forest tattooed on his eyelids left a residue of its presence in his vision. The expanding eye, staring at him from his monitor, filled the screen until his monitor went black. Then something else started to happen.

He rolled his chair closer to his desk, leaning in to look at it.

Condensation appeared to be forming on the outside of the screen— dark drops of some sort of oily liquid was beading on the glass, then running down the surface of the monitor in trails to drip from the bottom onto his desk. Jackson reached a finger to touch one of the drops. Before he could, the static in his ears swelled into a roar. His monitor changed from a machine with a glass screen to an open window and a flood of the thick liquid came gushing out. It was as though his monitor had become the portal of a sinking ship already under the surface of the ocean.

He jumped up and back, sending his chair skidding, then lost his footing in the black pool that had already formed around his desk. He went down, flailing his arms.

Impossible. None of this was possible.

He mind refused to accept what was happening, but his animal brain fully believed and was in a blind panic.

When he tried to get back on his feet, the liquid was too slippery for him to find purchase. He fell again, face first into the liquid, and came up spluttering. He turned and caught a face-full of the oily liquid as it continued to gush out of the monitor.

Down he went again.

The force of the liquid pushed him in a tumble toward the door. He felt as helpless as he once had as a child, falling into a stretch of rapids while fishing with his father. His father had plucked him out of the water then, but there was no one to do that here.

He hit the door with enough to force to take the wind out of him and fell face forward into the goopy liquid again. It was almost a foot and a half deep now and showed no sign of letting up.

The static breeze in his ears had grown into a dull roar. Dimly, beneath its static rasp, he heard the voice from his dreams.

Find . . . can't find . . . can't . . .

He managed to grab hold of the door handle and haul himself up above the surface of the liquid, his feet still skidding from under him as he tried to stand. He spat to clear his mouth, but the goop clung to his gums and his teeth and the roof of his mouth. Getting a good grip of the door handle with one hand, he used the other to wipe at his face.

He froze when his hand came in front of his eyes. With numb fascination, he realized that he could see right through it as though he were fading. Or coming apart.

High school science classes came back to him, some teacher droning on about how everything was made up of molecules, constantly vibrating. Linked to each other to form matter.

Linked . . .

It was like the links that held him together were dissolving as surely as had the ones on the Wordwood Web site when he'd infected it with his virus.

This couldn't be happening.

Except he could see right through his hand. He could—

His other hand lost its grip of the door handle. Or did it simply go *through* the door handle?

It didn't matter anymore.

As he sank into the liquid, he could feel himself being absorbed by the black goop, molecule by molecule, all the links that held him together fading away, no longer able to do the job they were meant to do.

The last thing he thought was, if a Web site has a spirit, this must be what it feels like when a virus takes it down . . .

Holly Rue

To: "holly rue" <hollyl@cybercare.com>
Date: Sat, 26 Aug 2000 22:38:19 -0700
From: "thomas irwin pace" <tip@lunaloca.com>
Subject: WW down?

Hey Holly

Quick question: Have you been able to log on to the Wordwood site lately? I haven't been able to connect to it all week long, and it's not just me. Everybody I've talked to says the same thing. I don't think it's been on-line since Monday—at least that's the last time I was able to connect. Wasn't a great connection either. Pages took forever to refresh. No real-time dialogue with whoever's running the site these days. All the streaming video and sounds were down.

Any ideas?

Tip

P.S. Aiden says you'll really like Monkey Beach by Eden Robinson. She wrote that collection Traplines a few years ago, remember?

Holly hadn't been able to connect to the Wordwood all week either, but she hadn't considered that the site itself might be down. She'd simply assumed it was yet one more problem with her own service provider. CyberCare had been great when she'd first signed up with them a few years ago, but the ISP's service had been getting dodgier ever since, especially over the past couple of months. She was seriously considering switching ISPs, for all the hassle that would entail in terms of having to move her store's Web site and change its Internet address.

After rereading Tip's e-mail, she tried to log on to the Wordwood again herself and received the same message she'd been getting all week:

This page cannot be displayed.

She stared at the useless screen, wishing her partner Dick was as good at solving computer problems as he was at keeping the bookstore tidy. She was hopeless with either. She used to think she was pretty good at keeping the store neat and running smoothly all on her own, but that was before she discovered she had a hob living behind the furnace in her basement. A real hob, mind you, like in a fairy tale. Not some little man pretending to be one.

Dick Bobbins wasn't much more than two feet tall with curly brown hair, large dark eyes and a broad face creased with laugh lines. He now lived in her spare bedroom. He was the one who kept the store so shipshape, spending his evenings dusting and filing new arrivals, organizing and straightening the books on the shelves, and generally being more efficient in one day than Holly could be in a week. Though he'd share a cup of tea and meals with her, he really seemed to get his sustenance from the books he read.

Holly had no idea how that was even possible, but she supposed when it came to logic, magic marched to its own drum.

She hadn't even realized that beings such as Dick existed until she first met him a year or so ago. He'd been her own secret fairy-tale housekeeper—so secret, even she hadn't known he lived with her. And when she did find out, it seemed that real life followed the fairy tales when it came to hob lore—thank them, or give them a gift, and off they'd go. Dick had his bags all packed and was sneaking out the door until she made him an offer of partnership in the store. Ever since, she'd felt guilty because Dick worked so hard while she continued with her usual slow-mo puttering. But it was hard to *make* Dick relax. He loved to read, of course, and he read prodigious amounts of books. Which is why he'd chosen her store as a residence in the first place. But his idea of relaxing was endlessly dusting, sweeping, tidying, cleaning . . .

Fairy-tale being or not, Dick was definitely suffering from an obsessive-compulsive disorder.

She'd given him a book on the subject, but after reading it, all he said was, "Yes, Mistress Holly, that's me all right," and kept right on doing it. She guessed that breaking him of the habit of leaving a place after he'd been thanked was at least a good start—she'd just have to work on this compulsive need to be constantly cleaning. Though, really. If it was left up to her own haphazard approach to store maintenance, she didn't want to think what the place would look like.

"What do you think, Snippet?" Holly asked, turning to look at her Jack Russell terrier. "Am I taking advantage of him the way Christy says I am?"

Snippet regarded her with one eye and gave a desultory kick at the air with a hind leg. All it would require was the smallest hint of encouragement and she would bound up from the front display window where she was lying and into Holly's lap. When Holly returned her attention back to the computer, Snippet gave a heavy sigh.

"Oh, I'm not forgetting your walk," Holly said over her shoulder. "Just let me answer Tip's e-mail."

What could have happened to the Wordwood?

Anything, she realized. Almost from the first—when she and Tip, Sarah, Benjamin and Claudette had first started it up—the site had been one anomaly after another.

They'd all attended Butler University together, going their separate ways after graduating. Still, they'd stayed in touch—with e-mail it was easy—and got together whenever they could, which usually worked out to be once or twice a year since they all still had family in Newford. It was at one such get-together a number of years ago that they hit upon the idea of putting together a site specializing in literature—which had quickly gone on to encompass writing of all kinds as they couldn't agree on what should or shouldn't be considered literature.

The initial vision was to collect as many bibliographies, biographies, and public domain texts as they could, sharing the storage space on their various servers, linking to other sites such as Project Gutenberg and First

Chapters to save themselves from having to input information that already existed elsewhere on the Net.

They soon had an enormous surge in enthusiastic help from e-mail correspondents across the globe, making suggestions, pointing out errors, e-mailing new links and material. The Wordwood quickly grew from a hodge-podge of a Web site—a personal vision brought to life and existing on five separate servers—to something else again. Something they couldn't have predicted and still didn't understand.

For the site took on a life of its own.

It didn't happen overnight—or at least they didn't realize it overnight.

First they began to find texts on one or another's servers that none of them had put up. This shouldn't have been possible since, like most Web sites, theirs was password-protected and only the site owners were supposed to have access. Initially, they treated it as an anomaly, something that the more computer literate among their number tried to figure out in their spare time, but nothing they actually felt they needed to worry about.

"Strange things happen on the Net," Sarah, the real computer guru of the site's original founders, liked to say. "There's all kinds of voodoo in cyberspace. Ghosts and spirits, haunting the wires."

The unauthorized text additions didn't become a real problem until copyrighted material began to show up. Not wanting to be sued—and besides they had a healthy respect for the rights of authors, two of their number making their living as writers—they removed this material as soon as they became aware of it. But to no avail. It would simply reappear.

And then the storage sites disappeared from their servers.

You could still access the material by pointing your browser at www.thewordwood.com, but the Wordwood site itself now existed in some impossible limbo in between computers.

That's where magic happens, Christy had explained to her. Not here or there, but in between the two.

Holly was uncomfortable with the word magic, but there was no other word to explain what had happened with the Wordwood. It was now possible to have real-time conversations through the site with somebody who always seemed to be on-line, no matter what time of day or night you accessed it. More curiously, this somebody's style of communicating often echoed the voice and conversational mannerisms of someone the user had known. In Holly's case it was her grandmother, five years dead.

The Wordwood grew in enormous leaps and bounds, bibliographies and texts appearing on it at a prodigious rate. The copyrighted material all had some sort of complex protection on it so that while you could access it on-line, you couldn't read a work in its entirety, and you certainly couldn't download it.

If you tried, the Wordwood cut off your access to it. A message of explanation appeared on your screen:

> You have attempted to access copyrighted material beyond what is considered fair use. For that reason your privileges on this site have been terminated.

You lost a week's access for a first offence. A subsequent attempt to download copyrighted material barred you from the site permanently. And there was no getting around it. Logging on with a different user name, or even from someone else's computer using their I.D. and protocols, made no difference.

Sarah was unable to explain it.

It wasn't simply a text-based site anymore, either. The opening splash page had a background of what appeared to be real-time video now. It depicted an impossible forest, inhabited by the sorts of things you'd expect to find in the woods—squirrels and mice, songbirds and insects—but there were odder creatures in it as well. Sometimes you caught glimpses of hybrid beings—an owl with a man's face, a chipmunk with tiny human hands and fingers, a woman with moth wings. Or there were people that, when you saw them in context with a robin or a red squirrel, say, appeared to be no more than six or seven inches high.

The trees in the forest weren't of any species anyone could recognize— a simple enough feat if they'd simply been created on a computer and then animated. But Sarah said their details were too complex and random for animation—even with today's CGI technologies—and swore there were no loops in the video streaming. What they saw in the Wordwood's opening screen was real-time video—although real-time video of what forest, or where, she couldn't say.

And now it was gone.

Holly turned away from the computer and looked out the store's front window. She should be putting out the stock that had come in today— before Dick took it upon himself to do it for her—but she couldn't seem to muster the energy. Saturday was always a busy day in the store and today had been no exception. Helpful though Dick was behind the scenes, he left it to her to deal with the public. There were times today when it had gotten almost frantic, there were so many people in the store, each with a question, or wanting their purchase rung through, or change for the bus, or wanting her to go through their want list and recommend where they could get this or that title if she didn't have it in stock.

Many customers didn't seem to understand that in the secondary book market, she could only carry what people brought in to sell or trade. She couldn't simply order a book for them from Ingrams. Well, she could, but it would be a new book and they'd expect to buy it at a used price, and that wasn't going to happen in this lifetime. At least not in her store.

Most of the time, the book they were looking for was long out of print.

"How can it be out of print? I love this book."

She heard variations on that at least once a week, if not more, and wasn't unsympathetic. There were times when she, too, felt that a particular book being out of print was a personal affront. Still, there was nothing she could do about it except to explain the vagaries of the secondary book business and do a search for the book if the customer wanted her to, both of which took up time.

Dick didn't help with the on-line customers either, though he was happy to package the books to get them ready for Holly to take to the post office. Though that still left Holly working into the evening answering e-mail on days like today, when it had been too busy to get on the computer during store hours.

But she was almost finished now. She patted her lap and Snippet rose from her bed in the front display window and jumped onto her.

"Hey, you," she said, scratching the little dog behind the ear. "Just let me send these e-mails and we'll go for that walk."

The browser window explaining that the Wordwood site wasn't available was still open when she turned back to her computer.

Maybe the pixies were causing this current problem, Holly thought. They were certainly the reason that Dick wouldn't go near the store's computer. He was too afraid that they'd come bursting out of the screen once more to wreak havoc and mischief up and down the blocks neighbouring the store as they had the last time.

If Holly hadn't seen them with her own eyes, she might not have believed that they could exist. But she had. And they did. Though she didn't know why she should be so surprised. After all, she had a hob for a business partner. And then there was the whole mystery of the Wordwood . . .

Send the e-mail, she told herself. Go for a walk and then to bed.

She started to reach for her mouse, to bring the window with her e-mail program back on screen, then stopped. Something was happening in her browser window. Right in the middle of the screen, a small black dot had appeared. As she watched, it began to expand like the eye of a camera. On her lap, Snippet lifted her head. Whining, she returned to the window seat. An inexplicable uneasiness came over Holly.

She set Snippet back in her bed in the front display window and looked around for Dick—not directly, but out of the corner of her eye. Dick had this trick where he could sit so still, he as much as became invisible to people. Even Holly wasn't completely immune to it and she'd known him for ages now, though once she caught a glimpse of him from the corner of her eye, she could hold him in sight thereafter. Strangers simply didn't register his presence.

This time she found him curled up in the club chair that stood at the end of one of the bookcases, reading, of course.

"Dick," she said. "Come and look at this."

He put down his book and joined her behind the desk—as usual, making it obvious how reluctant he was to be this close to the computer. Holly took off her glasses and gave them a quick cleaning on her shirt tails. Making room for Dick in front of the monitor, she put them on again and looked over his shoulder. The dot on her screen was still growing bigger.

Dick appeared to be mesmerized by it. He started to reach a hand toward the monitor.

"What do you think it is?" Holly asked. "Because I'll tell you, it's giving me the creeps and I don't know why."

Her voice made him start and he pulled his hand away from the screen as though he'd been about to put it on a hot stove burner.

"Dick?"

He gave her a worried look that made her uneasiness grow.

"Oh, this is bad, Mistress Holly," he said.

He dropped to the floor, scrabbling around in the nest of wires that were clustered around the power bar under the desk. Behind them, Holly could hear Snippet growling from her bed in the window.

"Which cord is it?" Dick muttered.

"Which cord is what?"

Holly glanced at the monitor to see that the black dot filled almost two thirds of the screen now. When Dick looked up and followed her gaze, he grabbed the power bar itself and gave it a wild yank. The computer went dead. The monitor, now blank, tottered on the edge of the desk—pulled off-balance because its power cord was still plugged into the bar in Dick's hand. Holly made a grab for the monitor, but she was too late. It fell to the floor, its cheap plastic casing exploding on impact.

Snippet bounded out of the window and circled the broken monitor, barking and growling at it.

Dick stood up again, still holding the power bar. His big eyes had gone bigger than ever, his lips forming an "O." He turned to Holly with such a woebegone look on his face that she wanted to bend down and give him a hug. But though Dick was small, she knew better than to try to comfort him as she might a child. He was older than her. A lot older. How much, she couldn't begin to guess. Yet there was still a childlike innocence about him, especially in moments such as this.

"I . . . I didn't mean . . ."

"It's okay," she told him.

The monitor was broken now and its tumble off the desk couldn't be taken back. There was no point in making Dick feel worse about it.

"What was happening?" she asked. "Why did you have to kill the power to the computer so quickly?"

Dick let the power bar drop to the floor.

"There . . . there was something trying to get out," he explained.

"What kind of something?"

Having once had that gang of pixies come flooding out of her monitor, Holly wasn't about to argue the impossibility of something else trying to get out as well.

"I don't know for sure," Dick said. "Not exactly bad. But wild. And hungry for . . . something."

"Like the pixies."

He shook his head. "Whatever this was, it was far bigger and stronger than a pixie." He turned to her. "It had me charmed as sure as a snake can charm a bird, Mistress Holly. If you hadn't spoken up and broken the spell . . . I don't know what would have happened. But nothing good. I can tell you that."

"But it's gone now?"

"I think so. I don't feel it anymore—do you?"

Holly shook her head. "But I didn't feel anything in the first place. Just a kind of uneasiness. Snippet, come here!" she added, calling to where the dog was still growling at the monitor.

"I think maybe you shouldn't use your computer for awhile," Dick said.

Holly nodded, not bothering to mention that, without a monitor, she couldn't anyway. Dick was only just starting to look a little less distraught about having broken it in the first place.

Snippet stood expectantly at her feet. Sitting down, Holly patted her lap and the little dog jumped up.

"This something you're talking about," she said to Dick, soothing Snippet with a scratch behind the ear. "It's loose in the Net, isn't it? Like the pixies were."

"Except if it gets free . . ."

"We're in bigger trouble than we were then. Okay. So we stay off the Net. What about phone lines? Do you think it'd be safe to make a call?"

"You could try."

Holly reached for the phone. She felt nervous picking up the receiver, then stupid for feeling nervous, but that didn't stop the uneasiness. She held the receiver so that both she and Dick could listen to the dial tone.

"What do you think?" she asked.

"I don't sense anything—not like I did when the computer was on-line."

"Okay, then," Holly said and she began to punch in a number. "Time to call in an exorcist—or at least the closest to one that I know."

Christy Riddell

I've really been caught up with a new book these days that's got me doing research into the mysteries inhabiting the World Wide Web: everything from spirits and ghosts to the new urban legends that have grown up around the use of computers—especially when they're connected to each other through the Internet and e-mail.

Jilly says I should call it *Spirits in the Wires,* but that doesn't strike me as accurate enough for my purposes. I don't see spirits haunting the hardware—the circuits and wiring, the actual technology—so much as using the hardware to get around. They ride the software, cables, and telephone lines, and make homes for themselves in the spaces that lie in between the various computers that the technology connects. Science fiction writers call those territories cyberspace, but I think of it all as a kind of voodoo. *Les invisibles* finding a more contemporary host to ride.

For these aren't new spirits—at least not from what I can tell. They're the same magical beings of the woods and fields and waters wild that first made a journey from their rural origins to more urban settings, and have now moved into the technologies of the future. They'll probably follow us into space.

Not all of them, of course. Just the more adventurous, the strongest— those with the same characteristics that human explorers need when they leave the safety of the Fields We Know to strike out into unknown territories.

I first started keeping notes on these more recent phenomena after I became aware of the anomalies surrounding the Wordwood and Saskia's connection to it. Holly's adventure with the pixies only served to convince me I was on the track of something new and worthwhile of my interest.

It's funny. The more computer literate among my friends have been telling me odd stories about the Internet and new technologies for years, but it's only in past few months that I'm paying attention to them. I almost feel like I'm coming too late into the game, since any number of urban legends have already grown up on the Internet, spreading as quickly as wildfire viruses. Or at least warnings about viruses. But people studied fairies and ghosts for centuries before I took it up and I'm still finding new things to write about. Better late than never.

Considering how much I've always loved legends—urban or ancient— I don't know why I didn't clue into these contemporary changes in folklore and myth sooner. Even when I was a kid I was drawn to this sort of thing. For a long time, cataloguing and tracking the stories that slip between the cracks of fact and history was my only real escape from a boyhood that was otherwise filled with unhappiness and discouragement.

But I guess I have a bit of a Luddite's aversion to technology. When I finally start to use something new, it's already old hat for everybody else. Or at least everybody on the cutting edge. By the time I got a fax machine, everybody else was using e-mail. My tech friends all have cell phones and handheld computers like Palms and iPAQs. I still prefer to use a phone booth if I'm away from home and write in the hardback journal that goes everywhere I do.

But now that I've found the connection to my earlier, more traditional studies of the odd, curious, and just plain strange, I've become completely absorbed by technology and its own particular take on the paranormal. It's all I want to think about and research. So, of course, just as I'm starting to get some real leads on new avenues to explore, a set of galleys shows up from Alan that he says he needs back last week.

Probably the worst thing about the business of being a writer is correcting galleys. These are the typeset page proofs the publisher sends to you for final corrections that are supposed to incorporate all of the corrections and changes that were made during the various editing and copyediting processes. At least it's the worst part for me. I like everything else, from researching and tracking down sources, through the actual writing and editing, to finally sitting in some bookstore and chatting with my readers. But the galleys . . .

By the time I'm at this point in the procedure, I've seen the words too many times and find myself wanting to change things simply for the sake of having something different to look at. You can't of course. Instead you sit there, bored stiff while you go through the mind-numbing task, trying not to get too cranky.

I'm not very good at the not getting too cranky part. Which, I guess, explains why Saskia's "I'm just dropping by the café for an hour or so" earlier in the evening was actually code for "I'm going out for the night; I hope you've finished this by the time I get back."

I wish I could be, but no such luck. I may not enjoy correcting galleys, but I take the time to do the job right. I'll be at this through next week. So when she gets back to the apartment—close on midnight, by the clock on my bookshelf—I've only got another couple of chapters done.

"How's it coming?" she asks from the door of my study.

"Swimmingly," I tell her.

"That bad?"

"No, it's just tedious. You know what it's like."

She nods, having gone through this with her poetry collections and the freelance writing she does.

"But I'm done for today," I say.

I straighten the stack of loose galley pages I've been working on, tapping them on the top of the desk to get them all aligned, then set them down in a neat stack. I'm terrible about that sort of thing, which is probably why Jilly got me that T-shirt that reads "Is there a hyphen in anal-retentive?" I don't wear it. I keep it folded up with all the other joke T-shirts people give me that I'll probably never wear. And yes, I see the irony in that. But I've always been somewhat of a compulsive tidier. I might have all sorts of books lying around, waiting to be read or put away on the bookshelves, but they're all stacked in orderly piles, often sorted by category and in alphabetical order.

Saskia settles in one of the two club chairs by the bookcases and puts her feet up on the ottoman. I turn off the light on my desk and join her, sitting in the other chair, sharing the ottoman with my own feet.

"So how was your evening?" I ask, tapping a foot against hers.

"Interesting. I met your shadow at the Beanery Café."

"Really? That seems like an odd place to run into her."

Though when it comes to my shadow, odd is usually the norm. She's the sort of person that you can never figure out what she's thinking, what she'll say, or where you'll meet her next. Even when she's forthcoming, I still usually come away from our conversations wearing a cloud of confusion. It's part of the reason I call her Mystery.

"I know," Saskia says. "It's weird to think of her hanging out in such a mundane place, isn't it? Though of course she fit right in."

I have to smile. "She fits in wherever she goes. I think environments adjust themselves to suit her rather than the other way around."

"I wish I could do that," Saskia says. "I feel like it's just the other way for me."

I give her a puzzled look.

She sighs. "Your shadow and I got talking about where we came from and that reminded me of that first morning I woke up in this world and how hard it was for me to fit in."

I nod. We've talked about this before.

"And it started me thinking again about who I am and where I came from. If I'm even real."

"It doesn't matter where you came from," I tell her. "You're real now."

"Am I? Isn't part of being real knowing where you came from? I'm like an adopted kid. It doesn't matter how happy your life is, if you don't know your parents—if you don't know *anything* about your origin—you're living with this black hole underlying who you are. And not all the platitudes in the world can make it go away."

"But you know your origin. You've said you were born in the Wordwood."

She nods. "And how weird is *that*? How *real* is that? How can a real person be born in a Web site?"

"I don't know. But you're here now." I touch her arm. "You feel real."

"Your shadow thinks I should go to the source with my questions," she says.

"You mean to the Wordwood?"

"Where else?"

"I guess. It seems to answer any question you put to it." I put my feet down from the ottoman. Sitting up, I look at my computer over on the desk. "I suppose we can see if it's come back on-line again."

"What do you mean?"

"The site's been down all week."

Saskia shakes her head wearily. "And I never even knew. What does that say about my so-called connection to it?"

"You said it cut you loose."

"Or I cut myself loose. But going on-line wasn't exactly what I had in mind. Your shadow says she can take me into the otherworld. That we can find the Wordwood on its own ground."

"Wait a minute. The Wordwood exists in the otherworld?"

"She seems to think it does."

"As what? A place? A person?"

Saskia shrugs. "Who knows? Maybe as some combination of both."

"This is getting too weird."

"And me being born in a Web site isn't?"

"You know what I mean. The Wordwood's a human construct—the product of software and HTML language. How can it exist in the other-world?"

Saskia just looks at me. "Maybe it doesn't—at least not most of the time. But if it has spirit, then the spiritworld would seem to be the easiest place to find it."

"Yes, but . . ."

"It's just a kind of magic," Saskia says. "The same magic that allowed me to walk in the world, clothed in flesh and bone."

"I guess . . ."

Truth is, I'm never one hundred percent certain that Saskia's origin is quite so exotic as she accepts it is. I know that she believes it. And there are days when I believe it, too. All I have to do is to remember how it was when I first met her. She used to be like a walking encyclopedia, able to quote amazing references at the drop of a hat, but not seeming to have had first-hand experience with something so simple as hot chocolate.

But for my all normally ready acceptance that there's more to this world than we can see—than we *expect* to see—I have a cynic living in my head as well as the believer. He's the one who insists that ghosts and spirits are delusions. That what we have here, is all there is. There's more? he asks. Then prove it. Show me.

When I listen to him, I can't imagine a Web site giving birth to a living, breathing human being. For that matter, there are times when Saskia's as much a skeptic as the cynic in my head. But this, apparently, isn't one of them.

"Okay," I say after a moment. "But let's at least check out the source by more conventional means first."

I get up and cross the room to my desk, starting up the computer. The machine's up and running by the time Saskia joins me. She stands behind my chair, hands on my shoulders. I click on my dial-up icon, the modem dials the number, and soon we're listening to the familiar squawk and buzz of the computer connecting to my ISP.

After I open Explorer and enter the Wordwood's URL, the error message I've been getting all week comes up in my browser window. I start to close my connection.

"What's that?" Saskia says.

She leans over my shoulder, the point of her index finger going to a small black dot that's appeared in the middle of my browser window. I have this flash of premonition, but before I can stop her, her fingertip touches the screen.

Have you ever seen a firecracker fuse burn? That's what it's like with her, except the detonation comes first. There's this flash of—I don't know what. Like an electrical discharge. It blows me off my chair, against the wall, and knocks the breath out of me. But I can still see what's happening to her from where I'm lying.

A flare of white hot light runs up her finger, her hand, her arm, her shoulder, travelling the length of her body. Like a fuse. But instead of leaving behind a string of ash, it leaves behind a pixelated version of her, like she's no longer solid and I can see all the molecules of her body. It's like the difference in seeing a painting, then seeing a photo of it in a newspaper where it's made up of thousands of little dots of colour.

I try to scramble to my feet, but my limbs are numbed and jellied and they won't hold me.

Saskia gives me a look—a haunting, desperate look. Then the computer just shatters and collapses into itself. One moment the monitor and keyboard are on my desk, the tower on the floor beside it, the next they're just the heaps of broken plastic, circuitry, and wiring.

Saskia reaches for me. But it isn't Saskia anymore. It's this human shape made up of thousands of flickering tiny pellets of shadow and light.

I call her name, try again to get to my feet. I hear a telephone dialing, as though somewhere in the wreckage of my computer the modem's trying to reconnect to my ISP. Then Saskia's gone and the room is so still the silence hurts.

I manage to crawl to where she'd been standing, stupidly patting the floor as though she's hidden on the carpet like a fallen pin or paperclip. But there's nothing there. She's gone. Swallowed back into the Internet from which I'd only half-believed she'd been born. Swallowed back into the Wordwood, and I don't have the slightest idea how to get her back.

The loss of her swells through me like a tsunami, threatening to tear me apart, and all I can do is press my forehead against the carpet where, only a moment ago, she was standing.

Christiana

I'm pretending to sleep when the phone rings.

I suppose that sounds odd—not the phone ringing, but my pretending to sleep. The thing is, I don't need to sleep, or even eat, but I do both anyway. It's one of the first things Mumbo taught me when I strayed over into the borderlands.

"It will help make you feel normal," she told me. "And if you feel normal—if you act and appear normal—then other people won't treat you differently."

I didn't think it was so important then, but being treated like a freak gets old fast. So I learned to eat and drink. And while I don't need the sustenance, I love the flavours that tickle across my taste buds when I do partake. A basil and tomato sandwich. Hot Mexican salsa. Squash soup. Strong coffee. A glass of red wine.

And more rarely, I sleep.

When I do, I think I actually *am* sleeping, because sometimes when I close my eyes, I go away. Time vanishes into the same black hole it does for people whose bodies require them to sleep. And sometimes, when I'm in that black hole of sleep, I dream.

That's what's happening when the phone starts to ring. I feel thick-headed and confused as the beep-beep of the cell phone pulls me out of a confusing mélange of images and sensations. Traces linger in my head as I look for the phone. Something to do with monkeys having a high tea and the Vegas Elvis, sweaters being worn backwards and flying—no I can't fly, though I'd dearly love to be able to. Even the talent to shapechange into a bird would be welcome.

The monkeys were humming an off-key rendition of a Beatles song—"Strawberry Fields," I think—and Elvis was ignoring them as he dipped a deep-fried scone into his tea. I remember being fascinated by the oily film that formed on the surface of his tea and trying to figure out why. When he took the scone out, it made this sound like a truck backing up.

But it was only the phone.

I finally spot it across the meadow, lying on the fat arm of the club chair where I tossed my clothes before going to sleep. Getting out of bed, I shuffle barefoot across the grass to the chair, wondering who it could possibly be. I hardly ever get calls on it because only a handful of people know the number. Maxie. Tom Stone—the only lover I ever managed to stay good friends with. Mumbo—though she never calls. And now Saskia.

I pick the phone up, find the "on" button, and lift the phone to my ear. It takes me a moment to recognize the odd sound I'm hearing. It's like a bad recording of wind blowing through the topmost branches of a forest—rasping and harsh, full of pops and crackling.

"Hello?" I say.

"..."

The response is so faint I'm not sure I actually heard anything.

"Hello?" I try again. "Is anybody there?"

The voice comes to me as though from a radio station that's not quite tuned in. Raspy, unrecognizable.

"Please . . ."

I press the phone more closely to my ear, as though that's going to make the voice louder.

"Let . . . me . . . in . . ."

I know enough about the hidden worlds beyond the World As It Is to know that it's not only vampires that need permission to enter a safe place. And though I also know better, I still find myself saying, "Yes."

There's this one dark moment where everything feels wrong. I find myself remembering a conversation I had with Christy once about the odd motivations of the characters in fairy tales, when there even is a motivation.

"Why do they do these things?" I said. "Why does the third son go on what he believes is a doomed quest? Why does the farmer boy want to marry the princess? What could they possibly have in common?"

"Who says they have a choice?" he told me.

That's what my saying "yes" feels like. Like I had no choice. Like some enchantment came through the phone's receiver and I had to welcome it into me.

I have time to think of all of that, with the underpinning impression that something's very wrong. It's like an accident, where everything's speeding up and slowing down at the same time. It's going so slow that you're aware of every nuance. You have time to replay a conversation, look across the meadow that carpets your living room floor to the fields beyond. But it's also happening so fast that you can't even begin to stop it.

There's no time for me to drop the phone. I can't take the word back.

Something like an electric shock erupts from the receiver and flashes into my ear. My hair stands upright—all my hair, from the tangle on my head to the tiny ones on my arms. My head fills with the radio static, amplified to such a volume that it's a hurricane of white noise.

Then everything goes away, me included.

Holly

Dick was miserable.

Holly had tried to cheer him up. She'd taken him with her when she went out to let Snippet do her business and even let him do the honours with the plastic bag after said business was done in the empty lot at the end of the block. When they got back, she let him clean up the mess that the monitor had made when it crashed to the floor. But not even cleaning and tidying seemed to help. So she made him a mug of tea, English Breakfast with a splash of whiskey in it, just the way he liked it. That didn't seem to help either.

He was convinced the whole business was his fault—though how that could be, he couldn't explain.

"You saved the day," she told him for about the tenth time.

They were sitting behind the desk in the store, drinking their tea.

"If it hadn't been for you," she went on, "whatever that thing was would have come right out of the monitor and swallowed us both."

She wasn't sure if that was exactly the case. She just knew that magical beings were able to step out of the Internet into the real world, as witness their invasion by a gang of vandalizing pixies a year or so ago. So if something dark and scary had been about to pounce forth this evening, Dick really had saved the day. The trouble was, Dick found any number of things dark and scary—from television shows and certain kinds of pies, to the customers that patronized the store. Considering some of the odd birds that came in, Holly could sympathize with the latter.

"But I broke your monitor, Mistress Holly," Dick said.

"Thereby saving us."

"But it's all broken and now you can't do your work on the computer."

"Hello? I can't do any work on it anyway because of creepy things that are just a modem dial-up away, waiting to pounce on us."

"But still—"

"But still, nothing. You're a veritable hero and I wish you'd stop feeling otherwise."

Dick only gave his head a mournful shake and stared into the inch or so of liquid left at the bottom of his cup. Holly sighed. She gave the phone a look, willing it to ring, but it was obstinately silent.

Dick had lent a hand when it came to figuring out a way to get the pixies out of Holly's neighbourhood and back into the Internet, but he hadn't been Holly's main source of help. That had come from a woman named Meran Kelledy, one half of a musical husband-and-wife duo who had been playing for years around the city, when they weren't touring further afield. Holly had met her the same week that all the trouble with the pixies began, and they'd become friends since then.

She was a lovely woman, attractive and smart. The sort of woman who turned heads as much for her charisma as for her trim figure, dark, wise eyes, and her waterfall of brown hair with its surprising green streaks. Dick seemed to think of her as some sort of faerie royalty and was in awe of her whenever she came by the store, but Holly didn't see her that way at all. Meran was simply good company, easy to talk to and as normal as anyone else, except she seemed to know an inordinate amount about things magical and folkloric, and how they were presently colliding with the modern technological age.

So it was Meran that Holly called from the store after the computer monitor had smashed on the floor, but no one had picked up at the other end of the line. She'd had to leave a message on the Kelledys' answering machine.

"What will we do?" Dick said, still not lifting his gaze from the bottom of his mug, although Holly noted that it was now completely empty.

"Replenish our drinks?" she asked. "Or go to bed and see if everything looks the same in the morning?"

"The monitor will still be broken."

"Yes, I know. I just meant perhaps things will feel different in the morning. We can call some other people and—"

Holly broke off as someone rapped on the glass of the door behind them. Turning, she expected to see Meran. It was something Meran would do—come directly by, rather than return Holly's earlier phone call. But a stranger stood there under the outdoor light on the other side of the store's front door. A wonderfully handsome stranger. He looked like Holly's romantic notions of a Gypsy: dark-eyed, with a tangle of shoulder-length, crow-black hair pushed back from his brow and small gold hoop earrings in each lobe. His baggy white cotton shirt added to the Romany look, even if it was tucked into a pair of ordinary blue jeans.

When he caught her gaze, he gave her a rakish smile and lifted his hand in greeting. Holly felt like melting. She wasn't the sort to be swayed so easily by a handsome face—she saw at least one good-looking man every day, operating a store that was open to the general public as she did—but something about this stranger had her all flustered and warm. She brought a hand to her hair, all too aware of how the red strands were spilling out every which way from where they'd been gathered in a loose bun at the nape of her neck this morning. She wasn't wearing any make-up—not even lipstick. And why in god's name had she changed into a pair of old cut-off jeans and her oldest flannel shirt after the store had closed?

Because, common sense said, as it did its best to quiet the sudden jump in her pulse, she wasn't expecting visitors. It was late at night. And handsome though the man was, he was still a stranger and it was long past store hours. He could be anyone. He could be dangerous.

Holly was aware of that and more. Still, she put her glasses down on the desk, got up and went to the door all the same.

"Yes?" she asked through the glass. "Can I help you?"

She couldn't hear a word he said in response, but then she doubted he'd heard her either. It was more a matter of them reading each other's lips. When she saw his—very full for a man, but not remotely effete, and oh, just look at the lashes above those gorgeous eyes—shape Meran's name, she happily threw caution to the winds and unlocked the door. Opening it just enough to pop her head out, she caught a strong whiff of apples and cinnamon. God, he even smelled good.

"What were you saying?" she asked.

"I'm taking care of Meran's place," the stranger said. "While she and Cerin are out of town."

"And that brings you here because . . . ?"

"The message you left on their machine. You sounded pretty upset so I thought I'd come by to see if you needed a hand."

His voice was perfect, too, warm and resonant. Then she realized what he'd said. Oh god. He'd heard her babbling about pixies and something weird trying to come out of her monitor?

"Are you all right?" he asked.

Only mortified, she thought. But she gave a quick nod.

"So everything's under control now?"

"Yes. I mean, no. I mean . . ." She sighed. "How do you know Meran?"

"We're sort of distant cousins."

"Sort of?"

"On her husband's side."

"So then you're not really related."

"Well, in a way I am. To Cerin's Aunt Jen. But I'm not really blood kin to any of them." He gave her another one of those rakish smiles. "It's more of a tribal thing."

Holly regarded him for a long moment. The only way he could have heard her message was if he was in the Kelledy's house. And if he was in their house, she supposed he must be trustworthy. Burglars and serial killers didn't take the time to listen to their victims' answering machines, did they?

She stepped aside and held the door open for him.

"You might as well come in," she said. "The least I can do is offer you a cup of tea after coming out all this way at such a late hour."

"Thank you," he said.

He looked past her to where Snippet was sitting up, alert, but showing no signs of alarm at the stranger coming in. That he passed whatever test it was that the Jack Russell had for strangers boded well. Snippet was good during the day—you never heard a peep out of her. But once the store was closed for business she became fiercely territorial to anyone she didn't like, or at least didn't recognize.

"Hello, dog," the stranger said.

Holly was surprised to see Snippet's tail begin to wag. Then she was surprised even more when the stranger's gaze continued to where Dick was sitting.

"And good evening to you, Master Hob," he added.

Dick gave him a small nervous nod in response.

"You can see him?" Holly said.

The stranger turned to look at her, eyebrows lifting. "You can't?"

"Of course I can. It's just that most people . . ."

She let her voice trail off and covered up the increased awkwardness she was feeling by closing and locking the door once more.

"We're having tea with whiskey in it," she said when she turned back to him.

"Sounds perfect," the stranger said. "Although perhaps I'll forgo the tea part, if I may. Tea usually keeps me up all night."

Holly smiled. "I'm Holly," she said and offered her hand. "Though I guess you already know that from the phone call."

"Borrible Jones," he told her.

His grip was firm, his hand callused, both distracting Holly until she realized what he'd said. She couldn't have heard that right.

"I'm sorry?" she said.

He grinned. "I am, too. But what can you do? My friends call me Bojo."

"But—"

"The name. I know. There are any number of theories as to its origin. One is that my father was a poet who didn't like children so he named me to have something to rhyme with 'horrible.' Another is that he was too fond of Michael de Larrabeiti's books."

Holly gave him a blank look.

"You know," Bojo said. "The author of the Borrible books? Borribles were these fictional residents of London? Sort of like little feral Peter Pans?"

Holly nodded. "I knew that."

"Of course you would. You own a bookstore."

"So you don't know who your father is?"

"Never met the man," Bojo said.

"That seems very sad." Holly'd had a wonderful relationship with her own father until he'd passed away a few years ago. "I'm sorry."

"Me, too. I'd love to have known what he was thinking."

"And your mother . . . ?"

"Would rarely speak of him."

Holly didn't know what to say. Finally she settled on, "Let me get you that whiskey."

She felt she needed a whole tumbler of it herself.

There wasn't room for all of them behind the desk, so they took their drinks and went upstairs to Holly and Dick's apartment above the store. There were as many books on shelves, in piles and boxes and hidden under furniture, up here in her living room as there were downstairs. The difference was, these weren't for sale. At least not yet.

Bojo settled into an easy sprawl on the sofa, reminding Holly of a cat, the way he could so quickly look as though he'd been relaxing there for hours. Dick perched on the other end of the sofa, holding his mug in both hands. Though he appeared to be using it to warm himself, it hadn't been refilled yet. Holly made some more tea, then pulled a chair over from the dining room table and sat down herself. Snippet, after following Holly from room to room as she made the tea, settled now under Holly's chair, curling up in a ball with her head turned so that she could watch Bojo.

"So you're having pixie trouble," Bojo said.

Holly shook her head. "Had. Do you know much about pixies?"

"Well, that depends. They're like a kind of bodach, aren't they? But malicious rather than tricksey."

Holly had no idea what a bodach was, but Dick was nodding in agreement.

"All their fun's mean," he said. "I've never heard of one with a kind thought or doing a kind deed."

"Whereas a bodach can be quite friendly—like a brownie or you hobs. At least that's what they're like where I'm from."

Holly was good at picking things up out of context and felt she was safe in assuming that a bodach was yet another kind of little fairy man. But the conversation between Dick and the stranger made her wonder where it was that such knowledge was so common.

"Where exactly are you from?" she asked.

"Where? Everywhere and nowhere. We were always travelling, and I still do. We Kelledys have always been a travelling people."

"You're tinkers, aren't you?" Dick said. "Like in Ireland."

Bojo shook his head. "We're tinkers, but of an older tribe than the Irish."

"But you said your name was Jones," Holly said.

"It is. Kelledy's a tribal name, used by most of us. But my mam was a Jones when Aunt Jen adopted us, and I stay a Jones in her memory."

Holly had a hundred more questions. Even the normally shy Dick appeared to be bubbling with curiosity for a change. But before either of them could speak, Bojo sat up a little straighter. He took a sip of his whiskey, regarded the pair of them for a long moment, then said, "Tell me about the pixies."

So Holly did, with Dick filling in the bits she left out. And when they were done with that story, they moved on to what had happened earlier in the evening.

"I guess we just got spooked," Holly said when they got to the end of that story. "After the business with the pixies and all, I mean. You wouldn't believe the havoc they created around here in just one night."

"Oh, I can imagine," Bojo said.

"So you *have* seen them before."

He shook his head. "Only the messes they've left behind. And I've heard the stories, of course."

Like that was the sort of thing that ordinary people talked about around the water cooler. The weather, the stock market, pixies . . . Not that she could ever imagine Bojo standing around a water cooler or holding any sort of a regular job. Though she supposed he must. Everybody had to do something for a living.

"I think you were wise to be careful," Bojo said, making Holly bring her thoughts back to the matter at hand. "I smelled the otherworld as soon as I stepped into the store, and it wasn't because of you, Master Hob."

"Oh, it was a spirit, all right," Dick said. "All set to come popping out of the screen. Old and dark and powerful."

Bojo shook his head. "Powerful, yes. But I sensed something young. Something new. Something the world has never seen before."

"Is that good or bad?" Holly asked.

"I don't know that it's either. Most spirits are like the weather, neither good nor bad. They simply are. They live their lives without concern for us. We're the ones to complain about a storm blowing down our barn, a drought ruining our crops."

So, Holly thought, still looking for clues about her visitor. If he was using farms as analogies, maybe he was from a rural background.

"But they're not all like that," Dick said.

"No," Bojo agreed. "There are also a number that delight to interfere in the lives of the likes of you and me. And unfortunately, they're usually . . . the less pleasant of their kind."

"But what do they want?" Holly asked.

Bojo shrugged. "Who can tell? Sometimes we're simply in the way, and they deal with us the way we would a gnat—brushing us away, squishing us between their fingers. Sometimes they're hungry."

Holly didn't like the sound of that at all.

"They want to *eat* us?"

"It's more a matter of the spirit," Bojo said. "You know, our life energy. Some spirits consider it sustenance."

This was getting worse by the minute.

"Can you help us?" she asked. "Is there anything we can do to get it out of the Internet and back to wherever it came from?"

Bojo had some more of his whiskey.

"I know next to nothing about computers," he said. "But I do know spirits. The first question we need to ask ourselves is, did it, in fact, come from somewhere else, or is it native to the Internet?"

"What do you mean?" Holly said.

She glanced at Dick and saw her own confusion mirrored in his face.

"Well, from what I understand," Bojo said, "the Internet is much like a realm unto itself. Would that be a fair assessment?"

"I guess . . ."

"Then it would seem logical that it would have its own life forms and spirits."

"But we're talking about a place that doesn't exist except as code in the files of a service provider's computers. Bits and bytes. It's nothing tangible."

"And yet the pixies have managed to find a way to travel in that realm. And then there's the whole matter of the Wordwood and the spirit you said had come to inhabit it."

Holly gave a slow nod. "I guess that's what makes me feel I have to do something. We—my friends and I—created the Wordwood. If it somehow gained sentience through what we did, then we're responsible for that as well."

"So the other question we need to answer is this," Bojo said. "Has the Wordwood gone feral, or is it under attack itself?"

"When you put it like that . . . it sounds so insane."

Bojo nodded. "It's a long way from anything I understand, too. But we'll just have to do what we can. There are people who should be able to help us. It's only a matter of tracking them down and seeing what they know."

"And I'll do the same with Sarah and the others that were in on the Wordwood from the start." She paused for a moment, then added, "I'm really glad you came along. My friends might know a lot about computers, but when it comes to the other stuff, we're in way over our heads. This sort of thing is too weird to deal with on our own and with Meran out of town . . . I guess I just want to say thanks. Really."

"I couldn't very well walk away, leaving the friend of my cousin to face this on her own." He held up his glass and added, "You wouldn't have any more of this lovely whiskey, would you?"

Holly went to fetch the bottle and poured a splash into each of their cups, this time forgoing the tea in hers and Dick's.

"I feel good about this," she said. "Like we have a real chance to beat this thing."

Bojo smiled. "We can only try."

They clinked their glasses together in a toast.

Holly was still smiling when she came back upstairs from letting Bojo out. She said goodnight to a somewhat bleary-eyed Dick and scooping up Snippet, went into her room. She paused for a moment, then went and unplugged her phone. She doubted anything would come across an ordinary phone line—and after all, she'd used it without any problem earlier to leave the message on Meran's machine—but why take chances?

Christy

There's nothing in the research I've been doing on the Web to explain what's happened to Saskia. That's not so surprising, I suppose, since there's also nothing to explain the mystery of her origin—something I'm not even remotely questioning now. The only big question for me now is, how do I get her back?

I still can't believe she's gone.

I've spent the past hour torn between despair and determination and not really able to do a lot about either. All my notes were on the computer that's now lying in pieces all over my desk and on the floor below it—a war zone, in miniature. I have backups of everything on Zip discs—multiple backups, since I'm as organized about that as I am about everything, especially after the time Sophie managed to crash my computer and I did lose a few weeks of work. But I don't have a computer to access the discs.

I need another computer.

I need Saskia back.

I need help.

But it's almost three A.M. Who am I going to call at this hour—especially with the story I've got to tell? Where are the Ghostbusters when you really need them?

I've got a long list of like-minded colleagues and friends, but their expertise lies mostly in the more traditional forms of the paranormal and folklore, and many of them have less access to modern conveniences—like a phone—than I do. There's also my new network of research sources on the Web—folks I've only met electronically through newsgroups—but I need a working computer to contact any of them. The worst thing is that, at this point in time, I'm the only one I know who's pulled together so many disparate threads of techno rumour, folklore, and gossip, and tried to find a correlation between them all.

I'm my own best expert and I don't have a clue what to do next.

I could call Jilly. She's been playing with the professor's computer since her accident, poking around with her usual intuitive sense that lets her home in on things strange and different, but I hate to bother her while she's still recovering. It's been over a year now since the accident, but she still tires quickly and needs her rest. And besides, much as I love her, she's a bit too scattershot for the kind of focus I need right now. Not to mention that she's even less technologically inclined than I was before I got into this current research. She knows how to turn the computer on and go on-line. She can use a Web browser and e-mail. She's been playing with a paint program that Wendy installed on the machine for her. But she hasn't a clue how any of it actually works. So she's out, too.

Anybody else is just going to think I'm crazy.

I decide on my brother Geordie. He'll still think I'm crazy, but at least he'll listen because of Saskia. Not only did he first introduce her to me, but he knows as well as I do that it's because of her that he and I have been a lot more successful at keeping the lines of communication open between us.

It's not that we didn't talk before Saskia came into my life. We just didn't talk about anything important. We were going through the motions of being brothers, desperate to not have our relationship be as screwed up as it is with the rest of our family, but not having the first clue how to go about it with any real success. Honesty was missing from the equation. Along with an inability to express the fact that, even after all we've been through—or maybe because of it, since we at least came out of our messed up childhoods relatively intact—we really cared about each other.

That's something we never got to do with our older brother Paddy. He died in prison. They say he hung himself, and all the evidence points towards it, but all these years later, it's still hard to believe. Of the three of us, I always thought he was the most resilient. The one who'd carry on and make something of himself. Instead he ended up in jail and died there. Just goes to show how little you can know about someone supposedly so close to you.

I'm still a wreck when Geordie arrives at my door. In the time between calling him and his arrival, I've been to the corner store and bought a pack of smokes. He gives the smoldering cigarette in my hand a look, but to his credit, he doesn't say anything. He knows I'd given quitting another shot—six months and counting this time. He also knows I have to be pretty messed up to have started up again.

"So what happened?" he asks as he comes in.

I close the door behind him and follow him into the kitchen. I've already got a pot of coffee brewing. That's what the Riddells do when there's a crisis. Head for the kitchen and make coffee.

I don't know how to start, so I pour us each a mug of the coffee and bring them over to the table where he's already sitting. I light a new cigarette from the stub of the old one and grind the butt out in the saucer I'm using for an ashtray.

"Did you have a fight?" Geordie asks.

All I told him over the phone was that Saskia was gone and I didn't know if she'd ever be back. He didn't ask any questions. He just said, "I'll be right over." But I know what he's thinking.

My therapist used to call the way our relationships fall apart a self-fulfilling prophecy that was rooted in low self-esteem—yet one more holdover from our childhood, where nothing we could do was right, or good enough. Geordie and I both have this problem with women: We set our sights too high—or at least on women we perceive as too good for us. It's like we need the pedestals and can only yearn after the impossible women. In school it was the prom queens and cheerleaders who had no time for kids like us, hicks bussed in from the country. And we just carried that misconception along with us after high school.

We weren't completely pathetic. But even when we did find some special woman who wanted to be with us, in the end, they always left—often under weird circumstances.

For Geordie there was Sam, pure cheerleader material, but also smart and hip. She fell into the past one day—literally. She got swallowed into the early part of the century so that we weren't even born by the time she died in her new life. Then there was Tanya, a movie star with a one-time drug problem. Geordie was there for her when she could have slipped back into her old junkie ways, got her on her feet and back doing what she loved to

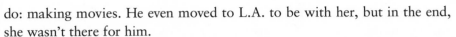

do: making movies. He even moved to L.A. to be with her, but in the end, she wasn't there for him.

Of course everybody knows he should be with Jilly, he's been carrying a torch for her forever and they'd be a perfect couple, but he waited too long on that and now she's with Daniel.

Before Saskia, I wasn't doing much better. The archetypal Christy Riddell romance was with a woman named Tallulah. I called her Tally. Everything was perfect, except she turned out to be the literal spirit of the city. She left me because she said the city was getting to be too hard, so she needed to be hard, too, to survive. Loving me was making her too soft.

Of the three of us, only Paddy had normal relationships—at least so far as we could tell. "Yeah, and look where that got him," I said to the therapist when she brought that up. She just shook her head and asked me, did I want to talk about that?

"No, it was nothing like that," I tell Geordie now. "We don't fight."

"Then what? There has to be some reason that she just up and left you."

"I don't know how to tell you this," I say. "You're going to think I'm putting you on."

The way I did when we were kids, always talking about fairies and the Wolfman and what-have-you like they were real—because I knew it'd get a rise out of him. It only got worse when I came to understand that there really *is* more to the world than what we can normally see. Not that he hasn't had a few brushes with the inexplicable himself, but that kind of thing always seems to wash off of him the way water does from a bird's wing.

"Just tell me," he says.

So I clear my throat and do as he asks.

I don't look at him while I'm talking. I don't want to see his reaction. I just want to get through it—get it all said before I have to deal with the disbelief that'll be plain on his face.

I wish I could be writing this down. That's what my writing really is—therapy. Doesn't matter if it's my journals, my occasional forays into fiction, or the volumes of case studies and oral collections bound for the "Isn't life strange?" section of the bookstore. When I write something down, it starts to make sense for me. It doesn't solve my problems. But at least I start to understand them.

"Jesus," he says when I'm done.

"Look," I start, but he gets up and leaves the table.

I think he's heading for the apartment door, that he's walking out on me and my weird take on life, once and for all. But he heads for my study instead. He stands there in the doorway and looks at the wreckage of my computer. I wait in the hall behind him, smoking yet another cigarette, staring at the back of his head, the set of his shoulders.

"She told me about that connection she had with the Wordwood," he says, not turning around. "I can't remember where we were, but it was after the two of you had moved in together. She said the same thing you did tonight—that I wouldn't believe her."

"And did you?"

Geordie shakes his head. He moves over to the desk, touches the wreckage of the computer with trailing fingers. Finally he turns to me.

"She didn't seem completely convinced herself," he adds.

"You don't have to explain," I say. "The further she got from being 'born,' the less real that connection felt to her as well."

"It was just so weird."

"I know."

I look around for somewhere to put the long ash at the end of my cigarette and settle on tapping it into my free hand.

"And now?" I ask.

He sighs. "What possible reason could you have to lie to me about something like that?"

"I wish I *was* making it up."

I return to the kitchen to butt out my cigarette and get another. When I return to the study, I bring the saucer with me. Geordie's sitting in the chair Saskia occupied a couple of hours ago. I take the other one, but we don't tap our feet against each other on the ottoman like I did with her.

"So what do we do?" he asks.

"I don't know where to start."

"You could talk to Joe."

Joseph Crazy Dog's a friend of Jilly's who, by Jilly's accounts, spends most of his time in the spirit lands that lie just beyond the borders of the world that the rest of us live in. According to her, that's where he's originally from—not the Kickaha rez like everybody thinks.

"He's not exactly a techno kind of guy," I say.

"What about the professor?"

Ah, the professor. Bramley Dapple. Taught at Butler U. for years, retired now. My compadre in exploring the mysteries of the world—Don Juan to my Castaneda. He was the first adult I met that took this interest of mine seriously. He used to teach art history, but his heart was always in mythology and folklore. "They should teach Mystery 101," he used to say. "The real things. Fairies and spirits, ghosts and hobgoblins and all. It's a parallel history to what's actually taught, but no less pertinent."

"He's even less computer literate than I am," I say. "I mean, he writes on a computer, uses the Internet for research and belongs to god knows how many obscure and arcane discussion groups, but he doesn't understand the hardware any better than I do. And don't get me started on him and software. I've never met anyone so incapable of doing a simple install the way he is. Anyway, according to him, computers and the Internet are a necessary evil that he's only using by sufferance."

"But what about the stuff you've been researching lately? Doesn't that intrigue him?"

"He doesn't believe it's relevant. Or . . . real. Or at least not as real as the oral tradition of folklore and stories."

I've been trying to avoid paying any attention to my desk and the computer lying in pieces on top of it. Whenever I do, the loss just hits me so hard that my chest gets tight and feels like it's going to implode. But I glance at it now, then back to Geordie.

"I guess what I need is access to another computer. Maybe someone in one of my newsgroups can help me."

"I've got that laptop that Amy lent me," Geordie says.

"Does it have a modem?"

He nods. "But I don't know how fast it is. I only use it for e-mail."

"It'll do. Is it at the loft?"

He gives me another nod.

Geordie's apartment is actually our friend Jilly's old studio. He's subletting it from her because the crash that left her in a wheelchair also makes it impossible for her to navigate the stairs. The building has no elevator.

It's funny. He's been staying at Jilly's loft for almost a year now, but none of us think of it as his place. It's still "Jilly's," or "the loft"—even though she's been staying at the professor's house for all this time. She's a long way from being able to navigate stairs, so Geordie moved in when he got back from L.A. When you step inside, you can hardly tell that he's been living there as long as he has. There are a few instruments scattered around, some of his books and clothes, but otherwise it's pretty much the same as when Jilly was living there. Except it's neater. And the fairy paintings are all gone.

"Do you want to come over and use it?" he asks.

My gaze tracks back to the part of the room where Saskia disappeared and the vise closes in on my chest again. I know she's not going to simply pop back into existence. I can *feel* her absence and it's total. But at the same time, I don't know that she isn't going to pop back, either. Once you entered the world of the impossible, how can you say anything's unequivocally this or that?

Geordie stands up.

"Let me get the laptop and bring it back here," he says.

I give him a grateful look. He's gone before I can even get out of the chair. I stand by the front door for a moment, feeling completely adrift in the waves of loneliness and despair that wash over me, then slowly make my way back into the kitchen. I pour myself some more coffee. I light another cigarette. I try to empty my mind of everything, but that doesn't work so well. Worries and fears and half-made plans bounce around in my head until it feels like a pinball machine.

Mostly I just wait.

Christiana

I'm not aware of falling. Of losing my grip on the phone. Of how long I lie there in the grass that carpets my little meadow apartment, my mind a blank slate. Big time *tabula rasa*. Like all I really am is a shadow—a shadow cast on the ground and you can make anything of me you want, depending on how and where you shine the light.

<Christiana.>

The sound of my name pulls me back from the empty place into which I fell. It goes echoing and echoing through this black void where I'm floating until I finally make the connection.

Christiana. That's me.

I use my name like a line to pull myself out of the dark.

The sunlight is harsh on my eyes, making them water, and it seems to take forever to sit up, twice that for the world to stop spinning.

I've never fainted before. Somehow I thought it'd be different. You see it in the movies, the damsel swoons and someone's there to catch her. People flit about and fuss and finally she opens her eyes with a becoming flutter of long lashes and gives the male lead a dreamy look. It's all so romantic.

In my case, the ground caught me—luckily the grass is soft and I didn't whack my head on the end of the bed or something. Coming out of it, I'm disoriented and sweaty. There's a bad taste in my mouth and my head feels fuzzy, like it's too full, if that makes any sense. There's a pressure in between my temples, as though something is shifting or stretching inside my head.

You know how the first time you sleep with someone new in your bed—doesn't matter if you've made love or you're just lying there together—you're very aware of the other person's presence in what's normally a solitary place? Every movement they make is exaggerated. Every sound is magnified.

That's what this is like.

And as for romantic feelings, I feel more like crawling into bed and pulling the blankets over my head than making goo-goo eyes at some guy, just saying there was anybody around in the first place.

<Christiana.>

Scratch that. Somebody's here. And now I remember how hearing my name brought me out of the dark.

This time I look around, but there's no one here. At least no one that I can see. Whoever it is has to be hiding in the trees that border my meadow.

"Who's there?" I say.

But as the words leave my lips, I've already matched the voice against the catalogue in my memory. I know who's speaking to me.

"Where are you, Saskia?" I ask. "How come I can't see you?"

My gaze stops on the cell phone lying in the grass nearby. I remember the phone call that pulled me out of sleep. I remember the blast of white noise that came from the speaker. I remember falling. Nothing else.

I pick up the phone and bring the speaker to my ear, thinking Saskia's on the other end of the line. But the phone's dead. I turn it on and get a dial tone.

<Don't freak out on me.>

I don't like this at all. Nobody knows how to get to this place. Hardly anybody even *knows* about it.

I turn off the phone and look around some more. Wherever Saskia is, she's doing a good job of hiding.

<I didn't mean to do this, but I didn't seem to have a choice. It was either this, or oblivion.>

I'm starting to get a really creepy feeling. I realize that I'm not hearing her voice the way I should be. It's not coming to me through my ears.

<I did ask before I came in.>

The voice is in my head.

<You said yes.>

"Get out of my head," I tell her.

<But you said—>

"This isn't funny."

I want to bang my head against the end of my bed or a tree. I can't physically feel her inside me—there's just her voice, and the impression of something else, something foreign in my head—but it's giving me the major willies having her inside my skin the way she is.

"I don't know how you did this, but you'd better just get out."

<I can't.>

"I'm serious."

<I am, too. I can't get out. I didn't even know I could get in until it actually happened.>

"So what? This is some science experiment?"

<No. I had to hide in somebody.>

"Why didn't you just go into Christy's head?"

<I tried that first, but I couldn't get in. There was no . . . I don't know what to call it. Conduit, I suppose.>

"And there is with me?"

<There was with the phone line. I can't explain how it happened. It all went so fast—this expanding dot appearing on Christy's computer screen, me touching it. It was like something shorted out inside me. Like I've been an illusion all along and whatever was growing on the screen made it come apart.>

"You were never an illusion."

<Then how come I'm here in your head? This doesn't happen to real people.>

I didn't know what to say to that. There's a long pause, then she continues.

<But at the same time everything was happening in such a rush, I felt the way . . . I guess a computer would feel if it could feel. I could do a hundred things at the same time. Try to hold myself together. Try to use Christy as an anchor. Try to fight whatever it was that was taking me apart, pixel by pixel.>

"You're not made of pixels," I say.

<Molecule by molecule, then.>

"Whatever."

<And some part of me reached for you, but the only way I knew to contact you was from the phone number you left me.>

"But how did you come across the phone lines and into me?"

<I don't know. Like data, I suppose. The way you send data. Because

that's all I am. Some data that the Wordwood gussied up into a simulation of a human being.>

"Stop saying that," I tell her.

Except then I start to wonder, maybe she is just data. Maybe that's all she's ever been. Data that got more real as it began to accumulate its own life experiences. Just like a shadow does . . .

Even with my own origin in mind, even with all the strange beings I've met in the borderlands and beyond, this still feels too crazy. She was too real for that.

But then I think of myself as real, too, don't I? What's the difference between a being created out of shadows, and one created out of data?

I need to think, but I don't know where to start. It's too mondo, big-time bizarre, having her inside me. What's she doing in me? Going through my memories? Does she have control over my body? Are we sharing it in more ways than one?

"This is totally freaking me out," I tell her.

<I'm not exactly comfortable with it myself.>

"What can you see . . . you know, inside me?"

<Nothing.>

"What do you mean, 'nothing'?"

<I have no sense of a body whatsoever—at least not of my own. I can see what you see, hear what you hear, but it's like a movie with smell and taste and tactile senses thrown in for good measure. There's no sense of immediacy—of my actually being able to experience this on my own. It's all secondhand.>

"You can't read my mind? You can't access my memories?"

<No.>

Can you hear me if I specifically aim a thought at you like this?

<Yes. But it feels very strange. Like there's a ghost in my head.>

"Welcome to the club."

<Christiana . . . I'm sorry. I was desperate, grabbing at anything I could. And you . . . you said I could come in.>

"I did."

And I don't know why.

"What are we going to do?" I ask her.

Saskia's silence is all the reply I get. I understand. I don't have a clue either. How do you fix something like this? Where do you even start? It would sure help to have somebody step up and offer some advice right about now. I mean anything from "I know a good systems analyst who also

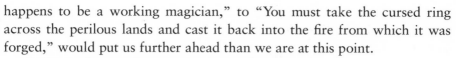

happens to be a working magician," to "You must take the cursed ring across the perilous lands and cast it back into the fire from which it was forged," would put us further ahead than we are at this point.

It doesn't have to be easy. Just *some* direction.

I sigh and look off across my friendly little meadow apartment. I remember coming home last night and how comfortable I was, puttering around, reading a little bit, finally going to bed. Now everything feels different. Well, duh. I've got somebody else living in my head. But it's more than that.

<It's starting to get dark,> Saskia says.

"Yeah."

I'm too caught up in all of this to really pay attention to what she's saying. But then it registers. I realize that it *is* getting dark.

"This isn't possible," I say.

Like so much else about today is.

<What do you mean?>

"I told you how I made this place. I grabbed a perfect memory and stuck it away in this nook of the borderlands. It only has two faces—a sunny day and a twilight evening, depending on how much light I want. It doesn't have weather. It can't change."

<Well, it looks to me like there's a storm coming.>

It does to me, too. From the west. I walk toward the western edge of the meadow and step into the trees. There's really nothing past them. Walk far enough and you'll simply pop out somewhere else—into whatever place happens to be in your mind at the time, even if it's only in your subconscious. The only rule seems to be that you have to have been there before, or have a really good image of it from a photograph.

That's how most people build their memory holes. There's a clear demarcation between your private place and all the other places you can access from it. When I made mine, I added views that you'd expect to see from a meadow—rolling hills, forests, some distant mountains. But they're not really there. And they're completely static. Like a painting. Like a photo.

So it's particularly weird to see storm clouds gathering in the western skies. It'd be like you looking at a landscape on a wall in your home—some beautiful sunny hillside, say—and as you look at it, a storm starts to form in one corner of the picture. It shouldn't be able to happen.

But it does. It's happening here.

Why am I so surprised? People aren't supposed to take up residence inside your head, either.

"I'm getting a bad feeling about this," I say.

I feel like I'm reading from the script for some B-movie—a tacky horror flick or an action piece.

There's no reply for a long moment, then I hear Saskia say softly in my head, <I think it's the Wordwood.>

"What makes you say that?"

<I'm getting the same worrisome feeling from that build-up of dark clouds as I got from the expanding black dot that showed up on Christy's computer screen. I didn't know what it was then, but I recognize it now.>

"What makes you so sure it's the Wordwood?"

<I . . . I don't know. I'm not. Christy said something about the Wordwood site having been down all week. So maybe this isn't the Wordwood. Maybe it's whatever took it off-line.>

"You mean like a virus?"

<I guess.>

"How could a computer virus show up like a storm in the borderlands?"

<I don't know. How can data show up in the World As It Is and take human form the way I did?>

"Don't start in on that again," I say, but my heart's not really in it.

Maybe she was just data. Maybe she was never real. Maybe I'm not either. It would make sense. Why else would Mumbo always be showing me things to help me pass for normal among real people? The key word here is "pass." You have to pass for human when you're not.

I start to feel a little sick again, and I guess I finally understand why this has all been such a concern for Saskia. I haven't thought about this—*really* thought about it—in a long, long time. I wish I wasn't thinking about it now.

<We should get out of here,> Saskia says.

It's *so* hard to get used to this voice in my head.

"Why?" I ask her.

<Look what happened to me when I came into contact with that thing earlier tonight.>

"But I'm not made of data. It's not going to be able to affect me the way it did you."

<We don't know that.>

"No. We don't know much about anything. And we're not going to find out by running away. If this storm is an aspect of whatever it was that took away your body, then it's the very thing we have to face to get it back."

<And if it does something worse?>

"What could be worse?"

There's a pause before Saskia replies. <Are you really this brave?>

I laugh. "Maybe I just don't know any better."

But I do. The thing is, when I get into a situation like this, I almost always go forward, into the darkness. I don't think of it as being brave or foolhardy. It's just what I do. Because I don't like hiding. I get scared just like anybody else does. But I refuse to let my fear make me back away. When you do that, the darkness wins.

I take a step forward, expecting Saskia to try to pull me back. She doesn't. So she was telling the truth about that. Because I know that she wouldn't let me do this if she could stop me. But all she's got is words.

<Christiana,> she says, her nervousness plain in her voice.

"Don't worry," I tell her. "I'm the queen of getting out of trouble."

Big words. I'm good with words. Not as good as Christy, but I've always got something to say. Trouble is, words aren't really much of a help right now.

I keep walking. We're well past the border of my little memory hole. We should be somewhere else now—in the borderlands, the otherworld, even what the professor calls the World As It Is—except we're continuing across a field that lies on the other side of the line of trees demarking my memory hole. A field that shouldn't exist because it's only an image. But I can feel the grass brush against the bottoms of my jeans. The wind in my face. That invisible crackle in the air of the gathering storm that's just about upon me.

<It's getting closer.>

"I can see that."

I can *feel* it. All the little hairs on my arms and at the nape of my neck are standing straight up.

The dark clouds are rolling in fast, turning what was already twilight into something that's even closer to night. The wind's picking up and there's a sound under its bluster. It takes me a moment to figure out what it reminds me of. Then I have it. Static. Like there was on the telephone line just before Saskia came into my head. Except this time it's not coming to me through the phone. It's all around us. We're in the middle of it.

I lift my gaze to the horizon where the clouds are darkest. The light's poor, making details hard to pick out, but I find if I look hard, the landscape flickers. Distant mountains, clouds, the horizon. One moment they're in sharp focus, the next they're a pulsing storm of pixels, then they firm up again.

Maybe Saskia's right, I find myself thinking. Maybe this really is the

Wordwood. Or maybe we've been pulled into some cyber realm where the Wordwood exists and everything has different rules from the ones we know.

Maybe coming out here wasn't such a good idea.

I see a sheet of rain coming across the fields toward us, darker than any water I've seen before. I consider a hasty retreat. I know, I know. I said I like to face the darkness. But there's a right time and a wrong time to make a stand. Like if someone's got a gun in your face, it's not a good time to crack wise. And if the world falls apart and you find yourself in a place like this—real, not real, can't make up its mind—it only makes sense to fall back to firmer ground and rethink the situation.

I start to turn. Too late.

The wall of rain's right on us. Not water. Something else. Heavier, thicker. Like oil.

It hits me and pounds me into the ground.

I try to stand. I can't even get to my knees.

The impact of the black rain drives me down and keeps me there.

I feel myself losing my grip on consciousness again. I find myself thinking that I'm beginning to make a real habit of this fainting business, but then—

Saskia

I thought that losing my body the way I did was the most awful thing I could experience. I was wrong. This is worse. Way worse. I can't bear to be so helpless—an ineffectual spirit locked in Christiana's head, while my faceless enemy pounds her into the ground.

And there's nothing I can do to stop it.

It's my fault this is happening to her. All my fault.

She's gone now. I can't find even a spark of her consciousness anywhere inside this body we're sharing. The black rain continues to beat on her limp body and I can only pray that it's battered her into unconsciousness. That she's not dead.

But if she's not already dead, she soon will be. The rain turns to an oily goop on the ground, forming puddles around her that rapidly grow into a small pond of the thick liquid. When she collapsed, it was into a small hollow in the field. It's shallow, but deep enough for her to drown if the level of the goop rises much more.

I try to take control of her slack limbs, but it doesn't seem to matter that she's unconscious and unable to use them herself. I'm still just a passenger and nothing will move for me. Not even an eyelid. I focus on the task like I've never focused on anything before, but all my effort is of no more use than trying to stop a river overflowing its banks with only your hands.

The rain keeps pouring down and the little pond around Christiana continues to rise. If this keeps up . . .

I don't want to think about it, but it's all I can think about.

Until, through the oily film that covers her eyes, I see a blur of movement.

There are shapes moving in the black rain. Human figures, but they're like Spielberg aliens—all smooth, without edges.

I redouble my efforts to take control of Christiana's limbs with about as much success as before, which is none.

The oily water keeps rising. It comes up to her mouth. Her nose. The figures are all around us now, leaning closer with strange blurred features. I scream in Christiana's mind, trying to rouse her. Trying to move her. But it's no use. She won't wake and I can't move her. There's nothing I can do except sit inside her head while she drowns.

The liquid pours into her nostrils, into her mouth, down her throat, filling her lungs.

And then I go into the same black space I guess she did.

Christy

It's only been three-quarters of an hour, but it feels like a week before Geordie finally returns with Amy's laptop. He doesn't have a carrying case for it, so he brings it in his backpack.

"The battery's kind of wonky," he says as he sets the old machine on my desk. "So you have to run it off the power cord."

Which, happily, he remembered to bring along. I give the machine a quick look-over. It's a 386—still running Windows 3.1, Geordie tells me—but it has a PCMCIA modem card so that I can get on the Internet and the processor should be plenty fast enough for what I need it to do. All I want to do is send some e-mail.

While Geordie was gone, I smoked I don't know how many more cigarettes. But I also cleaned up the mess in the study, picking up all the various bits and pieces of my computer and stowing them in a cardboard box that I grabbed from the recycling container on the back balcony. I wasn't able to do much with the top of the desk. The scratches and burn marks needed more than a sponge or cloth to clean up, but they were the least of my worries.

As I worked, all I could think about was Saskia. She's all I can think about.

I didn't know what to do with the debris from the computer so I put the box beside my desk. I realized that I couldn't throw it out just yet. I have this weird idea that since Saskia disappeared into the machine just before it exploded, she's still tied to it somehow. If I throw it out, it'll be like throwing her out. I know. It makes no sense. But nothing about the night makes any sense.

"Thanks for going to get this," I tell my brother.

"No problem."

He sits in the extra straight-backed chair near my desk, watching as I finish setting up the laptop and plug it in. I pick up the phone cord that I used with my own computer, but the end got melted, so I go looking for a fresh one. Finally I give up and take the cord off the phone in the bedroom.

"It's kind of weird out there," Geordie says as I make the final connection. "On the streets, I mean."

I lift my head to look at him. "What do you mean 'weird'?"

He shrugs. "I don't know. There's just a feeling in the air. Like the shadows are too dark and . . ." He gives me an uneasy smile. "And maybe there's things moving in them."

"What did you see?"

"I didn't see anything. It was just a feeling. Like this is about more than Saskia."

I'd never took that into account. Considering Saskia's claims concerning her origin, I simply assumed this was about her.

"Why don't you check the news," I say, "while I try to get a couple of messages out."

"As if it'd be on CNN."

"So try the local stations first."

"Christy," he says. "I can't count the number of weird things that happen in this city, but when was the last time you saw a mention of any of them on the news?"

I just give him a look.

"Okay," he says. "I guess it can't hurt to check it out."

I go back to what I'm doing. Now that the hardware's all connected, I boot up the laptop and wait forever for this old version of Windows to load and give me the Desktop screen. Then I go searching for Geordie's e-mail program. Once I find it, I make a note of his sending and receiving protocols. I replace them with my own and I'm ready to go.

I don't remember the e-mail addresses of all my regular correspondents—it's like putting numbers into the automatic dial-up directory of your telephone. You get so used to simply pushing a button that your memory doesn't retain the actual numbers anymore. But I do remember the

addresses of the newsgroups. The hard part is figuring out just what to say.
I start typing.

I don't really know where to begin . . .

I keep it simple and don't get too specific. I don't mention Saskia's ori-
gins or how she got swallowed by the computer. Instead I talk about the
Wordwood and ask if anyone's experienced any oddities with the Web site.
I hesitate, then clarify that by adding:

. . . oddities with the Web site that cause actual physical
anomalies in your real world environment.

I finish up by asking anyone who might have experienced anything
along those lines to contact me and put my phone number under my name
at the end of the message. Lighting up yet another cigarette, I read it back
to myself. There's so much more I could say, but I want to leave this clear
enough that someone with a genuine experience will contact me, yet vague
enough that I don't get inundated with calls from the cranks on those same
newsgroups. Satisfied, I queue it up.

Now comes the part that I've been worrying about ever since Geordie
went out to get the laptop: connecting to the Internet again. I don't know
what to expect, but I'll tell you this. The first hint of anything weird and I'm
just pulling the phone jack out of the computer, never mind shutting down
the connection.

But I needn't have worried. Everything acts the way it's supposed to.
Dial-up, connect. I hit send and watch the progress bar as the e-mails go off
into the pixelated ether.

I'm shutting down the e-mail and Internet connection when Geordie
comes back into the room with an expression on his face that I can't read.

"You have to come see this," he says.

"See what?"

"It's on CNN. Saskia's not the only one that's disappeared into a computer."

"What?"

"Just come look at this," he says and leaves the room again.

I turn off the laptop and follow him into the living room. We sit side-
by-side on the sofa watching the calm, perfectly-coifed anchorperson coor-
dinate her own commentary with cuts to correspondents in various parts of

North America and abroad. There's live footage, of course, but it consists mostly of the exteriors of various houses and apartment buildings that look perfectly normal except for the police cars and emergency vehicles parked outside.

While all the incidents happened at approximately the same time—and also, not coincidentally, I'm sure, at the same time that Saskia disappeared—it took the authorities a while to realize that the rash of 911 calls were connected.

"The count of those missing now stands at one hundred eighty-six," the blonde anchorperson is saying. "Authorities believe that the final figure will be much higher, as the information they have to date doesn't take into account those living alone with no one to report their disappearance."

There's no actual mention of www.thewordwood.com. I can't decide if they're keeping that under wraps, or if they simply don't know. From the footage of the interior of one of the disappeared's homes, it must be the latter. There's a camera pan across a study and the brief glimpse I get of the computer shows that it's a mess. Not shattered like mine did, but it's dripping some kind of black oily goop. The emergency workers in the room are wearing bio-hazard containment suits, giving the video an even more surreal quality.

The reportage cuts to a woman being interviewed outside of her home. As she starts talking about this flood of thick black oil pouring out of her husband's computer screen, I turn to Geordie.

"That's not what happened to Saskia," I say.

He nods. "But there's no way it's not connected."

"No question," I agree.

"So we should tell someone," he adds.

"What for?"

"So that it doesn't happen to anyone else who tries to log on to the Wordwood."

I shake my head. "I'm pretty sure we don't have to worry about that."

"But—"

"Weren't you listening to what they were saying?" I ask, nodding at the TV. "It all happened around the same time. I'm guessing it was a spike of . . . I don't know, some kind of energy or whatever. It happened, now it's done."

"We don't know that. If we can save other lives by—"

"Nobody's dead," I tell him, needing to believe it myself. "They were taken away to . . . well, I don't know that either. Someplace else. And if we let the 'proper authorities' deal with it, we'll never get Saskia or any of them back. They'll just screw it up."

"We can't take that chance."

I sigh. "Okay, I'll prove it," I tell him.

I get up and go back into the study where I boot up the laptop again.

"What are you doing?" Geordie asks.

"We're going to run a test. If nothing happens, we keep the Wordwood connection to ourselves. If it looks like there's going to be a problem, I'll pull the plug and we phone the police or whoever will listen to us."

When the Desktop shows up on the screen, I double-click on the Internet connection icon.

"Wait a minute," Geordie says. "Amy only loaned that to me. If you blow it up she's going to kill me."

"Nothing's going to get blown up."

The connection's made and I start up the Internet browser, an old version of Netscape.

"This is just being stupid," Geordie says. "It's too dangerous."

"I know what I'm doing," I tell him as I type in the Wordwood's URL. "If that dot shows up, I'll unplug it so fast it'll make your head spin."

"My head's already spinning."

I hit return and the browser goes searching for the Wordwood.

"We're going to end up sucked away into wherever along with the rest of them," Geordie says.

I think about that. Think about how Saskia was stolen away. I've gone over it a million times, how I could have forestalled all of it if I just hadn't suggested we go on-line to check with the Wordwood. But no. I had all the answers.

Turns out I didn't have any.

"Maybe that wouldn't be such a bad thing," I say.

"What?"

"Nothing."

"We can't just—"

"Too late," I tell him. "We're already there."

The familiar "This page cannot be displayed" dialogue comes up on the screen. I realize I'm holding my breath as I wait for the black dot to reappear, but the seconds tick away into a minute, two, three. Nothing changes.

I close the page and take the computer off-line.

"You see?" I say as I shut it down. "It's just a dead link again."

"You really think you can figure this thing out?" Geordie asks.

"Not by myself. But with the right input from some of the others in my newsgroups, we've got a fighting chance."

"And if that doesn't work?"

"I don't want to think about that right now," I say. "Let's try to keep a positive spin on things."

"But—"

"Please?"

He nods and we go back into the living room. I light another cigarette. Geordie makes some more coffee and we watch the TV, where all the experts fumble to make sense of what's going on. What I find most interesting is how everybody avoids any consideration of the supernatural being involved. Reporters, police and government spokespeople, the experts. None of them bring it up. They're postulating terrorist biological attacks, bizarre cult conspiracies, anything but what actually happened.

We're still watching TV when the phone rings. Geordie lowers the sound with the remote.

"Is this Christy Riddell?" a woman's voice asks after I say hello.

"Yes. And you are . . . ?"

"It's Estie. From the alt-mythology-computers newsgroup. Is your computer still on-line?"

"No, but I don't think it matters. I figure it was a one-time anomaly. I've been back on-line since . . . since the incident and all I get is the dead link."

There's a moment of silence, then I hear her take a steadying breath.

"Okay," she says finally. "Do you want me to go first or do you want to tell me what happened to you?"

"Have you got your TV on?" I ask.

"No. Why?"

"Maybe you should have a look at what's on CNN."

I figure she's on a roam phone as I can hear her moving around, probably from one room to another. I hear her TV come on—it sounds like a commercial until she punches in the channel number for CNN, and I get a tinny echo through the phone's receiver of what's playing on low volume on the TV set in my living room.

"Oh my god," she says after a minute or so. "This is worse than I thought."

I give her a moment to digest what she's seeing, though a moment isn't going to be nearly enough. At least it hasn't been for me.

"Tell me what happened," I say.

There's a long pause, where all I can hear from the receiver is the sound of her TV set coming over the line.

"My name's Sarah Taylor," she says finally.

I know that name and say as much, though I can't remember where I know it from.

"We have a mutual friend," she says. "Holly Rue."

"Wait a minute." I start to make the connections. "Does that mean you're—"

"Yes. I'm one of the original founders of the Wordwood."

I get this immediate sense of relief. She'll know what to do. We're going to get Saskia and all those other people back.

But my relief is fleeting.

"But that doesn't mean I have the first clue as to what's going on," she adds.

The grin that was starting to pull at my lips dies.

"So what do we do?" I say.

I pull another cigarette out of the pack and frown. It's almost empty.

"Well, to start with," she says, "we can compare our stories. I was on-line with Benny—Benjamin Davis. Do you know who he is?"

Now that Estie's made the connection to Holly for me, various conversations Holly and I have had about the Wordwood are coming back to me.

"He's another of the cofounders," I say.

"Right. I keep in touch with him more than the others. No real reason. Maybe just because I've known him the longest, or because he's like me: more of a techie than the rest."

"I know how that goes."

"Anyway," she says. "We were just trying out some new software for our Web cameras, chatting to each other through instant messaging while we screwed around with the settings. Then we got sidetracked by this e-mail we got from Tip about the Wordwood."

She doesn't stop to explain who Tip is, but I remember Holly talking about him. She means Tom Pace, another of the founders.

"Neither Benny nor I have much to do with it anymore . . . not since, you know."

"It became sentient."

She gives a nervous laugh. "I guess that's one way of putting it. Anyway, we didn't even know that the site had been down, so Benny decides to go have a look. He aims his browser at the Wordwood, but we still have our Web cameras on."

She goes on to describe the images the Web camera put on her monitor's screen, how he has this puzzled look and leans closer to the screen then suddenly jumps back. She gets a glimpse of this gush of black liquid issuing from something in front of him. Sees him fall into it. He goes down, out of camera range, and then nothing. He doesn't get back up. Frantically, she sends him an instant message, then an e-mail. No answer. Finally she phones him and gets his boyfriend Raul on the line.

Raul's in a total panic. The story she manages to get out of him, and that she now relates to me, is pretty much the same as what Geordie and I have been hearing on CNN from the few eyewitnesses that reporters have managed to track down: black goop pouring out of the monitor in an impossible flood, enveloping the victim, then slowly dissolving away to leave not a trace.

I don't want to get into Saskia's origins—not even with one of the Wordwood's founders. Maybe especially not with one. So I make like it happened pretty much the same way for Saskia as it did for Estie's friend Benny.

"How's something like that even possible?" Estie says. I can hear the strain in her voice. She's feeling the same shock I did when Saskia was taken away. "What could that stuff be?"

"I think it must be a kind of ectoplasm," I say.

"You know, I've heard that term before, but when I think about it, I really have no idea what it means."

"In spiritualist terms, it's this thick, sticky substance that supposedly flows out of the body of a medium to produce . . . I guess you could say manifestations. Living forms that usually have some relationship to the spirit being called up."

There's a pause and then she says, "Do you buy this?"

"I've seen stranger things."

She gives that nervous laugh again. "Yeah, I keep forgetting who I'm talking to. We were all surprised to have a celebrity like you show up on our newsgroup."

"I'm no celebrity," I say.

"Well, you've got a higher public profile that all the rest of us put together." There's another pause. "So who was having the séance?"

"What do you mean?"

"Well, isn't that where you'd find a medium?"

"I suppose the medium could be the computer," I tell her. "Or perhaps even the Internet."

"And the spirit that got called up is whatever took over the Wordwood way back when?"

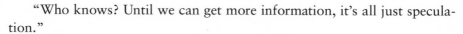

"Who knows? Until we can get more information, it's all just speculation."

"So what happens to the people that get taken?" she asks.

"I don't know. I figure that what happened was a flare-up of some sort, though what could have caused it is anybody's guess. Whoever happened to be trying to log onto the Wordwood at that instant got caught up in it and taken away."

"Taken where?"

I'm slow in responding. It's just now occurring to me that the flare-up could well have been caused by Saskia's trying to get in touch with the spirit of the Wordwood. Something as simple as a spiritual short-out brought about when creation and creator come into unexpected contact. Like when wires cross, except here it was spirits in the wires.

"I don't know that either," I finally tell her. "I'd say the spiritworld, but I don't know that technological spirits would exist in the same world as fairies and goblins."

Now it's her turn to be quiet.

"Are you still there?" I ask after a few moments.

"Yeah. I was just thinking. Growing up, I was never much of a one for fairy tales and such. But ever since that business with the Wordwood taking on a life of its own, I've just known that there's something lurking in cyberspace. Not just whatever took over the Wordwood site, but other spirits, too. Maybe lots of them. Which is weird, when you think about it. Because cyberspace doesn't really exist. It's more just a concept that we created. A label for us to put on what goes on when the vast nets of data crisscross over the wires and in the computers that house Web sites.

"It's something we made up. So I guess we made up these spirits, too."

"Maybe," I say. "There's certainly a line of thinking that believes that gods and fairies and the things that go bump in the night exist only because we believe in them. That we created them to explain the confusing mystery of the world."

"But you don't," she says.

"Not entirely, no. I think some of the mysteries of the world can be explained that way, but not all of them. Not even most of them."

"This is so frigging weird."

"Uh-huh." I wait a heartbeat, then ask, "How come you never talk about this kind of thing in the newsgroup?"

"Have you ever noticed how you *can't* really talk about it on-line?" she says. "I know people who have tried. They've written articles, or even just done like you said. Talked about it in newsgroups, or tried to start new ones. But those spirits are jealous of their privacy. You watch. By six or seven this morning, CNN's coverage isn't going to even talk about the computer connection anymore."

"You're probably right. The human mind is very good at forgetting what it can't explain."

"I'm not saying it will be people, forgetting in order to hang onto their sanity," she says. "Those spirits don't let it happen."

"But—"

"It's something all the hackers know. There are things you just don't talk about on-line. Hell, you can't talk about it on any medium that's connected to computers, which is pretty much every medium we have, except for word-of-mouth or handwriting. Come at it from any other way—anything that touches a computer—and the words, the videos, the whatever you used to try to get the message out just gets erased. I can tell you about chapters disappearing from books. Scenes from documentaries. It's been going on for years."

"I've come across some of that in my research," I say.

"But only face-to-face research, right?"

I light yet another cigarette and think about that for a long moment before agreeing with her.

"So where do we go from here?" I ask.

"I've got a flight booked," she says, "that'll bring me into Newford midmorning tomorrow. Before I leave, I'll try to get Tip and Claudette to fly in as well and meet me at Holly's store. Raul told me he's coming, too. He's enough of a techie that he'll be useful and I know he needs something to get his mind off of what happened to Benny. To feel like he's doing something to bring him back."

"I know exactly how he feels," I tell her.

"We could use your help, too. You know more about the whole spirit side of this than any of us."

"You've got it," I say. "But what is it that you're planning to do?"

"I don't know exactly. Brainstorm, I guess. I've got this idea that maybe we can start over again with the Wordwood, see if we can't make another connection with the spirit that stepped into it, except this time show that we're benevolent. That we don't mean it any harm. I figured if we do that, we should use Holly's old 386—the one we used to make the Wordwood in the first place."

"I'd think you'd want to use a faster machine."

"But what if the magic's in that particular machine?"

I think about all the times I've hung around in Holly's store, sitting behind the desk with her and yakking about books, the computer monitor casting its light on the various papers, magazines, and books scattered about on the surface of the desk.

"She doesn't use that computer any more," I tell Estie.

"I know that. But I'm pretty sure she's still got the old one stashed away in her basement. You know Holly. When does she throw anything away?"

"Have you checked that she still has it?"

"I was hoping you would. I haven't been able to get in touch with her. I've tried calling her a number of times in the last hour or so, but there doesn't seem to be any phone service at her apartment, and downstairs in the store, the machine just picks up."

"You don't think something's happened to her?"

"No. Her computer's in the store. If something had happened to her like it did Benny or your friend Saskia, it would've fried the phone wires the way it did at Benny's place. The only reason I was able to get through to Raul was because they have a second line in the house for Raul's business. He imports clothing and furniture from Mexico and wholesales it to stores."

"I'll go by Holly's as soon as I get off the phone," I tell her.

I'm starting to feel a little worried about Holly now. Because the thing is, while the one phone cord got wrecked in my study when Saskia disappeared, I didn't lose my phone service. All I had to do was replace the cord to get back on-line and the phone was never out. But to bring that up now with Estie means I'd have to explain about Saskia and why I didn't tell her earlier. I'm still not ready to get into that.

"Great," Estie says. "I'll see you sometime in the morning—noon at the latest."

"I'll be there." I hesitate a moment, then add, "Have you talked to the authorities yet?"

"And tell them what? They'd think I was insane. And if they didn't, they might just lock me away for being one the people who started up the Wordwood in the first place. I won't be able to do anything to stop it from a jail cell."

"Good point," I say, as though it hadn't occurred to me.

"And you?" she asks.

"I'll follow your lead in this."

When I hang up, Geordie gives me a quizzical look so I take him through a much shortened rundown of Estie's side of the conversation.

"I notice you didn't tell her much about what really happened with Saskia," he says.

"I couldn't."

"Why not?"

"Because I've got this bad feeling that maybe Saskia was the catalyst for all these disappearances."

"Oh, come on now," he says. "Saskia'd never do anything like that."

"I didn't say she'd do it on purpose. I'm thinking it was more like . . . I don't know, the computer version of a chemical reaction. Or the way a pin can burst a balloon."

Geordie's still shaking his head.

"You know the Wordwood was already down before any of this happened?" I say.

"Yeah, but—"

"So something happened to it. Something *changed* it. That being the case, her contacting it could easily have set off a chain reaction."

"You don't know that."

I shake my head. "No. But until we *do* know more, what really happened to Saskia's going to stay between you and me. It has to, Geordie."

"Okay."

I start to get up, but he grabs my arm.

"Wait a sec'," he says. "You need to see this."

He turns up the sound as CNN replays some of the interview footage from one of the witnesses.

"All I know," the middle-aged woman on the screen is saying to the reporter, "is that he was down in the rec room. I don't pay any attention when he's down there, but then I hear this strange burbling sound coming up the stairs. So I get up to go have a—"

Geordie thumbs the "Mute" on the remote, cutting her of in mid-sentence.

"Estie was right," he says. "It's already starting to happen."

"I'm not following you."

"That woman's quote," Geordie says. "I've heard it a few times now. The first couple of times she said, 'He was down in the rec room messing around on that stupid computer of his.' But the part about the computer's been cut out now."

"Are you sure?"

Geordie nods.

I give the TV a worried look.

"Jesus," I say. "I wish I knew whether this really is the doing of spirits like Estie said, or if the authorities have caused a blackout because they've decided to sit on that information."

"Well, you could give the police a call," Geordie says. "Tell them you're this expert on computer myths . . ."

His voice trails off when he sees the joke's not going anywhere.

"Come on, Christy," he says. "You can't seriously believe that these spirits can be monitoring all broadcasts, the Internet, satellite feeds, cable . . ."

"What are computers better at than we are?" I ask. When he shakes his head, I say, "Multitasking and crunching data. They do it as easily, and probably with about as much attention, as you or I breathe."

"But to believe they're eavesdropping—"

"I know."

Probably the biggest bullshit paranoia dealing with computers is the myth that people—the government, aliens, your neighbours, it doesn't matter who—can watch what you're doing through the screen of your monitor. It's not even a new idea. I've heard it applied to TVs, as well. It's something you laugh off when you hear it, but now, thinking that perhaps there really are spirits in the wires—jealous of their privacy, as Estie put it—I'm wondering if maybe it's not such a farfetched notion after all.

Considering what happened to Saskia, and now this business with how the spirits are able to protect themselves by erasing any mention of them in electronic media, who's to say they *aren't* watching us from the screens of our computer monitors and TV sets? Maybe they're not simply inhabiting cyberspace. Maybe they can move through any technology that uses electricity or phone lines.

And how about satellite feeds? They could be listening and watching us from the skies, from our household appliances, from anything that's plugged in or utilizes power . . .

I should call Estie back, I think. Warn her that the spirits could have been listening to us over the phone lines. But I don't have her number. And—

I give my head a shake and force myself to stop thinking about this kind of thing before I drive myself crazy.

"You want to take a ride up to Holly's store with me?" I ask Geordie.

"Sure. It's not like I'm going to be able to sleep."

Borrible Jones

Bojo stood alone in the library of the Kelledys' house, feeling over-whelmed. The ceiling was almost fourteen feet high, as befit an old mansion such as this, but such heights also gave a room far too much wall space, so far as Bojo was concerned. He stood looking at floor-to-ceiling book cases that lined each wall except for the doorway where he stood, and a space across from him on the west wall, where the bookcases were broken up by a lead-paned bay window that had a seat underneath large enough to hold two people comfortably.

There were simply too many books. He walked slowly around the room, reading the spines. It was an eclectic selection—music books, fiction, histories, biographies, fairy tales, and esoteric texts, some of the latter writ-ten in languages so obscure that Bojo couldn't even recognize the alphabet they used. He wondered if the cursive marks and ideograms were, in fact, languages and not some sort of arcane code like the *patteran* of his own people—the ideographic marks they left on the sides of buildings and on roadsides as messages for each other.

It didn't help, either, that the books appeared to be filed in haphazard order. Nor that, when it came down to brass tacks, as his Aunt Jen would say, Bojo didn't really have a clear idea as to what he was looking for.

He wasn't really a book person—that was the main problem here. Bojo came from an oral tradition where advice was taken from tribal elders, or found in the tribe's stories and histories that had been handed down through the years. He knew how to read, but had rarely opened a book since learning to do so. Books, subsequently, had acquired a somewhat mystical connotation in his mind, this library being a perfect example.

He knew they were divided into two basic categories: those you read for entertainment, and those used for reference. Over the years of visiting the Kelledy house, he'd often seen either Meran or Cerin come into the library with a problem, take down a book, and there, as magically as he might read trail signs in the wild hills, they would have the solution.

But they knew what they were looking for, or at least where to look. And to further complicate matters, they as often found what they needed in the fictional books as they did in those that were more obviously kept for reference.

Sighing, Bojo stood in the middle of the room for a while longer, hands in the pockets of his jeans, gaze scanning the bewildering array of titles. Finally, he decided that whatever gift the Kelledys had for finding just the right needed book lay in them, not the library, and he called it quits. He would have to find what he needed in his own way.

He left the library, left the Kelledys' house with its gables and tower, and walked under the oaks in the front yard until he reached the sidewalk. There he looked up and down Stanton Street before lifting his gaze skyward, eyes half-closed. For a long moment, he stood, quiet and attentive, silently sifting through an overabundance of impressions.

Anyone without his understanding of the steady traffic between this world and those it bordered would be unaware of the greater percentage of whom and what Bojo sensed. He was looking for magic, and there was plenty to be detected in this rambling city, but he was also looking for wisdom, and that wasn't as readily found.

He was conscious of any number of bodachs and spirits, shadowmen and border folk, faerie and ghosts, all going about their business. They were under the trees behind him and up in the boughs of those same oaks. They wandered along the streets, keeping to the shadows. They slept in gardens, poked through dumpsters. They scurried about in the sewers and alleyways, crept along rooftops or along windowsills, peering into people's apartments.

Bojo wasn't particularly surprised to sense them out and about the way they were. The hidden people were always present—as much at the height of noon as in the middle of the night. But it was easier to spy them now, when the streets were quiet. Glimpses caught from the corner of the eye, rustles heard from an apparently empty corner.

Tonight the streets seemed very busy, as though this was a holy day when the bone fires burned high in the parks and empty lots. Beltane. Or All Hallows' Eve. Nights when the hidden folk ran in packs and troops, full of mischief and song. But though they were out in large numbers, they were subdued.

And there was a sense of something unfamiliar in the air, as well. As though the shadows in alleyways and along the sides of buildings were casting loose from their moorings. The power lines hummed louder than usual, and there was a scent like an electrical fire when wires short out—faint, but present. Bojo's curiosity itched, but whatever this new thing might be, abroad tonight, he didn't have time to investigate it.

He forced himself to concentrate on the inquiry at hand. He cast the scope of his search farther and wider and finally brushed up against an indication of the sort of magical sage he required—a faint and flickering spark that came from a good distance away.

Closing his eyes, he focused on that spark, trying to get a better impression of who or what it represented. All that came back to him was a whisper of old power and shadows. And that it was a man—or at least male. He couldn't get much more than that. It was as though a cloak of darkness lay upon the man, and it was impossible to tell if the shadows it cast grew from the one he was looking for, or were pressing in upon him.

It didn't matter. Whoever he was, he was the only presence Bojo could find tonight who might be strong enough for their purposes. For better or worse, the tinker knew he would have to find this man or go back to Holly empty-handed, and that, he was unwilling to do.

Thinking of Holly made him smile. Don't get involved, the uncles and the aunts were always telling him. That isn't your world. But how could he not be attracted to someone like Holly? She was so pretty and smart, and that red hair.

Bojo had a weakness for red-haired women. Especially when they rode a motorcycle. He wondered if Holly had one stowed away in a shed behind her shop. A Norton or an Indian. Perhaps a Vincent Black Lightning.

Concentrate on the task at hand, he told himself. Fail in this and he wouldn't be able to show his face back at the bookstore to find out. Women liked men who kept their word. He said he'd help, so first he'd help, then he'd determine how she felt about motorcycles.

Like the hidden folk with whom he shared the night, he kept to the shadows. His route took him east on Stanton where the estates became steadily more rundown before finally giving over to brownstones and storefronts. He ducked into doorways or alleys whenever he saw a vehicle approaching, or—more rarely—another pedestrian. He carried no papers, nothing to identify himself at all, so he was wary of being stopped by one of the city's authorities and having to answer questions about what he was doing out so late at night. Keeping a low profile was almost second nature by now.

It didn't matter what world one was in, tinkers were used to unwanted altercations with the law. The sheriffs and police of any place—village, town, or city—could never make up their minds if they wanted to lock you up or move you along, but they were united in their dislike of the rambling men and women of the tinker clans. That was no longer news for Bojo.

Once he reached Palm Street, he didn't need to be so cautious anymore. He passed more than one parked police cruiser, engine idling, the officers inside barely giving him a glance. They had far more to interest them here than one footloose tinker.

Palm was the main through street of the Combat Zone, this less reputable part of the city, the streets lined with pool halls, diners, strip joints, nightclubs, hotels, the Men's Mission, and innumerable small stores specializing in discount merchandise that were locked up so tightly at this time of night with graffiti-festooned metal sheeting that one might be forgiven in thinking they actually had something valuable to sell.

Even at this hour, cars drifted slowly by, drivers and passengers checking out the lively assortment of bikers, transients, drug dealers, prostitutes of both sexes, not to mention the slumming regular citizens drawn by curiosity or, more likely, the hope of conducting a transaction. The developers hadn't yet cleaned up the Zone the way that they'd Disney-fied Times Square in New York City, but that was only because no one had yet stepped up with enough cash in hand. Still, that time was coming and the gentrification had already begun at the south end of Palm, where it ran along Fitzhenry Park.

Bojo liked this part of town. He felt he could relax here where identification papers or one's station in life were of far less concern than how much money you had in your pocket. He'd spent time in some of the jazz clubs and pool halls and even sat in on a few back room card games, never drawing too much attention to himself, but still able to be himself.

But he didn't have time for amusements tonight.

The spark grew steadily stronger. It led him north on Palm, up to Grasso Street where he took a right, until he finally stood across the street from a diner that was obviously closed for the night. If it wasn't for the spark, he would have walked right by. He stood watching the darkened windows for a long time, but saw no movement, no indication at all that there might be anyone inside.

He waited a little longer before he finally crossed the street. He tapped on the glass door. There was no response. But when he pressed his hand against the cool pane, the door moved under the pressure.

He pushed it open, just enough to poke his head in.

"Hello?" he called, his voice pitched low, but loud enough to carry. "Is anybody here?"

Still no response.

He pushed a little harder, widening the opening until he could step inside.

"Hello?" he called again.

The pull of the spark towed his gaze to left side of the diner. There, in the middle of a row of booths, was a silent figure, a man sitting so quietly that he would have remained invisible except that his aura of potent energy drew Bojo's attention to him as surely as movement might have.

Walking slowly to show he meant no harm, he approached the man's booth. It was hard to make out his features in the poor streetlight coming in from the windows, but Bojo put him in his early twenties, a slender black man in a pinstriped suit, small-boned and handsome, with long delicate fingers and wavy hair brushed back from his forehead. An old Gibson guitar stood upright on the seat on the other side of the booth, as though the two of them were having a visit, sharing confidences.

Bojo opened his mouth to speak. Before he could, the black man's hand lifted from where it had been hidden under the table and Bojo found himself looking into the muzzle of what appeared to be a very large revolver.

"So you found me," the man said. "Don't think I haven't felt you sniffing me out for the past couple of hours. But the question you've got to answer is, now that you're here, what am I going to do with you?"

Christy

When we step outside, I see what Geordie meant about there being an odd feeling in the air tonight.

Tonight? What am I saying?

I shake my head as we walk down the block. It's almost dawn and the night's pretty much gone. Though it's still dark here in the narrow canyons between the brownstones, the skies are already lightening in the east. But the dawn's not quite here yet and there's a *mood* on the streets that I can't quite put my finger on. I walk around a lot at night—a habit I first picked up from Jilly—and I'm used to the otherworldly air that the city streets can take on at this early hour when there's hardly anybody about. At least not in Crowsea. Other parts of downtown—like Palm Street, or up on Grasso—it's busy twenty-four/seven. But in Crowsea, the buildings themselves seem to drift off some time after midnight.

Here, you get a breathing space between when the last stragglers from the clubs have gone home and the morning rush hour starts, with its first trickles of commuters passing through on their way downtown. Movement in the corner of your eye could be an alley cat, could be some little man, hauling his goods to a goblin market. It doesn't matter. Everything just feels open and deep and . . . possible.

But tonight it's different. I spy flickering hints of electric foxfire along the edges of roofs and around distant manhole covers, blue-white and crackling. The transformers on the power and telephone poles are humming louder than usual, and I keep catching an echo of that same smell that filled my study when the computer imploded.

There's definitely something in the air and it's not something I recognize from other late night excursions on the streets. I don't know whether it's because my mood's been coloured by what happened to Saskia, or if there really is something new in the shadows, something dark and maybe a little hungry. But I can feel a warning prickle at the nape of my neck that's usually not there. It's like someone—*something*—is watching us.

My car's parked a couple of blocks away in a garage I rent from the owner of a dollar store over on Williamson Street—what we used to call dime stores back when Geordie and I were kids. There's a sign of inflation that I never thought of before. The car's an old Dodge stationwagon. Give me a North American car any day. These K-cars might not look like much when you've put the years on them like I have this battered old beast, but they just won't die. Stick the key in, winter or summer, and the engine turns over, pretty much every time.

I don't drive it often—maybe once or twice a week—and my apartment building doesn't have parking, but I don't like leaving it on the street, even if it's only the rust that's keeping it together. Sure, it's too beat-up to get stolen, but it would definitely get ticketed during the day, and it's a royal pain to have to keep moving it around every few hours, just to stay ahead of the parking control officers. I know people who do it, people who can easily afford the cost of renting a parking place, but they'd rather play the parking spot game. Takes all kinds.

We finally reach Mr. Li's building. I unlock the garage door and roll it up, metal sheets rattling loudly as they fold away. The Dodge starts right up and I pull it out, idling by the curb while Geordie shuts the garage door behind us.

"So what do you really think about all of this?" he asks as I pull away and turn onto Williamson Street. "This idea of Estie's, I mean. Trying to make a new connection to the Wordwood seems like clutching at straws."

"I don't know what to think."

"Well, I think we should call in someone like Joe, who can walk between the worlds. I mean, this whole cyberspace thing—it's like another world, right? A variation on *manidò-ak*—Joe's spiritworld."

I give him a quick glance before returning my gaze to the street.

"I still can't get used to hearing you say something like that," I tell him.

"I mean, considering how hard you've always fought the idea of there being anything more than what we can see and feel in the World As It Is."

"I've seen too much not to believe anymore, starting with how these days we've got Wendy and Sophie happily crossing over whenever the fancy takes them." He gives a small laugh that holds more discomfort than humour. "I've actually gotten used to seeing someone step into a doorway and disappear instead of going on into the room the way logic says they should."

"You've never been tempted to go over yourself?" I ask.

He nods. "But I'm waiting for Jilly to get better so that I can do it with her. It doesn't seem fair to go on my own—not when it's something she's always dreamed of doing."

I think about how sad it is that the two people in this world that couldn't be more perfect for each other, always seem to have something keeping them apart from being more than friends. Before Jilly was with Daniel, it was Geordie with Tanya. They never seem to get it right.

"What about you?" he asks.

I take the time to light a cigarette before responding, cracking the window open on my side to let the smoke out.

"I've thought about it," I say. "You know, asking Wendy or Sophie, or even Joe, to walk me over, but something always stops me. I think it's because everything that interests me about these kinds of phenomena centers around how they interact with the World As It Is, and how those of us living here react to these intrusions. To just cross those borders and be someplace where everything's magical, where anything can happen . . ." I shake my head. "I suppose I'll go one of these days, if only to have the experience. But I'm not in any hurry."

Geordie nods. "It's funny. I always thought you'd be over there in a flash. That you were like Jilly and this was something you'd spent your whole life looking for."

"I thought the same thing," I tell him. "Until suddenly it was possible. Now I worry that if I do go over, this world will pale too much and it won't satisfy me anymore."

"You think it's that much better?"

I shake my head. "That much more intense. I like this world too much to take the chance lightly."

"You just don't like change."

I smile. "That, too."

"But what if we have to do it now?" Geordie asks. "To get Saskia."

"I'd cross over in a flash."

We fall silent for a couple of blocks, Geordie looking out the passenger's side window, while I keep my attention on the road ahead. There's next to no traffic. A few cabs and delivery vans. A police cruiser that followed us for a couple of blocks before it turned off onto Gellar Street.

"Do you really think we'll get them back?" Geordie asks. "These . . ." He hesitates, then uses the term CNN coined for their coverage. "The disappeared."

I nod, light another cigarette. "Of course we will."

"I don't see how," he says. "What are we supposed to do? Download them from a Web site?"

"If they were able to vanish into their computers, then there's a way to pull them out again. Remember those pixies that caused all that trouble for Holly a couple of years ago? They stepped in and out of her computer."

From the corner of my eye I can see Geordie just shaking his head. I suppose that even with all he's seen, Holly's pixel pixies are still too much like a storybook for him.

"Okay," I say. "Think of the computers as portals—you know, doors to the otherworld—no different from the ones that Wendy steps through."

"She has to hold some little red stone that this Cody guy gave her."

"You know what I mean. It's a similar principle. Something has to act as a catalyst to open these hidden doors. In Wendy's case it's a magic stone. With the disappeared, it's something else—something to do with the Wordwood. We just have to figure out what."

I don't know who I'm trying to convince more—him or me—and we fall quiet again as we cross Gracie Street and head into the Tombs, what the runaways call Squatland.

This part of town just depresses the hell out of me. I can't believe the city council ever let it get this bad. Or that after it had, they haven't done something to make it right. It's a whole condemned section of the city, block after block of abandoned buildings and empty lots. Except for a few through streets, mostly running north/south, the side streets are all blocked with rubble from collapsed buildings, the wrecks of rusting cars and trucks, and other, often less identifiable, debris. The rats grow as big as cats here, hunted by small packs of wild dogs that were originally family pets before they were cast aside and went feral.

It's not just an eyesore, it's dangerous. The wild dogs aren't the only things running feral in Squatland. This is where the bikers have their parties, where the dealers and outlaws hide out, because once you make your way into the Tombs, you disappear from the cops' radar. It's where the lost and the hopeless go to make their last stand—the runaways, the homeless, the junkies and winos.

I believe that everything has a spirit—people, animals, plants, minerals, water. Everything. Even places, like parts of a city. The one that hangs like a cloud over these streets is despair. When I'm as close to it as we are now, I can feel my own old depressions start to press against the walls of my chest. Maybe that's what starts me talking again—anything to distract myself, even if it's to tell Geordie things I've probably told him before. But we didn't really talk to each other for years and I can never remember what I have or haven't shared with him.

"But getting back to the otherworld for a moment," I say, "I guess maybe the real reason I hold back from visiting it is that I have this feeling that once I cross over, that'll be it. This journey I've been on for my whole life will be over."

Geordie gives me a puzzled look.

"The thing people chasing magic forget," I tell him, "is that catching the magic isn't what it's all about. It's how you conduct yourself while you're along the way."

"Like with Tao," he says. "It's the journey that's important."

"It's like everything, if you stop and consider it. I can't think of one process that an individual might undertake where it wouldn't hold true."

Geordie nods. "It's why I don't really care about making the big time. I just want to make music."

I'm surprised—here's more of what we don't know about each other. And I never thought of it like that . . . how his single-minded pursuit of his music might be the same as my chasing magic. That they're just different ghosts wearing the same coat.

We leave the Tombs behind and get back onto more civilized territory, though now Williamson is increasingly lined with fast-food outlets, muffler and body work shops, discount retail outlets. The older buildings still have apartments above them. The newer ones sport parking lots in various shapes and sizes. But they all back onto older parts of the city: tenements, and clapboard and brick houses set snug against one another with the odd driveway in between. We're still a few miles from the suburbs with their scrubbed houses and lawns.

I light another cigarette and find myself thinking about my shadow, that elusive piece of my childhood self, part Nimue, part Huckleberry Finn, who went walkabout when she was separated from me. They don't come any more free-spirited than her. I wonder if Geordie's ever met his shadow, and if he has, what she's like. Or maybe he doesn't even know that he has one. Most people don't. If they do interact with their shadow, it's in dreams, or they're unaware of it.

Then I realize that in a lot of ways, Jilly could fit the bill for him. She could easily be his shadow. Maybe that's why they connect so well as friends, but it never goes any further. I almost bring it up, but then we're turning onto Holly's street and the moment's gone.

"Holly's probably not going to appreciate this," Geordie says.

I pull into a parking spot right in front of the store. There's no jockeying for a good spot at this time of the morning. I look at the darkened store. The apartment upstairs shows the same lack of lights.

"I don't know if appreciate's the right word," I say. "But she'll want to know. They were all really tight in university."

"Only one way to find out," he says.

I step out of the car and up to the front door, Geordie trailing along behind me. I reach up to about a third of the way down from the top of the doorframe and move aside a false brick that's on a hinge. There's a buzzer hidden in the alcove that was behind the brick. I give it a couple of jabs, then cover it over again with the brick.

"Cute," Geordie says.

"Holly got tired of customers ringing the apartment at all hours of the night and day, looking for a particular book that they needed *right now*. This is so her friends can buzz her. The other one—" I point to the regular buzzer on the exterior that's a foot or so below the hidden one. "—only rings in the store."

"Having worked in retail," Geordie says, "it makes sense to me. I can't believe the things that customers will assume."

I'm peering through the door as we talk.

"Here she comes," I say.

We both step back while Holly unlocks the door and opens it wide enough to look out at us. She's barefoot, dressed in a fluffy coral terrycloth robe held closed at the neck with one hand, her hair mussed, her eyes sleepy behind her glasses as she peers at us through the crack.

"Christy," she says, looking from me to my brother. "Geordie."

Geordie nods. "Hi, Holly."

"What do you get when you've got double the Riddells?" she asks.

I smile. "I'll bite. What do you get?"

She blinks then shrugs. "I thought I had a joke going somewhere but I'm too sleepy to find the punch line. What time is it anyway?"

"Going on six."

"And *what* are you doing here?"

"We need to talk and your phone seems to be out of order."

"I unplugged it earlier." She gives me a considering look, the sleepiness in her eyes starting to fade. "So what couldn't wait until a decent hour?"

"It's about Benny," I say.

"Benny . . . ? *My* Benny?"

I nod. "There's been some trouble with him and the Wordwood."

I don't recognize the look that crosses her face—not until later when she tells me about her own evening's adventures. For now, she opens the door wider and steps back.

"You'd better come in," she says.

Saskia

If Christiana's in this place, I can't find her.

First I fall into a black void—it's like that moment between when I lost my body and got into the phone lines, just before I willed myself to the number that Christiana gave me when I first met her in the Beanery Café. It was only last night, but it already feels like a lifetime ago.

That void seemed to draw every molecule of my essence toward . . . something. I'm not sure what. A cage, a trap, a place from which there would be no escape. I didn't know what it was, only what it would do to me. It manifested itself as a tiny, invisible maelstrom that I could sense was no bigger than a pinpoint, but it had the inexorable tow that lies at the heart of a black hole. Those dense remnants of a supernova can swallow millions of tons of matter every second. If I'd let myself go, I would have immediately vanished into that maelstrom and been lost forever.

This void is the exact opposite. It's just as overwhelming, but here every piece and particle that makes me who I am is being pulled in a hundred thousand different directions. If I let myself go here, I'll never be able to find all those pieces and put myself together again.

Maybe I'm in the heart of that black hole this time. Maybe I'm already lost.

I can't accept that.

I won't accept that.

I do what I did the last time. I search for a pulse, a wave, some kind of energy in motion that I can latch onto. Something I can focus on that will get me out of here, though that's not the only reason I focus with such determination. I need to escape this place, but I also know that the very act of concentrating so intensely upon release will help keep me in one piece, giving my efforts a two-fold purpose.

There are no clues to time's passage so I've no idea how long I'm lost in this utter darkness, searching for a way out, fighting the tearing pull that yanks at me from every direction. Maybe there is no way out. Maybe this is what death means for someone like me, born in pixels and data. Maybe I should stop fighting; just let myself go and return to the anonymity where the spirit that inhabits the Wordwood site found me before it brought me into physical existence.

There's no pain involved in my struggle. How can I feel pain when I don't have a body? There's only this mental panic that doesn't even feel real because there are no physical symptoms to back it up. But the strain on my spirit is slowly eroding my will to survive.

I'm so tired.

I'm so close to letting go.

But then I hear—no, what am I saying? I don't have ears. I can't hear anything. I become *aware* of this humming. It's long and narrow, like a thin wire of sound, cutting though the darkness.

It's there.

No, there.

No, *there*.

I fling a net of my thoughts towards it, wrapping myself around the invisible drone of its passage through this place.

And suddenly there's motion. I realize that there must be air here, because sound couldn't exist without it. The droning sound wave is putting pressure on the air, like ripples in water, and I'm riding the rise and fall of its passage. I'm a part of the variations it causes in the atmosphere, staying with it as it turns into an electrical sound signal where the voltage varies at the same rate that the original drone created its ripples in the air. And I'm still a part of it as voltage converts into binary numbers, a bewildering flicker of on-off electrical pulses that change so quickly it's impossible to focus on a string of them, never mind one.

Each measurement is changed into a 16-bit number.

Coded into digital sound.

And now I know where I am.

No, not *where* I am, but *what* I'm in. I'm somewhere in a computer processor. Or I'm a part of a signal travelling between processors. I'm back in the digital womb where I was born, except this time I'm aware of being here. I know who I am. I don't know what I am, but I know who.

And now I have hope of finding a way out. It won't be easy. The digital domain is immense. The bits that make it up aren't simply patterns stored in one computer any more. With Internet connections, they can cross vast distances, lodging in distant processors and memory stores. Millions of computers communicate with each other throughout the world. I could be anywhere.

But machines operate on logic. I may be lost, but if I can figure out how to access HyperText Transfer Protocol, I can direct this signal I'm hitching a ride on to take me where I need to go.

I visualize the URL in my mind.

www.thewordwood.com

That's where all of this started—my trying to contact the pixelated spirit that brought me into this world. That's where *I* started, in the domain it carved out for itself from the World Wide Web. So that's where I need to return. I don't just need answers anymore. I need my body back. The spirit gave it to me once. I'll have to convince it to give it to me again.

I put all my concentration into the Wordwood's site.

I can't be sure, but I think I detect a slight variation in the signal's passage. I concentrate harder.

Time passes—in a confusing blur now, I'm moving so fast. But it's no easier to judge how long I'm riding on the back of this digital signal than it was trying to measure how long I was floating in the earlier darkness.

Then suddenly my awareness explodes with a dazzling array of strings of blue-white light. I'm flying at immeasurable speeds over a bewildering grid work of crisscrossing lines. It's circuitry, I realize, only viewed not from a physical viewpoint, but in terms of the energy it emits.

The signal takes me faster. Faster.

I focus harder on the Wordwood's URL, but I can't muster the strength to hold onto it anymore. I can't hold onto anything. No matter how much I try, how determined I am, everything slips away and my consciousness is gone again. . . .

Bojo

"Wait a minute," Bojo said.

Staring into the muzzle of the enormous handgun pointed at his face, all Bojo seemed able to do was hold his hands out in front of him, palms forward. He wasn't sure if it would look like he was hoping to stop a bullet with his hands, or showing that he was unarmed and presented no danger. It didn't matter. Just so long as the man didn't shoot.

It was hot in the diner, with a close smell in the air—a mix of old grease from the kitchen and whatever had been used to clean the countertop, tables and floor. But under that was a faint, pleasant scent, like a fruity cologne smelling of apples and roses. Or maybe lilacs with a hint of citrus. Whenever Bojo thought he recognized it, the scent shifted into something else.

He tried to muster up a smile, but it was hard. His mouth was dry and he swallowed hard as he considered the best way to frame an explanation of what he was doing here. It turned out he didn't need to.

"You're no hellhound," the man said, lowering his arm.

"No," Bojo agreed. Whatever a hellhound was. "I'm just a simple tinker who's come looking for advice."

The man smiled. "Advice. I should see about getting myself a column, maybe have it syndicated."

He got up from his booth and shifted the revolver from his right hand to his left.

"I'm Robert Lonnie," he added, offering his free hand.

Bojo shook hands with him, noting that for all his slender frame and his long, delicate fingers, Robert had a firm grip—more like that of a man who worked with his hands, than the besuited gangster dandy he appeared to be.

"Pleased to meet you," he said. "I'm Borrible Jones, but most people call me Bojo."

Robert's eyebrows lifted. "Unusual name to give a kid."

"Well, the story is that when the midwife lifted me up, my father took one look at this bloody baby, wailing its lungs out and dripping all over the floor, and he said, 'That's horrible.' Except he had a speech impediment, so it came out, 'Bat's borrible.' For some reason, the name stuck. I suppose it didn't help that I wasn't a very well-behaved child."

Robert regarded him for a long moment, amusement flickering in his eyes.

"Have a seat," he finally said, motioning to the side of the booth he'd just vacated.

He sat down beside the guitar, laying his revolver on the table between them.

"They call it a Peacemaker," he said when he saw Bojo's gaze settle on the large handgun. "A single-action Colt, .44 caliber. But the only peace it makes is if you shoot the person that's troubling you. My daddy took it from a dead man who'd been considering a lynching before his own premature demise."

Bojo wasn't sure he'd heard that right.

"They still lynch people around here?" he asked.

"Oh, that was a long time ago—another part of history that folks'd sooner forget, though it's hard when it's your own people that were hanging like strange fruit from trees and lampposts."

Bojo's gaze had adjusted enough to the bad lighting in the diner that he was able to see the something in Robert's eyes that said he'd been around for generations—not the way tinkers circumvented time, by stepping through worlds, but simply by living through the years, ageless.

As the knowledge came to Bojo, he saw a smile pull at one corner of Robert's mouth, as though the bluesman could read his mind. Robert picked up the Gibson and began to pluck a slow walking blues from its strings, right-hand thumb keeping the bass rhythm, those long fingers of his left hand travelling the fingerboard like the legs of a spider.

"So what's this advice you need?" he asked.

"It's kind of a long story."

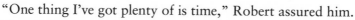

"One thing I've got plenty of is time," Robert assured him.

"I guess you would," Bojo said.

That crooked smile stayed on Robert's lips. He didn't speak, but a simple hammer-on on the bass string, followed by a bluesy slide of notes on the high E, seemed to say, Why don't you tell me this story of yours?

So Bojo started in, beginning with the telephone message that had brought him around to Holly's store and finishing with what he'd sensed on the streets on his way to finding Robert here in this diner. The guitar laid a counterpoint rhythm to the cadence of his voice, making Bojo feel as though he was delivering a talking blues rather than simply telling a story.

"And the advice you need is . . . ?" Robert asked when Bojo's voice trailed off.

He made the high strings call a quizzical note while the bass line continued, faint but keeping the rhythm.

"Because I've got to tell you," Robert said, "I don't know the first thing about computers or the spirits that might be sitting there somewhere inside them. What do they call those places—virtual worlds?"

Bojo shook his head. "No, those are the ones that aren't real."

"Depends where you stand, I suppose. Probably real to those living in them."

"I suppose."

"The way I see it," Robert went on, the guitar continuing to play a counter rhythm to the flow of his voice, "is maybe what you've got here is more like the Native take on things. See, with my people there's always a lot of trading going on when it comes to the spirits. Baptist minister or gris-gris man, everybody's trying to cut themselves a bargain, doesn't matter if they're figuring out how to get into heaven or working on some piece of hoodoo. But for the Indians it's more like a tree. You see the trunk and foliage, but all the important stuff's going on underground, out of sight."

"A tree."

Robert smiled. "I just mean things are hidden. That there's more sitting in front of you than you can see. It's not like an onion where you've got to peel back layers to see what's going on. Or even like those Russian dolls where each one's got itself a smaller one inside. It's more you see the one thing, but there's a whole invisible world going on behind it. One you don't even know is there, never mind being able to see it."

Bojo nodded to show he understood.

" 'Course maybe we're talking words here," Robert went on. "They have to use words to tell the computers what to do, right?"

"I think they call it code," Bojo said, remembering what Holly had told him about it. "Programming languages."

"Which is still words and words . . . well, words are an old magic that goes right back to the first days. The ones they're using for their computers are just that old magic dressed up in some new technological jacket." He paused for a moment, the guitar still playing. "There's a lot of people believe that the universe was created with just a word, but I guess you know that."

"Like the Word of God in the Bible," Bojo said.

It was something he'd heard about, but he was hazy on the details.

"Right," Robert said. "Logos. Though Christianity's not the first religion, and I doubt it's going to be the last, to slip that bit of old history into its stories about how we all came to be. You know how it usually goes?"

Robert didn't wait for an answer. The music from his guitar shifted into a minor key.

"Way I heard it," Robert says, "is that this one word that jump-started the world became a language and that language started up a conversation that gives everything its shape and meaning—a conversation that's still going on to this day. The trouble is, over time, that original language went and fragmented into a thousand thousand variations and dialects. Before you know it, none of us can really speak to each other anymore. Animals, plants, people, the dirt under our feet—everything has a different language now. Hell, these days we can't even be sure that some word we use is even close to what it means to the person we're talking to.

"But bits and pieces of that original language still remain. Some of those old words. And we're talking powerful mojo here."

Bojo nodded. "I remember Meran talking to me about that. I think she even knows some of those old words."

"Everybody's got a few of them floating around in the old parts of their minds—the places inside them where instincts still work and the soul spends its time. Most of them just don't know it, which is probably a good thing. You speak one of those words and things . . . change."

"You know any of those words?" Bojo asked.

"Only one. It's what keeps the hellhounds circling around, but they never can quite find me."

Bojo nodded. He wanted to ask about these hellhounds Robert kept mentioning, but his years on the road had taught him that you didn't ask after personal information, you only took it when it was offered. So instead he sat there on the other side of the booth and listened to the music his companion pulled out of that old Gibson. It had shifted back into a major key, but when exactly that had happened, Bojo hadn't noticed.

"So I take it you like this girl," Robert said after a few moments.

His fingers never stopped their spiderwalk up and down the neck of his guitar, his right hand pulling the notes.

"What do you mean?"

Robert smiled. "Well, for someone you just up and met, you seem pretty fixed on wanting to make a good impression. You know, save the day, have her in your arms when the story's done."

"It's not like that."

"Every time a mention of her comes up, your heartbeat tells me different."

Bojo shrugged. "Can you help us?" he asked, wanting to steer the conversation back to something that might be useful.

"Don't know that you want my help, exactly," Robert said.

"Why's that?"

Robert shrugged. "Trouble's always got an eye out for me—it's why I keep a low profile. I come along to your friend's store and I could be bringing more problems than we're trying to solve."

"You mean these helldogs you keep talking about."

"Hellhounds," Robert said. "And they're not necessarily dogs. They come in all shapes and sizes. The only thing they have in common is their interest in me."

Since Robert had started the personal questions by asking how he felt about Holly, Bojo thought maybe he could satisfy some of his own curiosity without appearing impolite.

"Why are they chasing you?" he asked.

Robert smiled. "You might say we had us an altercation. That was a time ago, but there's some that don't know the meaning of either forgive or forget."

"Old spirits."

Robert nodded.

"Well," Bojo said, "I think the ones we're talking about here are new ones. Technological spirits, I suppose we could call them."

"Unless it's old spirits wearing new clothes." Before Bojo could comment, Robert added, "But you're right. It doesn't feel like it, does it? Because that's the thing about spirits—they get more set in their ways than we do."

"Maybe because they've been at it a lot longer."

"Could be," Robert agreed.

"So will you help?"

"How about if the most I promise is that I'll come along and have a look-see?"

They took a cab up to Holly's store, the two of them sitting in the back with the guitar in its case on the seat between them. Bojo hadn't seen where the handgun had gone. One moment it was on the table in the diner, the next it wasn't, and the classic cut of Robert's suit didn't sport any new bulges to show where it might have been hidden. For all Bojo knew, it could be under the fedora that Robert had put on before they left the diner, locking the door behind them.

"I know this store your friend owns," Robert said as the cab took them north. "Though I don't think I ever went in. I'm not much of a book reader."

"Me, neither."

"But there used to be a coffee shop I liked a few doors down. I spent many a morning sitting in there, drinking my coffee and looking out the window. I'd read the papers, play a few tunes."

"What made you stop?"

Robert shrugged. "It got to be a pattern and I try to keep patterns out of my life."

"Because of the hellhounds."

"Partly. Partly I just don't like to acquire habits. And then that coffee shop went all upscale on me. I don't blame Joe—Joe Lapegna, the guy who owns the place. He saw which way the wind was blowing and had to stay competitive, what with all the high-end cafés coming into town and all."

He looked out the window as the cab turned onto Holly's street.

"Guess what I'm trying to say," he said, "is that I miss the place."

Holly

"She really just . . . disappeared into your computer?" Holly asked when Christy finished his story.

The part about Saskia's disappearance had come early on, but Holly was still trying to get her head around the idea of it. Even with the pixie infestation that she and Dick had experienced, not to mention living with the hob for the past two years since then, what had happened to Saskia and Benny still seemed impossible.

But Christy nodded. "Like she never existed."

Holly heard the catch in his voice and reached out across the table to put her hand on his.

"We'll get her back," she said. "Saskia and Benny and all of them."

She knew they were just words, but sometimes people needed words, even when the promise held in them couldn't necessarily be fulfilled.

They were sitting around in her apartment—just as she'd sat with Dick and Bojo earlier, except the tinker had been replaced by the Riddell brothers, and they were in the kitchen rather than the living room. She got up now to make a second pot of coffee and pulled out a tin of day-old, homemade scones that were still fresh enough to serve to company if you slathered them with jam. The coffee went quickly, but no one seemed to have much appetite.

There was a restlessness in the air—a need to be doing something, *any-thing,* but no one knew what. The only one who appeared to be immune was Geordie, but Geordie was always able to put a calm face on things. As Jilly would say, "It's just this gift he has." But Christy kept opening the screen door and standing out on the fire escape to have a cigarette, and Dick was wearing a path in the floor between the kitchen and the front room windows that overlooked the street, though what he was expecting or look-ing for he didn't say.

Holly was feeling a bit jittery herself. It looked like she and Dick had come *so* close to getting pulled into the computer themselves. If Dick hadn't accidentally broken their Internet connection, not to mention her monitor . . .

Don't think about it, she told herself and poured herself another half-cup of coffee.

"So they're all coming?" she asked. "Estie and Tip and all?"

"Apparently," Geordie said. "Do you still have that old computer stored away somewhere?"

Holly looked to Dick, but he was in the front room again.

"I think so," she said. "Dick'd know better."

Geordie stirred at the sound of the hob's name and looked around. Holly knew exactly what was happening to him: magical being that Dick was, his existence kept slipping Geordie's mind, the way it did for most people. You'd forget, then you'd hear his name or see him again and you'd wonder how you'd ever forgotten.

"It's okay," she told him. "Dick has that effect on pretty much every-body until you get to really know him."

Geordie nodded. "That's what Christy keeps telling me. But it's still disconcerting when it's actually happening to you. Makes you wonder what else you're missing."

"Who's missing what?" Christy asked, coming in after having another cigarette.

Geordie shrugged. "Me. Missing all the hidden things in the world."

"It's not your fault," Christy said. "You just don't have the trick of it yet, that's all. You need to immerse yourself in—"

He broke off as Dick came running back into the room.

"The tinker's back," Dick said. "And he's brought a friend."

"Tinker?" Christy asked.

"He's that fellow taking care of Meran's place," Holly said. "I told you about him."

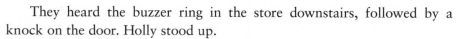

They heard the buzzer ring in the store downstairs, followed by a knock on the door. Holly stood up.

"I'll get that," she said.

She was happy that none of the others had come down with her because she immediately started to blush at the warm smile Bojo gave her when she unlocked the door and let them in. His companion was a dapper black man with a relaxed look about him, belied only by his penetrating eyes. He was easily as striking as Bojo, though his neat suit and fedora were a far cry from the tinker's more Bohemian look, and he carried a battered guitar case in his left hand. He took off his hat, tucking it under his arm when he came into the store.

"You'll be Holly," he said, offering her his hand. "I'm Robert Lonnie."

They shook hands, then Holly stepped aside to let them by. She closed the door behind them and locked it again. When she turned, Bojo laid a hand on her shoulder and gave it a squeeze.

Be still my heart, Holly thought.

"I told you I'd be back," Bojo said. "With help in tow and all. Robert here—"

"Doesn't know much about anything when it comes to computers," Robert broke in, "but he's seen a thing or two that doesn't make sense in this world." He paused, then smiled. "He also hates it when people talk in the third person about themselves, so I'm going to stop right about now."

"There've been some complications since you left," Holly told Bojo.

"You and Dick are okay?"

Holly nodded. "We're fine. But—well, you should just come upstairs and I'll let the others fill you in."

She started for the stairs to her apartment, pausing when only Bojo followed.

"Aren't you coming, Mr. Lonnie?"

"It's Robert," he said, looking up briefly before his gaze tracked through the store, settling on the desk again.

"Are you looking for something?" Holly asked.

Robert shook his head. He continued to study the desk for a long moment, then finally turned and joined them at the foot of the stairs.

"I was just taking in a sense of this place," he said. "Getting a feel for things. Something almost came through here tonight—from the other side, I mean."

Holly nodded. "If Dick hadn't been as quick as he was, we could've been sucked away just like all those other people."

"What other people?" Bojo asked.

The question was repeated in Robert's eyes.

"That's what I was trying to tell you," Holly said. "It's not just me and my weird little computer woes anymore. But Christy can tell you more."

"Lead on," Robert told her at the same time as Bojo asked, "Who's Christy?"

"Christy Riddell," Holly said over her shoulder as she started up the stairs. "He and his brother Geordie lost someone to a computer last night and there have been other disappearances, too. Apparently it's been on the news and everything. Christy thinks it's all tied to the Wordwood site."

"Wordwood," Robert said, repeating it as though he was tasting the way the two words came together into one.

Before Holly could explain more, they were upstairs and she was too busy introducing everybody. Geordie and Robert had already met, though only in passing. Everybody else needed an introduction. Robert appeared to be particularly delighted to meet Dick.

"I've never met one of the little people before," he said, then paused. "Do you mind being called that?"

Dick shook his head. "Oh, no, sir. You've been calling us that for hundreds of years now, just like we've been calling you big folk, or tall folk."

"Well, I'm very pleased to make your acquaintance," Robert told him.

"Borrible," Christy said to Bojo. "That's an unusual name. I'm a bit of a collector of names and I've never come across it before. Is it a given name?"

Bojo nodded. "It comes from the time before we became a travelling people. We lived in a mountainous area of our homeland and when the traders first came to our villages, they referred to us as aboriginals. Later, when relationships became more acrimonious between us, they started to call us borribles instead. My father, apparently, decided that we should reclaim the term and replace its negative associations with positive ones. So he changed his name to Borrible and named me the same. I'm told he hoped that I'd name my firstborn son the same, but I don't have a cruel streak in me."

Holly shot him a hurt look, disappointed to find out that he'd lied to her, but Robert only laughed.

"Sounds like you've got a different story for everyone you meet," he said.

Bojo shrugged. "Depends on how you look at it. Somewhere, some-when, each of those stories is true."

"I don't understand," Holly said.

"It's how the tinkers circumvent time," Robert explained. "Travelling in and out of worlds, they have many lives, rather than just one. It makes it hard for the years to catch up with them."

"Is this true?" Holly asked.

"My Aunt Meran notwithstanding, we're a restless people. Few of us settle down the way she and Cerin have."

"Though," Geordie put in, "the pair of them are still away touring for half the year or more."

Bojo gave a slow nod. "I hadn't thought of it like that."

There was a brief lull in the conversation then. Christy went out onto the fire escape for another cigarette. Dick got up as well.

"What do you keep looking for out there?" Holly asked him.

This time he had an answer.

"Pixies," he said over his shoulder.

Bojo poured himself and Robert another coffee, the others declining when he offered the pot to them. Robert took his mug and returned to the chair in the corner. He slipped his guitar out of its case and began to noodle on the strings, the unconnected notes finally falling into a simple twelve-bar blues.

"From the residue I sensed downstairs," Robert said when Christy and Dick had both returned to the kitchen, his voice following the rhythm of the music, "and with what I've been hearing now, I think Bojo is right. This is a deep magic, but it's not an old one."

"Does that mean there's nothing we can do?" Holly asked.

The bluesman shook his head. "On the contrary, the fact that it's not an old spirit works in our favour. It'll be less experienced and that means we'll have a better chance to get it to do what we want—so long as we do it right. But we're going to need some way to start up a conversation with it."

"Without a monitor, the store's computer isn't going to be much use," Holly said. "But if we can find my old one . . ."

This time when she looked at Dick, he was still in the room.

"It's still in the basement," he said. "Behind all those boxes of *National Geographic*."

"So, should we set it up?" Holly asked.

Robert nodded. "But since it doesn't seem like any of us is particularly computer-adept, we should probably wait for your friends before we try to use it. When you're working a mojo like this, you pretty much only have the one chance to get it right. Spirits learn fast. We won't get a second shot."

"But we do have a chance?" Christy said.

"Oh, yeah," Robert told him. "People always have a chance. Only trouble is, once we get that thing we need so bad, it doesn't always work out the way we thought it would."

"What's that supposed to mean?"

Robert slipped from the E♭ blues pattern he was playing into a minor key.

"Come on now," he said, his gaze mild as it lifted from the Gibson's strings and settled on Christy's features. "I know who you are. You've studied on this for years. Don't tell me you can't be surprised anymore."

"I don't understand," Holly said.

"What he means," Bojo explained, "is that some spirits just have it in their nature to play unfair. Maybe you asked for wealth. So you find you've got a cave full of treasure stashed away somewhere safe. Except you're sitting on Death Row and there's nothing you can do to get to it."

Holly glanced at Dick and the hob gave her an unhappy nod.

"It's true, Mistress Holly," he said. "Some of the old ones delight in thinking up new ways to keep their word but at the same time make it impossible for you to benefit."

"I've still got to try," Christy said.

" 'Course we've got to try," Robert said. "We've just got to step up to this with our thinking caps on. Figure out what the spirit wants. Figure out how we can guarantee we get what *we* want with no strings attached."

"But you're telling us it'll be hard," Geordie said.

Robert nodded. "Oh, yeah. It'll be hard. But hard doesn't mean impossible."

Aaran

One of the great side benefits of being the newspaper's book editor, so far as Aaran was concerned, was that he got an endless supply of freebies. And it wasn't only books and galleys that got packed away in his briefcase every day to be taken home. Because he made a point of writing reviews for other parts of the entertainment section, he got to cherry pick all the various promotional items that arrived at the paper. Prereleases of new CDs, videos, and DVDs. T-shirts, stickers, mugs, shooter glasses, watches, posters . . . whatever a company might use to promote their product.

It was a running joke at the office that Aaran would take home anything. What they didn't know was that he made a tidy little profit on the side, selling the various items on eBay, or to a few select record and book shops in Crowsea. Like he'd actually ever wear an Eminem T-shirt, or put a signed poster of Mariah Carey up in his living room. Or drink his morning coffee from a mug with the characters from *The Simpsons* printed on the side.

He also got to snap up tickets to concerts, films, and shows, which was what had brought him out to the Standish Hall last night for a concert by the Australian country singer Kasey Chambers. She was obviously a huge success with the sold-out crowd that had filled the 3000-seat concert hall, though Aaran couldn't understand why. He just didn't like this kind of music—alt-country, Americana, whatever you wanted to call it. But attending the odd dud concert such as this—or at least the first twenty minutes or so of the headliner's set, which was invariably enough for him to write a review—was the price he paid for also being able to score front-row Elton John tickets.

He sat now in his study, face and hands tinted blue from the glow of his computer screen as he composed his review of the show. He restrained himself from being too nasty—the entertainment editor had a different philosophy from Aaran's own in the book pages and preferred her reviewers to focus on the positive elements of what was being covered—but he couldn't resist slipping in a few digs about Australia, a country he'd never visited but instinctively disliked, and the idea that Chambers could have any sort of real experience on which to base her songs of heartbreak and country life.

And really, what was with the twang in her voice? Chambers should take a page from real country artists like Shania Twain, or Faith Hill's more recent work.

Melissa Lawrence, the entertainment editor, would probably edit out the digs, since she was a fan of Australia in general and Chambers's music in particular, but at least Aaran got the satisfaction of bringing her blood pressure up a notch or two. Especially since she hadn't been able to attend the show last night, which was how he got the job. It was never a bad thing to have people owe you favours.

The real highlight of last night's concert hadn't been the music, but a conversation he'd overheard while waiting in line to get into the Standish Hall. He'd recognized the pair standing ahead of him to be a couple of Saskia's friends and couldn't hold back a grin as he listened to them lament the fact that the Wordwood site was still down. He'd been very tempted to tap them on the shoulder and brag about the part he'd played in bringing its collapse, but common sense prevailed.

There was no point in making a scene.

Some of the people in that crowd of Saskia's were very high-strung and argumentative. It seemed to be one of the prerequisites of being an artist. That celebrated creative temperament.

When he was finished writing the review, he saved it on a disk then shut down his machine. Pocketing the disk, he set off for the newspaper's offices. He could as easily have e-mailed it to Melissa, but this was Sunday, when the Arts & Living offices would be pretty much empty, which made it a perfect time to go rooting about in the week's new promotional arrivals to see if there was anything he might have missed.

The office was a hubbub of conversation when Aaran stepped out of the elevator. Clusters of the newspaper's employees gathered around various desks, caught up in animated conversations, or sat in front of their monitors, fingers tapping on their keyboards. CNN was on the television set in the corner, but from where he stood, Aaran couldn't make out what its earnest news anchors were discussing. Either some big story had broken, or something had happened to one of the staff. His coworkers never got this interested in much else.

Big story, he decided when he spied a few of the hard news guys working at their terminals. Chuck Tremaine. Barbara Haley. Rob Watley. You never saw any of them in the office on a weekend unless there was a story well worth their time. And then, as though to confirm his suspicions, his gaze went to the glass windows of Kathleen Winter's office. There was a meeting underway in the news editor's office with a half-dozen production people sitting or standing around her desk. Which probably meant she was shooting for an extra edition and needed to work out the logistics.

"What's going on?" Aaran asked of the three reporters talking around the desk closest to the elevator doors.

Harold Cole turned to him. "Christ, Goldstein," he said. "Are you living in a cave? CNN's been running the story for hours."

Aaran shrugged. "I was out late last night and didn't turn on the TV this morning."

"So was she good?"

That was Mark Sakers, fresh out of journalism school and always eager to hear Aaran's stories of sexual conquest. Aaran never disappointed him, even if he had to make the stories up.

"They're always good," he told Mark, before turning back to Harold. "Seriously, what's up?"

"CNN's calling them 'the disappeared'—which should piss off anyone who lost relatives to South American dictators. But I suppose it's as descriptive a term as any, seeing how a few hundred people just up and vanished from their homes last night."

"What do you mean 'vanished'?"

"As in gone without a trace," George Hooper said. He was the third of the reporters standing around Harold's desk, an old hippie with his grey hair tied back in a ponytail. "There one moment, gone the next."

"But . . . how's that even possible?"

George smiled. "It's not—hence the big story."

"How many people are we talking about here?" Aaran asked.

When Harold turned to look at the television set, Aaran's gaze followed, but he couldn't make anything out beyond the blonde anchor looking into the camera with her patented serious expression.

"I think it was just tipping three-fifty," Harold said. "The last time I looked."

"All from the city?" Aaran asked.

George shook his head. "From all over the country, and abroad, too."

"We lost one of the nerd squad," Mark put in. "Disappeared right out of his apartment last night. Very *X-Files*."

Aaran got an eerie feeling in the pit of his stomach.

"Who was it?" he asked, though he was pretty sure he already knew. It just came to him in a flash, the way a good phrase did when he was writing a review.

"Jackson Hart," Mark said. "Did you know him?"

Aaran shook his head. "Just to see him around the office. What did you mean about it being very *X-Files*?"

"This is where it gets good," George said. "Apparently his landlady heard something dripping outside her apartment door. When she looked in the hall, there was this black goop dripping down the stairs, coming out of the crack under Hart's door. She stepped around it and banged on his door—no answer. So she uses her master key, opens the door, and this flood of the crap comes flowing out."

"Black goop?"

George shrugged. "Who knows? Anyway, she beats a hasty retreat and calls the cops. No sign of Hart inside—though she swears she heard him up there a few minutes before and he never went out. And then, get this, over the next fifteen minutes or so the goop just fades away like it never was. Now you tell me. If that isn't weird, what is?"

"No kidding," Aaran said. "I'm still trying to take it all in."

Not to mention trying to figure out how he'd known it was Jackson that had disappeared. And why he also knew—as clearly, if as inexplicably—that it had something to do with the little blackmail task he'd set Jackson. What, he didn't know. But somehow the disappearances were connected.

"Thing like this," Harold said. "I'll bet it makes you wish you were a real reporter."

Aaran gave a slow, distracted nod, not rising to the bait.

"You guys all have assignments?" he asked.

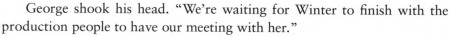

George shook his head. "We're waiting for Winter to finish with the production people to have our meeting with her."

"Well, good luck with it," Aaran told them.

He went into Melissa's office. Pulling the disk with the Chambers review out of his pocket, he dropped it on the entertainment editor's desk, then left the office without even bothering to go through the promotional materials that were on the bookcase behind her desk, or piled up in boxes along one wall.

After leaving the paper, Aaran went straight home and switched on his TV. He sat down on the couch, punched in CNN on his remote, and watched the story unfold. To anybody who'd been tuned in to the channel for awhile, this would be the umpteenth repeat of their coverage, but it was all new to Aaran as he watched in disbelief.

The truth was, back at the office, he hadn't really taken his coworkers seriously. While he'd known that there was something major going on— that was obvious—he hadn't really believed it to be some massive disappearance of people, figuring that Harold and the others had just been having him on. All he'd known for sure was that it had something to do with Jackson Hart, and therefore it could possibly be connected to him. How, he wasn't sure. What exactly it was, he hadn't known either, but was willing to wait until he got home rather than make a fool of himself by asking someone else in the office.

But there it was on the screen, and unless CNN had taken a page from Orson Welles and was doing their own version of *The War of the Worlds*, this had really happened.

The disappeared.

According to a little box in the corner of the screen, the number of people confirmed to be missing stood at eight hundred sixty-three, worldwide. Half that number had disappeared from North America.

At least there was nothing about computers, he thought, as the anchor woman completed her update. Nothing to connect any of this to me. It was just coincidence that Jackson Hart was involved. That little frisson of alarm that had made him think it had anything to do with blackmailing Jackson was obviously wrong.

But he still couldn't completely quell the uneasiness that had gripped him ever since he'd heard the news back at the paper. And questions kept rising to jangle his nerves.

Like, what if the authorities were merely withholding the fact that computers had been involved?

That was exactly the kind of thing they'd do, hoping some schmuck would trip himself up by showing he knew more than what was reported in the media. Just asking about it could get you into trouble.

But Aaran still had to know.

He sat awhile longer, staring at the TV but no longer hearing the anchor's voice or seeing what played out on the screen. Finally he shut it off, got his coat and went out again.

Don't do this, Aaran told himself as he made his way to Jackson's apartment.

But he went all the same.

"I've already talked to someone from the *Journal*," Jackson's landlady said.

She started to hand Aaran back his press I.D., then gave it another look.

"I know you," she said. "Jackson's talked about you."

The hand of fear tightened its grip inside Aaran.

"Did he now?" he said, managing to keep his face far calmer than he was feeling.

The landlady nodded. Although he put her age at not much more than his own thirty-eight, she gave him the impression of being older, like someone from his parents' generation rather than his own. It was something in the cut of her skirt and blouse, and those sensible brown shoes. Her makeup and the nondescript styling of her short, already greying hair only added to the impression.

"Nothing bad, I hope," Aaran said.

"Oh, no. He seemed to quite admire you. All the books you read and how you're able to write about them in a manner that's both intelligent, yet accessible to the lay person."

"Really?"

Jesus, Aaran thought. No wonder Jackson had opened up to him in the bar that night. And what had he done? Turned around and blackmailed him.

The landlady was nodding again. "Yes. Though he hasn't spoken of you in a while. I take it yours was more of an office friendship."

"The truth is, I didn't really know him all that well."

"Then it's all the more commendable for you to have come by to see about him now."

Aaran blinked in surprise. He felt as though he'd stepped into some surreal alternate dimension where dowdy tenement landladies turned out to be well-spoken and people only seemed to have nice things to say about him. That didn't normally happen. He wanted to be liked, but he also knew that he sabotaged any relationships—romantic or otherwise—with his constant need for control. To be the one on top.

Occasionally, he even made an effort to change, but it never lasted.

"Well, I just hope nothing bad's happened to him," he managed to say.

"So do I," the landlady said. "Jackson's a good man. He worked hard to make a success of himself. Most people with his unfortunate background don't."

Aaran had no idea what she was talking about. But while he was curious about what she meant, right now all he wanted to do was get away.

"If—*when* he comes back," he said. "Will you tell him I was by?"

The landlady nodded. "Keep him in your prayers, Mr. Goldstein."

"I will. Thank you for your time."

"The pleasure was mine."

Aaran backed away. He lifted a hand by way of goodbye and made his retreat through the front door of the building, feeling the weight of the landlady's eyes upon his back with every step he took.

Halfway down the block, he stopped and turned around to have another long look at the building. He wasn't really sure what had happened back there, or even why he'd come in the first place. What had he expected to find out? Yellow police tape had sealed the door to Jackson's apartment and it wasn't as though the landlady would have let him in anyway. Nor could he have asked about a computer connection to Jackson's disappearance, or what Jackson might have said about the Wordwood site.

He hadn't learned anything about the strange fluid that the landlady had noticed before Jackson's disappearance. Hadn't learned anything at all, except for what he already knew on nights when he was sitting in his own apartment with nowhere to go, no one to call: He was a heel.

Sighing, he turned his back on the building and continued on his way. God, but it was turning into a miserable day. And with not much improvement to look forward to, either. You'd think that he could just—

"Spare change?"

Aaran hadn't even seen the panhandler, tucked away in the doorway of the store he was walking by.

No, but I've got some spare saliva, he wanted to tell her, and then maybe he'd spit in her hand. Or at least tell her off.

Street people just annoyed him, from the big scary drunks trying to browbeat a few dollars out of you, to whiny runaways who left perfectly good homes and then expected people like him to support them.

But when he turned to look at her, his displeasure got swallowed by a rather earthy curiosity. Behind her dirty face, this ragged gamine with her short spiky blonde hair was actually pretty good-looking. And she also had what looked like a fine body under her baggy T-shirt and skateboarder's cargo pants—a little on the thin side, maybe, but an excellent lung capacity all the same.

His attraction to her was instant, but it was tempered with a vague uneasiness that he couldn't quite identify. He supposed it had to do with her age, which was hard to tell. She might be in late teens or early twenties, which would put her at about half his age.

He'd have to be careful here; she could be underage. But he'd long carried around a fantasy of picking up one of these little street girls, bringing her home and cleaning her up. . . .

Play this right and he could just get lucky.

Looking for an opening, his gaze went to the face of the native man on her T-shirt. Under it a slogan read, "Remember Dudley George." It took Aaran a moment, but then his eidetic memory kicked in and he connected the face to the relevant news story: Thirty-five natives peacefully protesting land seized during the Second World War—native land that contained an ancient burial ground—were confronted by two hundred and fifty heavily armed policemen. The resulting clash left George dead and ruined the career of the cop that had shot him. It had happened over five years ago, but the civil lawsuit was just going to court now.

"You think his family will win their lawsuit?" he asked.

Her look of surprise and the sudden interest in her eyes told him he had the hook in. Gently now, he told himself.

"What?" she said. "And ruin the government's record of successfully screwing indigenous people?"

Aaran nodded. "There's that. I've never understood why they don't just bite the bullet and do what's right."

"Money," she said, rubbing the pad of her thumb against her index and middle fingers. "Someone's making a buck, or we'd see a change." She smiled at him. "So what are you, an activist?"

"Not really," Aaran said. "I just believe we have to stand up against injustice."

And he supposed he really did believe that, so long as it didn't interfere with his own quality of life.

He let a pause hang for a moment between them, then turned the conversation to more personal concerns.

"I guess you've hit some rough times?" he asked.

She shrugged. "They say there's no recession, but . . ."

"Tell that to the people who can't get a job," Aaran filled in for her. "Not to mention how they make it so hard to collect welfare that a lot of people don't even try anymore."

She gave him a considering look.

"So what are you?" she asked. "A social worker?"

Aaran laughed. "No, I'm a book editor for a newspaper. My name's Aaran."

She shook the hand he offered her. Her hand was small in his, but her grip was firm.

"I'm Suzi."

"Pleased to meet you, Suzi," Aaran told her, "though I wish it was under better circumstances—for you, I mean."

"Oh, I get by."

"You been on the street a while?"

"Long enough to know the score."

"What do you mean?"

"Well, you're hitting on me, aren't you? Except you're going easy 'cause you're thinking I just might be jailbait."

Aaran shook his head. "No, I'm not—"

"Well, I'm not jailbait," she went on, "but I don't fuck for money, or whatever else you're offering."

"You've got me mixed up with someone who did you a bad turn," Aaran said. "I just stopped for some conversation, though I can't help but wonder how you got into your present situation. And I can't help feeling bad about it."

She studied him again. "So you weren't trying to figure how to get into my pants? Maybe offer me a shower and a meal back at your place in exchange for a fuck and a blowjob?"

She was turning him on, but he didn't let it show.

"I'll admit the thought crossed my mind," he said. "I mean the part about giving you the chance to clean up and have a good meal."

"Well, you can just—"

"But I wasn't going to," he went on, cutting her off, "because as soon as the thought came to mind, I realized exactly what it would sound like, and I didn't want to insult you or make you feel bad. I figure you've got it tough enough as it is without having to worry about my intentions."

"Yeah, right. As if—"

"I would have just given you some money," he lied, "but I don't think I've even got a quarter in my pocket at the moment." He added in a rueful smile. "Spent a bit too much last night and I haven't had the chance to hit a bank machine."

She shook her head. "Man, you sound almost genuine."

"Look," Aaran said. "I should just go."

But she put a hand on his arm as he was turning away. If she hadn't, he would have found another excuse to dawdle.

"So you're a book editor," she said, dropping her hand.

He nodded. "For *The Daily Journal*. Though I actually edit the book pages—you know, reviews, author features, that sort of thing. Not the books themselves."

"And you're not some old guy with a thing for young little street girls?"

"Hey, I'm not that old."

She nodded. "Yeah, I guess you're not."

"I should go," he said. "If I've got some money the next time I see you, I'll—"

"Wait," she said. "Look, it's rough. I've been fighting off straight guys with hard-ons for the past few months that I've been on the street. And all the classy businesswomen just sneer at me—when I even register at all."

He nodded to show he was listening.

"Thing is," she went on, "I haven't had a decent meal in ages and I'm dying for a shower. I'd go to the shelter, but the last time I was there I almost got my face cut by some butch top thinking I was hitting on her sweet young thing. So . . ."

Aaran waited.

"So you're on the level? You're really just offering me a chance to clean up and get something to eat?"

"Nothing's going to happen that you don't want to have happen," Aaran assured her. "You can even get a good night's sleep—though I'm really going to insist that you have that shower first. But I'll make up a bed for you on the sofa."

She gave a short laugh. "Yeah, I guess I'm not exactly debutante material right now."

"You're fine," Aaran said. "You've just had a few bad breaks."

"So . . ." She had to swallow, before going on. "If your offer's still open . . ."

"Of course it is."

She hesitated a moment longer, then turned to pick up her duffel bag from where it was lying against the door.

"Let me get that for you," Aaran said.

He knew she was nervous. He knew she wanted to take this at face value and was determined not to have to pay for it with her body. But he had faith in his ability to sweet-talk anybody into anything. He could maintain a charming face for an evening. It was the long-term that always undermined his relationships. Like anything longer than a weekend.

The only thing that worried him was that flash of disquiet he'd felt when he'd first seen her. Because it hadn't gone away. Though it hadn't gotten any stronger, either, which he couldn't say for his hunger to hold her, to feel her hands on him . . .

He figured he had a right to feel on edge. The last time he'd felt this combination of intense attraction and vague unease had been with Saskia, and look where that had gotten him. But he'd be cool this time. Besides, it was probably just nerves from this business with Jackson. Or the worry about her age.

"So, are you from the city?" he asked as they walked along. He carried her duffel bag slung over a shoulder and maintained a body's distance between her and himself.

She shook her head. "I don't think I'm from anywhere, we moved around so much when I was a kid. . . ."

Holly

Holly woke with a start to find that she'd dozed off right there at the kitchen table. She wondered if anyone had noticed.

Dick had gone to his room earlier—to lie down, he'd said, but Holly knew he was reading. Reading and tidying were the two things that sustained the hob, especially when he was feeling stressed. Christy was gone as well—probably out onto the fire escape for another cigarette. Bojo smiled at her when she looked in his direction. *He*'d noticed that she'd dropped off there for a moment and that made her blush again, pleased that he paid attention, but annoyed with herself for acting like some young schoolgirl around him. Robert and Geordie hadn't, however, and she tuned in to what they were saying.

". . . are true?" Geordie asked.

"How many?" Robert shrugged. "Depends on which stories you're talking about. I'd say not so many." He smiled. "But enough to keep some people's lips flapping."

Holly liked the cadence of his voice. Set against the soft melody he seemed to draw without thinking from his guitar, it lent the air of an old ballad or blues song to everything he said. She looked over the top of her glasses at the clock on the wall above the stove. It was almost nine. They'd already set up her old computer on the dining room table, after first clearing away tottering piles of books and magazines. She and Dick invariably took their meals in the kitchen.

Almost nine. In a few hours, Estie and the others would be here. For now, all they could do was worry and wait.

"But you know," Robert went on, "if you stick around long enough, there's always bound to be stories. Trick for someone like me who doesn't care for the limelight is to keep to the shadows. When you're not easy to see, and harder to find, people tend to forget there was some puzzle about you."

"Out of sight, out of mind," Holly said, joining the conversation. Maybe it would keep her awake.

Robert nodded. "Though it's more than that. We've all got something in our heads, like a dial on an old radio set, that lets us turn down the memories of things we see that don't make sense. Some of us turn them down and only remember them at times when we're alone. Maybe it's in the quiet of the night, when we're lying in bed, looking for sleep, and we hear a creak we can't place. Or maybe it's when we're walking by a boneyard. Others are so good with that, they can dial those memories right out of their heads."

"So the story about the crossroads . . . ?" Geordie began.

Robert's smile widened. "Is one that just won't go away."

"But *was* it you who—"

"Oh, I've been to a crossroads or two in my time," Robert said. "I'd say they were overrated. Mysteries often are."

"Except when they're not," Bojo said.

Robert just laughed.

"So, have you ever run into anything like this before?" Geordie asked.

Both Robert and Bojo shook their heads.

"But there's a thousand things I've never heard of in this world," Robert said. "And a thousand more for each and every one of them. Some days just about everything can surprise me."

Geordie nodded. "But this still seems new. I've listened to Christy and Jilly and the prof go on and on about stuff like this. But not *like* this, if you know what I mean."

"I suppose I do. So let me put it this way: Whatever spirit we're dealing with here is unfamiliar, but the disappearances aren't."

"They're not?"

"Nope. You go back through history and you'll find a long list of large groups of people disappearing overnight. Armies in China. The Aztec civilizations. Ships in the Bermuda Triangle. Indian tribes in the American southwest. A village in New England. Another in Scotland."

They were all staring at him now. Robert laid his hand upon the strings of his Gibson, stilling its sound.

"See," he said, "the thing is this, spirits—certain spirits—thrive on attention. Some swell up with prayers and rituals. Others have to find more dramatic ways to get us to be mindful to them. I don't have an explanation for where the people they take go, or even why the spirits take them, but it's happened before."

Geordie glanced at the kitchen door. They could see Christy leaning on the railing, still smoking.

"Do they ever come back?" he asked.

Robert hesitated a moment, then shook his head. He waited a few beats, then began another twelve-bar blues progression, fingers so light on the strings that they didn't so much hear the music as sense its presence.

The bluesman's final words lay heavy on all of them.

Holly sighed, closing her eyes again, head propped by her arms. Why couldn't he just have lied? Left them some hope.

As though he'd read her mind, Robert added, "But like I told Christy earlier, that doesn't mean we shouldn't do our best to find them and bring them back."

"But—"

"Just because something's never been done before, doesn't mean it can't be done. There's always got to be a first time."

Suzanne Chancey

Coming back to some stranger's apartment to have a shower wasn't high on Suzi's list of things she would do. But so far, this wasn't so bad. Aaran was easy to talk to. He might be a little flirty—she could see his interest every time he looked at her—but he hadn't actually hit on her yet. And god, she'd needed a shower.

She came out of the bathroom now, hair tousled and still wet, wearing an oversized Heather Nova T-shirt under a terrycloth bathrobe. Aaran told her she could keep the T-shirt—"you wouldn't believe how much merchandise shows up in the office every week." The dirty clothes she'd been wearing and that were in her duffel bag were all in Aaran's washing machine.

It was a little bit like heaven.

Aaran came out of the kitchen with a cup of tea for her. "I thought we'd eat in, considering you don't have anything to wear."

"That's cool," she told him.

"An omelet sound good?"

She smiled. "You guys and your bachelor food. I think cooking eggs is hardwired into you from birth."

"We could have something else."

"No, I love eggs." She took a sip of her tea. "Say, would you mind if I checked my e-mail while you're cooking?"

He gave her a look of surprise.

"Yes," she said. "Street people have e-mail. All we need is a Hotmail account and a couple of bucks for one of the Internet cafés. Hell, some public libraries even offer access for free."

"Of course. The machine's over in the corner there."

Suzi turned and saw the slim notebook computer sitting closed on a beautiful antique writing desk in a corner of the room. The desk appeared to be mahogany, with turned legs and little slots for envelopes at the back of the desk's surface.

"Would you mind connecting to the Net for me?" she asked. "I don't want to screw anything up on your machine. Don't worry," she added when she saw him looking a little anxious. "I'll be fine once I'm in a browser. It's just that every machine seems to be a little different in how it connects."

"No problem," he said.

She followed him over to the desk and watched as he went through the protocols. Finally he double-clicked on the Explorer icon and the browser window came up to fill the screen.

"There you go," he said, standing up.

She took the seat. "Thanks."

She typed in the Hotmail URL and Aaran went back into the kitchen. While she was waiting for the page to come up, she glanced at the kitchen door, then quickly checked the "Favorites" drop-down menu, scanning the sites he'd bookmarked.

Okay, she thought. This was another good sign. No porn or weird sex sites. No "My Favorite Serial Killers" Web sites bookmarked.

Maybe he really was on the level. That'd be a first. But she'd been so dirty and was still so hungry, that she'd had to take the chance. People just didn't much care in this city, and Sundays were the worst for panhandling.

She'd actually been looking forward to this weekend. The week had been rough, but she'd done well in the Market on Saturday, cadging enough money to splurge on two nights at the hostel with enough left over for a laundry and a couple of decent meals. If she stuck to the soup and sandwich specials at the donut shop, that is. It would have left her nothing to start out the week, but at least she'd have been clean, well-rested, and fed. She would have been able to spend most of Monday applying for jobs before she'd have to start panhandling again.

Everything would have been fine except her good fortune hadn't gone unnoticed. On her way to the donut shop, a couple of guys dragged her into an alleyway. The knife one of them stuck in her face had her digging in her pocket and handing over the handful of small bills and change she'd managed to collect through the day. The one without the knife took the money. The one with the knife gave her an ugly little grin, then punched her in the stomach with his free hand.

She stumbled back into some garbage cans, lost her balance, and fell to the ground. By the time she got up, they were gone.

She supposed she was lucky they hadn't done worse. Really beat the crap out of her, say. Or even raped her. But she didn't feel lucky last night, huddled in a doorway, stomach sore and growling with hunger. And she hadn't felt lucky this morning, either.

So she'd taken the chance with Aaran and it looked like it was paying off. Hell, she might even take him up on the offer of his sofa for the night.

She took another sip of her tea as she logged onto her Yahoo account. There were a handful of new messages, but they were all spam. Still nothing from Marie.

Suzi sighed. She'd been so hoping to be able to open the lines of communication with her little sister again, but it had been almost three months now since that terrible day, and Marie still wouldn't respond to either phone calls or e-mail. Suzi wondered if they'd ever talk again.

She could understand Marie being upset. Traumatized even. The two of them had been sitting around the kitchen in the house Suzi had shared with her husband—so far as she was concerned, her *ex*-husband—Darryl. Darryl had been drinking that evening. Nothing hard, but he'd gone through the six-pack that had been in the fridge. When he came in looking for another beer and found they were all gone, he'd flown into a rage.

That had been new. Not his anger, but the fact that he wasn't controlling it in front of Marie. He was usually so careful when there was anyone else around and he knew Marie adored him, so he seemed to take special care when she was present. But not that day. That day he'd backhanded Suzi so hard, he knocked her off her chair. When she started to get up, he hit her again. Swore at her. Swore at Marie when she started to cry. Told her she'd get the same if she didn't shut up, which only made Marie cry harder.

He took a step toward her, hand lifted, but Suzi'd managed to get in between him and her little sister. She took the blow. And something snapped inside her. Her fear and weakness shattered, and she was surprised to find courage waiting for her. Or maybe he'd just pushed her so far that she was past being afraid or feeling weak. She just didn't care anymore. Or maybe it was for Marie, to protect her little sister from the monster that her husband had become.

Whatever it was, he read something in her face that made him back away. He gave her one long look, the promise of pain to come lying in his eyes, then he stormed out the front door, slamming it behind him.

Suzi had turned to Marie then, wanting to comfort her. But Marie pushed her away.

"How could you?" she'd cried. "What did you do to him?"

And then she fled herself. Out the back door.

Suzi had stood for a long time in the kitchen, leaning heavily against the kitchen counter before she'd finally picked up the phone. She started to dial 911, but then slowly cradled the receiver. She made her way into the bedroom. Every breath she took made her wince. She'd taken the old duffel bag that had accompanied her on many a camping trip and stuffed it with a few essentials. Took the grocery money. Then she left, too.

It wasn't the first time she'd left her husband. But it was the first time it stuck. The first time the old love she'd felt for him hadn't managed to smooth over her hurts and anger. The love was finally gone.

But so was any support she should have received. She didn't know what Darryl had told their friends and her parents—or maybe it was Marie who had talked to Mom and Dad—but overnight she seemed to have become a pariah in their eyes.

So she set aside enough money for meals and a couple of nights in a motel, then took a bus as far as what was left would take her. Which is how she ended up in Newford, basically broke and all too soon living on the streets. Funny how fast that could happen. Funny how prospective employers could read your desperation no matter how well you thought you'd hidden it.

Pimps tried to recruit her, but she'd managed to keep them at bay. She could have worked in a strip club, but she preferred the indignity of panhandling to dancing naked to a room full of Darryls.

She rubbed her face, then pinched the bridge of her nose with her forefingers.

Her gaze remained on the computer screen, but she hadn't really seen it for quite a few minutes now. She was focused on some far-off, unseen summation of her life that scrolled by in her mind's eye.

It was odd, how distanced she felt from it all. Had three months on the street already made her that hard? It seemed so easy to look at the story of her life as though it belonged to someone else, as though she was hearing about it, rather than having lived it herself. Is this what she had to pay to be strong enough to be free? She was happy that she'd proved resilient enough to make it on her own—even just living hand-to-mouth the way she did at the moment—but had to wonder at the cost.

She used to *feel* things so intensely. And she supposed she still did. But what she felt was *now*. The relief of being clean again. The warmth of the tea. The chance to relax for a moment, instead of having to be focused on her safety in dangerous surroundings.

She couldn't feel her past in the same way.

She didn't like Darryl, but she didn't experience that residue flash of anger or hatred when she thought about him. She didn't even feel the fear anymore. She believed that her parents and Marie had treated her unfairly, but the hurt she felt was intellectual, not in her gut.

How could all of that have just faded?

Sighing again, Suzi tried to put all of this out of her mind and focused on the computer screen in front of her. She deleted the spam unread, then composed her usual message for her sister.

I miss you, Marie. Please write.

She sent it and was about to close the browser when a small window popped up in the middle of the screen. She expected an ad and was already moving the cursor to click on the little "X" in its corner when the image registered.

It was a grainy, black-and-white photo of a young, good-looking black man standing in some kind of forest that looked like it had been built out of old circuit boards, wire, and other electronic litter. His face was tilted up so that she felt as though she was looking down at him from a higher perspective.

She waited to see if anything was going to happen, finger hesitating on the mouse button that would make the window disappear. But the message, when it started to scroll across the bottom of the window, wasn't an ad.

. . . aaran . . . help . . . me . . . aaran . . . help . . . me . . .

For a long moment she stared at the words as they continued to scroll across the bottom of the small window. Finally she raised her gaze to the kitchen door.

"Aaran," she called.

He popped his head out the door.

"You better come see this," she said.

She got out of the chair to make room for him in front of the computer.

"What is it?" he asked as he took her place.

But then he looked at the screen, took in the picture, read the words scrolling under it. His face drained of colour. He turned to her.

"How did . . . what did you . . ."

"I didn't do anything," Suzi said. "Honest. That window just popped up."

She bit at her lower lip, trying to figure out what she'd done, why this was freaking him out so much. He looked like he was about to have a stroke.

"Do . . . do you know that guy?" she asked.

Aaran gave a slow nod, his gaze returning to the screen.

"His name's Jackson Hart," he said. "He works at the paper and . . . he's one of the disappeared."

"I don't get you. What are 'the disappeared'?"

Aaran started to answer, but then shook his head. He got out of the chair and picked up the TV remote. He switched on the TV, and CNN came up on the screen. Suzi came and sat beside him on the sofa and tried to make sense out of the bizarre story that the anchorwoman was reporting.

Christy

I've come out onto the fire escape for another smoke, but it's mostly just to get away from all the planning and conversation going on inside.

It's quiet out here, almost peaceful, if it wasn't for the anxieties pressing on my heart. The city's just beginning to wake up—Sunday mornings it always takes its time. Even most of the stores don't open until noon. I lean on the railing and look down the alley that runs behind Holly's building. Nothing's moving here, only a cat sniffing at the base of the dumpster behind Joe's café, a few buildings down.

I start to take another drag from my cigarette, but pause, my gaze caught by the red ember burning at its end. It's funny, how quickly you get back into these things. And what do you get? A momentary calm. Something to do with your hands. But mostly it leaves your mouth tasting like crap and you get to carry the stink of the smoke around with you. Lovely. I can almost see Saskia wrinkling her nose, the frown marks forming between her eyebrows.

I flick the butt away, watch as it explodes in a shower of sparks on the pavement below.

I miss Saskia so much it's a constant pain in my chest.

I've never had a lot of luck in my relationships—at least not the romantic ones. I always pick the women who are different, I mean *really* different.

Spirits and ghosts and those that are just *other*. But it's not the same with Saskia, for all her otherness. I mean, we're all mysteries to each other anyway, aren't we? So, she's a little more mysterious, that's all.

What I do know is that we've made a good life with one another, snugly fitting together the separate pieces of who we are, but remaining individual at the same time. How often do you get *that* in a relationship?

I can't bear the idea of her being gone forever.

Whoever or whatever's responsible—man, woman, or some damned spirit in the wires—they'll pay.

Funny, I'm beginning to sound like my older brother Paddy. Violence was the way he solved most of his problems. Me, I prefer to find more peaceful solutions. Usually. But right now . . .

I guess it's true that most anybody can go over the edge, if you push them far enough. If you push them hard enough. Because right now, I just want to hit something. If I had whoever took Saskia away from me in front of me right now, and there was no way to bring her back, I think I could kill them. I could . . .

I shake my head. She's not gone forever, I tell myself. We'll get her back, one way or another. We have to.

I find myself remembering a dream I once had. I was at a book signing, opening a book to sign it for a reader, and all the words slid off the page and fell onto the floor. A couple of people were standing to one side—one of them was Aaran Goldstein, *The Daily Journal*'s book editor. He turned to whoever he was with and said, "I've always said that his words don't really have any staying power."

It has nothing to do with my life right at this moment, except for the helplessness I felt in the dream.

I stand and stare down the alley, watching Joe from the café down the street step out his back door to throw a garbage bag in the dumpster. The cat that was there earlier is long gone. The door closes with a bang behind Joe as he goes back inside.

I listen to the other sounds of the city, the traffic over on Williamson, a distant siren, but it hardly registers.

I think of Saskia.

The world of hurt I carry twists inside my chest again.

Eventually, I light up another smoke.

Aaran

"So what does any of this have to do with you?" Suzi asked, finally turning away from the screen to face Aaran where he sat on the other end of the sofa.

Aaran muted the sound on the TV and regarded her for a long moment. Sometimes when he looked at her—surreptitiously, when her attention was focused on something else, rather than like this—an unaccountable feeling rose up to collide with the other, more earthy, hunger of his libido.

He didn't know exactly what it was, but he could feel it now. There was this subtle something different about her that set her apart from the other people he knew. Something that rose from her like an almost visible aura. If he had to describe what it felt like, the first word that came to mind was blue—a warm, electric blue, if that was possible with such an inherently cool colour.

Maybe it had something to do with him seeing her through this growing infatuation he had for her. Maybe it was her living the way she did. He couldn't remember ever really talking to a street person before, never mind spending this much time with one. But whatever it was, she seemed to have a different take on everything, a different way of looking at the most simple thing. Like with this business on CNN.

She didn't seem to be in the least perturbed by what she'd just seen on the TV screen. Maybe once you were homeless, events beyond the ragged borders of your street life didn't really register anymore. Or matter. But it mattered to him. And the longer he sat here thinking about it, thinking of the enormity of what he'd gotten himself involved with, the more of a need he had to talk to someone about it.

Suzi was here. She was also so divorced from any other part of his life, that talking with her felt like it would be easier than with someone he actually knew. And it wasn't like there was anyone else he could turn to. But he *had* to talk about it.

"It's all my fault," he said.

"I don't get it."

"That guy in the computer," Aaran said, jerking his head to the desk. "I got him to run a virus to bring down this Web site called the Wordwood."

"I still don't follow you."

"Something must have gone wrong. Don't you see? All those people got sucked into their computers. I knew this was connected to the virus the first time I heard about it. I just *knew* it. Jackson sitting there in my notebook only confirms it."

"That's not a person," Suzi said. "It's just an image—and not a very good one, either."

"No. He's in there. Maybe not in my notebook, per se, but somewhere in the Internet. They all are. Jackson told me about these, I don't know, things that live in the wires. They're like voodoo gods or spirits or something. And they don't like people messing around with them. They don't even like people talking about them."

He could see what she was thinking, how she thought he was crazy. She was probably seriously regretting that her clothes were still in the dryer and she couldn't just bolt from the apartment. He didn't blame her. He felt a little crazy himself.

"Hold on a minute," Suzi said. "First of all, nothing *lives* on the Internet. That's just impossible. And secondly—" She pointed to the muted TV screen. "Nobody's saying anything about computers on the news. When you cut through all the bullshit, they're not really saying much of anything."

"And you know what makes me feel the worst about all of this?" Aaran went on as though she hadn't spoken. "His landlady told me that he used to admire me. I'm such a shit."

"Listen to me," Suzi said. "Computers don't swallow people."

"Then where did they go?"

"I have no idea. But they're not on the Internet."

"But these spirits . . ."

"Web sites are set up by people," Suzi said. "Living, breathing people, no different from you or me."

Aaran shook his head. "I don't know . . ."

Neither of them said anything for a time. They sat on the sofa, watching the talking heads on the silent TV screen. The dryer stopped its cycle in the laundry room and Suzi got up. She took her clean, dry clothes into the bedroom and closed the door. A few minutes later she came back out again. Aaran noted that she was still wearing the T-shirt he'd give her under a zippered fleece jersey.

"Okay," Suzi said as she sat down beside him again. "Let's not talk about where these people have gone or spooky Web sites because we're never going to agree on that. Instead, let's deal with where you're at. You feel responsible. So what are you going to do?"

"What *can* I do?"

"Well . . . you could go the police and tell them what you've told me."

Aaran nodded. "And they'd believe me as much as you do. I know how crazy it sounds. To tell you the truth, I don't know if *I* even believe what I've been saying."

"No," Suzi said. "You don't talk about boogiemen on the Internet. You talk about the site. How this guy—"

"Jackson Hart."

"How Jackson Hart brought it down with a virus. How maybe the people running the site have found some weird way to take their revenge on him."

"Not to mention how many hundreds of other people."

She shook her head. "No, just stay focused with this. Talk about what you do know. Nothing more. Let them make connections and try to sort it out."

"I'll probably spend the rest of my life in jail by admitting to any kind of involvement. This is a big deal now. Way bigger than anything I was really trying to do."

"But all those people . . ."

Aaran bent over, his hands against his face.

"I know," he said, his voice muffled.

How had it come to this? It had seemed so simple a week or so ago— just a way to get back at Saskia and her too-cool crowd.

"Well," Suzi said. "I guess the other thing you could do is contact the people who run the site. Do you know who they are?"

"Not really . . ."

"You must know something about them to have enough of a grudge to have your friend write a virus that would take down their Web site."

Aaran sighed. He really didn't want to get into any of this. But he felt committed now, having told Suzi as much as he had. Besides, what would it matter? It wasn't like they knew anybody in common. What made him hesitate was that he didn't just want to get into her pants anymore. However improbable it might seem to anyone who knew him—including himself— he was beginning to care about what she thought of him. But he was into this too far to hold back now.

"It wasn't with them, per se," he said. "There's just this woman. She treated me like shit and then she got all her friends to do the same."

Suzi gave him a funny look. "I know how that feels."

"You do?"

"Maybe we'll have time to exchange war stories later, seeing how we're sharing all these confidences. Right now let's focus on the problem at hand."

Aaran sighed again. "God, I feel like such a shit. When I think of all those people . . . it makes me feel like a monster."

"Did you ever hit a woman or a kid?" Suzi asked. "Did you ever beat on someone not as strong as you? Someone you should have been protecting?"

He shook his head.

"Then you're not so bad." She smiled. "Or at least not entirely bad. So tell me what this ex-girlfriend of yours—I'm assuming she's an ex?—"

Aaran nodded.

"What do she and her friends have to do with what's happening now?"

"They were all really into this Wordwood site," Aaran explained. "So I thought a way to get back at them would be to have Jackson take the site down with a virus. I wasn't planning anything permanent—and certainly not on this scale. It was just supposed to be an inconvenience."

"But you don't know any of the people who actually own the site?"

"I'm not sure who's running it now, but one of the people who started it up lives here in town."

"Then start with him."

"It's a her. She owns a bookstore up on the north side."

"Then we should start with her."

"I guess . . ."

Suzi stood up. "So come on."

"What, now?"

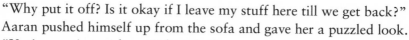

"Why put it off? Is it okay if I leave my stuff here till we get back?"

Aaran pushed himself up from the sofa and gave her a puzzled look.

"You're coming with me?" he asked.

"Sure."

"Why?"

She smiled. "I've got a bunch of reasons. The first is, well, you seem to be a pretty good guy. I know you'd like to jump my bones—oh, don't deny it. You don't think I can tell from the way you've been looking at me? But the thing is, you've been polite and you haven't pushed or anything. After what my life's been like for the past few months, I appreciate that."

Aaran was going to protest, but then he simply shrugged. He'd started out with the truth when they started talking about Jackson. He might as well stick with it.

"Secondly," Suzi went on, "I get the feeling you don't have a whole lot of friends, and I know what *that's* like, as well. Especially when people you thought were your friends turn on you."

Aaran caught something, not so much in her voice, as passing over her features, that told him there was more to it than that. A world of more. He wanted to ask her about it. He wanted to know why this whole conversation, why *everything* about Suzi was making him the feel the way he did. He'd never talked to anyone the way he was talking to her.

"I wasn't all that nice to her, either," he said instead. "To Saskia, I mean. The woman I was trying to get back at when I started all of this."

"But we've already established that you weren't hitting her or anything, right?"

"Words can be almost as hurtful," Aaran said.

Suzi's eyes clouded. "Yeah, don't I know that. But you regret it now, don't you?"

Aaran nodded. Surprisingly, he actually did. Not because of the trouble it had ended up getting him into, but because it had been wrong.

"Who are you anyway?" he said. "You've got me saying things and feeling things no one else ever has."

She smiled. "Maybe I'm your guardian angel. I mean, we're all supposed to have them, right? But who says they have to be these celestial beings floating around with harps and halos? Maybe they're just someone you happen to meet by chance and that meeting changes your life. Hell, if that's the case, maybe you're *my* guardian angel because I'm sure feeling a lot more human than I have in a long time. You know, being able to have a conversation like this where the other person doesn't think you're just some loser or freak."

Aaran could only shake his head.

"Which brings me to my last reason," she said. "I've been living on the streets for three months now. I know that's not a long time in the overall scheme of things, but when you're actually *doing* it, it feels like forever. Every damn *day* feels like forever. And the worst of it is how you just feel so worthless. But I don't feel like that right now. I feel like I'm helping you, that you appreciate my support, and that makes me feel like maybe I'm not as useless as people make me feel when I'm trying to get a job or panhandling."

She paused. "I'm talking too much, aren't I?"

"No. And you're right on all accounts. But let's eat first and then I'll call a cab."

"Let's take the bus. Does it go as far as we need to go?"

Aaran nodded. "We can take the subway up as far as Alicia and Moore and transfer from there. But what's wrong with a cab?"

"We'll probably still be talking about all of this and when you're in a cab, you don't think the driver's listening to every word you say?"

"But there'll be even more people on public transport."

"That's true," she said. "But only ten percent of them actually pay any attention to what the people around them are talking about. We'll just sit among the other ninety percent."

"And we'll know the difference because...?"

"I'm good at noticing that kind of thing."

Aaran laughed. "Okay. You want to make some toast while I finish cooking us brunch?"

"Love to," she said as she trailed into the kitchen behind him.

She touched his arm before he could pick up the whisk to beat the eggs.

"This'll all work out," she said. "That's why doing the right thing is always the right thing to do."

"We'll see," he told her. "But these people dislike me something fierce. And . . ." He hesitated, then added, "I guess with good cause."

"Don't be so hard on yourself."

Aaran shook his head. He couldn't believe this woman. She was living under the worst circumstances he could imagine—penniless, homeless, and apparently, though he found this hard to believe, friendless—and yet she was still so upbeat and positive.

"I'm beginning to really like you," he said.

"It's always good to be liked," Suzi told him, "but don't go getting any ideas. It could never work out between us."

"Why not?"

"Because no matter what happened, I'd always be the homeless woman you took in off the street. That simple truth would lie under everything else. You don't think it would matter, but you'd never forget it either."

Aaran started to protest.

"And neither would I," she added.

Christy

It's midmorning and we're still playing the waiting game, killing time until Estie and the rest of Holly's computer friends show up. Dick's finally come out of his room, but it's only to go downstairs and dust the already immaculate bookshelves. It's how he deals, Holly says. The rest of us sit around in the kitchen, drinking too much coffee and tea while Robert noodles on his guitar, though for me to call it noodling is a real injustice. Somehow he can take the most simple progressions and infuse them with all these layers of nuance and meaning. I know that. I know he's good. Normally I'd be captivated, but today the magic he's waking from that old Gibson of his just disappears into the background, the way everything else that doesn't concern Saskia does.

Occasionally one of us starts to talk, and somebody else joins in, but after a few moments the conversation always comes around to the problem at hand, and there's nothing new we can add to that. All we can do is speculate. Too much speculation and you begin to feel crazy.

We end up with a lot of big holes in the conversation—not the comfortable kind you have when you're together with friends, but they aren't entirely uncomfortable, either. They're just . . . periods of waiting. Stretches of silence, where time slows down until minutes feel like days and hours never seem to finish. But it's not like we can really do anything. Everything we can do has already been done. It wasn't much. We cleared all the books out of the dining room and got the old computer out of the basement and set it up on the table in there. Checked to make sure it's still working. Plugged the modem in and checked it as well, though not by logging on to the Wordwood site.

And that was it. Now there's nothing to do but wait.

I'm not good at waiting, so I keep coming out here onto the fire escape. I'm not entirely sure why. Having yet another smoke is only an excuse, it's not the reason. I don't think I'm specifically trying to avoid the people inside. After all, Geordie's my brother, Holly's a very dear friend, and I've really come to like Dick over the past year. The two strangers to me, Bojo and Robert, are the kind of people I'd normally want to listen to for hours, taking notes in my head while they talk. But right now I can't seem to spend more than ten minutes sitting with the group of them in the kitchen before I start getting all antsy and have to come out here on the fire escape again.

I hear the screen door open behind me and turn to see Geordie coming out to join me.

"How are you holding up?" he asks.

I shrug. "Okay, considering."

He leans on the railing beside me and looks off down the alley the way I've been doing for the past few hours whenever I've been out here. Mostly nothing happens except for that one scrawny alley cat making his rounds, and people from the shops that back onto the alley stepping out for a smoke, or throwing their garbage into the dumpster. Once, a couple of kids in their late teens did a furtive exchange at the far end of the alley, standing close to each other, looking about as suspicious as you can as one of them passed something to another. Probably a drug deal. But who knows? Maybe they were just trading a different kind of crack—registration codes for bootlegged software. Though you'd expect them to do that on-line.

"It's funny," Geordie says after we've been standing there awhile, "but I'm not even tired."

"I know what you mean," I tell him. "It's been a long time since I've pulled an all-nighter."

Geordie nods. "I've got that taste in my mouth and a bit of a burn behind my eyes, but that's about it. I keep expecting to crash, but I guess the adrenaline's still got me firing on all cylinders." He gives me a small humourless smile. "Even though we're all just waiting around like this, doing nothing."

I think about what I can add to that and come up empty. I consider lighting up another cigarette, but that doesn't have any immediate appeal either. The silence starts to drag out, but before it becomes uncomfortable, we hear the door open again. I turn and think there's no one there until I lower my gaze and see Dick standing in the doorway, looking anxious. It must be hard to get noticed sometimes, when you're barely two feet tall, never mind having that whole "most people can't see you" fairy thing going for you.

"Master and Master Riddell," he says. "Mistress Holly says you'd better come quick."

I squat on my haunches so that I'm not towering over him.

"What's happening?" I ask. "Is Estie here?"

I'm surprised that we hadn't heard them arrive—or at least Snippet's welcoming barks.

He shakes his head. "Other guests have come," he says. He hesitates, then adds, "Maybe not so welcome."

I don't like the sound of that at all.

When he turns, Geordie and I follow him through an empty kitchen, then down the stairs where we can hear voices ahead. I don't know who I'm expecting as we step into the store, but if I'd had to guess, Aaran Goldstein would have been the last person on the list. He's standing just inside the front door by the recent arrivals shelf with a briefcase in his hand and a pretty girl I don't recognize at his side. She's short and slender and I can't place her age. Her blonde spiky hair, the faded green cargo pants and grey hooded jersey make her look younger than I feel she is. What I do know is that she's not the kind of person I'd expect to see in Aaran's company.

Holly and Bojo are talking to them, with Snippet staring at them from around Holly's legs. I have to look around to find Robert. He's standing down one of the aisles, just out of the line of vision of Aaran and his friend.

"What the hell are you doing here?" Geordie says as we approach the group.

He's got a glare fixed on Aaran, and I can hear the anger in his voice. I give him a surprised look. Geordie's such an easygoing guy that I can't remember the last time I actually heard him raise his voice. But he's loyal almost to a fault, and I guess the way Aaran's treated both Saskia and me over the years just pushes all the wrong buttons, even for a gentle soul like my brother.

Then we find out what Aaran's been telling the others, and I have to put a hand on Geordie's arm as he takes a sudden step forward.

"Let him talk," I say. "It's not like he meant for this to get as out of hand as it has."

I'm surprised to find myself defending him. It's funny. Aaran's such an officious little prick, and I've never liked him, but I can't even seem to find the energy to get mad at him right now. And there I was, out on the fire escape a few hours ago, ready to do physical harm to whoever was responsible for this nightmare. I guess in the end I'm more like Geordie usually is than like our older brother Paddy was.

Geordie gives me a surprised look. "But—"

I shake my head. "No. This isn't about bad reviews or how much we hate to see dipstick here strutting around like he owns the world. This is about Saskia. It's her life that's at stake and I'd deal with the devil if that's what it'll take to get her back."

"Not sure I'd recommend that," Robert says stepping out of the aisle where he's been standing. "Dealing with the devil," he clarifies. "I'm behind you on every other count."

We go upstairs and crowd into the kitchen, bringing in extra chairs from the dining room so that everyone can have a seat. The woman with Aaran is Suzi Chancey, a street person he's just met today. For those of us who know Aaran—which would be Holly, Geordie and myself—the idea that Aaran would stop to talk to a street person, never mind bring them home, is almost as surprising as finding Aaran knocking on Holly's door. What doesn't surprise us is what we learn when he goes back through his whole story and we find out why he was getting this Jackson Hart fellow to sic a virus on the Wordwood site. That's the pure, mean-spirited Aaran Goldstein we know, through and through.

But I'll give him this. He seems genuinely regretful for what he's done—especially when he finds out that Saskia was one of the victims.

"Wait a minute," Suzi says to us. "Are you trying to tell me that you actually believe that people have disappeared into the Internet?"

"I know what I saw," I tell her.

"And if pixies can come out of the Internet," Holly adds, "I'm not surprised that people can get trapped in it."

That comment requires a sidebar. Neither Aaran nor Suzi seem completely convinced by Holly's story, though when Dick does his sudden "I've been here all along" pop into view, I can see the cogs of reconsideration start to turn in their heads.

Bojo, Geordie, and Robert have been quiet through all of this. Geordie still has his mad on. He sits at the table, arms crossed, obviously distrustful of Aaran and his motives for coming here. Bojo's relaxed, slouched in his chair and giving the appearance that he's only barely paying attention, but I get the sense he's not missing a thing. I notice that Robert hasn't touched his guitar since we came back to the kitchen and I wonder about that, just as I wonder about why he stayed out of sight when Aaran and Suzi first arrived. I guess if the stories about him are true, he wants to be cautious about who hears his music, and whom they might tell.

At one point Aaran takes his laptop out of his briefcase and shows us the image of Jackson Hart that had appeared on his screen while Suzi had been using the machine to check her e-mail. He'd saved it as an HTML document so that he could bring it back up at any time, even when the computer's off-line.

Bojo sits up then and gives the grainy image a careful study before slouching back in his chair.

"Recognize the place?" Robert asks.

Bojo shakes his head. "But there's not much to go by from that picture."

"Why would he recognize it?" Suzi asks.

He smiles. "I travel a lot."

I can tell she feels she's missing things here, that there are undercurrents she's not getting. And let's face it, there are. When she introduced herself, telling us so forthrightly how she lives on the street, almost making it a challenge, I think she expected us all to tell her more about ourselves in return. But no one did. For my part, I just wondered, why's she with Aaran? And what's her stake in all of this?

I can accept Good Samaritanism—I wish the world had a lot more of it—but she came in a package with Aaran Goldstein, and while I'm willing to hear him out—hopefully to find something that will help us reclaim Saskia and the others—I don't particularly like or trust him now any more than I ever have. Maybe it should be different, but the sad truth is, you're always judged by the company you keep.

There's more talk and we finally start drifting into speculation again. I'm just about to make another retreat to the fire escape when we hear a banging on the front door downstairs. Snippet jumps up from under Holly's chair and goes to the head of the stairs, ears twitching, a small growl rumbling in her chest. I glance at the wall clock. It's a quarter to twelve.

"Maybe this'll be Estie," Holly says as she gets up to go have a look.

Snippet goes down the stairs, claws clattering on the wood, with Holly right behind her. Bojo waits a beat, then seems to not so much rise as drift out of his chair to follow them. The rest of us wait in the kitchen. From the happy sounds that come from downstairs, it's obvious that the welcome the new arrivals are getting is far different from Aaran and Suzi's. Bojo reappears and returns to his chair, dropping back into his slouch as though he'd never gotten up in the first place. Moments later, Holly leads her friends into the kitchen and for a few minutes chaos reigns as introductions are made all around.

Sarah Taylor—Estie—turns out to be a tall, dark-haired woman with grave eyes and an air of quiet grace. Her girlish voice on the phone last night had put such a different image in my head that I wouldn't have come close to recognizing her today without an introduction. She gives me a warm, sympathetic smile when we shake hands.

"Have you heard anything from your friend?" she asks.

I shake my head. "But we've got some new leads."

The dark-haired Hispanic man standing beside her perks up at that. I've already heard him introduced as Raul Flores, which would make him Benny Davis's boyfriend, Benny being the one of the Wordwood founders who disappeared while on-line with Estie.

"What have you heard?" he asks.

I start to answer, but then Holly's introducing me to someone else. I see Estie put her hand on Raul's arm. She leans over to him and murmurs something in his ear, and he nods, but with obvious reluctance. I don't blame him. If someone had even a scrap of information about Saskia, I'd say be damned to politeness and want to know right away as well.

But Holly's introducing me to Tom Pace—the one they call Tip—and I don't have the chance to tell Raul what we've found out so far. Tip's taller than me, a lean and lanky throwback to the old hippie days with his ponytail hanging past his shoulders and long, wispy beard. His eyes are serious, peering at me from behind wire-framed glasses, and his features are thoughtful, but I can tell by the laugh lines around his eyes that he's not always like this.

The last of the newcomers is Claudette Saint-Martin, a full-figured black woman in a business suit with a delightful French accent. Apparently she was on her way to work when she got the call from Estie and simply had the cab she was in take her to the airport instead of the office where she'd originally been bound.

There's not nearly enough room in the kitchen, so we take what chairs we need and set up command central in the dining room where the computer's waiting for us. The newcomers are startled when Dick seems to appear out of nowhere, but while they're plainly intrigued, they're too polite to ask about him. Holly and Bojo bring in a new round of coffee, tea, and soft drinks as we get settled. There's a lot of cross-conversation, different people talking at once, but somehow everybody gets brought up to date.

An awkward silence follows the revelation that Aaran was responsible for the virus that started all of this, and all heads turn in his direction. I actually feel sorry for him, but Suzi's the one who speaks up for him.

"Okay," she says. "So he messed up. Didn't any of you ever mess up? And at least he's had the balls to come here to try and make amends."

I notice that Holly's friends aren't particularly impressed with that. They don't seem too taken with Suzi herself, either, but I don't have to wonder about that. She seems very nice—too nice to be in Aaran's company, and that's the problem. Aaran's not exactly on anybody's favorite people list that I know, though I have to say he's doing a very good job of acting like a normal person today. Maybe he really is sorry about what he's done and genuinely wants to make up for how badly he's messed things up.

Then the conversation turns to the mechanics of how they set up the original Wordwood site and speculations on how they might be able to recapture those original configurations. Estie reaches into her purse and pulls out a stack of floppy disks held together with a rubber band.

"I managed to dig out my copy of the first back-up we did," she says.

"That's good," Tip says. "I couldn't find mine. But the thing is, if there *is* an actual spirit in the Wordwood, won't it have evolved since it was first created? I'm not sure there's any point in starting at the beginning again."

"What we really need to do," Claudette puts in, "is establish some sort of communication with whomever or whatever is running the show on the other end of that URL."

"You don't have to play coy," Estie says. "Not with anybody that's here. We all know we're dealing with the spirit that lives in the Wordwood."

"But we don't know *what* it is," Holly says.

Claudette nods. "That's true. But we still have to find some way to contact it."

"Except basics is still the best place to start," Raul says. "You strip away all the fancy flash and plug-ins, and everything's still built on that original HTML you guys wrote way back when."

I listen to them brainstorm, but even with all the research I've been doing lately, they soon get so esoteric that they lose me. After a while I turn to Holly who's sitting beside me, Snippet asleep on her lap.

"Are you following any of this?" I ask.

She shakes her head. "Even though we used my computer to initially set up the site, I was always just one of the content people. Back in those days, all I did was collect the material and pass it on to one of the others to format. I've since learned to do HTML, but I don't really understand it."

On the other side of Holly, Claudette turns around and grins.

"That's because you never tried," she says. "And besides—"

"I had you all to do it for me," Holly finishes.

It's obviously an old joke between them.

I listen awhile longer, then go out onto the fire escape for another smoke. When I return, the conversation's in another lull. Raul and Tip are studying the picture of Jackson Hart on Aaran's laptop. Estie's loading the data from her floppy discs onto Holly's old 386. Everybody else is just sitting around, looking tired.

I try not to let my frustration show, but none of this seems to be getting us anywhere. I want to say, let's just get *on* with it. Hook the damn computer up to the Internet and let's go.

Except I don't know where to go any more than the others do.

That's when Bojo clears his throat.

"I don't know much about computers," he says, when he's got everybody's attention, "so correct me if I'm heading down the wrong road here. But this virus that got sent to the Wordwood site—does it work the same way that a virus you or I could get would work?"

There's a moment's silence, then Estie shakes her head.

"Not really," she says. "This is something that only affects computers."

"The software, to be precise," Tip adds. "You know, the protocols that tell the hardware how to work and where to look for information. It doesn't physically affect the hardware, except that your operating system doesn't know where to find it anymore—depending on how the virus was set up, of course."

Bojo nods. "I was just thinking, when someone gets sick among my people, we use herbs and cures . . . the way your doctors will prescribe antibiotics. So I thought if a computer virus worked in the same way, maybe there might be some sort of an antivirus we could send to the Wordwood site to combat the virus that Hart created to bring it down."

The computer experts among us exchange glances.

"Maybe," Estie says slowly. "If we knew *what* the virus was . . ."

"We'd need to get into Hart's computer," Claudette says. "But what are the chances of that? The police have probably impounded it by now."

Raul nods. "Or at least sealed off his apartment because it's a crime scene. We'd never be able to get in."

"I think I can help with that," Aaran says.

Everybody turns to look at him.

"I mean, so long as the police really haven't taken it away."

"I thought you hardly knew him," I say.

"I don't. But his landlady seems to like me, and if I told her it would help us bring him back, I think she'd let us in."

I look at Estie. "What do you think?"

"It's hard to say without actually seeing what he's written," she says. "But I like this a lot better than trying to sort out mystical mumbo jumbo. At least I understand programming languages."

"So some of us can work on that," I say, "while the rest of us can work on trying to set up some kind of communication with the spirit that runs the site."

"And if we can't get it to come to us," Robert says, speaking up for the first time, "maybe we can go to it."

His words hang at the table for a long moment, and everybody just looks at him.

"You're talking about a place, right?" Robert asks. "Am I hearing this right? You're saying that this spirit's got its own place, out there in the wires somewhere?"

"I suppose . . ." Estie says. "I mean, there's the Wordwood site."

"And that's on the Internet? Or at least it's in some computer connected to the Internet?"

"Well, logically . . ." Tip begins, but then he laughs. "What am I saying? There's nothing logical about this. You're right. The files that make up the Wordwood site *should* be housed in a computer somewhere. But that's where the site got really strange. Not only did it develop this personality of its own, but it also disappeared from the computers where we were storing it."

"And took up residence out on the Internet somewhere?" Robert asks.

"I don't see how that's possible," Claudette says. "It's got to be housed in a physical computer. There's no physical *place* for it in the wires or satellite feeds or however people access the Web."

"Tell that to the people that have disappeared," Estie says.

Claudette nods. "Point taken. Not understood, but taken."

Something starts niggling at the back of my mind. A conversation I had, maybe. I'm not sure what. I start to think out loud, hoping to catch the memory unaware.

"The way I see it," I say, "is that these spirits might use the Internet as a means of getting from one place to another—travelling pretty much the same as the data we send—but they *exist* somewhere else. And if I had to guess, I'd say it was *between*."

That's not quite it, but I can almost taste myself coming up on that elusive memory.

"I don't follow that," Estie says.

"*Between* is where magic is strongest," I explain. "The spaces between one thing and another. Not day or night, but dusk or dawn. Not the land on either side of a river, but the bridge that connects them. The boat that will take you from one side to the other."

"So you're saying that the Wordwood site exists someplace in between the routes we use to connect our computers to the ISPs housing Web sites?"

I nod. And now I've got the memory that had just been out of reach.

"And what's more magical than the spiritworld?" I say. "Just before Saskia disappeared, she was telling me about a conversation she had with . . . with a friend of ours. It doesn't matter who. But this friend believes that the Wordwood site exists in the spiritworld. Or at least that it can be accessed through the spiritworld. I don't know how I could have forgotten that."

"The spiritworld," Claudette repeats.

I see Geordie giving me a puzzled look. I want to tell him that Saskia was talking to my shadow, but that's something I don't even want to start to get into with this group. They're all looking at me with varying levels of confusion.

"Not the spiritworld, Master Riddell," Dick says. He blushes when everyone looks at him, but gamely goes on. "The spiritworld isn't *between*. But the borderlands are."

Bojo nods. "And the borderlands can take you anywhere—so long as you know what you're looking for."

"These are actual places?" Estie asks.

"Oh, yeah," Robert tells her. "You don't get more actual. Some people will even tell you that this world we're living in is just one echo of what you'll find across the borders."

After telling his own story, Aaran's been sitting quietly through all of the various conversations we've been having around the table. But he leans forward now, his gaze fixed on me.

"And is that a place you can take us?" he asks. "We can go there and get these people back?"

"I can't," I say. "But I know people who can cross over. The big problem's going to be figuring out *where* to go once we do cross over. You can't begin to imagine how vast the spiritworld is."

Suzi laughs. "I can't even imagine *it.*"

That wakes smiles from many sitting around the table.

"You don't have to go looking for more people to bring into this," Robert says. "What you're talking about now is pretty much my own take on the problem. I can't see people disappearing into a machine. But if that machine's a gate into the otherworld? Oh, yeah. That's more than possible." He looks from me to Bojo, to Dick. "And it makes sense, doesn't it?"

"Now wait a minute," Claudette starts. "I can't believe any of you are taking this fairy-tale nonsense seriously. What we need is a real solution to—"

But Raul puts his hand on her arm.

"Let's hear this out," he says. "I'm willing to listen to anything that offers up a chance of getting Benny back." He turns his attention to Robert. "You can do this? You can get us into this place?"

Robert nods. "Like Bojo said. I don't know much about computers either. But I know the spiritworld. I figure between those of us who've got some familiarity with the place, we won't be shooting completely blind."

He looks to Dick who gives a sad, negative shake of his head.

"Not me," he says. "I've no sense of direction and I've never gone very far into the borderlands." He shoots Holly an apologetic look. "Hobs hardly ever do."

Robert's gaze travels on to Bojo.

"I'd need more to go on than guesswork," he says. "Christy wasn't exaggerating," he adds, looking up and down the dining room table. "It's a big place. Anything you've ever imagined, exists somewhere in there. And that goes for everyone who's ever lived—they might die and travel on, but the places and people they imagined stay behind. There are worlds upon worlds upon worlds in there. They're not all hospitable. And they're mostly dangerous. And the borderlands are even more confusing for those who don't know exactly where they're going."

"I might be able to call up the right door," Robert says. "Everything's got its own signature, and I've been hearing enough about this place that I figure I can find a piece of music that'll get us close, if not right to where we want to go. Though it's not something I care to work on for too long."

"Why's that?" Estie asks.

Robert shrugs. "Let's just say that there are all kinds of spirits over there on the other side of the veil separating this world from the otherworld and not all of them have taken a liking to me. They know the sound of my Gibson. They know *my* signature—the way I pull a tune from its strings. I play too long and they'll come sniffing around. And when they come, we'll be in a whole mess of new trouble."

"You get us close," Bojo says, "And I'll take us the rest of the way. I don't need music."

"Just like that," Claudette says. "We're just going to up and step into Never-Never Land, following you like you're the Pied Piper."

"You're mixing up your fairy tales," Holly says.

"You know what I mean."

"Once we get there," Tip asks. "Can you bring us back again?"

Bojo hesitates, but he nods. "Like someone once said, there and back again. But only so long as you do what I say and stick to the paths I take you on. Take even one step off the way I lay out for you, just to look at a flower or pick up some bauble that catches your eye, and I might never be able to find you again."

"Though something else might," Robert says.

"Why are you trying to scare us?" Tip asks.

"Because it's *dangerous*," Robert tells him. "Truth is, I'd just as soon none of you go, but once we get there, we're going to need at least one person that's familiar with this spirit."

"But none of us are really familiar with it," Estie says. "None of us know what it really is. I'm not trying to back out of this," she adds. "It's just . . . we know computers. We know *this* world." She looks at her friends. "None of us know about spirits and . . . you know, magic."

"You've talked to it," Robert says.

He's not asking a question, but Estie and the others nod in response all the same.

"So that'll be a job for one of you," Robert tells them. "To recognize the spirit and put your case to it. The others are going to go to Hart's apartment to see if they can figure out a way to undo his virus."

"What about Saskia?" I ask. "And the other disappeared?"

"If we're right," Robert says, "and this spirit's made a hidey-hole for the Wordwood site on the other side, then I don't figure it takes much guesswork to expect we'll find them there, as well."

"You said none of the people from these other mass disappearances ever came back," Holly says.

"That's right. I did say that. But I also said that shouldn't stop us from trying. And who knows? Maybe some folks did escape before, but they just didn't want to go around talking about it after. Time was that every big story didn't have to end up on the news. Some people like to keep things to themselves."

"Or maybe they turned the radio dials in their heads *way* down," Holly says, "and just made themselves forget."

Robert smiles. "Maybe so." He looks around the table. "So now you need to decide. Who's coming with us, who's going to Hart's apartment, who's staying to hold the fort. Those of you who are going, you're going to need travelling gear: good footwear and at least a couple of pairs of socks. Clothes that can take some hard living. Bedding. Water. Food. Don't forget a hat."

"What about weapons?" Raul asks.

"Bring what you want. But I'll warn you, keep it simple. A lot of things made in this world don't work the same on the other side. It's iffy in the borderlands, but if we have to go into the spiritworld itself, you'll find no use for a compass, or a walkie-talkie, and you can just plain forget about your fancy automatic pistols and the like."

"You really think we can do this?" Geordie asks.

"I don't know," Robert tells him. "But at least you'll be doing something. The way it stands now, you don't know how to bring all these people back from wherever they've been taken—at least not from this end. But maybe, if we can get you to the right place, you can work it out from the other end."

I stand up.

"What time is it?" I ask.

Raul looks at his watch. "Almost four-thirty."

I didn't realize we'd been talking that long. No one says anything for another long moment and then I realize something.

"Why's everybody looking at me?" I ask.

Robert smiles. "The troops need a general."

"I'd think you'd be better suited than me."

He shakes his head. "I'm not good with people."

"What makes you think I am?"

"You can be," Geordie puts in. "I'm with Robert on this."

Holly agrees, which has Bojo and Dick nodding their assent. Then one by one the others agree as well, even Aaran.

I sigh. I don't feel prepared for this. It's not like I've got a military mindset or have ever coordinated anything more than a book signing before. But then I think of Saskia. Lost somewhere. Counting on me.

"Okay," I say. "Here's how we'll do it."

I divide us up into teams.

Dick's too nervous to come across into the spiritworld—that's easy enough to tell. I know he'd come if Holly was going, but with Bojo and Robert, I figure we already have the experts we need for the trip, so I have him stay at the store with Holly and Geordie. Geordie protests until I tell him that I'm counting on him to be our backup.

"If anything goes wrong," I say, "you know people to contact."

"Like Joe."

I nod. "Just don't go borrowing that stone Wendy uses to cross over. You won't know where to start looking for us."

For the trip into the otherworld, no one argues when I say that Bojo and Robert will be coming with me. It's only when I include Raul that the questions arise.

"But he wasn't part of the original group," Claudette says. "Not that I'm saying I want to go. But don't we need one of the founders?"

"I don't think we'd be able to stop him from coming," I say.

"You've got that right," Raul says. Then he looks at the others. "And maybe I wasn't in at the beginning, but at this point I've logged as much or more time on the site than any of you."

I see something in his eyes and I guess Estie does, too.

"Whose voice does it use to talk to you?" she asks.

"My grandfather's."

She nods. "I hear my cousin Jane's inflections." She looks around the table. "She died in a car crash when she was eighteen. Drunken driver."

"Abuelo—my grandfather," Raul says. "He's dead, too."

"Why do you think the Wordwood uses the voices of dead people to talk to us?" Tip asks.

"It's not using those voices," Robert says. "That's just the way you're hearing them. Spirits like to make a quick personal connection to you. I don't know how they do it, but they're good at sounding like someone you once knew—especially someone you had feelings for."

The rest of them I send off to accompany Aaran. Estie's the real computer expert—so I don't doubt that she'll be doing most of the work—but I wanted her people to outnumber Aaran and his new sidekick Suzi, just in case Aaran has a change of heart. Naturally, I don't say that. But I don't have to. Estie's group leaves first and as soon as they're out the door, Holly turns to me.

"Do you really trust him?" she asks.

"You mean Aaran?"

She nods.

I shrug. "Yes and no. I think he's genuinely appalled at what he's done."

"Yeah, but how long's that going to last?" Geordie says.

"I don't know. He's never been one to sustain any one thing for very long. But I don't think he's actually evil. He's just what he's always been: self-centered and more than a little mean-spirited."

"And this Suzi?"

I shake my head. "I really don't know about her."

I find my gaze going to Robert, who's finally taken his guitar out again and started to play.

"There's something about her," he says, "though I couldn't tell you what. She's just *more* here than most people you meet. That doesn't mean she's dangerous or supernatural or anything," he adds when he sees our worried looks. "Just means she's living *now* instead of carrying around the baggage that most of us do."

"But she could be trouble?" Holly asks.

Robert just smiles. "Anybody can be trouble. You haven't figured that out yet?"

"Well, we've got enough to do with the trouble we already have," I say as I get up from the table again. "I'm not going to go looking for more."

"Good advice to remember," Robert says. "Though not always so easy to put into practice. The world has a habit of deciding that kind of thing for us."

I nod, then look at Geordie. "Do you want to come back to the apartment while I pick up some gear?"

"Sure," he says, rising from his seat.

I know him well enough to see he's still got something worrying at him.

"What're you thinking about?" I ask.

He shrugs. "I was just wondering who told Saskia that the Wordwood site might be in the spiritworld."

I hesitate for a moment, then say, "My shadow."

"Your shadow."

A world of unspoken commentary wakes in his eyes. We've been through this before. It's just another trip down all those roads where I believe things and he doesn't. But he doesn't say anything. Maybe he's finally coming around to actually believing the things that so many of our circle of friends have experienced, himself included.

"Now that's interesting," Robert says. "You don't meet many folks that have a working relationship with their shadow."

"I wouldn't call it a working relationship," I tell him. "She pretty much comes and goes as she pleases."

"Well, what do you expect, you being the one that threw her out and all?"

"*What* are you talking about?" Holly asks.

"I'll tell you later," Geordie says.

I study Robert for a moment. There's something in the way he was defending my shadow that tells me he's had his own experiences with the phenomenon. I'm curious about it, naturally—truth is, I'm curious about everything to do with the bluesman—but now's not the time to get into any of it.

"You guys need anything in the way of gear?" I ask instead.

Bojo shakes his head. "I travel light."

"I don't go anywhere without my girl," Robert says, running a hand down the neck of his Gibson. "Otherwise, you could say the same for me."

"Does she have a name?" Bojo asks. "Your guitar?"

"Everything's got a name," Robert replies, "but she's never told me hers and I haven't asked."

Bojo nodded. "Among my people, the instruments all have names. But I think they're given to them by their players."

"I don't go around handing out names. Things have got enough personality of their own without my hanging another tag on them that they've got to live up to."

"How about you?" I ask Raul. "Anything we can get for you?"

"I've got everything I need except for food and water," he says, "and Holly says we can get that at a grocery store down the street while you're gone. But I wouldn't mind a knapsack to carry my stuff in. All I brought was a carry-on for the plane."

"I've got a spare," I tell him, then I turn to Geordie. "We should get going."

"We'll be ready to go when you get back," Bojo says.

I nod. I know why he's with us—it's obvious that he's got a thing for Holly. But Robert's still a mystery.

"Why are you helping us?" I find myself asking before I can leave.

Robert smiles. "I don't know. I guess it's for the same reasons that always get me into trouble. Curiosity, plain and simple. I get this need to find out what a thing is. I have to know how it all turns out."

I suppose that's as good a reason as any. I know I've stepped into a hundred situations because of my own insatiable curiosity.

"Well, I want you to know we're grateful," I say.

"Tell me that again if we survive this trip."

Aaran

"I haven't felt like that since high school," Aaran said.

He and Suzi were waiting in the lobby of the hotel while Estie and the others checked in at the front desk, then went up to their rooms to drop off their luggage and change. They sat side by side on a fat leather couch in the lobby, an island of stillness as the hotel staff and guests bustled around them.

"I can barely remember high school," Suzi said.

Aaran laughed. "That's all I *can* remember some days. It set the tone for the rest of my life."

She glanced at him. "What do you mean?"

"You remember the fat, pimply kid with the Coke bottle glasses that no one ever wanted to talk to?"

She nodded.

"I'm the grown-up version of him. You may not see him when you look at me, but he's still sitting there inside me."

Now it was her turn to laugh.

"That's funny," she said. "I was your typical popular cheerleader type—you know, most likely to succeed and all that."

"Why's that funny?"

"Well, look at us now. You're a big success and I'm living on the street." She touched his arm. "But don't take what happened back there too hard. You did the right thing and they know it."

"I suppose."

"And they didn't all hate you. What's his name—Christy. He stood up for you."

"Yeah. That really surprised me. I used to see him a fair amount before he started going out with Saskia. We got along pretty well, but I always thought he was just sucking up to me to make sure his books would get a good review. Now I'm beginning to realize that he's actually a decent guy. I mean, his girlfriend's one of these disappeared. I doubt I'd be as fair-minded about all of this if I were in his shoes."

"Hopefully, this'll all be over soon," Suzi said. "Estie and her friends seem really smart. I'm sure they'll figure it out once we get to Hart's apartment."

"*If* I can get us in."

"Think positively," she said. "It's always better to put out positive energy. Otherwise you're just going to attract bad luck."

Aaran smiled. "This from the woman who doesn't believe any of this is possible in the first place."

"You believe it's real, don't you?" Suzi asked. "I mean Web sites with spirits and other worlds and everything?"

Aaran shrugged. "The evidence has moved way over to the 'hard not to believe' side of the scale for me."

"Then I do, too."

Holly

"I feel like I'm in the middle of some Looney Toons cartoon," Holly said to Christy.

She'd come downstairs with the Riddell brothers as they left the store. Geordie had already gone ahead to the car.

"But you know this stuff is real," Christy said.

Holly gave a slow nod. She bent down and picked up Snippet as the terrier tried to slip past Christy's feet and have an impromptu solo walk.

"But that doesn't make it feel any less weird," she said. She hesitated for a moment, then added, "You were awfully nice to Aaran, all things considered."

"Don't make more of it than it was," Christy said. "I wanted to know what he could tell us, and he wasn't going to tell us anything if we treated him the way he deserves to be treated. And while it turns out it wasn't a lot, well . . ." He shrugged. "We're further ahead knowing about Jackson Hart and this virus than we were before Aaran showed up."

"And it might even be useful—if Estie and the others can figure something out." She paused for a moment, then added, "You don't think you should wait to see if they can?"

Christy shook his head. "I don't know how much time we have, but in my heart, I can feel it running out on us."

"You'll be careful."

He smiled. "You can count on it." He waited a beat, then added, "And I'll make sure Bojo is, too."

Holly couldn't stop herself from blushing.

"I hardly even know him," she managed to say.

Christy bumped a feather-light fist against her chin. "Doesn't mean you shouldn't get the chance to know him better."

He leaned over and gave her a quick peck on the cheek, then he was out the door. Holly closed it behind him and engaged the lock. Her gaze fell on what was left of the store's computer. Even if they managed to succeed at stopping the Wordwood spirit and were able to get all those missing people back, she didn't know how she was ever going to use the machine again.

Shadows in the Wordwood

Skin spun off,
stripped of
flesh and bone,
spirit singing,
free at last.

Come my turn
to take the journey,
will there be anything
left of me
to go on?
—SASKIA MADDING,
"Death Is for the Living"
(*Spirits and Ghosts,* 2000)

Christiana

I come slowly out of this second blackout of mine, drifting from complete unconsciousness into a dreamy state where I'm not fully aware of my body. I'm not sure that I even have one. Whatever I am is floating through a meadow, dotted with trees, that sits on the edge of a dark forest, but it's a confusing place because everything is made of words.

The grass and wildflowers are narrow phrases, swaying in the wind, punctuated with blossoms whose wordy petals radiate from clusters of vowels. The trees are thick paragraphs, dense with description, that lighten into shorter sentences and finally simply words as they follow the natural progression of trunk to branch to twig to leaf. Small verbs and nouns scamper along the branches or in amongst the roots of the trees. Others sit in the topmost branches, trilling sweet wordsongs, or soar by on wings of poetry.

It's all very strange, but I'm completely accepting of it, the way you are in a dream. My spirits are buoyant and light.

I don't know how long I'm in this place, but after awhile it starts to drift away—or I drift away from it. A sharp pang of disappointment goes through me. I felt safe and happy there, even with some of those darker stories I spied hiding in the shadows under the trees where the forest of legends and fairy tales began in earnest.

But then I feel a tingling in my limbs. I realize I have limbs. I have a body again. I hear one last trilling song from a small yellow-breasted verb perched high in a paragraphing oak—

Catch as catch as catch as can!

—before it's all gone and I'm waking up.

When I open my eyes, the world's spinning. I imagine all these faces crowded close, peering down at me, blurred and colourless. But when the spinning stops, the faces are still there, still blurred and leeched of colour. There's no colour anywhere, which is a real shock after the brightly-hued world of words I've just left behind.

I sit up and see that the faces are attached to bodies as ill-defined as the out-of-focus features on the heads above them. They drift away from me whenever I turn to look at a particular group, the ones not in my view taking the opportunity to crowd closer behind me.

"Back off!" I tell them.

I get to my knees, waving my hands at them. They do what I tell them and give me some space, watching me from a distance. The effort of chasing them off makes me dizzy, but I force myself to put one foot on the ground and push up until I'm standing, though swaying would be a better description of what I'm doing.

"I mean it," I say as the ghostly figures begin to move closer again.

That's when I realize that I still have my colour. I lift one hand, then the other. They're the same coppery brown they always are. I look down at my sweater and jeans. I'm far more *here* than the ghost people are. I'm far more here than the place *itself* is. The pale rose of my sweater, the faded blue of my jeans, the scuffed brown leather of my walking shoes—they all vibrate with presence and colour.

Well, I guess they would, here in this chiraoscuro world, where everything's just black and white and the shades of grey that lie in between. Standing here, I jump out like a spot of tinted colour in a black-and-white photograph.

But that's not the strangest thing about this place. The setting could be the same as my dream of the word world, except this meadow borders a forest that looks like a sculpture made out of junk metal and old electronic parts: trees, branches, leaves, undergrowth and all. It's all circuitry and wires and bits of metal and cast-off scraps of god knows what.

Everything's like that. I bend down and touch the vegetation underfoot. It looks like its made up of hundreds of tiny wires, soft and pliable like grass would be.

But I think it's the lack of colour that gets to me the most.

I've been in colourless worlds before—or ones that were as close to it to make no difference. A lot of the borderlands exist in a perpetual twilight that lays a grey hue over everything. But they're nothing like this. There's something in the air here that feels heavy. That makes me feel heavy. Maybe it's the lack of colour. Maybe it's all the metal and electronic junk. More likely, it's those ghostly figures that drift around as easily as mist.

But if this is one of the strangest places I've ever been, it does have this much going for it: it's still a place. I'm not sure where it is—somewhere in the spiritworld, I suppose—but if I'm here, that means I'm not dead.

"Is this weird or what?" I say to Saskia.

There's no reply in my head and I realize that the slight pressure of her presence is gone.

That figures. Just when I could really use someone to talk to—if only in my head—she's found somebody else to inhabit. Or maybe she got left behind when I . . . when whatever happened to bring me here.

I try to remember and it slowly comes back to me. The storm that shouldn't be able to exist. Me going out into it. The black rain beating me to the ground . . .

I guess Saskia was right. Maybe I should learn to be a little less head-strong. Can't see it happening, though. If Mumbo hasn't been able to convince me after all these years, I doubt anything can.

I study the ghosts some more, wondering what they want from me. I suppose it could just have been curiosity, the way they were all hovering around me when I was coming to. They don't seem particularly menacing. In fact, they're all keeping their distance now. Though they haven't lost interest in me—not by a long shot. I think the weight of their observation is adding to this heaviness that's settled over me.

I thought they were all the same at first, but I can see differences now. Even as out-of-focus as they are, their features are individual when you look at them long enough. Men and women of all races. Teenagers, pensioners, and all the ages in between.

Since they still haven't made any threatening moves in my direction, I decide to try open up the lines of communication between us.

"So," I call out to the nearest group of them. "What's this place called?"

That bunch immediately backs away. I hear an odd sound coming from them which sounds like radio static. It takes me a moment, but after I try another two or three times with other groups, I realize it's their voices.

Scratch communication with the natives.

I look away from them and try to get my bearings. The meadow I'm in is actually the scrub between the forest and a sweep of grasslands that goes all the way to a line of low hills that I can see on the far horizon. There are probably dips and valleys, but from where I'm standing it appears to be one big, flat expanse of open land.

That direction seems less than promising, so I turn back to the forest. I know I'm probably going to have to go into there, but I'm not looking forward to it. I don't like the idea of being in such a confined space, not with all those ghostly creatures floating about.

I fasten onto that word. Ghosts. Maybe I am in some land of the dead. Since I'm so solidly present, I guess I'm still alive. But *they* could be spirits of the dead. Or lost souls.

I immediately think of Saskia again.

Lost soul pretty much sums the state she was in the last time I—I want to say "saw her," but she had even less physical presence than the ghostly figures I've got floating around me here. Could she be one of them? Is that what I'm doing here? She got pulled into this place and I got dragged along with her?

I call her name. Once, twice, and again. I call as loud as I can, letting my voice ring, but all I succeed in doing is totally scaring off the ghosts that have been watching me. That's okay. I can live without the weight of their attention.

I listen hard, hoping for a response, but I don't get one. I realize that there's next to no sound here. No birdsong. No wind. Nothing except this faint hum that seems to come out of the ground underfoot.

I try calling for Saskia some more, keeping it up until my throat gets raspy.

There's still no response.

So I give up. I have a last look at the grasslands, then slowly turn to the forest. I can't see anything worth my attention in the grasslands, but the forest . . . the forest could be hiding anything. That's the trouble as well as a possible solution to my situation, of course. That anything waiting for me under those strange, junk metal trees could just as easily be dangerous as helpful. But I really don't see that I have a choice beyond standing here like a dummy, doing nothing.

So. I take a deep breath. I start forward the way you do any journey, big or small. You put one foot in front of the other.

I get maybe a dozen paces closer when something hits me in the head with enough force to bowl me over and send me sprawling in the wiry grass.

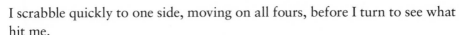

I scrabble quickly to one side, moving on all fours, before I turn to see what hit me.

There's no one there.

I lift a hand to my head and feel around through my hair. But there's no sore spot. There's no blood. Nothing. Only this pressure in my head. A familiar pressure . . .

"Saskia?" I say. Then I repeat it as a thought. *Saskia, are you in there?*

<Christiana?>

She sounds totally surprised.

"Are you here because I was calling you?"

<That was you?>

"I don't see anybody else here. Where've you been?"

<Lost,> she says. <Lost somewhere in cyberspace. I was trying to follow this URL, but it was just taking me in circles and—>

"Hold up there. What's an URL?"

<It's like an address. On the Internet.>

"Ohh-kay."

<It doesn't matter. I was just in this loop and until I heard something calling to me . . . my name, I guess . . . > Her voice trails off for a moment, then she adds, <The next thing I knew I was back in your head.> Another pause. <Sorry about the hard landing.>

"No problem. I'm happy to have the company."

<So I guess that's twice I owe you my life now—if you can call this living.>

"Oh, don't go all mournful on me. This place is depressing enough as it is. Speaking of which, do you have *any* idea where we might be?"

<Well, I was aiming for the Wordwood site . . . >

"I think I was there," I say and tell her about the dream I had just before I regained consciousness.

<I don't know what that place was,> she says, <but I don't think that was it. I think this is.>

"*This?* Come on. This is just a junkyard—a creative one, I'll grant you, but really. This other place was *made* of words. There were even animals and birds that were somehow both words and themselves at the same time, if that makes any sense."

<Not really. But this place *feels* right. Remember, I was born here.>

"So you recognize it?"

<No, it's just how it feels. Though obviously something's gone very wrong with it.>

"Okay, say this is the Wordwood. Any ideas where we go from here?"

<I don't know. What have you found so far?>

"Pretty much nothing," I tell her and then I fill her in on what little I've seen since I found myself waking up here in a field of grassy wires.

<These ghosts wouldn't talk to you?> she asks when I'm done.

"They seem to scare pretty easily. I think that static-y sound they were making was their language, but I couldn't make out a word."

<Probably because we're from two different operating systems.>

"Say what?"

<You know, like a Windows PC trying to talk to an iMac.>

"I don't have the first clue as to what you're talking about."

<It's like people from different countries who can't understand each other.>

"If that static I heard even was a language." I get another thought then. "Are you the only one the spirit sent out into the consensual world?"

<The what?>

"Where we met—what Christy calls the World As It Is. I was just wondering if the spirit sent others like you out into it."

<I never even thought of that. They'd be like my brothers and sisters.> She's quiet for as moment, then adds, <But if the Wordwood did send others out, I sure hope it prepared them better than it did me.>

"I guess if you were the first, it would have learned from that until you . . . what? Stopped broadcasting information back?"

<That worked two ways,> Saskia says. <I also had access to everything that was in the Wordwood. Which was strange, but useful. I could give you an historical overview of chocolate, but I had no idea how it actually tasted.>

"That would be handy right about now."

<You mean some chocolate?>

"No. Some more background info."

<Oh.>

I take another look at the forest. "Well, I say we should get a move on. Are you ready to do a little exploring?"

<I guess . . . >

I start forward, my gaze sweeping the shadows under the trees for I'm not sure what. Ghosts, I guess. Danger.

Something in here worries me.

The undergrowth isn't thick—this forest is too old and overgrown for much light to get through the thick canopy above. Then I have to laugh. I touch the bark of one of the first trees—it's like running my hand over a sculpture made up of circuit boards pasted together. Does this stuff even grow?

I'm about to ask Saskia what she thinks when, from the corner of my eye, I catch something move, like a figure ducking behind a tree. It looked like a man—still black and white, but much more substantial than the ghosts I saw earlier.

Did you see that? I ask, then I feel foolish. Of course she did. She sees everything I see.

<It looked like a person.>

If I can grab him, maybe we can convince him to tell us a little something about this place . . .

<Be careful,> Saskia says. <Remember where your last bold move got us.>

I know. Here. But now we really have nothing to lose, do we?

<But . . . >

Don't worry. This is something I'm good at.

It's true. I lead an active life, which surprises some people who only see this delicate creature the way Christy does. I've always been more tomboy than debutante. Maybe it's because I started life out as a boy.

I keep walking, as though I never noticed the figure ducking out of sight, slowly shifting my direction until I'll pass right by the tree that he's hiding behind. When I come up to its fat bole with all the circuits and wires hanging from it like bark, I dart around the opposite side from where he'd be expecting me to pass. He has his back to me, but he senses me and starts to turn. Too late. I charge at him like a defensive line back. My shoulder hits his chest and he goes tumbling down in a sprawl with me on top of him.

I'm stronger than I look, but he's bigger than me and he pushes me off, scrabbling backwards until his back comes up against another of these weird circuit board trees.

"Don't hurt me, don't hurt me!" he cries as I move toward him.

I hold my hands up, palms out.

"I'm not going to hurt you," I say. "What makes you think I want to hurt you?"

"You jumped on me, didn't you?"

"Yeah, but that was only after you started stalking me."

"I wasn't stalking you. I was just . . . observing you."

"Sounds like stalking to me."

"I was just trying to figure out who you are," he adds quickly. "To see if you're dangerous or anything."

"And?" I ask. "Am I dangerous?"

"Jesus, I don't know."

The look in his eye tells me he thinks I am, but I don't call him on it.

He's solid flesh and bone, for all that he has no colour. From his features and the darker grey tones of his skin, I figure he's of African descent. Mid-twenties and good-looking. Kind of twitchy, but I think that's more to do with me surprising him than any natural inclination on his part.

<At least we can understand him,> Saskia says.

Yeah, but did you notice that there's a bit of static when he talks? Like hearing a radio that's not quite on the station.

<Was that what it was like with the others?>

No, I couldn't make out a word they were saying—if they were saying anything. And this guy's a lot more solid.

"Who are you?" I ask out loud so that he can hear me.

"My name's Jackson. Jackson Hart."

"And do you live around here, Jack?"

"I prefer Jackson."

"Okay, Jackson it is. Do you live around here?"

He shakes his head.

"So where are you from?"

"A place called Newford. I . . ."

His voice trails off as he cocks his head to listen to something. As soon as he does, I hear it too.

<What a strange sound,> Saskia says.

No kidding.

I can't quite figure out what it is. It's not high-pitched, but it's still got that quality of a fingernail on a blackboard mixed with a dull, um, I guess I have to say wet whine, if that makes any sense. You'd have to hear it. There's also a hissing sound, like water boiling, maybe.

"Oh, Jesus," Jackson says. "It's the leeches."

I'd put a mild panic in his eyes when I knocked him over, but now they hold pure, unadulterated terror.

"Leeches?"

"That's just what I call them," he says. "Land leeches." He gives another anxious glance in the direction the strange sounds are coming from, then turns back to me. "I don't know who you are or what you're doing here, but you *don't* want to meet these creatures. And with the way you look, they're going to be all over you."

"What do you mean the way I look?"

He holds out a black and white hand, then points at my own.

"You're in Technicolor—that makes you stand out in a black-and-white world."

"Sure, but—"

"There's no time to explain. Just do what I do."

He starts to tear at the forest floor, peeling back layers of matted wires, circuitry, handfuls of what looks like thin, small pieces of sheet metal, but is far more pliable.

"I'm serious," he says when he realizes I'm still just standing there.

The sound's a lot closer now and it's starting to hurt my ears.

<Maybe we should do what he says, Christiana.>

I guess.

He's dug himself a hole and now here's something even weirder. Under all this crap we've been walking on is a mess of words—a great tangle of them, like a thick undercarpet of leaves and weed clippings. I flash back to the word world I was dreaming about before I woke up here. But these are different. They're like dirt, dark, with a smell that's a mix of ink and something metallic.

Jackson lies down on the words and starts to cover himself up.

<Christiana!>

I stir at Saskia's sharp cry.

I'm on it, I tell her.

And none too soon. I scrabble in the debris, getting I-don't-even-want-to-think-about-what under my nails as I dig my way down under the rubbish to the layer of words below. They feel odd against my skin. Warm and dry, for all that they look so damp. I feel almost cozy as I burrow down among them and cover myself over with the junk that was covering them. I leave myself a small hole to peek out of. Saskia makes a gasping sound inside my head and she doesn't even have lungs.

But I understand.

If this world is hard to describe, and the sound the approaching creatures make is even harder, I'm not sure where to begin with the creatures themselves. Imagine some weird combination of a snake and a garden slug, with a shark's fin on the hump of its back. They're solid black, fast and slick, and I see why Jackson calls them land leeches, because there's something like a leech in them as well, for all that they're flowing over the land instead of in water. They're just skimming along, but you can't see any legs and their body doesn't undulate. Electricity seems to flicker on their oily skin, running from one end to the other.

I don't know how many of them there are. I see two, three, then I look away, afraid that they'll feel the weight of my gaze.

I'm sure they know we're here. They ooze menace and have eyestalks on their front ends that are constantly in motion, checking everything out with a field of vision that encompasses a full three hundred and sixty degrees, and probably above them as well.

I burrow deeper and try not to breathe.

Nothing here, nothing here, I chant in my head. No need to stop and check this spot out.

This close, the sound they make sets my teeth on edge. And then there's their smell. Like burnt wiring and sulfuric acid. Like when an outlet fries an electric cord, along with something organic and rotting.

I don't know how long I lie there—Saskia and I don't even talk to each other—but after what feels like forever, I hear something moving in the debris around my hidey-hole. I tense up, ready to go down fighting, when I realize that the sound of the creatures has been steadily receding and the smell's not nearly so pungent any more.

What do you think? I ask Saskia.

But before she can reply, I hear Jackson's voice.

"Hey," he whispers. "Are you okay down there?"

I push up through the circuits and matted wiring and other junk and sit up.

"They're gone?" I ask.

He nods.

<Thank god,> Saskia says.

Ditto, I tell her.

"What *were* those things?" I ask Jackson.

"I think they're a manifestation of the virus."

"What virus?"

"The one that took down the site," he says. "The Wordwood site."

"So this *is* the Wordwood."

He shrugs. "I guess. I just assumed it was when I got here. The damn place was haunting me the whole week before . . . you know . . . ever since it went down."

He looked like he was going to say something else, but I don't push.

Right now he's the only one here who has even a vague clue as to what's going on, so I'll let him dole out the information in his own time. At least for now.

I look over to where the leeches went by and see they've left behind a wake of slagged debris. Some of it's still smoking the way metal will when you drop acid on it.

"How did you figure out how to hide like this?" I ask.

Though I realize even that wouldn't have helped if the creatures had come oozing by right on top of where we were hiding.

"I was desperate," he says. "The first time I heard them, I didn't know what was making that sound. I just knew it would probably be dangerous. They caught me out in the open or I would have tried to climb one of these weird trees. Instead I just dug at the grass—I guess I was going to try to cover myself with it—but when I pulled at it, I found all this code underneath."

He brushes some of the debris from the hole I'd been hiding in, and pulls out some of the words.

"Code?" I say.

He nods. "Yeah. HTML. The code you use to build Web pages. See?"

He's holding what's like a transparent ribbon with words on it. This one says:

Dickens, Charles

"Dig far enough through this stuff and it's all binary," he says. "A big mess of zeros and ones."

"I don't know what you're talking about," I tell him.

<He's means the programming languages that tell a computer how it's supposed to operate. It's what lets us talk to the machines, and to each other.>

"This place is like an old DOS program," Jackson says. "Everything's really basic and it doesn't have any of the graphics or scripts we can access today. I think the virus is what's brought it back to this primitive state."

I give a slow nod, like I know what he's talking about.

"How did you get here?" I ask.

"I don't know for sure. One moment I was sitting in front of my computer, and the next, this flood of black goop came bursting out of my monitor and I was drowning in it. Or I thought I was. I guess I just blacked out, because I woke up here." He gives me a weak smile. "Unless this is the afterlife."

The liquid black goop sounds like the storm that knocked me off my feet, back in the borderlands. Looks like I came the same way. The only difference is, I haven't lost my colour. The first explanation for that doesn't do anything to lighten my spirits: It's probably because I'm a shadow. I've been listening too much to Saskia, I guess, but I can't help feeling like there's something missing in me. And since I don't really exist in the consensual world, why should it be any different in this one?

"How long have you been here?" I ask.

Maybe it's not just me, I find myself thinking. Maybe it's something that happens over time. You lose colour, then substance, until finally you're like the ghosts I saw when I first came to.

"I don't know that either," Jackson says. "It feels like forever."

"We . . ." I begin, then correct myself. No need to let on there's more than one person inside my head. "I just got here. And there were these ghosts . . ."

"They're like us—they're not from here. Or they're like me, anyway. People that got sucked into their computers. The way it seems to work is, you're like a ghost when you first get here, and you stay like that, too, it seems, until you start to figure things out. At least the more I've explored and worked out stuff, the more solid I've become." He gives me a kind of yearning look. "But I'm still black-and-white."

So it works the opposite from the way I thought.

"Are there others like you?" I ask.

He nods. "But they all seem to keep to themselves. And here's something really weird: Some of them don't even speak English. You have to wonder. What were they doing, accessing an English language database?"

<The Wordwood's not just English,> Saskia says. <It automatically translates into whatever language you're using.>

I repeat what Saskia just said so that Jackson can hear it.

He starts shaking his head. "That's not possible."

"We're not talking about a program," I tell him. "We're talking about an entity. A spirit. Something that's alive and lives in . . . wherever we are. Cyberspace, I guess. It communicates with us through the Internet. Or at least it did."

"But—"

"Okay, maybe this is simpler. You remember your classical mythology—how there was a god or goddess for everything?"

"Vaguely," he says, but he nods at the same time.

"So the Wordwood site was the home of the god of something like electronic books. Pixelated words."

"A god."

"I'm just trying to put this in terms you might be able to relate to," I say.

"But a god."

"Maybe that's not the best analogy."

"And he'll be pissed off at me."

"Maybe it's a she," I say, thinking of Saskia. The spirit could have made her in its own image. Then I realize what he said. "Why would it be mad at you in particular?"

"You want to know the truth?"

"No, I prefer it when people lie to me."

<Christiana,> Saskia says. <Maybe we can learn something here.>

Now you're my conscience?

<I'm sorry, but—>

No, you're right. I shouldn't be taking it out on you. Or him.

"So why's the spirit of the Wordwood mad at you?" I ask, gentling my voice.

He's shaking his head again.

"You know, it figures," he says. "Forests have creeped me out for years, so naturally, if I'm going to piss off a god, it'd have to be one that lives in a forest. Even if it's a metaphorical forest. Though weird as this place is, it feels pretty real."

"Jackson," I say, trying to get him back on track. "It's not a god. It's just a spirit. Yes, they can be powerful, but they're only another kind of being, like the difference between, oh, a bear and a gnat. No, that's another bad analogy," I quickly add when I see the stricken look on his face.

Help me here, Saskia.

<Tell him they can be reasoned with.>

Yeah, right. Have you met any of the really old—

<I know,> she says, cutting me off. <But he hasn't. It'll make him feel better.>

So I tell him, and sure enough, Saskia's right. I can see him relax a little.

"Maybe I can just explain to it how it was all a mistake," he says. "Well, not exactly a mistake, but I didn't have a choice."

"I need for you to back up a little here," I say. "I don't know what you're talking about."

"This," he says, waving a hand. "It's all my fault."

"Maybe you should start at the beginning," I say.

So he tells us the whole sorry tale of hacking into this bank's computer, how Aaran Goldstein blackmailed him into sending a virus to the site. How he was haunted by visions of this forest, hearing a static-y wind. How he kept losing chunks of time until one day he lost the world and ended up here.

We listen to it pretty much without interruption, except for the first time he mentions Aaran.

Is this the same guy that—

<God, I hate him,> Saskia breaks in before I can finish my question. But it doesn't matter. She's answered me all the same. <Of *course* he'd be involved in something like this.>

"Is he here?" I ask aloud.

"Who, Aaran? I doubt it. I don't think he spends much time on the computer. And especially not the Wordwood site. I mean, why would he want me to take it down, if he did? I figure it's mostly a bookish lot that got pulled over. Librarians. Avid readers."

<I doubt Aaran Goldstein even likes books,> Saskia says.

Something had to get him started as a book editor.

<I suppose. But I don't think he likes them anymore. Christy says he hates writers because he tried to write himself, and it was a complete disaster.>

Yeah, well, Goldstein isn't exactly one of Christy's favorite people.

<Is he anybody's?>

I'm just saying there's a lot we don't know about him—you know, why he is the way he is.

<Why are you defending him?>

I'm not. I'm just trying to get a full picture.

Jackson has no idea about the conversation going on in my head, so he's just been talking away.

"What did you say?" I ask.

"I was just saying that the few people I have talked to since I got here were all on their computers, trying to access the Wordwood site when . . . whatever happened went down."

I nod and he goes on, telling us about how he sent an e-mail to the site's Webmaster—"I guess I was talking to the spirit itself, right?"—explaining what he'd done and how it could be fixed.

"But right after that . . . boom. Here we are."

<Boom,> Saskia repeats. <Though in my case, it was more like fire-works gone awry.>

There's so much loss in her voice that I start to feel bad about the way I was talking about Goldstein earlier. I really *wasn't* trying to defend him, but I can see how she might take it that way.

When we get all of this sorted out, I tell her, *we'll find a way to make him pay.*

But now it's her turn to be the voice of reason.

<I don't necessarily agree with the idea of revenge,> she says. <I think the bad you do comes back on you, no matter how justified you might think you were to do it.>

We don't have to do anything ourselves. We can just tell the Wordwood spirit where it can find him.

<I don't know . . . >

"Jesus," Jackson says, distracting us from our own silent conversation. "You know what's happening here?"

My sympathies are more with Jackson than Goldstein in this mess, but after listening to his story, I'm not feeling particularly charitable to either of them.

"Yeah," I tell him. "You were playing show-off computer nerd and you screwed a whole bunch of people."

"No. I mean, that's true. But he forced me to do it."

"You could have said no."

"And gone to jail."

"I'm just saying you had a choice."

I see in his eyes that he knows this all too well. That it's been eating at him ever since he got here. Not just because of what's happened to him, but because of how many other people have been hurt as well.

"I shouldn't have said that," I say.

He shrugs. "Why not? It's true."

"Okay. It's true. But we need to move on now. You were saying some-thing about knowing what's going on?"

It takes him a moment to shift gears, but then he nods. "It's just that, if the Wordwood is a being rather than a Web site, then my virus hit it like a disease. I wrote it to screw up all the HTML links in the site. But if it hit a person—or at least a being of some sort—then what it's doing is playing havoc with their metabolism. It's not letting the various parts of its body communicate with each other. At the very least, it's not going to be able to form a coherent thought—or at least not one that has any correlation to anything else it happens to know."

<He's probably right.>

Probably.

"How does this helps us?" I ask.

"I don't know. But maybe if I can access a computer . . ." He looks around himself and his excitement dies. "What am I saying? We're *inside* a damn computer."

He bends down and tears up a handful of the words we burrowed in to hide from the sliders. I get a flash of that binary code he was talking about earlier—zeros and ones flashing by at an incredible rate, almost too fast to see.

"What we really need," I tell him, "is to find some of these other people. Or . . . have you seen anything that could be the place where the spirit would be staying?"

He sighs and looks deeper into the woods.

"There are the ruins," he says.

"Ruins? What kind of ruins? And where are they?"

"Deeper in the forest. It looks like the foundation of some old building, but all that's left of it is the fieldstone base on which it was built. The only weird thing there is the glass coffin with the girl in it."

"What?"

"You'd have to see it. It's like out of *Snow White and the Seven Dwarfs.* Before you, it was the only piece of colour I've seen in this whole place."

"The coffin's in colour?"

He shakes his head. "No. The dead girl inside is. Or maybe she's not dead. Maybe she's only sleeping. All I know is she doesn't move. She just lies there with her hands folded on her chest and her eyes closed. You can't get into the coffin and you can't wake her up. I've tried."

"Show us," I say.

I've no way to gauge how long we tramp through the woods. The light never changes. Actually, nothing really changes except that the land underfoot rises steadily. It's a long gentle slope, so it's not too arduous, but it's hard to get a sense of where we are, or where we're going. For all their size and the lack of real undergrowth, the circuit board trees grow too thick to allow for much of a long view.

That plays in our favor when it comes to the land leeches. We can't see them from far off, and they can't see us. But we can certainly hear them coming.

Twice on the way to the ruins we have to hide from them. The first time we hear that unmistakable sound of their approach, I don't even wait for Jackson to say a word. I just stop where I am and start digging.

I've seen a lot of strange things in my travels through the spiritworld and the borderlands, but these things are definitely the scariest. I think it's because they appear to be so utterly implacable. I can't imagine reasoning with them, or outwitting them, which are pretty much the only two tricks in my repertoire when it comes to beings that are much more powerful than me. How would you even talk to something like that in the first place?

So I follow Jackson's example. I hear them coming and I'm gone, burrowed as deep as I can get into forest floor before their arrival. I've seen the smoking slag they've left behind when they're gone. And Jackson tells me he's seen them absorb ghosts that are too slow to get out of their way. Not for me, thanks.

Anyway, it's a while before the trees start to thin out and the ground gets steeper. But finally we come out of the forest into an open field. There's more of that strange wiring here, pretending to be grass and gorse and who knows what kind of weed. As we keep climbing, I look around and see that the forest stretches as far as I can see on all sides. Here and there, other bare peaks rise from the forest.

I try to see them as a pattern, the way you'd expect inside something as logical as a computer, but their placement appears to be completely random. Here a pair close to each other. There three in a cluster. Between them a huge expanse with nothing to break up the forest.

After a good long look on my part, we continue up.

I'm a little worried about those leeches catching us here, out in the open, with nowhere to hide. But I don't see any of their trails and Jackson assures me that the grass will pull up as easily here as the carpet of metal leaves and crap does in the forest. I believe him, but I have to give it a try anyway. He's right. Under the layer of wiry grass I peel back, I find more of those dark code words that pass for soil in this place.

When we reach the summit, I take a close look at the stones that make up the ruined walls of the foundation. I can't tell what they're made of, but it's some kind of metal, discoloured and patterned just like field stones would be.

"She's in there," Jackson says.

The wall's too high here for me to look over, so I follow him around to an opening where I guess a window would have been. It's easy to climb over the sill and jump down onto the vegetation inside. It's spongy underfoot—like a thick bed of lichen.

The inside of the ruins is broken up into a maze of rooms. Walls marking the boundaries of the rooms and halls, with no roof, no floor or furnishings.

<I wonder who lived here?> Saskia says as we look back out through the window.

Maybe you did, I say. *Before you were born in the consensual world.*

<Maybe . . . >

Jackson leads the way through the rooms, two right turns, a left, another right, then he stops in the doorway of an enormous room and moves aside. I step by him, my gaze immediately going to the explosion of colour that's the dead girl he was talking about. Her coffin's in the center of the room.

For a moment I can't make out any detail. Seeing this much colour after all these hours of monochrome makes my eyes hurt. It's like looking directly into the sun. Spots dance in front of my eyes, but they adjust quickly.

It's right out of a fairy tale scene all right—a blonde woman lying on her back in a glass coffin, hands folded over her stomach—except she's wearing blue jeans, a white T-shirt, and running shoes, which kind of takes some of the romance out of the image. Then I focus on her face and I'm sure all the blood drains out of my own.

<That's . . . >

You, I agree.

<Me.>

Sarah "Estie" Taylor

"So what's the deal with her?" Claudette said.

Estie shrugged. The two of them walked side by side as they made their way down the block to Jackson's apartment, trailing behind Aaran and Suzi who were in the lead, with Tip in between. It reminded Estie a little of the old days when they'd go wandering through the city, sometimes two or three of them, usually all five of the original Wordwood founders. In those days, they'd been pretty much inseparable.

"Suzi?" she asked.

"Who else?"

"I've no idea," Estie said.

"There's something off about her. I don't know exactly what, there's just *something . . .* "

Estie nodded. She knew what Claudette meant, though she wouldn't have put it exactly that way. For her, Suzi's presence was more confusing than anything. She understood why she and Tip and Claudette were here—if it wasn't for them, the Wordwood wouldn't exist in the first place. And if the Wordwood hadn't developed this spirit of its own and then gone wrong, Benny and Saskia and all these hundreds of other people would still be safe in their homes, happily surfing the Internet instead of having been kidnapped into some pixelated corner of it.

She also understood Aaran's wanting to atone for the part he'd played in the recent crisis.

But Suzi had no stake in any of this. So far as Estie could tell, she was just tagging along.

"Maybe she feels grateful to Aaran," she said. "You know, for taking her off the street."

"She doesn't look like any street kid I've ever seen."

"Well, she's had a chance to get cleaned up. . . ."

"And besides," Claudette went on. "He's old enough to be her father."

Estie smiled. Trust Claudette to zoom in on that. She'd been the worst gossip, back in the old days.

"We don't know that they're sleeping together," she told Claudette. "Not that it's even any of our business."

"But still . . ."

"She could be in her mid-twenties," Estie said, "and I doubt Aaran's forty. So it might not be *that* huge an age gap."

"Well, if they're not sleeping together," Claudette said, "then what *is* she doing here? I don't buy her being all super grateful for a meal and a shower."

"Why not?"

"It's just weird. And I don't trust her. I don't trust him either, mind you, but I *really* don't trust her."

Estie nodded. "I suppose it's just—you know how sometimes you meet somebody and they're perfectly okay, but you still don't click anyway?"

"I guess . . ."

"Well, that's probably what this is. For whatever reason, we're not clicking with her. It doesn't have to mean anything more than that. There's enough weird stuff going on without us looking for more."

"But that's just it. We weren't looking. The weirdness came to us and—"

"Shh," Estie said.

The others had stopped ahead of them and were going up the stairs of a brownstone, indistinguishable from the rest of the buildings on the street, but obviously their destination. Claudette followed them up onto its stoop, but Estie paused on the sidewalk to look up at the sky. There wasn't a cloud in sight and the sun was almost directly overhead, beating down on the city's streets. She'd forgotten how hot August could get in Newford. It got hot in Boston, too, but the breezes that came in from the ocean usually kept it from getting too unbearable.

"Are you coming, Estie?" Tip called down from the top of the stairs.

Estie look up and saw that he was holding the door open for her. The others had already gone inside.

"I was just remembering why I moved from Newford. God, it's hot."

Tip grinned. "I had The Weather Channel on in my hotel room while we were changing. It's going up into the nineties today."

"Still," she said. "It's not the heat—"

Tip laughed and they finished in unison: "It's the humidity."

"But if you think this is bad," he added, "don't come down to Austin in the summer. There are days it's still this hot at midnight."

"So why do you keep inviting me?"

"Can't beat the music."

Smiling, she stepped by him and entered the foyer.

It was cooler inside the brownstone, but not by much. The relief Estie felt after first getting out of the sun quickly faded and she found herself wishing that she'd stopped to buy a bottle of water at one of the grocery stores they'd passed. She felt dehydrated and the way they were all crowded together in the narrow hallway outside the landlady's door wasn't helping. She shifted the carrying case for her laptop from one shoulder to the other while they waited for the landlady to respond to the knock on her door.

Mrs. Landis surprised her. When Aaran explained that they wanted to access Jackson's computer in hopes of finding some clues as to where he'd gone, she seemed to take it as an everyday request.

"If you think it will help," she said. "Only why does it need so many of you?"

The landlady gave Suzi a particularly searching glance as she spoke. Claudette caught Estie's eye and gave her a "you see?" look. Estie shrugged in response, then returned her attention to the conversation between Aaran and the landlady—or rather the lack thereof.

Mrs. Landis appeared to have caught Aaran off-guard with her simple question.

"We . . . um . . ." he began.

"It doesn't need all of us," Estie said, jumping in. "I'm the one who knows about computers and Aaran knows Jackson and will be the best one to sort through what we do find. The rest of us can wait outside."

The landlady shook her head. "No, that's all right. It's much too warm for anyone to be sitting out in this hot sun. It's just . . . do you really think this will help you find Jackson . . . ?"

"I sure hope so," Aaran said. "But we won't know until we see what's actually on the computer."

"Then how could I not let you have a look at it?"

Estie couldn't remember the last time she'd met someone so trusting. She realized that Mrs. Landis was worried about Jackson and only wanted to help, but Estie was happy all the same that her own landlord back in Boston was the grumpy Mr. Morello, who would barely exchange more than a couple of words with his tenants, never mind someone he didn't know. It was comforting to know that even if she ended up vanishing herself, there wouldn't be gangs of strangers traipsing through her apartment. Or at least not until the police were called in.

Mrs. Landis went into her own apartment to get her keys, then led them up the stairs to Jackson's.

"I don't know that you'll even be able to start his computer," she said as she unlocked the door to the apartment. "It's not in very good shape after . . . after what happened last night."

"It's probably not as bad as it looks," Estie said. "If the hard drive's intact, we'll be able to access his data."

"I still don't understand what you hope to find."

Estie shrugged. "We thought if we looked through his agenda and his e-mail, we might find something. Perhaps he made an appointment to see someone. Or there could be e-mail about some plans he might have made. We really won't know until we look."

"I'm surprised the police didn't think of this," Mrs. Landis said.

"I'm sure they would have eventually," Claudette said.

"And whatever we find out," Aaran added, "we'll make sure to pass along to them."

The landlady got the door open and stood aside to let them in.

"It's all so mysterious," she said.

Mysterious didn't begin to describe it, Estie thought. She wondered what the landlady would think if they explained what they really believed and why they were really here.

She'd have the police here in minutes. Or at least the men in white coats from the Zeb with their one-size-fits-all straightjackets.

Estie slipped past Mrs. Landis and walked into the middle of a familiar room. It wasn't that she'd been here before—she'd simply been in a lot of apartments much like this where bachelor computer geeks set up shop with all their computer paraphernalia, stereo equipment, oversized TV sets, and other tech toys. There was no room left over for traditional furnishings.

Though she shouldn't talk. She might keep her living room relatively geek-toy free, but the rest of her own apartment wasn't much better.

"Do you see what I mean?" Mrs. Landis said, pointing to the main desk. "I really don't see how you'll ever be able to get it up and running again."

Estie's heart sank when she turned her attention to the main computer. It really *was* a mess. It looked as though it had been through an electrical fire—much the same as Raul had described the condition of Benny's computer to be. The faint scent of burnt wiring still hung in the air. The monitor was especially scorched, the glass webbed with dozens of tiny hairline cracks, the beige casing streaked with dark burn marks.

"I thought there was some kind of oil," she said.

Mrs. Landis nodded. "There was. An awful black liquid."

"This looks like it's been in a fire."

"That's the way it was when I came in last night. I haven't touched a thing and neither did the police." Mrs. Landis paused, looking at the mess. "I suppose it's hopeless."

Estie wasn't sure they'd get anything out of this machine, but she put on a good face.

"We don't necessarily need to actually get it up and running," she said. "We just need to access the hard drive and see if the data on it is salvageable."

Mrs. Landis gave a slow nod, but though Estie could tell she had something else on her mind, the landlady didn't say anything more. If anything, she seemed nervous, even uncomfortable. Estie might have put it down to Mrs. Landis having second thoughts about letting all these strangers into one of her tenant's apartments, except she felt something, too. There was a *feeling* in the room. A sense of wrongness that appeared to originate from the area where the computer sat. It was as though the machine was casting shadows, the way a bulb casts light.

Estie stole a glance at Suzi, curious as to what her reaction would be. The small blonde woman stood very quietly beside Aaran, her gaze slightly unfocused.

"God, it really is a mess," Tip said.

Estie blinked, his voice pulling her out of her reverie. Tip had walked over behind the long desk and bent down now to look at something that was below her line of sight.

"There are two more towers down here," he said, "all connected to each other and the one on top of the desk through a cable router. Even if their hard drives are only twenty gig each, we've got our work cut out for us."

Estie joined him. She cleared a space on the desk so that she could set down her laptop's case, then studied the setup herself.

"Looks like there's an ADSL line connected to the router," she said.

Tip nodded. "Yeah, here's the modem."

Estie was happy to see the cable router. That was going to save her a lot of time. Instead of having to try to set up a dialogue between her machine and the towers with the gear she'd brought, she could just plug the cable from her network card directly into the router and access Jackson's towers the way she would any other drive connected to her laptop.

Tip leaned a little closer to the modem.

"Okay, this is weird," he said.

"What is?"

"See that little green light? The system's still on-line."

"So now we know why he's got three towers," Estie said. "He must be running a little service provider business on the side."

"Or he just does a lot of FTP exchanges."

Estie nodded.

"But when Benny got taken," Tip said. "Didn't you say that it fried all the phone lines?"

"That's what Raul said. But it didn't at Christy's place."

"Okay. Still, maybe we should unplug the modem anyway . . . just to be safe."

"I suppose."

She stood up and was about to start unpacking her laptop when she glanced at Claudette and the others. They were all standing around by the doorway, obviously unsure as to what they should be doing.

"I've just made some iced tea," Mrs. Landis said when Estie's gaze went to her. "Can I bring up a pitcher?"

Estie smiled her thanks at the offer. "We don't want to be a bother," she said, but she was only being polite. She was absolutely parched.

"It's no bother."

"Then that would be lovely," Estie told her.

"Let me help you," Claudette said.

The landlady smiled at Claudette and the two left the apartment. Now it was only Aaran and Suzi standing awkwardly by the door.

"You guys should find someplace to sit," Estie told them. "This could take awhile."

Aaran nodded. Before Estie could turn away, Suzi spoke up.

"Do you feel . . . nervous at all?" she asked.

Estie gave her a puzzled look. "Why should we be nervous?"

"I don't know. There's just something in the air. I felt it as soon as we stepped into the apartment."

"I did, too," Estie told her. "I think it's just some residual . . . I don't know. Vibes, I guess. Left over from what happened."

Suzi gave her a doubtful nod.

"Estie?"

She turned from Suzi to look at Tip. He was holding up the end of a phone cord.

"What is it?" she asked.

"The outside phone cord going into the modem. I've unplugged it."

"So?"

"So the modem's still working."

Estie bent down to see that he was right. The small green light on the modem was steadily pulsing. She started to reach for the cable connecting the modem to the router, but Tip stopped her.

"I don't know," he said. "I don't think you should be linking up with Jackson's system while it's still on-line—especially considering that it shouldn't even *be* on-line anymore."

Estie nodded. "You think it's the Wordwood."

"What else?"

"Well, we wanted to talk to it. This could be our chance."

"I don't know if that's such a good idea."

Estie smiled, trying to project a confidence she wasn't really feeling. Perhaps she was being foolhardy, and certainly she understood and felt some of Tip's nervousness, but if this was an opportunity for them to communicate with the spirit of the Wordwood, she didn't see how they could pass it up.

She took the Ethernet cable coming from her laptop and plugged it into the router, then stood up.

"Only one way to find out," she said as she turned on her laptop.

Christy

Now that we're actually ready to go, Raul seems to be getting cold feet. I don't blame him. This isn't like taking the subway downtown.

We're in the basement of Holly's store, the two of us with our backpacks and wearing more clothes than I'd normally have on in this heat: good walking shoes with thick socks, jeans, T-shirts, flannel shirts on top of that, jackets, baseball caps. Normally it'd be shorts, sandals and a T-shirt for me. But Robert told us to be prepared because we wouldn't necessarily find the same hot August weather where we were going and I took him at his word.

Mind you, neither he nor Bojo have changed, though Bojo does have a leather shoulder bag with a jacket lying on top of it. Robert's still in his suit, fedora tilted at a jaunty angle. All he's carrying when we come down to the basement is his guitar case.

"I don't know about this," Raul tells me. "I'm feeling really nervous."

"Me, too."

I'm not just saying it to make him feel better. I had a nervous prickle at the nape of my neck the whole ride from my apartment with Geordie. We had to park a couple of blocks away from the store—there's not much in the way of close parking for anyone at this time of day. Walking back to the store in the sun, even with the temperature having climbed into the nineties the way it has this afternoon, my skin goose-bumped thinking about this trip I'm about to take.

"Have you ever . . . you know, been over there before?" Raul asks.

I shake my head. "But we'll be with guides who have," I say, glancing over to where Robert's laying his guitar case down on the floor.

"Don't look at me," Robert says. "I've crossed over into the borderlands a time or two, but I like to stay clear of the spiritworld itself."

"Keeping your low profile," Bojo says with a smile.

Robert flashes him a quick grin. "Keeping myself alive."

I can feel Raul tensing up even more beside me at that. I guess Robert notices, too.

"Don't worry," he tells us. "You'll be okay. There's nothing actively hunting you."

The others have come down to see us off: Holly, with Snippet in her arms. Dick and Geordie. None of them look particularly happy to see us going. When Robert takes his old Gibson out of its case, Holly pushes her glasses back onto the bridge of her nose.

"Why do you need music to cross over?" she asks.

"It doesn't have to be music," Robert says. He adjusts the tuning on his guitar while he talks. "It's whatever you need to help you focus your will."

Holly's gaze goes to the tinker. "But I thought Bojo could just step in and out as he wanted."

"I can," Bojo says. "But only to places I've been before. If I don't have the familiarity, I have to do the same as anyone else. Make my own way by foot or whatever transportation I can find until I get to that new place."

"So that's where the music comes in," Robert explains. "Music can take you to places you've never been before. I guess any kind of art can, when you do it right. I got a good sense of the spirit we're looking for from the traces it left behind in your store. What I'm going to do now is let the music reach out and find us a way to get to wherever that spirit might have hidden itself away."

"That sounds too easy."

Robert smiles. "The world's a pretty simple place. We're the ones that make it so complicated."

I can see she's got more she wants to ask, but Robert starts to pull a twelve-bar from the Gibson, a slow bluesy number in some minor key, and then no one wants to say a word. We're caught, listening, mesmerized, just like that, no more than a couple of chords and a handful of lead notes into the tune. I may not have Geordie's ear, but I can tell right away there's something different in this music.

"Mmm-mmm-mmm."

Robert's humming. It's not a melody, more like a soft, growling counterpart to the melody that the guitar hints at, like a fragment of conversation that only he and the instrument understand. But if I can't be privy to that conversation, I am aware of a change in the air.

One moment we're in an ordinary basement under Holly's store. An old oil furnace crouches in the corner, like a hibernating bear, drowsing the season away until it can be useful once more. There are boxes floor-to-ceiling along one wall, full of books and magazines, I assume, from the black marker itemization scrawled on their side. "National Geos," one reads. I glance at some of the others. "Sci. Amers." "Hist.—pub pre-60." "Ace doubles."

Another corner holds a tall pile of cardboard flats. Under the stairs is a tidy array of snow shovels, rakes, skis, a bicycle with a flat tire and other, less readily identifiable objects. There's a long worktable set against the wall near the stairs going up to the store, with tools hanging above it. Its surface area is covered with material necessary for shipping books: more box flats, padded envelopes, shipping tape, address labels and the like.

The four of us would-be travellers are in a clear space in the middle of the floor. Dick and Holly are sitting on the stairs with Snippet on a riser between Holly's knees. Geordie leans up against the worktable.

One moment, that's all there is. The next, nothing changes physically, but suddenly the air is thick with . . . possibilities. I can't think of any other way to put it. I just know that the music has opened the potential for us to be anywhere. Perhaps Bojo and Robert are seeing these doors to the otherworld that they spoke of earlier. I don't know. I can't see anything other than what was here when we first came down the stairs. But I can *feel* the difference.

I suppose time passes, but I don't know how much. But now I begin to see flickers in the corners of my eye. Still not doors. They're more like heat mirages: ripples in the air that are gone before I can turn and give them my full attention.

"We're getting close," someone says.

I'm not sure who. Either Bojo or Robert, I assume, because who else among us would know? I turn to look at them.

"Just tell me when," Bojo says.

So it was Robert who spoke earlier.

I'm not that familiar with blues music, but this sounds darker and, at the same time, full of joy and more languid than any I've heard before. And I'm not always sure that it's just Robert playing. Sometimes I think I hear the whisper of another instrument, here one moment, gone the next. A scratchy fiddle. The soft wail of a blues harp. Another guitar. A banjo—or some banjo-like instrument playing softer, almost muffled notes. Robert isn't using a slide on the strings, but occasionally the notes he's playing ease, one into the other, the way they do on a dobro.

It's confusing and satisfying all at once. And so full of promise.

"Get ready," Robert says.

I see Bojo nod. He gives Raul and me a look and we both stand a little straighter, waiting for I don't know what. One of these invisible doors to open, I guess. I take a look behind me and see the wall has a shimmer to it, like it's not quite solid anymore.

And then we hear something else. Another faraway sound, but this one grates against the music.

For a long moment, I can't place what it is.

"You better stop," Bojo says.

Robert doesn't look up, but he shakes his head. "No, we're almost there."

"And so are they."

Then I recognize that new sound. It's the distant baying of dogs. And I know what it must mean.

Robert's hellhounds have caught his scent.

Christiana

"Do you know this woman?" Jackson says.

I walk slowly toward the coffin and lay my hands on the cool glass. This woman, he says, like she's some picture we've come across while flipping through a magazine. That's Saskia lying in there. Of course I know who she is.

"What makes you ask that?" I say, which is no reply at all.

It's just the kind of thing you say when you have nothing you can or want to say. I'm sure not telling him more than he needs to know.

"You had this look on your face," he says. "Like you'd seen her before."

I shrug. "It's just . . . pretty surprising."

<Does this mean . . . am I dead?> Saskia asks.

Of course not, I tell her.

But all I can give her are words. Neither of us knows anything for sure. Not anymore. Because this is beyond understanding.

I stare at the body lying there under the glass and try to figure out where we go from here. Whatever I expected to find in this cyber world, this isn't it. But I suppose it figures. The Wordwood is loaded with fairy tales, so why wouldn't it use a fairy-tale touchstone as a motif for what it's done to Saskia? Only what happens now? Do we have to find a way to get Christy into this world so that he can give her the traditional prince's magical kiss? Or am I supposed to do it?

There are no seams in the glass, at least none that I can see. The body's lying on a covering of crimson velvet. Maybe the casket opens from underneath. I wonder if we can tip it over to see.

I rap on the glass with my knuckles.

Or we could just break it open with a rock, though Jackson says he's already tried that without any luck. Obviously.

Then there's the whole question of, what if her being in this glass casket is what's keeping her alive? *If* she's even alive.

No, I tell myself. Don't even go there.

But I can't stop thinking about it. That she's already dead and I have a ghost in my head. Or that if I break into the coffin, she really will die. She'll disappear from my head and be gone forever.

Christy would never forgive me.

I don't know if I would.

I haven't known her for very long, but I like her. For a lot of reasons. And because we've both got these strange origins of ours, because of our connection to Christy, I feel as though we're family. Sisters.

<What . . . what are we going to do?> Saskia asks.

I don't know, I tell her.

I wish I did.

I turn to look at Jackson.

"There's got to be something you aren't telling me," I say, although I'm one to talk. "Something else you've seen. Something someone's told you."

He shakes his head.

"What about these other people you've met? Where can we find them?"

"I haven't seen anybody for a while," he says. "Except for the ghosts. And you."

"And there are no other buildings or ruins like this? No other . . ." I stop myself from saying bodies. ". . . mysteries you haven't told us about?"

"No. There's just the leeches."

I don't even want to think about them.

<We have to find the spirit itself.>

I'm open to suggestions.

<Maybe we could just . . . I don't know. Invoke it.>

Well, since, best case scenario, Jackson's virus has made it a little crazy,

*worst case, this whole world's steadily disintegrating right under us, I don't
know how much help it would be even if we could find the spirit.*

<Jackson's a programmer,> Saskia says. <Maybe he knows how.>

But—

<That's what we came for, right? To talk to the spirit?>

That was the plan, I agree. *At least it was until we got hijacked into
this mechanical fairy-tale wood. Now we're just trying to get back to the
status quo.*

<At least ask him.>

Okay.

When I turn from the casket, Jackson's got this strange expression on
his face which makes me wonder what I look like when I'm having these
internal conversations with Saskia. Do my features go all slack and I start
to drool?

I stop myself from lifting a finger to check. At least I can't *feel* anything
in the corners of my mouth.

"What?" I say.

"Nothing. You just looked like you'd gone away."

"Don't I wish."

"I mean gone away somewhere in your head."

"Let's focus on the other kind of going away," I say.

"Don't think I haven't tried."

I lean my hip against the glass casket, stick my hands in my pockets.

"Okay," I say. "So what exactly have you tried?"

He gives me a puzzled look.

"You know," I say. "Did you try to figure something out with the other
people you met? Have you tried to contact the spirit? Where have you
gone? What have you done?"

"I told you. Nobody seems to know anything. And I didn't even know
there was a spirit until you told me."

"So, really, you haven't done anything?"

He frowns at me. "I haven't been this solid for very long."

"I'm not getting on your case," I tell him. "I'm just trying to find a
place to start looking for some answers."

"Yeah, well, good luck."

I go down on one knee and pull at the ground, grabbing handfuls of the
wiry lichen to reveal the dark loam of words underneath.

"Let's start with this stuff," I say. "You told me it was some kind of
code."

"HTML. Yeah."

I dig through that first layer until the binary code is revealed, the ones and zeros flashing by at an incredible rate.

"And this stuff," I say. "It's what runs a computer?"

"They're binary numbers."

"Another kind of code?"

He nods. "The numerals represent bits that are read like electrical charges—'1' meaning on, '0' meaning off."

"So everything in a computer comes down to these bits?"

"It's like a basic language," he says. "But it's not that simple. I can't actually do anything with it."

"Why not? You're a programmer, right? Isn't this what you do?"

"I need to write code to manipulate the binary numbers. And I need a keyboard to write the code. This is like trying to mix the ingredients to bake a cake while you're inside the oven. I can't work directly with the binary. I can't even read it. It's going by too fast."

<I can read it,> Saskia says.

What does it say?

<It's a story. A book, I guess. But all the words are jumbled together—no punctuation or paragraphing or even spaces between the words.>

Because of the virus.

<I guess.>

I focus back on Jackson. "So all those ones and zeros we see flashing by—that's just information?"

"It's raw data, yes."

"And there's no way we can tap into it?"

He starts to shake his head, but before he can answer, we all hear it. That now-familiar, high-pitched, hissing whine. Approaching.

Jackson's face goes pale.

"Leeches," he says.

"I thought you said they didn't come up here," I say.

"I said I hadn't seen them up here before. Come on. We have to hide."

<My body,> Saskia says at the same time as I turn to the casket.

"We can't leave her here," I tell Jackson. "Unprotected."

He just looks at me.

"I don't know who she is, or why she's here," he says, "but there's nothing we can do for her now. We have to look out for ourselves."

I grab his arm. "No, we can't just—"

"Hey, for all we know she's what they've been looking for all along.

Maybe she's in charge—directing them with her dreams or thoughts or something. Who cares? We have to get out of here."

He starts to pull his arm free, but I tighten my grip. That horrible sound of the leeches is getting closer.

<Why are they all coming here?> Saskia says, the growing panic plain in her voice.

I've been wondering the same thing, and I think I have an idea.

I don't know what you being in the casket means, I say. *But I'll bet our coming here—the proximity of your spirit—has set off some kind of alarm. You're either supposed to reconnect with your body, or it's the last thing they want.*

<How do we know which it should be?>

We don't. Not until we try it.

"Help me see if we can topple it over," I say to Jackson. "Maybe we can get into the casket from the bottom."

He gives his arm another yank. This time he pulls free.

"Work it out on your own," he says.

He goes over to the far end of the room and begins to pull up the wiry lichen.

"Every time you cover yourself up," I tell him, "I'm going to pull that crap off of you. And then I'm going to wave and yell and call the leeches over."

"What, are you *nuts*?"

"Just help me here."

He glances in the direction from which the sound is coming, but it's not coming from any one direction anymore. They must be coming up the hill from all sides, zeroing in on the ruins of this house.

"Jesus, we're surrounded," he says. "We're *completely* screwed."

"So help me."

"Don't you understand? I said—"

"You're wasting time."

He glares at me with a look I've seen before. He knows I'm not going to back down, knows there's nothing he can do about it but help me. But that doesn't mean he's going to be happy about it.

"Fuck you," he says.

But his heart's not in it and he joins me by the casket. We reach underneath, fingers scrabbling for purchase, and find an edge we can actually grab. Looks like it's flat on the bottom.

"On three," I tell him.

I count it out and we put our backs to it.

Nothing.

"You see?" Jackson says. "Now can we—"

"Stop wasting your breath," I tell him. "Again. On three."

From the sound of it, the leeches are almost at the walls of this ruined building.

<God, they're getting so close,> Saskia says.

Let me concentrate on this.

<Sorry.>

I count it out again. I feel like my shoulders are going to pop out of joint, I'm straining so hard. Still nothing. But just when I'm about to give up, I feel something. A shift in the casket. So miniscule, I could have imagined it. But I'm grabbing for hope here, and refuse to believe that.

"Put. Some. Muscle. Into. It," I tell Jackson.

He doesn't bother to answer. He doesn't have to. We can both feel it now. It's like when you've got your foot stuck in thick mud and you just can't pull it out no matter how hard you tug. You get that mild panic feeling, that you're never going to get it out, but then there's that feeling, no more than the hint of a promise, and the next thing you know, there's movement. The mud gives up its death grip and suddenly you're free.

That's how it happens with the casket.

One minute we might as well be trying to shift a ten-ton rock. The next the casket pops free from whatever was holding it down. Some kind of adhesive, I guess. It sure wasn't because the casket was that heavy, because it weighs next to nothing, we find out all too soon. When the adhesive gives, it's like somebody suddenly opened a door we were pushing on. The casket goes toppling over. I get a flash of the body tumbling from its velvet bed. It slides toward the top of the casket, which is now the bottom. Jackson and I both lose our balance and fall with it, adding to the casket's momentum. When it hits the edge of the faux stone platform it was on, the glass cracks.

All along I've been hearing that wet, fingernail-on-a-chalkboard whining of the leeches. But it's drowned out now as the casket breaks open and something—air, I guess—comes rushing out. More air than could possibly be in that small enclosed space. The roar of it fills my head—like standing beside a jet that's getting ready for take-off.

Jackson and I tumble onto the wiry lichen, falling in different directions. We regain our balance at the same time and stare wide-eyed as the casket breaks apart. The glass is in five or six pieces and Saskia's body falls out of it onto the ground. I want to go to her, but the body starts to glow.

Electric blue. A deep gold. Blue again. And then a pillar of light explodes skyward, going straight up into the monochrome sky.

No. Not light. Or at least not *just* light.

Inside it are those binary numbers. The code. The flashing 1s and 0s are a part of the strobing blue and gold pillar of light.

<What . . . ?> Saskia begins, but she can't finish.

I understand. I don't have the words either. But Jackson manages to get out a whole sentence.

"What the fuck have we done?" he says.

And then, over the roar of the burning pillar as it pierces the sky like a searchlight, we hear them.

The leeches.

I turn and see the first one coming through the nearest wall, the faux stones melting away like wax from the contact of its slick black body. The stench of sulphur and hot metal fills the air.

Suzi

Suzi was nervous as soon as she set foot in the tenement building from which Jackson Hart had so mysteriously disappeared the night before. It didn't help that, except for Aaran, everyone was making it pretty clear that they didn't much like her and were suspicious of her tagging along. Even the landlady, who'd had a friendly smile for everyone else, had given her a weird look. Aaran was good, lending her some moral support by staying close to her, but she knew that even he couldn't quite figure her out.

She couldn't blame him, not being entirely sure herself why she felt so determined to stick it out. It was no longer simply to be supportive of Aaran—at the moment she was getting more from him than he was from her. And it wasn't even a need to know how this would all play out, though that was certainly a part of it.

It was more as if she was being compelled to come here, that she *had* to be a part of it, for all that she was feeling progressively more nervous the closer they got to Jackson's building.

She was edgy entering the tenement. Going up the stairs to Jackson's apartment made all the little hairs stand up on her arms and once she actually followed the others inside, all she wanted to do was turn around and walk right out again. There was something too creepy about the place. It was nothing specific, nothing that she could put her finger on. There were no visible signs that this was other than what it was supposed to be: the home of a techie, filled with all the latest computer, stereo, and video gear. But from the moment she crossed the threshold, she sensed that they were all in danger.

She listened to the others make small talk. Watched Estie and Tip decipher Jackson's computer setup. When Claudette offered to help the landlady get the iced tea, she wished she had the nerve to ask if she could accompany them, but she knew she wouldn't be welcome. Not that she was particularly welcome here in the apartment, either. But at least going with them would have got her out of this room and let her think about something other than the inexplicable foreboding that had taken root in her head.

Finally she had to say something. Estie agreed with her that there was an odd feeling in the air when Suzi expressed her concerns, but then she went right back to talking to Tip about the computer connections. Tip hadn't even looked up.

"Don't worry," Aaran said. He spoke softly so as not to disturb Estie and Tip. "They sound like they know what they're doing."

Do they? Suzi thought.

It didn't feel like it. Nothing felt right about any of this.

"I just . . . I get the sense that something's about to open," she said. "In this room. Maybe in me. Or that . . . I don't know. That something's approaching. Something big, that can't be touched or held. Something . . . dreadful."

She managed to give him a half-smile to show that she knew she was overreacting, but Aaran returned it with a worried look.

Suzi sighed. "Look, I know how stupid this must sound—especially since I was pooh-poohing the whole idea of Internet spirits just a few hours ago."

"It doesn't sound stupid," he told her. "I'm just not sure I understand what you mean. Is it like a premonition?"

"I guess."

She could hear Claudette and Jackson's landlady coming up the stairs behind them. Aaran had turned away from her to listen to what Estie and Tip were saying to each other. It took Suzi a moment to register what the words meant. They rasped inside her like glass, sharp and brittle. The air in the apartment grew more close, almost oppressive.

"No," she said. "You can't bring it here."

But it was too late. She saw that Estie had already connected her laptop to Jackson's system and turned it on.

"Bring what here?" Claudette asked from behind her.

Estie looked up. "We've got another mystery," she said. "Jackson's computer is still on-line, but as Tip's discovered, the ADSL connection is broken."

Tip held up the outside phone jack that he'd disconnected from the router.

"But that's not possible," Claudette said. "Is it?"

Estie shrugged. "Apparently it is. Tip seems to think that by my having connected my laptop to the router, the Wordwood spirit is going to come to us." Her gaze went to Suzi. "And so, it seems, does Suzi."

Tip stood up from behind the desk. Claudette came into the room, with Mrs. Landis trailing behind her. The landlady looked from Suzi to Estie, plainly confused.

"I don't understand," she said. "What do you mean about a spirit?"

"Maybe we should ask Suzi," Estie said. Her gaze stayed locked on Suzi. "What *do* you know about all of this?"

Suzi wanted to bolt. The room was suddenly too small. Too close, too confining. The air too heavy.

"I . . . I don't know anything," she said. "I can just . . . feel something. Like . . . like there are things in the corners of the room that we can't see. Waiting. Watching us . . ."

Oh, just shut up, she told herself. You're sounding like a lunatic.

Except she didn't feel crazy. She *did* feel that they were in danger. It was just that the words to explain it didn't seem to exist.

"It *is* oppressive in here," the landlady said. "We should open a window and see where Jackson keeps his fans. We need to move the air around a little."

"Suzi's not talking about the heat," Estie said. "Are you, Suzi? At least not that kind of heat."

Aaran stepped in between them. "Stop bullying her. It *is* hot in here."

"Sure, it is," Estie said. "We're all hot. But we're not all hiding something."

Suzi's gaze darted from one face to another. They were all staring at her, even Aaran, though at least in his case, it appeared to be out of concern for her. The weight of their combined attention was almost as bad as the sense she had that there was something watching them from the corners of the room.

"I'm not hiding anything," she said. "It's just . . . can't you *feel* it?"

Mrs. Landis stepped forward. "Maybe if you have some of this iced tea."

Suzi stepped back as the landlady held out her tray, offering her a glass.

Why couldn't they feel it? It reached right into her, like it was trying to pull something out of her chest.

But from their expressions, the only thing they sensed was that she was losing it. Maybe she was crazy.

Except there *was* something in the corners of the room—though not what she'd thought at first. There weren't monsters or evil spirits coming for them. It was that the room itself was . . . fraying at the edges.

There was no other way to put it.

She couldn't see the dissolution when she looked directly at any part of the room, but seen from the corners of her eyes the walls and corners were shivering. No longer solid. Unraveling.

It was like the difference between a real photo and a picture in a newspaper. The walls weren't solid like a photograph. Instead they were made of hundreds of tiny dots of colour, all pressed in tight against each other. And now all those tiny dots weren't holding together anymore.

"Suzi . . . ?" Aaran said.

She focused hard on his face. Maybe if she didn't look at anything else, it would all go away. The fraying walls. And this new sensation . . . like something was grabbing at her, reaching deep into her chest . . .

Don't look away from him, she told herself. Focus.

But a mild vertigo slid through her. She swayed and then made the mistake of looking down to keep her balance.

And saw her hands.

She lifted them up, not quite sure what she was seeing.

"Jesus," someone said.

Her hands were unraveling, just like the walls. She could see the molecules that made up her flesh and bone, except they looked more like the pixels of a Web photo with really bad resolution.

She lifted her gaze back to Aaran's face. It was like looking through gauze, as though her eyes were shivering apart, just like her hands.

"What . . ." She could hardly speak. "What's happening to me?"

No one replied. She looked at them, one by one, but they only stared back at her with incomprehension, in horror.

Her own growing panic exploded full-blown.

Her legs crumpled beneath her, but before she hit the floor, a shaft of light burst out of Estie's laptop and darted for the three computer towers around Jackson's desk. Parts of it were blue, others gold, all of it woven together like a braid. In an instant all four machines were connected by it, forming not quite a circle, not quite a square. Then the braid of light sent out a shaft, straight as a laser beam, right for her chest.

There was no time to dodge. No time at all.

At the moment of contact, there was a brief instant where nothing existed for her. The light entered her like a flashlight beam cutting through shadows. It enveloped the pixels that her flesh had become, and she was gone, lost in a soundless void, devoid of any tactile sensation. But almost before she could react to her new environment, that void was gone as suddenly as though a switch had been thrown. She was back in Jackson's apartment, floating a few feet up in the air, and everything was changed.

The flesh and blood world was gone, or if not gone, utterly transformed. This new version of it was like finding herself transported inside a Saturday morning cartoon. Or some computer game with primitive graphics that was making a valiant, though less than successful, attempt at three-dimensionality.

Almost as strange was that her panic had disappeared along with the world as it was supposed to be. Here, in this new version of the world, she was the calm eye in a storm of garish colour, bold linework, and bad animation.

The looks on the faces of her companions now seemed exaggerated, almost comical. She wanted to laugh at Estie and Tip's big round eyes, the exaggerated "O" that was Aaran's mouth. Mrs. Landis appeared to have fainted. She lay in a slapstick sprawl that made her limbs seem to be out of proportion. Claudette stood with her back pressed up against the wall, cartoon hands held defensively in front of her.

But Suzi's humour faded as she returned her attention to the braided bands of gold and blue that still connected her to Estie's computer and Jackson's three towers. The ray had changed from a laser-straight beam to an undulating tendril that felt as much a part of her as her arms and legs. And now it connected her to . . . not so much an orb of light, as a portal of some sort, in which the beams of light had broken up to become pale swirls of blue and gold. Forming in the pattern they made was the impression of a figure, indistinct, but shaped like a human. Beyond the figure she could see endless rows of what looked like bookcases, hundreds of thousands of them disappearing into an infinity point.

"Child," the figure said.

The voice was soft, but resonant. It had a mother's strength, a father's warmth, and that one word it spoke was like a key, unlocking knowledge inside her. She knew who this was, half hidden in the swirl of blues and golds.

It was the spirit of the Wordwood.

At first she thought it was addressing only her, but the same inner knowledge that let her recognize the spirit for who it was also told her that she was only one of many. In other places—she didn't know exactly where, some close, some distant—other people floated in the air just like her, connected to the Wordwood spirit through the closest electronic device and by their own undulating braids of light. They were all individual, but once they had each been a part of this being in its library of light. The life history she remembered had been constructed for her, just as each of the others had had their own life histories constructed for them. They'd been sent out . . . sent out to . . .

It took her a long moment to pull her gaze from the world inside the swirling lights to focus on Aaran's cartoonish features.

They'd been sent out to track down those responsible for the virus that had crippled the Wordwood spirit. Sent out to track them down and bring them to a place such as this, where the spirit itself could have physical access to them.

"Our enemies are found," the spirit said. "You can come home now where I will deal with them, or you may keep your new life. The choice is yours. Consider it payment for how you have helped me."

"What will you do to him?" Suzi found herself asking.

The spirit's gazed settled on her and she knew that it was seeing only her now, not all the other pieces of itself that it had given individuality to and then sent out into the world.

"That remains to be decided," it told her. It paused a moment, then added, "He was not alone."

Suzi nodded. She knew. The spirit had probably found out about both Aaran and Jackson through her.

"I think," the spirit went on, "that I will bring the tenets of the Old Testament to bear upon them. I will do to them what they did to me. Sever all the ties that link their minds to their bodies. The ties that give their thoughts coherence. That link their cells to each other."

"That will kill them," Suzi said.

"Not necessarily. It didn't kill me."

"But you're not human."

"They should have considered that before they began this."

"They didn't know. They thought you were just a Web site."

The spirit regarded her steadily. "Ignorance is a state of being, not an excuse."

A state of being for Aaran and Jackson. And also for her.

A coal of anger began to smolder and glow in her chest. The spirit of the Wordwood had used her, her and all the others it had sent out. Given them lives, identities, made them think they were real. That they had been born, had families, friends. Or in her case, a family and friends that had dissolved into ruined relationships around her. But it had still been *her* history. Her life.

Except it hadn't, had it?

The Wordwood had created perfect moles with her and the others. Spies hidden so deep under cover that even they hadn't known who or what they were until they were activated by the one who had created them and then sent them out. To do what? In her case, it was to betray others the way she'd been betrayed herself. By a violent husband. Family and friends that turned their backs on her. A sister that hated her.

No, she told herself. Those memories weren't real. She had never been betrayed—not unless you counted what the Wordwood spirit had done to her.

Aaran might have been a little shit to other people—what was she saying? Of course he had been. But he hadn't been like that with her and he hadn't betrayed her. He hadn't known what was going to happen when he got Jackson to bring down the Wordwood site. *Who* could have guessed a simple computer virus would cause so much harm? And when he found out, he'd tried to make right.

But it was obvious that the Wordwood spirit didn't see it in the same way. The part of her that was connected to the spirit knew that it wasn't some bookish, kind-hearted being, merely defending itself. It was an amoral creature, reacting to how you interacted with it. Converse with it and it would happily converse back. Use its resources for research and it would open the doors of its virtual library to you.

But attack, and it would strike back. Hard, without consideration of extenuating circumstances.

She doubted that it had ever initiated a single random act of kindness in its life.

"And the others?" she asked. "The people that were pulled into . . . into your world?"

"They are not our concern."

But they were. At least *she* felt they were.

How could that be, if she was only an errant piece of this amoral spirit? Shouldn't she feel the same as it did? Or had she truly become her own person once the Wordwood had sent her out into the world, tied to it only by this service it had needed her to perform?

They weren't questions for which she had answers. She didn't have them now. She might never have them. But she did know one thing.

"You can't have him," she told the spirit.

"How can you stop me?" it replied.

She looked down at the rippling cord of light that bound her to the Wordwood. Reaching down, she found that the braided beams of gold and blue actually had substance. It was like holding onto warm, firm gel that squirmed in her grasp.

"How about if I do this?" she asked.

Tightening her grip, she gave a hard yank.

She hadn't known what to expect. She hadn't even really thought about what she was doing. It was an action born out of frustration and anger, not reason.

The beam broke in two.

Light flared so bright she was blinded and thrown violently backward. She hit the wall behind her, hard enough to knock the breath out of her before she slid down to the floor. But the pain of that was nothing compared to what exploded inside her chest. It felt like something was being torn out of her. Her heart. Her lungs. The hurt was so intense that she blacked out for a moment.

When she opened her eyes, stars flashed in her gaze. But the cartoon world was gone. As was the portal through which she'd accessed the Wordwood spirit.

She took a breath and almost cried at the pain it woke in her chest. Her hands hurt, too—from where she'd gripped the beam of light—but looking down she could see no physical damage. Just as there wasn't a hole in her chest for all that it felt like there should be.

Aaran finally stirred and moved towards her. He still looked a little stunned, but concern for her seemed to be bringing him out of his shock.

"Get . . . we have to . . . get out . . ." she managed to say as he knelt down beside her.

She tried to get up.

"Easy," he told her. "Maybe you shouldn't try to move just yet."

She looked past him. Didn't anybody feel the urgency she did? Tip stood staring at the space where the Wordwood spirit had opened its portal into this world. Estie was white-faced as she looked at her hands, turning them up and down as though to reassure herself that they were flesh once more. Claudette was helping Mrs. Landis to her feet. They acted as though they had all the time in the world.

Suzi wasn't connected to the Wordwood anymore, but that didn't stop her from feeling the approaching storm of the spirit's wrath.

"No, we . . ." She took another painful breath. "We have to get out."

"But—"

"Now!"

Talking so sharply hurt, but at least it galvanized Aaran, if not the others. He helped her stand up and she took a faltering step towards the door. That made Aaran follow her, if only to keep her from falling down.

"Get them out of here," she told him when they reached the doorway.

He nodded. Still holding onto her, he looked back into the room.

"Suzi says we have to get out of here," he said. "Right away."

Estie looked up from her hands to frown at Suzi.

"What did you do to us?" she demanded.

"She didn't do anything," Aaran said. "You saw what happened. It was the spirit of the Wordwood. Suzi saved your ass."

"Saved *your* ass, you mean," Claudette said.

Estie nodded, her hard gaze never leaving Suzi's face. "Where did you take us? What *was* that place?"

"I . . . I didn't . . ." Suzi began.

"Like hell you didn't," Claudette said.

She was supporting Mrs. Landis, much the way Aaran was helping Suzi stay on her feet, but the landlady was in worse shape. She appeared to be shell-shocked, unable to focus on anything. Beside her, Claudette glared at Suzi, the vague animosity she'd shown earlier now full-blown.

Suzi looked away and started to move out into the hall, using the door-jamb, and then the walls, to support herself. The pain in her chest was lessening but it still hurt to breathe too sharply.

"Just . . . just get them out of there," she told Aaran over her shoulder.

"You heard her," Aaran told the others.

"Screw you," Claudette said. "If she says leave, I'm guessing the safest thing we can do is stay right here where we are."

"Suit yourself," Aaran said.

He turned to go into the hall himself.

"No," Suzi said when she saw he was abandoning the others. "We can't just leave them behind."

"We can't force—" Aaran began.

He never got to finish.

Estie's notebook exploded—not in a shower of metal and plastic and circuitry, which would have been bad enough. Instead it was like it had turned into a geyser, spewing out a towering fountain of some thick black fluid. The liquid went straight up from the laptop, moving at such velocity that when it hit the ceiling, it sprayed out over everything in the room, drenching people and furnishings alike. Estie and the others cried out in panic, frantically wiping the black goop from their faces.

Aaran stood in the doorway, dumbstruck for a long moment. Then he started forward, only to be stopped when Suzi grabbed his arm. The sudden movement made her wince with pain, but she knew she had to stop him from going in.

"It's too late," she said. "Remember what happened to the others that got caught in that stuff."

"But—"

"We've got to find higher ground," she said, pointing at how the liquid had pooled onto the floor and was now flooding in their direction.

Aaran nodded, understanding now.

"You're right," he said. "Unless that stuff can move up hill, the stairs are our best bet."

He bent slightly, lifted Suzi behind the knees so that most of her weight was on his shoulder, then staggered to the stairs. He deposited her a few steps up, just before the liquid began to pool against the first riser. They couldn't see into the apartment any more, but they could still hear the sound of the gushing liquid and the cries of those they'd had to leave behind.

Then there was only the sound of the fountaining geyser.

The liquid rose to the top of the first riser and began to flood the second one.

Without speaking, they started up the stairs, Aaran supporting Suzi as they slowly climbed one riser after the other. The light was either turned off or burned out in the halls and stairwell, so their progress was slow and further encumbered by Suzi's pain. The next flight past the third floor wasn't any better.

They didn't stop until they reached the door to the roof. The handle wouldn't move and for a moment they thought it might be locked. Aaran cranked down hard on it, putting his shoulder to the door's metal panel. On his second try, the door popped open with a squeal, and then they were outside on the gravel rooftop. Aaran waited until Suzi was through before he slammed the heavy door behind them.

Twilight had fallen while they were inside, but even its half-light seemed bright after the dark stairwell. The air was humid, still holding the heat of the day, and they both began to perspire—as much from the close air as their recent exertion.

Suzi pressed her hands against her chest. It didn't stop the sharp pain when she breathed, but it helped ease the worst of it—or at least the physical aspect of it. She didn't know if anything would quell the hopeless sense of loss she was also suffering. She bore no love for the Wordwood spirit, had no idea of the connection between them until it had told her. But now that the link had been severed, there was an ache inside that felt ready to swallow her whole.

"Are you okay?" Aaran asked.

She nodded, then led the way to the edge of roof. There was a low wall running around the building and someone had laid down some bamboo mats—for sunbathing, she supposed. She let her knees sink down on them and leaned her forearms on the wall.

"That was horrible," Aaran said. "God, I can't believe how everything's gotten so out of control."

"Things just happen," Suzi said. "You'll go crazy trying to shoulder the blame for everything."

"Except I *did* set this whole thing off."

"You didn't know."

"Like the spirit said, ignorance isn't an excuse."

She couldn't see his face, but she knew how bad he was feeling from his voice.

"It's done," she said. "We should concentrate on what we're going to do now instead of worrying about blame."

"I suppose."

She understood how he felt. After what they'd just been through, it was hard to concentrate on much of anything. For her part, she just wanted to be held for a moment. To have some human contact. To know that she *was* flesh and blood, that she could feel and be felt. But knowing how Aaran had originally felt about her when he'd met her on the street, she didn't think it was such a good idea right now. It would only complicate an already messy day.

"You really did save my life back there," Aaran said suddenly.

Suzi turned from the view to look at him. "You pretty much carried me up the stairs, so I think we're even."

"I meant in the room when . . . when the world went all strange." He paused, his gaze steady on her. "That happened, didn't it? You were floating in the air and everything was like some kind of cartoon?"

She nodded. "I think the spirit pulled the room into some part of cyberspace."

"The spirit. That's what I was talking about. It was going to kill me, wasn't it?"

"It sure looked that way."

"So, thanks."

Suzi shrugged. "You'd have done the same."

"I hope so, but I don't know if I'd have been that brave." There was another pause and she could tell he was deciding whether or not to go on. Finally he did. "What the spirit was saying about you—was all that stuff true?"

"Apparently."

"So then, what . . . ?"

This time he didn't, or couldn't, finish.

"What am I?" she said for him. "I don't know. I feel like an ordinary person. I get dirty. I get hungry. I feel the heat. I feel—" She banged her hand on the wall. "I can feel pain."

"But it's weird . . ."

"No argument there."

Neither of them said anything for awhile. Suzi slid down the side of the wall so that she could lean her back against it. She was hot and sweaty and her heart still beat too fast from their recent escape. Just sitting here, she could feel it hammering in her chest. She wondered how long it would take for that black goop to dissipate so that they could go back downstairs and leave the building.

Aaran came over and stood beside her. He had his back to the roof so that he could take in the view.

"So you never knew?" he said.

She shook her head. "I didn't even have a clue, though I suppose I should have. I mean, I have all of these memories, but except for what I've experienced since yesterday morning, none of them feel . . . immediate. They're just facts with no emotional resonance." She gave a short laugh that didn't hold any humour. "Though who's going to guess that they were only born a day or so ago and that everything they know is only there because it's been loaded into them like software. And then there's the whole physical impossibility of translating something digital into flesh and blood."

"I don't know how you deal with it."

"By trying really hard not to think about it," Suzi said. "Whenever I do, I just want to curl up in a ball in some dark corner and hide away from everything. I mean, talk about being a freak."

"I don't think you're a freak."

"Then you're the exception. Everybody else seems to dislike me the moment they meet me."

She glanced at Aaran when he didn't reply. He was still looking out at the city, but he turned and smiled.

"I was just thinking," he said. "I got a bit of that weird vibe from you—right at the first. Nothing I could put my finger on, but I just knew there was something about you that's—"

"Not human."

"I was going to say different. A kind of dissonance. Maybe it came from the transition you made from digital to flesh and blood."

Suzi gave a slow nod. That made sense. It was something people would sense on an instinctual level.

"Funny thing is," Aaran went on, "the last time I felt that vibe was when I first met Saskia. And she had the same problem you have—people just taking an immediate dislike to her."

"I got the sense that people really like her."

"They do," Aaran said. "That vibe went away after awhile."

"So you think she's like me—born in cyberspace?"

Aaran laughed. "No, I'm guessing you're unique in that."

"But I'm not alone," she said. "The Wordwood spirit created others."

"Then maybe she is like you. Maybe all of the people who disappeared originated in cyberspace and that's why they got pulled back into it so easily."

"Software recall," Suzi said, her voice soft.

Aaran had been looking away again and turned back to her.

"What did you say?" he asked.

"Nothing. What is it you keep looking at out there?"

"Just all these lights."

"Yeah, they're pretty," Suzi agreed. "When you look out across the city at night, you never think of all the mess that's hidden under that pattern of lights."

"I didn't mean the lights from the buildings and street lamps."

She got up and leaned on the wall once more to see what he was talking about. It took her a moment before she saw what he'd been referring to—flashes of blue-gold light, sparking here and there. Not many, but enough, if they were what she thought they were. She noted a half-dozen, raising her count to nine when she spotted a few others she hadn't seen the first time. They were too distant for her to be able to confirm her suspicions, but as she watched, she could see that they were steadily coming their way.

"It's some of the others," she said.

"What others?"

"Like I said, the Wordwood didn't just send me out. It sent out a whole pack of searchers."

Aaran nodded. "That's right. I remember." He looked out at the lights and added, "So are they all like you?"

"Like I was—inside, I mean." She shrugged. "I've no idea what they'll actually look like."

"They're coming for us, aren't they?"

"I'm afraid so."

Aaran turned and sat on the edge of the parapet. "So what do we do now?"

"Get away from here and then don't go near any computer—even if it's off-line."

"But if it's not on-line . . ."

"Remember what happened downstairs?"

"Yeah. But . . . how's that even possible?"

"I don't know," she said. "I think it's like the way the Wordwood spirit made me and the others—as much magic as tech."

"Voodoo spirits," Aaran said.

"Whatever. But it looks to me that the Wordwood spirit can leave pieces of itself in computers that have accessed its site, which, in turn, lets it manifest in that machine whenever it wants."

"So we stay away from computers." He jerked his chin toward the edge of the roof. "What about them?"

"We have to avoid them, obviously. I don't think they can actually track us. I don't feel a connection to either them or the Wordwood anymore, so why would they have one to me? But this is the last place we were seen, so I guess it makes sense that they'd come here."

"We should see if the hallway's clear."

Suzi nodded. "And then make our way back to Holly's store. If nothing else, we have some new information to share."

"God, they're going to hate me even more now," Aaran said.

There was no self-pity in his voice, just a stating of the facts.

"They're going to hate us both," Suzi said, "once they find out the part I played."

"You had no choice—you didn't know."

"Neither did you when you got Jackson to send the virus in the first place."

Aaran nodded. "But that was still an act of meanness. I don't think you have a mean bone in your body."

Suzi wasn't so sure about that. The anger she'd felt earlier toward the Wordwood still frightened her. It had been *so* intense.

"It doesn't matter what they think of us," she said. "We still have to help all those people who've gotten caught up in this through no fault of their own. And the best way we can do that at this moment is to go back to the store and see if they've had any success."

Aaran nodded. "I'll check the hallway."

Suzi took the opportunity while he was gone to lift her shirt and assess the physical damage that breaking the link to the Wordwood had done, but her abdomen was smooth, the skin not even bruised. The hurt was all inside, physical as well as psychological. She dropped her shirt when Aaran came back out the door, the squeaking hinges giving her plenty of warning.

"It's still a mess down there," he said. "That goop's a couple of inches deep and pouring down into the lobby. But there's an exit to a fire escape just down this first flight of stairs. I had a look and it'll take us right into the side alley."

Suzi looked over the wall. Two or three of the approaching lights were little more than a block away now. Aaran came over as she got to her feet.

"It's okay," she said. "I can move a little easier now."

But she let him take her arm as they walked across the roof back to the door, gravel crunching under their feet. The exit to the fire escape was through a window at the foot of the stairs. Aaran had left it open and they both climbed through, making it down to the pavement without incident.

The alley ran the length of the building, connecting the streets in front and behind the building. Without discussing it, they both headed toward the street at the rear of the building, navigating their way around garbage cans, debris, and a junked car. When they were almost at the street, Suzi took Aaran's arm and leaned her head against his shoulder.

"Just be casual," she said.

"Right."

They ambled out of the alley and looked both ways. Cars were parked along the curb on either side of the street. A van idled by the mouth of an alley across from them and other vehicles were moving on the street. Residents sat on their stoops. A bunch of kids were playing with a hacky-sack, some others were sitting on the sidewalk with their backs against a tenement, sharing what was either a cigarette or a joint. There were no people with blue-gold auras pointing straight up into the sky like searchlights.

"Let's go," Suzi said.

She chose the direction in which she'd seen the fewest approaching lights, still leaning against Aaran's shoulder like they were a couple out for a stroll. They were between stoops when she saw the telltale blue and gold glow at the far corner. Grabbing Aaran, she pushed him against the wall of the tenement.

"Kiss me," she said. "Like you mean it."

"What makes you think I wouldn't?"

She smiled. "Just do it. Now."

She liked the way he held her. She liked the firmness of his lips against hers. She had memories of making out—with old boyfriends, with her husband before he'd turned mean and started treating her like a doormat—but thinking of those occasions called up none of the immediacy of the sweet, weak-kneed sensations she was experiencing now. Because they weren't real. But this was.

She'd almost forgotten why they were kissing when she realized that one of the Wordwood's searchers was standing on the pavement studying them.

She broke off the kiss to look at him. He was of medium height and build with pleasant, if forgettable, features. Without the blue-gold aura, no one would give him a second look. But right now, up and down the street, everybody was staring at him.

She felt nothing from him—no bond, no connection. But he seemed to sense something in her. She decided to brave it out.

"What's your problem, freak?" she demanded.

Aaran had turned with her to look at the man. When she spoke, the muscles in his arm went tight.

Trust me, she wanted to tell him. I know what I'm doing.

Or at least she thought she did.

"Okay," she added when the man made no response except continuing to study them. "You've had a good look, now why don't you go find somebody's birthday cake to stand on?"

"You're not . . . surprised to see someone like me?" the man finally said. "The others—" He indicated the people on the street that were all staring at him with varying degrees of surprise and wonder.

"Jesus," she told him. "You live long enough in this city and you'll see any damn thing. So what? A freak like you with a built-in spotlight is supposed to be something special? I've seen lots weirder."

The man blinked, obviously taken aback by her attitude, which was just what Suzi was aiming for. The Wordwood spirit would have sent its searchers out looking for a man and woman on the run, trying to hide and not make waves.

"I am looking—" the man tried, but she cut him off.

"To get your face rearranged. And you know, looking at you, I don't even think I'll let my boyfriend do it. I figure I can take you all on my own." She stepped away from Aaran and made a pair of fists. "So bring it on, spotlight boy."

The man took a step back.

"That's right," Suzi told him. "Bugger on off to wherever you came from." She linked her arm in Aaran's again. "Come on, Tommy. Let's find someplace we don't have to put up with shitheads like this."

She gave him a tug and they walked off in the direction from which the searcher had come.

" 'Go find somebody's birthday cake to stand on'?" Aaran said softly.

For all his obvious nervousness, she could see a smile pulling at his lips. And they were nice lips, she remembered.

"I didn't hear you complaining back there, 'Tommy,' " she said.

"I couldn't have come close to putting on a show like that." He started to look behind them.

"Don't check him out," she said. "We have to act like we couldn't care less. In fact, let's stop right here and have another kiss—just to show how carefree and guiltless we are."

She stopped and tilted her head.

Aaran smiled. "And is that the only reason?"

She grinned back at him. "That's for me to know and you to find out."

This time when they kissed she let herself melt against him, breasts pressed tight against his chest, her pelvis rubbing against his own growing interest. She almost forgot to steal a glance back the way they'd come. When she did, it was just in time to see the blue-gold aura of the searcher disappear into the alley that ran along Jackson's apartment building.

"God," Aaran said when they came up for air. "You're a complete wanton."

"But that's a good thing, right?"

He nodded.

"So, come on," she said, taking his hand. "We've got a bookstore to visit."

"Don't remind me," Aaran said, but he fell in step beside her.

They'd walked a couple more blocks without passing another searcher. Whether someone was following them was another matter, but Suzi'd been keeping an eye out and she didn't think anyone was.

"Back there," Aaran said.

"Was really nice," Suzi broke in before he could go on. "And who knows? Maybe when this is all over, we can find the time to sneak in a little romance, but what I said before still stands. It'd never work out between us in the long-term—especially not now. When I'm, you know, not just some homeless woman you brought home, but . . . well, who knows what I am?"

"That doesn't matter to me."

"I know. At least it doesn't right now."

He shook his head. "I don't know how to explain this, but ever since I met you, I feel changed. Like I'm a different person and I can't imagine doing the things I've done—not ever again."

"So I'm, what? Your epiphany?" She smiled to take the sting out of her words.

"Is that such a bad thing?" he asked. "But, no. It's more like what you were saying before we left my apartment. How maybe we're each other's guardian angels. At least, I know that you bring out the best in me."

"Maybe it's because I'm willing to believe in you. I get the idea nobody's ever believed in you before—at least not the real you."

He nodded. "That's exactly it. And to tell you the truth, I feel redeemed. I don't mean that suddenly everything's okay," he added quickly. "I know I've got a lot to atone for. I've left behind a history of a lot of damage and we're not just talking about the current fiasco. But now I *want* to do better. I want to make up for the wrongs I've done. And I don't want to repeat them. The only thing is . . ."

"You don't think you can do it without me?"

That earned her a smile. "No, I was going to say I don't know that I'll get the chance to make it up to a lot of people—that anybody's going to be willing to give me another shot."

"That's the hardest part," Suzi said. "Carrying on with your good intentions even when no one believes that you mean them."

Aaran nodded. "I guess it will be. But none of that's where you come in."

"Where *do* I come in?" Suzi asked.

She didn't mean to, but she couldn't help being flirty as she spoke.

"I just think we're good for each other," Aaran said. "That maybe we really can be each other's guardian angels. I don't mean or expect some life-time commitment. I'd just like to think that as soon as this is done, you're not going to just walk out of my life and I'll never see you again. I'd like to get to know you better."

"I'm not going to make any promises."

"No promises," Aaran agreed. "But tell me you won't close the door either."

Suzi smiled. "No door closings, either."

They were so busy talking that they didn't notice that they'd reached Williamson Street until they were right upon it. A northbound bus pulled into a stop directly ahead of them. Suzi looked around, but there were no blue-gold auras in sight. Maybe they'd toned them back down again. Or maybe all the searchers were still milling around in Jackson's apartment building.

"Will this take us up to Holly's store?" she asked.

Aaran checked the bus number and nodded.

"I think we should just leave things where they stand," Suzi said. "With you and me, I mean. Right now it's time to go face the music."

But she took his hand while they waited in line to board the bus.

Christy

I've been writing about the unexplained for over half my life now. Of spirits and mysteries, hauntings and haunted places. Of ghosts and fairies and goblins. Of hidden races of curious beings that live both in the wilds and right under our noses in the city—some whimsical, some dangerous, all strange.

But I don't have much actual hands-on experience.

Sure, Tallulah, one of my first serious girlfriends, turned out to be the literal spirit of this city. And Saskia was born in a Web site—maybe the same one into which she's disappeared again. But these are only words. Anyone can *say* they're whomever or whatever. I never actually saw Tallulah do anything more inexplicable than make me feel like I was floating on air whenever we were together—and you know, that's what love does. And until Saskia vanished right before my eyes, she never exhibited any mysteries that couldn't also be explained away with a more mundane rationale.

What I'm trying to say is that I don't hobnob with the otherworldly the way my readers think I do. The first time Wendy used that little magical red stone of hers, opening a threshold into the otherworld, where a doorway leading into the professor's kitchen was supposed to be, I was so overcome with the sheer impossibility of it that I literally went numb. For a long moment, I couldn't move, couldn't even think. My head felt like it was stuffed with cotton batting.

Wendy offered me her hand and said something I couldn't hear. But I understood. She was asking me to join her as she stepped through the arch of the kitchen door into this stunning vista of red rock canyons. It took me awhile before I was finally able to reply. But the bigshot writer, as Geordie likes to call me, so rarely at a loss for words, could only shake his head.

No one could understand why I declined to cross over, except maybe for Jilly. But it's like I told Geordie last night, what interests me about these kinds of phenomena centers around how they interact with the World As It Is, and how those of us living here react to these intrusions. I don't like the idea of a mundane world, devoid of wonder or mystery. But I know I wouldn't be any happier in a world where it's all wonder and mystery.

Up to that moment, I'd always been equal parts skeptic and believer. That might also explain the success of my books. My readers see that in me: The skeptics think I agree with them, but isn't it interesting to consider anyway? And the believers just assume I'm in their camp, only more experienced than most of them.

I guess now I am.

I hear the sound of the hellhounds again. Closer.

And once again I'd just as soon decline the invitation to step into the unknown territories of the otherworld. But I've got Saskia to think about now.

"Let it go," Bojo says.

Robert shakes his head and keeps playing his guitar. That music of his could make angels swap their celestial harps for a blues harp, just to try to capture even an echo of what he's calling up. It's earthy and slinky. It's a gospel choir wrapping their voices around a twelve-bar blues. It promises and it delivers. It reaches right inside to your most private place and says, I know you. I know your pain, but I know your joy, too.

I don't doubt that he can call up any damn thing he wants with it—not just some doorway into an errant Web site, hidden away in a digital version of Never-never Land.

Trouble is, we've just discovered that we're not the only ones listening.

The hellhounds bay, closer still.

"I'm telling you," Bojo says. "You've got to let it go."

Robert doesn't even look at him. "Hell, no," he says. "We're almost there. I can pretty much taste that Wordwood spirit."

"You don't stop playing," Bojo tells him, "the only tasting that'll go on here is the hellhounds taking a bite out of you."

I glance at Raul and he's looking more nervous than I am and that's not easy, considering how I'm feeling. Over by the stairs, Dick is hiding his face in his hands. Geordie and Holly are staring wide-eyed at the shimmering wall behind me. Snippet's trying to be invisible and fierce, all at the same time, and not doing a good job of either.

"We've got time," Robert says. "You just open that door when I tell you."

"Oh, yeah, time," an unfamiliar voice says from behind me. "Funny how it works. Sometimes it moves like molasses and you've got all you might ever need to do any damn thing at all."

I turn slowly, realizing now that Geordie and Holly weren't just looking at the shimmer of the wall. Three men are standing there—having stepped right out of the wall, I guess, because they certainly didn't come down the stairs.

Up until this moment, the biggest, darkest-skinned black man I've ever seen is Lucius Portsmouth, this friend of the professor's that Jilly says is the raven uncle of the crow girls, her personal favorite of the animal people that figure in local folklore and stories.

These men are as big, but where Lucius reminds me of a serene, black Buddha, our uninvited guests are grim-faced, with a mean look in their eyes, and they're built like weightlifters or linebackers, seeming as wide across the shoulders as they are tall. Their skin isn't just black, it's pure ebony—that absence of light you find in the heart of a shadow. Like Robert, they're wearing suits, only theirs are solid black broadcloth, with white shirts, narrow black ties, and fancy, tooled leather boots.

One of them shifts his foot and I hear what sounds like the low, deep-throated growl of a hunting hound. Snippet whimpers and burrows his head against Holly's leg.

"And sometimes," says that same unfamiliar voice I first heard, but now I can see it's coming from the man standing in the center of the three, "time goes by so fast you never can catch up with anything."

Robert holds his guitar by the neck and stands up to face the men.

"This has got nothing to do with anybody but you and me," he says. "Don't you go bothering these folks."

"They're with you, aren't they?"

There's absolute menace in that voice, despite its mild tone. Another of the men shifts his feet and again I hear a low, throaty growl. That's when I realize that *these* are the hellhounds. I don't know if they're shapechangers, animal people like Jilly loves to talk about, or something else again. The only thing I'm sure of is that they're dangerous and we're in big trouble.

But Robert doesn't concede one iota of defeat. He stands there stiff-backed, radiating strength, guitar dangling from his left hand. He slips his other under the front panel of his suit coat.

"I'm only telling you this one more time," he says. "Maybe we have ourselves a difference of opinion, but don't go dragging anybody else into this business."

"Or you'll what? Pull out that old Colt of yours and try to shoot me? After all these years, do you really think something like that can stop us?"

"That your final word?" Robert asks, his voice as mild, but as full of threat as the hellhound's.

"What do you think?"

"I just need to hear you say it, plain and clear."

The hellhounds' spokesman looks left and right, grinning at his companions, before he turns back to reply.

"Then I'm saying it," he tells Robert. "All your lives are forfeit."

Robert just smiles. "I was hoping that'd be the case."

That earns him as puzzled a look from the hellhounds as I know we've got on our faces, but Robert keeps smiling. The hand that we all thought was reaching under his jacket for a weapon comes out empty. He hefts his guitar in front of him and when he pulls a chord from that old Gibson of his, I swear the brick walls shiver around us. The concrete trembles at our feet. The hellhounds make like it's no big deal, but I can tell they're running down a list of what Robert's got planned. They know he's up to something, but they can't figure out what, any more than I can.

But Robert just pulls another chord from his guitar—a minor chord, rumbling with dark promise—and turns his back on them to look at us.

"I should explain something to you," he says. "What we've got here are some of *les baka mal*, hellhound spirits who like to lay proprietary claim to *les carrefours*—or at least they will at whatever crossroads they think Legba isn't watching. These particular ones have stolen the names of the three Rada drums for themselves. Guy in the middle calls himself Maman. The other two are Bula and Seconde."

I can't believe he's taking this time-out to fill us in. I give the hellhounds a nervous look over Robert's shoulder, but they still seem confused. The two on either side of the one Robert called Maman are trying to get his attention. He ignores them, his gaze fixed on the back of Robert's head. Behind his eyes, you can tell his mind is still in overtime, trying to work out what Robert's up to.

Well, the hellhounds and me both.

"They know about this engagement I've made with Legba," Robert's saying like none of this is any big deal. "I'm not going into the whys and wherefores. All you've got to know about that part of our pact is that I can't defend myself against *les baka mal*. It's why I work so hard to keep out of their way. They're not more powerful than me. My problem is that I can't break my word to Legba and raise a hand against them. If I do, dying's the least of my worries. Legba won't just have my soul, he'll have it in pieces."

Now he finally turns back to the hellhounds.

"But what you forgot, Maman," he says to the lead hellhound, "is that Legba never said anything about me not being allowed to defend somebody else from your kind."

The understanding comes to them at the same time as I get it. Whatever this deal between Robert and Legba is, it left Robert helpless against the hellhounds—*unless* they happen to threaten someone else.

I can see their indecision. Attack, or break and make a run for it? I wonder that they even hesitate. There's three of them. We might outnumber them, but except for Bojo, not one of us looks like much of a fighter. Doesn't mean we won't try—at least I know Geordie and I will. Our brother Paddy taught us a long time ago: You may get the crap beat out of you, but it's better to go down fighting than not stand up at all. Funny thing is, once or twice, I've even come out still standing on my own two feet.

But it doesn't come down to that.

"We're not alone," Maman says. "You know how many hounds are out there on the wild roads?"

Robert nods. "But you're alone right now."

"We can have a pack on your ass so fast—"

Robert breaks in. "But you've got to be alive long enough to call them down on me."

I don't see the man on the left of Maman draw the knife. One moment his hand's empty, the next there's a length of pointed steel flashing through the air at Robert. Robert manages to pull another chord and lift the body of the guitar at the same time. The knife bites into the wood, setting up a discordant echo to an already dissonant music. Something dark starts to take shape in the space between the *les baka mal* and Robert. The hellhounds hesitate a moment longer, then they turn and make their escape through the hole in the basement wall behind them.

"I can't let them go," Robert tell us. "I do and they'll be back ten times as strong and there'll be no finessing our way out of that encounter."

Bojo takes a step forward. "But you can't just go on your—"

"That place we're looking for is close," Robert says, interrupting. "You should be able to find it."

He pulls the knife from his guitar and drops it on the floor, then starts for the hole where the hellhounds disappeared.

"Robert!" Bojo calls after him.

The bluesman stops at the edge of the hole and looks back.

"You don't understand," he says. "That was my one ace-in-the-hole—that they'd come on me when I was with someone else and they'd threaten whoever I was with. Unless I stop those three, I can't use it again."

"But—"

Robert shakes his head. "They weren't lying. They've been hunting me a long, long time and now I've gone and put them on the run. That's something they'll never forget or forgive. Give them half a chance and they really will have an army down on us. And let me tell you, they'll be wanting you as much as me, seeing as you were here to witness it all."

And then he's gone.

Silence fills the basement.

You ever have that moment when you just *know* what's going to happen? I *know* everyone's going to start talking at once. We're going to be divided on whether we follow Robert or proceed with our initial undertaking. I can feel it coming and I'm trying to decide how to forestall it when we hear a hammering on the front door of the store upstairs.

Our reaction time is still molasses slow. Finally Geordie says, "I'll go see who it is."

I nod. When he starts up the stairs, I look over to where Bojo's picking up the hellhound's knife. His gaze rises from the polished blade to meet my own.

"We can't just let Robert go after them on his own," he says as he stands up.

"I don't see that we have a choice," I tell him. "There are a lot of people trapped somewhere in the Wordwood and I get the feeling that we're their only hope of ever getting back."

"Yeah, but—"

"He looked like he thought he could take care of it. I don't know much about Robert, but if the reaction of those hellhounds is any indication, I'm guessing he's not just some snappy dresser who plays a mean guitar. Those men were . . . if not scared, certainly nervous. I didn't see them sticking around."

"I suppose."

Holly comes walking up with Snippet in her arms. I get the sense that if she put the little dog down, Snippet would be up the stairs as fast as her legs could carry her. Dick's still sitting on a riser, shoulder pressed up against the wall, eyes large. Raul stands beside me and his eyes seem almost as big. I can feel the nervousness still coming off him in waves. Or maybe it's only my own anxiety that I'm feeling.

Holly steps by us to take a closer look at the opening in the wall with its shimmering edges. There's an odd optical illusion at work because not only can you see the wall, but you can also see what's on the other side of it, the two images seeming to occupy the same space.

The other side appears innocuous. We're looking at a moonlit cross-roads, but all that are crossing here are a pair of narrow footpaths with an old oak tree towering above the spot where they meet. There's a heap of stones under the tree and a hint of forest and fields beyond.

But the hellhounds came out of that world we're looking in on, so I know it's not as innocent as it seems. And being a crossroads . . . didn't Robert say Legba hung around them?

Voudoun's not a major study of mine, but I recognize the name. Legba is one of their *loa*—the god of gates and crossroads. All the ceremonies begin with a salute to him because he embodies the principle of crossing, of communicating with the divine world. He's usually depicted with a cane and a tall hat, and his brother is Baron Samedi, the *loa* of the dead.

I don't know that I want to meet either of them.

"I can't believe this is real," Holly says.

"Welcome to the weird world," I tell her.

She turns to look at me. "I guess this is old hat for you, but I have to tell you that it's giving me the major heebie-jeebies."

I shake my head. "I just write about it. I can count my actual experiences on one hand. Bojo's the only expert we have left."

But he shakes his head. "Keep a low profile is the tinker's way. When we're in your towns, we stay clear of the sheriffs and lawmen. In the other-world, we stay away from the spirits. The more powerful they are, the less I want to do with them, and *there's* the real trick."

"What's that?" Raul asks.

"Figuring out how powerful they are. Some of the smaller, more harm-less looking ones, are actually the most powerful. The best thing is to avoid them all if you can."

"That hole . . . portal," I say, pointing to the opening in the wall with its shimmering edges. "How long is it going to be there?"

"I can keep it open," he says. "Robert's music was like a cardsharp shuffling a deck, honing in on the place we want to get to. We needed the music to find the Wordwood because I've never been there, but that's not the only way. Trial and error works, too. It just takes a lot longer. The otherworld's a big place—you can't imagine how big a place. The worlds it contains fold in on themselves so that there are places where one step can take you through three or four of them, and you won't even know it without a guide."

"So without Robert, we're screwed."

Bojo shakes his head.

"If he says we're close, we should be able to find it now on our own, without magic. It'll take longer than it might have with Robert's help, but not as long as it would have without his getting us this far."

I feel a clock ticking in my head—it's been there ever since Saskia was taken away from my study. Each passing moment without her, this world, the World As It Is as the professor likes to call it, feels emptier and emptier. And I can't shake the fear that the longer she's gone, the less chance we'll have of getting her back. Of getting any of them back.

I nod. "We've got to go on."

"We will," Bojo tells me.

He's about to say more, but then we hear footsteps at the top of the stairs. We turn to see Geordie leading Aaran and his friend Suzi down to where we're all gathered.

"Apparently we've got more problems," Geordie says.

My heart sinks as Aaran and Suzi relate what happened at Jackson's apartment. And I have to admit that my earlier suspicions about them aren't put to rest by their story. Suzi's like Saskia, a part of the Wordwood? They managed to escape while the others were taken away? Aaran's genuinely remorseful?

"So you just got away?" Geordie says, putting into words what I guess we're all feeling.

"They wouldn't listen to us," Aaran says. "To Suzi."

I can see how it wouldn't have been their fault—*if* things went the way they said they had.

"And there are more of these . . . scouts?" Bojo asks.

Geordie gives me a look, and I know what he's thinking, but I only shrug. I really don't see what talking about Saskia's origin is going to add to the discussion at this point. But I can't let it completely go. Not when I know how it was for Saskia and seeing that strong suspicion towards Suzi that's on Holly, Raul and Bojo's faces. Dick's still on the stairs, so I can't judge his reaction.

"They aren't necessarily the enemy," I find myself saying. I feel confident telling them that, because Saskia certainly isn't. "I mean, think about it. They can only operate on the information that they've been fed by the Wordwood spirit. There's a good chance that, given the whole story, they'll come over to our side. Suzi's proved that."

Suzi gives me a grateful look, which just makes me feel guilty. I'm expressing a faith in her that I don't feel—it's based on Saskia and the fact that it seems as though they have a similar origin.

But they all accept what I'm saying—one of the benefits of being considered an expert in this sort of thing, I suppose. Though with all the complications that keep cropping up on us, and none of us with a clear idea as to what they mean or what to do about them, I feel about as far from an expert as any of them.

"What can you tell us about the Wordwood?" I ask Suzi. "Do you know if the spirit has any weaknesses we can exploit?"

"I don't really know a lot about either of them," she says. "It's . . ." She gives a small nervous laugh. "It's really weird. I mean, I only just found out what I am, that all these memories I have of a life have been put in my head. When I actually stop and think about it, I feel like I'm insane."

"I understand."

She cocks her head and studies me for a moment. "You know, I think maybe you do."

"So you can't give us anything that might help?" Bojo asks.

She sighs. "The problem is, once I found out what I am, I did gain some memories of what it was like in the Wordwood. But I don't remember it as an awful place. When I think about it, I get this really strong impression of knowledge and peace. I . . ." She looks at us, one by one. "You'll probably think I'm just saying this, but I don't think the Wordwood spirit is bad. The virus is doing this to it. Instead of making plans on how to fight it, we should be trying to figure out how to heal it."

"Any ideas on that?" I ask.

She shakes her head. "And the encounter I had with it in Jackson's apartment doesn't add a whole lot of credibility to my theory. But I can't shake the feeling that what I met there wasn't all of it. It's like the thoughtfulness and kindness I feel when I think of the place I came from have been buried by this new cruel and vengeful persona. That it's put the good in itself aside so that it can take its revenge without having to argue with a conscience."

I find myself thinking of the red-haired woman who visits me from time to time, the one who claims that she's all the pieces of me that I didn't want when I was a kid.

"Like a shadow," I say, and I explain Jung's theory without going into the experiences I've had with my own shadow.

Suzi's nodding as I talk.

"Isn't that possible?" She looks from me to the others. "Couldn't that be what happened to the Wordwood spirit?"

"Well, they say that spirits are much like us," Bojo says, "only the canvas of their lives is bigger."

I pick up my pack from where I placed it on the floor earlier and swing it to my back.

"We're just going to have to play it by ear," I say. "I don't want anybody to get hurt, but I'm not coming back without Saskia and as many of the others as we can find."

Bojo looks at the knife in his hand. He gets a shirt out of his own small shoulder bag. Wrapping the knife in it, he stows it away in his bag and stands up. Raul's already waiting by the portal in the wall. He doesn't look any happier than I feel, but just like me, he's got someone in there that he's not coming back without. I don't know if we're brave or stupid; I just know it's something we have to do.

"We're coming," Suzi says.

I hesitate as she and Aaran approach the wall, as well.

"I know you don't trust us," Aaran says, "or at least me, but it's something I have to do."

It's weird how his words echo my thoughts of a moment ago.

"Think of us as the spear-carriers," he goes on. "If you lose anybody on an adventure, the spear-carriers always go first. So that'll give you that much of a better chance to get out yourselves."

"If that's the case," Suzi says, "I wouldn't mind having an actual spear to bring along."

I look at Bojo and Raul and they both shrug, leaving it up to me. My gaze returns to Aaran and Suzi.

"Let's go," I tell them.

I don't want any long goodbyes. I don't want to think about what I'm doing, where we're going. So I give a quick wave of my hand to my brother, to Holly and Dick. Then I turn and step through the wall.

Christiana

I feel like we're caught between all that's good and all that can go wrong, that this ruined building in the Wordwood site stands right on some precarious border where Heaven meets Hell.

The spiraling rush of blue-gold light bursting out of Saskia's limp body pierces the sky like a searchlight, casting a shimmering glow over everything. Highlights sparkle and flicker in the wiry lichen underfoot and flash on the low metal walls of the foundations around us. It makes for an astonishing glamour, as glorious in its own way as some of the fairylands I've seen across the borders. But all its bright wonder is sharply contrasted by the virus, manifesting here in the shape of the leeches, black and slick, reeking of sulfur and burnt wiring and hot metal.

It doesn't feel right. Somehow it's worse being bathed in this amazing light as the virus is about to kill us.

As though echoing my own dismay, I hear Saskia cry in my head, a long aching wail. She was plugged back into the Wordwood when the light first burst from her—connected again, if only for a few brief moments, to that long-severed link that once bound her to the Wordwood's vast library of knowledge and the beatific spirit of the wood itself. It was as though she'd been taken back to those first few months after the spirit had created her, when she was still newly-arrived in the consensual world and could readily access the Wordwood's knowledge with no more than a thought.

The cry she makes at that brief familiar connection is involuntary. She tells me that it wasn't that she wanted to be a part of it again—surprise simply pulled it out of her—but at the same time, she can't deny a sense of regret for what's now gone.

I suppose it's like coming out of the womb a second time . . . when you want to stay where it's warm and safe, but you're longing for the world outside at the same time. I can still remember that feeling, back when I was a baby boy—or at least a part of a boy.

But Saskia says it's more like the comfort Christy knows when he's researching a project and finally has all the material on hand. He doesn't *know* it all, but he knows how and where to access it, and that's what gives him the confidence to actually start writing. When she was connected to the Wordwood, she had this unlimited access to pretty much anything she needed to know about the world, which, in the face of all the unpleasantness she faced in those first few months, was what helped give her the confidence to become who she is.

So I've got Saskia wailing in my head. There's the pillar of light, impossibly tall and bright and awesome. There's Jackson falling apart beside me, head whipping back and forth, desperately looking for some way to escape, only there's nowhere to go. And then there's the virus, slagging its way through the walls on all sides, coming right for us.

I hesitate for a moment, then reach into the light and cradle Saskia's body to my chest. That's when I discover that the light wasn't so much coming from the body, as somehow shining right through it, because the pillar of light continues to stream up just as it did before. The only difference is Saskia—or at least her body—isn't part of it anymore.

I rock the body gently and try not to think of much of anything. I know there's nothing I can do to stop the sliders, but they're still going to have to go through me first to get at her.

It's funny. I almost expected the light to burn, but it was cool to the touch. Saskia's body still is. It seems to weigh nothing—no more than a gentle thought, or a dream. She's gone quiet in my head as well, her presence like a feather.

I turn to face the nearest of the sliders. I've always said that when the time came, I'd look my death in the eye and not turn my face away. I'm a little surprised to find myself actually able to do it, now that the moment's here.

<I'm so sorry to have gotten you into all of this,> Saskia says.

I'm glad to have her back again.

It's been weird, I tell her—like having her talking in my head while her body lies limp in my arms isn't—*but I'm still glad I met you.*

And that should have been it. The virus should have been upon us and we would have come to the end of our story.

But a moment after I've taken the body in my arms, I feel a change in the light. I can't exactly explain what. It's not the temperature or brightness—more in its . . . mass, if that makes any sense. It goes from an intangible radiance to something with actual physical presence. But while that presence has no more physical weight behind it than the touch of a feather as it brushes my skin, its effect on everything around me is far different.

Glowing waves of the gold and blue light spill from the pillar, waves that undulate and wash over me before they travel on. Whatever they touch regains its normal form and colour. The lichen goes from dense fine wiring to vegetation, pale green and yellow. The stones change from metal to natural rock, mottled and patched with moss. Jackson becomes a regular black man, his dark hair tinged with highlights of red, his skin all these wonderful hues of mocha and chocolate brown.

And the river of light continues to spread out, wave after wave. A waxing tide of radiance.

The light envelopes the leeches, washing over their slick black bodies and melting the virus creatures away. The immense threat they presented only moments ago vanishes with their disappearance. And still the light continues to spread. The ruins of the building explode with colour—you never know how much colour there is in grey stone until you see it go from black and white to the way it really is. I guess you don't normally pay attention to that kind of thing, but I'm sure paying attention right now.

I lay Saskia's body gently down on the lichen and stand up. I'm about to ask Jackson to give me a hand getting her out of the building when everything shimmers, like in a heat mirage, and the building goes away, just like that. It dissipates into the ground, like it was never there. For a long moment we're still on the crest of that high hill we climbed what seems days ago. We can see the light washing over the forests on all sides, leaving wave after wave of colour in its wake.

Then, like it's all part of some stately gavotte, the hill begins to sink, its heights lowering until we're standing in a large glade that's at the same elevation as the rest of the landscape. Trees rise up out of the ground as smoothly and naturally as when the foundation of the building melted away earlier. It's like watching one of those time-lapsed nature documentaries where the bud opens into a full blossom in moments, except these are trees, growing from sprigs with a leaf or two, to what look like hundred-year-old giants in moments.

My legs have a bit of a jelly-feel to them—the way they can when you step back onto land after a long boat ride. There's a smell in the air of old forest. Mossy and a little damp, earthy. It reminds me of when I first crossed into the otherworld with Mumbo, when everything was still so marvelous and I was just a little tomboy of a girl, my ball-shaped companion rolling along at my side, propelling herself with her long spindly limbs. We spent a lot of time in that old forest in those days. Mumbo called it the Greatwood and told me it's the closest echo there is of the First Forest, that vast tract of ancient wood that Raven supposedly called up out of the darkness when he made the world.

This cyber wood feels like that forest did. It has the smells and resonance of a close echo to the First Forest, except I sense an undercurrent of something foreign running underneath what I can physically sense and feel. I suppose it's a digital pulse. The fact that I know everything I'm experiencing has its actual origin in binary code. But knowing that doesn't lessen any of the wonder I experience as this enormous forest forms around us.

<What . . . what's happening . . . ?> Saskia says.

I have no idea, I tell her.

I stand there with my mouth open for the longest time, then I finally turn to Jackson. But before I can speak to him, rooty vines come snaking from the ground to wrap themselves around our legs. They hoist Jackson up and tie him to the nearest tree, so that he's hanging there, limp. The bottoms of his feet are a couple of yards off the ground, and he's not even trying to get free. I guess he was already in shock from our escape from the leeches and the transformation of the ruined hilltop foundation into this forest.

I don't struggle either, although in my case it's because the vines can't seem to find a hold on my legs. They keep sliding off like my calves and ankles are covered with a film of grease, allowing them no purchase. But that doesn't stop me from being majorly creeped as they continue to writhe around my feet and try to crawl up my legs.

I step away from them, moving closer to Saskia's body which they're not trying to grab at all. They follow, new vines slinking their way out of the ground, but none of them can hold me.

Why can't they get a grip? I ask Saskia.

Not that I'm complaining. I don't want to suffer Jackson's fate, trussed up in a tree like a spider's prey.

<I don't know,> Saskia says.

Maybe it's because I'm not real.

<Or maybe it's because you began life as a shadow.>

Same difference, I want to say. And I'm still a shadow, no matter how much I like to pretend that my life is now my own. Considering my origin, how can I ever be anything but?

I keep my thoughts to myself. These days, neither Saskia nor I am all that strong on the self-confidence front—at least, not when it comes to what sort of beings we are. Animal, vegetable, mineral. Or just make-believe. Pick one.

So I just say, *Maybe.*

Neither of us is really feeling all that coherent either—or at least I sure don't. I've been in some strange places in the otherworld, but nothing to compare to this. It's like we've fallen down some cyber version of Alice's rabbit hole, where nothing makes sense anymore. I'm waiting on the Cheshire cat or an army of playing cards to drag us away to the Queen's court for judgment. All I get are the vines. They keep crawling up my ankles and I have to kick them away. I hate the feel of them as they crawl up under my jeans, the rough sound as they rub against the coarse fabric.

My gaze goes to where Jackson's hanging from the tree. He can't talk because his mouth is full of leaves now, but his panicked eyes are more than eloquent enough to get his message across. He reminds me of the Green Men, forest spirits I've met in the Greatwood from time to time. Root-and-leaf people like the Green Knight in his wooden armor, riding a red-flanked stag, or the Jill-in-the-Wood with her bird's-nest hair and cloak of leaves—except they're born of the green sap and they run free. They're not trapped and hanging from the trunk of some tree the way Jackson is.

His eyes plead with me to get him down.

I'm torn between staying with Saskia's body and going to see if I can help him. So far, the vines are still ignoring her limp body, but I'm not sure how long that's going to last. Do I want to risk losing her to them while I try to give Jackson a hand? It's not like I owe him anything. After all, he's the one that got us into this mess in the first place.

But he's a handsome man and I can be a sucker for a handsome man.

<We can't just leave him hanging there,> Saskia says when I put the question to her. As I expected, her heart's so big she's full of indignation that I'd even consider such an uncharitable course.

And if the vines go after your body while we're cutting him down?

<Oh, yeah . . . >

I've been standing, facing Jackson. Now that my initial surprise at the transformation of our surroundings is over, I realize that there's still a blue-gold glow on everything—cast by that pillar of light, I suppose. I turn to look at it, only to find that it's been transformed, as well.

There's a man there. Or at least the pillar has taken on the form of a man, but there's no way he's human, not radiating light the way he is.

There's only one person he can be: the spirit of the Wordwood.

I'm not sure what I expected him to look like, but it certainly wasn't this. Pressed, I'd have said an angel or a monster because, from other experiences I've had in the otherworld, that's the way these beings usually manifest. They come in all shapes and sizes, of course, but in the end they will invariably be something to either wake awe, or strike terror. Which is why I try to avoid them. Too many of them are just these big picture beings with little or no consideration for the small concerns of the likes of you and me. Unless we get in their way, and then they can be merciless.

I'm not saying they're always like that. And to be fair, most of the scary ones are more like forces of nature, so we really shouldn't try to put our own concepts of ethics and morality on them. That'd be like criticizing a tornado or the winter for being what it is. You can't, though it shouldn't make you any less cautious around them. I can understand a storm, but that doesn't mean I want to go out and tromp around in the middle of it.

But I'm getting way off the point. The real point here is that the Wordwood spirit has chosen to appear as the stereotypical image of a male librarian—you know, the lifelong bachelor—slight, a little stooped at the shoulders, wispy hair, white shirt with tweed vest and trousers, wire-frame glasses. I'd smile, but the fact is, no matter what he looks like, he's still made of blue-gold light. He's still a powerful spirit.

I find myself wondering if this is what he really looks like, or if it's just some mask he's put on—the same way that this forest around us masks the binary code lying at its heart. And if it is a mask, then what's it for? I doubt it's to put us at our ease, because he doesn't even acknowledge our presence. All of his attention is on Jackson, hanging there in the tree.

"So," the spirit says to him. "We have one of you, at least."

I look around to see if the spirit has companions, but except for the writhing roots and vines, he seems to be on his own. He must be using the royal we.

Jackson's only response to the spirit's attention is a glassy-eyed stare—that's all it can be, I guess, what with his mouth still full of leaves—but the spirit doesn't seem to care much about his captive's lack of response. And he certainly doesn't go on to acknowledge that I'm here either, standing a half-dozen yards away with Saskia's body lying at my feet and her spirit in my head.

It's probably better that he's not paying any attention to us. Unfortunately, I can't leave it at that. We have questions that need answers, and this spirit in his guise of a glowing little librarian man is all we have at hand to give them to us. Considering what happened to Jackson, I'd just as soon stay unnoticed. But I don't see it as an option. Not if we want to get Saskia back into her body and the both of us out of this place.

I take a steadying breath to gather my courage.

One thing I've learned about these otherworld spirits is, if you want them to take you seriously, you have to come to them like an equal. It's different if they're the figurehead of some religion that you follow. Then the respectful follower route is a good choice: bended knee, cast-down gaze, that sort of thing. But that isn't the case here. I like books, but I don't worship them.

"Hey," I say. "You with the glow."

It's a good thing I've never been shy. Saskia would probably add cautious and smart to that.

<Christiana!> Saskia says in my head. <Don't get him angry.>

There she is, right on cue.

Relax, I tell her. *I know what I'm doing.*

The spirit turns to me. More roots and vines burst from the ground at my feet, trying to wrap themselves around me, but they can't get any better purchase on me than the others did—the ones that were in automatic snatch-and-grab mode, I guess.

"This is curious," the spirit says.

I'm hoping he doesn't start referring to himself in the third person. I hate it when they do that, although it can be a good way to find out their name.

"You're telling me," I say. "One moment I'm home, minding my own business, and the next I find myself in this place, wherever *it* is."

"I was referring to your presence here."

"Yeah, well, it's not my idea of a good time, either. Think you can point me to the quickest route out of here?"

"What makes you think I will let you leave?"

I offer him my cockiest smile and give the vegetation still moving around at my feet a little kick.

"What makes you think you can stop me?" I ask.

I can feel Saskia vibrating in my head, just waiting for him to do something horrible to us. I have to admit, I half expect it myself. But I've got this going for me: there are a lot of different spirits in the otherworld, some, despite their appearance, far more powerful than others. No one knows them all. So even for a spirit such as the one glowing in front of me, it pays to be a little cautious. I could be just what I am, though he doesn't know it: the shadow of a seven-year-old boy grown up now in my own right. Or I could be some old creation spirit, slumming in the shape of a young woman.

You can't tell, just by looking.

The spirit's been studying me. Now his gaze drops to Saskia's body.

"I know that woman," he says.

"Wouldn't surprise me," I tell him. "I think she's from around here, originally. But right now there's nobody home."

The spirit nods. "But she is near. In the Web, if not somewhere in this particular site."

Close, but no cigar. Then I think about what he said and realize he's just confirmed that we're in the Wordwood site. I know, I know. No big surprise since we'd pretty much worked that out on our own. Still, it's good to have the corroboration. The question now is, is the Wordwood a part of the otherworld, or somewhere else again. And how do we get out of here?

But I figure since his attention's on Saskia at the moment, I might as well work on the other half of our problem.

"Have you ever seen this kind of thing before?" I ask him. "Where the spirit is gone, but the body's still alive?"

He gives me what I feel is a reluctant shake of his head and that makes me reconsider his standing. Maybe he's not such an old spirit. Maybe he just came into being when the Wordwood did. He could have been floating in whatever netherworld spirits float around in before they manifest, just waiting to attach himself to something. I remember Mumbo talking to me about that kind of thing, but she didn't seem entirely clear on the concept and I wasn't interested enough to ask her to clarify it at the time.

"I found her in a glass coffin," I say. "When this place . . ." I wave a hand around at our surroundings. "Was different."

The spirit's gaze goes to where Jackson's still hanging from the tree.

"We . . . I've been . . . ill," he says. "I don't remember a great deal of what has happened in the past little while."

I give him a sympathetic look.

"But the funny thing," I go on when he doesn't continue himself, "is

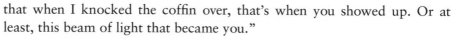

that when I knocked the coffin over, that's when you showed up. Or at least, this beam of light that became you."

"I really don't remember."

"It was as though breaking her out of the coffin was . . ." I hesitate. I was about to say "what set you free," but settle for, "the catalyst for your return to health."

<You're sly,> Saskia says. <But do you really think he'll feel beholden?>

I can't remember the last time I heard that word used in a sentence.

The spirit is studying me again, a careful look in his eyes.

"There did seem to be some sense of outside intervention," he finally says. "There at the end."

I open my arms expansively and say, "Ta da. That was us."

He continues to study me.

"It's hard for me to say 'you're welcome' when you don't say 'thank you' first," I tell him.

"So you want something from me," he says.

I shake my head. "Nothing for me. But for her . . ."

He closes his eyes and it's like he goes away. It's only when he starts to talk that I realize he must have been referencing some of the texts he has stored on the site.

"You need a soulstone," he says, opening his eyes again. "To allow her to return to her body."

<I've never heard of such a thing,> Saskia says.

Me, either, I tell her.

"A soulstone," I repeat aloud.

He nods.

"Which is?"

"It looks like an ordinary pebble, smoothed by a river's current or the ocean's tide, but when you place it in the mouth of someone whose soul has become detached from her body, it creates a conduit to allow the soul's return. They're quite difficult to acquire."

"Do you know how I can get one?"

He nods. "You must find the dawn branch of the Secret Road and take it eastward through the Hills of Morning. It's a long journey, but if you keep on the road, eventually you will see the tall crags of the Brismandarian Mountains to the north. You will come in time to a path that leads off from the road—I'm not sure if it's marked, probably not. But when you find it, it will take you cross country into the foothills and then into the mountains themselves.

"Once there, you have to look for a ruined goblin tower nestled in the lower peaks. Under it is the entrance to a dragon's cave where—"

"Oh, get real," I tell him, breaking in. I feel like I'm being read the dust jacket of some high fantasy quest novel. "What book did you steal that from? How about we skip over the bullshit and you just tell it to me straight? What's a soulstone? Does it really exist? And if it does, how do I get one?"

<Christiana,> Saskia says. She's been giving me free rein so far, but I guess she really doesn't like it when I get too pushy. <This isn't helping. You're just going to make him angry.>

So? He's not exactly endearing himself to me, either.

<Please.>

The spirit's looking a little pouty, which makes me question again how powerful he really is. Or at least how young. It's the look a kid gets when you call him on something he's not really sure about himself, but has presented with great authority.

"That's how it was described in the book," he says.

I sigh and try to keep the irritation out of my voice.

"What book?" I ask.

He hesitates a long moment, then finally says, "*Her Glorious Hoard.* By Caitlin Midhir."

"Which is a novel?"

He nods.

"So really, you have no idea."

He shakes his head.

"And you can't help us at all—at least not with this detached soul business."

"Sorry."

And he looks so full of regret.

"Well, can you at least show us how we can get out of this place?" I ask.

"I don't travel beyond this site."

Don't, he says, but I'm guessing can't. This makes me think that maybe the Wordwood spirit is a *genus loci*—the tutelary spirit of a place. One that's bound to his location, rather than obliged. The obliged can leave; they simply have to return from time to time—check in like a watchman on his rounds. The bound can never leave. Which would be why he'd send someone like Saskia out to experience the world for him. And that makes me wonder if he maybe he really does recognize her. Maybe he's being so unhelpful because he's got some other use for her body.

But I don't let any of this show on my face.

"No clues?" I ask. "Not even a hint?"

"I'd say the same way you arrived."

Great.

"I have to go now," he says. "Other business to attend to and all."

But he doesn't move. I'm guessing either he can't—either that pillar of light he was is bound to the spot where he's standing, the way the beam of a searchlight can't escape the mechanism that casts it—or he has nowhere to go, but he doesn't want us to know.

I think about that royal "we" he used when he first spoke, how he started to use it again during our conversation, but caught himself. Then there's the way he looks and his whole attitude. How he talks big, but he seems kind of weak and inexperienced.

What if he's putting up a bigger front than I am?

"You're not the Wordwood spirit," I find myself saying aloud.

I'm just trying the idea on, throwing it out to see what kind of reaction I might get. He gets this look—caught out, wanting to protest, knowing he hasn't got it in him to pull it off.

Bingo.

"So who are you?" I ask.

<Oh my god,> Saskia says in my head. <I think you're right. He must be another construct, except his job is probably something like administrating the day-to-day running of the site.>

What he says next only confirms it.

"Perhaps it's true," he says. "perhaps I am not the spirit of this place. Perhaps I am only *of* the spirit."

"So which is it?"

"When the site was still operational and we would be contacted with questions and requests, I was the one who found the information they required and furnished them with it."

<He's like a macro,> Saskia says.

Say what?

<It's a little program you can write that will handle some mundane computer task so you don't have to keep doing it over and over again yourself.>

"So you're like a macro," I say aloud, trying out the word on him.

He gets this affronted look. "I am far more than that. You could call me Librarius, the Master Librarian of the Wordwood. I am its administrator, in charge of all acquisitions and communications. Without my expertise and effort, this site would never have had any interaction at all with the myriad territories beyond its borders. It would merely be a pocket world—home to a Great One, it is true, but he would be alone. There would be no one to look after him. There would be no one to maintain the flow of and collect all the attention paid to him that he requires for his sustenance."

"Sustenance? What, you mean he eats e-mail?"

Librarius shakes his head. "Hardly. But like many gods, he requires attention. Without it, he will wither away and die."

I get it. I've heard of these spirits that buy into godhood—buy into it so much that their belief in how it works becomes fact. Eventually, they really do require the prayers and attention of their followers in order to exist. In the case of the Wordwood, all the e-mails that arrive at the site would be like prayers, sustaining him. Making him strong. Without them, cut off by the virus, he thinks he's dying.

"The virus hurt him bad," I say.

Librarius nods. "I've managed to purge the last of it from the site, but even with it gone, the Great One is still stricken."

"Can we see him?" I ask.

"Normally, I would say no," Librarius tells me. "Normally, all you see would be the Great One, for he would be part and parcel of everything that makes up this world. But now . . ."

He does something with his hands, some kind of ritualistic motion in the air in front of him, or maybe he's just touching controls we can't see. Whatever it is that he does, our surroundings change again, only this time it's as fast as you might snap your fingers. There's no gradual change from forest to this new place we find ourselves in. We're just *here*.

<Oh my . . . > Saskia breathes in my head.

No kidding.

We're in a library, an enormous chamber filled with shelves and shelves of books, a chamber that is so vast that I can't see an end to it, no matter which way I look. Everything is lit with a diffused version of the blue-gold light I've come to associate with the Wordwood, but I can't see a source for the light. The bookshelves tower up until they disappear into shadow. The top shelves are only accessible from rolling ladders that are so tall I can't imagine climbing up one and I have a good head for heights. There's carpeting underfoot, an Oriental pattern that, if handwoven, would take centuries to make by an army of carpet-makers.

I turn to Librarius and he looks like flesh and blood now. The soft light touches him, like it touches everything, but he's no longer made of light himself. Saskia's body is still at my feet. I look to where Jackson had been hanging from that tree, but he's in a leather club chair now, his arms and legs strapped and buckled to it so that he can't get up. His mouth is no longer full of leaves, but he doesn't say anything. He just sits there, looking scared, but a little angry, too. I don't blame him.

"Where's the spirit?" I ask, turning back to Librarius.

"This way," he says.

He starts off down one of the corridors between the bookshelves, pausing when I don't immediately follow.

"What's the matter?" he asks.

"I don't want to leave my friend just lying here."

He gives a slow nod and does something with his hands again, manipulating the air. Saskia's body and the chair that Jackson's sitting in float up, hovering a few inches from the carpet. I take an experimental step and Saskia's body keeps pace, floating beside me.

Librarius turns and sets off once more and this time I follow him, Saskia's body at my side, Jackson's chair trailing along behind.

<He's not just a servant,> Saskia says, referring to the librarian. <He's got access to power.>

His own, or the spirit's?

<Does it matter?>

I suppose not.

After a number of twists and turns through the maze of bookshelves, we come out into a cavernous space—it might even *be* a cavern for all I know. It's hard to tell because the diffuse lighting doesn't really allow you to get a real sense of distance. I just know we're on the shore of something. A river. A lake. Maybe even an ocean. It's hard to tell. The water stretches away from us, disappearing into shadow.

On our left, the bookcases march up to the shore. On the right, there's a jumble of rock that goes right into the water. Then I realize it's not rock. That enormous shape is a body, its lower torso and legs submerged in the water. I hear Jackson make a soft choking sound behind me when it registers for him. I can barely breathe myself, but I try not to let it show.

Instead, I walk boldly up to the body.

<Christiana,> Saskia says in my head.

There's the usual warning in how she uses my name, but what does she think I'm going to do?

I just want a closer look, I tell her.

I walk up to the head, Librarius keeping pace with me. I can't believe the size of the body. The head alone is as big as a city bus.

I just about die when one enormous eye opens and looks at me.

Aaran

From the moment that Geordie, wearing a thin veneer of politeness over his hostility, had led them down to the basement, Aaran hadn't been able to take his gaze from the wall. That was another world he could see through the shimmer. A real, honest-to-God other world. Even after their experience in Jackson's apartment, and given the evidence of his own two eyes, it still seemed too improbable to be real. But there it was all the same. So amazing, but at the same time, so ordinary as well. As though every Newford basement had a portal to another world in one of its walls.

He almost smiled at the idea.

Maybe they did. Maybe there was one in the basement of his own building. He wouldn't know. He'd only been down there a few times, and only so far as his storage locker. Past the lockers, there could be anything.

The portal continued to distract him as they all brought each other up to date, Christy and Suzi doing most of the talking. But he did tear his attention away from it later, when the discussion arose as to what to do next. He was surprised to find Christy not only defending Suzi, but allowing the two of them to join the group going into the otherworld. That required more than a little trust on Christy's part, and Christy was the one they had to win over, because the others appeared to be following his lead.

Considering how Aaran had treated Christy over the years—more to the point, considering how he was directly responsible for Saskia's disappearance—Aaran thought it was awfully big of him. He wasn't sure if the situation were reversed, that he'd have been able to do the same. Certainly not before he met Suzi and she did whatever it was that she'd done to him to make him see himself and the world in a different light.

Once the decision to go ahead with their journey into the otherworld was made, people began lifting their packs and moving toward the portal.

We didn't bring anything, Aaran realized. No extra clothes, no food or water. Nothing.

He was about to ask Suzi if she was okay being so unprepared for the trip when Holly approached them with a pack in her hand. She offered it to them.

"What's this?" he asked.

Holly shrugged. "I kept thinking that I'd wait until the last moment and then talk Christy into letting me join them, so I packed some stuff. Nothing that'll fit you, but Suzi should find things she can wear. There's also some bottled water, a first aid kit and matches, and some food."

"You sure you don't want to come?" Suzi asked.

Holly shook her head. "After seeing those guys that came for Robert . . . nope, I don't think so. I'm happy to stay here and hold the fort."

Aaran took the pack. "Thanks."

"Just bring them back. Saskia, my friends. Everybody."

"We'll do our best."

Holly fixed him with a serious look.

"And you'd better not be playing a game here," she told him. "Because if you are and you screw things up, I will personally—"

Suzi put her hand on Holly's arm. "No games," she said. "We want this to end as much as you do."

"Right. Of course, you do. I'm sorry. It's just . . ."

"Really hard," Suzi said.

Holly nodded. "I love those guys. If they're gone for good . . . I just don't know what I'll do."

"We'll bring them back," Suzi assured her.

You can't know that, Aaran thought, so why make the promise? He saw that knowledge in Holly's eyes, too, but he also saw how the promise helped, so he added his own to it.

"We won't come back until we do," he told her.

The others were waiting for them on the far side of the portal—three poorly-defined shapes seen through the shimmer. Suzi took his hand as they were about to step through.

"Nervous?" she asked.

Aaran nodded. "Guess this is old hat for you."

"I wish it was. I feel like I'm going to pee my pants."

Then, before she could lose her nerve, she stepped ahead, into the wall, into the shimmer of the portal. Every inch of Aaran's skin shrunk from the contact as they went through. But there was nothing there—only a thickening of the air—and then they were on the other side. Vertigo hit Aaran hard. Nausea rose up and he would have stumbled if Bojo hadn't caught his arm.

"It doesn't last," the tinker said. "Here, sit on this rock for a moment and put your head between your legs."

Aaran gave a dull nod and allowed himself to be led over to a jumble of rocks under a large old tree of some kind. He dropped his head between his legs when all he really wanted to do was lie down in the dirt. But Bojo had told the truth. The feeling went quickly away leaving only a slight queasiness in its wake. When he was able to look up he saw that Raul still looked a little ill, too, but the other three appeared unaffected.

"Apparently it doesn't hit everybody the same way," Suzi said.

She had the decency to look a little guilty as she offered him a hand up.

"And some people not at all," he muttered.

"What can I say? It's all in the constitution."

Aaran gave her a weak smile and looked around. So this was the otherworld. It didn't look a whole lot different from the landscape north of the city. Big fields. Mountains in the distance. A forest, mostly evergreens, to his right. When he turned the other way, the view was only a variation on what he'd already seen.

Two paths joined each other in the place where they were standing—dirt trails leading off as far as he could see in four different directions. The tree above was some kind of oak, he decided.

"It's not what I expected," he said.

"It changes," Bojo said. "That's probably the most disconcerting thing about the otherworld. One moment you're in a place like this, the next you're braving a winter storm on a tundra. The transitions can be that abrupt, or as gradual as they are in the consensual world."

Aaran gave a slow nod.

"Now, this is the most important thing you need to know for the moment," the tinker went on. "I can't emphasize this enough. Don't leave the path. It might change underfoot, it may seem to be taking you in the opposite direction than you want to go, but whatever you do, stay on it." He pointed to the open field in front of them. "You might be thinking, how can I get lost over there, well, trust me in this. You can and you will if you stray."

Aaran wasn't so sure it was as serious as Bojo was making it out to be, but he wasn't going to argue. Then he had a sudden thought. He looked around again.

"The portal," he said. "It's gone."

A sudden panic made his chest go tight. How were they going to get back?

"It's not gone," Bojo assured him.

He made a movement with his hands and the portal shimmered back into view. Aaran stepped closer to look back at the basement. Through the shimmer he could see Geordie, Holly and Dick standing by the stairs, talking. Sitting directly in front of them, staring at the wall was Holly's Jack Russell terrier. She barked when she could see them and the others turned around. Bojo waved to them, then let the portal close again.

"Don't worry," he said. "I can easily find my way back here."

Aaran nodded, but he made a point of memorizing the look of the tree and the stones that were jumbled under it in case something happened to Bojo and they had to get back on their own. Of course, then they'd still have to figure out how to open the portal.

"How does the portal work?" he asked.

"It's easiest to find a place like this," Bojo said. "A crossroads—some place where the border between the worlds is thin. And then it's only a matter of concentrating on where you want to be—holding it very clearly in your mind. That's why you need to have been there before. You can't make the same connection with a place you've never been."

"Which way should we go?" Christy asked.

Bojo stood for a moment, looking either way down the path, his brow furrowing as he concentrated on Aaran wasn't sure what. Every direction looked pretty much the same to him.

"This way," the tinker said finally, pointing to the right, where the path led toward the evergreen wood. "Robert's music took us past the worlds that lie back there."

"Any sign of him or the hellhounds?" Christy asked.

Bojo shook his head. "But they'd be many worlds away by now."

"Can't say I'm unhappy to hear that," Raul said.

"I hope he'll be okay," Christy said.

Bojo nodded. "Yeah, me, too." He shifted the strap of his pack to a more comfortable position. "Time we were going."

The trip proved to be as disconcerting as Bojo had described. The first time the landscape shifted, all of them except for Bojo stopped dead in their tracks. The fields and distant mountains were suddenly gone and the path they followed now took them along the top of a dune. A beach, with a vast body of water beyond it, lay on the left of the path. To the right was a heath that went on for miles until it disappeared into a haze on the horizon. High in the sky, a solitary hawk moved in slow lazy circles, riding the wind.

"Jesus," Raul said. "How'd that happen?"

Aaran nodded. The change had come between one step and another.

"The path we're following," Bojo explained, "takes us through an area where the worlds lie smack up against each other, sometimes even overlapping. Some of them are only a few acres in size, others as large or larger than the consensual world. What makes it confusing is that they shift their positions and sometimes their sizes. That's why the otherworld is impossible to map."

"And is there a Rip Van Winkle effect?" Christy asked.

"Time does run differently in some of the worlds—faster in some, slower in others. In some, time spirals, so that when you walk one way, it's into the future, another, and you step into the past."

"What kind of world are we in?" Suzi asked.

"We're not in a world," Bojo told her, "so much as walking along the edges of them. On this path, time runs the same as it does in the consensual world, perhaps a little faster. We won't return to find a hundred years have gone by, though we might be a little older than we're supposed to be, given the amount of time that will have passed. On the plus side, the air of the otherworld offers a measure of longevity as compensation."

"What do you mean by that?" Raul asked.

Bojo shrugged. "It can help you live longer."

"You're kidding."

"No, but it's not as simple as that. Unless you have the right kind of blood—the right kind of genes, I suppose you would say—staying too long in the otherworld can affect the stability of your mind."

"Like in the fairy tales," Christy said. "You come back a poet or a lunatic."

"Something like that."

If you come back at all, Aaran added to himself. In some of those same fairy tales, the characters never come back. Or if they do, as soon as their feet touch mortal ground, they crumple away into dust.

The changes in the landscape, especially the abrupt ones, took some getting used to for most of them. Considering all of his previous experience with the otherworld, it didn't surprise Aaran that Bojo wasn't affected. Suzi seemed to take it all in stride, too. Maybe that was because being newborn the way she was, everything felt new to her and she simply accepted the bizarre along with the mundane. But it was harder for the rest of them, even Christy. And that did surprise Aaran.

"But you've been writing about this stuff for years," Aaran said at one point, when he and Suzi were walking on either side of the writer.

Christy smiled. "You don't really read my books, do you?"

"What do you mean by that?"

"The short story collections are fiction, and yes, there are stories about otherworlds in them, but they don't come from personal experience. They're either based on other people's experiences, which I listened to with the proverbial grain of salt, or they came from my imagination."

"I wasn't talking about them," Aaran said. "And I *have* read your books—or at least the ones I've reviewed. The ones where you collect all those urban myths and make connections between them and old legends and folk tales. In them you allude to personal experiences as well, though you don't go as much into them."

"That's because until now, I could count my truly inexplicable experiences on one hand. I've always been a believer and a disbeliever at the same time."

"It never seems like that in your books."

Christy laughed. "That's because people tend to find what they're personally looking for in them—it's human nature. The believers believe, the skeptics focus on my own questions, and those with a personal axe to grind against me will find what they think makes me look foolish, even when the examples they inevitably pull out aren't actually in the text."

On the other side of Christy, Suzi laughed as well. "I'm guessing Aaran was one of the latter."

"Maybe I was a bit too enthusiastic," Aaran said, "but—"

"You had an axe to grind," Suzi finished for him, still laughing.

"Yeah, I guess I did."

"That's okay," Christy said. "It's not like you're alone. The very idea of the consensual world, never mind discussing what might lie hidden within or beyond its boundaries, pushes a lot of people's buttons."

Suzi gave him a curious look. "You sound pretty accepting of the negative press."

"Oh, I have my moments of bitterness, but really, what can you do? You can't—sometimes I think you shouldn't even try to—change people's minds. It just gets their backs up. Better to put the information out and let them deal with it in their own way, on their own time."

"And if they don't take the time to assimilate the information?" Suzi asked.

"You conduct your own life as a positive example. Always remain open-minded."

"People aren't going to believe in fairies just because you do," Aaran said. "They aren't even going to think seriously about it."

"I know. That's why in my nonfiction I'd rather focus on the World As It Is—as Professor Dapple likes to call it. The idea of a consensual world— that things are the way they are only because that's what we've agreed to. It's something that seems completely preposterous to so many people, but the funny thing is that chaos theory—which science *does* take seriously—is now catching up to the same ideas: how on a microscopic level, it's the presence of an observer that makes a thing be one thing or another. Until that moment of observation, they're simultaneously both and their possibility remains completely open-ended.

"And those same scientists are now actually considering the concept of parallel worlds as viable."

"Well, considering where we are," Suzi said, "that theory is pretty obviously true."

Christy shook his head. "These are *otherworlds*. The parallel worlds theory posits that every time a decision is made, a new world splits off from the original, making for an infinite number of alternate or parallel worlds. They start off very close to one another, but if you think about the decisions in your own life, even the smallest choice can start a ripple effect resulting in utterly changing your life."

"Like how the movement of butterfly wings in China," Suzi said, "can affect the weather here. Well, not *here*, maybe, but back in Newford."

Christy nodded.

Or like stopping to talk to Suzi had been for him, Aaran thought. It had begun with him thinking of himself as usual, wondering what he could get out of her, and ended up with him being here, in this place, risking his life for other people, most of whom he didn't even know.

Was there some other parallel world where he hadn't? Where he'd gone on the way he always did?

Was there a world where he hadn't forced Jackson Hart to write that virus in the first place?

Before he could follow that line of thinking too far he realized that up ahead, Bojo and Raul had come to a stop. He looked past them to see that the path they were following dipped under a freeway overpass. To their right, the highway was lost in a wide sweep of fields and far-off mountains. To their left, the ocean had long since vanished and he could now see a large city in the distance. Traffic sped by on the freeway in both directions, no one seeming to pay any attention to them.

"Okay, this is weird," Aaran said.

"Why's that?" Bojo asked.

"Well, look at this. What's a freeway doing here? I thought fairyland was supposed to be all pastoral, with maybe a castle or some little village."

Bojo smiled. "This isn't fairyland—it's the otherworld. Somewhere in its reaches you'll find every landscape you could possibly imagine, and some you can't."

"Yeah, but that city . . ."

"Is Mabon."

Aaran saw Christy perk up.

"Mabon?" Christy repeated. "Really? That's Sophie's city. Or at least it was when she was a little girl." He turned to look at the others. "She started imagining it when she was a latchkey kid and . . . well, I guess all of that grew up around the few streets she created."

"You know Mabon's creator?" Bojo asked.

Christy nodded. "Sure. She's a friend of mine."

"Wait a minute," Aaran said. "Are you talking about Sophie Etoile, the artist?"

When Christy gave another nod, Aaran was about to argue how that was impossible. *He'd* met Sophie and . . .

But he caught himself and just shrugged instead. Maybe nothing was impossible anymore—at least not in this place.

"I need you all to wait here for a few moments," Bojo said, "while I scout the lay of the land under that overpass."

"Is there something wrong?" Raul asked.

"Don't know yet," Bojo said. "But it looks like a place of power—what with that freeway and all those people travelling over what amounts to another crossroads. You've already had a brief introduction to what you can meet at a crossroads."

He was referring to the hellhounds, Aaran realized, which the others had confronted in Holly's basement. He and Suzi had missed them and he, for one, was happy to leave it that way.

"It won't take me long," Bojo said.

Aaran watched him go ahead, then looked at the city again.

"So Sophie made that," he said.

Christy nodded.

"Does your friend Jilly have a place here as well? When I think about how *she* goes on about fairies and magic . . ."

"No," Christy said. "But she's been to Mabon."

"Bojo's waving the 'all clear,' " Raul said.

Aaran took another look at the city before trailing along after the others. On the other side of the overpass, the landscape did another abrupt change and for a block or two they were walking in a derelict cityscape that reminded Aaran of the Tombs back home in Newford, but this area seemed far older than the abandoned buildings and empty lots of the Tombs. This city appeared to have been deserted for decades—or at least deserted by normal people. By the time they were halfway down the second block, Aaran got the sense that they were being watched, but by whom or what, he couldn't tell. He just had this prickle in the back of his neck, some vestige of alarm handed down from his own primitive ancestors warning of imminent danger.

But then they reached the end of the block and they were walking across a frozen field, snow crunching underfoot. Aaran shivered and wrapped his thin jacket more tightly around him. He was about to ask Suzi if she wanted to see if they could find something warmer for her to wear in the pack that Holly had given them, when the landscape changed once more and they were walking through desert scrub, where every plant seemed to have a thorn, even the trees. But at least it was warm, and the nervousness Aaran had felt in the deserted city had faded.

They'd fallen into a new order as they walked. Bojo continued to take the lead, but Raul was now walking on his own behind him. Christy and Suzi were next, the two of them still talking about consensual worlds and parallel universes. Tired of that conversation, Aaran stayed in the rear.

Trudging along, he continued to fall farther behind the others, distracted over and over again by the changing landscape. By the time they came to another of what seemed like a perennial English countryside, the others were well ahead of him and didn't hear him when he stopped and called out after them. He was surprised that none of them had noticed the little man he'd spotted just off the road. But perhaps he hadn't even been here when they walked by, the landscape changed so frequently.

Aaran studied him curiously, half-disbelieving what he saw.

He was more the way Aaran imagined a fairy-tale character to be than Dick, the hob he'd met back at Holly's store, had been. Barely a foot tall, this little man's features were all sharp angles, his limbs gangly and stick-like. He was wearing a red cloth cap and leather pants, but his jacket seemed to be made of burrs and leaves, held together with vines and braided grasses.

He appeared to have his foot snagged in among the protruding roots of the tree that towered above him. Aaran couldn't identify it. All he knew was that it was a solitary tree with a wide expanse of open fields spreading out from beyond it and some of its boughs overhanging the path. When Aaran stopped, the little man tried to make himself invisible, but without any real luck. He wasn't having much luck freeing his foot, either.

Aaran glanced at where his companions were still foraging ahead. He remembered Bojo's warning when they'd first crossed over.

I can't emphasize this enough. Don't leave the path.

But this wouldn't really be leaving the path. It was only a couple of quick steps to where the little man was trapped.

He gave a last quick look at the backs of his companions, two hundred yards or so ahead on the path, then stepped off, into the field. The little man's almond-shaped eyes went round with fear and he frantically started tugging at his foot again, his whole little body shaking and trembling.

"Take it easy," Aaran said, gentling his voice the way you did with a frightened child. "I'm not going to hurt you."

When he reached forward, the little man stopped moving. He lay there, terrified eyes staring at Aaran, nervous tremors making his limbs jump.

"Really," Aaran told him. "I'm here to help."

He dug with his fingers around the little man's foot, found where the roots had wedged around the tiny ankle. It only took him a moment to stretch the knotty roots far enough apart to pull the foot out. Even with his foot free, the little man continued to lie there on the ground, shaking with fear.

"It's okay," Aaran said. "You can go now."

He moved back, holding his hands open to show that he meant no harm.

"Or did you break something?" Aaran asked.

But as soon as he was an arm's length away, the little man jumped to his feet and went tearing off into the field. In a moment, all Aaran could see was the small wake the little man left behind in the tall grass and weeds. Then that, too, was gone.

"So I guess you're fine," he said, straightening up. "No need to say thank you."

He had a last look into the field, trying to see if he could spot the little man, before he turned around to get back onto the path.

Which was no longer there.

Don't leave the path.

Oh, come on, he thought. I only took a couple of steps.

But retracing those steps didn't bring him back to the packed dirt of the path they'd been following. Instead, he was still in the middle of this enormous field, knee high grass and weeds swaying in a light breeze, the expanse dotted here and there with large trees like the one under which he'd rescued the little fairy man.

And not at all a bright little man, either, Aaran thought. If the fairy hadn't panicked, he'd have discovered that all he had to do was push his foot the other way and he could have worked himself free.

Maybe fairies weren't all that smart.

Right. And look who's talking.

He turned back to look at the tree, trying to judge how many steps he'd taken from the path to get to the roots where the little fairy man had been trapped. He was about to go back and try to retrace his steps when a hand fell on his shoulder and he suddenly understood the cliché of almost jumping out of your skin.

Adrenaline slammed in his chest and he whirled, flailing his arms, only to have them both caught in firm grips. Then he saw who it was that held him. Bojo let go as soon as he stopped struggling.

"Jesus," Aaran said, heart still pounding in his chest. "You just about gave me a heart attack."

"I told you not to leave the path."

"I only stepped off for a minute."

"Maybe for you," Bojo said. "But you were gone two hours for us."

That didn't seem possible.

"Two hours?" Aaran repeated.

The tinker nodded.

"But . . ."

"Trust me," Bojo said. "You were gone for a while."

"But . . ."

Bojo smiled. "I thought a newspaperman would have a larger vocabulary than that."

"He should. I mean, I do. It's just . . ."

"Hard to get your head around. I know. It's always like that at first. But if it makes you feel any better, the four of you are doing much better for a first trip into the otherworld than most people do. Now come on. Let's get back to the others."

He did something with his hand again, a sideways motion, a twitch of his fingers, but Aaran couldn't concentrate on it. And then he didn't care about it anymore because they were back on the path and Suzi grabbed him in a hug.

"I thought we'd lost you forever," she said into his chest.

He put his arms around her and looked over the top of her head at the others.

"Look, I'm sorry," he said. "There was this little fairy man who looked like he was pretty much made of twigs and leaves. He had his foot caught in a tree root and I just stepped off the path to help him out. I really didn't mean to cause a problem."

"Did he have a red cap?" Bojo asked.

Aaran nodded. "Yeah, he did. Does that mean something?"

"Just that you were lucky. It must have been a brownie under the cap instead of a goblin. Goblins get their caps that colour by dipping them in blood, and they get their blood from people like you that they coax off a safe path."

"Jesus."

"But a goblin also wouldn't get itself into that kind of predicament in the first place."

Goblins and brownies, Aaran thought. Next thing you know, they'd see a dragon.

"But it worked out okay, I guess," he said.

Beside Bojo, Raul smiled. "Sure. You got to be like the hero in some fairy tale."

"What do you mean?"

"You know, stopping to help a spoon or an old woman, and later on in the story it turns out they're the only one that can help you?"

Aaran shook his head. "It wasn't like that at all. And I think that the point of those stories isn't that you should help someone now for a payoff later down the road. It's that everyone's important, no matter how insignificant they might seem." He let go of Suzi so that he could look her in the face. "It's like our guardian angel thing," he said. "You do it because you can. Not because you have to, or because you think you should, but because you want to."

Suzi beamed at him, but no one said anything for a long moment. Then Christy stepped up and gave him a light punch in the shoulder.

"Maybe there's hope for you yet," he said.

Bojo nodded. "Only next time, don't do it on your own. We were lucky we found you as quickly as we did."

"I tried calling after you guys, but you were already too far ahead."

"We were probably too distracted to hear you." Before Aaran could ask for an explanation, the tinker added, "We found the Wordwood, but . . . well, you'll have to see it for yourself."

He started off down the road again and the others fell in behind him. Suzi held Aaran's hand.

"You're really doing well," she said.

"High praise," he told her, "coming as it does from my guardian angel."

"Don't wear that into the ground," she told him, but she was grinning.

"So what's Bojo not saying about the Wordwood?" Aaran asked.

"There doesn't seem to be a way in," she said and pointed ahead.

For a moment, Aaran wasn't sure what he was supposed to be looking at. All he saw was the others ahead of them on the path, the path itself leading off into the greying distance. But as they drew closer, he realized that the greyness he saw wasn't in the distance. It was a thin wall of mist with pale, blue-gold lights playing deep inside it. Stepping right up to it, Aaran could plainly see a deep forest on the other side, the path continuing into it.

"You're sure that's the Wordwood?" he asked.

Bojo nodded. "It's giving me the same feeling that I got from the residue the spirit left behind in Holly's store."

"So what are we waiting for?" Aaran asked.

Bojo bent down and worked a small stone free from the border of the path. When he tossed it into the mist, they never saw it land on the other side.

"Where does it go?" Aaran asked.

"Damned if I know," the tinker said. "I guess into some between."

Aaran gave him a puzzled look. "Some between?"

"A space in between where we are and that forest we can see. It could be a few yards wide, it could be the width of a continent. It could drop us into the middle of an ocean or a volcano. Or it could just be an extension of this path we're following—a little detour of some kind."

"But we're sure that's the Wordwood?" Aaran asked.

"As sure as I can be without having a native of the place confirm it for us."

Aaran looked from him back into the mist.

"So I guess one of us should step through and find out for sure," he said.

"That's what we've been arguing about while we were looking for you," Christy said. "It's either step through into the unknown, or leave the path and try to find a way around."

"Which is also a big-time unknown," Raul put in.

Aaran turned to Bojo. "I guess you're the expert. What's your take on it?"

"I can't decide which way is the least dangerous."

"And while we're all standing here wondering about it," Aaran said, "who knows what's happening to the disappeared people, lost somewhere in there."

"Don't think that's not on our minds," Christy said.

"I wasn't saying it for that reason," Aaran told him. "I was just reminding myself." He glanced at Suzi, then shrugged. "I think one of us should follow the path, see where it goes, and I think it should be me."

Robert Lonnie

The hellhounds were travelling too fast to hide their trail, but it wouldn't have mattered if they'd had the time. Robert had developed such an awareness of them from all his years of avoiding their attention that he could have tracked them with his eyes closed and his fingers in his ears.

Their speed didn't help them either.

For every twist and turn they took, Robert knew a shortcut. When he finally caught up with them at another crossroads, he was there ahead of them, sitting on a low wall under the skeletal branches of a bare-limbed hanging oak, guitar on his lap, bones of those unfortunate enough to have been hung from the boughs above scattered among the clumps of dried grass by his feet. He waited until they burst through the rags of mist that surrounded the crossroads, let them get a look at him sitting there, calm and waiting, then he played some music for them.

The first chord dropped them to their knees.

The second chord snaked right into their heads and went rummaging around in their souls.

The third chord left them lying in the dirt as though they were dead.

Robert let that last chord echo and ring. When even the memory of it had faded, he finally laid his hand across the strings. He was about to stand up when a solitary clapping started up behind him.

Robert turned. There was a man leaning against the hanging oak, black-skinned and white-grinned, a gold cap sparkling on one of his front teeth. Like the hellhounds, he was dressed in a white shirt and black broadcloth suit, except he held a cane with an ivory head and had a tall top hat on his head. There was so little warning of his appearance, it was as though he'd stepped right out of the hanging tree. Knowing who this was, Robert wouldn't have been surprised if that had been the case.

"I didn't think you had it in you," the *loa* said.

"Didn't have what?"

"The balls to kill them."

"I haven't gone back on our bargain," Robert said. "They made the mistake of going after some friends of mine."

"I know that."

"And they aren't dead."

"I know that, too."

"I just took all the meanness out of them," Robert said.

"Which is pretty much the same difference as killing them," the *loa* said.

He pushed himself away from the tree and walked over to where Robert was sitting. His movements were stiff, as though there were only bones under that broadcloth suit—no muscle or flesh. He took his time lowering himself down to the wall beside Robert, using his cane to take the weight until he was settled.

"Not that I care," he added. "They were only under my protection if you killed them for yourself."

"Except I didn't kill them," Robert said. "All I did was take away the waste of their lives and give them a fresh start on things. Did them a favor, really."

The *loa* lifted a questioning eyebrow.

"Taking away their meanness," Robert said, "leaves them with less to work through in their next lives."

"Always thinking of others," the *loa* said.

"Well, I try."

The *loa* gave Robert another flash of that toothy grin of his. "And you're doing a fine job of keeping your soul out of my hands, too."

Robert shrugged. "Keeps me busy."

"But I'll have it in the end."

"I've never had an argument with that."

"You just haven't been in a hurry, either."

"Can you blame me?" Robert asked.

"I don't know," the *loa* said, answering what Robert had only meant as a rhetorical question. "I've never lived the way you do, so I've got no way of knowing if it's the kind of thing I'd want to hang onto or not."

Robert gave another shrug. "You hear people talk about immortality like it's a curse, but the way I see it, that only holds if you stop learning. I don't know that there's an end to what there is to find out in that world I'm living in."

"You're not immortal," the *loa* said.

"I'm working on it."

"I can make it happen."

Robert shook his head. "I've only got the one soul, and it's already sitting in that ledger book of yours, so there's nothing left to bargain with."

"Maybe I want you to do something for me."

"Isn't likely I'd be interested."

"You'd be surprised," the *loa* said. "You might find it of benefit to yourself, and I don't just mean me forgetting this engagement we've got concerning your soul."

Robert wasn't about to start working for him and they both knew it, just like they both knew he'd hear the *loa* out. He stifled the impulse to touch the strings of his guitar except to hold them still.

"So what is that you're proposing?" he asked.

"Interesting place, this Internet," the *loa* said.

"I wouldn't know."

"Then take my word for it. Interesting and busy."

"People have time," Robert said, "they do any damn thing with it except look out for each other."

"I suppose you're right. I don't know them as well as you do and it's not something I need to learn. But I'm learning about the Internet. I see a lot of spirits making a home for themselves in that place. It's getting to the point where if you need to contact one of *les invisibles,* all you've got to do is go on-line."

"You're right," Robert said, when the *loa* paused, and he felt he needed to at least indicate he was listening. "That is interesting."

"By which you mean, get to the point."

Robert shook his head. "I don't get a lot of time to sit around and yarn with someone like you. I'm enjoying this."

The *loa* gave him a considering look, them smiled. "Damn, if you're not telling the truth."

"So what's the Internet got to do with you?"

"Think about it," the *loa* said. "When people have a direct line to the spirits through a thing like that, there's not much need for an intermediary like me anymore."

"You really think it'll come to that?"

The *loa* shrugged. "Yes, no, maybe. It's hard to predict something that changes and grows as fast as technology. Ten years ago, mention the Internet and most people wouldn't know what you were talking about. Now everybody's getting on-line."

"Not me."

"Maybe you don't think so."

"What's that supposed to mean?"

The *loa* smiled. "See, the funny thing is, with all these spirits in the wires, the spiritworld's starting to bleed into the Internet. I can see a time— and I'm talking months, not even years here—when it's all going to be one big place."

Robert shook his head. "That's not going to happen."

"Turn a blind eye if you want, but it's already started."

Robert looked away, past the bodies of the hellhounds still lying in the dirt, to where he could catch glimpses of the world beyond the mists that pressed up against the edges of the crossroads. He'd see a shantytown, then the mists would shift, open to show him a hillside grey with rain, shift again and there was a graveyard.

He turned back to the *loa*. "What is it you're planning to ask me to do?"

"I just want to send a message," the *loa* said. "Take down one or two of the bigger spirits setting up house. Let everybody know that contacts between the worlds should be going through me."

"You've never had a monopoly on that sort of thing."

"Maybe not. Maybe that's what's wrong with the world. Maybe we need a little bit of order put back into it."

But Robert was shaking his head. "I'm not killing anybody—not for you, and especially not for my own gain."

"You don't even know the target."

"I'm not interested."

"Even when it was someone you were fixing to deal with anyway?"

Robert gave the *loa* a hard look. "What are you talking about?"

"The Wordwood spirit."

"What makes you think I'm interested in him?"

The *loa* laughed. "What makes you think I don't keep tabs on where you are and who you see? Oh, don't get that look. I play fair. I've never set anybody on your trail. And I'm patient—I can wait till you die. But surely you didn't think I wouldn't pay any attention to the doings of my investment?"

"I'm still not killing anybody for you."

The *loa* shrugged. "Did I use the word 'kill'? Maybe I just want you to play the meanness out of him, like you did with the hellhounds. Send that spirit back to wherever he came from. All I need is to send a message. The Wordwood spirit doesn't need to die for it to be understood."

"Why's he so important?"

"It's not so much that he's important," the *loa* said. "He's just so damn big."

Robert shook his head.

"I don't even need an answer," the *loa* told him before he could speak. "You just think on what we've been talking about when you're standing face to face with that spirit. Could be your need and mine will be the same. All I'm asking you to do is to consider it when the time comes."

"I don't know . . ."

The *loa* stood up, leaning on his cane.

"I'm not the bad guy," he said. "People come to me and I've got no say in what they do with the help I give them."

"I never said you were."

The *loa* nodded. "Just so we're clear on that. Remember, I didn't come looking for you, back when."

"I remember."

The *loa* gave another nod. He tipped a bony finger to the brim of his hat and turned away. Faster than should have been possible with his slow gait, he disappeared into the mists.

Robert sat there for a long time before he finally got up himself. It was time he looked into what kind of trouble the others had gotten themselves into while he was gone, see if he could help out.

He paused by the hellhounds. The one who'd been calling himself Maman was starting to stir. Robert knelt beside him as the big man's eyes fluttered open. He helped the hellhound sit up.

"Take it easy," he said.

"Where . . . where am I?" Maman asked.

"At the crossroads," Robert told him.

"But . . . how did I get here?"

Robert shrugged. "Don't really know. I just came upon you and your friends, lying here in the dirt. Are you going to be okay?"

The big man lifted a hand to his head. "I can't remember anything . . ."

Robert nodded. "How's that feel?"

"It's funny . . . it feels kind of good."

One of the other men made a groaning sound.

"Maybe you should see to your friend," Robert said.

When Maman turned to the other man, Robert stood up. He had stepped into the mists and disappeared by the time the big man looked back.

Christiana

That big eyelid lifts, the hidden gaze finds me, and it's an impossible moment. It's like a tree pulling up its roots to go walkabout. Like a mouth opening in a cliff face and speaking. Like a tidal wave rushing down the central concourse of a shopping mall on the commercial strip of some desert city. It already seems impossible enough that there could be the semblance of a man so immense—a giant statue, a land form in the shape of a sleeping man—but to know that he's alive, that his attention can focus on you . . .

Saskia gasps inside my head. My own pulse jumps into overtime, but it's not for the same reason that Saskia's so shocked. I'm as amazed as she is that the giant man is alive and aware of us, but when that eye opens and his gaze meets mine, I also recognize him. Not who he is, but what he is.

The realization is almost overwhelming. My legs feel weak, knees like jelly. His gaze pulls me in, and I'm about to go falling into the strange and immense mind that lies behind the eye, when the lid slowly droops, closes once more.

I take a steadying breath. I still feel like I need to lean against something.

<What is it, Christiana?> Saskia asks.

This is all wrong, I tell her.

<No kidding. The size of this guy. And when that eye opened, it was . . . I can't explain it, but it felt like we were going to be pulled right

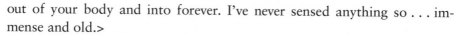

out of your body and into forever. I've never sensed anything so . . . immense and old.>

That isn't the Wordwood spirit.

<What are you talking about?>

I turn to the librarian. "That's a pretty old spirit," I say.

He nods. "And very powerful."

No kidding.

"Is this how he always manifests?" I ask.

"Oh, no," Librarius says. "As I told you before, until the virus struck, he was an invisible presence. He was *everywhere.*"

"And when the virus *did* strike?"

"First that body of water appeared, swallowing a few acres of the library. And then he came stumbling out of the water, dropping to the ground before he could get all the way up onto the shore. The impact when he struck was like a small earthquake. I was certain that the nearest bookcases were going to come tumbling down."

I turn to look at the collapsed giant once more.

<What's going on here?> Saskia asks. <What did you mean by saying this isn't the Wordwood spirit?>

It's a leviathan, I tell her.

I wish I had someone from the borderlands here to help me work this out. Mumbo or Maxie Rose. Or better yet, one of those scholars who would come to the parties at Hinterdale, clustered in gossiping coveys along the walls of the great ballroom in their black robes, arguing over obscure references that no one else would think of, and if they did, they wouldn't care. But that's exactly the kind of attention to detail I need right about now because I am so way out of my depth here.

<Okay,> Saskia says. <I know what "leviathan" means, but you're obviously using it in a context I don't understand. Unless you literally mean it's the spirit of a whale or some sea monster.>

No, no. The original leviathan are so much older, so much more incomprehensible than the word's come to mean.

<I'm not following you.>

Think of how the world came into being.

<Which version?>

The true version. How it was when Raven made the world.

<Can anybody even know the true version? I mean, every culture and religion's got its own take on it.>

I stifle a sigh and wonder what Librarius is thinking as I have this conversation inside my head. Because I know now that he's not the innocent administrator he's made himself out to be. But I don't want to turn to look at him. I want him to think I'm still mesmerized by the leviathan while I talk to Saskia.

<And besides,> Saskia is saying. <What does any of that have to do with what's going on here?>

The leviathan gave Raven the means to make the world—pieces of . . . I'm not sure exactly what. Themselves, I guess. Or the places where they come from. Some kind of energy that can be shaped into anything.

<Sounds like a lot of the world's concepts of God.>

I suppose. But the leviathan don't come from Heaven or Nirvana. They exist in some other place again. They're pure spirit and they shouldn't be here.

<Except this site *is* in the spiritworld.>

Yes, we call it that. And it is the place where people go when they dream, where spirits exist, but it's still a corporeal place. The home of the leviathan is somewhere deeper still, beyond physical matter.

<A spiritworld inside the spiritworld.>

Something like that. More like something that lies sideways or above or below any world in which the physical can manifest.

As I'm talking, some of the conversations I've had with the Hinterdale scholars are coming back to me. It's funny what you don't realize you remember until the information comes slipping up on you in a situation such as this.

The point, I tell her, *is that one of them shouldn't be here.*

<How do you even know this is a leviathan?>

I think of what Delian St. Cloud once told me when he and his brother Elwin were trying to explain the leviathan to me.

"If you should ever meet one," Delian said, in that distinct voice of his, half the scholar, half the amused gadabout, "and believe me, that's a thousand times less likely than Elwin acquiring a sudden penchant for women—you'll know. You'll just know."

I remember thinking it was a cop-out at the time—that neither of them really knew—but I understand now. There aren't words to describe what I met in this giant's eyes. But before I can relate any of this to Saskia, I hear the whisper of movement behind me.

Turning, I see Librarius stepping up to us. Behind him Saskia's body now lies on the floor beside one of those towering bookcases. Across the aisle from her is Jackson's chair, also settled on the ground. Poor Jackson looks a mental mess, staring at the leviathan more goggle-eyed than ever. I feel bad that he's got to go through all of this, tied up, on his own the way he is, but I can't spare the time to babysit him at the moment. Not with the suspicion I see taking shape in Librarius's eyes.

He tries to hide it, but I'm good at seeing through that sort of thing. Almost as good as I am at schooling my own features. I have such a good poker face that I can hardly ever get anyone together for a decent card game anymore.

"I learned something when the virus struck," he says. "A trick if you will."

I shake my head. "I'm not really interested. I'd rather know how you brought this spirit here."

"I told you, he has always been here. It was only when the virus struck that he manifested into what he is now."

"I don't buy it."

He shrugs. "It doesn't really matter what you believe. The truth is I've decided that you're not nearly as useful as I thought you might be. At least, not in your present condition."

I guess the sudden appearance of a blue-gold aura should have been the tip-off, but it takes me a moment to realize that he's starting up some spell. He begins to do something with his hands—the fingers twisting as he moves them through the air like some bad stage magician trying to distract you from what's really going on. I start for him, ready to do some damage. I've gone all the way from being totally in awe of him to wanting to give him a good smack in the head. But I should have moved more quickly. He speaks a word in no language that I know and it's like a lightning bolt strikes the top of my head.

I stand there vibrating, unable to move, every hair on my body standing on end, my eyes rolling back in my head. I feel like there's a hand inside my chest, rummaging around, trying to grab my spirit and pull it out of my body.

And then I get it—what he meant about this trick he learned from the virus. He's figured out how to remove the spirit without killing the body. I guess he watched how the virus short-circuited Saskia and drew only her body into this place.

But I can't imagine what use he has for *my* body . . . unless . . .

Unless he needs one to get out of here. If he's bound to this place, if he wants out . . .

And he does. I'm sure of it.

Saskia's body wouldn't work for him—originating as she did in the Wordwood—though I don't doubt he tried to use hers first. Maybe that's what that whole business with the glass coffin was all about. He must have been the prince that would give her the wake-up kiss, except she'd wake up with him inside her. The only reason he hadn't gotten to her before was because of the virus. He had to deal with the virus first. And then, I guess, he found out that he couldn't use her body.

But I'm different. I was born outside of the Wordwood and I didn't change like everybody else did when I got pulled into the site. He's probably thinking that I could be his ticket out.

There's only one problem, but he doesn't know it yet. There are two of us inside this body of mine.

<Let the spell take me,> Saskia says, and I realize that she's figured all of this out at the same time as I have.

But . . .

<There's no time to pull straws or argue,> she says. <Besides, this is *your* body—so you stay.>

So while I continue to struggle with the spell that's trying to rip me apart, she embraces it. There's this moment of confusion inside my head, then the pressure eases on me. The spell grabs hold of her, retreating from my body, pulling her out with it.

Everything snaps back into focus, but I pretend the spell worked and slump gracelessly to the ground, trying to land so that I don't get too hard a whack on my head. I shouldn't have worried. Librarius actually has the decency to catch me before my head hits the ground. Guess he doesn't want the goods damaged—not if he has to wear them.

He lowers me to the floor where I lie trying to figure out the best way to catch him off guard. I need a diversion and try to will Jackson to do something—anything—to attract his attention. But when the diversion comes, it's from a completely unexpected source, though maybe I should have figured this would happen when Saskia was pulled free. My eyes are slits. Through my lashes I see Librarius turn when he hears Saskia stir. I'm thinking it'll freak him, but it turns out he was expecting it.

"You see," he says to her. "I'm not entirely cruel. If I was, I wouldn't have provided your spirit with another place it can call home."

I don't know what Saskia's doing. Is she sitting up, everything back to normal? Or is she disoriented, trying to get her bearings?

It doesn't matter. All that matters is that she's providing the diversion I need.

I open my eyes wide, then rise soundlessly to my feet once I see that the librarian's back is to me. I guess this is where my boldness comes in handy. I don't even stop to think, I move in close to him and kick him from behind, the toe of my boot going between his legs right into where it hurts.

And what do you know? He's not a eunuch.

He doubles over and actually screams from the pain—not that I blame him. I kicked him hard, and I mean *hard*. But I'll give him this. He's not out for the count yet. Even hurting the way he is, that blue-gold aura of his starts to intensify. His fingers are still twitching. He's trying to spit out a word.

Can't let that happen.

I take down a nice heavy volume from the nearest shelf—an all-in-one volume of *The Golden Bough,* I note—and bash it against his head. It takes me three hits before he finally drops and lies still. My gaze lifts from him to where Saskia's sitting up, leaning for support against a bookshelf.

"Are you okay?" I ask.

There's no response except for a twitch of her lips. Her gaze tracks my voice, finds my face.

"You're in there, right?" I ask. "And everything's in working order?"

"G-give . . . me . . . a . . . minute . . ."

Her voice is raspy from disuse. I can tell that her vision's still swimming.

"Take all the time you need," I say.

I cross over to Jackson's chair and start to work on the buckles of the straps holding him in place.

"How about you?" I ask as I work the straps free. "Think you can stand?"

"Don't . . . know . . ."

He looks in bad shape, too, but I think he's coming back around, the shock starting to wear off. I get the last of the straps undone and he sits there, massaging where they'd rubbed against his skin.

"Is he . . . is he dead?" he asks.

I don't have to ask who.

"I don't know," I say.

I discover that the straps can be worked loose from the chair and I fuss with them until I've got all four free. I take them over to where Librarius is lying and set to work. I bind his wrists behind his back, then use another strap to bind his arms tight against his chest. The third goes around his legs. Tearing a piece of cloth from his shirt sleeve, I ball it up and stick it in his mouth, using the last strap to hold it in place.

"You think that can actually hold him?" Jackson asks.

I shrug. "Have you got a better idea? He seemed to need to move his hands and actually speak to get any magic done."

"But you said he was a god."

"No, I said he was a powerful spirit—*like* a god, but I was only using the word to give you some term of reference."

"But even a powerful spirit . . ."

"I know, I know," I tell him. "He'd still be way out of our league. But unless you can come up with something better, this is going to have to do."

"Throw him in the lake," Saskia says.

I turn to look at her. She seems all here now and back to normal—except for this sudden bloodthirsty turn of her mind. Maybe she's been hanging around inside my head for too long.

"We might still need him," I say.

"What for? He's the real cause of all our problems."

I shake my head. "I don't think he planned any of this. He just took advantage of how the virus screwed everything up."

"You still haven't said what possible use we could have for him."

Before I can frame a reply, never mind actually voice it, we hear a distant rumble. Not like thunder—it's more like the sound ice makes on a lake when it's cracking. Jackson's head whips around, his anxiety immediately flaring.

"What was that?" he asks.

I don't know why everyone thinks I've got the answers to anything.

"Beats me," I tell him.

I go over to where Saskia is and help her stand. I put her arm over my shoulder, my own around her waist, doing what I can to support her. She starts out kind of like dead weight, but as I walk her back to where Jackson's sitting, she quickly starts to improve.

"God, I'm thirsty," she says.

"There's a whole lake over there," Jackson says. I detect more than a touch of hysteria in his voice.

"I'm not drinking from that."

That rumbling crack comes again. It sounds closer, though it's hard to tell for sure. There are too many echoes. I leave Saskia half-sitting, half-leaning on the arm of the chair and turn my attention to the giant.

"We have to do something about the leviathan," I say.

They both look at me, puzzled.

"Its being here is all wrong," I tell them.

I can hear the voice of one of the St. Cloud brothers in my memory, answering my innocent question about what would happen if a leviathan were to appear in the physical world. They went on about cosmic balances and ruptures in space/time continuums which I didn't understand then any more than I'm able to make sense of now. I just remember that it would be a very, very bad thing.

"Our being here is all wrong, too," Jackson says.

He has a point. But I don't see that we can leave—even if we figure out how. We have to deal with the leviathan's presence. We have to make sure that Librarius doesn't get into some new kind of deviltry. We have to round up all the other people that were pulled into this site and try to find a way to get everybody home.

The rumble comes again, closer still. The echoes bounce off the ceiling, invisible in the dark somewhere above us. But this time it's followed by a weird gurgling sound. As one, we turn towards the lake and see the fissure that's appeared in the stone floor right at the shore. Water's pouring into it.

I guess the first thing we have to do, I realize, reassigning priorities, is figure out a way to stop this place from falling apart around us.

Christy

Aaran just keeps surprising me. He's acting so out-of-character, so *not* the cynical, self-serving Aaran Goldstein I've always known, that I can't help but wonder where Suzi's managed to trade him in for this new, improved version. It's either that or she's got to be a seriously effective role model herself.

Take the business with the little fairy man he stepped off the path to rescue. Or how right now he's offering to test whatever lies on the other side of the wall of mist before the rest of us go through. The old Aaran wouldn't have considered either of those courses of action as an option. He wouldn't have even stopped *to* consider them, never mind actually following through on one of them, unless there was some kind of profit in it for him.

"I don't think that's such a good idea," Bojo says in response to Aaran's offer. He turns away from where he's been studying the way the path continues on out of the mist to face us. "The last thing we want to do at this point is to split up."

"So everybody should take the risk?" Aaran says.

The tinker sighs. "Think about it. We don't know what's on the other side of the mist. More importantly, we don't know if, once we go across, we can even come back. Or if we *can* come back, if it'll be to this same place. So, let's say it is safe on the other side of the mist. What help is that to us if you can't come back to tell us?"

"But we don't know that."

"We don't know that it's unsafe, either," Bojo says. "That's why I've been saying that the decision we need to make is: Do we look for a way around, or do we continue on the path through the mist? Whichever way we choose, we should all go. And my vote is to stay on the path."

No one says anything for a long moment. The forest on the other side of the wall of mist draws our gazes. My memory holds the image of the pebbles Bojo threw earlier, the ones that never landed where the path continued on the other side of the mist. I'm not eager to find out where the pebbles went, but if that's the way to the Wordwood, then that's the way I have to go. I don't have a choice. Saskia's in there. And I suppose if I have to go, I'd just as soon have company. Especially Bojo's since he's the only one of us with any real experience in the otherworld.

"I'm with you," I tell him. "My vote also goes to staying together and following the path."

"Count me in, too," Aaran says.

"And me," Suzi says, then she frowns at Aaran and punches him on the arm. "I can't believe you thought you could leave me behind."

"It wasn't like that."

"What about you Raul?" Bojo asks.

"I've come this far," Raul says. "I'm not backing out now."

His gaze finds mine for a moment and I know just what he's thinking. His own lover's lost somewhere in there, just as mine is.

We turn back to the mist. It's so strange seeing that deep forest on the other side, knowing that when we step through, our feet will land in some *elsewhere*.

"Everybody hold hands," Bojo says. "Just for while we're going through. To make sure we all end up in the same place."

I have this sudden incongruous thought. I remember the galleys I was correcting when all of this started, how I never called Alan to tell him I'm going to be late turning them in.

"Christy?" Suzi says.

Her voice makes me blink and I'm back. I put out my hands. Suzi takes my left, Raul my right. We're strung out like beads on a necklace.

"Hold on tight," Bojo says.

Suzi's fingers press harder against my own as one-by-one we follow the tinker through the mist. I find myself doing the same to her and Raul.

Stepping through that wall of smoky grey air is one of the weirdest things I've ever felt. And following the others as they disappear before my eyes might be one of the bravest. I can't begin to describe the panic that tightens in my chest as I watch them go. Bojo, Aaran, Suzi. Then there's just an arm, free-floating in the air, gripping me hard, and it's my turn.

I don't want to go and it's all I can do to not dig in my heels, to pull free of Suzi's grip. But I force myself, wincing as Suzi's fingers are gone and now it's my own hand that's disappearing.

The mist doesn't so much touch my skin as go through my skin. It's like for one moment I'm myself, but I'm also the mist, all our molecules mingling. I hear a sound in my head like faint radio static. The temperature seems to drop ten degrees. I expected another bout of nausea, like when we first crossed into the spiritworld, but it's not like that at all. Instead I feel this intense, penetrating loneliness. An awareness that no matter how many people I surround myself with, in the end I'm alone in the universe.

Then I'm through, Raul right behind me.

For a long moment we all stand there on the other side, still holding hands, trying to see through the gloom. I feel like I have to learn how to breathe again, but at least that awful sense of isolation has eased. The air tastes stale, like in an old basement. There's just a hint of damp.

"Now that's something I don't want to make a habit of doing," Bojo says.

His voice breaks the spell that holds us. We let go of each other's hands and look around.

The light's poor, but once our eyes adjust, it's not as dark as it seemed when we first stepped through.

"Do you know where we are?" Raul asks Bojo.

The tinker shakes his head. "Somewhere underground."

As soon as he says it, I begin to really register our surroundings. We appear to be in a broad corridor or tunnel. The walls are brick, heavily patched with cement. The ground is a mess of rubble and junk: stones, pieces of brick, newspapers, and refuse of all kinds. I pick up the closest paper and squint at the words. Either the light's worse than it seems, or it's written in some language I've never seen before.

I look up, trying to see where the light's coming from. High up on the walls is a phosphorus glow. I can't see the roof. If the air wasn't so still and stale, I'd think there was only sky.

"Look at this," Suzi says.

She's moved a little further ahead and is pointing to what looks like a shelter of some kind: a crude lean-to, the supports made of obviously salvaged wood and covered with tarpaper and cardboard. Beyond it there's a whole village of lean-tos and cardboard shacks, running the length of either wall for as far as I can see.

"People live here?" Raul says.

"More like lived," Bojo says. "It doesn't look like anyone's been here for a while."

"But it's like a sewer."

"More like an old subway line," I say. I toe at the refuse underfoot. "We could probably find rails if we dug under this stuff. Or maybe it's like Old Town, back in Newford."

"Except nobody actually lives in Old Town," Aaran says. "Not since the quake dropped all those buildings underground."

"Are you so sure?" I ask.

Aaran gives me a weary look and shakes his head. "Come on," he says. "I suppose you're going to tell us about those goblins—what did you call them?"

"Skookins."

"Right. Are you trying to tell me they really live down there in Old Town?"

"That's what I've been told."

"And you've actually seen them?"

"No," I say. "But I've seen homeless people. It's safer than the Tombs because you don't get as many of the rougher elements down there—you know, the junkies and the bikers."

"What are you even doing down there?"

I give him a smile. "Looking for goblins."

Aaran shakes his head again.

"So what do we do now?" Raul asks. "Follow the tunnel?"

Bojo nods. "The path's still here. I can't see it, but I can feel it under all this crap."

I know we all have questions, starting with how can this tunnel even be here when all we could see through the mist was an old growth forest, but when Bojo sets off, we fall in behind him, just like we did when we first crossed over into the otherworld. This time Suzi and Aaran walk together behind the tinker, leaving Raul and me to take up the rear.

"You think we're actually going to find them?" Raul says after awhile. "All those people that disappeared."

He means, are we going to find his Benny.

I give him a quick glance. "We have to," I tell him. "Otherwise I'd go crazy."

"I feel like I already am crazy," he says, waving a hand to take in our surroundings. "All of this . . . all these different worlds . . ."

"Yeah, it's not like I thought it would be either."

"I don't know how Bojo makes sense of it all."

"It's what you get used to, I suppose," I say.

"Are you scared?"

I nod. "Though not as much for myself as I am for Saskia. That we won't find her. Or that we will, but . . ."

I can't finish the thought.

"I've been scared my whole life," Raul tells me. "Scared of pretty much everything, from the world at large to the kids beating on me back when I was growing up. I was a skinny little runt, always more interested in drawing than I was in sports or girls or hanging with the guys." He gives me a humourless smile. "They were calling me fag and fairy long before I actually realized my sexual orientation."

I think of Tommy Brown, this kid in junior high, and the chant of "Fairy, fairy, fucking fairy" that would follow him down the gauntlet of halls at the school. I didn't join in, but I didn't try to stop it. Nobody did. Of course I was having my own problems in those days, and not just with bullies, unless you can include your parents in that designation. They didn't treat Geordie or me any better than the kids in school did.

"I know what you mean," I say. "I didn't get to enjoy the golden days of boyhood either, except when I was by myself."

"Yeah, it's always easiest to be by yourself," Raul says. "But it's so damn lonely growing up like that, being on the outside looking in. Back then I'd have given anything to be able to get an erection from looking at a girl."

I have to smile. "I didn't have any trouble with that—not unless you count actually getting a girl to talk to you as part of the equation."

"You think that was tough?" Raul says, smiling with me. "How about having daydreams about the football team? Talk about your unrequited loves. One wrong word or look and they'd really have gone to town on me."

"I got beat up by a quarterback," I say, "but it was only because I was trying to make time with his cheerleader girlfriend."

"Which is acceptable. The law gets laid down, but you're okay because why *wouldn't* you want to score with his girlfriend?"

"Sure. Those guys loved having the girls everybody else wanted."

Raul nods. "Imagine what the quarterback would have done if it had been him you were trying to chat up."

"Your not doing it wasn't fear," I say. "It was just common sense. In those times . . ."

"I doubt it's all that different now."

"Probably not, more's the pity."

Raul shrugs. "But the funny thing is I'm not so scared now. I think it's because for the first time in our relationship, Benny needs me. For once our roles are reversed and he's the one that's counting on me to make everything right. I just hope I don't screw it up."

"We're doing everything we can."

"I know. But it still doesn't seem even close to enough."

I understand exactly how he's feeling.

The tunnel saps at our spirits. It's hard to see all these lean-tos and makeshift shelters, knowing that people have actually had to live like this. In some places they still do, under even worse conditions. Bojo can't explain where the tunnel exists—somewhere in between the worlds in a kind of borderland—but he says it echoes a real place in the World As It Is.

It's probably another half-hour of trudging through the litter and rubble before we see a different light, far ahead of us in the gloom. As we get closer, we hear a sound that it takes me a moment to recognize. Then I realize what it is. Rain.

Another few minutes brings us to the end of the tunnel and for a long moment we stand there under our shelter, looking out at a rain-drenched forest. I don't know if it's the same one we saw through the mist, or another one. It might just be a different view of that first one we saw. The rain falls heavy and steadily, the kind that would soak you to the skin in minutes if you were caught out in it. The leaves of the trees are all slick and dripping. The air smells so good—earthy and wet. The path that we haven't been able to see emerges from the rubble and junk underfoot and heads off under the trees.

"Is that the Wordwood?" Suzi asks.

Bojo nods. "Or at least it has the feel of that spirit. Let's rest up here for a few minutes. Maybe if we're lucky the rain will ease off."

I'm not happy about the idea—I can hear that clock ticking in my head—but everyone else seems in favor of a break, so I don't say anything. But once we do stop, I find my own body betraying me—all those days of sitting at my computer haven't prepared me for the long hours of hiking that we've already put in today. My calves and thigh muscles are aching. The small of my back and my shoulders breathe their own sigh of relief when I remove my backpack and set it on the ground.

We find places to sit in the mouth of the tunnel and break out granola bars and trail mix, washing them down with bottled water. There's not much conversation. Mostly, we watch the rain come down, listening to the steady drum as it hits the ground. I look into those dark, wet woods and think of how Jilly's always talking about the journeys the characters make in fairy tales, how their passage through the dark woods is an analogy for the struggle one has to go through to reach one's goal.

Right about now, I think I'd rather have an analogical wood than the real one waiting for us in the rain.

After a moment I pull out my cigarettes and shake one out. Light it. I see there are only a couple left in the pack and who knows where the nearest corner store is? Looks like I'll be giving up the habit again.

"How do you think Robert's doing?" Raul asked after a time.

Bojo shrugged. "Robert seemed to me to be the kind of man who can take care of himself."

"But those guys . . . the hellhounds . . ."

Bojo gives a slow nod. "Yes, I know. I've seen their kind many times before. Town sheriffs and tavern bullies. And those three were not only large and strong. They had real power to back up their threat." He hesitates for a moment, then looks around at us. "I have something to confess," he says after a moment.

I get a sinking feeling hearing those five words and my imagination goes into overtime, thinking of all the terrible things the tinker might be about to tell us.

"I remember the old stories from when I was young," Bojo says, and then he smiles as though we've caught him out at something. "Oh, I don't mean from books. I'm not much for reading now and was even less so then. But when I was a boy, there were always stories being told around the campfires and in the wagons, and like any boy, I was eager to hear them.

"They weren't about the heroes and kings like you might expect. They were about ordinary folk, usually tinkers like ourselves. What I liked the most were the stories about my namesake, Borrible Jones. Among the tribes, there are whole story cycles about him."

"Are we about to get another origin for your name?" Raul asks.

Bojo chuckles. "No, but it's interesting in that among other things, my

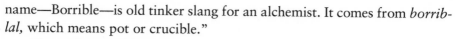
name—Borrible—is old tinker slang for an alchemist. It comes from *borrib-lal*, which means pot or crucible."

"So you're an alchemist?"

"No. But supposedly the Borrible Jones of story was. He was also a soldier of fortune, an itinerant musician, a wizard, and any number of other occupations, depending on the need of the particular story. But mostly he was a kind of Trickster, though I suppose saying he was a tinker is saying enough since there's a bit of the Trickster in every tinker."

"Does any of this have to do with your confession?" Aaran asks.

"Yes, no." Bojo sighs again. "It's just that I feel I've been leading you all on. You see, I'm no expert in any of this." He waves a hand out toward the forest. "It's not that I'm unfamiliar with spirits or the otherworld—I've spent the better part of my life travelling these roads among them. But I know about as much about dealing with one of these old spirits as any of you do."

My heart sinks. I thought between him and Robert, we had a chance. Then we went and lost Robert. . . .

"Then why *did* you offer your help?" Raul asks.

"Because of Holly." He ducks his head a moment, then looks at us. "I'm . . . interested in her and I suppose I wanted to impress her, so when she first mentioned her troubles, I promised her I'd help. The one thing a man shouldn't do is go back on his word."

"Well," Suzi says, "if you had to confess something, I'm glad that's all it is."

Bojo gives her a surprised look. "All? Don't you understand? *None* of us are prepared to go up against a being as powerful as the Wordwood spirit appears to be. But I let you believe that I had a solution."

Suzi smiles. "Well, you could have said you were in league with the spirit, and we were all your captives or something. Or that you've been deliberately leading us in the wrong direction."

"I would never do that."

"And," she goes on, "I think it's kind of sweet that you'd be doing all of this just because you have a crush on Holly, who seems very cute, by the way."

"I don't know what it is," Bojo says, "but it came on me like it never has before—just hit me from the first moment I saw her through the door of her shop. It was all I could do not to simply take her in my arms, right there and then."

"Just as well you didn't," Suzi says. "We like a little courtship."

"Of course," Bojo says. "But the way it came over me so suddenly was a curious thing, nevertheless. It's not as if I haven't met other attractive women before." He gives her a grin. "Like you, for instance."

Suzi laughs, but I see Aaran bristle at her side and realize that Bojo, Raul, and I aren't the only ones doing this for love. And it also explains Aaran's complete change of personality over the past day or so. Love begs changes from us—it can be as small a thing as our taste in music, to everything we are.

"Easy, cowboy," Suzi tells Bojo. "Don't waste that tinker charm on me."

With the riddle of Aaran's involvement solved—I never quite took to his claim that he just wanted to make amends—that leaves only Suzi's presence unexplained and gives me a new puzzle to worry at.

"The rain's letting up," Raul says.

He's right. The downpour's eased to a misting rain. Bojo stuffs his water bottle and the wrappers from his food back into his pack. He stands up and shoulders his pack.

"Good," he says. "It's time we were back to doing rather than talking."

I get to my feet as well, feeling nowhere near as spry as the tinker seems to be. I start to bend down to get my own backpack when we hear a loud rumbling in the sky overhead.

Thunder, I think. Not so odd, considering the rain we had earlier. Looks like we're in for another downpour.

But then the ground trembles in an echo to the thunder—enough that I have to hold out my arms to keep my balance. I hear the sound of shifting rocks and we all look back down the tunnel.

"Out, out!" Bojo cries.

He grabs Raul's arm and steers him to the mouth of the tunnel. Thunder booms once more and again we feel the ground shake. This time it knocks me down to one knee. I hear the grinding of stone from deeper in the tunnel and an ominous crack. I picture a fissure opening in the ground, racing toward us.

"Move!" Bojo calls to us.

I don't need to be told. I'm back on my feet, helping Aaran to his. Suzi grabs the backpack that Holly gave them and then the rest of us scramble out of the tunnel and into the rain to where Raul and the tinker are waiting for us. We only just get outside before there's another rumble of thunder, except this time it comes from the tunnel. We run for the trees. When we get under the canopy, I turn to look back. I'm just in time to see the mouth of the tunnel collapse in a deafening crash, spitting rubble and debris out onto the grass where we were standing a moment ago.

The misting rain puts a sheen on our faces and starts to work its way into our clothes. My hair's already wet and lying flat against my head. But all I can do is look at where the mouth of the tunnel had been. If we'd hesitated a moment longer, we'd be buried under that mountain of debris.

It's a long moment before anybody speaks.

"Jesus," Raul finally says. "That was too close."

Aaran nods. "But at least we all got out in time."

That's when we hear another rumble like thunder, and the fissure I imagined when we were in the tunnel comes snaking out of the rubble, darting to the left just before it reaches us. We all grab tree boughs and each other to keep our balance. We stare at where the ground has opened up, stare down into some unimaginable depth that wasn't there a moment ago.

"What . . . what's going on?" Suzi says.

"It's this world," Bojo says. "The Wordwood. It's collapsing."

There's another rumble and another fissure opens from the side of the one in front of us.

Nobody waits. As one, we turn and bolt into the forest, following the path.

Holly

Holly came back from walking the dog to find the bookstore empty. She wasn't surprised, although she had left Geordie and Dick on the main floor not fifteen minutes ago, sorting through and filing the new arrivals that had come in yesterday, before all of this began. She didn't bother to see if they'd gone upstairs to the apartment. Letting Snippet off her lead, she followed the little dog down the stairs to the basement where, as she expected, she found them sitting side by side on the bottom riser. The hob's toes just touched the basement floor, while Geordie's knees were raised high enough that he could comfortably rest his chin on them. They studied the blank wall that hours ago had been a portal into the otherworld. Now it was simply concrete once more.

Snippet squeezed in between the pair and went to sniff at the wall before returning to the stairs where she waited for Geordie to pay some attention to her.

"Watching that wall's not going to bring them back any quicker," Holly said.

Geordie nodded. He reached out and tousled the stiff hair between Snippet's ears.

"I know," he said. "But they've been gone so long."

It was well past midnight by now, closing in on two. The streets outside had been quiet while Holly took Snippet out to do her business. Holly liked to refer to it as Snippet "checking her pee-mail."

"It just seems like a long time," she told Geordie. "It's actually only been a few hours. We have to be patient—they could be gone for days."

"I know. Maybe we should have gone with them."

Holly sat down on the stairs a few risers above them. She thought about her friends, trapped somewhere in a world on the other side of that wall. Of the handsome tinker that she'd hardly gotten to know, gone looking for them with Christy, one of her best friends.

"Maybe we should have," she said.

"Oh no, Mistress Holly," Dick said. He turned to look at her, his broad face earnest. "It's too dangerous a place for the likes of us."

Geordie gave a short humourless laugh. "Well, doesn't that make me feel better about how the others are doing."

Dick got a horrified look. "Oh, I didn't mean—"

"That's okay," Geordie told him. "I know what you meant. We knew it was dangerous going in, but it wasn't like we had a choice. Somebody had to go."

"But the waiting's hard," Holly said.

"The waiting's really hard," Geordie agreed. "And I guess what has me worried the most is that it's not just the otherworld that they've gone into. There's also this whole business with Web sites. I mean, I can barely get my head around the idea that they can have a physical presence in the otherworld."

Holly nodded. She understood exactly what he was feeling.

"But if we accept that it's possible," Geordie went on, "then that means that part of Christy's and the others' safety is dependant upon computers, and I don't know about you, but I'm not exactly overjoyed with that idea. I mean, think about it. The damn things seem to crash if you just blink at them wrong. Would you trust your life to one? And that's without even adding magic into the equation."

"The Wordwood was always stable," Holly began.

"Until a virus took it down," Geordie said.

"You're not making me feel any better."

"I'm sorry, but this is just eating at me. When it comes to computers, you don't even need outside glitches like a virus to screw things up. Just think about what it's like when you're trying to install some new piece of software. You can do it ten times in a row and it's only on the tenth that it actually works, though nothing's changed and you've been following the exact same procedure each time. Magic doesn't even have to be there to screw things up, but we *do* have magic."

"Yes," Dick agreed. "Computers are very dangerous and home to pixies and goblins and every manner of unseelie creature."

Geordie sighed. "You see what I mean?"

"But there's nothing we can do," Holly said. "Is there?"

When Geordie shook his head, she turned her attention to Dick.

"I don't know anything about computers, Mistress Holly," Dick said.

Having had the hob as a roommate for more than a year now, Holly knew when he was being evasive. She could tell that he knew something, but just didn't want to say it.

"And?" Holly prompted him.

Dick wouldn't look at her. "Oh, don't ask me, Mistress Holly."

"Dick!"

"It's . . . it's just . . ."

"Just what?"

The hob looked miserable.

"Another kind of dangerous," he finally said.

Geordie was about to say something, but Holly held up a hand to stop him. By now, she'd become used to coaxing Dick to tell what he didn't want to share.

"And what kind of dangerous is it?" she asked.

Dick sighed. "Talking to Mother Crone kind of dangerous."

"That's her name?"

"No. You should know by now, Mistress Holly, that names hold power. Never give a fairy your real name. You'll notice that they only ever give you their *use* names."

Holly gave him a nervous laugh. "I haven't actually met enough fairies to be able to judge that. And I think I'm just as happy to leave it that way. Fairies and me seem to spell trouble—present company excluded, of course."

Dick nodded.

"So, *use* names," Holly went on. "I guess they're kind of like user names on a computer."

As Dick gave her another nod, she thought of Bojo with all the different origins of his name, depending on who he was talking to.

No, she told herself. She shouldn't think about him, because that just led to the confusing welter of the immediate attraction she'd felt for him when he came to her door; the fact that he and the others were gone, most likely into some terrible danger; and the worry that she might never see him again . . .

"So, why should we talk to this Mother Crone?" she asked Dick.

"She's a seer. She might be able to help us—for a price."

"Why does there always have to be a price?"

"I don't know, Mistress Holly. There just does."

"I wonder if it's a good/bad fairy thing," Holly said. "When Meran helped us, she didn't want anything in return."

"What kind of price would Mother Crone want?" Geordie asked.

"I don't know that, either," the hob said. "I just know that the bigger the favour, the more dear the price will be."

"Maybe this Mother Crone can tell us why there's always got to be this trade-off," Holly said.

"Oh no," Dick said. "You mustn't ask her questions the way you do me. Most of your Good Neighbours have no patience for them and consider prying to be an insult."

Holly nodded. "I won't pry," she assured the hob. "So tell me, where can we find her?"

"At the mall."

"At the mall?" Geordie said.

Holly had to laugh. "Well, it stands to reason, doesn't it? If there are going to be pixies on the Internet, why not a seer at the mall?"

"Which mall?" Geordie asked. "The Williamson Street Mall?"

Holly knew why he'd picked that one. It was the oldest one in the city and it stood to reason that if some old fairy seer lived in one of their malls, it would be in the oldest one they had.

But Dick shook his head. "No. She lives in the new one up on the highway." He turned an anxious face to Holly. "But you have to understand, Mistress Holly. Someone like Mother Crone uses a widdershins magic. No good can come of it in the long run."

"But you think she could help."

"If she doesn't turn us all into toads."

Holly shivered. "She can do that?"

"Someone like Mother Crone can do that and more," the hob said. "It's why going to her is a last resort."

"Well, I think we've pretty much entered last resort territory, don't you?" Holly looked from Dick to Geordie. "I mean, look at where we stand. We have a Web site that's gone feral and has swallowed a big chunk of the people using it, including a whole bunch of our friends. Christy and the others could be lost forever by now, for all we know. And then the real magic worker we had on our side has gone chasing big scary men and still isn't back."

"Meaning, Robert," Geordie said.

Holly nodded. "The bottom line is, we're now down to three and not one of us really has a clue as to what's going on or what we should do next. So I'm ready to talk to some seer."

Geordie nodded.

"What should we bring to give her?" Holly asked. "I've probably got a couple of hundred dollars in petty cash. Or maybe she'd like a book . . . ?"

"It will probably be something more personal that that," Dick told her. "A favour, to be called in later."

"What kind of favour?"

"I don't *know*."

"It's okay," Holly said. "I know this is upsetting you and I'm sorry. But you see where we're going crazy doing nothing?"

The hob nodded. "Just remember," he said. "Being around widdershins magic puts your shadow behind you, out of your sight where anyone can steal it. So if you do nothing else, keep a good hold of it."

Holly blinked in confusion. "My shadow? You mean like Christy was talking about earlier?"

Dick shook his head and pointed to where the basement light was casting her shadow on the stairs behind her.

"That shadow," he said. "The one that guards the door to your soul."

"Now I'm really confused," Holly said. "How am I supposed to hold onto it? There's nothing to grab."

"It's more that you have to stay aware of it," Dick explained. "Even if you can't see it, remember that you have one and imagine what it's like, how it stretches from you, dark against the light."

"Because if we don't . . . ?" Geordie asked.

"Some errant spirit could use it to step into your body."

Holly sighed. "Lovely."

"So you've changed your mind?" Dick asked, hope rising in his voice. "We can stay here and wait for the others to get back?"

Holly shook her head. "You can. Just tell me how to find Mother Crone once I get to the mall."

Geordie stood up and smoothed his jeans down where they were bunching at his knees.

"I'm coming, too," he said.

"Oh, why is it always the one thing or the other?" Dick said, standing up as well.

"You don't have to come," Holly said.

"But I do. You'd never find her on your own, Mistress Holly."

"Okay. We can go now, right? Even though the mall's closed for business?"

"Nothing is ever closed to fairies," Dick told her.

As Holly started up the stairs, Snippet went scrabbling by her, claws clicking on the wooden risers.

"What about Snippet?" she asked Dick. "How's she going to know that she's supposed to keep thinking about her shadow?"

"She should stay here in the store," the hob told her. "Not all fairies like dogs the way I do."

That managed to pull a small smile from Holly. It wasn't so much that Dick and Snippet didn't get along. But they didn't exactly seek out each other's company either. It also told her that Dick was reasonably certain that they wouldn't be gone for long.

Woodforest Plaza, situated in the southeast corner of where Richards Road intersects Highway 14, had once been the shopping centre pride of the city's northern suburbs. But early last year, developers had bought up the farmlands north of Richards Road, leveled the fields, including a sixty-year-old crow roost, and before you could say "shop till you drop," they had constructed a two-storied glass and concrete shopping centre so big that it could easily be its own small town. There were certainly people who spent their whole days there, from when the doors opened first thing in the morning until they finally closed at night.

Geordie drove Christy's old Dodge wagon around the Cineplex at the south end of the mall to the shipping bays in the back. He pulled into a parking spot by the eight-foot retaining wall that had been constructed to keep the still-untouched farmlands at bay. When he turned off the engine, they all got out. The banging of the car doors when they were closed seemed loud and to echo forever.

"This is creepy," Holly said. "I've never liked shopping centres at night. There's just something about these huge empty parking lots that doesn't seem right."

Geordie nodded. "I used to have a friend that lived on one of the farms that's now somewhere under all this concrete. I think it was over there, by the grocery store."

"And that's another thing," Holly said. "All those old farms gone—plus the roost."

"Yeah, the crow girls were really ticked off about that. Someone told me that, after it happened, they stole one of those huge cement mixer trucks, drove it to the home of one of the developers, and dumped the whole load of wet cement in his living room. But I don't know. There was never anything in the news about it."

He turned to Dick, who was standing close to the car. The hob's already large eyes seemed bigger than ever as he stared at the folding metal doors of the closest shipping bay. New as the mall was, the door was already covered with graffiti.

"Where do we go?" Geordie asked him.

The hob pointed to the doors. "In there."

"Okay. So what do we do? Just go up and knock on them or something?"

"Or something," Dick said.

Squaring his little shoulders, he set off across the parking lot, the leather soles of his shoes clicking softly on the pavement. Holly and Geordie exchanged glances, then followed the hob.

Holly wasn't sure what she expected when they reached the metal doors. She had little enough experience with magic or fairies, for all that she had a hob for a partner in the bookstore. It wasn't as though Dick's friends came by for a visit—at least they never came around when she was there—and Dick never did anything more magical than his bit where he sat so still he became invisible. So when the hob laid his hand on a part of spray-painted spiral, opening a portal like the one that had opened in her basement, she let out a gasp.

"Is . . . is that the otherworld?" she asked.

Dick shook his head. "It's just a bodach door to take us inside the mall."

"Right. And a bodach is?"

"Like me, a hob. Or like a brownie."

Geordie was still looking at the big metal door.

"Doesn't the iron in the metal bother you?" he asked.

"No, Master Geordie. I've lived among men too long for it to trouble me the way it would my country cousins." He started to step through, then paused, looking at them. "Are you coming?"

"Right, um, behind you," Holly said.

She closed her eyes as she stepped into what her mind still told her was a great big solid metal door, but her hands met no obstruction and then she was inside, Geordie behind her. When she opened her eyes, she saw that they were in a receiving facility of some sort. It must be for one of the department stores, she decided, because all around them were stacks and stacks of cardboard boxes holding everything from kettles to lawnmowers.

Dick took her hand.

"Come on, Mistress Holly," he said. "Mother Crone is supposed to hold court in the main courtyard. Where the swans fly."

It took Holly a moment to understand what he was talking about. Then she remembered the sculptures of the great white birds hanging from the big domed ceiling by the mall's central doors, their long necks stretched out, metal wings outspread, as they appeared to soar across the vault of the dome. She couldn't recall how many there were—a fairy-tale seven?

Dick led them to the far side of the warehouse and out into a hallway that eventually took them into the mall itself. Holly had always thought that it might be fun to have the run of one of these places at night, but right now it felt as creepy as the empty parking lot outside. Plus all the individual stores were locked up, so it wasn't like you could go rummaging around in them or anything.

"Do you hear something?" she asked as they walked down the cavernous hallway toward the central court.

They walked by shuttered carts, wooden benches, waste dispensers and small temporary kiosks, locked up for the night. Their reflections, caught in the windows of the dark stores, kept pace on the other side. Holly glanced behind her, looking for her shadow. Because the light came from above, it was pooled around her feet. But still there.

"It's music," Geordie said. "Something with a hip-hop beat."

Holly nodded. At first she'd thought it might be coming from the mall's sound system. She supposed there was no reason for them to turn the Muzak off at night. But then she realized it came from further up the hallway, growing steadily louder as they approached the courtyard.

"It's revel music," Dick said.

Holly was about to ask what he meant, but then she could see them ahead of her, figures of all shapes and sizes dancing to the music, and from their enthusiasm, the word "revel" became pretty much self-explanatory. It was only when they got right to where the hallway spilled into the courtyard that she saw that the source of the music was a prosaic boombox. Considering the dancers, she would have expected it to be far more exotic: some sort of outlandish elfin creatures creating the music live, rather than having it come from a simple recording.

But the dancers made up for the mundane source of the music.

There were little people half Dick's size that seemed to be made of twigs and moss and grass, although here and there she spied a few similar creatures that looked to be made of wiring, with sparkplug noses and circuitry board torsos.

There were tall men and women with pointed ears, dressed in stately gowns and Victorian waistcoats and suits. Others the same size in rough fabrics with vests and cloaks that were as much leaves and moss and feathers as they were cloth. Others still, in skateboarders' baggy cargo pants and T-shirts.

There were beings that seemed as much animal as human. Gangly monkey creatures with bird-like features. Tubby pumpkin bodies topped with the faces of raccoons and badgers. Straw-thin beings with lizard and snake faces.

There were creatures that Holly recognized from the illustrations of fairy-tale picture books. Goblins and brownies and pixies, and even what seemed like a small trow dressed in rustic browns and greens, with a nose too big and legs too squat and short.

There was, in short, every sort of fairy that Holly had ever imagined, and many she couldn't have begun to. But one thing they had in common: they were all light-footed and graceful—even the stiffest looking of them, which was a creature that appeared to be nothing so much as an ambulatory log with spindly arms and legs and a face that pushed out of the bark at the top. And they were quiet on their feet.

Holly spied soft-soled slippers and running shoes and bare feet, which might have explained the quiet to some degree, but surely there should have been some sound. Whispers and scuffles, the slap of a bare foot on tile or even the faint pad of paws. But the soft-stepping fairy revelers made no sound at all when they moved. There was only the music, the infectious groove of a hip-hop beat that seemed to allow for any kind of dancing, from ballroom to break, all of which were evident.

The revelers completely ignored them until Dick cleared his throat. Then the music continued, but all the dancers stopped and turned to look in their direction. Finally a little twig and leaf girl standing close to the boombox, her vine-like hair pulled back into a thick Rasta ponytail, reached over and turned off the music. Utter silence fell over the courtyard and they were looking into the dozens of fairy gazes turned in their direction.

At that moment Holly felt very exposed and not a little afraid. There was something about the eyes of the fairies that woke a shiver at the base of her spine, that had the hairs standing up on her arms and at the nape of her neck. There was nothing threatening about them—not yet, at least—but nothing human either. They were cat eyes and hare eyes and bird eyes. They were the eyes of wild things, but a sharp, knowing intelligence burned in them as they did in no ordinary animal.

"Well," someone said, breaking the tableau. "I've been expecting you."

She came walking through the crowd, a tall woman with her dark hair hanging halfway to her waist in a dozen or so thick braids. Holly couldn't figure out why she hadn't noticed her among the dancers earlier, she was such a striking woman, with her piercing gaze and fine-boned, narrow features. She wore black cargo pants, platform sneakers, and a tank top that was sized so small it lay like paint against her skin and bared her midriff.

"You . . . have?" Holly managed to get out. "But how could you know we'd be coming?"

"She's Mother Crone, Mistress Holly," Dick said.

"*You're* Mother Crone? But you don't look at all . . ."

Holly let her voice trail off.

"Cronish?" the woman said.

Standing in front of her, the woman towered over Holly.

"I guess," Holly said. "I was going to say 'old.' "

Mother Crone smiled. "It's only a name. You're not made of holly, are you?"

"Well, no . . ."

Though right at this moment, Holly wouldn't have been surprised to find that she was, in fact.

"Why were you expecting us?" she asked.

"I'm a seer."

"Oh, right," Holly said. "Of course."

Mother Crone laughed. "But that said, I'll admit that I only knew someone was coming. Not who, or what you might want from me."

She lowered herself so that she was sitting cross-legged on the floor—a quick, graceful movement that made it appear as though she'd simply floated down. Holly hesitated a moment, then took a seat on the floor herself, although she didn't feel nearly so graceful doing it. Geordie and Dick sat down on either side of her.

"So tell me how I can help," Mother Crone said.

The fairy woman seemed so friendly that Holly had to wonder why

Dick had been nervous about coming here. Then she remembered how he'd been around Meran, who he thought was a princess of some fairy wood.

"Don't be shy now," Mother Crone added.

Holly started, realizing that she let her thoughts drift. She gave Dick a quick glance, but he seemed to be content to leave everything in her hands. Great. And then she remembered something else he'd said about Mother Crone. Better get that out of the way first.

Holly cleared her throat. "Um, could you tell me what the price will be?"

"I need to know the problem first."

"Oh, right. Well, it's a little complicated."

"By the time a problem comes to me, it usually is," Mother Crone said. "It's best to start at the beginning."

So Holly did—but not right at the beginning, all the way back to when pixies had first come stepping out of her computer monitor. Instead, she started with Aaran Goldstein getting his friend Jackson to send a virus to the Wordwood, backtracking a little to explain her own connection to the Web site, then outlining the high points of all that had befallen since.

Mother Crone listened well, asking few questions, and then only to clarify something that Holly hadn't properly explained. But when Holly was done, she cocked her head and gave Holly a puzzled look.

"I understand the problem now," she said, "and it certainly is a messy one. What I don't understand is why you've come to me for help."

"Well, it's just that Dick . . ."

Holly gave the hob a glance and saw a look she knew well; it was the one where the last thing in the world he wanted was to have what he considered some higher class of fairy pay any sort of attention to him.

"I thought you might give us some advice," Holly finished. "You know, as to what we can do to help."

"Hmm."

Mother Crone glanced over her shoulder and singled out one of the little circuit and wire men.

"Edgan," she said "Do you know this place that our guest is talking about?"

The little man nodded. He scurried off, opening a bodach door in a nearby computer store. He returned with a laptop under his arm and set it down on the floor. While he got it up and running, the fairy with the Rasta ponytail who had been operating the boombox approached Mother Crone, handing her a wooden bowl and a plastic bottle of water.

"Thank you, Hazel," Mother Crone said.

Holly watched in fascination as Edgan pulled a credit card-sized circuit from out of the tangle of wiring and circuitry that was his chest. He stuck it in the PCMCIA slot of the laptop and pulled a little aerial out of the card. His narrow wire fingers danced on the laptop's keyboard, then he looked up.

"Here it is," he said.

Holly leaned forward so that she could see what was on the screen. All that was visible was the "This page cannot be displayed," message that they'd been getting ever since the virus had taken the site down, but Mother Crone gave a thoughtful nod.

"Better disconnect it," she said.

The little man hit a key, then removed the PCMCIA card from the slot and inserted it back into his chest. Holly blinked—that was just *so* weird—and turned her attention back to Mother Crone. The seer set the wooden bowl on the floor between Holly and herself. Untwisting the top from the water bottle, she poured the contents of the bottle into her bowl.

"Did . . . did you see something?" Holly asked. "On the computer screen?"

"Not exactly. Just enough to know that there's something very wrong there. I'm not much good at scrying with technology. But now that I have a touchstone to that place, I can use this—" She indicated the bowl of water. "—to look in on it through more traditional means."

Holly was beyond surprise by this point. "Will you be able to see our friends?" she asked. "Can you tell us how they are?"

"I can try," Mother Crone replied, which promised nothing.

She moved a hand over the water and a ripple in the water followed the motion, back and forth across the surface. Lifting her hand, she studied the water as it stilled.

"Hmm," she said.

Holly leaned forward as well but saw nothing, only water in a bowl.

"What do you see?" Holly asked.

The seer made no response. She pursed her lips, all of her attention on whatever invisible drama was being enacted on the surface of the water in her bowl. When she finally looked up, her gaze was troubled.

"I'm sorry," she said.

Holly's chest went tight. "Why? What is it?"

"There is . . ." She looked away, her gaze going inward. "I'm not sure how to explain," she went on when she focused on Holly once more. "Do you know much about the otherworld, how it isn't one place so much as many places—a patchwork of worlds, some large some small, but all connected like some enormous quilt?"

"Vaguely . . ."

"And that this Internet site has become one of those worlds?"

Holly nodded. "That's what—I can't remember who. I think it was Christy who figured that out."

Mother Crone gave a slow nod. "This Wordwood is closed from the rest of the otherworld at the moment and it's a good thing. There is something in it—I can't say exactly what. I just know that it's old, and it's dying. And as it's dying, it's taking the Wordwood with it. Or perhaps it's the Wordwood itself that is dying, taking everything inside it along with it. All I know for sure is that it's too late to do anything about it now."

"But our friends . . . ?"

"What's this thing inside?" Geordie asked.

Mother Crone turned to him. "I don't know. Something ancient. Something I've never met or seen before, though there are stories about its kind."

"And it's evil?"

She shook her head. "It's neither good nor evil on its own. But it's very powerful."

"I guess it doesn't matter," Geordie said, "whether it's the Wordwood or this spirit that's dying. We just have to get hold of the others and get them out of there. . . ."

His voice trailed off as Mother Crone shook her head.

"You won't help us?" he said. "Just tell me the price."

"It's not a matter of price."

"That's my brother in there. Our friends."

Mother Crone sighed. "I know. I understand. But to open any gate into that world at this time means allowing whatever's happening inside loose into the rest of the otherworld. I won't be responsible for that."

"But—"

"Would your friends . . . would your brother want to live at the cost of the death of the millions that would die in the otherworld if whatever this thing is gets loose? And that's saying you could even do anything at this point." She pointed at her scrying bowl. "All I sense in that world is the ancient one. We don't even know if there's anybody else even alive in there at the moment."

"But we can't just abandon them all."

Holly saw the pain in Mother Crone's eyes. "Yes, I know. Hundreds have been lost. But unless we leave the struggle contained as it is, it could truly be millions. It might even spread into this world."

Holly thought she was going to be sick. Geordie stood up beside her. For a moment she thought he was going to hit someone, but instead he stalked off to the glass windows that overlooked the mall's parking lot. He stood there, looking out into the night, his fists clenched at his side.

"I'm so sorry," Mother Crone said.

Holly gave a slow nod. "I . . . I understand. Not what's going on. But why you can't—why we can't do anything. But it's hard to just stand by . . ."

"There is nothing harder than a moment like this," the seer said. "When you would give anything to help those you love, but there is absolutely nothing that can be done."

Holly gave another nod. She wished they'd never come. Better to have stayed at the store, living with ignorance and the hope that ignorance allowed, than to have to deal with this awful feeling.

"There's got to be something we can do," she said, knowing there was nothing. "Someone we can talk to."

Mother Crone hesitated. "I don't know if it would make things better or worse," she finally said, "but we could go the edge of the Wordwood. Perhaps something'll come to us when we're standing there, seeing it firsthand."

Holly scrambled to her feet. "I'm ready to go. Geordie!"

Mother Crone arose as well.

"This could be harder on you than waiting here," she said.

"Harder than dying in the Wordwood like our friends are?"

Mother Crone shook her head.

When Geordie came back to where they were standing, Holly quickly explained what they were going to do.

"I'm in," he said as she knew he would.

"You should go back to the store," she told Dick.

The hob shook his head. "I won't, Mistress Holly. I won't let you go alone."

"I won't be alone," she said. "And someone needs to look after Snippet in case, you know . . ." We don't come back, she was about to say. "We're gone for a while."

Dick began to shiver, but before Holly could comfort him, Mother Crone stepped forward and put a hand on his shoulder.

"Don't worry, Master Hob," she told him. "I'll bring them back."

He gave a glum nod.

"I knew coming here was a bad, bad idea," he said. "I just knew it."

In the end, Mother Crone sent Edgan back to the store with Dick. Under the protests of some of the other fairies that had been following the various conversations and were determined to come as well, she would only allow Hazel to accompany Geordie, Holly, and herself into the otherworld.

"But if it's so dangerous . . ." one of the human-sized fairies began.

"It's not," Mother Crone said. "We're going to scout, not to fight a war."

"But if it's not dangerous," the fairy went on, "then there's no harm in us coming."

"I would prefer not to have a crowd," Mother Crone said.

She spoke in a tone of voice that was mild, but would brook no argument, and there were none. She turned to Holly and Geordie.

"Have either of you crossed over before?" she asked.

They both shook their heads.

"Then be forewarned," she told them. "The crossing can make you a little nauseous."

No more than she was already feeling, Holly thought. She couldn't stop thinking of the others, trapped in this stupid dying Web site/magic world that she'd had a hand in creating. It made her sick to her stomach. Her chest so tight it was hard to breathe.

"What do we do?" Geordie asked.

"Do?" Mother Crone said. "You don't have to do anything."

"Are you going to use this . . . this widdershins magic?" Holly asked.

"Widdershins to what?" Mother Crone replied.

"I don't know. I just heard . . ."

Holly's voice trailed off.

"You will be safe with me," Mother Crone said. "Just so long as you stay by me and don't go straying off on your own."

She lifted her hands above her head and brought them down with a sweeping arm-wide motion on either side of her body. When her hands touched just in front of her knees, there was a shimmer in the air, like the wall had shimmered in the store's basement, and then they were looking in at a place that shouldn't be there. Here in the middle of a mall, with the night still dark outside, they were looking through a portal at a sunny field, mountains in the distance beyond them.

Another world.

Mother Crone and Hazel stepped through, followed by Geordie. Holly bent down and kissed Dick on the forehead, then took a steadying breath and followed after.

Robert

It was a longer trek than Robert had thought it would be, walking to the Wordwood from the crossroads where he'd left the three transformed hellhounds. But he knew how to pace himself, and he knew how to make good time, taking shortcuts where he could, so it was a quicker trip for him than it might have been for another. Quick, but rough going in places. When he finally drew near enough to see the grey mists in the distance, his fancy shoes were scuffed and dusty, his suit wrinkled, with sweat stains growing under the arms and on his back where his guitar hung, slung from the thin braid of leather that he used as a strap on the odd occasions when he needed one.

He could sense the passage of the others where they'd made this same journey, hours ago. Saw where Aaran had left the road, where Bojo had gone after him, where they'd both come back on the road again. He paused for a moment, studying the fields, wondering what had drawn Aaran away. When he looked back in the direction of the Wordwood, he saw a figure on the road approaching him. He swung his guitar around in front to give him quick access to it and patted the holster under his coat where his Peacemaker hung. But as the figure drew nearer—and when he could finally reach out with his thoughts and read her—he knew neither would be necessary.

She was a big woman—easily as tall as Bojo and twice the tinker's weight. Her hair was thick and brown, a waterfall of curls and ringlets that splayed out over her shoulders and halfway down her back and chest. She walked with a rolling gait, her feet bare, the mass of her body covered with a brightly-coloured muumuu. Instead of the usual large flowers one might expect on such a garment, hers was decorated with large cabalistic symbols and astrological signs.

Everything about her was large, but especially her spirit. That spirit was so big that even a body her size was unable to contain it. When Robert looked at her, she seemed to shine as bright as a sun.

As they drew near enough to each other to exchange words, the woman lifted a meaty hand and favored him with a smile so infectious that he couldn't help but grin back at her.

"Hey there, stranger," she said. "I sure hope you're not on a pilgrimage today."

"Why's that?" Robert asked when they came abreast of each other. He gave a tug on the braid of leather that held his guitar so that it swung around onto his back once more.

"It's all blocked up a-ways from here," the woman told her. "Damnedest thing I've ever seen in this place. I don't think there'll be anything going in or going out for a while, which might be a good thing, considering."

"Oh?"

"I don't know what all's going on behind the wall of mist, but I know it can't be good. It just *feels* wrong, you know what I'm saying? Name's Lindy, by the way. Lindy Brown."

Robert lifted his eyebrows and she grinned back at him.

"Oh, that's just what people call me," she said. "I know enough not to be handing out to my name to just anybody, even a handsome stranger such as your own self. But it sounds so unfriendly saying, 'You can call me Lindy,' like we've got to drive home the fact we don't trust each other."

Robert smiled and held out his hand. "I'm Robert."

"Pleased," she said, giving his hand a shake. "It's been quiet on these roads, the past few weeks. Seems I've been meeting next to nobody, and I guess I've got what feels like a year's worth of words stored up in my head, just waiting to get out. Oh, don't you worry," she added, holding up a hand. "I'm not expecting you to hear 'em all out. I just mean it's nice to say how-do to somebody for a change."

"Did you see anybody up that way?"

Lindy shook her head. "'Fraid not. You lose someone?"

"Just had some people travelling ahead. I was hoping to catch up to them soon."

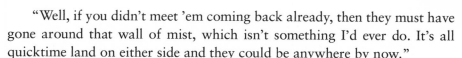

"Well, if you didn't meet 'em coming back already, then they must have gone around that wall of mist, which isn't something I'd ever do. It's all quicktime land on either side and they could be anywhere by now."

"I'm pretty good at finding my way around in here."

"I'll just bet you are. Me, I stick to the realtime routes I know. That's why I'm heading back to find me a cross-path that will take me around."

"Mabon's not that far back."

She nodded. "I know. I passed it coming in. But there's a footpath this side of the city that I mean to take. It'll save me a few hours that I'd lose going through the city. Not that I'm in a particular hurry. I'm just not partial to crowds, most of the time."

"I know the feeling."

"You're welcome to tag along with me, if you have a mind."

"Thanks," Robert said, "but I think I'll pass. I've got an itch to see this wall of mist up ahead."

"Just be careful you don't get too close. I surely mislike the feel of that place, damned if I can tell you why. It's just *wrong*."

"I'm always careful," Robert assured her.

But he understood her concern once he'd left her behind and reached the mist. It was definitely the Wordwood in there behind that grey wall. He had no trouble recognizing the feel of the place from the little of it he'd tasted back in Holly's store. And he could also see that Christy and the others had gone into it. He studied it for a long moment, then just as Bojo had done earlier in the day, he bent down, picked up a stone and tossed it into the mist.

And never saw it land.

He nodded to himself. He'd seen this before, some piece of the between cozied up along the borders of the world. He reached in with his thoughts to see if he could find any of the others, but this piece of the between was either too deep, or the others had already travelled out of range. He couldn't get a clear connection inside the Wordwood, either. The whole area behind the mist was swollen with an annoying buzz of static that made it hard to focus on any one thing in particular. But distracting as it was, he could still sense the presence of some enormous old spirit in there, and one other thing, another presence that reminded him of Papa Legba.

It took him a moment to figure out why. Then he had it.

It was because this second presence was also a gateway spirit.

Neither it nor the other, older spirit seemed healthy. There was a rot in the air of the place, a feeling that it was sliding into some deep and lasting darkness. Like Lindy had told him, there was something *wrong* in there.

Robert could fix it. He knew the notes he had to coax from his old Gibson, the music that would reach in and clean that place out. But he hesitated. He wasn't sure that it made much difference which gateway spirit nested in that place, the one that was already there, or Papa Legba. The trouble was, if the *loa* wanted him to do this thing, then there was probably something he was missing. A being like Papa Legba usually had more than one reason behind his side of a bargain. There was the one he'd tell you up front, all open about it. But more often than not there was another, or others, hidden and secret. Twisty reasons that would give the *loa* some extra advantage over you.

He went back over his conversation with Papa Legba. The bargain the *loa* had offered appeared straightforward. If he got rid of the gateway spirit inhabiting the Wordwood—allowing the *loa* to take the place over, Robert assumed—Papa Legba would renounce all claim on Robert's soul. Nothing complicated about that. If there was a trick, Robert couldn't see it. And he supposed that the advantage of being rid of this competitive spirit and the subsequent control Papa Legba would have over the Wordwood far outweighed his loss of one old bluesman's soul.

Robert studied the mist some more, peering through its grey haze at the forest of old growth trees that lay behind it. If he squinted, the trees lost some of their definition and he could see towering bookcases superimposed over them, with aisles in between that seemed to go on forever. He blinked and the library was gone.

There was still no sign of the others, but he wasn't sure if that was because they were elsewhere—taken by the vagaries of the between to some distant world—or if the static was stopping him from being able to sense their presence.

He swung his guitar around in front of him and closed his fingers around the neck. Muting the strings. Still thinking.

Did it really matter which gateway spirit used this place? One was pretty much the same as the other, at least so far as he could see. And if he did use a bit of gris-gris to clean this place out, did it matter if he was doing it for himself, or because he'd promised Bojo and the others to help fix what was wrong with the Wordwood?

That, he could answer. Of course it mattered. He wasn't so naïve as to forget that with magic, intent was everything. Using it for self-gain was never nearly so potent as a selfless act. Though that went with pretty much anything in life, and there was no rule against combining the two, was there?

Still, he hesitated.

"Having second thoughts?"

He turned to see that the crossroads *loa* had joined him. Papa Legba with his black hat, leaning on his cane, still playing up the fiction of his infirmity. Robert wasn't surprised that he'd missed the sound of the *loa*'s approach. Gateway spirits had the whole business of popping in and out of thin air down to a fine art. Robert could do it, too, here in the otherworld, but it wasn't something that came naturally to him.

"I'm just wondering what it is that you aren't telling me," Robert said.

"Well, now," the *loa* said. "Considering the few times we've had the chance to talk, there's a whole world of histories and stories we haven't even started to touch on yet."

Robert indicated the mist. "How about, specifically, what do you have planned for what lies behind this wall of mist?"

"What do you want to know?"

Robert regarded him for a moment. The complete lack of guile in the *loa*'s dark gaze. The half smile playing against that same apparent honesty.

"What do you hold sacred?" Robert said.

The question actually appeared to puzzle the *loa*.

"Sacred?" he repeated.

"You know what I mean."

"I suppose I do. I guess I'd have to say Kalfou."

Robert didn't know if the *loa* literally meant "crossroads," which was one meaning for the word, or if he was referring to the name that the Petro people gave to the more dangerous aspect of his spirit. Legba was the *loa*'s designation as a member of the Rada nation, the revered gatekeeper who provided the only means for voudoun practitioners to contact other spirits. Kalfou was his other aspect, a trickster who delighted in upsetting the natural order of things and caused unexpected accidents.

He supposed it didn't matter, so long as the *loa* held it sacred. He studied Papa Legba for a long moment, still considering. The *loa* returned his gaze with that deceptive mildness in his own eyes, his earlier half smile still tugging at his lips.

Robert gave a short nod. "That'll do. Swear to me on Kalfou that replacing the gateway spirit inside this place with you isn't going to hurt anyone."

"Besides that other spirit?"

"I can get rid of it without hurting it."

"I suppose you can," the *loa* said.

"So swear it."

"I can swear that it's not my intent to harm anyone, but you know how it goes. Supplicants come asking for favours, I can't guarantee what they do with them."

"Then swear that, to your knowledge—"

The *loa* interrupted. "Now I'm supposed to know everything?"

"You're being evasive," Robert said.

"And you're being excessively particular."

"I like to think of it as careful."

The *loa* nodded, but instead of responding, he changed the subject.

"Can you feel it?" he asked. "Something's gone bad in that place. It smells like a stagnant pond and it's getting worse all the time."

"What about it?"

"I can take it away," Papa Legba said. "Whatever's gone wrong in there, I can make it better."

"Out of the goodness of your heart?"

The *loa* smiled. "Yes. Oh, I stand to gain—I won't hide that. But surely you know this much about me: I can't abide disorder."

"Except when you're Kalfou—and then you're first in line to . . ." Robert hesitated a moment, looking for the least confrontational way to put it. "To make things interesting."

"Do I look like Kalfou?"

Robert shrugged. "I wouldn't know. I've never met you in that aspect."

"Well, I'm not. And time's wasting. Every moment we stand here and argue, the rot behind that wall of mist grows stronger."

That was certainly true. Even through the static that kept him from making clear contact with anyone behind the mist, he could tell it was worsening. The old spirit he sensed . . . its power was turning dark and restless. And he was inclined to believe that the *loa*'s intentions, at least in this particular instance, were honest.

"Just tell me," Robert said. "*Swear* that you don't intend to cause any harm."

"That I can do. On Kalfou, my shadow's name."

"Then I'll clean that place out," Robert said.

When he loosened his grip on the neck of his guitar, the strings gave a small hum of anticipation—low, almost inaudible, but there came an answering echo from deep underground. He shaped a chord, fingers stretching in for what most players would be an extremely awkward shape, but for him was as simple as a basic C chord.

"I learned this from an old woman," he said softly. "Back in the delta. She could sing a piece of this chord all on her own, harmonizing with herself."

"What did she use it for?"

"Cleaning out bad spirits from a place," Robert said.

Then he drew the thumb of his right hand across the strings. The chord he played rang out with far more volume and power than should have been possible from the small-bodied Gibson he played. It rumbled, deep and throaty, and that faint echo that had come a moment ago, from deep underground, returned and grew into a sound like distant thunder.

"You be careful," Papa Legba said. "That kind of music could do some real structural damage."

Robert nodded. The chord he'd played was a piece of the music that had sounded when old, black-winged Raven pulled the world out of nothing, back in the long ago. It was the sound of continents rising out of the sea, of mountains shifting and valleys shaping. It was the whisper of rain on the seedling first forest. It was the voice of water flowing, wind blowing. Of the first bird cries and a canid's howl. It was a lonely sound that called community into being.

In the long ago, language was still a part of the great mystery and every word held power. Speaking was a ceremony. What was said then had weight because its effects could carry on for generations. The world wasn't spoken about; the world was spoken into being, word by word.

But older than that ceremonial tribe of words, was music. The first music.

Robert had never played it before, hoarding the little he knew of it against a time just like this. But he hadn't been worried about using a chord of the first music. He'd put the right intent behind it, kept it focused and on the problem. It didn't even need to be repeated. It just kept on sounding, cutting into the mist and going deep into the world that lay behind it.

But what he hadn't taken into account was the static. The same static that made it impossible to get a clear picture of who all was in that world, was messing with the harmonics of the chord. Changing it.

Too late, he saw that it was doing something other than what he'd intended. He damped his guitar strings, but the chord continued to resound. It was out of his hands now and he couldn't take it back.

"This is a little more extreme than I was looking for," the *loa* said.

"I know," Robert said. "Something's changing it—something inside the world."

"Can you fix it—play something else?"

Robert shook his head. "If I couldn't control what happened with one chord going through that mist, playing anything else is only going to make things worse."

"So we wait."

"And we pray."

Papa Legba laughed, but there was no humour in it.

"Yeah," he said. "Like it's something I've ever done before."

Robert closed his eyes. "Then I'll do it for both of us."

Saskia

It's weird being back in my own body like this. But I'm not really allowed the luxury of getting used to it. Because on top of all the rest of our problems, it looks like the Wordwood's about to come apart right under our feet.

We all stare at that huge fissure that's opened at the edge of the lake, the way the water is pouring into it. I hear more thunder, coming from deeper in the library. I'm not sure if it's another of these fissures opening up or the sound of these enormous bookcases collapsing. Maybe a combination of both.

"We need to get out of here," I say.

Jackson gives a quick nod of agreement, but Christiana only shakes her head.

"There's nothing we can do," I tell her. "We're so far out of our depth, I wouldn't know where to begin to look for a way to fix any of this."

"Maybe . . . in the books . . . ?" Jackson says.

"We don't have that kind of time," I tell him.

As though to underscore that, there's another huge clap of thunder, and this time the ground shifts right underfoot, making us all struggle to keep our balance.

"Maybe we don't know how to fix it," Christiana says, "but I'm betting I know someone who does."

She gets this look on her face that I recognize. It's the same look that Christy gets when something that should have been obvious finally slips into place—but this is only after hours of worrying at the problem. With Christy, it's usually a matter of research and he just takes a blue pencil to his manuscript. With Christiana . . . well, with Christiana I'm beginning to realize anything can happen.

I've spent time inside her skin, but I was a passenger in her body. I was able to tap into her physical sensations—what she heard and saw and tangibly felt. But I never touched her emotional landscape. All I know is that she can be impetuous and volatile. And unlike Christy, who'll talk a thing out, she makes snap decisions and then follows through on them immediately.

I want to say something now. I don't know what's come into her mind, but I want her to try to be a bit more like Christy for a moment. I want her to stay calm, to talk to me.

But she's not Christy. She looks from the leviathan to Librarius, whose eyes are open, watching us. Christiana stalks over to where we've left him lying, tied up and helpless. Undoing his gag, she picks him up and slams him against a bookshelf. I've forgotten how strong she is.

"Start talking," she says, her voice low and dangerous.

"I don't know anyth—"

Before he can finish, she steps back, then slams him against the bookshelf again. A couple of books on one of the higher shelves come tumbling down, not two feet from where they're standing. Christiana doesn't even look in their direction.

"Maybe you don't get it," she says. Her voice is still quiet, almost conversational. "I don't want to hear any more of your bullshit. What I *want* to hear is exactly what you did to this place."

"You can't—"

She slams him again.

"You get one more chance," she tells him, "and then I'm going to start taking you apart, piece by piece. Look into my eyes. Read what you see there and tell me I'm making idle threats."

She's starting to scare me now. If this is a part of Christy's personality that he gave up when his shadow stepped out of him, I'm just as happy that he did. But I think she's bluffing. I *hope* she's bluffing, but that Librarius will believe her. But he thinks she's bluffing, too.

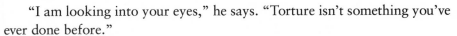

"I am looking into your eyes," he says. "Torture isn't something you've ever done before."

I find myself letting out a breath of relief that I hadn't been aware of holding. I didn't want to think that she could be that harsh. But my relief doesn't last long.

"So you think I'm not capable of it?" she asks. Her voice is dangerous now, as though she wants him to push her too far.

There's a long moment of silence, then he slowly shakes his head.

"N-no," he finally says. "You could do it."

She lets him go and he falls to the ground, unable to keep his balance because of how he's bound. He curls into a fetal position as though he thinks she's going to hit him. Instead she puts a foot on one of the hands tied behind his back. I see him wince when she applies some pressure.

"I don't want to see those fingers moving," she says. "And all I want to hear coming out of your mouth is the truth."

"I . . . I . . ."

She crouches down, her foot still on his hand. "Now, tell me what you've done."

I don't like what's happening, but I understand why she stepped on his hand. He needs to move his fingers when he speaks a spell. And then I think about how a few moments ago I was ready to just throw him into the lake, bound and all. I guess I'm not so immune to violence as I'd like to think I am.

"I did tell you the truth . . ." He flinches as she applies some more pressure on his hand. "Just . . . just not all of it."

"So do it now. Tell me about the leviathan."

He swallows thickly and looks in my direction. I school my features to remain expressionless.

"The leviathan *was* here already," he says, looking back at Christiana. "I didn't lie about that. He was the spirit called into this place when the Wordwood took shape."

"That's not possible," Christiana says. "I may not know a lot about leviathans, but I do know they don't physically manifest."

"He didn't," Librarius tells her. "He *was* the Wordwood. At least until the virus struck."

"So what happened?'

"You have to understand," Librarius says. "A place like this, so easily accessible to anyone . . ."

"Through the Internet."

He nods. "It's very desirable real estate. It's hard for spirits to develop—let's call it a constituency—these days. Few people have the desire or time for rituals and devotions. The Wordwood is like a gold mine. Every visitor lends credence and potency to the one who controls it."

"You're saying the leviathan wanted to be worshipped?"

"Not the leviathan. Me. Any being such as me."

"And you are?"

"A gateway spirit."

"Ah."

"What does that mean?" I ask.

Christiana turns to me. "People are always reaching for the Great Mysteries," she explains, "but few of them can make contact with them on their own. So they go through intermediaries. It can be religion. It can be private rituals that they create on their own or with a small group of like-minded friends. It can be sacrifices and devotions made to a gateway spirit who will connect them to the spirits they wish to contact. Usually it's some combination of all of that—whatever will take their invocation and deliver it to the appropriate spirit."

"Sort of like using a search engine," Jackson says.

Christiana gives a slow nod. "I suppose. Though it's more personal than that, because—"

She breaks off as another crack of thunder shakes the ground. I grab the nearest bookcase to keep my balance. When the shivering ground settles down once more, Christiana turns her attention back to our captive.

"So you wanted the Wordwood," she says, "and when the virus incapacitated the leviathan, you stepped in and took over."

"Something like that. Except the leviathan wasn't incapacitated by the virus. He was just disoriented. I'd been eyeing this place for ages. When the virus struck and I saw what was happening, I took the opportunity to . . . contain him."

I don't get it, but Christiana nods before I can ask.

"You gave him a physical body," she says.

"I thought it would work. It's not like I—or anyone—has the power to cast something like a leviathan out of a place like this."

"And it's killing him," Christiana says. There's that dark tone in her voice again.

"I didn't *know,*" Librarius tells her. "I swear I didn't know."

"And that's why the Wordwood's falling apart around us."

Librarius shakes his head. "The leviathan's dying is turning this place into a shadow world. Anyone looking in on it from the outside would see a place of darkness and despair. Already, steps would have been taken to close off access to it from the rest of the spiritworld—not by any entity, but by the spiritworld itself."

"Because?" Christiana asks.

"If the Wordwood is accessed—if any gates are opened by those departing or entering—the miasma that rules this place now would spread into other worlds."

"So what's causing the Wordwood to fall apart?"

"I don't know. Perhaps someone is attempting to exorcise the spirits from it. I can feel a pushing inside me, a demand, in no uncertain terms, that I leave. It resounds inside me like a piece of the old music, the first music that helped the old ones create the world in the long ago."

Christiana gives a slow nod. "Where will it send you? Back into whatever void spat you out in the first place?"

"Not exactly. I had a life in the spiritworld before I took on this guise. But if this is an exorcism and it takes hold, it could dissipate my essence. It would take me a very long time to pull the parts of me back together once more."

"Well, that wouldn't be any great loss," Christiana says. She studies him for a long moment. "But you don't seem particularly worried about it."

"Why should I be? Whatever is working the spell against me and the leviathan is breaking up against the fact that the leviathan's immense spirit is contained in a physical form. We're all going to die before the exorcism can work on me."

"And dying's a better thing?"

Now Librarius smiles. "It is for me. If the exorcism was to work on me, I might never be able to collect enough of the errant pieces of my spirit to regain this particular life I wear. But I've died before. It takes me no great effort to return from the dead—I am a gateway spirit, after all." His smile widens slightly. "Pity you can't say the same thing."

"Yeah, it's a real shame," Christiana says.

She starts to stand up, but another tremor rocks the ground. We all have to grab onto the bookcases. When the thundering echoes finally start to fade, Christiana gets to her feet.

"One of you put his gag back in," she says. "And watch his hands. If he starts wiggling his fingers, don't screw around. Just break them all, including his thumbs." She looks from Jackson to me. "Do you think you can do that?"

I know why it has to be done, but I don't think I can do it. But Jackson nods.

"Yeah, I can do it," he says.

I guess he finally found some backbone, though maybe I'm not being fair. In some ways, he's had it the roughest of all of us, starting with having to carry the guilt of being responsible for all of this in the first place, however inadvertently it came about.

"What are you going to do?" I ask Christiana.

"Find something I can use to kill the leviathan," she says, then walks away before I can ask her more. A half-dozen paces down the corridor between the bookcases, she breaks into a run.

Christy

It's impossible to find steady footing as we follow the path into the wet forest, but we go slipping and sliding anyway, splashing through mud, banging up against the trunks of these big trees that sometimes, out of the corner of your eyes, seem to shift into enormous bookcases. But when you look at them straight on, they're trees again.

I don't know how long the panic has a hold of us, but Bojo finally grabs my arm, stopping me. Raul collides into us. He starts to fall except Bojo and I each catch an arm and haul him to his feet. Suzi and Aaran come to a skidding stop and only just miss sending us sprawling in the mud.

We're all breathing hard. I don't know about the others, but I've got a stitch in my side that makes me bend over and lean against the nearest tree. I stare at the bark. I don't know what kind of trees these are, but they're huge. Some have trunks so big that all five of us couldn't touch hands around it. And they go up forever. Redwoods are the closest I've seen like them in the World As It Is.

After we stand there for long moments, catching our breath, Aaran starts to say something, but Bojo holds up a hand. He walks a few paces back the way we've come, cocking his head to listen. We hear more thunder, but it sounds like it's a long way from us.

"I think we've outrun the worst of it," Bojo says when he comes back to us, "but let's keep moving."

He sets off and I fall into pace beside him.

"Does anybody else keep seeing bookcases instead of trees?" Raul asks from behind us.

"They really are bookcases," Suzi says.

That brings us all to a stop.

"What?" I say.

"And they're trees at the same time," she adds. "They both exist at the same time. Don't forget, I was born in this place."

Like Saskia, I think, and I feel the sharp pang of loss that comes every time I think of her.

"Do you know which way we're headed?" Bojo asks. "What we can expect?"

She shakes her head. "I just know we're in the Wordwood. It feels very familiar." Then she shrugs. "And very different at the same time. Something's really wrong with the Wordwood spirit."

"Yeah," Raul says. "It's trying to kill us."

"I don't think so."

"Let's keep moving," Bojo says. "We can talk while we're walking."

"How can they be trees and bookcases at the same time?" Aaran asks as we set off again.

"I don't know," Suzi says. "They just are."

"I think I know," I say. "It's a perceptual thing. We see what we're expecting to see."

Aaran chuckles. "So, what are you saying? That this is more of your 'the world is the way it is because that's what we expect it to be' business?"

"Pretty much."

"Except none of us knew what to expect," he goes on, "so why would we all see it as a forest?"

"Maybe because of the name?" Raul offers.

Conversation falls off after that and we keep walking. Slowly our environment begins to change. The ground firms up underfoot. The mud's gone, turned into dry, packed dirt—the way the path was before we entered the mist. The trees are just as big as they've always been, but the constant drip of water from the leaves has stopped. It's like it never rained here.

I don't know about the others, but I keep getting more and more flashes of the ghostly, here-then-gone-again bookcases, of flooring underfoot instead of dirt, like we're walking through the stacks of some huge, deserted library. I'm about to ask if anyone else is feeling the same way, when Bojo brings us to an abrupt halt again.

"What is it?" I ask, pitching my voice low.

"I hear something," he says. "Footsteps. Something's approaching, and moving fast."

We all hear it then. It sounds like one person, running full out. To us, I wonder, or from some new peril? Then she bursts into view, a half-dozen yards ahead of us on the trail, coming out from between the trees . . . no, from a side corridor as the trees suddenly disappear and the bookcases firm up all around us. It's a completely disorienting moment—for all of us, but especially for me. Not just because of the abrupt shift in our surroundings, but because I recognize the woman. When she turns in our direction, I see the same shock of recognition in her features.

"What are *you* doing here?" we both say at the same time.

"Whoa," Raul says. "Is this Saskia?"

I hear the hope in his voice. Because if it is, then mightn't his Benny be somewhere near, as well? I hate to bring him down.

"It's my shadow," I say as she walks toward us.

I've never seen her this disheveled before. She's often scruffy, but I get the sense that's from choice, on a particular day, just as I know that right now she's been too busy to care about her appearance. She looks like she's been sleeping in her clothes, though I'm sure none of us look any better. Especially not after our trek through that old subway tunnel.

Her gaze goes from me to the others. "Do any of you have a weapon?" she asks.

As usual, there's no preamble with her. She just cuts right to the chase.

"What do you mean, she's your shadow?" Aaran asks.

But it turns out I'm not the only one to recognize her.

"I know you," Bojo says. "You're one of Maxie's friends."

My shadow nods. "Yeah, I've seen you around, but I can't remember where. Maybe in Hinterland?"

Who's Maxie? I wonder. Where's Hinterland? What I don't know about my shadow could fill this library.

"Say," she goes on. "Do you have one of those tinker blades you guys are known for?"

Bojo shakes his head. "But I've got something that might be better. A hellhound knife."

"You're kidding."

Bojo sets his pack on the ground and pulls out a shirt that's been rolled into a bundle. Unrolling the fabric, he takes out the knife that the hellhound threw at Robert's guitar, that Robert dropped on the floor back in the basement of Holly's store. I'd forgotten that Bojo had picked it up and stowed it away in his pack.

"Perfect," my shadow says when he hands it to her.

"Who are we fighting?" the tinker asks as he stuffs his shirt back into his pack and reshoulders the pack.

"*We're* not fighting anybody," she says. "But I'm going to try to kill a leviathan."

Then she takes off again, back down the corridor she burst out of. We all stand around like dummies for a long moment, then hurry after her, but she's already way down the corridor, far ahead of us. Too far for us to catch up to her. I wonder why she doesn't do the fade away bit that she normally does with me back at home, then realize it's not even necessary, considering how easily she's left us all behind.

"Okay," Aaran says. "What the hell was all that about?"

Bojo sets a brisk pace and we follow as we can, straggling behind him. We're already so beat it's hard to muster the energy we need. I explain what I know of my shadow's origins as we go along.

"This is insane," Aaran says.

"You can still say that after the past couple of days?"

"I know," he says. "But, come on. Your shadow can go walkabout on its own?"

"Were you sleeping during Philosophy 101? Jung says—"

"I *remember* what he said. But he was talking metaphorically, not literally."

"Give it up," Raul says. "Just because something's whacked, doesn't mean it's not true. Not anymore. And besides, what about Suzi here? What makes her origin any easier to understand?"

Aaran sighs. "I know. It's just . . ."

"It's all still new for a lot of us," Suzi says. She tucks her arm into the crook of Aaran's. "Don't think I'm not feeling a little nuts myself."

"So, what's your shadow doing here?" Raul asks.

"I have no idea," I say. "The truth is there's more I don't know about her than I probably ever will. I don't even know her name."

"It's Christiana," Bojo says over his shoulder.

"How do you—" I begin, but then I remember that he's met her before.

"You tend to make a point of getting her name," the tinker says in response to the question I didn't finish, "when a woman's as attractive and lively as Christiana."

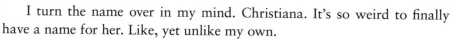

I turn the name over in my mind. Christiana. It's so weird to finally have a name for her. Like, yet unlike my own.

I want to ask Bojo what else he knows about her and her friend Maxie and anything else he'd care to share with me about her life, but Aaran brings up a new concern.

"So she expects to kill a whale with that knife you took from the hell-hounds?" he asks.

Bojo shakes his head. "No, a leviathan."

"That's what I said."

"It means something different here," the tinker says. "Though to tell you the truth, I didn't even think they were real."

"Or that they can have a physical presence," Suzi adds.

"Can we back up here a moment?" I say. "What's a leviathan?"

"They're big, old-time magic," Bojo says. "Precreation spirits. Legend has it that they're the ones who gave Raven the music that let him create the world. And like Suzi said, they're not supposed to be able to manifest in the physical world."

"So they're the gods that made god," Aaran says. "See, I'm getting with the program now. I'm not freaking out or shaking my head."

"Raven's not a god," I tell him. "The way he tells it, it was like you or me starting a car. He just happened to be there and had the key in hand."

"So now you've talked to God?" Aaran says.

I shake my head. "No. He's just this guy that everyone else keeps referring to as Raven. As *the* Raven."

"Man, have I been leading a sheltered life," Aaran says.

I'm about to say something like, that's what I've been trying to tell you all these years, but there's this huge cracking sound that I remember all too well from the subway tunnel. This time it comes directly from the other side of the bookcases to our right. No one stops to argue or even think about it. We just run, and none too soon. Behind us, in the part of the corridor where we just were, a fissure appears, splitting the floor. The bookcases on either side come crashing down, raining books. Except for Bojo, who's further ahead, we all lose our balance and fall against each other, sprawling to the floor.

Bojo returns and pulls Raul up. The rest of us scramble to our feet and then we're all off and running again.

It's funny. Moments ago I could barely keep up with Bojo as we chased after my shadow. But right now I'm running full tilt, fueled by adrenaline and fear.

Holly

The otherworld wasn't anything like Holly had expected. She'd expected . . . well, magic. For everything to be strange and different, like walking into a Dali painting or one of those confusing Escher pieces, where down was up but it was also down, when it wasn't going sideways. The place Mother Crone had taken them to didn't even have some Bavarian-styled castle off in the distance, or the deep ancient woods that Sophie and Jilly were always talking about.

Instead, they stepped from the mall concourse out onto a wide dirt path. Ordinary grass fields stretched away to either side of where they stood, with mountains in the far distance. Some hawthorns and brambles grew along the verge.

The shopping mall with its dancing fairies had been far more magical. The only really strange thing here was the wall of mist that rose up a couple of hundred yards ahead of them, blocking a clear view of what looked like some enormous forest. Holly smiled when she saw the trees. Now *that* was more like Jilly's Cathedral Wood. Her gaze tracked down from the heights of the trees to where the path they were on disappeared into the mist.

Standing on this side of the mist were two men.

"Stay behind me," Mother Crone said, stepping forward to place herself between the strangers and her companions.

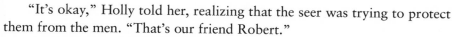

"It's okay," Holly told her, realizing that the seer was trying to protect them from the men. "That's our friend Robert."

"And the man with him?"

Like Robert, the stranger was also dressed in a dark suit. He had a hat, too, but instead of a guitar, he had a cane.

"We don't know him," Geordie said.

Mother Crone nodded. "But I do."

Holly didn't like the sound of that. There was something in Mother Crone's voice that said they might have just stepped into a whole world of trouble. Maybe we should go back, she wanted to say, but then the men turned and an unnoticed retreat, at least, was impossible.

Geordie came up from behind to stand beside Mother Crone. He lifted his hand.

"Hey, Robert!" he called.

When he started forward, Holly trailed along behind him. Mother Crone waited a beat, then followed with little Hazel staying close by her side.

Robert gave them a welcoming nod. "You're about the last bunch I expected to meet here."

"We got so worried," Holly said.

"Well, you've got good cause."

Holly sighed. She hadn't actually wanted to hear that. For all Mother Crone's certainty, Holly had still been holding on to the hope that the seer had made a mistake in her reading of the situation.

"What *is* going on in there?" Geordie asked.

"That world in there is going to pieces," Robert said, "and it's pretty much all my fault. I was trying to exorcise the bad spirits that had taken it over, but once my first chord got into that place, the music left my control and it's not coming back."

"Christy's in there," Geordie said. "And the others. Bojo and Raul. And all those other people that disappeared."

"I know," Robert told him. "Don't think I don't know that."

"But if the world's going to pieces—"

"It won't necessarily be completely destroyed," Robert's companion said. "I think the chaos will last just until the spirits are banished. And they will be banished. This is only a little messier than we'd expected."

Robert gave him a sharp look.

"Fine," the stranger said. "Than *I* expected. But once they're gone, I'll slip in and lay down some order. Any of your friends that found themselves a hidey-hole, they'll be right as rain once I'm done."

"Except we don't *know* that it'll work out that way," Robert put in.

Mother Crone had slipped by them and stood inches from the mist—peering in, Holly thought, until she went over to stand by Hazel and the seer, and saw that Mother Crone's gaze was turned inward.

"It's extremely unlikely that anything is going to survive in there," she said finally, turning around to face Robert. "That's a leviathan you've got going to pieces in there."

Robert's eyes went wide. "What?"

"Oh, yes," Mother Crone said. "I've never actually seen or met one—I don't know anyone who has. But that spirit is so ancient and strong . . . what else could it be?" Her gaze moved to Robert's companion. "What do you think, Kalfou?"

"You've got me mistaken with someone else," the man she'd addressed said. "My name's Legba."

Mother Crone nodded. "Today perhaps."

"Look," Legba said. "I don't know what stories you've been listening to, but I'm just a spirit, same as you, trying to get by. I don't look to cause trouble. All I like to do is see that there's some order in the world."

Mother Crone continued to nod. "Not to mention broadening your influence a thousandfold once you're ensconced as the gateway spirit of that world."

"It wouldn't hurt anybody."

"Probably not. But you can't just work your mojo on a leviathan. That's like trying to keep a tornado locked up in a teacup. It can't be done."

"I know that," Legba said. "Don't think I don't. But I didn't know there was a leviathan in there."

Robert was nodding in agreement. "They don't take on physical shape."

"Then *you* tell me what's in there."

"A gateway spirit," Robert said. "Nobody I know or ever heard of before."

"And?"

"Something old and potent," Robert added with some reluctance. "I could sense that much when I got here. But . . . come on. How could anybody have known it was a leviathan?"

"You couldn't have, I suppose," Mother Crone said. "But to have used a piece of the first music on it . . ."

Her voice trailed off and her gaze went inward once more, but Holly couldn't see what had distracted her. Her and the other two men. They were all three staring into nothing now, and so intently.

Holly sighed. The whole conversation between them had gone way over her head and when she turned to Geordie, she saw only the same confused expression on his face that she knew was on her own. Her gaze tracked past him and found Mother Crone's companion, the little twig girl Hazel.

"How about you?" she asked. "Do you have a clue as to what's going on?"

Hazel shook her head. "Something bad."

"Yeah, we got that part," Geordie said. He turned to look at the wall of mist. "It's so damn frustrating, knowing they're somewhere in there and there's nothing we can do."

Holly nodded. "I was really hoping that somehow we'd turn out to be the cavalry."

"Some things can't be changed," Hazel said. "You shouldn't even try."

Holly hated this stoic acceptance that they all seemed to subscribe to.

"Like this whale everybody's freaking about," she said.

"It's not a fish," Hazel said.

"Mammal, actually," Geordie put in.

"It's one of the ancient spirits that the world grew out of," the twig girl went on, as though she hadn't been interrupted. "Like the Grace."

"I've heard of her before," Geordie said, turning to Holly. "She's this spirit that embodies all that's good in . . . well, pretty much anything."

"So, what . . . what does this spirit embody?" Holly asked. "The leviathan that Mother Crone says is in the Wordwood."

Hazel shook her head. "I don't know. I don't think they actually embody anything. They're more like doors into the medicine lands—the place we all came from when the world was being formed."

Holly was still trying to get her head around that when Mother Crone stirred.

"That's odd," the seer murmured.

Then her eyes flashed open. She and Legba looked at each other in shock.

"Oh, shit," Robert said. "We need to get out of here!"

Mother Crone grabbed Hazel by one hand and Geordie by the other and pulled them away from the wall of mist. Before Holly could ask what was going on, Legba had her by the hand, and they were racing down the dirt path after Mother Crone and the others, Robert taking up the rear.

If she'd been looking back, Holly knew she'd have been blinded. As it was, the flare of white light that came from behind them was still a shock to her eyes, leaving her blinking, tear ducts welling. There was no sound, just that awful, searing light. Then a blast of wind picked them up like they were so many leaves and twigs and scattered them along the length of the path.

Christiana

It's getting worse, I realize, as I go tearing back to where I left the others watching over Librarius and the leviathan by the lakeshore. All around me I can hear the thundering crashes of bookcases toppling as fissures open underneath them. A huge one comes from just behind me. I hope Christy and his friends are okay, but I don't have time to go back and look. Then one of the crevices opens right in front of me.

I jump over it, clearing it easily, but the ground's still moving when I land and it's enough to throw me off balance. I crash into a bookshelf, hitting it with my shoulder. Books come flying off, tumbling around me as I fall to the floor. I don't know how, but I manage to hold on to that hellhound knife I got from the tinker.

I start to get to my feet, then see the fissure widen and the bookcases on either side of me begin to slide into it. I put an arm over my head to shield myself from the falling books and scrabble out of the way. The books that hit me are falling from the nearest shelves, but I know that any minute the ones higher up are going to be coming down. If one of them hits me, I'm going to have worse than bruises to worry about.

It's hard to make progress. The floor's at an odd angle, sloping back. Like it's trying to funnel me back into the fissure. I only just make it back to a level section when the bookcase on my right goes sliding into the crevice. I allow myself one look back, hear an ominous, stony crack from almost directly underground, and take off again.

I don't realize how far I'd come in my search for a weapon until now, when I'm making my way back. I don't know how big this place is, but I've been running for miles. I've always had a lot of stamina, but I have a stitch in my side by the time I finally reach the lakeshore where I've left the others. Saskia turns around, eyes widening at the big knife I'm carrying. Jackson's still standing watch over Librarius.

"Don't let him so much as twitch," I tell Jackson as I angle my course to where the huge body of the leviathan lies sprawled, half in, half out of the lake.

"You've got it," he tells me.

I guess I misjudged him because he's proving to be a lot more capable than I would have guessed from when I first met him.

"Christiana!" Saskia calls.

"Don't worry," I tell her. It's easier to pretend everything's under control. "I saw Christy and some other folks back there. It's going to take them awhile to work their way here, what with all those bookcases coming down, but they shouldn't be too long."

She's trailing after me. Now she turns to look back the way I've come.

"Christy's here? Is he okay?"

"He looked fine."

"Who's with him?"

"I didn't recognize anybody, but I guess they're all here on a rescue mission."

"But—"

"There's really no time," I tell her.

I speed up a little to put some distance between us, but I needn't have bothered. She's still looking back to where I came out of the bookcases and not following me anymore. She's obviously thinking about Christy.

And then I'm by the leviathan, his immense bulk rearing up above me.

I can believe how big he is. I mean, I *know* how big he is—you can't miss it, up this close—but he's so enormous that unless he's right in front of me like this, I lose the size reference. It's as though my memory can't hold his immensity, so it brings him down to something manageable—you know like twenty feet tall instead of the two hundred or so he really is.

But he's not twenty feet tall. He's a mountain, lying there. A behemoth.

I look at the knife in my hand.

Yeah, like it's going to do the trick.

But there's nothing else. Until I ran into Christy and his friends, the only thing I could find were books. Lots of books. So what was I supposed to do? Tear out some pages and paper cut him to death?

Though I'm not planning to actually kill him. I just want to set him free of the weight and burden of the flesh that *is* killing him. Semantics, I suppose, but it makes sense in my head.

I take another look at the knife, then put it between my teeth—which feels really weird—and start up the side of one enormous arm.

I've experienced worse things in my time, but not many. Quickly heading the list is this: grabbing fleshy handfuls of the putrid skin of this monstrous man to haul myself up onto his chest, handhold by handhold. It's making my stomach do little flips.

I keep expecting him to rouse. Not get up and lumber around—I think he's too far gone for that. But to lift a giant hand to brush away some bothersome insect crawling up his arm? I can see that happening. I can really see that happening. My imagination's way too good.

But I get up onto the slope of his chest and he doesn't even twitch. There's just the slow rise and fall of the spongy flesh underfoot to tell me that he's still alive. Barely.

I take the knife from between my teeth and slowly make my way up to his throat, arms held out to keep my balance against the movement of his breathing. I get right up to the collarbone, then slide carefully down into the hollow of his throat. I don't have any trouble identifying the twinned carotid arteries I need to sever. I touch the edge of the hellhound knife with my thumb—just enough to feel the edge of the blade. It's sharper than a razor.

I bring it down toward where the arteries pulse just under his skin.

And then I can't do it.

It doesn't matter that I have only his best intentions in mind. I feel too much like I haven't weighed enough other options. Sure, he's dying. And the Wordwood is falling apart around us as he goes. But who's to say that my killing him will free his spirit to go back into the Wordwood the way it was before Librarius bound him? For all I know, I'll just bring about the Wordwood's destruction all that much more quickly.

The Wordwood, and us in it.

I wish I knew what to do.

I wish someone else would step up and take charge.

It's funny. I'm the most independently-minded person I know, but right now I really would give almost anything to have somebody else here to make the decision for me. Or at least for them to give me some informed advice. How come Mumbo didn't prepare me for a situation like this? Some days it felt like she was readying me for everything and anything, up to and including fixing a kitchen sink. But while I know all about passing as human and getting around in the borderlands and the otherworld, when it comes to leviathans, I've got nothing to fall back on.

I look away, over at the rest of the library. It's really getting bad now. The cracks of fissures splitting the stone floor, the crashing of the bookcases coming down, are a steady cacophony that doesn't let up. From my vantage point on the leviathan, I can see great gaping holes where bookcases used to stand.

I think of what Librarius told me. Of how he wasn't afraid to die, because dying he'd just be born again as himself. What he was afraid of was if whatever's destroying the Wordwood also tore *his* spirit apart, because then there was no telling when, or even if, he'd be himself again.

I guess that's what answers my dilemma. If the leviathan dies—if I can summon the courage to use this knife—he'll get to go on as himself. But if I don't kill him, then he'll be torn apart like Librarius when the Wordwood completely falls to pieces around us.

I know that I can't let that happen. The leviathan doesn't deserve it. For all I know, he's the very one who gave Raven the tools to make the world of which this little corner of the otherworld is only a tiny part. Wouldn't that be horribly ironic?

Before I can chicken out, I take a deep breath, then plunge the knife down into the artery and tear it across. The knife goes into his skin like I'm cutting a pudding. There's no resistance at all. And then the hole I made explodes. Blood fountains out, a grotesque, red geyser. The immense body underneath me shifts and I fall down, sliding across the blood-slick skin.

It's weird. My perceptions go slow-mo, like in a car accident. I feel a huge change . . . in the air, inside my chest. Something shifts inside me. Deep. Bone marrow deep.

The blood rains down on me. I'm covered in it. Sliding in it.

I'm going over the edge of the leviathan's shoulder. I try to grab a hold of something, anything, but his skin's covered with blood and too slick.

Then I'm airborne.

Falling.

And everything goes white.

Christy

We almost lose Bojo in the next fissure. It starts to open under our feet, separating Suzi and Aaran from the rest of us. Aaran makes the leap across, then turns back to help Suzi, Bojo at his side. The gap keeps widening, stones grinding deep underfoot. The bookcases are tottering, sliding into the fissure. Suzi makes the jump and Bojo and Aaran each catch her by a hand, pulling her to safety. But before they can get to level ground, the floor does a dip under their feet.

Bojo gives Aaran and Suzi a shove to where Raul and I can grab them, but he goes sliding down into the fissure. All that saves him is that he manages to grab on to a bookcase that's wedged into the crevice at an angle. Books are falling, hitting the floor and sliding past him into the growing gap. Bojo starts to climb back along the bookcase, but it suddenly drops another foot and he almost loses his grip.

"Hang on to me," Raul says.

He stretches out on the floor and flings his knapsack toward Bojo. Aaran, Suzi, and I hold on to his legs. One of the straps on the knapsack reaches Bojo. Raul's holding on to the other with both hands. Another shower of books comes down—luckily slim folios. It's pretty much a miracle that no one's gotten a concussion yet from one of the larger books.

Bojo grabs the strap and then we all start hauling Raul back, which also pulls Bojo toward higher ground. We manage a couple of yards before

Bojo finds some purchase for his feet. He pushes himself forward and crawls to safety. And we all scramble to our feet on the level ground. I don't know about the others, but my heartbeat's doing double-time in my chest.

But there's no chance for us to take a breather.

There's another crack of splitting stone.

"Look out!" Suzi cries.

Another fissure is opening right in front of us. We dart down a side corridor to avoid it. The gap widens faster than before and the bookcases are crashing down, swallowed into it in moments.

"This way," Bojo says.

He leads us down the side corridor. We cross, one, then another passage. At the third, he has us heading back in the same direction that we'd been going earlier, the direction that my shadow took. All around us we can hear the grind of stone, the thundering crashes of the bookcases coming down.

"This is the way I've always figured things would end," Raul says as we trot behind Bojo. "If a person was to get caught up in something as big as this, I mean. You can be brave, and you can do your best, but in the end all your efforts prove to be ineffectual."

"I don't believe that for a moment," Suzi says from behind us. "When we expend the effort, we make a difference. We might not solve the big problem, but at least we'll have done something to improve the small aspects of it that lie closer to home."

"Which is really comforting when you're dead," Aaran puts in. Then he adds, "Ow," and I assume Suzi's given him a whack.

I want to add something to the argument, but then Bojo calls out from ahead of us.

"I think it's opening up!" he says.

We all look forward. In between the bookcases, far ahead, I get a glimpse of what seems to be an impossible sight. A lake, in the middle of the library. A giant man with blood fountaining from his throat.

Then there's a flare of white light. Blinded, we stumble into each other and fall in a tangle of limbs.

As I try to stand up, I realize that my eyes are still open, but I can't see anything.

And then the world goes completely away.

Holly

Holly picked herself up from the dirt, moving gingerly. It took her a long moment to remember where she was and what had happened. Her body still held an echoing tremor of the blast. Her mouth was full of dust and stars flashed in her eyes, blinding her. There was a ringing in her ears and her whole body felt bruised, although the bruising seemed to be on the inside of her skin. But after a brief spell of dizziness, the stars finally faded and she was able to find her glasses. She put them on and looked around.

Not far from her, Legba was already standing up, brushing dust from his suit with a gloved hand. When he bent lower to get at a patch on the pant legs below his knees, the sleeve of his jacket rode up. Holly's eyes widened. Instead of an arm, there were only bones there, held together by she didn't know what.

I didn't see that, Holly thought and she turned away. But she couldn't forget that he'd taken her hand earlier. It had certainly *felt* real.

On the other side of her, Geordie was helping Mother Crone stand. Little Hazel sat in the middle of the path, her legs splayed in front of her, her eyes unfocused and a confused expression on her pixie features. Past them, Robert was using the sleeve of his jacket to clean the dust from his guitar. He looked up and caught her gaze.

"She's taken quite the beating this trip," he said. "Between a hellhound's knife and a handful of new cracks from this fall, we're talking some serious repairs."

Holly nodded, not knowing what to say. She felt guilty about what had happened to his guitar, but the guitar was the least of their worries. She felt guilty about everything. Except for Legba, everybody was here because of her. Not to mention Christy and the others, trapped in the Wordwood.

She finally let her gaze go to where the wall of mist had been veiling their view of the Wordwood's forest.

It was different now. Completely opaque. She had no idea what that meant, but it couldn't be good.

"What . . . what happened?" she asked as she got to her feet.

Mother Crone shook her head. "It's changed," she said. "But how, or from what, I have no idea."

She turned her attention to Hazel, stroking the little twig girl's locks of Rasta vines until Hazel finally blinked and came back from wherever the blast had sent her.

"I can tell you how it's changed," Legba said. "The leviathan's left his physical shape and swelled to fill the world behind the mist. He's that world and it's him. There's no place for a gateway spirit in there now because there'll be no going in or out anymore."

"Making it useless for you," Robert said.

Legba shot him a quick humourless smile. He gave his sleeve a last brush—

Don't think of what's under the cloth, Holly told herself. Or better yet, what's *not* under it.

—and picked up his cane.

"I doubt I will see any of you again," he said. His gaze went to Robert. "Except for you, of course. We'll meet at least once more."

He touched the brim of his hat with gloved fingers, tapped his cane in the dirt, then stepped away, disappearing. Holly blinked in surprise.

"What did he mean by that?" Geordie asked.

Robert shrugged. "Oh, you know these old spirits. They like to be cryptic."

Holly didn't bother trying to work that out. There was only one thing that concerned her at the moment.

"Can you tell what happened to our friends that were inside?" she asked Mother Crone.

The seer had trouble meeting her gaze.

"I'm sorry," she said. "I can sense the leviathan, but nothing more."

"So they're all . . . gone . . ."

An enormous ache filled Holly as the realization hit home. All those people who had disappeared. Christy and the others . . .

Their deaths opened a deep pit in her chest and she didn't know if she'd be able to stop herself from falling in. She didn't know that she could bear the weight of this much sorrow.

"I don't know," Mother Crone replied, her voice gentle with sympathy. "It's like Legba said. It's impossible to reach inside and see anymore. I can't ignore the leviathan—he has such an enormous presence—but nothing else is clear."

"But . . ." Geordie had to clear his throat before he could continue. The anguish in his features was too much a mirror of what Holly was feeling and she had to look away. "The danger you were talking about earlier . . . ?"

"That, at least, has passed."

The seer took Hazel's hand. She looked as though she was about to add something more, but Robert caught her attention. Holly turned to see him cocking his head. What now? she was about to ask, not sure she could bear anything else. Not sure she even cared. But then she heard it, too. It was like in the basement of the store—the sound of a distant howling. She was surprised to discover that she could still feel afraid for herself with all that had been lost.

"I really thought he'd give me a little bit of grace," Robert said.

"Legba's rarely generous," Mother Crone said.

"Tell me about it."

"Those are the hellhounds, aren't they?" Geordie asked.

Robert nodded.

"But I thought you dealt with them."

"I dealt with one batch of them, but the otherworld's thick with crossroads spirits, looking to cut their own deal with the *loa*. There will always be more."

He slipped the strap of his guitar over his shoulder and let the instrument hang at his back.

"They'll follow me," he said. "But that doesn't mean you should still be here when they arrive."

Holly looked down the path. She had a long view, but while she could still hear the howling, there was nothing in sight yet.

"What will you do?" she asked.

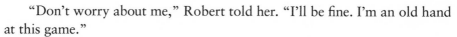

"Don't worry about me," Robert told her. "I'll be fine. I'm an old hand at this game."

Then, just as Legba had done, he stepped away and disappeared. Here one moment, gone the next.

"He's right," Mother Crone said. "We should go."

"But our friends . . ." Holly began.

"There was nothing we could do for them before," the seer told her, "and even less now. They've either escaped or . . . or not."

Holly turned to look at the wall of mist. Nothing had changed. It was still impossible to see through.

"Come," Mother Crone said.

She held Hazel by one hand and took Holly's hand with the other.

"Stay close to us," she told Geordie.

"Can . . . can you just take us back to my store?" Holly asked.

Mother Crone nodded. "Keep an image of it clear in your mind."

"I'll try."

Holly looked back at the wall once more, trying not to think of their friends trapped or dead behind it, unable to think of anything but.

The sound of howling rose up, closer now.

"I'd rather not have to confront those hellhounds," Mother Crone said.

Holly wanted to say, "Right," or "Of course," but she couldn't seem to shape the words properly, so she simply nodded.

Mother Crone repeated what she'd done back in the mall, lifting her hands above her head and bringing them down with a sweeping arm-wide motion on either side of her body. The air went iridescent when her hands came together and then they were looking through a shimmering portal. They could see the bookstore, lit only by the streetlight coming through the front window.

"Is this the place?" Mother Crone asked, taking Hazel and Holly's hands once more.

"That's it," Geordie said when Holly still couldn't speak.

Her grief was unbearable.

She let Mother Crone lead her and Hazel through, Geordie following close behind. The portal closed behind them as silently as it had opened, and with it, all their hopes of ever seeing their friends alive again.

Christiana

I was pretty sure I was dead when I went sliding off the shoulder of the leviathan and that flare of white light blinded me. I remember thinking it was a version of the light you sometimes hear people talk about, the one they see at the end of some tunnel when they're dying. It starts out like a dot, burning far in the distance. They're rising up to and falling into it at the same time. Then they finally disappear right into it and everything goes white.

I don't know. I didn't see a tunnel. But I was falling, spilling right off the leviathan's giant shoulder, and everything did go white.

And then I came back.

I'm completely disoriented at first and become aware of things all jumbled out of their order of importance:

I realize the blood's all gone. I was drenched in it, but there's not a drop on me now.

I have a really sore shoulder, like I landed on it when I fell from the leviathan.

The lake is gone.

The *leviathan* is gone.

The library . . . the library is different. I sit up and look around. The rows of bookcases still go on forever, but I can see a tall, vaulted ceiling now, with chandelier lights hanging at regular intervals. Carpets with an

Oriental pattern run on forever, up one corridor, down another. The rows of bookcases are broken by various little reading islands made up of two or three leather club chairs with ottomans, reading lamps, and side tables.

I look back to where the lake had been. I get up slowly and walk to the bookcase that's right where the shore should be. When I touch the bookcase, it's solid. I pull a book off the shelf, flip through a few pages, then replace it. Same deal. The books are real.

So then the leviathan . . .

Intellectually, I remember his sheer enormity, but my memory calls up a figure in the twenty-foot range. Still improbable. But not the sheer impossibility that I clambered up and stuck with a knife . . .

I see the hellhound blade, lying on the carpet.

And then I remember my companions.

I turn around, but I'm alone. Saskia and Jackson are both gone, like they were never here. Librarius is gone, too, but I see a heap of cloth where I remembered him lying before the world went white on me and everything changed yet again.

I walk over and toe the fabric with my foot. It's his clothing. Mixed up in the folds of cloth are the straps I used to tie him up.

I guess he got taken apart after all.

I can't say I'm sorry, but what does that mean for Saskia and Jackson? And if they got taken apart, too, then where are their clothes? And why am I still here?

It's so quiet in this place that every sound I make echoes loudly—the shuffle of my feet on the carpet, the sound of my breathing. I don't know why I should worry about it. It's not like anybody's going to come along and *shush* me. Then I hear voices. Somebody—a bunch of somebodies—are approaching. It takes me a moment to figure out what direction they're coming from.

I wonder if I should hide, but then it's too late and I realize it doesn't matter anyway, because I recognize them. It's Christy and the tinker and three other people I don't know—the ones that were also there when I got the hellhound knife from the tinker. They all look pretty much as bewildered as I'm feeling and stop dead when they see me.

I figure I must look a sight, but then I remember that the blood's all gone.

Did any of that even happen? Was there a lake and a leviathan? Did I actually kill him?

I remember the blood fountaining from the wound and my stomach does a little flip.

Then I remember something else, how this strange sensation swelled inside me as the leviathan died. Something shifted in me. Changed me. But I'm not sure exactly what. I just feel different. I'm aware of every cell in my body, from my skin to the blood in the marrow of my bones.

Christy and the others have started walking toward me again. They stop a half-dozen feet away.

"Christiana," Christy says. He pauses. "Is it okay if I call you that?"

I have to smile. Trust him to keep a sense of propriety, even in the midst of all of this. He's wanted a name for me forever, but I never wanted to give him that box to put me in. I guess the tinker must have told him. It doesn't seem to matter anymore.

I might have been born as his shadow, but for all I don't know or understand, I do know that I'm my own person and have been since I stepped out of him, this seven-year-old tomboy shadow that got taken under the wing of a ball with arms and legs all those years ago. He can't put me in a box, except for one that he carries in his own head. It's not going to change who I am inside of *me*. He can't know me any more than I know him, except for the things we tell each other, and the trust we have to hold on to to believe that what we're saying is true.

The only box I can be in now is the one I make for myself.

"Sure," I tell him. "You can call me that."

"Are you okay?"

I nod. "How about you guys?"

Now it's his turn to nod.

"Have you seen anybody else?" I ask.

They shake their heads. We're doing real good in the nonverbal communication department here. But I don't blame them. Something like this is so big that it's hard to get your mind around it. I don't know if you ever can.

"Who else was here?" the tinker asks.

At the sound of his voice, I find myself remembering his name. Bojo, short for Borrible Jones. He had this really funny story about why his father gave him that name.

"Saskia was with me," I say. "And this guy named Jackson."

Christy and one of the guys with him both speak at the same time.

"Saskia was here?" Christy says.

"Jackson?" the other one says. "Jackson Hart?"

I nod a yes to both of them and then we do a quick catch up on how Saskia and Jackson and I got here, on who they all are and what brought them.

I give Aaran a hard look, trying to see the monster in him that Saskia told me about, but he's wearing a congenial mask and it's not slipping.

Christy smokes a cigarette, his hands shaking a little while he lights it. It must be hard for him to have been so close to her and then lose her again. He seems pretty messed up, but I don't know what to tell him. There's nothing I can tell him.

Raul asks after some friend of his, but all I can say is that I never saw him. At least, not that I know. He could have been one of the ghosts I saw when I first got here, the ones with voices like radio static.

I find Suzi fascinating. She's got the same energy as Saskia, except she's . . . I don't know. Edgier. I think of the story Saskia told me, about how hard it was for her to fit into the world at first. To assimilate herself with all of its complexities. That's what's different with Suzi. She's not as integrated with the world as Saskia is now.

Bojo's been along for the ride, like me, but he hasn't come close to seeing what I've seen. Doing what I had to do.

"So this librarian," he asks, then pauses. "He actually called himself Librarius?"

I nod.

"He was the one that caused all the trouble?"

"Not the virus, but otherwise, yes. Though to be fair, I don't think he meant it to get so out of hand."

"Do you believe it happened the way he said it did?"

I nod. I don't explain how I was ready to beat the information out of him. It's not something I'm particularly proud of. I don't mean my threatening him. I mean that I was completely ready to go through with actually hurting him if I had to.

"And the Wordwood spirit," Bojo goes on. "He was really a . . . leviathan?"

"I think he still is," I say.

The words come out of my mouth without me even thinking about what I'm saying. But as soon as I do, I realize I'm right. I don't know how I know. I just do.

"When those friends of yours," I say, looking at Christy—I'm working it through as I speak. "When they were making the Wordwood site, either something they did drew him into it, or there was something about it that just appealed to him. So he came . . . across, I guess. From wherever the leviathan exist."

"Like Isabelle's numena," he says. When I nod, he looks at the others, explaining. "A friend of ours has this . . . gift that lets her paintings literally come to life."

"Are you talking about Isabelle Copley?" Aaran asks.

Christy nods.

"So all those weird abstracts she does . . . ?"

"No, this was before them," Christy says. "When she was doing stuff like Jilly used to do. Fantastical creatures and portraits."

"So they just stepped off the canvas?" Aaran says. He holds up his hand as Christy starts to answer. "I'm not arguing," he adds. "After everything I've seen recently, nothing much can surprise me anymore."

"They didn't step off the canvas," Christy says. "What happened was that as she painted, spirits were drawn to inhabit the same shapes as what had been depicted in the final versions of Isabelle's paintings. They were separate from the paintings, but still connected to them."

"Connected how?" Aaran asks.

"You remember the big fire on the island when her studio burned down? When she lost all her studio and all that art?"

Aaran nods.

"The numena died when their paintings went up in flames," Christy says. "They all died, except for the few whose paintings weren't at the studio."

The look Aaran gets really makes me wonder about the things Saskia had to say about him. There's so much honest empathy and distress coming from him—it's nothing like you'd expect a freak to be feeling.

"Jesus," he says. "So when she switched to abstracts . . ."

"It was so that she wouldn't be responsible for any more numena deaths," Christy says.

"I get it," I say then. "So, if Holly and her friends brought a leviathan across in the same way, then whatever happened to the Web site, also affected him."

"Except," Raul says, "I thought you said that a leviathan couldn't take on a physical presence."

"I didn't think so either," I tell him. "And maybe he still can't. Look what happened to him when Librarius forced him into a shape."

"But if he's the Wordwood—"

"Except," I break in, "it's not really physical either, is it? I mean, we're standing inside it, but it's really just digital information."

"I guess," Raul says, but he doesn't look convinced. Or maybe he's just confused. I know I am.

"Who knows, really?" I say after a moment. "I don't want to say anything's possible, but I've seen enough things in the spiritworld to know that whether or not something actually exists isn't a question that comes to mind. If it's in front of you, you believe. And think about it. There's so much that we don't know about the consensual world—you know, the one we all came from. You have to multiply that a thousandfold when it comes to spirits and this world."

We all stop to digest that for a moment. I'm thinking of Mumbo and how quickly it didn't seem weird to have a ball with arms and legs to be my friend. How I still don't think it's weird. She's not this freak. She's just Mumbo.

"So it—he's still here?" Bojo asks, bringing us back to the question of the leviathan.

"I can feel him," I say. "Can't you?"

Except for Suzi, they all shake their heads.

"I feel something," she says. "But it's not the same as it was before."

"Maybe that's because Librarius was the one who gave you a shape and then put you out into the world."

"I guess," she says.

But she doesn't sound sure. Or maybe it's that she doesn't want that to be the case. I can't say I blame her. Given a choice, I'd much rather be thinking of the leviathan as my daddy than to know I'd been put into the world by some freak like the gateway spirit that called himself Librarius.

"Can we talk to him?" Christy asks. "I mean, the spirit of the Wordwood. Can we ask him what happened to the people that disappeared?"

What he really means is, how can we find Saskia?, and I'm with him on that. The trouble is . . .

"I don't know," I have to tell him.

"Maybe we need to be connected through a modem," Raul says. "Well, that's how it worked before," he adds, when we all look at him.

"So," Suzi says. "Anyone bring a laptop?

I can tell she's joking. How would you dial up to a server here? What would you plug the phone jack into? Unless you had a cordless connection, you wouldn't be getting on-line, and I doubt there are any communication satellites floating around in the skies beyond the vaulted ceilings of this library.

"Maybe there's some ritual that will work just as well," Bojo says.

He looks at me, like I'd know, but I can only shrug.

"Maybe," I tell him. "Or maybe we just need to open our thoughts to him."

I see Aaran shaking his head.

"What?" I ask him.

"Nothing," he says. "I'm just not going to be any help if you start getting into the woo-woo stuff, that's all. No offense."

I have to smile. "I know what you mean," I tell him.

"But you're . . ."

"A shadow. Yeah. I know. But Christy's the one who puts all that stuff up on a pedestal. I just take it on a day-by-day basis."

I'm about to expand on that when I get distracted. I lift my head. I thought I heard something, but I'm not sure what. Then I realize that I'm still hearing it except it's not so much a sound—or *just* a sound—as a feeling. A pressure inside me. The more I concentrate on it, the less I can tell if it's something in me, trying to get out, or something outside of me, trying to get in.

I look at the others, but it's as though time has stopped. They're frozen in place—Christy lifting a hand to brush his hair back from his brow. Aaran turning to say something to Suzi. Her eyes are half-closed, in the middle of a blink. I can't see Bojo or Raul and that's when I realize that I can't move either. All I can see is what's directly in front of me. All I can hear is that whisper feeling of pressure, a sound that's not a sound.

This is too weird.

For some reason I don't panic. I'm pretty sure that the Wordwood spirit is doing this. The leviathan. Librarius told me that before its spirit was contained in the body I killed, the leviathan was everywhere, permeating this place. Maybe he's trying to contact me.

Hello, I say, shaping the word in my head the way I talked to Saskia when she was in me. *Is anybody there?*

There's no response.

But the pressure continues to build.

They say our largest organ is our skin, which I always thought was a bizarre concept, because you don't really think of your skin as an individual thing, an organ like your heart or your liver. But I believe it now. I can feel every cell and pore of my skin, all at once, trembling like a drum's membrane in sympathetic vibration to some bigger sound that I can't actually hear.

It's an eerie feeling. Like turning a familiar corner, but everything's changed—not the way it is in the borderlands, where you expect that sort of thing, but how it works in the consensual world, where everything's locked into what it is by the agreement of a hundred thousand wills.

It's like I'm tuning in to something, dialing through the static.

Or like something's tuning in to me.

I remember the shift I felt inside me just before the leviathan died and the white light blinded me. Something changed for me then, but I still don't know what. I can only recognize that a change occurred and that maybe what's happening to me right now is a result of that subtle transformation—a transformation so subtle that I can only sense the results. I can't connect to what it is.

But I don't want to change. I don't want to be someone else. Truth is, the idea of it kind of scares me. I remember, growing up, how I'd hear other people wishing they were someone else—and I still overhear that in conversations—but I've only ever wanted to be me. Me, with all my faults and scraped knees and bruised heart and all. I know I've done some dumb things, and gotten into more trouble than I should have, but those mistakes and escapades helped shape who I am.

And I like who I am. Or was. I don't feel like I know who I am right now.

Because there's something else inside me. It's not like it was with Saskia, a recognizable foreign presence. It's something that's not me, but it's me at the same time, if that makes any sense. It doesn't to me, but that doesn't stop it from happening all the same.

At some point—

Moments? Minutes? Hours?

—I find my—

Attention? Gaze?

—turning inward.

I can't see anything anymore. I feel like I'm floating in water, but under the surface. Encompassed in . . . I don't know.

Thick air? Some kind of gel?

I just know it's peaceful. So serene. I could float here forever and not worry anymore about who I am or if I've been changed.

But then the sound that's not a sound, the *pressure,* builds inside/outside me again, a choral rhythm that thrums on both sides of my skin, and this time I can sense a sort of communication. It's not like how you or I talk to each other . . . with words, in sentences. Instead, I suddenly acquire all this information that I didn't have before, all at once—like a data dump, Jackson would say—and I understand that—

The leviathan is changed, too.

He's been damaged by either the virus, or what Librarius did to him—it doesn't matter how it happened. What matters is that the leviathan is . . .

I'm not sure how to explain it. He's expanding. That's what the pressure I feel is. It's the leviathan, his spirit swelling, pressing against the borders of the Wordwood. He needs us—or at least one of us—to stay here and provide an ongoing conduit to the world outside the Wordwood, allowing the pressure building up inside him to dissipate at a regular, steady pace instead of all at once.

Without that conduit, he'll implode like a black hole, sucking the spiritworld with him into the wormhole the implosion will create. Eventually, the whole of spiritworld will be gone and when that happens, the consensual world, *our* world, will start to be sucked in along behind it.

Cause and effect, domino-style.

So the leviathan needs to ease the pressure in small amounts through contacts outside of the Wordwood, and he can't do it himself because he has no connection to either the spiritworld or ours. But those of us trapped in here with him at the moment . . . we do.

I think of Librarius. It figures. While this wasn't the case before I freed the leviathan from his fleshy prison, a being like Librarius is now necessary: a gateway spirit, opening lines of communication between the worlds. Librarius was just planning to go about it the opposite way from how it needs to be done. He wanted the attention, the input of the people in the worlds outside the Wordwood to feed him. The leviathan needs to send his own attention *out* of the Wordwood.

Through one of us.

But I'm not a gateway spirit, I find myself saying. *None of us are.*

The reply comes, not in words, but I understand it all the same:

Gateway spirits don't have to be born; they can be made.

He means one of us.

One of us needs to stay.

I run through the options in my mind.

It can't be Christy—he needs to be with Saskia. He's been willing to sacrifice everything to see her safe and be with her again. We couldn't possibly ask this of him.

The same goes for Raul who's here for his lover Benny.

Suzi can't do it because she hasn't got a strong enough connection to the consensual world yet, and no connection at all to the spiritworld.

As for Aaran, not knowing his history, you'd think he was a good man. But I can't forget what Saskia's told me about him. How could he possibly be trusted for something this important?

That leaves only Bojo and me.

And it's obvious who it has to be. Bojo's far more of an innocent by-stander than I am. He only got pulled into this because he likes Holly and wanted to help her. I started out the same, wanting to help Saskia figure out who she was, but then I started messing around like I always do. Breaking Saskia's glass coffin. Busting Librarius. Freeing the leviathan from his prison of flesh.

But the most important difference between Bojo and me is that he's not a shadow.

He's real.

And I'm not, no matter what I try to tell myself.

I mean, think about it. The truth has been sitting there right from when I was that little seven-year-old girl cast off from Christy, and Mumbo came along to show me the ropes. She was teaching me to how to *pass* for human.

I hate to give up my independence, but really, who's got the least to lose? Except for Suzi, at least the others stuck in here with me are all real. And Suzi's too newborn to be of any use to the Wordwood spirit, for all that she looks like she's in her twenties. I'm the only one of the two of us with the right kind of connection to the outside world.

After coming to my—admittedly reluctant—decision, my head fills with directions on how the others can leave the Wordwood and what I need to do here once they're gone. It's like the leviathan's monitoring my thoughts and isn't *that* creepy.

You know, I say. *If we're going to have any kind of a decent working relationship, the first thing we need to do is work out some boundaries. It's bad enough I'm going to be stuck here like this. The least you can do is allow me a little privacy. Because really, nobody likes—*

I don't get to finish. As suddenly as I found myself unable to move and ended up wherever it is I am, it all goes away, and just like that, I'm back in my body.

My eyes feel dry and I blink. I see Bojo making the sign of horns, thumb holding down his two middle fingers, the remaining two standing straight out. It's a tinker's ward against bad luck. The others just look the same way I feel: stunned.

"Wow," Christy says after a moment, Mr. Words reduced to the vocabulary of a doper.

Aaran gives a slow nod. He looks around at each of us, gaze finally settling on me.

"Was that . . . was that *him*?" he asks. "The Wordwood spirit?"

Suzi answers before I can. "I think so. It must have been. But it didn't feel like the spirit I knew . . ."

"He was right inside my head," Raul says. "No, he was totally a part of me, but separate at the same time."

That's when I realize that everybody's had the same experience as me. Good. It makes what I have to do easier.

"That was the leviathan," I say. "And I take it you all know what has to be done?"

Raul nods. "Someone has to stay behind, or he . . . what? Implodes? Did I get that right?"

"Pretty much," I tell him. I look at the others. "And you all learned how to leave?"

Christy finally finds his voice. "We open a door back to our world—" He starts to shape the spell with his fingers, but stops before the sequence of finger movement is complete. "—staying focused on where we want to go while we're doing it."

"But who stays?" Raul asks.

"That's easy," I say. "It's going to be me."

I see the looks that cross their features: relief that someone else has stepped forward, which then shifts into guilt. Christy's the first to argue the point.

"Why does it have to be you?" he asks.

"Because I've got the least to lose," I tell him. "I might as well be here as in my little hidey-hole in the borderlands. Being here's not going to make that big a change in my lifestyle."

"Bullshit," Christy says. "You're the original free spirit. This'd kill you."

He's right. It might. But I'm not about to admit that. Not till they're gone and the deal's done.

"No, I should do it," Suzi says. "I don't have a life to lose—not a real one, at least. All the memories in my head were put there, except for what's happened in the past day or so."

"And that's the problem," I tell her. "You don't have a strong enough anchor to the consensual world. A day or so in here, on your own with the leviathan, and you could completely lose what little connection you have."

"Not if I stayed with her," Aaran says.

She gives him a warm look. I can't tell from Christy's expression if he trusts Aaran or not, but I still don't.

"Or I can stay on my own," Aaran adds. "After all, what's happening here is my fault."

"I'll give you that," I tell him. "But do you have the background or stamina for this kind of thing?"

He shrugs. "I could ask the same of you. I know books."

"This isn't going to be about books."

"No, but it will be about spending a lot of time in this place and it looks like the only distraction will be the books. My whole life's been about books." He glances at Christy. "Even if I could never write one worth a damn." He turns back to me. "And as for stamina, none of us know how well we'll do until we give it a try. Unless you've done this kind of thing before?"

"Yeah, right."

He nods. "So there you go. I should be the one that stays."

"No," I say. "I'm doing it and I'm not arguing about it anymore. Like I said, I've got the least to lose."

"What about me?" Bojo says.

I shake my head. "You've got something to go back to—or at least the potential for something, which is more than I'll ever have."

"Playing the martyr doesn't become you," Christy says.

"I'm not playing at anything. Now go. You know how to leave. The leviathan showed you, the same as it did me."

There's a long moment of silence. I look at them, one by one, trying to stare them down into agreeing with me. When I get to Christy, I can tell he's about to start in again, but Aaran interrupts him before he can get the first word out.

"No," Aaran says. "She's made her decision. Who are we to argue the sacrifice she's willing to make? It's a hard enough thing she's got to do as it is, without our making it harder by not giving her our support."

I really don't see the creep in him that Saskia does. Who knows, maybe he's changed for real. Whatever. I'm just happy to have someone backing me up. And one by one the others come around.

It's hardest for Christy, I can tell. He's torn between wanting to be with Saskia and stopping me from doing this. We've always had a weird relationship—I mean, just consider how I came into the world. He probably thinks he's alone in this endless fascination he has for his shadow twin, but that's only because I've never shared my own curiosity for him. I just go sneaking through his journals and observing him from a distance instead of asking questions the way he does of me.

"You can always e-mail me, care of the Wordwood," I tell him. Then I smile. "Just think, you'll finally have a way to contact me whenever you want. Won't that make a change."

"But I'll never see you again."

"Oh, this gig won't last forever," I say.

Everybody knows I'm lying—including him. After all, we all got the same telepathic message from the leviathan. Whoever stays becomes a gateway spirit and there'll be no coming back from that. For all I know, the change already started for me, back when I fell off the leviathan and into the light. Something happened to me then.

So we won't be seeing each other again.

But he doesn't call me on it—he knows how stubborn I can be once I make up my mind about something—and neither does anyone else.

"Say hello to Saskia for me," I say.

He nods. "Thanks for keeping her safe."

"It was my pleasure," I tell him and I mean it.

Then we all say our goodbyes and they open a door in the air to take them back into the consensual world—a one-way trip back. I want to look away, but I find I need this one last glimpse of what I'm leaving behind. All I see is some basement. A worktable. Stairs leading up.

I lean closer as they start to step through, one after the other. Then, just as the door's starting to close, I feel a shove from behind me and I'm falling through, arms flailing for balance.

And the door in the air whispers shut behind me.

This, Too, Shall Pass

*Were we always
strangers,
or did we only
learn to become
this way?*
—Saskia Madding,
"Strangers" (*Mirrors*, 1995)

Christiana

We land in a tangle of limbs on a cement floor. I suppose I should be grateful that I'm not on the bottom, but all I'm really concerned with is figuring out who gave me the shove and took my place back in the Wordwood. I have my suspicions.

Because I'm on top, it's easier for me to extract myself from the pile. I do a quick head count. Christy. Raul and Bojo. Suzi.

I was right and I get a little nervous twitch in the pit of my stomach.

It was Aaran.

No wonder he was so helpful and ready to take my side when we were arguing about who should stay. He must have had this planned from the moment the leviathan came into our heads and told us what we needed to do. What *one* of us needed to do.

And it wasn't me after all.

I can't tell what's stronger: relief that I'm not stuck back there in the Wordwood with the leviathan, or the worry about what Aaran will get up to in there.

Christy and Raul regard me with some confusion, but Bojo and Suzi get it right away.

"Oh, you fool," Suzi says softly, and I know she's not talking about me.

"He made his choice," I say.

I'm feeling a little weird. Do they all feel that way? That I was supposed to be the one to stay behind?

Suzi seems to understand what I'm thinking because she looks right over at me and gives me a half-hearted smile.

"He means well," she says. "But from everything I've come to know about him, he hasn't had that much experience at playing the good guy. And I don't know that he's strong enough to take on something like this. He's not like you in that way."

I've never been good at compliments so I don't acknowledge it. But it sure makes me feel better.

"This is going to be hard on you," I say. "You two had a thing going, didn't you?"

She shakes her head. "We had the start of something, but I'm not sure what. I like him—I like him a lot, actually—but we met under circumstances that could have gotten in the way of a long-term relationship. You know, once we got past the rush of getting to know each other."

"Like your being born in the Wordwood."

"Not to mention his picking me up while I was panhandling."

"That wouldn't make a difference," Christy says. "Not if you care about each other."

Suzi looks away from me, but not before I see the wet shine in her eyes.

Way to go, Christy, I think. Here we are trying to downplay Suzi's feelings for Aaran, and you have to come out with something like that. But I know he didn't mean to make her feel bad. He's thinking about himself and Saskia, trying to show how this kind of thing can work out. Trouble is, we're way past the chance of that happening.

"So does anybody know where we are?" I ask.

Adding anything to what we've just been talking about is only going to make Suzi feel worse, so I opt to change the subject.

"The basement of Holly's store," Bojo says.

I've been in the store before, but never down here. There's something in the air I can't quite place. A hint of the otherworld that goes beyond the fact that the basement has been used as a place to cross over. Now that I think of it, I got that same feeling upstairs the few times I've come into the store. I just put that down to all the books. They've always seemed like magic to me. I mean, talk about your doorways into other worlds.

"I need to use the phone," Raul says. "To call . . . home . . ."

That makes Christy perk up. Raul wants to check on his lover Benny. Christy needs to see if Saskia made it back. Because none of us know what

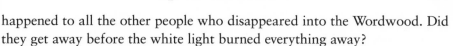

happened to all the other people who disappeared into the Wordwood. Did they get away before the white light burned everything away?

We troop up the stairs just in time to see yet another otherworld door open in the middle of the bookstore. Holly and Geordie come through it, along with a tall woman dressed like a skateboarder with a little twig girl by her side. I recognize the woman from revels in Hinterland. Her name's Galfreya, but I think she calls herself Mother Crone when she's here in the consensual world.

There's all sorts of confusion as our two parties meet—which is only heightened when a door opens at the back of the store and a hob and a little yapping Jack Russell terrier are added to the mix. As soon as I see the hob, I realize what that hint of the magic I feel here is. Holly's got a bookstore hob living in her store.

While Holly picks up her dog and tries to calm it down, I catch Galfreya's eye. She nods hello and has the same "funny to see you here" look in her eyes that's probably in my own. Then I do a quick fade into the borderlands and leave them all to sort it out.

I just want to go home, but first I have to check in at Christy's apartment to make sure that Saskia's okay.

I don't know why I assumed that Saskia was back, safe in the apartment she shared with Christy. I just did. So I have a moment's panic when I slip in—stepping sideways from the borderlands as I always do—and she isn't there.

I call her name. Soft. Then louder.

My heartbeat becomes a quick thunder in my chest as I go from room to room in the apartment.

The sudden ringing of the phone makes me jump. Christy, looking for Saskia. I don't pick it up. What could I say to him?

I remember the white flash when I was falling from the leviathan's shoulder. Had it burned her away?

Then I see clothing scattered on their bed. The jeans and T-shirt she was wearing in the Wordwood the last time I saw her.

She just got cleaned up and went out looking for Christy.

The sense of relief that floods me is almost physical. I find myself sitting on the edge of the bed and reach over to touch the jeans as though to assure myself that they're real.

I wonder if she knows he went to Holly's store? Probably not. So, where would she go? Geordie's place, I decide. Or the professor's house, where Jilly's still recuperating from the car crash that took her out of commission last year. I decide to try Geordie's first because it's on the way to the professor's house.

I take another shortcut through the borderlands and step back into the consensual world in the alley behind the apartment, startling an old orange tom with a torn ear. He goes skittering off through a hole in the fence of one of the yards backing onto the other side of the alley, while I walk around to the front. My heart lifts when I see Saskia going up the steps of the building. She jumps when I call her name. A huge grin lights her features when she sees me and she hurries over to give me a hug.

"You made it," she says as she steps back. "I was so worried about you."

I nod. "I was worried about you, too."

"I was just looking for Christy . . ."

"I figured as much. He's at Holly's store."

She turns to look for the bus stop, but I take her arm and walk her back into the alley with me.

"I really have to see him," she says.

"I know you do. That's why I'm taking you the quick way."

I step her into the borderlands, get my bearings, then pop back out with her into the consensual world at the same place I left Holly's store a few minutes ago. Christy's on the phone—calling home again, I guess. Everybody else is still talking a mile a minute, except for Bojo, who's leaning against the front door, a half smile on his lips as he takes it all in.

Saskia turns to me. "You'll have to teach me that trick."

"Any time," I tell her.

Then I leave her to run over to where Christy's trying to reach her by phone, and I finally get to go home.

Okay, here's what happened, or at least what I remember and was able to find out later. Some of it's been confirmed by news reports, back in the consensual world. A lot of it, for obvious reasons, can't be. The funny thing is what people actually remember, which isn't a lot. You can still find the original reports of the disappearances in newspaper morgues and on-line, but there isn't any of the follow-up you'd expect from a story this big. If you were paranoid, you might think it was a government cover-up, or if you know what I know, you might think the leviathan had something to do with it through his on-line resources now that he's got Aaran on board to make contact with the outside world again.

But *people* don't remember. It's like there was some little blip in reality and now that it's over, no one's willing to even think about it anymore. No, that implies choice. What we have here is like it never even happened in the first place.

All those people who disappeared reappeared from wherever they'd originally vanished. At least, I think they all made it back. I know Holly's friends did, but they don't remember any more of what happened than anybody else does. Even Jackson's clueless. I went by to see him and he just stood there in the doorway of his apartment looking at me—the way you do when you've opened the door on a stranger and you're not quite ready to let them in, but you're still willing to see what they want.

I'd have turned around and walked away, except for the faint puzzle of recognition I see in the back of his eyes.

"You don't really remember me, do you?" I say.

He shakes his head. "You seem a little familiar. . . ."

"Guess I really made an impression."

"I'm sorry, I just—"

"It was a joke," I tell him.

He still doesn't seem too big in the sense of humour department.

"It was a long time ago," I say. "We met in a library."

He shakes his head again. "I can't remember the last time I was in a library." He pauses for a moment, then steps aside. "Do you want to come in?"

"No," I say. "I just wanted to see if you were okay."

He gets a nervous look. "Why wouldn't I be?"

I wonder at his nervousness, then I remember him telling us about the prank he played on some bank, the one that let Aaran blackmail him. So he remembers that much.

"No reason," I tell him. I start to turn away, then look back at him. "A word of advice: Next time someone tries to blackmail you into sending a virus anywhere, maybe you'd be better off owning up to what you did and taking your medicine."

"What do you know?"

I smile. Not "What do you mean?" but "What do you know?"

"Nothing that's going anywhere. Just remember what I said."

"But he—"

Jackson stops himself.

"Don't worry about Aaran," I say. "He's out of your life now. Just don't get into any more trouble."

"Who *are* you?"

I shrug. "Maybe I'm your conscience," I tell him.

"Do you have something to do with the bunch of people I found in my apartment when I . . ."

"When you what?"

I can see the confusion deepening in him as he tries to work it out.

"I was going to say when I got back," he says, "but that's not right. I haven't been anywhere . . ."

"Don't give yourself a headache," I tell him. "And maybe try to find yourself a better hobby than hacking bank computers and sending out viruses."

"Wait a second . . ."

But then I do walk away, down the stairs and out of his life.

Christy has a theory about all of this forgetfulness. Of course, Christy has a theory about everything, bless his heart, but this one makes a certain amount of sense. I can't remember how we got to talking about it. I wasn't even planning on having a conversation with him that morning. The shades and curtains are all drawn, and it's comfortably gloomy inside when I slip into their apartment. I thought they'd both still be asleep—I just came by to stand at the end of their bed like the shadow I am, reassuring myself that, yes, they're still safe. I don't realize that Christy's awake and lying on the sofa in the living room until his voice comes to me from out of the darkness.

"I wanted to thank you again for rescuing my girl," he says. "I was so worried."

He's not being disrespectful, calling Saskia his girl. No more than she is when she refers to him as her boy. I think they'll still be doing it in their eighties. At least I hope they will.

"You don't have to," I tell him. I sit down in the wing-backed chair so that we can see each other without Christy having to get up from where he's lying. "I like her and I wouldn't want to see anything happen to her either."

"You do? Like her, I mean."

"Why wouldn't I?"

"Well, you're my shadow. I just assumed you wouldn't."

"Because I'm supposed to be all the things that you're not?"

He nods his head.

"Jeez, will you get with the program," I tell him. "That happened when we were seven years old. You've had plenty of time to reacquire all sorts of bad traits since then. Just like I've had the time to acquire some good ones."

"So, do you think we're more the same than not these days?"

What I want to say is: No. You're real and I'm not. But I don't feel like getting into a discussion about that at the moment. And I don't want to make it sound like I'm feeling sorry for myself.

"I think we're like twins," I say instead. "We're individual, but we still have this birth thread linking us to each other. We know how the other thinks and feels. We can feel each other's presence in the world, no matter the distance between us."

And that's true, too.

He smiles. "I never have the slightest idea as to what you're thinking about."

I laugh. "Yes, but that's only because I'm so mysterious."

"Christiana Tree," he says, and laughs with me. "Which makes you Ms. Tree." At my raised eyebrows, he adds, "Saskia told me."

"Has she left me any secrets at all?"

"You'll be happy to know that she was most circumspect. She said your secrets weren't hers to tell."

"I'd just as soon people didn't think about me at all," I say.

"Why's that?"

I shrug. "Life's just easier when you're anonymous—when people have no expectations about you."

"You're not exactly forgettable," he says. "Look at Bojo. He only met you the one time, but he remembered you right away."

"Maybe I was doing something outrageous."

He smiles. "Were you?"

"I don't know. Probably not. I find that people remember me more when I act just like them. Half the time I can step away into the borderlands right in front of someone and the next time I see them, it's like it never happened." That makes me stop and think for a moment. "Which," I go on, "is pretty much like what's happening with this whole business of the people who disappeared."

"It's a mental self-defense mechanism," Christy says, "that seems to have been bred into the species. Sometimes it works just on the level of individuals, other times, society itself convinces itself to forget."

"Is this more of your 'consensual world' theory?"

He nods. "The World As It Is exists the way it does for most people because they've agreed not to accept exceptions to what's been decided is impossible."

"So who decides?'

"No one person," he says. "It's something that becomes ingrained in the fabric of society as a whole. And there will be variations. It's why religious sects exist. They've all agreed to a different take on some aspect of the accepted canon of how the world's supposed to be. That agreement—that view into a different version of the World As It Is—becomes a rallying point for their beliefs and draws them together."

"So nobody remembers that all these people disappeared because it contradicts the way the world's supposed to be."

It's not a question, but Christy answers it as though it were with one of his own.

"Can you think of a better explanation?"

"Besides some vast hidden conspiracy?" I say.

He nods.

"Not really," I say. "But why do *you* remember?"

I don't have to ask about myself because I already know the answer: I'm not part of the consensual world in the first place. Considering my origin, my life, and where and how I live, I'd be in therapy forever if I didn't accept that little bit of information as true.

"There are different reasons why people remember," he tells me. "Someone like Jilly just expects the world to be more than it is, so she's never surprised when reality strays from the acceptable norm. Holly won't be forgetting because there's too much magic in her life now, starting with having a hob for a business partner and friend.

"As for me, writing it down has helped a lot in the past, but it's not foolproof. Looking at the words on paper is often too great a distance from what they're describing and rationality kicks in, convincing me it probably didn't happen."

"But in your books . . ."

"For some reason, the anecdotal evidence I collect for the books is easier for me to accept than what I experience myself. I mean, how long did it take for me to accept that you're real?"

"I didn't help."

He smiles. "No. But then we also *expect* the supernatural to be mysterious and speak in riddles."

"And now?" I ask.

He shrugs. "I'm starting to have more and more hands-on experience with the supernatural. It's coming to the point where I can't *not* believe, the whispering voice of reason inside me be damned."

I start to snicker and a puzzled frown crosses his features.

"What?"

" 'Hands-on experience,' " I repeat and then start to giggle. When he gives me a blank look, I manage to add, "You. Saskia," before I dissolve into laughter.

"Oh, for God's sake."

But he has to wait until I can get myself under control again.

I don't know why I'm feeling so giddy. It must be relief that even though we were all so far out of our depth, we not only managed to survive, but we also set things right again. How often does that happen, in this or any world?

Finally I'm able to stop, though laughter's still bubbling up in the corners of my bones, just waiting for any silly little thing to set it off again. I wish that for just once Christy would loosen up and let himself go. But though he's smiling with me, he doesn't lose it the way I do. Maybe he just doesn't think it's very funny, but I'm guessing it's more because he's always so in control of himself. It's funny, we're the same age, but sometimes our relationship seems more like parent/child. Right now he's looking at me the way a father might his errant daughter.

I clear my throat and try to feel serious.

"So Saskia's okay?" I say.

He nods. "She must be. She's able to sleep while I'm still sitting up. I thought I'd work on those galleys for Alan, but I can't seem to concentrate on anything."

"I can't help but feel that all of this is my fault," I tell him. "If I hadn't convinced her to try to make contact with the Wordwood spirit, none of this would have happened."

Christy shakes his head. "It was in motion long before that."

"I guess. But would *we* have been involved?"

"Maybe not. But think where that would have left the people who disappeared."

I give him a slow nod. "Not to mention the leviathan."

Christy closes his eyes for a moment. When he opens them again, I see they're filled with wonder.

"I only caught a glimpse of him," he says. "Before the flare. But he seemed immense."

"Like a mountain. I can't imagine him standing up."

Christy nods. "I don't think I've ever experienced anything so *other*."

"Me, neither," I say.

"Even with living in the borderlands and all you've done?"

"Even with that."

"That was a pretty brave thing you did," he says.

"Or pretty stupid. It could have all gone wrong. But I was running on instinct and there just didn't seem to be anything else I could do."

We fall silent awhile then, Christy lying on the couch, me slouched in the chair. He lights up a cigarette and offers me one. I shake my head. I feel like I should go and let him get back to bed, but I don't want to be alone yet. And he doesn't seem to be in any hurry to get up.

"So how is everybody else?" I ask.

He shrugs. "Oddly enough, Geordie's taking it the best of all. Considering his past history as our resident skeptic, I would have thought he'd be the quickest to put it all behind him, but the experience seems to have . . . I don't know. Loosened him up, certainly. He was talking about how much he was going to relish telling Jilly about all of this." Christy pauses for a moment, then adds, "And I think there's a little mutual attraction thing happening between him and Mother Crone."

I lift my eyebrows. Everybody knows that—his last long-term girlfriend notwithstanding—Geordie's always carried an unrequited torch for Jilly. Well, everybody except for Geordie and Jilly. But one of them always seems to be in a serious relationship when the other's not. At the moment it's Jilly. So Geordie being interested in Galfreya could be a good thing. Especially if she's interested in him.

"How mutual?" I ask.

"Well, when Holly asked her what payment she required for helping them cross over, she said his coming to play at one of their revels." Christy smiles. "Then added that she'd also consider it a favour and an honour."

I nod in understanding. Knowing Galfreya, she'd only offer such an invitation to a potential lover.

"I guess everybody's pairing up," I say.

"Traumatic experiences can do that. When you make it through, you find you just want to hold on to someone—you know, to feel grounded again."

That probably explains why I'm here.

"And how about Holly?" I ask.

Christy shakes his head. "You'll have to ask her yourself. But Bojo was still there when we all left."

After awhile I sit up from where I've been slouching. I uncurl my legs from under me and set them on the floor. Christy sits up as well.

"I should go home," I say.

"Home."

"I do have one."

"I never doubted it. It's just . . ."

I smile. "You're curious about where and what it is."

"Saskia said it was like a room in a meadow."

"It is," I say. "But she wasn't actually there. That was when she was riding around inside my head." I hesitate for a moment, then say, "If you're not doing anything, I can show it to you."

"You mean right now?"

"Why not?"

"I . . ." He looks to the closed bedroom door. "I'd love to," he says, "but it's too soon since all of this happened. I know Saskia's sleeping, but I want to stay close in case she wakes up. It's all I can do not to pull up a chair by the bed and just sit there, watching her sleep."

I wonder what it's like to have someone feel like that about you.

"It's okay," I tell him. "Some other time."

I reach over to the coffee table and pick up the notepad and pencil that are lying there. I write my phone number on it and put it back down.

"Call me when you're ready," I say.

"You've got a phone?"

"A cell phone."

"And it works over there?"

I nod. "I had to trade to get an ever-charge spell for the battery and rewire it. Don't ask me to explain what satellite the signals are bounced off of now, but yes, it works just fine."

"An ever-charge spell."

"Don't start banging up against the idea of magic again," I tell him. "Not with all of what we've been through."

"I'm not. It's just . . . you don't expect magic to be used for something so mundane."

"Here's a news flash," I say. "Most magic is used to enhance the mundane."

When I stand up, he does, too. He starts to put out his hand, but I give him a hug instead. I've never been very demonstrative with him for a whole bunch of reasons. I want to maintain my air of mystery with him and I know all too well that he's not one of your touchy-feely people. And then there's also that warning of Mumbo's not to get into physical contact with the person whose shadow you once were.

But nothing happens except he hugs me back.

"Don't be a stranger," he says into my hair.

"I never was," I tell him.

Then I let myself fade away into the borderlands and he's left holding only air.

Holly

It seemed to take forever before the last of them left the bookstore. Not that Holly was unhappy to have them here—these were her friends, after all. Or at least most of them were. And those that weren't—Mother Crone and Hazel, Benny's boyfriend Raul—were the sort of interesting people she could easily become friends with. But right now Holly was tired and the crowd of people—talking over each other, using the phone, vying for her attention as they retold some part of the story she already knew too well . . . it was all too much for her.

She needed to come down from the adventure, not relive it.

But finally it was simply Dick and Bojo still in the store with her. She stood holding Snippet, the little dog drowsing in her arms. Bojo leaned against her desk, looking handsome as ever, while Dick appeared asleep on his feet. When Christy closed the door behind him and the crowd that was going back to the mall to get his car, the hob blinked suddenly. He gave Holly and Bojo each a considering look.

"It's time for this old hob to get himself to bed," he said.

Which seemed odd to Holly, because she had the impression that Dick never slept. When he retired to his room, it was only to read until the morning when he could get up and go about his business in the store— when he wasn't dusting and organizing in the middle of the night. But then she realized what the considering look had been about and found herself blushing.

"I'm glad you're back, Mistress Holly," Dick told her.

There was a knowing smile in his eyes, reminding Holly once again that while Dick might be no larger than a child, he was actually much older than her. And probably far more experienced, too. She remembered seeing little men not so unlike him, dancing close to pretty little fairy maids at the revel in the mall concourse. There had been nothing innocent in the way they rubbed up against each other.

Dick turned from her.

"And goodnight to you, Master Borrible," he said.

He gave Bojo a nod, tipped a finger against his brow, then turned and went upstairs to the apartment. When the apartment door closed behind him, Bojo and Holly looked at each other.

There were a hundred things Holly wanted to say, but all she could think about was how handsome the tinker was.

"Well," Bojo after a moment. "Here we are."

Holly nodded.

Speak, she told herself.

But she was too shy.

"I should probably go see what the bodachs and piskies have been up to at Meran's house," the tinker added. "I was supposed to be looking after the place, after all."

But he made no move to leave.

Or you could stay here a little longer and kiss me, Holly thought.

But she seemed to have lost her voice again.

"So I was wondering," he said, "when I was off with the others on our adventure. Do you have a motorcycle?"

Holly shook her head, but the question was curious enough to surprise words from her. "Whatever for?"

"A red-headed girl in black leather on a motorcycle . . . could there be anything more a tinker could ask for?"

Heat rushed up Holly's neck, but she still managed to smile and keep her voice.

"The hair I've got," she said after a moment. "And the leather's doable—at least the look is. I think I'd prefer pleather." At his blank look, she added, "It looks and feels like leather, but you don't have to kill an animal to wear it."

"Not killing is good."

She nodded.

"What about the motorcycle?" he asked.

"You're going to have to settle for a bicycle."

He studied her for a long moment, then smiled.

"If I just had the red-haired girl," he said, "I wouldn't feel like I was settling for anything. I'd already have it all."

Something seemed to melt, deep inside Holly. Her pulse quickened.

Whoa, slow down, she told herself. Think this through.

Granted, there seemed to have been an immediate attraction between them from that first moment when he came through the front door in response to the call she'd left on Meran's answering machine. And she couldn't remember the last time a man this handsome had seemed so interested in her—it surely hadn't been in this lifetime.

But she also knew that surviving danger made people feel the need to be close to each other—and what was closer than sex?

And then there was the fact that he was a tinker. A travelling man. He could leave for parts unknown—*very* unknown—at any time. It could be tomorrow morning. And if not tomorrow, then next week. Next month.

And that, her heart asked her, was relevant to the moment at hand . . . how?

She took his hands and tilted her head.

"Don't make any promises," she said as he leaned down to kiss her.

He stopped, those gorgeous eyes of his with their long lashes so close to hers.

"I always keep my promises," he said.

"I know. You've told me that. But I don't want you to be bound to anything beyond right now. We don't even know each other."

"We know what's important."

Holly smiled. "No, we just know that, right now, we want to be close. We don't know anything beyond that."

"So, what is it that you look for in a man?" he asked.

"Someone who can stick around," she said. "Who can be here for me."

"Ah. Now I—"

Holly reached up and put her finger against his lips.

"No," she said. "No promises, no figuring anything out."

She took her finger away.

"But—" he began.

This time she stopped him from talking by pressing her own lips against his.

Suzi

They were kind and they meant well. There had been offers to give her a place to stay—from the couch in the apartment upstairs to the spare room at Christy and Saskia's place. And that feeling of being disliked for no reason except that she didn't seem to belong in this world, appeared to have faded—at least among these people. But Suzi still needed to get away and be on her own.

There was too much to think about.

She had a head full of memories—not simply from the past few days, the ones that she knew were real, but a lifetime of others that had been implanted in her upon her creation. When she considered them—the abusive husband, her family turning on her—she felt they must have come from a novel, filed somewhere in the Wordwood. Something teary and a little over-the-top, but nevertheless absorbing for all that it was fiction.

But knowing that didn't stop the memories from feeling real. It also created a whole other world of confusion, because now she had to live with the idea that underneath the implanted memories there was only a blank slate of a life. There was *no* life. She'd been "born" full-grown, just the way she was now.

She didn't know how to begin to deal with it. And since she didn't know where to start in understanding and getting along with herself, how could she possibly interact with others right now, no matter how well-meaning they might be?

It would have been different with Aaran. She might have told him that there wasn't much hope for a relationship between them, but that didn't mean there couldn't have been once she'd had the time to figure out who she was, which would, in turn, let her figure out who they could be.

But the chance for that was gone.

She had only herself.

And that became increasingly clear as she listened to Raul's side of his conversation with his returned lover Benny.

". . . know what I'm doing here," Raul said. Then he laughed. "I know. It is pathetic, isn't it? But I'm on my way home. I'll be on the first flight to Boston in the morning."

He didn't remember—not anything of what had happened. Neither did Holly's other friends who'd found themselves inexplicably in Jackson Hart's apartment. Listening to Holly's side of the conversation when Estie called the store, Suzi made up her mind. She slipped upstairs and retrieved Aaran's laptop, then said her goodbyes and left the store. They had protested—especially Saskia, who'd mysteriously arrived out of thin air when everyone had their backs turned.

"I know how hard this can be," Saskia said.

Suzi knew she meant well. And there was a kinship between them, considering their origins. But she was only interested in one piece of information from Christy's girlfriend.

"Can you show me how to step between the worlds the way you just did?" she asked.

Saskia shook her head. "I have no idea how it's done. Christiana brought me here."

And Christiana had already stepped away again, back into the other-world.

"I tried to adjust on my own, too," Saskia went on. "Trust me. It just makes it harder."

Suzi nodded. "I'm sure you're right. But I still feel like it's something I have to do on my own."

"If you need help—you'll call us, right?"

She found a piece of scrap paper on the desk and scribbled her name and a phone number on it.

"I will," Suzi told her.

Suzi was impressed. It was an awfully generous offer for Saskia to make, considering how she felt about Aaran herself, and what she must know of Suzi's own friendly relationship with him.

"Really," Suzi added when Saskia gave her a dubious look. "I will."

And then she was finally able to escape all of their good intentions, stepping out of the store and onto the quiet street. It was early morning—she wasn't sure exactly what time it was, but the skies were still dark and there was very little traffic. She walked briskly down to Williamson Street, not stopping until she got to the bus stop. She wasn't sure if the subway ran this far north, but she wouldn't have taken it anyway. She only knew her way back to Aaran's now-empty apartment from how they'd gotten here. By bus.

That was her big plan. She had to go back to collect her duffel bag anyway, but she might as well stay in the apartment for a little while. Why not? Nobody else would be using it. Not Aaran—that much was certain. It was near the end of the month, but surely no landlord would come looking for his rent cheque for at least a few days. She might even have a week. All she really needed was a quiet refuge while she tried to figure out what she was supposed to do with her life.

Sitting on a bench while she waited for the bus, she closed her eyes and tried to make a connection back to the Wordwood. But it was still gone. Severed as though it had never been.

She thought about Raul back in the bookstore, confused as to what he was doing here in Newford. Not to mention Holly's other friends, who'd not only found themselves far from their homes, but in some stranger's apartment with no clue as to how they'd gotten there.

The past was real for them, except for the last couple of days. *Those* they didn't remember at all. She, on the other hand, remembered the recent past as true, and all the rest of her life as a lie.

How were you supposed to be absolutely sure what was real and what wasn't? What if the past few days were the false memories? What if she really had walked out on Darryl after one physical attack too many? What if she really had a sister who now hated her because of that? A family that had pushed her out of their lives?

How were you supposed to know for sure?

She opened her eyes and stared across the street.

Maybe you weren't. Maybe people who grew in their mothers' wombs could get just as confused.

A southbound bus arrived then and she got on, finding a seat among the sprinkle of sleepy-eyed early morning commuters already on board. She sank back in her seat and tried to remember if there'd been a fire escape outside of any of the windows at Aaran's apartment. At least there hadn't been an alarm system.

Christy

All things considered, there's an unspoken decision made to take a bus over to the mall to pick up my car. I don't know what it would do to Raul if we suddenly took him on a shortcut through the otherworld. He's already forgotten everything that's happened in the past couple of days. He doesn't even register Dick—the hob disappearing from his awareness in that way that Faerie can do so well. Mother Crone's little friend Hazel doesn't register for him either, while Mother Crone just looks like a skateboarder, albeit one in her twenties. He never questioned Saskia's sudden appearance in the store.

Saskia.

I can't believe how my heart swelled to see her standing in front of me. Real. Unhurt. I took her in my arms and didn't want to ever let her go again. We might have still been there if she hadn't patted my back.

"Time for me to breathe now," she said in my ear.

I let her go, but after that it was hard for me to concentrate on much else of what was talked about until Geordie said something about getting the car from the mall's parking lot.

I know we tried to convince Suzi to stay here with Holly, or in the guest room at Saskia's and my apartment. I was aware of Estie and the others calling from Jackson's apartment, totally messed up about what they were doing there. Suzi left. Raul booked a flight that needed him to get to the airport in a couple of hours. Holly told Estie what hotel she and the others were staying at. She told them they could come over, but they, too, were intent on returning to their own homes.

"They're going back to their hotel to check out," she said when she got off the phone. "Then they're also going to book the first flights they can get out on."

Which is when Geordie mentions that we should pick up the car and I realize that we really should go. I'm dead on my feet.

I let go of Saskia's hand long enough to give Holly a hug and to shake Bojo's hand.

"Do you need a ride?" I ask the tinker.

He shakes his head. "I don't have far to go. I'm looking after the Kelledy's place."

"But that's—"

All the way downtown, I was going to say. Miles from here. But Saskia nudges me in the ribs and I get it. Holly and Bojo. They've been making moony eyes at each other ever since we got back.

"A good gig," I say. "They've got a beautiful house."

I glance at Saskia and she smiles approval at my recovery. She hooks her hand in the crook of my arm and gives me a little tug toward the door where Geordie and the others are already waiting. She's probably worried that I could still put my foot in my mouth.

I nod to Dick and then we all troop out into the early morning air, leaving the three of them behind in the store.

We trail along the sidewalk as we make our way down to the bus stop on Williamson Street.

"Oh, I never thought," Geordie says to Mother Crone. "Will you be okay on the bus?"

He worried about Faerie and iron—never a good combination in the old stories. But I figure any Faerie living in the city must have acclimatized themselves to the metal by now.

"We'll be fine," Mother Crone says.

"You don't like buses?" Raul asks.

"I'm just not used to them," she says and manages to sound sincere. "They don't have them where I come from."

"Jeez, where's that?"

"The place that they don't have buses," she says, but she smiles in a way that lets him know that she just doesn't want to talk about it. She's not mad or anything.

Raul shrugged. "I think I'd like it there," he says. "I've always hated public transportation."

The bus comes then, sparing us any further conversation. Hazel goes scrambling up the steps as soon as the doors open, invisible to Raul and the bus driver alike. I dig in my pocket for change, but Geordie produces a handful of tokens and pays for all of us.

I hand the car keys to Saskia when we finally reach our old beast. I know I'm too tired to drive and for all she's been through, she seems a lot more alert. Raul gets in the back on the driver's side, while Saskia slides in behind the wheel. I walk around to the other side.

Mother Crone takes Geordie's left hand and runs a finger over the calluses his fiddle strings have left on his fingertips.

"I meant what I told Holly," she says, her smile, her eyes, promising more. "Come play music with us—any time. Tap on the shipping bay doors that Dick took you through. The revels usually start after midnight."

"I will," he says. "Should I bring any other musicians?"

"So long as you bring yourself," she says.

She leans forward and says something that I can't hear, then she gives him a kiss on the brow and a little push towards the car. Hazel's sitting on the hood, staring in through the window at us and making faces. She jumps down when Saskia turns the ignition and then we're heading for the airport.

A couple of hours later we've dropped Raul off, then fought the growing commuter traffic back into town. Saskia pulls the car up in front of Jilly's building where Geordie's staying. I lean over the seat to look at him before he gets out.

"You okay with all of this?" I ask him.

He gives me a slow nod.

"I went to an actual Faerie revel," he says with a grin. "And I've been invited back."

"So you're not freaking anymore about things that aren't supposed to exist?"

"No. Should I be?"

"Not in my book," I tell him.

"What do you think of Mother Crone?" he asks.

"I think she needs a new name," I say.

"She has another one," Geordie says.

"What is it?"

He shakes his head. "I don't think I'm supposed to tell. You'll have to ask her yourself the next time you see her."

I shake my head. "She's no better than the rest—all riddles and mystery."

Saskia gives me a look but I can tell she's only mildly exasperated. "I think she's nice," she tells Geordie. "A little spooky, but nice."

"She's a seer."

"That would explain the spooky." She looks as if she wants to add something to that, but then she reaches back to ruffle his hair and only says, "Be careful."

"Because of Faerie glamours?" he asks.

He's still grinning. Saskia smiles in return.

"Because of whatever," she says. "Thanks for coming to look for me."

"Hey, you're like my sister. I couldn't *not* come."

He leans forward to kiss her cheek. Then, giving me a light punch on the shoulder, he gets out of the car. Saskia pulls away from the curb and we're finally alone.

We don't say much on the drive home, but I guess we don't need to.

Later, our positions are reversed. Usually I'm the one who drifts off after we've made love, but this morning I'm wide awake and she's the one who's fast asleep. I lie there beside her for a long time, marveling that I could be so lucky as to have her in love with me, but finally I get up.

I'm feeling restless and I don't want to disturb her. I wander around the apartment a bit and half-decide to do some work on those galley corrections that I owe Alan, but eventually I just lie down on the couch and think about all the strangeness that's filled my life these past few days.

I'm still awake when my shadow arrives. I smile as I see her slip into the apartment. I have a name for her now. Christiana. Christiana Tree.

"That makes her Ms. Tree," Saskia said before she fell asleep. "Get it?"

Suzi

Everything fell together for Suzi as though arranged by some higher power. Not God, of course, but when it came to manipulating data and finances electronically, the Webmaster at the Wordwood was certainly more than humanly efficient. She wanted to call him Aaran, but that was only who he'd been.

Now he was an anonymous Webmaster.

She hadn't needed to break into Aaran's apartment. There was a fire escape outside the bathroom window and the window had been open, covered only by a fine-mesh bug-screen. The window was too small for a regular-sized burglar to crawl through, but she'd been able to push in the screen and squeeze through without too much trouble. There were benefits to being small.

She searched through the drawers in the kitchen, then through the two in the maple washstand in the hall by the front door. One of the drawers in the latter rewarded her with a set of Aaran's spare keys. This was good. The next time she entered the apartment, she could come in through the front door.

Once she had the apartment key, she went back out to the alley and climbed up the fire escape to retrieve the laptop. She set it up on the mahogany writing desk in the corner where Aaran had kept it. Finding the right place to plug in the phone jack had her puzzled until she realized that the back of the machine opened up to reveal a hidden panel of sockets, one of which fit the phone jack. It took her longer to figure out how to get on the Internet. She couldn't remember the protocol Aaran had used and she wasn't computer-savvy enough to figure it out on her own. In the end, she tried simply opening Explorer, then clicking on "Yes" when the prompt came up asking her if she wanted to work on-line.

As soon as she was connected, she typed the Wordwood URL into the address bar near the top of the screen. After a moment's pause, a new window opened with a still picture of a forest rather than the streaming video that used to normally be there. There were no options to click on and no matter where she moved the cursor, it never changed from an arrow to the hand with a pointing finger indicating a link that could take her elsewhere.

She stared at the screen for a while, then returned the cursor to the address bar where she typed in the URL that would take her to her Hotmail account.

Besides the usual spam, there was only one new message.

Her pulse quickened when she saw whom it was from: Webmaster@ TheWordwood.com. But her happiness dampened as she read through the businesslike list of what had been provided for her:

The apartment was now in her name. Rent and all utilities were covered and would continue to be covered if she decided to move elsewhere.

A bank account had been opened in her name. A debit card was on its way to her by mail. If she needed money now, she could go to the bank to withdraw it from a teller. There was also some cash in the nightstand drawer on the left side of the bed.

She blinked when she looked at the amount that was in the account. Where had all that money come from? As though Aaran had expected the uneasy feeling rising up in her, the source of the funds was described in the next paragraph, something about skimming fractions of interest accrued on hundreds of thousands of accounts—each on its own amounting to nothing, but collected together it became a very tidy sum indeed.

The e-mail ended with the hope that she'd be happy in her new life and was simply signed "the Webmaster."

It was like getting a letter from a lawyer. Just the facts, ma'am.

Her first impulse was to walk away from it all. But reason prevailed. Yes, it made her feel like she was a kept woman, but there were no strings attached here. And really, did she want to go back to the streets and its dangers?

You never really lived on the streets, a part of her argued. That was only an implanted memory.

True. But that didn't make living on them any safer or easier.

She reread the e-mail and sighed, remembering an early conversation with Aaran when they'd decided that maybe they were each other's guardian angels.

He was certainly hers now.

Her distant, unapproachable guardian angel.

Because there hadn't been any warmth in the message. She supposed she should take comfort in the knowledge that seeing to her welfare had been one of the first things he had done once he'd established contact with the world outside the Wordwood, but why couldn't there have been something personal?

Something. Anything.

Because Aaran needed to cut himself off from human concerns, she realized. It would be the only way he could survive in the alien symbiotic relationship of which he was now a part.

She supposed she understood.

But it was small comfort, alone as she was in the world.

In the days that followed, she avoided everyone who'd been involved with the events that had led up to Aaran's disappearance into the Wordwood. Mostly, she stayed in the apartment. Reading, watching TV. As often as not, she simply pulled a chair up to a window and sat staring at the view. No one knew she was here—no one besides the Wordwood's Webmaster, she supposed—so no one tried to contact her.

But eventually she had to get out more often than simply slipping off to the corner store for staples.

She knew her past wasn't real—she was an active person, not a reactive one, no matter how the memories she was carrying around in her head said otherwise. The Wordwood spirit might have created a background for her in which she had docilely accepted Darryl's abuse until finally standing up for herself, but that wasn't who she was. Or if it was—if that was how she was *supposed* to be—then the conditioning had failed.

Or she had overcome it.

There was no point in looking for a job. Aaran had provided enough money for her to make the simple earning of money not an issue, and she had no burning desire to follow any particular career. At least not yet. That might come, but for now she thought it best to concentrate on experiencing more of the consensual world firsthand. Build up a store of her own *real* memories.

So she visited museums and galleries. She went into cafés and ate out, watching people as they interacted with each other. She tried shopping, but she didn't need much, not with everything Aaran had in his apartment. She did shop for clothes, but found that after picking up some new cargo pants and T-shirts, a nice jean jacket, underwear and even a couple of dresses, she wasn't mentally equipped to do any more. She carried around a pocket full of change and parceled it out to panhandlers and buskers that she passed on the street.

She discovered libraries and found them fascinating, both for the people-watching they provided as well as for the books. Aaran had a whole spare room devoted to his own personal library, but it held mostly fiction and she was more interested in nonfiction. How things worked. How history unfolded. How people, famous or not, lived their lives.

It was on one such expedition to the Crowsea Public Library, walking by the computer room, that she spotted a familiar face. She stood in the doorway watching Christiana, her face bathed in the light of the monitor, her fingers tapping away on the keyboard. She almost turned and walked away, but at that moment Christiana sat back from the computer and looked up. Their gazes met.

Suzi hesitated. Christiana smiled a greeting, but she seemed to sense how close Suzi was to bolting and she made no move to get up and come over. Finally, Suzi closed the distance between them. She pulled an unused chair from another table and sat down beside Christy's mysterious shadow, not sure why she was doing it. Not sure she even liked the woman. Christiana was the only one of them, other than Aaran, who had argued to stay behind. She was the one who should have stayed behind.

"So, how are you finding the consensual world?" Christiana asked.

Suzi shrugged. "It's interesting."

She glanced at the screen. It showed an in-box from a Yahoo account with as many messages as her own. None.

"Funny how that word's changed," Christiana said.

"What do you mean?"

"Well, people used to say something was interesting when it really did grab their attention. It'd be something remarkable. Or appealing. Or at least out of the ordinary. Now it's just a polite way of being noncommittal and usually means you don't find it interesting at all."

Suzi blinked.

"So which is it for you?" Christiana asked.

"A bit of both," Suzi admitted. "There are a lot of things that can keep my attention, but at the same time I feel distanced from it all."

"What have you been doing?"

"Mostly just watching people."

Christiana gave her a knowing look.

"Well, what's wrong with that?" Suzi asked.

"Absolutely nothing. But when I was learning how to be real, the first thing I was told was that I needed to interact with people."

"I don't have to learn how to be real."

"I didn't say you did."

Suzi smiled. "No, but you inferred it."

"I suppose I did. I guess I just assumed you'd be experiencing some of the same problems with self-identity that Saskia and I have."

"You don't think you're real?"

"I don't know. I was born as the cast-off shadow of a seven-year-old boy. How real is that?" Christiana smiled suddenly, but the humour didn't reach her eyes. "But it's funny. Until I first ran into Saskia and we had the long talk that got us involved with this whole Wordwood fiasco, I never really questioned where I came from. That's just who I was."

"And now you do."

Christiana nodded. "I feel kind of adrift. Rootless."

"Well, I may not be so good at interacting with the world at large," Suzi said, "but I'm sure about this much: It doesn't matter where any of us come from, or even what we look like. The only thing that matters is who we are now."

Christiana didn't say anything for a long moment. Her gaze traveled away from Suzi's face, and Suzi wasn't sure if she was looking inward or across the library.

"That's pretty good," she said finally, looking back at Suzi. "It puts the onus on yourself, instead of on where you came from. It suits what I like to think of as my independent temperament with the added bonus of making good sense. How can your genetic history or your past even begin to compete with who you are today?"

Suzi took that as a rhetorical question, so she didn't worry about an answer.

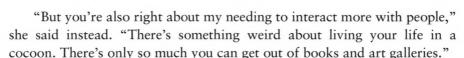

"But you're also right about my needing to interact more with people," she said instead. "There's something weird about living your life in a cocoon. There's only so much you can get out of books and art galleries."

Christiana nodded. "How are you doing for living expenses? Have you got a place to stay yet?"

"I'm in Aaran's apartment. He set it up so that everything of his is in my name, plus he's opened up a bank account for me with a ton of money in it."

"Probably ill-gotten gains," she said, but there was a smile in her voice that let Suzi know she wasn't not supposed to take it seriously.

"Only semi-ill-gotten," Suzi told her.

"Do you ever hear from him?"

Suzi sensed more than simple interest in the question.

"Just one e-mail that first day," she said. "It was very businesslike and just signed 'the Webmaster.' "

"That's harsh."

Suzi nodded.

"Have you ever run into any of the other . . . scouts the Wordwood sent out with you?" Christiana asked.

Suzi smiled at Christiana's momentary hesitation. She'd probably been about to say "spies."

"No," she said. "I can't sense their presence any more than I can the Wordwood's, but then I haven't been looking for them."

And she realized she wasn't particularly interested, either. That was all part of an old life. She wanted to concentrate on the new one. What she had now.

Christiana was looking at the monitor. "Funny to think how we were all right in there only a few weeks ago."

"In where?"

"The Wordwood. The Internet. Where it was a place instead of pixels on a screen."

"But it's nothing we have to worry about now," Suzi said.

Christiana nodded.

Suzi decided that she liked sitting here, interacting with someone other than the voice in her head. She also liked Christiana, even if it should have been her that stayed behind in the Wordwood.

"Do you want to go and grab some lunch?" she asked, surprising herself.

Christiana pretended she had to think about it. "But only if you're paying with those ill-gotten gains. It'll make me feel more piratical."

"And that's good because . . . ?"

"It means I can finally get a parrot and who knows? There might even be a treasure map tied to its leg."

"Except you'll have to change your name to something like Long John Silver."

"I suppose," Christiana said. "Say, did you ever wonder if he got that name because he always ran around in his underwear?"

That made them both giggle. The woman sitting at another computer station nearby shushing them only made it worse. So they got up and left before a librarian came over and threw them out, the two of them leaning against each other, bending over from having to stifle their laughter.

Christiana

So, remnants of our journey into the Wordwood continue to impact on my life.

I've got a new friend in Suzi—I love her observations about other people when we're out at a café or a concert, or just walking down the street. She can be serious and funny and she never hesitates at the thought of trying some new adventure. In that way, she's more like my friends in the borderlands than most of the people I meet here in the consensual world.

During that first lunch we had together, she asked me to teach her how to travel between the worlds. I knew why she wanted to learn, but I couldn't argue her out of it. She needed to talk to Aaran. So did I, but going back into the Wordwood didn't strike me as the answer.

Why did I teach her?

Partly because if I didn't, someone else eventually would. But mostly because I didn't see her getting into the Wordwood anyway. Even if Aaran—or what was left of Aaran in the Webmaster he'd become—wanted to let someone in, I doubt the leviathan would allow it to happen.

So I taught her how to find the borderlands by tricking them into existence in her peripheral vision. It's easy, really. What we actually observe is such a small part of what's going on around us.

Try this some time. Hold your hands out at arm's length and make a circle with your index fingers and thumbs that's about the size of a dinner plate. *That's* all you really see at any given point. Everything around it your brain makes up from its memories of what your eyes have taken in as you generally scan your surroundings. And that's why it's so easy to find the borderlands in your peripheral vision. All you have to do is to trick your mind into believing that they're actually there and then step sideways into them.

Though I guess that doesn't explain how you can catch something in your peripheral vision, like someone approaching, or a car as you're about to step off a sidewalk. But mostly it holds true. And I know for sure that the borderlands are always there, waiting for you.

The otherworld's tougher—at least crossing over to it from this world is. But it's simple to reach once you're already in the borderlands. The membrane, veil, whatever that lies on the edges of both our world and the spirit realm is so much thinner when you're looking through it from a vantage point inside the borderlands.

It took Suzi awhile to get the hang of it, but before too long she was moving through the worlds like a seasoned pro.

"I love this," she said the first morning she appeared in my meadow apartment.

She was polite enough to stand outside in the cedars and clear her throat, waiting for me to notice her and invite her in.

I smiled at her and beckoned her in.

"Yeah," I told her as she sat on the end of my bed. "It never gets old."

Christy and I treat each other more like brother and sister now. He's stopped putting me on a pedestal, and I try to be more straightforward with him and not feel like his weird little shadow. But there are still things I won't tell him. Like Galfreya's name. I side with Geordie on that one because when it comes to Faerie, names are a big deal. It's like that in most of the borderlands and the otherworld, too. Giving someone your name is a gift; it says "I trust you."

How come I know her name? That's a whole other complicated story involving whiskey and Maxie—never a peaceful combination—and this is neither the time nor the place for it. One thing at a time, Mumbo always tells me.

So as I was saying, mostly I try to be more forthcoming with Christy. We've even had these family dinners—Christy and Saskia, Geordie and me. I enjoy them more than I thought I would. There's none of the awkward tension of needing to make conversation that I was expecting. We just sit around and yak, stuffing our faces with some new wonderful meal that either Saskia or Geordie has put together. Neither Christy nor I can do much more than boil water and burn toast, though we make a fine clean-up team when the meal is done.

When Bojo's in town, I'll often hang out with Holly and him, though most of the time when I go by the bookstore I spend talking to Dick. We'll sit up into the middle of the night and talk about obscure books long after the others have fallen asleep. He loves the fact that I actually know a lot of the characters that started out their lives in the pages of those mostly forgotten stories. I think I've actually got him convinced to tag along with me to the next party at Hinterland, which is a big deal for a stay-at-home fairy man like a hob.

As for the others . . .

I never went back to see Jackson. He came through in the end, back there in the Wordwood, but I think knowing me would just cause him more problems than not. Every time he'd see me, he'd have that weird feeling of unwanted memories pushing up against the calm complacency of his life.

For some people that would be a good thing, but Jackson struck me as someone who expects to find order in the world, and knowing me tends to put a little chaos in your life instead. Look what happened to Saskia within a day of introducing herself to me in that café.

I didn't even meet the other Wordwood founders, but Holly tells me that they and Raul are fine. I did get her to ask if any of them had heard from Aaran, but they didn't know who he was and none of them will have anything to do with the Wordwood site anymore. When Holly asks why, they don't really have an answer and she doesn't press them.

I remember liking Raul—maybe because he was gay. He looked at me like I was an individual instead of evaluating my attractiveness the way so many men do with women. It's weird how refreshing a lack of sexual energy can be in this overly-charged world where even kids' cartoons seem to be selling sex, though it's not something I'd ever want to give up in the long term.

And it's not like I think Raul's some kind of prude. He's just got a different orientation. If I was a guy, he'd probably have been checking me out.

The only one I never met before the Wordwood business began was Robert Lonnie, but both Christy and Geordie talk so much about him that I've been keeping an ear out for that guitar playing of his wherever I go, whether it's wandering through the city or in the borderlands.

"You'll know it when you hear it," Geordie tells me when I ask him to describe it. "Trust me."

And he's right.

I'm on Palm Street late one night, walking past this run-down bar, when I hear a bluesy guitar playing a familiar twelve-bar like I've never heard it played before. I know exactly who this must be and stop dead in my tracks. The place has been closed for hours. It's dark inside and the door is locked—like that has ever stopped me. Drawn by the music, I step into the borderlands, then back into this world, but take a few steps so that when I reappear, it's inside the bar.

The guitar playing stops immediately.

I see this handsome black man sitting in a booth at the back of the bar, a guitar in his lap, a big revolver in his hand, the muzzle pointed straight at me. We stare at each other for a long moment before he finally lowers his hand and lays the weapon on the table.

"Either they're making hellhounds too pretty to resist," he says as he starts to play again, "or you've got some other good reason to come creeping around at this time of night."

"Can I sit?" I ask.

He smiles. "I don't know. Can you?"

I don't rephrase my questions into a "may I." I just take his smile as a yes and pull a chair from a nearby table and sit near his booth.

"I'm a friend of Christy and Geordie's," I tell him. "Kind of like a sister, really."

He cocks an eyebrow and his index finger does a hammer-on up around the seventh fret, bass string, that sounds like a question.

"Kind of how?" he asks.

"I'm Christy's shadow."

"You look pretty substantial to me."

I shrug. "He cast me off a long time ago—when he was only seven."

"How's that make you feel?"

"I don't know. Most of the time I never really thought about it, but lately . . ." I give him another shrug. "I just don't know."

Robert gives a slow nod.

"I've known a shadow or two," he says. "The one who usually comes to mind was cast off by this brother who ended up on death row for killing I don't know how many people. Back in my time they'd have just lynched him."

"What was he like?"

"Meanest mother I've ever had the misfortune to run across."

"I meant the shadow," I say.

"That's who I was talking about."

"But . . ."

"You don't really believe you're locked into whatever personality you were born into when you were cast off, now do you? That you've got to stay the opposite of the one that cast you off?"

It's the same argument I gave Christy. Somehow it seems to have more weight coming from someone else.

"Not really."

He nods. "In my limited experience, shadows have as much control in how they turn out as do the people who cast them off—and that's more than anyone thinks. Especially the people who like to use genetics as an excuse when they mess up."

"I'd like to think it's not all been laid out for me."

"Everybody makes their own way in this world," he says.

He falls silent then. Or at least he stops talking. His fingers make magic happen from that beat-up old guitar of his, and I just sit there and listen to him until the morning comes banging up against the windows of the bar.

Here's the one thing I can't seem to let go: Aaran in the Wordwood.

What's he *doing* in there?

I know it's partly morbid curiosity centering around the fact that it could have been me. That maybe it should have been me. But there's also a huge helping of worry in the mix because the Aaran I met doesn't jibe with the one Saskia and everybody else knew.

Christy said that Aaran appeared to undergo a genuine change of heart. He thought it had to do with Suzi, that somehow she got inside where no one else could. That just the example of her was enough—for whatever reason—for him to want to make amends for the way he'd been living, the way he treated people. That her coming into his life was an epiphany, though we shouldn't belittle his own efforts to change and make a difference either.

Suzi's in Christy's camp, though she thinks the changes in Aaran were all his own. That all he'd ever needed was for someone to accept him at face value. To look past the bullshit face he offered the world and just believe in him.

Saskia doesn't agree. She wants to be more generous, but I guess the wound he dealt her way back when cut too deep.

Me, I can't make up my mind. I need to talk to him some more first. So I keep e-mailing him in care of the Wordwood. I go on-line on Christy's computer when he and Saskia are out, or asleep. I become a regular at the Cyberbean Café, stopping in every other day for a cappuccino and to use their Internet resources. I slip into the Crowsea Public Library and use their machines, usually at night when everybody's gone home, but sometimes during the day, too.

Maxie says I should just get a machine of my own. Apparently there are ways to get them to work in the borderlands, the same way my cell phone does. But I don't really want one. Except for this one little cyber quest of mine, I've about as much interest in owning a computer as I do staring at the way little bugs scurry away when you lift a rock. No, that's not true. I actually like looking at little bugs.

So I keep borrowing other people's machines, and one day when I'm in the Cyberbean, there's finally a response waiting for me in my in-box:

To: MsTree@yahoo.com
Date: Tue, 26 Sept 2000 15:04:21 −0400
From: Webmaster@TheWordwood.com
Subject: Re: Are you there?

Hello Christiana,

I've been wanting to write for ages. And I would have gotten back to you much sooner, but . . . well, it's complicated. I've spent the last month or so completely caught up with the need to assimilate myself with this strange new reality I find myself in.

I guess the thing I really need to tell you . . . no, it's more that I need to share it with someone and, except for Suzi, you're the only one who keeps making an effort to contact me. I'd tell Suzi, but I don't know how to put it in the right words. And I know what she'd say, anyway: You make your own destiny, or some other positive thing like that. But I'm not sure she would actually understand. I'm not sure you will either, but it won't hurt as much if you don't. And maybe you will. You were inside the leviathan. Not just like the others, but like me. We were deeper inside him, I think. The others couldn't have been or they'd have put up a bigger argument to stay and do what I'm doing.

I'm not making much sense, I guess. It's funny, I can multitask like you wouldn't believe now. But it's all Wordwood business. Dealing with e-mail and downloads and running _serious_ scans for viruses on uploads. But when it comes to something personal . . . well, there's not a whole lot of personal left.

But what I need to tell you is this: Librarius lied to you. He didn't come from outside the Wordwood when the virus struck to take advantage of the situation. Oh, he was trying to take advantage, all right, but not like he let on.

He was trying to separate himself from the all-pervading spirit of the leviathan. He was in here all along, just like I am now. He was the Webmaster.

I guess what I'm trying to say is that I'm afraid that I'll give in just like he did.

I know it's different. I have foreknowledge. And I'll try to do this right like I've never tried to do right before. But I've only been here a month or so and I already know _exactly_ what Librarius was feeling. You don't get a moment's break. Not a moment to be yourself.

I don't feel real anymore. Hell, I'm _not_ real, am I? I'm no more than interactive software creating a conduit between the leviathan and the world outside.

So I guess what I'm really trying to say is, it could happen to me. Some new crisis like the virus Jackson sent could show up and, even though I know better, already I can see myself taking advantage of it and trying to figure out how to separate myself from the leviathan.

Not today. Or tomorrow. Or even in a year. Don't forget, Librarius was here for years before he broke.

I'm just scared that I'll break, too.

I don't know if I'm strong enough not to. I don't know if anybody is.

Aaran

http://www.thewordwood.com/

I realize as I'm reading his e-mail that he's not the only one having a crisis. I'm having one, too. An identity crisis, which is kind of funny when you think of how all of this started. Or at least how all of it started for Saskia and me: she was having the crisis and I convinced her to contact the Wordwood because it seemed the best way she could answer the question once and for all: Is she real or not?

But I'm the one who's been circling around that question ever since we got back.

No, that's not true. I've never stopped wondering about it from the moment I got pushed out of Christy. It's just that meeting Saskia—carrying her around inside me and with what I've been through with the leviathan and all—has brought it to a head and I don't know how to deal with it.

I'm still looking at the screen when someone sits down beside me. I look up and there she is. Saskia with her golden hair and sea-blue eyes, so effortlessly beautiful.

I get her to read Aaran's e-mail.

"You have to let this go," she says when she reaches the end and turns to me. "There's nothing we can do about it now."

"I know. It's just . . . worrisome."

She cocks her head and gives me a considering look.

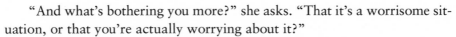

"And what's bothering you more?" she asks. "That it's a worrisome situation, or that you're actually worrying about it?"

How can she know me so well? Like Christy said, I'm the original free spirit. No cares, no worries. Something bad's happening? Tra-la-la. I'll go somewhere else where it's not.

"How much did you get out of me when you were inside my head?" I ask.

"Only what your physical senses told you," she says. "I couldn't read your mind or know what you were feeling about something unless you shared it with me."

"Well, that's a relief."

"And you're avoiding the question. Which of the two worries you more?"

"Both," I have to admit.

"Well, it's good that you can worry about it," she says, "but you still have to let this go."

"But . . ."

"What are you going to do? Figure out a way to get back into the Wordwood and take his place?"

"Maybe that's not such a bad idea."

She shakes her head. "And you wouldn't be affected by the same thing that's happening to Aaran because . . . ?"

"I'm a shadow?"

"Oh, please. What happened to that independent streak of yours?"

She reaches past me and pushes the delete button. Another e-mail pops up in place of Aaran's, some spam telling us that we really do want men's penises to be bigger. It's exactly what I need to put everything into perspective. There's *always* going to be someone or something that thinks it knows you better that you can know yourself.

We grin at each other. I exit my account and we leave the computer free for another customer. Saskia gets us each another cappuccino and we sit at a table by the window.

"With all our adventuring," I say. "We didn't really find anything out, did we?"

Saskia smiles. "You noticed?"

"So, are you okay with it? Not knowing for sure what coming from where you did means?"

"In terms of who I am now?"

I nod.

"I think so," she says. "I've decided that it doesn't really matter. That it shouldn't matter for anyone. Maybe this is sour grapes—you know, because *I* don't know what I really am any more than you do. Or maybe it's like a poor person saying money can't buy happiness because they don't have any themselves, but if we take it down to basics, it doesn't matter where we come from, or even what we look like. The only thing that matters is who we are now."

I smile. "That's almost word-for-word what Suzi told me."

"You've seen her?"

"Mmhmm. And I still do. I see all kinds of people in the consensual world now."

"You're becoming a regular little social butterfly."

"I always was."

"Only not here. Not in this world."

"Christy's world," I say.

"Why does it have to be his world?" she asks. "Why can't there be room for both of you in it?"

"No reason, I guess."

I feel a little lighter as I say it. Like actually using the words can make them true. Maybe that's the change I felt coming over me when the leviathan left his physical body. Maybe I'm finally accepting that I can have a place in this world, that I can make lasting relationships here, instead of always being the traveller, passing through.

I smile at her and repeat the words again, enjoying the taste of them as they leave my tongue.

"No reason at all."

Affirmations

for

Self-Healing

Self-Healing

Swami Kriyananda

CRYSTAL CLARITY PUBLISHERS
Commerce, California

© 2005, 1988 by Hansa Trust
All rights reserved. Published 2005.
First edition 1998. Revised edition 2005.
Printed in the United States of America
    6 8 10 12 14 13 11 9 7 5

CRYSTAL CLARITY PUBLISHERS
crystalclarity.com | 800-424-1055
1123 Goodrich Blvd. | Commerce, California
clarity@crystalclarity.com

ISBN   978-1-56589-207-1 (print)
           978-1-56589-630-7 (e-book)
           978-1-56589-812-7 (audiobook)
Library of Congress Cataloging-in-Publication Data 2005008190

Cover photography by Swami Kriyananda
Interior layout and design by Michele Madhavi Molloy

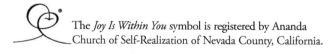

The *Joy Is Within You* symbol is registered by Ananda
Church of Self-Realization of Nevada County, California.

To my spiritual family,
with all love.

Contents

Introduction

The thoughts in this book are those by which
I have tried to live my life. They are the fruit of
experience, not of book learning. They represent
lessons learned—sometimes in sorrow, disappointment, and pain; at other times, in the thrill
of discovery and of expanding joy. Sometimes
I have quoted the wise words of my spiritual
teacher, for it might also be said that none of this
book could have been written, had it not been for
the guidance that I received from him.

There are fifty-two basic subjects covered.
Thus, they can be used for every week of the year.
But again, if you prefer, you can meditate on the
qualities that are the most meaningful to you,
turning to them at times of special need.

Affirmations for Self-Healing

An affirmation is a statement of truth which one aspires to absorb into his life. It has been said that we are what we eat. It would be truer to say, "We are what we think." For our minds express, and also influence, the reality of what we are far more than our bodies do. Our thoughts even influence, to a great extent, our physical health.

No real progress in life ever comes haphazardly. A sportsman must work hard to master the techniques he needs: throwing a ball, skiing down a difficult slope, jumping the greatest possible distance. And a pianist must work at least as hard to master the movements of his fingers, to play with ease the most intricate musical passages.

Living, too, is an art. Unfortunately, it is one to which most people devote little energy. They take life as it comes, and wonder why things keep going wrong.

Thoughts are things. Words, which are crystallized thoughts, have immeasurable power, especially when we speak them with concentration. The mere thought of fatigue is enough to sap our energy. To strengthen that thought by the words, "I'm exhausted," gives definition, and therefore added power, to the thought itself.

The opposite is true also. If one feels exhausted, but suddenly finds his interest drawn to something, his fatigue may vanish altogether! One *is* what one thinks. If, in addition to that sudden interest, he verbalizes it with the words, "I feel *wonderful*!" he may find that, instead of only feeling vaguely better, he actually feels as though he had acquired a new self-definition.

So many of our failures in life — to master new languages, to get along with others, to do well whatever we want to do — are due to the simple thought that what we want to accomplish is alien to us.

Again, many of our successes in life are the result of fully accepting the new as our own. French, for example, can be learned more easily by the student who absorbs himself in the thought, "I am French," than by him who says (as children in the classroom often do), "Those people talk *funny*!"

The difficulty is that our habits are buried in the subconscious mind. Thus, even when we resolve to change them, we find ourselves being drawn back repeatedly, and quite against our conscious will, into old ways.

Affirmations, on the other hand, when repeated with deep concentration, then carried into the subconscious, can change us on levels of the mind over which most of us have little conscious control.

We are what we think. But we are also far more than what we think consciously. We are the myriad conflicting patterns of feeling, habit, and reaction that we have built up over a lifetime—indeed, over lifetimes—in our subconscious minds. To heal ourselves, we must also set those inner conflicts in order.

Nor is it enough, even, to affirm change on conscious and subconscious levels. For we are part of a much greater reality, with which we must live in harmony also. Behind our human minds is the divine consciousness.

When we try to transform ourselves by self-effort alone, we limit our potential for healing and growth. Affirmation should be lifted from the self-enclosure of the mind into the greater reality of superconsciousness.

To be healed is to "be rid of an imperfection." To be perfect is to express the superconscious — the source of creativity and solutions. Therefore, in using affirmations we concentrate on positive qualities which are the solutions to our disease and imperfections.

The superconscious is that level of awareness which is often described as the higher Self. It is from this level, for example, that great inspirations come. It is through the superconscious that divine guidance descends and true healing takes place. Without superconscious attunement, affirmations, like any other merely human attempt at self upliftment, have only temporary benefits.

Affirmations should be repeated in such a way as to lift the consciousness toward superconsciousness. This they can accomplish when we repeat them with deep concentration at the seat of divine awareness in the human body, the Christ center, which is a point in the forehead midway between the two eyebrows.

Repeat the affirmations in this book loudly at first, to command the full attention of your conscious mind. Then repeat them quietly, to absorb more deeply the meaning of the words. Then speak them in a whisper, carrying their meaning down into the subconscious. Repeat them again, silently, to deepen your absorption of them at the subconscious level. Then at last, with rising aspiration, repeat them at the Christ center.

At every level, repeat them several times, absorbing yourself ever more deeply in their meaning.

By repeated affirmation you can strengthen, and, later, spiritualize your awareness of any quality you want to develop.

Affirmation is only the first step to self-healing. We must do our human part. Without additional power from God, however, our efforts are forever incomplete. Affirmation, in other words, should end with prayer.

Why should one pray only after repeating the affirmations? Why not before? Prayer is always good, certainly. But if it isn't uttered with an affirmative consciousness, it can easily become weak and beggarly: a plea that God do all the work, without man's active participation. Effective prayer is never passive. It is full of faith. It matures in an attitude of affirmation.

To become established in any new quality, it helps first to affirm it, following the sequence that I have described. Then, however, offer that affirmation up in loving prayer to God.

It is at the point of our deepest and most positive attunement with Him that He helps us the most. By divine attunement, our resistance becomes minimized, and our cooperation with His grace becomes fully open, willing, and super-consciously aware.

The Affirmations

1 *Success*

True success means transcendence. It means finding what we *really* want, which is not outward things, but inner peace of mind, self-understanding—and, above all, the joy of God.

Outward success means transcendence also. It means rising above past accomplishments to reach new levels of achievement. Success can mean accepting failure, too, when such acceptance helps us to transcend a false ambition. Every failure, moreover, can be a steppingstone to highest achievement.

Success should not be measured by the things accomplished, but by our increasing understanding, ability, and closeness to God.

Affirmation

I leave behind me both my failures and accomplishments. What I do today will create a new and better future, filled with inner joy.

Prayer

O Creator of galaxies and countless, blazing stars, the power of the very universe is Thine! May I reflect that power in the little mirror of my life and consciousness.

2 Love

One finds love not by *being* loved, but by loving.

We can never know love if we try to draw others to ourselves; nor can we find it by centering our love in them. For love is infinite; it is never ours to create. We can only channel it from its source in Infinity to all whom we meet.

The more we forget ourselves in giving to others, the better we can understand what love really is. And the more we love as channels for God's love, the more we can understand that His is the one love in all the universe.

Affirmation

I will love others as extensions of my own Self, and of the love I feel from God.

Prayer

O Infinite One, make me a channel for Thy love! Through me, reach out to sow seeds of love in barren hearts everywhere.

3 *Happiness*

Happiness is an attitude of mind, born of the simple determination to *be* happy under all outward circumstances. Happiness lies not in things, nor in outward attainments. It is the gold of our inner nature, buried beneath the mud of outward sense-cravings.

When you know that nothing outside you can affect you—no disappointment, no failure, no misunderstanding from others—then you will know that you have found true happiness.

Resolve strongly to keep this flame burning ever in your heart.

Affirmation

I vow from today onwards to be happy under every circumstance. I came from God's joy. I *am* joy!

Prayer

O Lord of Joy, fill me with boundless happiness. For I am Thy child, made in Thy blissful image. As Thou art Joy, so also, in my inner Self, am I.

4   *Energy*

Energy is ours not when we hoard our strength, but when we devote it willingly, joyously toward the attainment of that in which we deeply believe.

Faith and energy go hand in hand. If you have deep faith in what you are doing, you can move mountains. Energy is always highest when one's cause is just. The greater one's faith, the greater his will power. And the greater his will power, the greater his flow of energy.

Affirmation

Within me lies the energy to accomplish all that I will to do. Behind my every act is God's infinite power.

Prayer

O Cosmic Energy, vitalize all the cells of my body; recharge my mind with boundless inspiration; fill my soul with Thy inexhaustible joy.

5 *Sharing*

True happiness is found not in possessions, but in sharing what one has with others. Thus is one's self-identity expanded, as he learns to live in, and enjoy, a greater reality.

People who gladly share with others feel themselves bathed by a constant, inner stream of happiness.

Sharing is the doorway through which the soul escapes the prison of self-preoccupation. It is one of the clearest paths to God.

Affirmation

What I give to others I give not away, for in my larger reality it remains ever mine. I am happy in the happiness of all!

Prayer

O Infinite Giver, teach me to find happiness through others.

6 Work

Work should be done with a creative attitude—never for the sake of selfish gain, but for the chance it gives us to help create a better world.

Those who work with the thought of pay live in the future; they lose the habit of living here and now, where alone true happiness can be found.

Work should always be done as well as possible—not out of self-conceit, but in gratitude for the free gift of life, of sunshine, of water, of air—and in gratitude, simply, for our God-given power to be useful to our fellowman.

Affirmation

I will do my work thinking of Thee, Lord. I offer to Thee the very best that is in me.

Prayer

Beloved Lord, who so wonderfully created the high, snowy mountains; the bounding rivers; the colorful, fragrant flowers; the vast, heaving oceans; and the distant, glittering stars: Manifest, through me, Thy perfect joy.

7 Security

Man struggles all his life to store up treasures for himself, to insure his property against loss and his health against the devastations of disease. He rests his faith in outward measures, and sees not that such faith is like asking a wave not to move!

Security is his alone whose faith rests in the Lord. Most practical of men is he who offers his life to God, praying, "My safety is Thy responsibility, Lord." This does not mean we should not be conscientious. But after doing our very best, we should leave the worrying to God!

Affirmation

I live in the fortress of God's inner presence. Nothing and no one can break through these walls and harm me.

Prayer

I accept whatever comes, Lord, as coming from Thy hands. I know that it comes in blessing, for I am Thine, as Thou art ever mine.

8 Contentment

Contentment has been said to be the supreme virtue. Contentment means living to the fullest the good of every passing moment. Above all, it means living *behind* the present moment, in the Eternal Now.

How much is lost in life by people who perennially wish things other than they are! who complain unceasingly, and tell themselves that the world owes them more than it is giving them!

We must smile inwardly with God, knowing that life is His dream. Contentment is the surest way of drawing the very best out of every circumstance.

Affirmation

Through life's mightiest storms, I am contented, for I hold in my heart God's peace.

Prayer

Lord, as You live eternally at rest in Yourself, so let me live also, contented ever, that I may be worthy of living in Your joy.

9 Devotion

No good end is ever reached without devotion. No true success is achieved unless the heart's feelings are involved. Will power itself is a combination of energy and feeling, directed toward fulfillment.

In the quest for God, the unfolding of the heart's natural love, in the form of deep devotion, is the prime requisite for success. Without devotion, not a single step can be taken towards Him. Devotion is no sentiment: It is the deep longing to commune with, and know, the only Reality there is.

Affirmation

With the sword of devotion I sever the heart-strings that tie me to delusion. With the deepest love, I lay my heart at the feet of Omnipresence.

Prayer

Beloved Father, Mother, God: I am Thine alone! Let others seek Thee—or seek Thee not; it matters not to my love for Thee. Through all life's trials, my prayer is this alone: Reveal Thyself!

10 *Forgiveness*

Forgiveness is the sword of victory! When we forgive those who seek to hurt us, we rob them of their very power to do us harm. Better still, if they respond with love, they will unite their strength to ours, and so our strength becomes doubled.

But forgiveness should not be given primarily for its effect on others, but rather for the freedom it affirms in our own hearts. Let no outward circumstance condition your inner happiness. Be not pleased merely when man is pleased. Be pleased, rather, when you feel God's pleasure in your heart.

Affirmation

All that befalls me is for my good. I welcome any hurts that I receive as opportunities to grow in understanding.

Prayer

Lord, how often the hurts that I've sustained in life have grieved me! Strengthen my power of love, that I surrender all things to Thee, my eternal Friend.

11 *Will Power*

Will power, and not the vague abstraction *luck*, is the secret of true achievement. Will power, on subtle energy levels, generates what only looks like luck, by magnetically attracting to us opportunities. Our will is strengthened by removing from our minds the "no-saying" tendency: the obstructions of doubt, of laziness, and of fear—yes, even of the fear of success!

Will power is developed by persevering to the conclusion of whatever one attempts. One should start first with little undertakings, then proceed to bigger ones. Infinite will power comes from harnessing the little human will to God's infinite, all-powerful consciousness.

Affirmation

My will is to do that which is right to do. Part, all you mountains that stand in my way! Nothing can stop my progress!

Prayer

O Infinite Power, I will use my will, but guide Thou my will in everything I do, that it reflect Thy will.

12 Self-Control

If a lake is made to feed into too many streams, it will soon become drained. Similarly, if a person's heart energies are fed into countless streamlets of desires, he becomes drained, eventually, of even the power to feel. Sated with pleasure, he grows dry, blasé, and indifferent to even the greatest wonders.

The sensualist imagines that by giving up his pleasures he would renounce happiness. But in fact, the more one restrains his senses and learns to live in the peace of the inner Self, the more he finds himself glowing with happiness, good health, and a radiant sense of freedom and well-being.

Affirmation

I am strong in myself. I am complete in my Self. The joy and perfection of the universe await discovery within my inner being!

Prayer

I crave nothing that the world can give me, Lord. O Infinite Perfection, make me one with Thee!

13 *Patience*

"Patience," it has been well said, "is the shortest path to God." To attune the heart to the rhythms of Eternity, one must first adjust himself to life's longer rhythms. He should not allow his mind to become absorbed in concentration on the little ripples at the surface of the sea.

Patience means also adjusting to whatever *is* in life, rather than wishing it were something else. Patience is a prerequisite for every type of success. For it is when we work with things as they *are* that we can change them to whatever we might like them to be.

Affirmation

I am neither the ripples at the surface of the sea, nor yet the crashing waves: I am the vast ocean deeps, unaffected by mighty surface storms, untouched by any superficial change.

Prayer

Long have I called Thee, Lord, but Thou hast not answered me. Ah, but for what long eons didst Thou endure my fickleness! In this life, Lord, and if need be through eternity, I will keep calling Thee!

14 Good Health

Good health is more than the state of not being ill. It is a radiant state of inner well-being.

Physical illnesses may be cured by medicines. No medicine, however, can induce that state of boundless energy which comes when every cell in the body cooperates with the mind willingly, joyfully, in all that it seeks to do.

Such radiant well-being comes after the mind has been cleared of every shadow of unwillingness, of fear, and of doubt; when one has learned to say yes to life; and *when one has learned to love.*

Affirmation

My body cells obey my will: They dance with divine vitality! I am well! I am strong! I am a flowing river of boundless power and energy!

Prayer

O Mighty Source of all that is right and good, help me to see my strength as an expression of Thy infinite power. Let me banish the darkness of disease: It is forever foreign to Thy light!

15 *Enthusiasm*

Enthusiasm is the spirit of joy channeled through the power of the will. If we want to know joy, we must live always in the full expectation of it. Not even earthly happiness can come to those who demand it glumly, or who work for it with their eyes to the ground. To achieve happiness, one must work with happiness. To achieve divine joy, one must be keenly enthusiastic in everything one does!

Never presume. Never brush aside that subtle feeling of doubt which attends false, emotional enthusiasm. Try always to let God's joy express itself through you. Thus, your enthusiasm will grow, eventually to become His joy!

Affirmation

In everything I do, my enthusiasm soars to embrace infinity!

Prayer

O Perfect Bliss! Guide me, that I express Thee through my every feeling. May my enthusiasm be a channel for Thy joy.

16 *Willingness*

Willingness must be cultivated deliberately. It is an attitude of mind, and depends not on outward conditions.

Most people are willing or unwilling depending on their likes and dislikes. This habit tends to develop a bias toward unwillingness, which gradually becomes chronic, and attracts to itself chronic failure.

Don't wait for favorable circumstances to awaken willingness in you. Train yourself in the attitude of saying yes to life! Often by this simple attitude you will find Success arriving, unexpected, at your door!

Affirmation

I welcome everything that comes to me as an opportunity for further growth.

Prayer

Lord, help me to overcome the satanic pull of unwillingness. The more I embrace life in Your name, the more I feel Your joy.

17 Humility

Humility is not self-deprecation; it is self-forgetfulness! It is knowing that God alone is the Doer. It is the realization that nothing in this shadow-world of appearances is all that important, except as it draws us closer to the Lord.

Never tell yourself that you are sinful, or weak, or incompetent, or lazy, except as such a statement may help you to surrender joyfully to God's power. Then *live* by that power! Never wear the mask of false humility. Humility is self-acceptance, and self-honesty. You have a right to all power if you seek it in Infinity, and if you never hold the thought that it resides in your little self.

Affirmation

I live by Thy power, Lord. What I have is ever Thine — ever Thine!

Prayer

Thou art the Doer, Lord, not I. Express Thy perfection through me, as I strive ever eagerly to live in Thy light!

18 *Courage*

There are three kinds of human courage: blind, passive, and dynamic. Blind courage doesn't count the cost until it finds itself faced, horror-stricken, with the bill. Passive courage is the strength of will to adjust to reality, whatever it may be. And dynamic courage is the strength of will not only to accept reality, but to confront it with another reality of one's own making.

There is a fourth kind of courage: not human, but divine. Divine courage comes from living in the awareness of God's presence within, and in the realization that He is the sole Reality. Live more in Him, for nothing and no one can touch what you really are.

Affirmation

I live protected by God's Infinite Light. So long as I remain in the heart of it, nothing and no one can harm me.

Prayer

I look to Thee for my strength, Lord. Hold me closely in Thy arms of love. Then, whatever happens in my life I shall accept with joy.

19 Service

Service is ennobling. It is a way of offering our human littleness into the great Reality that is God.

Service should not be given with the thought that one is serving people, merely. It should be given with an inward consciousness to the Lord Who resides in all creatures. When we serve others in this spirit, we find our own spirits becoming freed from egotism. Peace then fills us, in the realization that there isn't anyone with whom we need compete.

What joy, to think that we belong to God!

Affirmation

I will serve God through others, and by my service to Him release the hold the ego has on me. I am free in God! In God, I am free!

Prayer

All that I do, Lord, I do for love of Thee. Accept the flowers of my service to Thee as I place them on Thy altar of Omnipresence.

20 Income

Money should be seen as an energy-flow, not as something that can be hoarded. For when money is treated as a material reality, it blocks one's creative flow.

Money, like matter, is only frozen energy. Energy is what creates matter. It is energy that forever moves, changes, and dissolves matter. Matter, untouched by energy, is inert.

If you need to increase your income, know that the energy you put out is more important than specific schemes for earning. Energy will *attract* opportunity. Recharge your energy from its cosmic Source, and whatever income you need will be ever yours.

Affirmation

The treasury of the Infinite is mine, for its wealth is energy, and I am energy!

Prayer

O Mighty Fountain of Infinite Light, from whose spray the countless galaxies are made: Let me wash away my worldly ambitions in Thy waters. Let me bathe in radiant eddies of Thy energy. Thou art my Wealth; Thou, my Treasure; Thou, my Security!

21 *Kindness*

When you can view all human beings as members of your own extended family—your brothers and sisters, mothers, fathers, and children—then you will find wherever you go that love awaits you, welcomes you! It is God who gazes back at you, when you behold Him in all!

Kindness is the recognition that all are truly our own. Kindness comes from not minding how others feel about us. It comes from the simple understanding that kindness is its own reward, worth giving out to others, because the source of so much sweetness in ourselves. For those of broad sympathies, the very universe is home!

The whole world is my home, and the human race, my family. With God's kindness I embrace all men.

Divine Mother, help me to see that by kindness to others I attract not only theirs in return, but Thy kindness as well. May I be kind to others always. May my kindness act as a channel of Thy unselfish love.

22 *Truthfulness*

Truthfulness is not caustic statements of unpleasant facts and unflattering opinions. Such statements are usually born of pride. But truthfulness is the effort always to see the *divine* truth behind appearances. It is the effort to express always that aspect of truth which may prove the most beneficial.

Truthfulness, as applied to ourselves, means not to hide behind self-flattering justifications: to look honestly at our real motives for doing anything, and not to flinch before unpleasant realities in ourselves. Truthfulness means seeing things as they really are, but then looking more deeply for ways to improve those realities.

Affirmation

Whatever is, simply *is*; I cannot change it for the mere wishing. Fearlessly, therefore, I accept the truth, knowing that, at the heart of everything, God's truth is always good.

Prayer

Heavenly Father, I will not fear the truth, for I know that Truth comes from Thee. Help me to see behind all appearances Thy smiling, all-compassionate gaze.

23 *Introspection*

People commonly delude themselves with easy rationalizations. "Maybe I wasn't as kind as I might have been," they'll say, "but wouldn't you have been unkind, too, if he'd treated you that way? It wasn't my fault. The fault was his." Thus, the blame for every wrong is placed at one's neighbor's door.

Introspection means to behold oneself from a center of inner calmness, without the slightest mental bias, open to what may be wrong in oneself—not excusing it, but not condemning, either. Introspection means referring what one sees to the superconscious mind, and detachedly accepting guidance, when it comes.

Affirmation

I am what I am; wishing cannot change me. Let me therefore face my faults with gratitude, for only by facing them can I work on them, and change them.

Prayer

Let me not delude myself with desires, Lord. Teach me to see behind the play of my thoughts Thy ever-calm gaze of wisdom.

24 *Calmness*

Calmness is perfectly achieved when life's little wave becomes absorbed into the cosmic sea, in divine ecstasy. In daily life, too, we can achieve calmness to a degree by keeping our awareness focused on the reality of the Spirit underlying all outward circumstances.

Calmness comes with the determination to live ever happily in the present moment, relinquishing the past, and not worrying about the future, but placing our lives firmly in God's hands, and knowing that He is fully in command. Calmness comes with non-attachment—with knowing that nothing in this world is truly ours.

Affirmation

Though the winds of difficulties howl around me, I stand forever calmly at the center of life's storms.

Prayer

With Thee beside me, I know that the tides of trouble can never sweep me away. Hold fast my hand, Lord; never let me go!

25 *Peace of Mind*

Peace of mind is the result, not of money in the bank, but of prayer and meditation. The more one contacts God in meditation, the more he feels descending upon him a blanket, as it were, of inner peace, cooling his body, calming his restless impulses, and thrilling his nerves with ever-new delight. Peace is like a weightless waterfall, washing away all worries, and bestowing a new, glad sense of confidence.

Peace of mind is his who knows that God is his only Treasury!

Affirmation

From pools of inner silence I sip the sparkling waters of
Thy peace.

Prayer

All that I own is Thine, Lord. Help me to know Thee as
the River of Peace, running silently beneath the sands of
my life's experiences.

26 Non-attachment

Nothing is ours. No one belongs to us. Mentally, we should make a bonfire of our love for God, and cast into it all attachments, all desires, all hopes and disappointments.

It helps mentally to examine one's heart every evening, and liberate it anew of all desires. Pluck out from your heart any burrs of new attachments that you find clinging there. Cast them joyfully into the fire of devotion.

Pray to God energetically, "I destroy all my attachments. They are no longer mine, Lord. I am free in Thee!"

Affirmation

Nothing on earth can hold me! My soul, like a weightless balloon, soars upward through skies of eternal freedom!

Prayer

I destroy all my attachments. They are no longer mine, Lord. I am free in Thee!

27 *Consideration for Others*

Consideration for others is one of the marks of a refined spirit. Many people on the spiritual path feel that, since it is within that they are seeking the kingdom of God, and since they are working at developing a spirit of non-attachment, it doesn't matter how they express themselves to others. Indeed, their inconsiderateness is an affirmation of their independence of the opinions and feelings of others. "If God is pleased," they tell themselves, "what matters the displeasure of man?"

Yet by unkindness we can never please God, who is all Kindness itself. Sensitivity to others is a way of self-expansion. One truly achieves freedom in himself when he can respect their realities, because he is wholly at peace with his own.

Affirmation

By sensitivity to others' realities, I keep myself in readiness
to perceive the truth no matter what garb it wears.

Prayer

Divine Mother, I worship Thee in all Thy forms, both ignorant and wise. Finding Thee within, may I behold Thee
enshrined in Omnipresence.

28 *Discrimination*

As science judges the relative speed of any object by one constant, the speed of light, so the devotee judges the relative merit of any idea by the one constant, God. Discrimination is clear only when it relates everything to the Eternal Absolute. Thus, while the intelligence may toy with ideas endlessly, discrimination asks, "Is this wisdom? Is it of God?"

True discrimination is not even the product of reasoning. It is soul-intuition. Reasoning, even from the highest point of reference, is uncertain compared to the inspirations of superconsciousness. To discriminate clearly, meditate first. Ask God to guide your understanding.

Affirmation

Resolutely I quell my inclinations, that my mind be open
to the wisdom-guidance of my soul.

Prayer

Guide me, Lord, that in all things I know Thy will, for I
know that only by Thy will are all things led to perfection.

29 *Renunciation*

Renunciation means turning one's back on non-essentials, that we may give our whole attention to the Lord. We might think of renunciation as an investment, which initially may seem a loss, but in time becomes multiplied to many times its original worth. The least gift that we give to God will return to us, in divine blessings, a thousandfold. Renunciation means nothing less than the gift to God of oneself.

Renunciation is of the heart. It isn't what you wear, or the outward rules you follow. When you renounce all for God, you hold that renunciation as a precious secret between you and Him. All your desires, all your ambitions, then, are for Him alone.

Affirmation

I spurn the tempting magic of this world, with its rainbow bubbles, ever ready to burst. See where I fly: high above the tall mountains. I am free! I am free!

Prayer

Lord, help me to see that in no outward experience will I ever find fulfillment. All that my heart has ever sought awaits me in Thee.

30 Non-injury

Non-injury is a fundamental rule in the spiritual life. It means primarily an attitude of mind. Outwardly, one cannot avoid doing a certain amount of injury — for example, to flying insects when driving one's car. The harm one does, however, by wishing harm to others hurts not only them, but even more especially, oneself. Spiritually, a harmful attitude separates one from the harmony and oneness of life.

Non-injury, on the other hand, embraces that oneness, and is in turn sustained by it. Non-injury is a powerful force for victory, for it enlists cooperation from the very universe, where harmfulness incites endless opposition.

Affirmation

I send out the rain of blessings to all, that love be nourished in hearts that, heretofore, have known only hate.

Prayer

Divine Mother, when others seek to hurt me, give me the wisdom to see that victory lies in blessing them, not in revenge. If I respond with anger, the loss will be mine, even if mine also is the outward victory, for inwardly I will have been hurt indeed. But if I return blessings for their blows, I shall remain ever safe within the impregnable walls of my inner peace.

31 *Concentration*

Concentration is the secret of success in every undertaking. Without concentration, thoughts, energy, inspiration, purpose — all one's inner forces — become scattered. Concentration is the calm focus of one's full attention on the purpose at hand. Concentration means more than mental effort: It means channeling your heart's feelings, your faith, and your deep aspirations into whatever you are doing. In that way, even the little things in life can become rich with meaning.

Concentration should not involve mental strain. When you really want something, it is difficult *not* to think about it! Concentrate *with* interest on whatever you do, and you will find yourself absorbed in it.

Affirmation

Whatever I do in life, I give it my full attention. Like a laser beam, I burn from before me all problems, all obstructions!

Prayer

Help me to see Thee, Lord, as the scriptures describe Thee: "the Most Relishable!" Help me to concentrate on Thee my gaze, my love, my aspirations, my entire being.

32 *Self-Expansion*

Self-expansion is the essence of all aspiration. Why do we seek to possess things? Because by acquisition we imagine we'll expand our dominion. Why do we seek to learn more? Because we think by enlarging our knowledge to expand our understanding. And why do we seek ever new experiences? Because we believe that, through them, we'll expand our awareness. When you stretch a lump of dough outward, it becomes not only broader, but thinner. Such often is the case when we stretch the mind only outwardly. Reaching out too far, we sacrifice depth in our lives.

The Self-expansion toward which all life aspires is of the spirit: an expansion of sympathy, of love, of the awareness that comes from sensing God's presence everywhere.

Affirmation

I feel myself in the flowing brooks, in the flight of birds, in the raging wind upon the mountains, in the gentle dance of flowers in a breeze. Renouncing my little, egoic self, I expand with my great, soul-Self everywhere!

Prayer

Beloved Spirit in all that is! Help me in my own nothingness to find myself one with all that is.

33 *Generosity*

Most people think of generosity as merely the giving of material benefits to others. More important, however, and much more satisfying is a generous spirit: a willingness to let the other person shine, even if it means being eclipsed oneself; a happiness in his good fortune, even if it means personal loss for oneself; a concern for his safety, even if, in an accident, one's own property has been destroyed.

Generosity means, above all, recognizing that everything we have and are belongs to God alone, and is His to dispose of where He will.

Affirmation

I am happy in the good fortune of all, even more than in my own, for in my happiness for them lies inner freedom.

Prayer

All that I have and am is Thine. Divine Mother, dispose of it as Thou wilt.

34 Alertness

There are two currents in life: One takes us downward toward unconsciousness; the other, upward toward cosmic consciousness. The first is an impulse born of the sense of past familiarity. Life, like a lotus, evolves out of the mud of lower consciousness toward the light of divine awareness. Subconsciously, we imagine ourselves comfortable with the stages we've traversed so far, but we are not always so ready for the adventure of further growth!

The second current in life is the soul's impulse. We cannot find happiness in turning back toward the mud. Fulfillment lies only in reaching up toward perfect divine awareness. To achieve it, we must be alert in everything we do. For in the flow of increasing wakefulness lies the joy we all are seeking.

Affirmation

I am awake! energetic! enthusiastic! I give my full, alert attention to everything I do, knowing that in absolute consciousness I shall find God.

Prayer

Let me pray always with alert, awake attention to Thy listening presence, knowing that Thou dost hear the merest whisper of my thoughts.

35 *Inspiration*

Inspiration is of two kinds: the rediscovery, or rearrangement, of thoughts that already exist in the subconscious mind; and the sudden appearance of new thoughts, or new insights, from the superconscious. This higher inspiration, certainly, is more to be desired than the lower, for it is based in truth and not in imagination.

It is not always easy, however, to recognize the difference between lower and higher inspiration, particularly when the lower is vitalized by the emotions. When inspiration comes, receive it with calm love, and see whether, untouched by emotion, its impulse grows stronger or weaker. Love is the water that nourishes true inspiration.

Affirmation

I hold my thoughts up to the calmness within; in calmness
I receive inspiration from my higher Self.

Prayer

O Spirit, Thou art all truth. In Thee lies the solution to my
every need. Inspire me now, Lord! Show me which path to
follow of the many that lie before me.

36 *Power*

Power is an aspect of God. Human beings often associate the word *power* with ruthless ambition and dominance over others. But it is a misdirection of power to exert it over others for selfish ends, and a misuse of it to exert it without care for their well-being. Rightly understood, power is the ability to command our own energies — above all for our own transcendence, but also for the good of others. Such power is important for spiritual growth.

Many people imagine that spiritual development is manifested as a sort of saccharine sweetness. The saints, however, are people of enormous inner power, before which others often tremble! Yet theirs is a power only for good. Its roots lie buried in the soil of pure love.

Affirmation

Mine is the power of the universe, channeled for my own awakening and the awakening of other sleeping souls!

Prayer

Help me to feel that Thy power runs through my veins, courses through my thoughts, and sets my noble feelings afire with love for Thee!

37 *Wisdom*

We often hear the expression "sadder but wiser." This is the mark of worldly wisdom, which people equate with disillusionment. Indeed, worldly hopes, sooner or later, all end in disappointment, and sometimes in great sorrow. Worldly wisdom often wears the garb of sadness.

Not so, divine wisdom! On the spiritual path, the expression should be "happier and wiser"! For true human wisdom means recognizing at last the pathway *out* of delusion, and toward the light of truth.

Divine wisdom is Omniscience itself. In such wisdom there is no shadow of sorrow, only bliss absolute, bliss infinite, bliss eternal!

Affirmation

As I learn the lessons that life teaches me, I grow toward ever-greater joy and freedom.

Prayer

I am grateful, Lord, for every test You send me. Each time I stumble, help me to learn. Each time my human weakness makes me fall, help me to grow stronger. May I realize behind every pain Thy calm, reassuring wisdom.

38 Joy

True joy is not an emotional state. It is not that which one feels when some desire is satisfied, or when everything at last goes well. It is inward; it is of the soul. It can be developed, first, by not reacting emotionally to outward things.

Don't be tossed on alternating waves of success and failure. Don't join, in their excitement, the buyers and sellers in the marketplace of this world. Be calm in yourself, even-minded and cheerful through the gains and losses of life. Then, in calm, deep meditation feel the joy of the soul. Hold on to that joy through all activities. Don't confine it, but try ever to expand it, until your little joy becomes the joy of God.

Affirmation

I am even-minded and cheerful at all times. I know that joy is not outside me, but within.

Prayer

In the calmness of meditation, at the heart of my inner peace, help me to feel Thy thrilling, joyful presence.

39 *Self-Confidence*

Self-confidence, as it is normally understood, recalls to mind images of army generals and cowboy heroes — people, in short, who know their blacks from their whites. But life's alternatives are usually much more complex.

Self-confidence on the spiritual path is of another order altogether. It means confidence in the inner Self, not in the ego. It means living from within, living by truth rather than by opinions. It means living by what God wants, not by what man wants. Thus, it means living by faith, in the sure knowledge that, although man is fallible, God is infallible.

Affirmation

I live in the assurance of God's truth within. In my inner Self, and not in the opinions of others, lies true victory.

Prayer

What matter, if people blame me? Of what importance is their applause? I live to please Thee, Lord, confident that when Thou art with me I am protected, though it be from an enemy horde.

40 *Awareness*

Awareness deepens, the more it is centered in itself. But the farther a person's interests extend outside himself, the thinner the supply line of his awareness becomes.

If a person's consciousness is centered outwardly in things, it takes on those qualities which it attributes to those things. Jewelers, for instance, often have bright eyes. People with no sense of higher values have dead eyes. Man needs to learn to change his focus from what he is aware *of* to what he is aware *with*. He needs to become more aware *at the source* of his awareness, at his deepest center, God. Through this awareness, his enjoyment even of the surrounding world becomes intensified a thousandfold.

Affirmation

I behold the world with eyes of calmness and of faith. For I know that, as I view others, so will I myself become.

Prayer

Infuse me, from my deepest center, with Thy joy. Make me aware of Thee, my divine Beloved, in all that I behold.

41 *Positive Thinking*

As we think, so we become. And as we think, so our lives and circumstances become also. From the divine consciousness come answers to all our questions, and solutions to all our problems. It is in lower consciousness that confusion reigns.

Think positively in everything you do, for in that way you help to attune yourself to the divine flow. One who is inwardly in tune with grace finds all things harmonious and beneficial being attracted to him. Positive thinking, combined with the sense of divine attunement, is never presumptuous, for it draws its power, not from the ego, but from the consciousness of God's joy within.

Affirmation

My outer life is a reflection of my inner thoughts. Filled with the joy of God, I express His joy and harmony in everything I do.

Prayer

Problems cannot exist, Lord, whenever Thou art near. Give me strength always to hold Thee in my heart.

42 *Humor*

A good sense of humor is an effective means of keeping a sense of perspective through the trials and difficulties of life. By not taking things too seriously, one develops non-attachment.

One should not laugh too much, however, lest the mind become light, and one's view of life, superficial. Thus, one needs to achieve a sense of perspective where humor itself is concerned. The best way to do so is to share one's laughter with God; to laugh with the sense of *His* joy, within. Never laugh at people, but rather *with* them. For humor should be kindly, not sarcastic. Laugh with pure delight, and everyone will join you in your laughter.

Affirmation

In laughter I recall my own mistakes. Merriest am I when, by laughing, I include myself!

Prayer

I delight in life's comedy, for it reminds me that true sanity exists in Thee alone!

43   *Even-Mindedness*

Many people confuse progress with movement and with outward change. Thus, the more dust of excitement they can stir up, the more productive they feel they are! The more they get swept up into a happy mood when things go well, the better, they imagine, things have gone. And their answer to every slump is to cast about for some other thing to sweep them high once more. Such lives are like cars driven over deeply rutted roads: Their movement is almost as much up and down as it is forward.

With even-mindedness, progress is a straight, not a jagged, line. Progress, however, should mean above all progressive understanding. Even-mindedness bestows clarity of perception, which is the ability to see things as they really are, undistorted by emotional bias.

Affirmation

I remain untouched by gain or loss. In the calm mirror of my understanding I behold Thy light reflected.

Prayer

When I rejoice, Lord, let it be with Thee. And when I grieve, help me always to see Thy sunlight through the mists.

44 *Acceptance*

One of the most difficult lessons in life is to learn to accept things as they are. How much energy we waste in trying to wish away the inevitable! "If only this hadn't happened!" "If only we had reached there in time!" The "if only's" and "might have been's" in life keep us from dealing realistically with what is.

Acceptance comes from knowing that reality lies within ourselves, and that all else is a dream. Acceptance of that one reality makes everything else acceptable. Instead of learning to come to grips with a thousand individual challenges, therefore, make the supreme effort to accept God unconditionally into your heart. Accept all that comes in life as coming from His hands. He will give you what is best for you, if you live for Him alone.

Affirmation

I accept with calm impartiality whatever comes my way. Free in my heart, I am not conditioned by any outward circumstance.

Prayer

Shine Thy delusion-cauterizing light into the hidden nooks of my heart's feelings, lest somewhere, without my conscious knowledge, I have not accepted Thee. If ever I err, strengthen me to accept Thy discipline, for in Thy will alone lies the happiness I am seeking.

45 *Openness*

Openness can be a great virtue, but only when it is exercised with discrimination. To be open to wrong ideas, or to people who would harm you, would be foolish. For it is not with openness that error can be conquered, but with love.

Openness of mind is a virtue when it is centered in the desire for the truth. Openness of heart is a virtue when it is centered in love for God. Both mind and heart, however, need filters to screen out what is not true, and what is not of God. This we can do by referring back for approval to the divine presence within whatever comes to us. We must be ever open to truth and to God, but ever closed, or at least indifferent, to error and delusion.

Affirmation

My mind is open to the truth, whatever its source. True statements remain valid, even if hurled in anger.

Prayer

Divine Mother, let me hear Thy melodies everywhere: in the laughing brooks, in the songs of nightingales—yes, even in the roar of city traffic! Behind all earthly sounds, let me listen for Thy voice alone.

46 *Moral Vigor*

Lack of moral vigor saps the will, and makes the intellect sponge-like, ready to absorb the prevalent opinion of the times. People with good intellects often suffer from the "Hamlet complex": the inability to come to any decision, or to commit oneself to anything. They justify their indecision by saying, "I want to be fair to all sides." But even an imperfect action is better than no action at all.

When you believe in something, stand by it! When you believe in someone, stand by him! Such loyal self-commitment is a higher law than "seeing all sides." Energy is needed to accomplish anything in life. With moral vigor, all things are possible. But without it, the end of every act is failure.

Affirmation

The decisions that I make in life come from within myself, from my sense for what is right. I am committed to the truth, and to channeling it outward to the world.

Prayer

Divine Mother, with every action of my will let me express Thy divine vitality, Thy truth, Thy perfection. Let me live to serve Thee alone, or else die in the attempt!

47 *Perseverance*

"Loyalty," my great spiritual teacher used to say, "is the first law of God." Most people are fickle. They change their jobs, their spouses, their friends, their beliefs, their ideas—not because of any new expansion of awareness, but because they lack the simple power of perseverance.

One must be loyal to one's principles, and not allow oneself to be ruled by sentiment. To be loyal to others, and to one's assumed goals in life—not for sentimental reasons, but in the name of principle—is the way of divine progress. Perseverance can be difficult, for in every undertaking there is a certain amount of dull routine. Don't be ruled, therefore, by likes and dislikes, but do whatever has to be done. If it is right, let *nothing* intervene until the job is finished.

Affirmation

I will finish what I set my mind to do before leaving it for something else. My word is my bond. So also is my resolution.

Prayer

Though the sirens of distraction call me to turn aside and relax the sternness of my dedication, keep me steadfast on my path, Lord. My goal in life is Thee!

48 *Gratitude*

Gratitude is a way of returning energy for energy received. Only a thief takes without paying for what he gets. And one who accepts a kindness without returning gratitude, as though the kindness were his by right, demeans both the giver and himself. He demeans the giver, because by ingratitude he implies that the kindness was inspired by selfish motives. And he demeans himself, because by giving nothing in return he breaks the cycle of creativity, without which prosperity's flow, both materially and spiritually, is blocked.

Accept nothing, inwardly, for yourself, but offer everything to God. Don't let yourself be bought by others' kindnesses. Be grateful to them above all in your soul, by blessing or praying for them. Give gratitude first of all to God, from Whom alone all blessings truly come.

Affirmation

I give thanks to the giver behind each gift, and to the one Giver behind all that I receive. My gratitude rises with devotion's incense to the throne of Omnipresence.

Prayer

I thank Thee, Lord, for all Thy blessings. But most of all, I thank Thee for Thy love.

49 *Immortality*

You are not your body. You are not your thoughts, your desires, your changing personality. Your body has a certain age, but you, yourself, have no age! Your body may tire or become unwell, but you yourself, the fatigueless soul, cannot tire, can never know disease!

Tell yourself always, "I am a child of eternity!" Don't be identified with your outward form, nor with change, but live in timelessness. It is our identity with change that creates the illusion of passing time. Feel that, through all outward changes, you, the immortal soul, remain the same. Death itself will be but one more change; be not identified with it. Then, when death comes, you shall rise in eternal freedom!

Affirmation

I am a child of eternity! I am ageless. I am deathless. I am the changeless Spirit at the heart of all mutation!

Prayer

Wherever my body travels outwardly, let me feel Thy changeless presence within. Wherever my thoughts take me, let them return always, like prodigal children, to find repose in Thee.

50 *Practicality*

Many spiritual seekers, and others with high ideals, lose sight of the need to make their idealism practical. Many even resent the suggestion that they try to put an ideal into practice—as though the very effort to do so would mean somehow lessening its purity!

But God is no idle dreamer! Were the universe not kept in a state of perfect balance, chaos, not harmony, would be the common state. We, too, should be practical in our idealism. Life, to be ever expansive, must be a search for truth. "Will it work?" is the preliminary question to, "Is it true?" The test of an ideal is whether it is practical or not. By practicality, we mature from the state of idle dreaming to become emissaries of the truth.

Affirmation

Though my spirit soars in the skies of consciousness, my feet and hands labor here on earth to make truth real to all.

Prayer

Let not my thoughts lift me up through beautiful clouds of imagined possibilities, unless You give me the power also to materialize my dreams.

51 God-Remembrance

To remember God means not only to think of Him constantly, but to realize that finding Him is an act of remembrance truly. For it is from Him that we have come. When the clouds of delusion evaporate from our minds, what will be left is what was there always, hidden behind the clouds: the blazing sun of divine consciousness!

One should not strain, nor reach outward mentally, to think of God. Know that He has been yours always—nearer than your nearest thoughts and feelings, nearer than the very prayers you offer Him! Think not merely *about* Him: Think *to* Him. Share with Him your passing feelings, your idlest fancy. Talk *with* Him. Practice His presence—at first, perhaps, for minutes a day, then for hours, and then all the time.

Affirmation

I will live in the remembrance of what I am in truth: bliss infinite! eternal love!

Prayer

Lord, Thou art always with me. Help me to feel, behind my thoughts, Thy inspiration; behind my every emotion, Thy calm, all-transforming love.

52 *High-Mindedness*

People often speak of cynicism as the mark of realism. In fact, in a universe without any visible center, one might justifiably develop his understanding of it from any conceivable starting point. One's understanding, however, will only reflect who and what he himself is. A view from the depths lacks the perspective that can be achieved from the heights. From the mountain top, all things are seen in their true proportion.

Strive always to be a channel for high thoughts and inspirations. Never cooperate with anything petty or mean. Remember, the universe is, for each human being, both a mirror and an affirmation. One who entertains high thoughts will be, himself, ennobled.

Affirmation

I will see goodness in everything. I will view the world around me, not from the depths of matter-attachment, but from the heights of divine aspiration.

Prayer

Lord, the universe was made in Thine image of perfection. Help me to bring out that image in others by blessing them in Thy love.

About the Author

"Swami Kriyananda is a man of wisdom and compassion in action, truly one of the leading lights in the spiritual world today."

—*Lama Surya Das, Dzogchen Center, author of* Awakening the Buddha Within

Swami Kriyananda (1926–2013) was a direct disciple of Paramhansa Yogananda (author of the classic, *Autobiography of a Yogi*). Kriyananda was trained by the great Indian yoga master to spread the life-transforming teachings of Kriya Yoga around the globe. He is widely considered one of the foremost experts on meditation, yoga, and spiritual practice, having authored more than 140 books on these subjects.

Kriyananda was the founder of Ananda, an international organization committed to the dissemination of Yogananda's teachings. In 1968 he founded Ananda Cooperative Village in Nevada City, California, the first spiritual community based on Yogananda's vision of "world brotherhood colonies." Today Ananda includes eight communities in the U.S., Europe, and India, and more than 140 meditation centers and groups worldwide.

Further Explorations

Dear Reader,

Ananda is a worldwide work based on the teachings expressed in this book—those of the great spiritual teacher, Paramhansa Yogananda. If you enjoyed this title, Crystal Clarity Publishers invites you to continue to deepen your spiritual life through the many avenues of Ananda Worldwide—including meditation communities, centers, and groups; online virtual community and webinars; retreat centers offering classes and teacher training in yoga and meditation; and more.

For special offers and discounts for first-time visitors to Ananda, visit: crystalclarity.com

Joy to you,

Crystal Clarity Publishers

We offer many additional resources to assist you in your spiritual journey, including many other books and audiobooks, a wide variety of inspirational and relaxation music composed by Swami Kriyananda, and yoga and meditation videos. Visit our secure website for our complete online catalog or to place an order for our products. To find out more information, please contact us at:

crystalclarity.com | 800-424-1055 or 530-478-7600

1123 Goodrich Blvd. | Commerce, CA 90022

clarity@crystalclarity.com

ANANDA WORLDWIDE

Ananda, a worldwide organization founded by Swami Kriyananda, offers spiritual support and resources based on the teachings of Paramhansa Yogananda. There are Ananda spiritual communities Ananda, a worldwide organization founded by Swami Kriyananda, offers spiritual support and resources based on the teachings of Paramhansa Yogananda. There are Ananda spiritual communities in Nevada City, Sacramento, and Palo Alto, California; Seattle, Washington; and Portland, Oregon; as well as a retreat center and European community in Assisi, Italy. Ananda supports more than 140 meditation groups worldwide, including many in India that are expanding rapidly.

For more information about Ananda's work, our communities, or meditation groups near you, please contact us.

530-478-7560 | ananda.org

THE EXPANDING LIGHT

The Expanding Light is the largest retreat center in the world to share exclusively the teachings of Paramhansa Yogananda. Situated in the Ananda Village community, it offers the opportunity to experience spiritual life in a contemporary ashram setting. The varied, year-round schedule of classes and programs on yoga, meditation, and spiritual practice includes Karma Yoga, Personal Retreat, Spiritual Travel, and online learning. The Ananda School of Yoga & Meditation offers certified yoga, yoga therapist, spiritual counselor, and meditation teacher trainings. Large groups are welcome.

The teaching staff are experts in Kriya Yoga meditation and all aspects of Yogananda's teachings. All staff members live at Ananda Village and bring an uplifting approach to their areas of service. The serene natural setting and delicious vegetarian meals help provide an ideal environment for a truly meaningful visit. For more information, please contact us.

800-346-5350 | expandinglight.org

AUTOBIOGRAPHY OF A YOGI
Paramhansa Yogananda

Autobiography of a Yogi is one of the best-selling Eastern philosophy titles of all time, with millions of copies sold, named one of the best and most influential books of the twentieth century. This highly prized reprinting of the original 1946 edition is the only one available free from textual changes made after Yogananda's death. Yogananda was the first yoga master of India whose mission was to live and teach in the West.

In this updated edition are bonus materials, including a last chapter that Yogananda wrote in 1951, without posthumous changes. This new edition also includes the eulogy that Yogananda wrote for Gandhi, and a new foreword and afterword by Swami Kriyananda, one of Yogananda's close, direct disciples.

PARAMHANSA YOGANANDA
A Biography with Personal Reflections and Reminiscences
Swami Kriyananda

Paramhansa Yogananda's classic *Autobiography of a Yogi* is more about the saints Yogananda met than about himself—in spite of Yogananda's astonishing accomplishments.

Now, one of Yogananda's direct disciples relates the untold story of this great spiritual master and world teacher: his teenage miracles, his challenges in coming to America, his national lecture campaigns, his struggles to fulfill his world-changing mission amid incomprehension and painful betrayals, and his ultimate triumphant achievement. Kriyananda's subtle grasp of his guru's inner nature reveals Yogananda's many-sided greatness. Includes many never-before-published anecdotes.

THE NEW PATH
My Life with Paramhansa Yogananda
Swami Kriyananda

When Swami Kriyananda discovered *Autobiography of a Yogi* in 1948, he was totally new to Eastern teachings. This is a great advantage to the Western reader, since Kriyananda walks us along the yogic path as he discovers it from the moment of his initiation as a disciple of Yogananda. With winning honesty, humor, and deep insight, he shares his journey on the spiritual path through personal stories and experiences.

Through more than four hundred stories of life with Yogananda, we tune in more deeply to this great master and to the teachings he brought to the West. This book is an ideal complement to *Autobiography of a Yogi*.

MORE RESOURCES FROM CRYSTAL CLARITY PUBLISHERS

The Essence of the Bhagavad Gita
Explained by Paramhansa Yogananda
As remembered by his disciple, Swami Kriyananda

Demystifying Patanjali
The Wisdom of Paramhansa Yogananda
Presented by his direct disciple, Swami Kriyananda

The Essence of Self-Realization
The Wisdom of Paramhansa Yogananda
Recorded, compiled, and edited by his disciple, Swami Kriyananda

Conversations with Yogananda
Recorded, with Reflections, by his disciple, Swami Kriyananda

Revelations of Christ
Proclaimed by Paramhansa Yogananda
Presented by his disciple, Swami Kriyananda

Whispers from Eternity
Paramhansa Yogananda
Edited by his disciple, Swami Kriyananda

The Rubaiyat of Omar Khayyam Explained
Paramhansa Yogananda
Edited by his disciple, Swami Kriyananda

The Art and Science of Raja Yoga
Swami Kriyananda

The Wisdom of Yogananda **series •**
Paramhansa Yogananda
How to Be Happy All the Time
Karma and Reincarnation
How to Love and Be Loved
How to Be a Success
How to Have Courage, Calmness, and Confidence
How to Achieve Glowing Health and Vitality
How to Awaken Your True Potential
The Man Who Refused Heaven

For Starters **series •**
Meditation *by Swami Kriyananda*
Intuition *by Swami Kriyananda*
Chakras *by Savitri Simpson*
Vegetarian Cooking *by Diksha McCord*

Touch of Light **series •**
Nayaswami Jyotish and Nayaswami Devi Novak
Touch of Light
Touch of Joy
Touch of Love
Touch of Peace

Secrets **series •**
Swami Kriyananda
Meditation and Inner Peace
Success and Leadership
Health and Healing
Spiritualizing Your Daily Life

God Is for Everyone
Inspired by Paramhansa Yogananda
As taught to and understood by his disciple, Swami Kriyananda

Timeless Tales told by Paramhansa Yogananda **series •**
Paramhansa Yogananda
Wisdom Stories from India (2021)

The Wisdom of Kriyananda **series •**
Swami Kriyananda
Building Spiritual Power Against Troubled Times (2021)

AUM: Melodies of Love
Joseph Bharat Cornell
  More titles featuring Sharing Nature*
    Sharing Nature
    Deep Nature Play
    The Sky and Earth Touched Me
    Flow Learning

How to Meditate
Jyotish Novak

Stand Unshaken!
Nayaswamis Jyotish and Devi Novak

Change Your Magnetism, Change Your Life
Naidhruva Rush

Loved and Protected
Asha Nayaswami

Transitioning with Grace
Nalini Graeber

The Yugas
Joseph Selbie and David Steinmetz

The Healing Kitchen
Diksha McCord

Walking with William of Normandy
Richard Salva

Religion in the New Age
Swami Kriyananda

Two Souls: Four Lives
Catherine Kairavi

In Divine Friendship
Swami Kriyananda

Pilgrimage to Guadalupe
Swami Kriyananda

Swami Kriyananda as We Have Known Him
Asha Nayaswami [Asha Praver]

Divine Will Healing
Mary Kretzmann

Ronald Millar was born in 1928 in Angus, Scotland, and was educated at Harrow and Oriel College, Oxford. He first became involved in *The Piltdown Men* while researching the Battle of Hastings. He has worked as a drover, journalist, ski-instructor, sailing-master and as a fisherman in Brittany, and has diverse hobbies including natural history, the sea, and old-style mountaineering.

He has also published: HEMINGWAY, KUT, and MATA HARI.

Ronald Millar

The Piltdown Men

PALADIN
GRANADA PUBLISHING
London Toronto Sydney New York

Published by Granada Publishing Limited
in Paladin Books 1974
Reprinted 1979

ISBN 0 586 08134 8

First published in Great Britain by
Victor Gollancz Ltd 1972
Copyright © Ronald Millar 1972

Granada Publishing Limited
Frogmore, St Albans, Herts AL2 2NF
and
3 Upper James Street, London W1R 4BP
866 United Nations Plaza, New York, NY 10017, USA
117 York Street, Sydney, NSW 2000, Australia
100 Skyway Avenue, Rexdale, Ontario, M9W 3A6, Canada
PO Box 84165, Greenside, 2034 Johannesburg, South Africa
CML Centre, Queen & Wyndham, Auckland 1, New Zealand

Made and printed in Great Britain by
Richard Clay (The Chaucer Press) Ltd
Bungay, Suffolk
Set in Monotype Ehrhardt

Granada ®
Granada Publishing ®

Contents

List of Illustrations

Plates

1 Palaeolithic flint implements ranging from the Clactonian scraper through the more sophisticated examples from St Acheul (Archeulian), Le Moustier (Neanderthal) and La Vallois-Perret, Paris (Lavalloisian)

2 Forged flint implements from Moulin Quignon

3 The skull of the Rhodesian Man: 'Cyphanthropus' or Stooping Man according to the ornithologist W. P. Pycraft, head of the British Museum (Natural History) Anthropology section

4 Heidelberg Man – a massive jaw discovered at Mauer, near Heidelberg, in 1907 which later prompted Charles Dawson to at first suspect an association with his thick-skulled 'Piltdown Man'

5 A reconstruction of Peking Man (female) – one of the skulls that vanished sometime in 1941 when the Japanese occupied Peking, China

6 Australopithecus (africanus). The missing link which now occupies the place in evolution formerly occupied by Charles Dawson's 'Piltdown Man'

7 'Piltdown Man' (Eoanthropus dawsoni)

8 A comparison of skulls in descending order of refinement from front to back: Modern Man (Caucasian); Neanderthal Man (Generalized); Peking Man (adult); Gorilla

9 The Piltdown Men: (Left to right) Front Row: W. P. Pycraft, Arthur Keith, A. S. Underwood, Ray Lankester. Back Row: F. O. Barlow, Grafton Elliot Smith, Charles Dawson and Arthur Smith Woodward. (From a portrait painted in 1915 by John Cooke, R.A., and later presented to the Geological Society by Dr C. T. Trenchman)

10 Piltdown Man's jaw now attributed to a 500-year-old orangutan

11 The fossil elephant thigh-bone implement from Piltdown

12 The Piltdown molars showing the non-alignment of the flat crowns. This unnatural placement cried out for notice in 1912 but oddly escaped attention for some forty years

13 The skull and fragment of jaw of Galley Hill Man – Britain's 'Neanderthal Man' – now thought to be a recently-buried woman

14 An 'eolith' from Piltdown, Sussex. Whether human workmanship – ancient or modern – was employed is conjectural

All photographs are reproduced by courtesy of the British Museum (Natural History)

Diagrams

Introduction

Piltdown man was unveiled to a densely-packed and excited audience at Burlington House, London, on 18 December 1912. Piltdown man – or to give him his correct scientific title, *Eoanthropus dawsoni* – was the fulfilment of the half-century-old prophecy of the famous biologist Charles Darwin. He was the ideal 'missing link'. His noble brow postulated high intelligence but his most astonishing feature, an ape-like jaw, was a direct link with man's ancestors. Here was an ape halfway across the evolutionary bridge towards man.

Piltdown man was greeted in Britain with great enthusiasm. His arrival was long overdue. For many years now British archaeologists had cast envious glances across the Channel. It seemed that the French had but to dig anywhere in their native land to find a Neanderthal man. But Piltdown man not only gained redress. Crude flint tools and the bones of long extinct animals found with him in the Sussex gravel pit proved that he had lived many thousands of years before Neanderthal man. But compared with Neanderthal man, Piltdown man was an intellectual. Only Piltdown man could be the true ancestor of modern man. The brutish-looking Neanderthal man was a biological freak, it was thought, which had evolved in some remote backwater during the terrible Ice Age and had died out without issue.

Piltdown man was highly acceptable. And he was British. He transfused life into a British palaeontology feeble from the proliferation of discoveries of Neanderthal men and other prehistoric artefacts across the Channel. It was due directly to the fossil man from Sussex that London was now preferred to Paris as the seat of the study of fossil man. It was to London that the world looked for acceptance of Peking man. It was to London that Arthur Dart came to seek acceptance for his South African ape-man. It was London that rejected him.

Small wonder then that Piltdown man's discoverer, Charles Dawson, a Sussex solicitor, was congratulated and fêted. Only his death in 1916 robbed him of a knighthood and a civil list pension. But many years later the famous Piltdown site in Sussex was scheduled as a National Monument. A suitably inscribed stone was erected to the memory of the famous amateur. In the forty years of Piltdown man's credibility it is estimated that some five hundred essays were written about him. This does not take into account the myriad allusions to the Sussex relics in books of the 'highways and byways of rural Sussex' genre. The Piltdown site attracted visitors as new-laid concrete does dogs.

Then came the shock. In 1953 – some forty years later – it was announced that Piltdown man was a forgery. He was an amalgam of a modernish skull with the jaw of a modern orang-utan. Obviously the human fragments, ape's jaw, flint implements and bones of extinct animals had been 'planted' at Piltdown. It was obvious also that the forger was Charles Dawson. He had duped Science and got away with it for forty years. Outraged Science tore his reputation to shreds. At the same time there was a great rush to explain that no one had really believed in Piltdown man anyway. Science, particularly the British Museum which had long sheltered Piltdown man, closed its ranks (an almost unprecedented event) and adopted a defensive posture. But the scientists need not have worried. Thanks to a long-established indifference to the study of prehistory among British educationalists, few could see the real joke. But the spectacle of the learned hoodwinked by the layman appeals to the vulgar sense of humour. An otherwise disinterested public picked on this aspect alone. Like the Australian bushranger Ned Kelly, Charles Dawson became a folk hero for a very brief period. Then he was forgotten.

The name 'Charles Dawson' meant nothing to me. I became acquainted with the spectre of Piltdown through another of the trickster's nefarious activities – a two-volume work, *The History of Hastings Castle*. In fact a considerable amount of time elapsed before I was made aware of the fact that the historian Charles Dawson was none other than the solicitor Charles Dawson; that I was in the literary presence of the 'Wizard of Sussex', the archduper and perpetrator of history's greatest archaeological fraud. By this time the damage had been done.

It is irrational but not unusual for one's good opinion of a work to be transferred to its author. The good opinion I had formed of the author of *The History of Hastings Castle* outlasted the discovery of his true identity. But even a superficial examination of the facts which surround the mysterious Piltdown forgery reveals that the assumption that because Dawson got the fame he should receive the blame is by no means unassailable. One other person got at least an equal share of the glory. Of the three main participants in the dig which brought Piltdown man to light there were two who were placed beyond shadow of suspicion merely because of their respective standing in Science and the Church. Another, who I firmly believe was the hoaxer, is never mentioned at all.

With this realization other issues began to intrude themselves. Who else could have been concerned with Piltdown? Why had the forgery remained undetected for forty years? Piltdown man so neatly fitted into the accepted evolutionary pattern, but why? What was this accepted evolutionary pattern?

As another layman I realized that to place Piltdown man in his correct historical perspective I should have to go back in time – to before the first fossil man astounded the scientific world. In order to understand Piltdown man's implications it was necessary to trace the history of the discovery of fossil man back to before the middle of the nineteenth century; to when it was never even suspected that such a progenitor of man had existed.

This then is a lay appraisal of the great fossil man hunt. It covers a period which is wishfully called (by scientists and encyclopaedias) a hundred years of scientific achievement. In fact it was a turbulent era of controversy, precipitate opinion, extravagant claims, fear, confusion and dilemma.

The present author gratefully acknowledges the kindness and patience with which Sir Wilfrid Le Gros Clark and Dr Kenneth Page Oakley assisted his inquiries about the Piltdown episode, and in the case of the latter, supplied him with the latest information on the Piltdown specimens.

He would also like to thank Williams and Norgate, Collins, Pitman Publishing, the British Museum, and the editor of *The Times* for their kind permission to use material, tables, diagrams, etc.

Westhampnett,
Sussex
1972

I

It is almost impossible for us to gain an adequate conception of the incredulity with which the majority of early Victorians received the first insinuations about the vast age of mankind. Unfortunately for our purpose we are too inclined to think of the Victorians as people like ourselves without the benefits of electricity; thus we mistake the acceptances of the latter end of a lengthy reign for the rejections of a major part of it, and interpret the contributions of the Victorian scientists as part of the Great Era of revelation when at the time these were often considered to be contentious hypotheses, even outrageous speculation.

It is unjust to single out the Victorians as uniquely antagonistic to new ideas and resistant to change, for they were not. Superficially, man is adaptable but he becomes notoriously ungymnastic when the rejection of attitudes based on fundamental principles is involved. For example, we too readily doubt the possibility of life on other planets without pausing too long to consider that some organisms might rejoice in an atmosphere of boiling sulphuric acid. It is not too much of an exaggeration to claim that a similar intellectual barrier was being assaulted by the early Victorians who were proposing that the Biblical conception of man's place in Creation might be entirely false. Such an insinuation at any time in the previous centuries would have been outrageous, even dangerous. Not much more than a hundred years had elapsed since unorthodox interpretations of the Bible had been purged in the fires of Smithfield. No such fate threatened the scientific heretics of the early nineteenth century but it was the view of the leaders of the Church that the exponents of this heterodoxy would be accorded the same fate at the Last Judgement.

There is no doubt that Victorian Britain was experiencing a religious backlash. Five years before Wellington's victory at

Waterloo, George III, after one more lapse into insanity (although his critics say it was the reverse), retired to Windsor leaving his realm at the mercy of the Prince of Wales. The Prince Regent was the least reputable of a family whose common stock of virtue was not superabundant. He was not devoid of ability, as his frequent clashes with Parliament bear witness, nor lacking in dignity, and he possessed considerable personal charm; nevertheless, he was a shameless voluptuary, reckless spendthrift, rake-hell, hard drinker and compulsive gambler. The Regent's conduct was an embarrassment to his ministers and a terrible example to his subjects, who slavishly followed it with an acquiescence and zeal which must have relieved its instigator of any feeling of responsibility. The brief reign of William IV brought some relief but there was a marked calming of the turbulent *mores* when the young Victoria, schooled in order, punctuality, obedience and self-sacrifice, succeeded to the throne in 1837.

The degree of profundity with which Religion smote the early Victorians is open to suspicion. Certainly a considerable proportion of the lower-class town dwellers were flagrantly lawless with but a thin veneer of religious observance and much hidden superstition. The effect of religious belief was most marked in the influential middle classes. But this manifested itself more in the form of a high-minded bigotry than in humanitarian uplift. A great age of social reform was ushered in but at its beginning, at least, Charity was dispensed with an ostentatious piety which raises doubts as to whether it did its donors or beneficiaries the more good. The workhouses to which the itinerant paupers were sent seemed to have been devised to rid the rich of the depressing sight of them. Not a few recipients of the grudging largesse of the New Poor Law designed to fight 'the growing evil of pauperism' wished they were dead and free of it.

The profundity of the early Victorian religion however need not concern us but its manifestation does. Having overcome the adversity of the previous reigns, the richly endowed and privileged Church of England now wielded authoritative power. But it was weak on the intellectual side. Its leaders were too obsessed with the temperature of Hell and the furniture of Heaven. Too much of their zeal came from belief in the eternal punishment of uncorrected sinners. They held too narrowly to a literal interpretation of the Bible. From all this stemmed a conviction that the swollen foot of scientific revelation could be squeezed into the narrow shoe of Biblical convention. This had a stifling effect on the teaching at the universities, which historically were religious foundations. Entry into the universities of Oxford and Cambridge was by way of religious tests which were not abolished until 1871. Most of the chairs of learning were occupied by men who were churchmen first and scientists second. Small wonder, then, that when the attack came it was extramural, from ex-university men to some degree emancipated from the theologio-scientific strait-jackets of their mentors.

By definition the prehistorian's material is unwritten and inscrutable. He creates his history of man out of the dumb evidence of tools and weapons, tombs, monuments, and indeed from his rubbish. For this reason much of the early study of prehistory was highly vulnerable to individual interpretation, fancy and invention. The equivocal material lends itself to all kinds of speculation. Anyone who could raise an audience used the relics as hooks on which to hang the most fanciful, astonishing and fallacious theories as to their nature and origin. This interpretation could be denied by the next describer. The ensuing debate, controversy, nose-pulling and name-calling seems to have added to the fascination of the subject for a great deal of it was indulged in for its own sake.

The historical study of man's development was by no means new even at the beginning of Victoria's reign. The Renaissance scholars of Italy studied not only the classical literature of the Greek and Roman Empires but also their archaeology. At the same time such men as William Camden explored Britain's ancient monuments with a view to discovering the nature of their builders. But in the main the study was more acquisitive than philosophical. It was the age of collectors of 'antiquities'. Great collections of antiquities were common. Most of the great houses had them. But, alas, it seems that at least some of the proud owners were none too scrupulous as to the qualities which distinguished a genuine artefact of pre-history from that which was not. Almost anything placed in a glass case assumed a value far beyond its intrinsic worth.

The year 1707 saw the formation of a club of enthusiasts who had met regularly at the *Young Devil* and *Bear* taverns in the

Strand, London. From this bibulous beginning was born the Society of Antiquaries. Horace Walpole, it seems one of the more aesthetic members, cast considerable doubt on many antiquities which were extolled in the Society's journal (published for the first time in 1770). He condemned the collectors for their lack of discrimination, writing to a friend: 'Mercy on us. What a cartload of bricks and rubbish and Roman ruins they have piled together.' He also described his fellow club members as 'the midwives of superannuated miscarriages'. Any lampooner short of a target invariably kept his hand in with a tilt at the Society. The hilarious highlight of a play by Samuel Foote performed at the Haymarket Theatre in 1772 was a visit paid to the Society of Antiquaries by the Nabob, who was preceded by Negro slaves bearing 'the twelve lost books of Livy', a piece of lava from the last Vesuvius eruption, a box of bones, beetles and butterflies, and a large green chamberpot described as a Roman burial urn dug up from the Temple of Concord.

The Rev. James Douglas was no doubt referring to this sorry state of affairs when he wrote, in the foreword to his *Sepulchral History of Great Britain*:[1] 'If the study of antiquity be undertaken in the cause of History it will rescue itself from an approach indescriminately bestowed on works which have been deemed frivolous.'

But how old was antiquity? The Christian religion provided the answer to this question. Early in the seventeenth century James Ussher, Archbishop of Amagh, occupied himself with the numerology of the Old Testament from which he deduced that mankind originated with Adam in the year 4004 B.C. The capacity for survival of the immediate descendants of Adam, which ranged from the 365 years of the comparatively short-lived Enoch to the 969 years of Methuselah, would render incredulous anyone not firmly committed to complete faith in Biblical chronology, but not so Ussher. He published his findings in 1650[2] and Ussher's calculation was widely accepted and considered as inspired as the Holy Writ itself, the year 4004 B.C. being duly marked in the margin of the relevant passages of the Authorized Version of the Bible.

The archbishop had supplied the missing element in a problem which had vexed theologians for centuries. Bede in the eighth century had considered that the Creation must have been

accomplished in the spring, for how else had God so easily succeeded with the agricultural part of it? Vincent of Beauvais,
writing in the thirteenth century, supported Bede. Later it was
successfully argued that on the contrary there had been much
water about at the time of the Creation, the passages in Genesis
which lead up to the Dawn of Mankind were full of it, so
surely this would indicate a wetter period of the year, say September at the Equinox.

One of the subscribers to this last view was Dr John Lightfoot, Master of St Catherine's College and Vice-Chancellor of
the University of Cambridge. Further consideration prompted
Lightfoot to amend the month to October. He declared in 1642
that he entirely endorsed Archbishop Ussher and that 'Heaven
and Earth, centre and circumference, were created all together
in the same instant and clouds full of water . . . this took place
and man was created by the Trinity on October 23, 4004 B.C.
at nine o'clock in the morning.' This precision owed nothing to
the Biblical text. It says much for Lightfoot's view of his calling
that he attributed the Dawn of Mankind to the date and time
of the commencement of the academic year.

Within the confines of this arbitrary chronology – let it not be
doubted that the Ussher–Lightfoot view was generally accepted
throughout the eighteenth and into the nineteenth century – it
seemed that little if anything remained to be discovered about
mankind's past. It was generally agreed that the great Assyrian,
Persian, Greek and Roman Empires had flourished before
Christianity. These would take up most if not all of the available
four millennia. But surely Britain, it began to be argued, must
have had some prehistory? What had happened in these islands
during the times of these great Empires? And there was the
evidence of the antiquities, the barrows, earthworks and stone
monuments which still stood in remote rural areas. Who were
the 'ancients' encountered by Julius Caesar and Claudius when
they came to Britain?

Scholars pondered this uncomfortable void but, gaining no
help from the monuments themselves, they resorted to inspiration and invention. The only rule of this game was that
whatever race was selected as suitable inhabitants of this country
during prehistoric times it must have some relation to what was
known of the other prehistoric civilizations.

Nennius, writing in the ninth century A.D., settled the Trojan Brutus, grandson of Aeneas, together with his followers, in Britain at the height of the Greek Empire. Belief that the early Britons were the descendants of Greeks or Romans was strong until well into the seventeenth century. As late as 1674, the Oxford *Almanack* headed the list of the kings of England with Brutus. Then Brutus was swept from power by a preference for a more Biblical origin and we became descendants of Noah. Japhet and the sons of Japhet were said to have peopled Britain very soon after the Flood. Then the Phoenicians, one of the Lost Tribes of Israel, even the Egyptians, were in turn canvassed and took their place as ancestors.

The supposed identity of the builders of Stonehenge, that conundrum on Salisbury Plain, varied with the prevailing ancestral wind. Inigo Jones was commissioned by King James I to make a study of Stonehenge. He declared in 1620 that it was a Roman temple. Dr Carlton, a court physician, countered that Jones was mistaken and that it was in fact built by the Danes as a place in which to consecrate their Kings. John Twyne and Aylett Sammes, strong for Phoenician settlement of these islands, saw no difficulty in recognizing strong Phoenician affinities in the stone pillars. Bishop Nicholson did not doubt that it was Saxon. Dr Bolton knew it as the tomb of Boadicea. The Elizabethan diarist John Aubrey and many others thought it the work of those conveniently ubiquitous mystics called 'Druids'.

At the beginning of the nineteenth century, amongst the more sober students of prehistory, at least, a certain frustration is discernible. After a study of New Grange, the megalithic monument in Ireland, thought in turn to be Mithraic, Danish, Egyptian and Phoenician, Sir Richard Colt Hoare wrote:

I shall not unnecessarily trespass upon the time and patience of my readers in endeavouring to ascertain what tribes first peopled this country [Ireland]; nor to what nation the construction of this singular monument may be reasonably attributed for, I fear, both its authors and its original destination will ever remain unknown. Conjecture may wander over its wild and spacious domains but will never bring home with it either truth or conviction. Alike will the histories of those stupendous temples at Avebury and Stonehenge which grace my native country, remain in obscurity and oblivion.[3]

Thus one of the foremost archaeologists of those times summed up the extent of real knowledge by confessing his despair. In the imaginations of his contemporaries the phantoms of long-dead civilizations still flitted among the ancient barrows and earthworks. Scholars still detected Egyptian hieroglyphs and Phoenician daggers carved in antiquity on the sarsens of Salisbury Plain. But Colt Hoare's statement marked some improvement. One archaeologist was admitting humbly that the study of antiquities was based on little more than guesswork, that he had been unable to wrest from these evidences of prehistory any positive information, that the happenings of four thousand years were obscured by darkness.

Perhaps this was too gloomy a view. By the beginning of the nineteenth century there had been one palpable achievement, although it was by no means widely accepted as such. For centuries mysterious stone objects had been turning up. The triangular wedges of chipped stone, usually of flint or chert, were at first dismissed as metaphysical phenomena such as thunderbolts or elfshot. Ullisses Androvandi, an eminent seventeenth-century zoologist, thought they were due to 'an admixture of a certain exhalation of thunder and lightning with metallic matter, chiefly in dark clouds, which is distilled from the circumfused moisture and coagulated into a mass (like flour with water) and subsequently indurated by heat, like a brick'.

But others took a more practical view. Sir William Dugdale was convinced that the flints were 'weapons used by the Britons before the art of making arms of brass or iron was known'.[4]

At the end of the century a stone axe together with the remains of an elephant were found. Unfortunately, the association allowed an entirely false interpretation to be placed on it. The stone axe and a portion of a molar tooth were recovered from building excavations in Grays Inn Lane, London, by William Conyers, an apothecary and antique dealer. The finder did in fact cherish the belief that he had stumbled across evidence which suggested that elephants could once have inhabited Britain and that the weapon must have belonged to an Ancient British hunter. His view caused great hilarity. John Bagford, a friend who delivered an account of the find to the Society of Antiquaries, confined himself to the observation that the elephant must be attributable to the Roman occupation of this country, in fact a Claudian import. The flint was presented to the British Museum.

The first recorded hint from a scientist at the probable vast antiquity of man was made by John Frere, F.R.S., in a paper read to the Society on 22 June 1797. Of several flint implements recovered from twelve feet of earth at Hoxne, near Diss, Suffolk, he said that they 'were fabricated and used by a people who had not the use of metals ... The situation [depth] at which these weapons were found may tempt us to refer them to a very remote period indeed, even beyond that of the present world'.[5]

One wonders what Frere's fellow members made of his attempt to attribute his stone axes to a hitherto unsuspected region of time. It is probable, however, that the inference was ignored completely for the paper lay dormant until the mid-nineteenth century when it was held up as evidence of British pre-eminence in archaeological discovery.

At the commencement of the Victorian era prehistoric archae-ology can usefully be likened to a fly in a bottle, ever buzzing for release. The bottle was its elder sister science – geology. If geology insisted that there was no time for prehistory, then it was useless for archaeology to propose events to put into it. But at this time geology itself was engaged in internecine strife. To-wards the end of the eighteenth century began the rift between those geologists who uncompromisingly believed in the Creation as described in Genesis and a few who had come to doubt whether what they saw in the rocks could be accomplished in the mere six thousand years allowed by the Ussher–Lightfoot chronology. Instead of rejecting Bibilical exegesis, the new school proposed that as the many strata of rocks could not have been produced by conditions which prevailed in modern times, then the past terrestrial energy must have operated at a higher intensity. They argued that at some time there must have been general catas-trophes, of which the Biblical Flood was but one example, an age of geological chaos which had exalted the mountain ranges and folded the valleys, natural phenomena which had anni-hilated, and made chalk of, countless millions of sea creatures. The rival factions split into Diluvialists, Catastrophists and Fluvialists, each battling for general acceptance of theories involving the multiplication or permutation of any number of floods and other kinds of natural catastrophes.

The greatest Catastrophist of them all was Georges Cuvier (1769–1826), geologist, naturalist and foremost member of the

French *Académie des Sciences*. Cuvier held that the many strata of rocks could only be interpreted correctly in the light of several catastrophes, the Noachian Flood of Genesis being one of many. He was the constant adversary of prehistoric archaeologists who claimed that man could have existed at the same time as the extinct animals. The science of geology, and its kindred science palaeontology, was advanced and advancing. That monstrous and strange animals, now extinct, once inhabited Western Europe was no longer denied but it was the entrenched belief of men such as Cuvier that these had perished during the age of catastrophes. According to these authorities time could be divided into three main epochs: the Antediluvium – that of the monstrous, now extinct fauna, and of catastrophes culminating in the Flood of Genesis; the Diluvium – during which were deposited the strata of rock in which the remains of these extinct species might be met with; and the Modern Age – that of mankind and the modern species of animals. At the Dawn of Mankind, it was believed, Adam and Eve had been born into the physical and moral perfection of the terrestrial Paradise. Therefore suggestions that man had once lived at the same time as the extinct fauna in a state of primitive destitution, as postulated by the crude flint implements, was preposterous, and anathema to men such as Cuvier.

But cautious claims that this might have been so were being made with increasing frequency. Men excavating in the *Midi* of France had found the bones of bears, hyenas and reindeer; many, they said, clearly bore the cutting marks of the flint tools found with them. Indeed, some advanced to the view that they had found the bones of the primitive men themselves. But against them all stood Georges Cuvier. Playing with skill one game with the rules of another, with gusto he threw himself into the task of demolishing these alleged human relics. His objective approach was exemplified by what almost certainly is an apocryphal story of a jape perpetrated on him by one of his young students. Clad in red costume, horns and hooves, the pranker burst into the bedroom of the father of palaeontology crying: 'Wake up, thou man of catastrophes. I am the devil. I have come to devour you.' Cuvier regarded the frightening apparition with cold and critical gaze. He said: 'I doubt whether you can. You have horns and hooves. You only eat plants.'

To Cuvier's Paris laboratory came the supplicants. Each bore his remains of 'antediluvian man'. The 'pope of bones' examined each case with care, then rejected it for what it was – the remains of an elephant from Belgium, fragments of cetacean from Cerigo, part of a tortoise from Aix-en-Provence and so on. If the remains were undeniably human they were dismissed as 'modern', as bones which had by some freak of nature intruded into the deposit where the extinct-animal bones were found, or judged wanting in corroborative evidence in the form of witnesses. A significant coup in 1811 was the destruction of an exhibit that had been going the rounds of laboratories and scientific exhibitions for ninety years as *Homo diluvii testis*. Cuvier incorrectly identified this human witness of the Flood as a slab of Miocene rock[6] in which was embedded the fossilized vertebra of the extinct reptile *Ichthyosaurus* to which was added the human skull of a recently deceased sufferer of hypertosis – an overvigorous activity of the pituitary gland causing malformation of the cranial bones. Cuvier summed up his ethic in a final verdict in the year of his death on a human skull recovered with the remains of extinct mammals in what was thought to be ancient mud at Lahr on the banks of the Rhine. He wrote: 'All the evidence leads us to believe that the Human Race did not exist at all in the countries where the fossil [animal] bones were found, at the period of the upheavals which buried them.'

Such was Cuvier's reputation for infallibility that a grateful nation offered him the post of Minister of the Interior, but death intervened. But his work did not die with him. His disciples within the *Académie* drew up a list of twenty-seven successive acts of creation with intervening catastrophes which were said to have obliterated certain animals and plants, by which geological time could be measured. Similar tables were compiled in England at about the same time. William Smith, known as 'Strata Smith' (1769–1839), drew up a table showing thirty-two such layers of strata. He found distinguishing animal and plant organisms in each.

The Catastrophists, Diluvialists and Fluvialists were in command but a faint voice now called for a more rational interpretation of the succeeding layers of strata. This doctrine, which came to be known as Uniformitarianism – the basis of modern geological thought – had as its apostle James Hutton. He held no brief for catastrophes, extraterrestrial energy or heavenly fire-works. Hutton's *Theory of the Earth*, published in 1785, instead saw the layers of sand, gravel, clay and limestone as the normal, undramatic successive deposits of water, both river and sea. He argued that nothing more was needed than ordinary sedimentary deposition over an immense length of time. 'No processes are to be employed,' he wrote, 'that are not natural to the globe; no action to be admitted except those of which we know the principle.'[7]

Uniformitarianism made nonsense of Biblical convention and, as might be expected, Hutton's contribution was received with anger and abuse by the seemingly impregnable phalanx of theo-logio-scientific geologists. Hutton, however, was soon forgotten. The Diluvialists returned to haggling with the Catastrophists and both raged against the Fluvialists. Thus frustrated by the Biblical politicking of the mighty Catastrophists, the prehistoric archae-ologists and palaeontologists sought another way to plead that man and the extinct animals had at one time been coeval. This impossible task was attempted by tricks of terminology of a kind best illustrated by the following example.

During the clearing of rocky hazards to navigation from the bed of the Jumna river in Bengal, North India, a large quantity of fossil animal bones were dredged up together with a few which were strongly canvassed as being human. A lively discus-sion took place in the British–Indian scientific journals of 1833 before it was proved that the human relics were nothing of the kind. Although this debate was a waste of time it did, by attract-ing the attention of correspondents with similar interests, grease the wheels for one of importance. Two years later, while interest in the Jumna dredgings was still alive, Hugh Falconer, super-intendent of the Honourable East India Company's botanical gardens and an enthusiastic archaeologist then excavating ancient deposits in the Siwalik Hills, uncovered the remains of a *Colossochelys atlas* – a gigantic extinct tortoise, some twelve feet long, eight feet broad and six feet high.

The enthusiasts seemed only too aware that a giant tortoise figured prominently in myth and folklore. In the Pythagorean cosmogony the infant world is placed on the back of an elephant which itself is sustained by a huge tortoise. In Hindu mythology a mighty tortoise grapples with an elephant. The dimensions of both animals were expressed in terms of extravagant magnitude. The tortoises of modern India are small. It would have been as legitimate to speak of an elephant contending with a mouse as with any of these. Could man then, ran the speculation, remember the days of these giant reptiles?

On this debate the Proceedings of the Zoological Society of London for 1844 commented:

The result at which we have arrived is, that there are fair grounds for entertaining the belief as probable that the *Colossochelys atlas* may have lived down to an early epoch of the human period and become extinct since.

In this careful way archaeological papers of the early and mid-nineteenth century pushed at the firmly closed door of Biblical conception. Many years later Falconer commented that if it were true that the giant tortoise may have *lived down* to man, then it must follow that man was alive on the earth at the same time as the tortoise. This way of expressing the relation was simply a semantic device calculated to minimize the likelihood of academic ridicule. A similar subterfuge was the statement that the primitive flint tool user was 'lived down to' by the extinct fauna of 'the *later* diluvium'. By such equivocation early nineteenth-century man was able to preserve his beliefs from direct conflict with established orthodoxy.

But the theologio-scientific cadre was not to be hoodwinked by such methods. Departing from its usual tactics of indifference or the swatting of reactionary gnats it closed its ranks. In 1802 William Paley[8] had published his *Natural Theology; or Evidence of the Existence and Attributes of the Deity collected from the Appearances of Nature*. Paley has been described as one of the most original thinkers on natural phenomena but his *Natural Theology* was a cringing testimonial to the old dogma. Dedicating the work to the Bishop of Durham 'to repair in his study his deficiencies in the Church', he had written that although the world teemed with countless animal and plant 'delights' it could not have done so for more than six thousand years. Everything was part of a splendid, precise design by God, the arch-watchmaker.

This was like balm to the sensitive hides of the theologio-scientists. It was thought that more needed to be done in this vein. In 1833 the Trustees of the Earl of Bridgewater commissioned a number of 'tame' scientific authors, selected by the President of the Royal Society in consultation with the Archbishop of Canterbury and the Bishop of London, to write treatises on the departed Paley's theme. The brief was that the account of the Creation in Genesis was literally exact and that Noah's Ark and the Flood were facts of prehistory. The contributions reached expectations, particularly that of William Buckland,[9] Dean of Westminster, a former Reader in Mineralogy in the University of Oxford.

Buckland's academic performance was superb from the point of view of the ecclesiastics. He had spent a lifetime equating his religious faith with the contrary evidence supplied by his geological excavations. The doyen of university lecturers, his eloquence packed the lecture halls to overfilling. He insisted on a Universal Deluge, holding that geology proved it beyond doubt. As in the case of Cuvier, the stories about Buckland were legion – how he disinterred the heart of a French king from Sutton Courtenay churchyard and ate it, how he kept a pet orang-utan in his rooms at Christ Church, and how he breakfasted Ruskin on toasted mice. It was claimed that his field geology was so profound that when lost one day on a horseback journey from Oxford to London, he dismounted, scooped up a handful of earth, and remarked: 'Ah, yes, as I guessed, Ealing.'

Buckland's immense authority was instrumental in disposing of the claim of Father J. MacEnery, a Roman Catholic priest. MacEnery recovered from Kent's Cavern, near Torquay, Devon, a rhinoceros tooth and a 'flint weapon'. He hopefully communicated the find to the Dean only to be told that he was mistaken in his interpretation. Buckland said that the Ancient Britons must have scooped ovens in the cave floor, thus allowing the weapon to intrude amongst the fossil animal bones below. MacEnery argued that the floor was of unbroken stalagmite and that there were no such ovens – but in vain. The priest then enlisted the support of a local schoolmaster named William Pengelly and through him that of the Torquay Natural History Society. But Buckland's strong opposition was enough to convince MacEnery that he had better not publish. Many years later the British Association for the Advancement of Science was attracted by the story and conducted a new series of excavations at the cavern. In 1867 a human jawbone was brought to light.

But the Bridgewater Treatises were becoming an anachronism. Already the tide of opinion was making strongly against the Catastrophists and the Uniformitarianists were growing in number. The year 1833 saw the publication of the third and final volume of Lyell's *Principles of Geology*. It has been rightly commented that no scientific work except Charles Darwin's *Origin of Species* has during the author's lifetime exerted such a powerful influence on its subject. It is one of those ironies of life that Sir Charles Lyell claimed to have been attracted towards geology by William Buckland's brilliant Oxford lectures.

Lyell was an example of that quite common nineteenth-century phenomenon – the amateur turned expert. Destined by his father for the legal profession, Lyell took a Master of Arts degree at Exeter College and was duly called to the Bar. But the seed implanted by Buckland exerted a powerful influence. Lyell was shortly off on a series of geological excursions to the Continent, principally to France with Roderick (later Sir) Impey Murchison. This was the turning point in his life. He wrote to his father that after the fullest consideration he had decided to give up law and devote his life to geology. He did so to such effect that by 1824, three years after leaving Oxford, he was secretary of the Geological Society, and two years later he was elected to the fellowship of the Royal Society. The first volume of his *Principles* was published that year.

To geologists who had gained their view of the formation of strata from Georges Cuvier's *Theory of the Earth* the work was a revelation. Instead of early convulsions and a higher intensity of terrestrial energy culminating in periodic catastrophes, Lyell proposed that the natural forces now existing were strong enough to produce stupendous changes in the earth's crust provided they were given sufficient time. The earth, Lyell argued, was millions of years old and not just a few thousand as suggested by the Catastrophists. Lyell's offering was not original. Hutton had said the same sort of thing at the end of the previous century, but it is a sad truth that a prophet out of his time rarely prospers. Only when the minds of men are conditioned to the reception of a new and strident hypothesis does it stand a chance of acceptance. Hutton was swept out of sight by the tremendous opposition. Lyell was lionized: knighted in 1848, honoured with the doctorate of Civil Laws by Oxford in 1855 and the Royal Society's Copley Medal in 1858.

Many Catastrophists, Diluvialists and Fluvialists joined the ranks of Lyell's supporters; later many more were brought round to his point of view. A notable English convert was the Rev. W. D. Conybeare,[10] Dean of Llandaff, a renowned geologist who not so long before had been postulating three deluges before that of Noah. He now claimed that Lyell's work was 'in itself sufficiently important to mark almost a new era in the progress of our science'. But Lyell by no means had it all his own way. Powerful men, such as William Buckland and Adam Sedgewick, Woodwardian Professor of Geology at Cambridge in 1818, came out strongly against the *Principles*. John Kidd, Buckland's former teacher, was possibly typical of the majority who merely allowed the salt of Lyell's work to flavour the old Biblical mess of pottage. In his Bridgewater Treatise, published in the same year but subsequent to Lyell's *Principles*, he wrote that in the previous century it had been generally considered that shells and other organic remains found in chalk and other strata were proof of the Deluge of Moses. But today, he continued, without prejudice to the credibility of the Scriptures these same men were admitting that the shells and remains may have been deposited after the Deluge. Who can say, he asked, that this later view will not be adopted in respect of the extinct mammals found in gravel and caverns?

So the theologio-scientists of Britain began to admit that there might be some truth in assertions that the extinct species of animals had bridged the Deluge. By this admission the road was opened for eventual acceptance that man himself might have done so, but by crossing the Deluge in the other direction, by reaching backwards in time instead of forward.

But this minimal concession was open-handed by comparison with the uncompromising attitude across the Channel. By its nature British Protestantism is far more liberal than French Roman Catholicism and this manifested itself in the staunch rearguard action fought on behalf of Biblical convention and chronology by the *Académie des Sciences*, particularly in the way that body spurned men such as Boucher de Perthes.

Jacques Boucher de Crèvecoeur de Perthes[11] is invariably described as a retired customs official, even a mere lock-keeper. In fact he was a frequently published author of travelogues which described visits not only to the British Isles but also to Italy, Scandinavia, Russia and North Africa. But at this range Boucher de Perthes is an enigmatic character. It is by no means certain that he himself made the visits he described. His activities described later in this book suggest also that he was either an innocent victim of enthusiasm or a downright charlatan.

Boucher de Perthes was absorbed in the archaeology of his native Abbeville, then a small out-of-the-way town in Northern France. In 1846 he published *Antiquités celtiques et antédiluviennes: De l'industrie primitive ou des artes à leur origine*, the results of many years of excavation. He made no attempt at compromise, writing that he had found at various depths in the gravel pits about Abbeville numerous stone tools and the bones of extinct animals. There was no doubt in the mind of Boucher de Perthes that in spite of their imperfections these rude stone tools proved the existence of man as a contemporary of the extinct fauna.

It is traditional that the *Académie des Sciences* was outraged by the publication and that he was the scientific laughing stock of Paris. The renowned palaeontologist and foremost French commentator on the history of this science, Marcellin Boule, has written that 'contradictions, sneers and scorn' were forthwith heaped on Boucher de Perthes' head. But there seems no evidence to support this dramatic view of the reception. It is more likely that the *Académie* accorded Boucher de Perthes the treatment usually reserved for radical amateurs. It completely ignored him. For many years he and his work remained undignified by official rebuttal.

But if Boucher de Perthes lacked worldly fame he was not entirely unrewarded. He had achieved a great deal of local importance. His future scientific papers continued to delight his fellow members of the *Société d'Emulation d'Abbeville* and were widely circulated in the historical societies of rural France. Abbeville became the centre of a vigorous and profitable trade in stone axes. Boucher de Perthes established a museum which attracted a large number of visitors. One of the many Englishmen who later made the pilgrimage to Abbeville described this 'impressive' collection. According to Hugh Falconer, the museum was housed in a hotel which 'was from ground floor to garret, a continued museum filled with pictures, mediaeval art, and Gaulish antiquities, including antediluvian flint knives, fossil bones, etc.'. He also reported that there was a not inconsiderable admixture of natural freaks such as water-perforated stones, and strangely-shaped pieces of glass and brick.

But the *Académie* was forced to notice Boucher de Perthes in time. In 1854, Dr Rigollet of Amiens innocently likened some stone axes found by himself in the sandpits of nearby St Acheul to those found by Boucher de Perthes at Abbeville. Rigollet was a member of the *Académie*, but instead of abusing the scientist it turned on Boucher de Perthes.

It was not unusual even up to modern times for a scientific body to castigate an outsider while at the same time overlooking similarly offensive views when expressed by a fellow scientist.

Why this peculiar form of injustice was practised so frequently is not obvious. The usual clannish intolerance of unwarranted intrusion by outsiders does not seem to be the whole answer. It is possible, however, that it was a kind of diplomacy. By this means an authoritative body could warn a member that he had transgressed without directly offending him. In this way the risk that a faction might be formed about him would be greatly reduced.

Whatever the reason, undoubtedly Boucher de Perthes received the sniggers which by right should have been directed at Rigollet. Like the Londoner's attitude to the Society of Antiquaries many years before, Boucher de Perthes became the target for Parisian humour. But Paris is a long way from Abbeville.

Speculation on both sides of the Channel about the probable antiquity of man was a step forward. But no one yet doubted that these distant ancestors of mankind, if indeed they had ever existed at all, could have been anything other than like us in appearance. The Bible said, and the Church and Science, laity and geologists and amateurs, devoutly believed it, that God created man in His own image. This much was sure. When a fossil man was found at last nobody recognized him.

The unearthing of Neanderthal man in 1856 – renowned as the first discovery of a genuine fossil man although events show that in fact he is not entitled to this distinction – and the uproar which followed the discovery span a decade. In this decade speculation on man's antiquity received several shots in the arm in the form of the Darwin–Wallace paper to the Linnean Society in 1858, the publishing of the former's sensational *The Origin of Species* the following year and Huxley's *Evidence of Man's Place in Nature* in 1863. The story of Neanderthal man shows how little the minds of men responded to these historically momentous works.

The Neander valley (*thal*) lies near the town of Wuppertal about seven miles east of Dusseldorf in what then was called Rhenish Prussia. The valley, through which flows the Dussel river, gained its name from the seventeenth-century hymn-writer and recluse Joseph Neander. By 1856 however the 'sweet flowery bower' of the hermit had been mostly destroyed by the relentless quarrying of limestone for building. Neanderthal man was dug out of a deposit of mud on the floor of a cave some sixty feet above the river. How the quarrymen found the bones is clear but why they attached any importance to the remains is not so evident for it appears that similar discoveries were common. But in this case Neanderthal man, a skull with the facial bones entirely missing, a clavicle, a scapula, two ulnae, five ribs and a pelvis, was handed to Herr von Beckensdorff, the quarry owner. He presented the remains to Dr J. C. Fuhlrott of neighbouring Eberfeld who in turn passed them to H. Schaafhausen, professor of anatomy in the University of Bonn.

The choice was propitious. Three years before, in 1853, Schaafhausen had rejected the Catastrophists, even propounding a crude theory of evolution, writing that:

living plants are not separated from the extinct by new creations, but are to be regarded as their descendants through continued reproduction.

A year after the discovery Schaafhausen published a paper on the Neanderthal remains. He said that they were undoubtedly human but had pecularities of conformation. The skull appeared to Schaafhausen to be of unusual thickness with exaggerated eyebrow ridges. The thighbones were strangely curved but none of this could be due to deformation by disease. The brain-size, suggested by the capacity of the cranium, could not have been much less than 1,033 c.c. (cubic centimetres) and so not much lower than the average capacity of the average modern skull.

But how old did Schaafhausen think the bones were? He found that the skeleton was of the same colour as other fossil animals' bones. The remains stuck to the tongue and when a fragment had been partially dissolved in hydrochloric acid no gelatine remained. When examined under a magnifying glass the bones were found to be covered with minute black specks. All this, wrote Schaafhausen, proved that the bones were genuine fossils.[1]

All this, Schaafhausen found himself able to conclude, pointed to the fact that the remains were those of

an individual of a savage and barbarous race derived from one of the wild races of north-western Europe, spoken of by the Latin writers and traced to a period when the latest animals of the diluvium still existed.

Considering the professor's advanced views on evolution this finding is disappointing. His reluctance to make an ambitious claim for Neanderthal man, his lack of audacity, robbed him of any notable niche in history. But he had said enough, too much for some.

A colleague at Bonn, Professor H. von Meyer, immediately wrote to Schaafhausen that his allusion to the diluvium was nonsense for it was evident that the remains were of recent origin. If Schaafhausen cared to look at the notepaper on which the letter was written he could see the black specks which he had mistakenly attributed to vast age. The writer said he had in his possession the skull of a dog which was as recent as the Roman occupation of northern Europe and certainly not as old as the diluvium of which Schaafhausen had written. This skull stuck to the tongue and it did not differ in colour from the animal bones discovered in French caves, also erroneously lauded as being of vast age.

Professor F. Mayer, also of Bonn, thought that Schaafhausen's enthusiasm had carried him away. A little quiet reasoning, he said, would show him that the so-called ancient man was nothing of the kind. Over the years Mayer had examined many human remains for which claims of antiquity had been made. None, said Mayer, had lived up to the expectations of the discoverers. Mayer had a theory which accounted for the peculiar shape of the ribs and limb bones. A protuberance on the left elbow, said by Schaafhausen to be the scar of an old injury, was none other than a symptom of advanced rickets. The protruding eyebrow ridges confirmed this diagnosis. The owner was in fact a Mongolian Cossack on his way through Prussia in 1814 in pursuit of Napoleon's fleeing army. The pain of the disease had furrowed the forehead of the horseman, for such he was as only a professional equestrian would have such bowed legs. The Cossack, said Mayer, had crawled into the Neanderthal cave and succumbed in agony. Mayer did not explain how the stricken man had managed to climb up sixty feet of vertical rock to the cave, nor did he even mention this fact.

Another colleague, J. A. Wagner, was convinced that the remains were modern but, unkindly, those of a Dutchman. Schaafhausen had to wait until 1872 to be told by Dr R. von Virchow that the Neanderthal skull was that of 'a pathological idiot'.

The French *Académie des Sciences* pointedly ignored Neanderthal man entirely. In England the discovery passed almost unnoticed except for a brief mention in two journals of a semiscientific nature. One, the *Westminster Review*, however, described the fossil as

the ruin of a solitary arch in an enormous bridge, which time has destroyed and which may have connected the highest of animals with the lowest of men.

The anonymous writer of these courageous words was not known. He anticipated scientific publication in England by almost four years, and general scientific thought by many more.

It is more than likely, however, that the prophet was Thomas Henry Huxley, for he was a regular contributor to the *Review*.

Huxley has that indefinable quality of being able to travel well through time. This is despite the efforts of many of his biographers who, with the best intentions in the world, tend to play up his idiosyncrasies. In 1856 he was just into his thirties but already of considerable authority. Of Huxley it can be fairly said that he had more talent than two lifetimes could have developed.

Of lower-middle-class stock, after a grammar-school education Huxley won a free scholarship to Charing Cross Hospital where he took prizes in anatomy, chemistry and physiology, winning the Gold Medal of the first University of London medical examination.

But his scholarship did nothing to obtain him a medical post and having to support himself he was forced into the only opening that was offered. He became an assistant surgeon in the Royal Navy, a turn of events which saved him for ever from a medical career, for his first – and only – appointment was to a survey ship with the unprepossessing name H.M.S. *Rattlesnake*.

With young Huxley aboard, the ship left England in December 1846 for a prolonged cruise of Australia's Great Barrier Reef and then up through the Torres Strait. This voyage would have been a major setback to the scientific pretensions of a lesser man, divorced as he was from instruction or guidance and with few books. Instead Huxley turned it to advantage. With the aid of a net adapted from a wire-mesh meat cover Huxley engrossed himself in the study of the anatomy of marine creatures. His scientific papers on the subject were of such peculiar brilliance that on his return to England in 1850 many established marine biologists sought to make his acquaintance. Within a few months he was elected to the membership of the Royal Society, and embarked on the first of the innumerable controversies which he provoked throughout his life.

Huxley blandly informed his Admiralty employers that he considered they were obliged to pay for the publishing of his scientific description of the voyage. The Admiralty refused, considering that it had been more than generous in allowing the biological questing at all, for he had not accompanied the survey as official naturalist but as a doctor. He was informed that furthermore it was his duty as a naval officer to rejoin the Fleet immediately.

The argument between Huxley and the Admiralty raged on and off for three years, culminating on 1 February 1854 with a direct order to proceed aboard H.M.S. *Illustrious*. Huxley refused, applying first for a postponement, then a cancellation, of the instructions. The Admiralty told him to report for duty or be struck from the Navy List. He did not and he was.

Now deprived even of the half-pay of the reserve fleet Huxley was penniless. Meanwhile he had married and necessity forced him to consider going to Australia to become a brewer. Nothing had come of his application for posts at the universities of Aberdeen and Cork or at King's College, London. But just before the effects of his expulsion from the Navy became too catastrophic he was offered the post of professor of palaeontology and naturalist at the Royal School of Mines, Jermyn Street, London, at a salary of £200 per annum.

Huxley's scientific papers were in great demand, and so was his writing for popular readership. Never was there a more potent purveyor of science for the layman. Although by training a physician and by inclination a biologist, Huxley embraced every related scientific subject and many that bore no resemblance. But all his articles were masterpieces of lucidity. The writer G. K. Chesterton remarked that Huxley was more a literary than a scientific man.

Huxley, however, did have an abrupt way with triflers or those he thought to be such, which has led to the charge of arrogance. But it would have been hard for the possessor of his staggering intellect to have been otherwise. Already he was developing a reputation for absent-mindedness. But it was noticeable that the suffering caused by his non-attendance at a scientific gathering was small compared to that caused by one of his surprise appearances at another where he was unlooked for. It is more than likely, therefore, that this feature was nothing more than a sudden change of mind precipitated by the last-minute discovery that adversaries more equal to his metal were to be found elsewhere. For Huxley dearly loved controversy. He was never better than when on his feet dealing with some famous transgressor. He described himself as 'a peace-loving, good-natured man' and declared that 'controversy is as abhorrent to me as gin to a reclaimed drunkard'. In justice to his own case he could have added 'and just as irresistible'.

As might be expected Huxley made many powerful enemies and friends. Amongst the latter were the geologist Sir Charles Lyell and Sir Joseph Hooker,[2] the famous systematic biologist who with his father built up the magnificent botanical collection at Kew. Both men remained lifelong friends of Huxley. Amongst the enemies was Sir Richard Owen,[3] professor of comparative anatomy and palaeontology at the University of Oxford. Owen was a staunch theologio-scientist, a man of immense prestige and influence and equal quantities of arrogance and vanity. He was sometimes called 'the British Cuvier'. Huxley said privately that this was like comparing British brandy with cognac.

Owen had at first earned Huxley's gratitude by interceding with the Admiralty to prevent his untimely recall. But when Huxley at last spurned the Navy it seemed to the professor to be neither a reasonable nor a proper act. The next encounter was even more disastrous to the relationship. Huxley solicited a written testimonial from the great man who obliged with a condescension which stung the young biologist into a fury. It seems to have been of the 'not a *bad* sort of fellow' colour. Huxley said his first impulse had been to seek out the professor and knock him down.[4] Relations deteriorated further in 1856, the year of the Neanderthal discovery, when Owen arrogated Huxley's title of professor of palaeontology, as a repayment for being allowed the use of laboratory facilities at the Royal School of Mines. Huxley got something of his own back in his Croonian lecture to the Royal Society that year by describing Owen's contention that skull bones were modified vertebrae – then a widely accepted belief – as absolute rubbish. Owen never forgave him.

So far as England was concerned Neanderthal man had to be content with two notices, both of a non-scientific and philosophical nature. He certainly was not noticed by the British Association, the Royal Society, the Geological Society, all directly concerned bodies, or in the Press.

In France however the situation was considerably worse. Not only was the Prussian fossil man ignored completely but the proponents of the view that man had existed in the times of the extinct species of animals had made no headway. It is one of those paradoxes that the main scientific body of the country where stone axes and tools were being found in the greatest abundance persisted in ignoring the fact.

Marcellin Boule blames Elie de Beaumont,[5] disciple of Cuvier, geologist and permanent secretary of the *Académie des Sciences*, for this state of affairs. He was certainly the leading figure in the conspiracy to ignore Boucher de Perthes. But the men within the *Académie* who respected the Abbeville amateur's view, such as J. L. de Quatrefages, Edouard Lartet, André Prevost and Jean Gaudry, did not strive for his recognition. They certainly encouraged Boucher de Perthes but it was well behind the back of de Beaumont and the other spiritual leaders of the *Académie*.

Boule attributes the *Académie*'s eventual tolerance of Boucher de Perthes to the intervention of British scientists, writing:

Before the intervention of British archaeologists and geologists had deprived this great question of its wholly French bearing, for so long the entire French Academy followed its Permanent Secretary like a flock of sheep.

This view is anachronistic and unfair to the French believers. British support for Boucher de Perthes did not begin until 1859 and by this time many French Academicians themselves were publicly supporting their countryman although, it must be admitted, with little success.

Would Boucher de Perthes have fared any better in England in 1846 – the year of his apostasy? The answer is in the affirmative but with a qualification.

There was no exact equivalent in Britain of the French *Académie*, to which only the most distinguished men of science and letters were invited as members. The nearest equivalents, the British Association for the Advancement of Science and the Royal Society, were again solely the platforms of the professional expert and beyond the range of the amateur. But lower down the order the views of Boucher de Perthes would certainly have received an airing on a scale that far exceeded that of the *Société d'Emulation d'Abbeville*.

The long, hot summer of Victorian prosperity, born of the Industrial Revolution, was at its height. As a result, for the middle and upper classes, came much time in which to do little. This idleness and the Victorian love of getting outdoors for some semi-scientific pursuit and talking about it indoors afterwards brought about a unique era of vernacular discovery. Many new societies were formed as escape valves for this energy. The already established learned societies received inrushes of new members, each one, it seems, with a view crying for release.

One of this latter kind was the Geological Society, with rooms at Burlington House, Regent Street, London. The interchange within this society was much freer from the strictures of religion than that within the French *Académie*. As has been observed earlier it was not too unusual for a speaker in pressing for the extreme antiquity of a find, to claim that this or that flint implement had been found with the bones of extinct species of animals which had somehow survived the Deluge. It is also certain, however, that such assertions were made in innocence of their implications, for what was being said would, within the still current interpretation of Biblical convention, send their authors posthumously to Hell.

So Boucher de Perthes would have certainly got a hearing. But such was the demand that the relentless 'papering' of the society tended to militate against itself. A paper almost invariably brought several against it, the proposition it contained often vanishing without trace in a confused sea of persiflage.

3

The *Beagle* took up her moorings at Falmouth, Cornwall on 2 October 1836, and Charles Darwin[1] returned home to Shrewsbury after five years. His father remarked that the shape of his head had 'quite altered'.

Darwin's output was enormous. With the help of Professor Sir Richard Owen, within six months of his arrival he had sorted his collection of specimens and arranged for them to be described by experts under his editorship in the official *Zoology of the Voyage of the Beagle*, and had written his own account, *Journal of Researches*. Then came three more books, *The Structure and Distribution of Coral Reefs* (1842), *Volcanic Islands* (1844), and *Geological Observations on South America* (1846).

While secretary of the Geological Society from 1848 to 1851 he studied and offered a solution to the problem of the origin of the 'parallel roads' – mysterious rock formations at Glenroy in Scotland. He erroneously attributed them to ancient marine beaches later divorced from the sea by land subsidence. Beaches they were but formed in a land-locked lake by glaciers. Several eminent geologists told him so with varying degrees of sarcasm. But Darwin also made the acquaintance of Sir Charles Lyell and Sir Joseph Hooker. It was to the latter that he first confided his theory of evolution by natural selection.

In an autobiographical sketch published in 1887 by Francis Darwin as part of *The Life and Letters of Charles Darwin*, the great man wrote that his main problem was how the changes in plant and animal species were brought about. He could see that man successfully applied artificial selection to animal and agricultural husbandry in farming, but how could this selection take place in the wild, with plants and animals living under natural conditions? Then the answer occurred to him. He read 'for amusement' Thomas Robert Malthus[2] who had written that animal populations increased in geometrical ratio unless checked. Darwin pondered the reason. Offspring in their early stages are always far more numerous than their parents, but in spite of this tendency to progressive increase the numbers of a given species actually remain more or less constant. The missing key then was the powerful and restless struggle for survival. Since all organisms vary appreciably only those advantageously equipped for the struggle can survive. Of this deduction Darwin wrote in a notebook: 'One may say that there is a force like a hundred thousand wedges trying to force every kind of structure into the economy of nature.'

This force was exerting itself just as powerfully on Darwin for he proposed to and was accepted by Emma, a daughter of Josiah Wedgwood, the potter of Maer Hall. The Wedgwood family had long been friends of the Darwins. Charles had known Emma since childhood. But it is typical of Darwin that before he took the plunge into matrimony he carefully weighed on paper the advantages and disadvantages of such a step. It is not even known whether Emma had come to mind before or after the favourable conclusion was arrived at. On 24 January 1839, the thirty-year-old lover was elected to the fellowship of the Royal Society. Five days later the couple were married but there was no honeymoon; the nuptials merely inspiring a wedding-day note on plant-breeding.

In 1842 Darwin wrote a thirty-two-page abstract of his theory of evolution, or 'transmutation' as he called it. Two years later he had enlarged this to an essay of 250 pages. At first only Sir Joseph Hooker was informed of these developments but in 1856 Lyell was allowed to join the conspiracy.

Lyell and Hooker repeatedly urged Darwin to publish, for to delay, they advised him, was to risk being beaten to the post by someone else. In the case of Lyell there might even have been an element of self-interest in the whip-cracking, for the same vast quantities of time were required for the working of the Darwinian theory of evolution as Lyell had claimed for his history of the earth. Darwinism was likewise a direct negation of the word of God as interpreted by the theologio-scientists.

But Darwin fussed and prevaricated. He began to draft an epic work to be called *Natural Selection* which, on his own estimation, would have been some 2,500 pages in length. Two years later the Lyell–Hooker prophecy was fulfilled. On 8 June 1858, to Darwin's complete consternation, he received a letter from Alfred Russel Wallace[3] which in twelve pages gave a brief but entire summary of Darwin's own theory of evolution by natural selection. According to Darwin, Wallace asked for help to get the paper published. Wallace, then in the Moluccas engaged in a biological survey of the Malay Archipelago, had been confined to bed by a bout of fever, during which he had set down his conclusions.

Darwin wrote plaintively to Lyell:

Your words have come true with a vengeance – that I should be forestalled. I never saw a more striking coincidence; if Wallace had my MSS sketch written out in 1842, he could not have made a better short abstract! Even his terms stand out as heads to my chapters . . . So all my originality, whatever it will amount to, will be smashed.

In truth Darwin – and Alfred Wallace – had been anticipated by over forty years. In 1813, while Lyell was still a young man collecting data for his *Principles of Geology* and Darwin was not much more than a baby, a most extraordinary paper had been delivered to the Royal Society by an expatriate American physician named Charles Wells.[4] The paper, misleadingly entitled *An Account of a White Female, Part of whose Skin Resembles that of a Negro*, contained an almost complete condensation of Darwin's main thesis – natural selection. Speaking of artificial as opposed to natural selection Wells had said: 'What is done here by art (in the case of domestic animals) seems to be done with equal efficacy, though more slowly, by nature, in the formation of varieties of mankind, fitted for the countries they inhabit.' Wells then proposed that some stocks might better resist disease and multiply at the expense of others in particular areas.

A correspondent of Darwin's drew his attention to the Wells paper in the 1860s. Darwin mentioned it in the historical preface to later editions of his *The Origin of Species* but said that Wells had confined his study to natural selection in the human races while he had extended his to embrace all organisms. Darwin was mistaken. Wells applies his remarks generally. He actually uses the phrase 'amongst men, as well as among other animals, varieties of a greater or less magnitude are constantly occurring'.

There is little doubt, therefore, that although Wells expressed his view more timorously and did not accompany it with such a wealth of evidence as Darwin did, a strong claim can be made for the former's priority. Like the geologist Hutton he suffered from being before his time.

On receiving the news about Wallace, Lyell and Hooker counselled Darwin that in fairness the only course was a joint publication. Darwin agreed and the paper was delivered to the Linnean Society on 1 July 1858. The reception seems to have been non-committal for there was no report of any explosion. Possibly the implication of the paper was not realized. Darwin, however, now threw himself into his task with energy. Within fifteen months he had completed his *Origin of Species by Means of Natural Selection*. It was a much shorter work than he had originally intended, being only 502 pages long; but still a magnificent achievement.

Alfred Wallace's own account differs somewhat from the above widely accepted version of the events which led to the joint paper. Some forty years later, writing of his cordial relations with Darwin he pointed out that in 1854 he had already published *On the Law which has Regulated the Introduction of New Species*, a paper which set forth a reasoned denial that new species of animals were the result of direct and separate works of Creation. Wallace said also that he had briefly met Darwin in the Insect Room of the British Museum at the beginning of that same year just before his departure for Borneo. So Darwin must have been aware of a similarity of view on transmutation of species. He had written Darwin 'a very long letter' with special reference to his article. Darwin had replied at similar length telling him that he agreed with 'everything in my article' and that it was evident that both had been thinking very much alike on the subject. Darwin had also informed Wallace that 'this summer will be my twentieth year since I opened my first notebook on the subject'. Wallace further commented:

But never in this nor in any other letters did he give me a hint of his having already arrived at the theory of Natural Selection; while in December 1857 he wrote: 'My work will not fix or settle anything; but I hope it will aid by giving a large collection of facts, with one definite end. Yet he [Darwin] had already written a sketch in 1842, and in 1844 enlarged this to 230 folio pages giving a complete presentation of his arguments set forth in the Origin.'

But although he was outshone by Darwin, Wallace was not complaining. Indeed, he claimed that Darwin's work had secured for himself 'full recognition by the press and the public'. Wallace was merely thankful that his work had compelled Darwin to write and publish without further delay.[5]

From abstract to completion it had taken Charles Darwin seventeen years to write *The Origin of Species*. Even taking into account the complexity of the subject this is about four times the length of time normally required for such a project. It is usual to attribute this prevarication to Darwin's earlier error over the 'parallel roads' of Glenroy, which made him wish to collect such an overwhelming mass of evidence for his new hypothesis that a repetition would be impossible. Lately it has been suggested instead that Darwin may have suffered from Chagas' disease, a chronic infection which produces lassitude and later affects the heart.

Chagas' disease is endemic throughout South America and it is known now that it can be contracted through contact with the armadillo, which is infected by the *Benchuca*, a bug which infests its burrows. Darwin could not have known this and he had certainly handled the armadillo, even eating its flesh. He had also encountered a *Benchuca* during his visit to Chile in 1853, allowing it to inflate itself with blood drawn from a finger. There is little doubt about Darwin's chronic invalidism, for soon after his marriage he started a daily log of his ill-health.

But it must be more than just coincidence that at this time he also began to rough out his *Natural Selection*. It could be that he prevaricated because of a deeper affliction – one of conscience. That he feared to publish. After rejecting medicine as a career at Edinburgh, Darwin had read for Holy Orders at Cambridge. He admits in *Life and Letters* that:

I did not then in the least doubt the strict and literal truth of every word in the Bible, I soon persuaded myself that our Creed must be fully accepted.

Darwin obtained a good pass degree in Theology, Euclid and the Classics. As a student he spent a considerable amount of his spare time with his mentor in botany, the Rev. John Steven Henslow. It was Henslow who obtained the budding biologist a place aboard the *Beagle*. Darwin's father, a deeply religious man, was not at all pleased at this advent. Only the personal intervention of 'Uncle Jos' Wedgwood had overcome Robert Darwin's determination that his son should make a career in the Church. Darwin's wife Emma had very strong religious beliefs.

It is therefore not beyond the bounds of reason that Darwin was none too happy about the philosophical escalator on which his perception had placed him, that he would have been only too pleased to get off but for Lyell and to a lesser degree Hooker. He may well have feared that publication of his hypothesis – his affront to the word of God – would lead to damnation.

Darwin even made a last-ditch attempt to prevent publication. He wrote to his publisher, John Murray, 'If you feel bound to say in the clearest terms that you do not think it [*The Origin*] likely to have remunerative sale, I completely and explicitly free you of your offer.' But Murray thought that it would, and it was published on 24 November 1859. The first edition of 1,250 copies was sold out on the first day.

It is usual to account for the astounding success of *The Origin* on a happy chance which made the regular scientific book reviewer of *The Times* ill, his substitute being T. H. Huxley. This view is erroneous. In fact Huxley arranged for his review to be printed in the newspaper to the neglect of the staff writer. He told Lyell that 'the educated mob who derive their ideas from *The Times* shall respect Darwin and be damned to them'.

Huxley respected Darwin's hypothesis but it is debatable just how much he believed in it. Controversy was meat and drink to Huxley, and Darwin had handed him an intellectual bombshell which would explode inside those sepulchres of the theologio-scientists – the universities of Oxford and Cambridge. He had met Darwin in the autumn previous to the publication of *The Origin* and had been allowed to read the final draft. He was enthusiastic, had been flexing his muscles for the fray ever since, but he was by no means an uncritical evolutionist. 'I by no means suppose,' he informed Lyell, 'that the transmutation hypothesis is proved or anything like it, but I view it as a powerful instrument of research. Follow it out and it will lead us somewhere.'

To Huxley, then, Darwinism was a working hypothesis; the current theologio-scientific view seemed to him to be no explanation at all. Of Darwin's contribution he said: 'Either it would prove its capacity to elucidate the facts, or it would break down under the strain.'

There can be little doubt, however, that no small element of the appeal of the Darwinian hypothesis to Huxley was that he knew it would be abhorrent to his old enemy, Sir Richard Owen. Darwin enjoyed protection, Huxley enjoyed giving it. He called himself 'Darwin's bulldog'. A palpable truth, for the principal evolutionist did precious little barking or biting himself. After reading *The Origin* Huxley told Darwin that the work would be greeted 'with considerable abuse and misrepresentation'. On the eve of publication he had written gleefully to the author: 'I am sharpening up my claws and beak in readiness.'[6] This bloodthirsty attitude must have alarmed Darwin more than it gave him pleasure. But Huxley had to wait until the next year before the bloodletting.

As early as 1858 Hugh Falconer had visited Abbeville. What he saw convinced him that Boucher de Perthes' claims were valid; that the chipped flints were indeed the tools of primitive man. On his return to England he urged the geologists Sir John Evans and Joseph Prestwich and a Mr Flower to make a similar visit.

On 26 May 1859, Prestwich proudly told the Royal Society the results of the visit, on 2 June the Society of Antiquaries was informed, the following day it was the turn of the Geological Society. Prestwich had to tell that his own digging at Abbeville had produced nothing but he had been able to purchase thirty flint implements from the locals. They were so well known to the peasants, said Prestwich, that they were referred to, by men, women and children alike, as *langues du chat* (cat's tongues).

All the flint implements, said Prestwich, were formed in the same rude way, a blunt hand-hold at one end from which extended two rude cutting edges which converged to a point. As the meeting could observe, the cutting edges and points of the tools were as sharp as if they had been made yesterday. The unworked portions however had a high yellow discoloration which suggested long exposure to weather and which was probably due to some chemical change. Prestwich concluded that some interesting points were raised by the tools. Who were the manufacturers of the primitive tools? Why had not the remains of their manufacturers been found with the implements? But these problems, said Prestwich, were the province of the archaeologist and not that of the geologist.

Two points emerge from Prestwich's concluding remarks. There was not even the barest suspicion that the flint tools could have been the work of a man of the kind represented by Neanderthal Man. Over three years had elapsed since the discovery of the Prussian fossil, but no one at any of the meetings of three of the foremost scientific societies in England had the faintest inkling of the possibilities of the discovery. The other point of interest is that Prestwich relegated the problem of the identity of the manufacturers of the flint tools. By doing so he made the first contribution to a state of affairs which profoundly hindered the study of fossil man.

As the years passed and the flint tools in the company of human bones were encountered with increasing frequency, the four most directly interested sciences – archaeology, palaeontology, anthropology and anatomy – developed four entirely different sets of terminology and methods of classification. The result was a proliferation of individual theories, unheeding controversy and unique interpretations. Until comparatively recently any attempt to gain a coherent picture of the study as a whole was like attempting a crossword puzzle while the clues were continually being changed.

The archaeologist differentiated flint implements by what he saw as cultural divisions, an ascending degree of refinement in manufacture. These were Abbevillian, Chellean, Clactonian, Acheulian, Levalloisian, Mousterian, Chatelperronian, Aurignacian, Solutrean and Magdalenian. The group names were derived from the localities where that type of flint was found in abundance. But as with other human products the flints by no means neatly dropped into strictly definable cultural pockets. This provided great sport and internecine conflict between individual archaeologists who could see 'great' differences between the flints they had excavated and any others hitherto discovered.

The palaeontologist had a different method. He dated flints or human bones according to the suspected age of the geological deposit in which they were found. As the progress of the science advanced and views changed as to the age of these sections, then of course the age of the flints or bones changed. Once again there was by no means a general view on the age of a deposit and so the dating, usually given in hundreds of thousands of years, varied with the individual palaeontologist. The anthropologist attributed finds to cultural patterns of races and suspected racial migrations. The anatomist dated human fossils according to his individual view on the fossil's place in evolution.

But at the time of the Prestwich meetings the stampede into disorder was just beginning. The year 1859, the *annus mirabilis* as it has been called by enthusiasts for its recognition of fossil man, was marked by a declaration before the British Association meeting at Aberdeen by Sir Charles Lyell. He said that he was 'fully prepared to corroborate the conclusions recently laid before the Royal Society by Mr Prestwich'. The year also saw some astonishing activities on the part of the *Académie des Sciences* to prevent the spread of the flint-tool cult.

The Geological Society was honoured by the presence of Edouard Lartet whom Marcellin Boule has named as the chief founder of the science of palaeontology. Lartet was another lawyer turned scientist, awakened to his true calling, Boule said, in 1834 when he saw the molar tooth of a mastodon found by a peasant of his native village of Gers, Armagnac, south-west France. He began to explore the local ancient deposits and discovered the remains of a fossil ancestor of the modern gibbon, which he named *Pliopithecus*.

In 1850 Lartet forsook Gers for Paris on being elected to the famous *Académie*. The next few years were spent writing up his many discoveries of extinct animal bones, and tactfully supporting Boucher de Perthes. But he went too far. In 1858, he upset the *Académie* by writing that it was an abuse of the technical language of science to use high-sounding expressions such as upheavals of the globe, cataclysms, universal disturbances, general catastrophes and so on, for they gave exaggerated significance to phenomena which were, geographically speaking, very limited. This sounded remarkably like Lyell, but in the eyes of the *Académie* repetition was as big a crime as original sin and Lartet was shunned.[7]

But already Lartet had been forced to look to London for an audience. During his visit to the Geological Society he showed pieces of bone of the long-extinct European wild ox, found in Paris during construction of the Canal de L'Ourcq. The deep incisions in the bones, said Lartet, were made with crude, unfinished flint tools usually discovered in the sandpits of St Acheul near Amiens. Similarly marked bones found at Abbeville seemed to have been made with flint tools of greater refinement. The marks on the bones, declared Lartet, established beyond all doubt the use of flint tools like those discovered by Boucher de Perthes and 'your learned countrymen, Prestwich, Evans and Flower'. Lartet concluded that the primitive people of Amiens and Abbeville might even have crossed the then dry land between France and England.

In this way Lartet included his English listeners in the great happenings across the Channel. What had been found at Amiens and Abbeville might be found in Britain. Could Lartet have detected in his British audience the first awakening of what was to become a general feeling that something was not quite right? Deeply rooted in each member of his audience was the conviction that their homeland was the priscan fount of knowledge, the epicentre of humanity. Inherent in every one of Lartet's listeners was the belief, never expressed, that if indeed God was not British then he at least had the nation's interests at heart. Where then were the British stone-implement makers? Why did not England have an Abbeville or St Acheul? This was the commencement of a unique era in which two nations vied with each other as to which of them had the most primitive ancestors.

But Lartet's departure from Paris was not undetected by the *Académie*. At the conclusion of Lartet's lecture the president of the Geological Society, Leonard Horner, read a note of denial from the *Académie*, which was a masterly confection of both concession and rebuttal.

The note read to the meeting by Horner described the Canal de L'Ourcq excavations in greater detail than had Lartet, then launched into a lengthy exposition of how the tongue test and the hydrochloric test had been applied to the wild-ox bones which had failed to come up to snuff. But, conceded the *Académie*, this was an instance of the unreliability of these tests, for the bones as proved by the species type were of no small antiquity. The *Académie* was prepared to go even further. The saw marks, read Horner, were too crude to have been inflicted with a modern blade. Lartet was correct to suggest that the marks had been scratched with flint implements. From this, said the *Académie* pointedly, it might be possible for some to argue that man was contemporary with the extinct animal in question. But when had the scratches been made? asked the *Académie*. They could have been made yesterday. Surely it was more likely that someone had chanced across the bones in modern times and had scratched them. Lartet's conclusions, therefore, were nonsense.

Before Lartet had a chance to reply to this disconcerting conclusion there was a rustle at the back of the hall and the president announced that the author of the *Académie*'s note had just arrived from France and wished to make a statement. Whether the *Académie* distrusted the postal service or just wished to gain a first-hand report of the encounter is not known, but here in the flesh was the distinguished Academician, Professor Delasse.

Delasse told the awed meeting that the note read by Horner expressed the *Académie*'s views precisely. He wished to reiterate, however, that the presence of gelatine in bone proved neither its antiquity nor its modernity. After a long series of tests conducted by Delasse nothing had been proved either way. Depending on the nature of the deposit in which they were found, some bones of high antiquity possessed gelatine whereas some comparatively recent bones had none. Delasse explained that his presence in London was entirely due to the *Académie*'s profound wish that the fullest possible evidence should be placed before such an illustrious gathering. Delasse did not doubt that the correct interpretation of Lartet's evidence would be made in any case.

Edouard Lartet appears to have been somewhat shaken by the *Académie*'s surprise intervention. Rising to his feet, he said that he was forced to agree with Delasse that the presence or otherwise of organic matter such as gelatine in bone was an unreliable indication of antiquity. But Delasse, he said, must agree that in this case the geological evidence proved that the bones could not be anything other than of vast antiquity. The Abbeville bones and flint implements had actually been found in 'diluvial' gravel which itself had been covered by an ancient deposit of loess. The Canal de L'Ourcq bones were found at a depth of twenty-eight feet. Only ages of time could have placed the bones so deep in these deposits.

Lartet said he had deliberately chosen the instances described in his lecture from a host of many such discoveries. He could, he said, have cited many instances of marked bones from caves but he had been on his guard. Critics of the evidence of marked bones would have doubtless used the accessibility of cave bones to destroy the value of the argument. But this accessibility certainly did not apply in the case of deeply buried bones, for how could they have been got at?

The contemporary accounts of such conflicts neglect to supply colourful details and therefore there is no record of the precise effect on Lartet of this intervention from Paris other than his words. But the bare fact that the *Académie* was prepared to send a representative to London shows that it went to great lengths to prevent its distinction being used by radical members to promote scientific hypotheses abhorrent to its inflexible view of the Creation.

The direct result of this collision was that men such as Prestwich, Evans and Flower reserved their verdict on bones of extinct animals alleged to have been marked by flint tools. But the general enthusiasm for the tools themselves continued unabated. In Britain, however, it was in the main an unrequited passion. Later in 1859 another Frenchman, Dr Rigollet of Amiens, told an envious Geological Society audience how flint tools were being recovered in large numbers from the Somme, Seine and Oise valleys of his native country. The lecture merely served to make the members even more jealous. Prestwich must have thought it necessary to bolster flagging morale.

Early in 1860 he told a meeting how an antiquary named S. Hazzledene Warren of Ixworth, Suffolk, had been handed a 'peculiarly worked flint' by a workman who said he had found it at a depth of four feet. He also described how twenty-five years had passed since a Mr Whitburn discovered a flint tool in a bed of sand between Guildford and Godalming in Surrey. Whitburn had not known what the flint was until he heard of the recent finds at St Acheul and Abbeville. He had now presented the flint to Prestwich.

Prestwich urged his fellow geologists to seek out the St Acheuls and Abbevilles of England in the brickfields of Kent,

Essex and Wiltshire, and the gravel and clay pits of Somerset, Oxfordshire, Cambridgeshire, Middlesex, Surrey, Sussex, Hampshire, Gloucestershire and Berkshire. All that was required, exhorted the speaker, was diligence. Even at St Acheul the search had been long before it had been rewarded with the find of a single specimen. Prestwich concluded that, judging from such a precedent, 'our motto should be *Nil desperandum*'.

Oddly enough, the next find reported to the Society had taken place in one of the Essex brickpits actually named by Prestwich in his harangue. But it was no flint implement.

The Rev. O. Fisher produced from what he grandiosely described as 'a cemetery of pachyderms' a 'singular red stone which looked as if it had been baked by fire'. The churchman had propounded an astonishing theory to account for its appearance. He said that it was possible that the kind of clay pots used by primitive hunters would not stand the heat of fire, so to boil water he was forced to heat stones and drop them into the pot.

Fisher's romantic explanation for his stone was adopted for future finds of stones which appeared to be blackened or cracked by fire. It was the first of an almost countless number of similar discoveries which have been reported ever since. The genuineness of these 'pot-boilers', as these stones came to be called, is still debated when nothing more pressing commands attention. Many who have experimented with this method of water heating seriously doubt whether there is any truth in the theory. The resultant explosions and the scattering of stone fragments smack more of warfare than cuisine.

T. H. Huxley's review of Charles Darwin's *The Origin of Species*
saw it as a work of genius. But Darwin had short-changed his
readers. He confined the scope of the work to the non-human
part of Creation. In but one passage did he mention man, saying
that 'light will be thrown on the origin of man and his history'.
From this it is clear that Darwin did not wish to be exemplified
as the holder of the torch.

Nothing is more indicative of the repressive theological atmosphere of the time than Darwin's reluctance to include man in
his observations. His old collaborator of the Linnean Society
paper, Alfred Russel Wallace, seems to have been somewhat
dismayed by his neglect. Prior to the publication of *The Origin*
Wallace had written to Darwin asking whether it was the
author's intention to include the evolution of man in the work.
Darwin had replied, 'I think I shall avoid the whole subject, as
so surrounded by prejudices, though I fully admit that it is the
highest and most interesting problem for the naturalist.'[1] He had
confessed to his friend, the Rev. Leonard Jenyns, that, 'With
respect to man, I am very far from wishing to obtrude my
belief; but I thought it dishonest to quite conceal my opinion.'[2]

In fairness to Darwin it is necessary to point out that with but
one discovered example of fossil man available for examination,
the author of *The Origin* was wise to delay, to administer the
medicine in swallowable doses. Indeed, it is quite possible that
Neanderthal man was unknown to Darwin. If Huxley was the
author of the advanced view expressed in the *Westminster Review*
in 1856 his later scientific writings seem retrogressive. In the light
of these he would hardly have been likely to commend Neanderthal man to Darwin's attention as definite evidence of the
pattern of evolution of humanity. There was little other evidence.
Hugh Falconer had recovered the fossil bones of a primitive ape,

Ramapithecus, during his excavations in the Indian Siwalik Hills, and there was Edouard Lartet's *Pliopithecus* – but that was all.

Though the vast majority of early nineteenth-century scientists did not suspect an actual genetic link between man and the ape they were conscious of some sort of connection. Travellers were inclined to confuse primitive races with the apes and *vice versa*. Many accounts show that there was by no means any clear standard by which one could be divided from the other. For example, the place in nature of the Hottentots of the Cape of Good Hope, whose low state of technology and language – desscribed as 'a farrago of bestial sounds resembling the chatter of apes' – was the source of great speculation. The primitive was often considered to be a kind of ape and the ape a sort of man.

But Darwin did not have to state coldly the evolutionary connection. The implication of his work appeared clear to all. As the other animals had evolved, so had man. He had affronted the theologio-scientists and cast grave doubt on their view that God created man in His own image.

It is overstating the case to suggest that the entire body of the Church was outraged. Many churchmen greeted *The Origin* with sympathy and understanding. Darwin's father did not disinherit him. On the contrary, he seemed rather impressed by his son's impact on science. But Darwin made many enemies in the Church.

Philip Gosse, a Plymouth Brother and another reviewer, said that although the work was rated as an hypothesis by a misguided few, it had done nothing to alter his own implicit faith in the Biblical interpretation of Creation. Gosse published a refutation of Darwin entitled *Omphalos*, in which he maintained that the world and all its works were created perfect. Adam and Eve, he wrote, were the sole parents of humanity and as direct children of God would have been born complete with navels, as in terrestrial birth. According to Gosse, in a similar manner trees would have been created with the annular rings which marked the season's growth. They had appeared on the earth as adult trees and not as seeds. Rocks had been created complete with fossils.

Gosse had neither originality nor Darwin's scientific standing. The real opposition came from a coalition between the theologio-scientists and the Church. The geologist Adam Sedgwick, a devout churchman and one of Darwin's Cambridge acquaintances, bitterly attacked him for deserting the only scientific method – that of Baconian induction. The Presbyterian geologist Adam White said that *The Origin* was 'a lapse into pernicious error'. The ecclesiastical botanist Henry Triman thought that Darwin was the most dangerous man in England.

Darwin's most malignant opponent, however, and it must have brought Huxley intense pleasure, was his old collaborator Sir Richard Owen, the foremost comparative anatomist in England. Owen believed, and said so, that Darwin's conclusions were outrageous, incondite, incompatible with the Christian teaching on Adam and Eve, the Fall from Grace, the established time scale of the heavens and the earth, and the date of Creation, which was 23 October 4004 B.C.

Owen is often seen as the scientific shadow behind the orator and Bishop of Oxford, Samuel Wilberforce.[3] He certainly supplied him with scientific ammunition. But the whole-hearted way in which he countered Huxley proved that he was by no means a behind-the-scenes manipulator.

The warfare between the exponents of Darwinism, or the 'evolutionists' as they came to be called – a name which seems to have rapidly acquired the same connotation as 'abortionists' – and the theologio-scientists was so far confined to heavy literary cannonade, Darwin keeping well out of sight, Huxley in his natural element. He successfully drew the fire on himself, choosing the *Westminster Review*[4] for a long and insulting article thinly disguised as a review of *The Origin of Species*.

He wrote that the 'species question' had overflowed the narrow bounds of purely scientific circles and was 'dividing with Italy [Garibaldi] and the Volunteers' the attention of general society. Everyone, he said, whether they had read Darwin's book or not, had given their opinion on it and 'pietists, whether lay or ecclesiastic, decry it with the mild railing which sounds so charitable; bigots denounce it with ignorant invective; old ladies, of both sexes, consider it a decidedly dangerous book, and even savants who have no better mud to throw, quote antiquated writers to show that its author is no better than an ape himself'.

Huxley said that all competent naturalists, whatever their ultimate opinions of the doctrine put forth, acknowledged that the work was a solid contribution to knowledge and that it inaugurated a new epoch in natural history. But he attacked what he described as 'the mistaken zeal of the Bibliolaters', among whom he named Owen, and recommended that these should read and attempt to understand the book before they condemned it.

This kind of writing was hardly likely to commend itself to the 'old ladies of both sexes' or to the 'savants who quoted antiquated writers'. Huxley was a marked man. The protagonists met face to face at the British Association meeting at Oxford in June 1860, at the traditionally famous debate between the 'apes' and the 'angels'; between the exponents of two books, one of which was alleged to have profoundly stimulated scientific thought and the other to have stifled it.

There can be no doubt that Huxley seized the Darwinian hypothesis and used it as a club with which to belabour his scientific adversaries. His altruism was suspect. Already he doubted the existence of God. Huxley did in fact coin the word 'agnostic' to describe his lack of belief. Just before the Oxford debate Huxley's four-year-old son Noel, his first-born, died of scarlet fever. This tragedy introduced an element of bitterness into everything that Huxley said henceforth on the subject of religion.

The Sheldonian Theatre at Oxford on 27 June 1860 was well filled except for the upper gallery which, according to a witness, could have accommodated twice the number. A third of those present were ladies.

The theatre had begun to fill soon after three o'clock in the afternoon; at ten minutes past four the great doors were thrown open and the grand procession entered. First came the university bedels, then Albert, Prince Consort, Lord Derby, Chancellor of the University, then Dr Jeaune, Vice-chancellor and Master of Pembroke College. Members of the royal suite brought up the rear.

His Royal Highness Prince Albert was greeted with prolonged applause which he repeatedly acknowledged. He said that as retiring president of the British Association he wished to express the hope that the interests of Science had not suffered in his hands. He then paid a compliment to his successor.

Lord Wrothesly, duly installed, delivered his address, the burden of which has not come down to us. The report in *The*

Times from which this account is taken says little more, three-quarters at least of the paper being taken up with a verbatim account of the debate in Parliament on the European Forces (India) Bill, a direct result of the Indian Mutiny. Indeed there is a complete abstention from public reporting of the famous debate. The *Proceedings of the British Association* was pointedly mute although the scientific paper which was used as the excuse for the *fracas* was printed fully. There does exist, however, a small number of private eye-witnesses, and hearsay accounts from which a glimmer of what took place can be sifted.

On the morning following the grand opening the Association's Section D, that of the zoologists, met at a lecture room for the first of the week's meetings. In the chair was Sir Richard Owen. Among the hundred or so scientists present was T. H. Huxley. Darwin was absent.

The first item on the programme was a Dr Daubeny's paper *On the Final Causes of the Sexuality of Plants with particular reference to Mr Darwin's Work on the Origin of Species*. The reading of the paper by its author passed off quietly enough, but a Mr R. Bowden rose and began to relate a series of anecdotes concerning monkeys. One was a pet which was fond of playing with a hammer, but although the animal was partial to oysters it could never be taught to crack the shells itself. From this, it was quite clear to him that the monkey was intellectually inferior to other animals, particularly dogs and elephants which could be trained to win food for themselves. The monkey, therefore, was no relative of man.

A flutter of anticipation greeted Bowden's final observation. Owen drew attention to the absence of Mr Darwin and wondered if anyone cared to reply on the biologist's behalf. No one felt so disposed and the president was forced to call on the sacrificial goat directly.

Huxley rose at last but to everybody's disappointment he said he considered that a general audience where sentiment would interfere unduly with intellect was the wrong sort for such a discussion. He resumed his seat.

But Owen would not allow the matter to be dropped so easily. He said he 'wished to approach this subject in the spirit of a philosopher' and that 'there were facts by which the public could come to some conclusion as to the probabilities of the truth of Mr Darwin's theory'. Bowden's point, said Owen, was in fact that the brain of man differed vastly from that of the monkey. As an anatomist of no mean distinction Owen begged to be allowed to draw Mr Huxley's attention to a feature of the human brain, the third lobe of the posterior horn of the lateral ventrical, called the *hippocampus minor*. This feature was unique to the brain of man, said Owen, for no gorilla possessed it.

Huxley thanked Owen for the anatomical instruction. He had nothing to add to his previous remarks except to draw Owen's attention to a major difference between man and gorilla. This was, he said, the power of speech.

Owen glowered but he seems to have considered that as Huxley had refused to come out of his corner the 'angels' had won a tactical victory. A Dr Wright, who seems to have entirely missed the drift of the discussion, and the atmosphere, innocently said that a friend had a pet female gorilla which he took to the sea-shore for the purpose of feeding on oysters, which the animal broke open with ease. But Owen cut the speaker short. He guessed that Huxley was not to be drawn on the issue of seafood-loving gorillas and he called the meeting to a close.

The zoological section's meeting the following day, a Friday, passed off uneventfully but it was common knowledge that the great confrontation would take place on the morrow. Huxley made no secret of the fact that he would attend. Nor did Samuel Wilberforce, Bishop of Oxford, Fellow of All Souls, nicknamed 'Soapy Sam' from his habit of rubbing his hands together when winning a point in debate, which he did very frequently and brilliantly. Wilberforce was pure churchman and orator extraordinary of Biblical convention as applied to science. Like Hindenburg and Falkenhayn, Wilberforce and Owen offered an unassailable front to theologians and scientists who might wish to transgress.

According to Sir Charles Lyell, the Saturday battle opened with 'redoubled fury' over a paper by an American, Dr Draper of New York, on *Intellectual Development, considered with Reference to the Views of Mr Darwin*. The excitement was tremendous. The audience proved too large for the lecture room and so the meeting adjourned to the library of the university museum, which was crammed to suffocation long before the champions entered the lists.

Professor Stephen Henslow, old comrade and now enemy of Darwin, was in the chair and 'wisely' announced that no one should be allowed to address the meeting who did not have a valid argument for one side or the other. This was a necessary precaution, Lyell's account continues, as the audience had now been swollen to some seven hundred by an influx of cheering and counter-cheering students. Four scientific combatants were already shouting vague declamations over the general din.

Then Bishop Wilberforce was on his feet and launched into a speech which was described later (by an 'ape') as 'full of emptiness and fairies'. It was evident to this witness that the bishop had been crammed to the throat by Owen and knew nothing at first hand. But 'he ridiculed Darwin savagely but in dulcet tones and with such persuasion and well-turned periods that I [Lyell] who had been inclined to blame the president for allowing a discussion which would serve no scientific purpose, forgave him from the bottom of my heart! Unfortunately for the bishop, hurried along by the current of his eloquence, he so forgot himself as to push his advantage to the verge of personality in a telling passage in which he turned round and addressed Huxley.'

The bishop, polishing his hands, asked Huxley whether he was related on his grandfather's or grandmother's side to the ape. Huxley rose and replied to his opponent's scientific argument with, said the witness, 'force and eloquence'. He then passed to the personal remark.

'With remarkable restraint he said, "A man has no reason to be ashamed of having an ape for a grandfather or grandmother. If I had a choice of an ancestor, whether it should be an ape, or one who having a scholastic education should use his logic to mislead an untutored public, and should treat not with argument but with ridicule the facts and reasoning adduced in support of a grave and serious philosophical question, I would not hesitate for a moment to prefer the ape." '

The impact of this remark was described as 'tremendous'. Huxley himself said that there was 'inextinguishable laughter'. A lady is reported to have fainted, the usual Victorian metaphor for high drama. According to Lyell many blamed Huxley for his irreverent freedom but many more whom he had heard talk of the affair, including Hugh Falconer, assured Lyell that Vice-chancellor Jeaune declared that the bishop 'had got no more than he deserved'. Falconer said that the bishop just sat down and said no more, that 'although he had been much applauded, before the meeting was over opinion had quite gone the other way'.

According to Lyell, when Huxley informed Darwin of the outcome of the debate he tittered nervously: 'How durst you attack a live bishop in that fashion? I am quite ashamed of you. Have you no respect for fine lawn sleeves?' But Huxley himself could not see what all the fuss was about. On the subject of the relationship of the gorilla with man, he said that to call man a modified gorilla was no more harmful, surely, than the Church's insistence that man was modified dirt.

But had the debate achieved much else? Huxley himself limited his popularity in Oxford to just twenty-four hours. No great philosophical sluice gates were swung open. There had not been one reference to Neanderthal man during the entire Oxford meeting. Huxley had not mentioned him and he was currently working on a scientific description of the Prussian fossil man. Darwin's hypothesis still had a lengthy uphill grind and many were the backslidings, even amongst his most devout followers.

Men were much more preoccupied with God in those days. By the majority it was thought to be far better to wait and see. Some were amazed at the longevity of Darwin, and Huxley even. That God did not strike them down forthwith amazed them. Not a few pulpits cried out for Heavenly retribution. As the years passed and the cries remained unanswered, it came to be considered that a profounder punishment awaited the leading evolutionists in Hell.

Possibly the most palpable achievement of the debate was, as in the case of the Jumna river fossils, that it threw open the windows of discussion with the maximum publicity. The next few years saw a heightening of the controversy between Huxley and Owen which raged in the scientific journals of the time. Bishop Wilberforce watched helplessly while Huxley relentlessly undermined his scientific colleague's authority.

Owen's statement that the *hippocampus minor* only occurred in the brain of man – it is in fact a feature common to all mammals – left him wide open to attack. As Huxley put it in a letter to the editor of *Natural History Review*:[5]

Owen had declared the structure known to anatomists as the *hippocampus minor* as occurring only in the human brain. The fact is he made a prodigious blunder in commencing the attack, and now his only chance is to be silent and let people forget the exposure ...

But Owen would not keep quiet and the lengthy dispute resulted in the printing of a series of comic verses in *Punch*. One, contributed by a 'Gorilla from the Zoological Gardens' and entitled *MONKEYANA*, read:

> Then HUXLEY and OWEN,
> With rivalry growing,
> With pen and ink rush to the scratch,
> 'Tis brain versus brain,
> Till one of them's slain;
> By Jove! It will be a good match!

The final two verses were:

> Next HUXLEY replies,
> That OWEN he lies
> And garbles his Latin quotation;
> That his facts are not new,
> His mistakes not a few,
> Detrimental to his reputation.

> To twice slay the slain
> By dint of the Brain
> (Thus HUXLEY concluded his review)
> Is but labour in vain,
> Unproductive of gain,
> So I shall bid you 'Adieu'.[6]

Many similar verses appeared over the next three years and to the public the controversy seems to have been of absorbing interest. In 1863 an eight-page burlesque pamphlet for the not so sophisticated was on sale which bore on the cover '*A Report of a Sade (sic) Case Recently Tried Before the Lord Mayor. Owen versus Huxley. In Which Will be Fully Given the Merits of the Great Recent Bone Case.*' An extract must suffice:

Policeman X—: 'Well, your Worship, Huxley called Owen a lying Orthognatheous Brachycephalic Bimanous Pithecus; and Owen told him he was nothing but a thorough Archencephalic Primate.'
Lord Mayor: 'Are you sure you heard this awful language?'

The most enduring relic of the Great Debate, however, was the churchman-novelist Charles Kingsley's delightful fantasy for children, *The Water Babies*, published three years afterwards, in which he described how:

The Professor got up once at the B.A., and declared that apes had hippopotamus majors in their brains just as men have. Which was a shocking thing to say; for if it were so, what would become of the faith, hope and charity of immortal millions?

But as Huxley wrote to Joseph Hooker after Oxford: 'Take care of yourself, there's a good fellow ... We have a devil of a lot to do in the way of smiting the Amalekites.'[7] Owen was but one of many. But eventually the relationship between man and ape was passed down from science through the music-halls to become an accepted part of modern lore. It is hard for the late-twentieth-century mind to grasp the extent of the resentment which greeted the first suggestions that there was such a relationship. Owen was considered to be, and in fact was, an advanced thinker compared with many of his contemporaries. At the time there were many who did not believe that there was any such animal as a gorilla. Following the publication of Paul Chaillu's *Explorations and Adventures in Equatorial Africa* in 1861, the traveller exhibited a stuffed gorilla at the Ethnological Society. There was an uproar. One of the audience, T. A. Malone, denounced the gorilla as a fiction of Chaillu's imagination and his *Explorations* as a pack of lies. The author knocked him down with a blow. Sir Richard Burton, the African explorer, defended Chaillu in a letter to *The Times*.[8] Burton commented lustily that the gorilla was fact and that Chaillu was justified in striking his detractor.

5

British science discovered Neanderthal man in 1861. George Busk, Hunterian Professor of Anatomy and Physiology at the Royal College of Surgeons, was a tireless translator of German scientific papers. One was the Schaafhausen description.

On the centenary of the discovery of Neanderthal man in 1956 Bernard Cambell wrote[1] that Busk's 'versatile mind immediately saw the importance of the discovery'. He saw Busk as the English discoverer of the Prussian fossil. But the view could also be taken that translation was all in a day's work to Busk and the role of pioneer was neither intentional nor within his control.

Busk was an insatiable tongue-tester of fossil bones; his hydrochloric acid had disenchanted many a finder of his find. His perception can certainly be called into question. Almost definitely a Neanderthal skull had lain undetected in his own collection at the Royal College of Surgeons since about 1848.

This skull has a peculiar history. It is believed that the discoverer was a certain Lieutenant Flint, Royal Artillery, then stationed in Gibraltar. The officer found the skull at Forbes' Quarry, North Front, and he presented it to the Gibraltar Scientific Society. There is a minute to this effect in the society's proceedings for 3 March 1848. The skull then disappears into the shadows until the 1864 British Association meeting at Bath, where Busk stated that the skull was part of the Hunterian Museum collection. It is therefore probable not only that an Englishman found the first Neanderthal skull, for the Gibraltar find was such a fossil, but also that Busk failed to notice it in his own collection until long after the Prussian find had attracted notice.

The British Association was much impressed by the Gibraltar skull and voted a grant of £165 so that Busk and Hugh Falconer could sail to Gibraltar to encourage further excavation. The governor of the military prison on the Rock, Captain Broome, himself a keen archaeologist, was an immense help to the visitors. On his return to England Falconer wrote to the Governor of Gibraltar, General Hugh Coddrington, recording the two scientists' appreciation of the work of Broome. He praised Broome's eagerness, energy and vigour, which had immensely helped the scientific enquiry. Coddrington forwarded the letter to the Secretary of State for War in London, and as a direct result Broome was cashiered for allowing military prisoners to be employed in private excavations.

Shortly before he died in 1865 Falconer wrote sadly of 'that unfortunate soldier Broome'. Of the troublesome Gibraltar skull itself he said at the same time that its owner was representative of 'a very low type of humanity – very low and savage, and of extreme antiquity – but still a man and not halfway between a man and a monkey and certainly not the missing link'.

With this denial Falconer was the first to use an expression which became a tradition and fascination for archaeologists, palaeontologists, geologists and anatomists. The Gibraltar skull, however, the rejected 'missing link', remained quietly in the Hunterian Museum until rediscovered by Arthur Keith in 1906.

The first Englishman to attack Neanderthal man was a geologist named C. Carter Blake. In an article in *The Geologist* the same year as the Busk translation, Blake wrote that the great Cuvier had doubted whether human remains of the same age as those of extinct species of animals had ever been found. This was precisely his own conclusion, Blake said, and, despite the anatomist Schaafhausen's claims, the united opinion of German geologists. The English anatomist Busk had also said that there was no doubt about the vast antiquity of the Neanderthal bones but this theory too remained uncorroborated by any British geologist.

The singular characteristic of the Neanderthal skull, suggested Blake, was the large prominent eyebrow ridges. But these were also present in the modern gorilla, giving the animal its 'penthouse-like scowl'. So, challenged Blake, wherein lay the antiquity?

Busk replied that Blake's reasoning was at fault for many modern savage and barbarous races had considerable foreheads but had no eyebrow ridges.

But Blake was not after Busk. In a subsequent article[2] he said that he had hoped the appeal to English geologists in his first article would have thrown light on the age of the Neanderthal remains, but as this had not been forthcoming he had decided to give his own view. This was:

The apparent ape-like but really maldeveloped idiotic character of its conformation is so hideous and its alleged proximity to anthropoid *Simiae* of such importance that every effort should be made to determine its probable date in time. The fact had not been conclusively demonstrated to English geologists that the Neanderthal skull is of high antiquity.

Blake said that the deposit of mud in the Neanderthal cave might have been modern. Also, he argued, there were several suspicious factors connected with the skeleton, for example, the bump on the elbow. The curvature of the ribs reminded Blake of those of carnivorous animals and might not belong to the skull at all. Most probably, concluded Blake, the skull belonged to 'some poor idiot who died in the cave'.

The anatomical content of Blake's tirade could suggest that its target was T. H. Huxley, whose part in the Oxford debate had by now been inflated by hearsay to the proportions of swashbuckling. Certainly at the time he was writing his *Evidences of Man's Place in Nature*, which contained an appraisal of Neanderthal man. But he was calling for a geologist to answer him. It is likely, therefore, that Blake was trying to come to grips with Sir Charles Lyell.

Not content with having caused a revolution in geological thought Lyell had now turned his attention to the nature of man. At the time of the Blake articles Lyell had just returned from a visit to Neanderthal. He had met Dr J. C. Fuhlrott of Eberfeld, into whose hands Neanderthal man had first come. He had been presented with a plaster cast of the skull and a brief description of the discovery. Lyell passed on both to Huxley for his anatomical opinion which he wished to include in his new work *The Antiquity of Man*.

Huxley's performance on this occasion was disappointing. Of the Neanderthal skull and a similar one from Engis in Belgium – which like the Gibraltar skull had been brought from some museum cabinet by the Prussian bugle-call – he maintained before the Royal Society, and Lyell faithfully reproduced his view in *Antiquity*, that neither seemed much different from the skull of the modern Australian aborigine, the scientist's low water in human intellect.

Blake may possibly have sensed from Huxley's performance before the Royal Society that the Evolutionists were finding themselves on insecure ground. If he could get Lyell to confess that the Neanderthal skull could not be proved to be antique, then this would be a strong blow on behalf of the Bible. Blake was a friend and staunch ally of Sir Richard Owen.

Huxley did however make some kind of redress in his own account of Neanderthal man in his *Evidences of Man's Place in Nature* (1863). He wrote that he had obtained a fuller description of the skull and therefore was able to reconsider his earlier remarks. The skull, he maintained, was unknown even amongst the most savage and barbarous races which existed on the earth in modern times and possibly was that of a representative of the race dimly remembered and described by the Celtic and Germanic inhabitants of Europe to the Latin historians as '*autochthones*'.

Beyond all doubt, wrote Huxley, the race represented by the Neanderthal skull could be traced back to a period in the earth's history when the latest extinct animals of the diluvium still existed.

Then Huxley faltered. In no sense, he wrote, could the bones be the remains of a human being intermediate between man and ape. At most they demonstrated the existence of a man whose skull could be said to have reverted back to the ape type.

This passage lacks Huxley's usual courage. The modern interpretation is that Huxley was proposing that Neanderthal man was a reversion towards a previous simian ancestor, that he was a throwback.

Lyell let matters rest, relying entirely on Huxley. But Neanderthal man at last found a firm friend in Professor William King of Queen's College, Galway, Ireland. In a paper to the British Association in 1863, King said that the mud on the floor of the Neanderthal cave must have been deposited at the end of the glacial period of the earth because of its similarity to deposits of the Meuse valley described by Lyell.

Here, said King, was an early forerunner of man. But because of his small cranium he did not believe that the 'brute' could have been capable of any moral or theological conception or inductive reasoning. King therefore proposed to distinguish him from his modern descendant by giving him the name *Homo neanderthalis*.

King's step was a bold one. No one before him had thought of creating a distinct species for the fossil human. He also started a new name-game which has been the constant source of much anthropological preoccupation ever since.

At a meeting of the Anthropological Society in London on 16 February 1864, came a collision between the friends of Neanderthal man and his enemies. Darwin's collaborator on the Linnean Society paper, Alfred Russel Wallace, was present but there were notable absentees. Darwin and Huxley were invited but Darwin always kept clear of such turmoil and Huxley forgot to attend. It was reported that Huxley set off for the meeting, but he never arrived.

C. Carter Blake opened fire with a paper *On the Alleged Peculiar Character and Assumed Antiquity of the Human Cranium from Neanderthal*. Blake said that some authorities were declaring that we had discovered the 'missing link' which binds together man and the apes. The speaker did not think so and he was, he said, strongly supported by the *Medical Times and Gazette*.[3] He begged leave of the meeting to read a portion of the article. It said:

'We strongly suspect that Mr Blake is right in his conjecture he throws out, that this skull belongs to some poor idiot. The description strongly reminds us of Sir Walter Scott's *The Black Dwarf*. A theory of rickets and idiocy, we suspect, goes some way towards unravelling the mystery.'

This, said Blake, was firm medical opinion. Nobody else, he said, seemed to agree about anything to do with Neanderthal man. King of Galway had said that a wider gap than a mere specific one separated the human species from the Neanderthal one. Schaafhausen disagreed with Busk on the issue of the enormous eyebrow ridges. Busk had said the cause was enlarged frontal sinuses. Schaafhausen said they were nothing of the kind. Huxley agreed with both that this peculiar conformation could not be pathological or artificial but that it suggested an ancient race. Then he said that the skull more resembles that of an ape than any race yet known. M. Pruner-Bey of Paris had recently said that the skull certainly belonged to a large Celt but he was unable to say for sure whether it was of an idiotic Celt or not. What, cried Blake in exasperation, was one to make of it all?

The next speaker was M. Broca of the *Société d'Anthropologie* of Paris. Broca said that he thought he could easily demonstrate that the Neanderthal skull was not that of an idiot, and launched into a long and intricate anecdote about a mental institution at Bicêtre where he had encountered an idiot with an enormous head. But at an autopsy, continued Broca, it was found that the brain was extremely small. So, said the Frenchman, skull size was no indication of idiocy.

Why Broca thought the case of the large-skulled but small-brained idiot of Bicêtre was relevant to that of the small-brained and small-skulled Neanderthal man, he did not explain. This contribution seems to have dumbfounded the meeting for there was no discussion on this point.

Blake returned to his feet next to attack King's statement that he doubted whether Neanderthal man was capable of moral or theological conceptions. This did not surprise Blake. Belief in God was not an inherent idea in the mind of all savages nor, if the claims that were being made for the so-called human fossil of Neanderthal were any guide, in some Englishmen. The skull was undoubtedly that of an idiot, said Blake. He did not belong to the diluvium at all.

A general discussion then followed. A Mr Redie said that whatever the opinion of the Neanderthal fossil's intellectual development and however low the state of man this might indicate, the skull was definitely that of a man not of an ape. The distinction between man and ape in intellectual capacity could not be mistaken. A gorilla had enough sense to warm itself by a fire made by Negroes but did not possess enough sense to put more logs on the fire to keep it burning. It was a pity, said Redie, that a similar test could not be applied to the Neanderthal fossil.

Alfred Wallace was the next speaker. He told how he had compared the skulls of aborigines of New Zealand, Australia and New Guinea. Some, he said, were very similar to the Neanderthal skull, others not at all. He was satisfied, however, that the Neanderthal skull belonged to a member of a very savage race in a low state of development. It was certainly not that of an idiot.

Blake replied that George Busk had recently drawn attention to the Gibraltar skull in the Hunterian Museum in London, so it was beyond him why Wallace had to cite places as far away as Australia for skull forms which corresponded to that of the Neanderthal skull. It seemed to Blake that all sorts of evidence was being gathered together from the most unlikely places to lend weight to Charles Darwin's hypothesis.

The speaker said that nothing was further from his mind than to cast doubt on the transmutation theory. Indeed he considered it a very rational hypothesis. But what had the Neanderthal skull got to do with such an hypothesis? Blake was convinced that the misunderstandings, as he called them, had only arisen from original misrepresentations by Germans, who had possibly made the whole thing up. What was wanted, declared Blake, was real proof to confirm or deny the transmutation theory.

On this note the meeting ended. It cannot be doubted that Blake had no brief for the transmutation theory and merely made his spoken concession in deference to the presence of Wallace.

The debate on the antiquity of Neanderthal man was to continue for many years. The old arguments, indeed the old angers, were perpetuated until replaced by new ones, until the sheer weight of numbers of Neanderthal men made it impossible to reject them as isolated freaks. This meeting took place in 1864, eight years after the discovery of Neanderthal man, and four years after the famous Oxford debate which popular legend maintains changed men's minds and opened them to a new insight into man's place in nature.

Certainly Blake seems to have been outnumbered at this meeting but his stand did credit to his Biblical belief, which was at least unambiguous and single-minded.

6

In confining our attention to events which bore directly on the belated discovery by British scientists of Neanderthal man, we have missed a *cause célèbre* which is now little publicized but which the Piltdown affair strongly echoed ninety years later.

While English enthusiasts were carrying out fruitlessly the Prestwich formula for archaeological success, the *Abbevillois* newspaper of 9 April 1863 announced a momentous discovery. Into the possession of the local amateur Boucher de Perthes had come an ancient human jaw which contained a molar tooth. According to the newspaper, the human remains together with a number of flint implements had been recovered by workmen from a unique 'black bed' of earth discovered in the side of a gravel pit near Abbeville at a site known as Moulin Quignon. At last, Boucher de Perthes had told the newspaper, here was the primitive manufacturer of the flint tools for whom Science had searched for so long.

No flint tools had ever come from the Moulin Quignon gravel pit until the year of the discovery of the human jaw. Many times Sir John Evans and Joseph Prestwich had travelled to Abbeville, visiting this very pit on some seven or eight occasions, but they had neither been able to find a flint there nor been offered one for sale by local workmen.

But in 1863 things began to happen. Many finds of flint tools at Moulin Quignon were reported. Boucher de Perthes gave two specimens to Prestwich, and M. Marcotte, a local enthusiast, presented one to Evans.

But the flints from Moulin Quignon possessed some peculiar characteristics. Instead of the dark yellow or brown coloration displayed by the flints from the Abbeville district, the Moulin Quignon variety were bright yellow. This was explainable by the fact that the natural gravel of Moulin Quignon was much brighter in colour than was usual in the area, due to a local abundance of natural iron oxide in the soil. Another characteristic, however, was not so readily explained. No flints encountered anywhere else in France were so crudely manufactured as those from Moulin Quignon. This could only mean that the ancient humans of Moulin Quignon had occurred earlier in time than those living about the other Abbeville gravel pits. But this answer presented something of a conundrum to the British geologists. As Lartet had pointed out during his visit to London in 1859, Abbeville flint tools were more refined than those produced by the ancient toolmakers of St Acheul, near Amiens.

So it was with a sense of wonder that Evans and Prestwich, on hearing the news, hurried to France, arriving at Abbeville after a difficult journey, on 13 April to a cordial welcome from Boucher de Perthes. The Englishmen examined the ancient jaw-bone with care and were greatly impressed.

A pilgrimage was made to the Moulin Quignon gravel pit. The Englishmen gazed in awe at what must have been holy ground. But the famous black bed from which the human remains had been recovered was now obscured by a fall of gravel. As the pair were about to leave, a workman who had offered his services as guide took two highly coloured flint implements from his pocket and handed them to Prestwich. He said that he had found the flints while working in the Moulin Quignon pit. They were crude, badly-shaped and smeared over with a deeply iron-stained clay. With intense excitement the Englishmen realized that the dark soil must have come from the black bed. They eagerly gave the workman the two francs he demanded. It was while washing the dark earth from the flints at the first cottage they reached that Evans and Prestwich realized that they had been hoodwinked. Not only the earth came away but most of the colour as well.

The Englishmen hastened back to Boucher de Perthes. They asked him to wash some of his Moulin Quignon flints and watched in anguish as the high colour faded, then disappeared. Prestwich and Evans warned Boucher de Perthes of the serious doubt now cast on the jaw. The Frenchman does not seem to have replied or if he did neither Englishman bothered to report it.

With sad hearts Prestwich and Evans returned to England. The story of the bogus flints was conveyed to a meeting of the Royal Society on 16 April. On 19 April the *Académie des Sciences* rejoiced at the downfall of one of its minor enemies. An anonymous contributor to *The Times* of 25 April added that there was little doubt that the jaw was a forgery as well.

Neither Prestwich nor Evans seems to have entertained for a moment the possibility that Boucher de Perthes might have been behind the forgeries. But a batch of highly scurrilous stories began to be circulated about London and Paris concerning him. According to one of these, an unnamed Englishman staying at an Abbeville hotel was driven from his bed early by the sound of hammering. He came across a peasant chipping a flint, who replied to the obvious question: 'Why, making a *langue du chat* for M. Boucher de Perthes.' Another, on being reprimanded for selling a dishonest flint to a visiting Englishman, was supposed to have replied in exasperation: 'But what am I to do? The Englishman asks me for a flint. I say I have not got one. He insists. He does not believe me. So what am I to do? I make him one.'

Hugh Falconer told Prestwich that he had further evidence that not a few of the flints obtained from other sites at Abbeville were forged as well. Falconer had been experimenting with chipping flint and had made a surprising discovery. When pieces of flint are struck from a block by hammering with similar material, as would be the case with primitive man, the detached flakes leave behind facets that are broad and shallow, with rounded dividing ridges. If the flakes are detached from the parent block by striking with a metal hammer, however, the facets are deeper, narrower and more pronounced and the intervening ridges are more elevated and sharp.

The Geological Society unofficially communicated its views on the Abbeville flints to interested members of the *Académie des Sciences*. The result was a 'congress' which opened in Paris on 9 May and closed at Abbeville on the 13th, at which a large number of flints and the Moulin Quignon jaw could be tried. The French contingent comprised men who had devoted a major part of their lives to the excavation of their country's prehistoric sites – men such as De Quatrefages, Desnoyers and Lartet, all of whom had at one time or another incurred the wrath of the *Académie*. Also present was Lartet's old adversary Delasse, who appears to have undergone a change of heart since his surprise appearance in London. The Englishmen were Prestwich, Falconer, a Dr Carpenter, and George Busk, the translator of Schaafhausen's paper on Neanderthal man. Evans could not attend and sent his apologies. Boucher de Perthes was not invited. This must have been a time of extreme bitterness for most of the delegates. They were about to play devil's advocate for their bitter adversaries within the *Académie*. They were to try to prove that at least some of the flint tools – their objects of faith for many years – were modern forgeries, and at least partially to destroy what the *Académie* still insisted was an invention – antediluvian man.

Some forty flints were produced by the delegates. Some came from St Acheul, some from Abbeville, some from Moulin Quignon. In front of the assembly they were scrubbed in hot water. The St Acheul flints remained unchanged but some from Abbeville and all from Moulin Quignon soon lost their colour, changing from bright yellow to bronze and then to natural flint grey.

The facets of the suspect flints now presented the dull appearance of recent fracture, without 'glimmer' – the patina caused by ages of weathering. They were deep with sharp dividing ridges suggesting that a metal hammer had been employed to produce them. When a flake was struck from a flint the fresh facet differed in no way from the others. Another surprising feature was apparent. The suspect flints exhibited a striking similarity of pattern, as if all were produced by one person or at the most by two.

The English detachment was forced to conclude that although the St Acheul flints and most of those from Abbeville were genuine, a few Abbeville flints and all those from the black bed of Moulin Quignon were false. De Quatrefages, Desnoyers and Lartet were not convinced. They held that the appearance of newness exhibited by the flints was no proof of falsity.

Attention now passed to the Moulin Quignon jawbone with its single molar. To act as a 'control' two fossils of undoubted antiquity were produced; one was a molar tooth of some unknown species of animal, the other was a molar of the extinct cave-dwelling hyena (*Hyaena spelaea*). Delasse embarked on a series of tongue tests, considerably confusing the issue with a lengthy demonstration which proved that absolutely no reliance could be placed on it.

A debate ensued in which the Englishmen insisted that the human jaw could not have come from the black bed of Moulin Quignon because it showed little sign of staining by iron oxide – the great feature of the deposit in which it was found. To enforce this opinion Busk then demonstrated how irreverently fossils were handled in the mid-nineteenth century The anatomist sawed the Moulin Quignon jaw in half. This produced, according to Busk, the distinctive odour of limb amputations performed on live subjects, a feature he would hardly expect of so-called ancient bones. The colouring, which was found to be superficial, was easily scrubbed from one of the portions of bone, revealing a surface which bore little of the erosion common in old bones.

Busk produced a human lower jaw loaned by a Dr Robert Collyer which he had found in a pit near Ipswich, Suffolk in company with coprolites – roundish fossils resembling stones supposed to be the petrified excrement of an animal. Busk said that this jaw was presumed to have preceded the Roman conquest of Britain. He showed how the bone was infiltrated throughout with iron from the soil from which it was recovered. This infiltration, said Busk, was typical. He had seen bones from Bolivian coppermines which had been filled with threads of native copper. The Moulin Quignon jaw was virtually unstained, so the jaw could not have come from the black bed. Busk doubted whether it was older than any other old bones that could be obtained from cemeteries.

But the French would not give in. The implications of fraudulence would allow the *Académie* to laugh them to extinction. They considered that none of the evidence was conclusive and that the jaw and the flints could be genuine relics of antediluvian man. Desnoyers then proposed a simple method of proving whether the Moulin Quignon flints were genuine or not. Whether colour came off the flints when washed, the evidence of crude workmanship, the depth of the facets, said Desnoyers, really proved nothing at all. The only real test was a search of the Moulin Quignon pit conducted by themselves, secretly and without giving prior warning to the locals. If only one flint was discovered *in situ* which displayed similar characteristics, it would prove beyond all doubt that the rest was genuine. This logic was irrefutable and the motion was carried.

The congress, now joined by a large number of French *savants* but, according to Prestwich, proceeding 'under utmost secrecy', arrived at Abbeville and travelled undetected to the Moulin Quignon pit. The archaeologists almost ran from their coaches to the edge of the gravel but the famous black bed was no longer to be seen. A workman explained that the bed had been a very local deposit and had been quarried away.

This stage in the proceedings was chosen by an eminent *Académie* geologist, Professor Hébert, to deliver an impromptu address. He said that it was obvious to him that the Moulin Quignon deposit was comparatively modern. It certainly did not belong to the diluvium. Notwithstanding this oration, a large party of local workmen was set to work under the close supervision of members of the congress and the *savants*. To the surprise of the English and delight of the French 'believers' in the party the search was rewarded almost immediately. Five flint implements virtually sprang from the gravel. Falconer himself saw two revealed by a fall of gravel undermined by a pickaxe. All the newly-recovered specimens exhibited the usual strange Moulin Quignon features. The facets were deep and the ridges sharp and the colour could be removed by washing in hot water. But the conclusion was thought to be inescapable. All the Moulin Quignon flints were genuine. Prestwich hurried to Boucher de Perthes with the glad tidings.

The French 'believers' likewise wasted no time in transmitting the results to the *Académie*. But it availed them nothing. The permanent secretary, Elie de Beaumont, refused to accept that the Moulin Quignon was older than the 'modern age'. It was certainly not older, he said, than the Somme valley peat beds which had been found to cover the remains of a Roman road in the Département de Nord. De Beaumont added:

I do not believe that the human race was contemporary with *Elephas primigenius*. M. Cuvier's theory [to this effect] is born of genius. It is still undemolished!

Meanwhile Prestwich had communicated the favourable result of the Moulin Quignon 'dig' to the Royal Society and the

Geological Society. Falconer followed suit in the August issue of *Natural History Review*.

Could this be the British support for Boucher de Perthes to which Marcellin Boule refers? If so, it must have escaped him that the British shortly had second thoughts. And with good reason.

Although convinced at first by the Moulin Quignon demonstration both Prestwich and Falconer soon began to wonder whether it had really proved anything. As a result, Prestwich again visited Moulin Quignon and conducted a test which had been omitted by the congress. He washed 135 fragments of flint which he personally recovered from the gravel. Unlike that of the flint implements, the high colour of the fragments could not be washed off no matter how hard they were scrubbed. It was now obvious to Prestwich that the Moulin Quignon flints were forgeries. Some unknown person or persons had manufactured the implements using modern tools and then dyed them to match the surrounding gravel.

To his enthusiastic paper in the Geological Society's quarterly journal which had already gone to the printer, Prestwich added a note rebutting it dated October 1863. He wrote that further and deliberate enquiry on his part had led him to revert to his opinion that the Moulin Quignon flint tools were forgeries. The entire congress, said Prestwich, had been mistaken in concluding that no fraud had been practised. He continued:

Our verdict respecting the flint implements (leaving apart the question of the jaw) will, therefore, I fear, have to be reconsidered. The precaution against imposition by the workmen seemed to have made this impossible, but although it remained undetected, I cannot continue to accept the authenticity of the flints.

However, he concluded that the occurrence of genuine flint implements at Abbeville and Amiens continued to receive fresh confirmation with every fresh investigation and these placed Boucher de Perthes' original finds at Abbeville beyond all doubt.

So this then was the outcome. The Moulin Quignon flint implements were demolished, bringing down with them the jaw of antediluvian man. As far as the flints were concerned, Boucher de Perthes' failure to detect the imposition seems inexplicable unless, contrary to his many biographers' opinions, he was simple-natured. The weight of opinion at the time, however, seems in favour of the proposition that Boucher de Perthes was the innocent dupe of some unscrupulous workman who took advantage of the amateur's gullibility.

Certainly neither Prestwich nor Falconer attached any blame to Boucher de Perthes. No doubt it was at their instigation that Boucher de Perthes was, on 17 June of that year, honoured by the Geological Society by being elected 'foreign correspondent'. One wonders, however, whether the wheels had been put into motion before the deception had been detected.

But Boucher de Perthes was never elected to the *Académie des Sciences*. He was still laughed at in Paris. It was also rumoured that shortly before the jaw was brought to him by a workman, he had offered a reward of two hundred francs for any human remains found in the gravel.

Boucher de Perthes died five years later, in 1868, and because of strong opposition by the *Académie* his family withdrew all his scientific papers from sale. Even in 1875, A. V. Meunier's *Les Ancêtres d'Adam*, which contained an account of what he described as 'the martyrdom' of Boucher de Perthes, was withdrawn by the publishers after they had been informed that the work was offensive to the *Académie*. It was published at last, however, in 1906.

7

The modern geologist employs aerogeophysical and seismic survey, and chemical and radiological assay. The Victorian geologist had only his eye and a geological hammer. We can gain some idea of the magnitude of the problem of the earth's crust for the Victorians by considering it in the light of what modern technology has revealed.

Unfortunately for the study of fossil man, particularly for the early attempts to date him, the Pliocene, the closing period of the Tertiary Age, and the Pleistocene, the first period of the Quaternary, which saw the emergence of man, man-ape and ape-man, are the most geologically turbulent.

During the early part of the Cenozoic Era, which culminated in the Pleistocene, much of Europe, North America and Asia was sub-tropical, with temperate forests of giant redwoods, elm and beech extending far north into Alaska, Greenland and Siberia. There were no mountains but instead monotonous rounded hills which offered little variation in either landscape or climate. Such humpbacks do not make for windward rain slopes or leeward deserts.

There had once been mountains, indeed the previous Mesozoic Era, that of the giant reptiles, had been one of mountain building, but these had eroded away during the first forty million years of the Cenozoic.

During the second half of the Cenozoic however, to the accompaniment of volcanade and convulsions of the earth's crust, the Rockies, Andes and that great spine of Eurasia, the Alps and Himalayas, uplifted themselves.

This geological change was equalled climatically. The onset of the appalling Ice Ages of the two million-year-long Pleistocene is attributed to the immense height of these new mountain ranges. Certainly a similar upthrust of mountains in the Permian, the final period of the Palaeozoic Era, some two hundred million years before, was accompanied by a similar but not so severe freeze-up. With the mountains came the glaciers.

Forming high in the Scandinavian mountains and fed by the increased precipitation of altitude, the glaciers pushed downwards. These glaciers met others formed in the foothills, uniting to bury entire mountain ranges, and pushed outwards. The build-up of ice produced its own impetus as it reflected back as much as eighty per cent of the sun's heat. The ice sheet now crept east, joining a similar one spreading from Siberia, and then west across the North Sea converting the water into ice as it went, to join the glaciers produced by the mountains of Britain. Thus one ice sheet covered two million square miles. In the region of the Gulf of Bothnia it was ten thousand feet thick. Similar sheets formed around the Pyrenees, Apeninnes and Carpathians to the south and in North America to the west. Thus a belt of ice girdled the earth down to about 50 degrees north of the Equator. At its greatest extent the ice locked up enough ocean to make the world sea level fall by four hundred feet. The northern ice-fields caused the belt of rain-bearing westerly winds to swing inwards towards the Equator by fifteen degrees of latitude, both north and south. Africa, the Mediterranean, Asia Minor, the south west of North America and South America experienced 'pluvial' periods: heavy and protracted rainfall with swollen rivers, rising lakes and floods.

At least three more times in the years of the Pleistocene the freeze was repeated. Three more times the ice-field pushed east, south and west. There was, it is believed, a similar encroachment by glaciers of the southern hemisphere but the effect on this area is difficult to plot, as it is mainly ocean.

Each of the four main Ice Ages, which occurred irregularly at intervals of roughly one hundred thousand years, was separated from the next by a warm period or 'interglacial'. During interglacials the ice contracted, but the retreat north was interrupted several times by checks and readvances.

With each climatic pulse there was a massive migration of animals, the less adaptable or less resistant species perishing. The considerable fall in sea level enabled the animals to move freely across desiccated sea beds. These land bridges connected Britain with Western Europe; Alaska with Siberia; Japan with Siberia;

Tasmania with New Guinea; and the Asian mainland with the Celebes and the Philippines.

Each pulse of the ice, each advance, check, readvance, retreat, check, readvance, and retreat, left a legacy – massive ice-scarred ridges, banks and moraine, wide spreads of clay, gravel and wind-borne loess. Each change of climate left the bones of its own distinctive fauna.

Then some twelve thousand years ago the ice retreated for the last time. There was a wild see-sawing of land and sea levels. First came the floods as the melting ice released vast volumes of water. Then land surfaces, long crushed down by the weight of ice, popped upwards. This left a legacy of raised beaches, drowned forests and submerged land surfaces.

It is not surprising, therefore, that the nineteenth-century geologists, aided only by observation and percussion, could make little sense of it all. At first it was not realized that the Great Ice Age was not one but four Ice Ages. As knowledge advanced and more than one Ice Age was detected, there was much strife between factions that accepted and factions that rejected them. It was the glaciations which gave the Pleistocene its distinction, therefore estimates of its duration and the distance in time from the previous Pliocene period varied according to the number of Ice Ages postulated. For the geologist who subscribed to two Ice Ages the Pleistocene was twice as long as the Pleistocene of the geologists who could only see evidence of one.

Edouard Lartet was but one of a number of palaeontologists who proposed a chronological classification of fossil man by fossil animal remains found with his tools. He wrote:

'Thus in the period of Primitive man we shall have the Age of the Great Cave Bear, the Age of the Elephant and the Rhinoceros, and the Age of the Reindeer, and the Age of the Aurochs (wild ox); much after the names recently adopted by archaeologists in their divisions of Stone Age, Bronze Age and Iron Age.'

The Englishman Sir John Lubbock was the first to refine the Stone Age into two main cultural groups. In 1865 he wrote in his best-selling book *Prehistoric Times* that the polished flint tools now being encountered represented the work of a more culturally refined and therefore later kind of humanity. He proposed that this group should be called the Neolithic or

New Stone Age. The crudely chipped flints belonged to the Palaeolithic or Old Stone Age.

But Lubbock's 'Palaeolithic' and 'Neolithic' were no more than broad labels for successive flint cultures. What was wanted by the archaeologist and palaeontologist was a more accurate chronology based on numbers of years. How long in years were the Palaeolithic and Neolithic Ages?

The geologists responded to the question with vigour. Not fully aware of the geological contortions of the Pleistocene, at first they thought the answer straightforward. The chipped and polished flints seemed to align themselves with two distinct groups of fauna. The chipped flints were to be found in deposits which also contained the bones of mammoth, rhinoceros and hyena; the polished flints were usually accompanied by the bones of reindeer and wild ox. These Palaeolithic and Neolithic groups of animals were to be found in certain kinds of deposits. All that was necessary then was a calculation of just when in the Pleistocene, at what phase in the movement of the ice sheet, the deposit had occurred.

But at this point in the mental exercise, concordance ceased. The above principles had long held good for the science of geology. An animal or plant fossil could be reliably ascribed to the Cambrian, Ordovician, Silurian or Devonian periods because it was actually found in that kind of rock. The depth in the rock gave an indication of age. But it was not a critical classification. The Devonian, for example, had lasted for fifty million years. A million years or so error meant little. Faced with the short Pleistocene, it was a different matter. A suspected error of say ten thousand years would set one geologist howling for the blood of another. The main trouble was that opinion varied widely about how long it took a deposit to be deposited. Nor was it realized that the glaciers had bequeathed different legacies to different areas at the same time. For example, gravel in one geological section, hill wash in a second, loam in a third, lake sediment in a fourth were considered to be evidence of different geological periods, whereas they could have been placed by different glaciers at the same time.

So it was that one worker found from deposits around Geneva that the Neolithic began seven thousand years ago while another reported at the same time that he had calculated from Egyptian deposits that the Neolithic began thirteen thousand years ago. Sir Charles Lyell, working in the Somme, considered that the Palaeolithic began not less than one hundred thousand years ago, and the Pleistocene Ice Age endured for two hundred and twenty thousand years, while in England Joseph Prestwich considered that the Palaeolithic lasted but twenty thousand years.

But one man held the key to the problem. In his 1862 address to the Geological Society T. H. Huxley stressed that geological deposits occurring in the same order and bearing the same fossils were not necessarily contemporaneous. In doing so Huxley endorsed the principles of stratigraphy, a relatively workable method of dating deposits. Much subsequent confusion and name calling could have been avoided if more people had taken notice of what he said. But they did not.

Even today the prehistoric archaeologist is criticized for his folly in ascribing flints to time-divorced flint cultures, to the neglect of pure geological dating. This may be true of present times, but if he had done so before modern geological techniques had sorted something out of the great natural puzzle then commensurate chaos would have resulted. Frederick Zeuner, a leading authority on the turbulent Pleistocene, calculated that before the adoption of stratigraphic principles the chances of success by such methods would be of the order of one in a thousand.

There was yet another problem which vexed many geologists from the mid-nineteenth century onwards. The geological hammer had its limitations, it was thought, but it was an instrument of precision compared with the methods of the students of fossil man. Animal and plant fossils embedded in rock which could be reliably dated were one thing; flint implements found in association with the bones of extinct animals in caves were another matter entirely. In its enthusiasm, human palaeontology was far too prone to relate the age of the container to the age of what was found in it. Never or seldom was it asked, the geologists complained, whether the flint tool had arrived in the cave before or after the animal bones were deposited. No palaeontologist seemed to consider that the cave was merely a datable box in which fossil bones and flints were placed by later eventuality.

But the evidence was slowly accumulating. In 1866 another representative of Neanderthal man – a jaw – had come to light in a cave called Trou de la Naulette, in a wooded hill at the conjunction of the Meuse and Lesse rivers near Dinant, Belgium. Found by a Belgian geologist named Dupont, the human remains were accompanied by the first tangible evidence of the antiquity of Neanderthal man, the bones of rhinoceros, mammoth and bear. This was a distinctly Quaternary collection. No bones were found with the Neanderthal man of Rhenish Prussia.

Rather strangely, the jaw was described by M. Pruner-Bey to the *Société d'Anthropologie*, Paris, as being extremely ape-like with huge, projecting canine teeth. C. Carter Blake, to prove Neanderthal man was an anthropoid ape, also spoke of enormous teeth. Even the methodical Darwin, quoting Blake, mentioned them later in his *The Descent of Man*, published in 1871. In fact, when discovered the jaw contained no teeth at all.

A third Neanderthal man was discovered in Belgium the same year in a limestone cave in a wooded hill above the Orneau river, near Spy. Evidently the site had been well dug over a number of times before and a number of implements of a type which came to be called Mousterian, in deference to the French (see page 98–9), had been found.

But Marcel de Puydt, a member of the Archaeological Institute of Liège, and M. Lohest, assistant geologist at the University of Liège, noticed a large neglected terrace in front of the cave. A four-foot trench was dug at this point, revealing a deep layer of bones and flints. The skeletons – there were two – were accompanied by animal remains which also related the find to the Quaternary.

Edouard Lartet was elected to the newly established chair of palaeontology at the Paris National Museum of Natural History in 1869, but he died some months later without having delivered a lecture. Lartet had however struck a last blow for the credibility of fossil man.

Late in the year before his death Lartet had been called to Cro-Magnon, near Les Eyzies in the Dordogne. Here railway excavations of a limestone cliff had uncovered a rock-shelter containing skeletons of five adult humans. But these remains were neither modern nor those of the Neanderthal brutes. The best-preserved skull had a steep forehead with faint eyebrow ridges. Indeed his cranial capacity of some 1,590 c.c. was well above the modern average of 1,350 c.c. The other bones suggested a tall individual possibly in excess of six feet, exceedingly muscular, definitely *Homo sapiens*, but with primitive features which placed him slightly apart from modern man. It was supposed by some that because of his extreme muscularity 'Cro-Magnon Man' could outpace a horse and bull-wrestle with ease, although he was not in fact a Stone Age superman.

With the human remains at Cro-Magnon were a large number of flint tools and sea shells, some pierced for use as necklaces. This suggested a ritual burial after death. The high degree of refinement of the tools, called Aurignacian, and bones of bison, reindeer, mammoth and primitive horse found with the human remains later led to the opinion that the Cro-Magnons had lived some time in the late Pleistocene, probably during the fourth and last glaciation known as *Würm*. Lartet found himself able to ascribe these fossil men to the Late Palaeolithic Age.

The impact of these discoveries on scientific thought would be hard to overestimate. The Belgian Neanderthal men swept aside the suggestions of idiot or imbecile hermit or rickety Cossack. One imbecile at Neanderthal was feasible but several similar imbeciles in Belgium not so. Even more important, coincidentally the men of Neanderthal and Cro-Magnon supplied two separate links in the chain of human evolution. For the first time Charles Darwin's *The Origin of Species* began to bear fruit. Maybe, it began to be thought, man really did have primitive forerunners in the same way as the beasts of the field. It was at least a beginning.

But as it is true that all winds blow some good, sadly the reverse is the case also. The excitement induced by Abbeville and St Acheul, and Cro-Magnon and Neanderthal, started Britain off on a great fossil man hunt. Flint implements were found in vast numbers but not the kind easily recognizable as such.

The Geological Society accords to a newly adopted president the right to devote his inaugural lecture to his particular interest. In 1857 Sir John Evans took this opportunity to cry out against the new craze. He said that formerly the antiquity of the human race could be proved by the class of fauna recovered with the remains and the geological changes which had taken place in the surface conformation since the human relics had been deposited. But today, complained Evans, increasingly it was becoming usual to consider as evidence of early man pebbles on which the finder could see the traces of human workmanship. He warned his listeners to be wary of the evidence of these alleged worked pebbles. No doubt Evans' disappointment over Moulin Quignon made him highly suspicious of those stones. He had reason.

The latest craze was due to Benjamin Harrison of Ightham, Kent. Inspired, it is said, by Lyell's *Principles* and not so evidently by Gilbert White's *The Natural History of Selborne*, Harrison, a general grocer, had begun to cast about for something to collect, to search the hills about Ightham for flint implements. The result was the 'eolith' – stone implements of such simplicity that human participation is barely detectable or, as Evans complained, extremely doubtful.

The authenticity or otherwise of the eoliths was enough to split British archaeologists into rival camps. The eoliths were considered by believers as something equivalent to the biological 'missing link'. The pebbles, it was claimed, bridged the gap between sticks, which possibly were the first tools of humans, and the easily recognizable chipped flints found at Abbeville and St Acheul. The evidence of human workmanship, said the owners of vast collections of eolithics, was there for all to see if only it were looked for. Chipped, scratched, marked pebbles formed the focal point at many a historical society's winter evening gathering.

The disbelievers assigned the manufacture of the eoliths to Nature, to the dashing by waves of one pebble against another, to the grinding of pebbles by earthquakes, to the crushing of cart wheels. Indeed, cried the disbelievers, it was almost impossible for a pebble to remain whole when the number of debilitating forces at work down the centuries was taken into account. Oddly enough, one of the most telling arguments against eoliths was used as overwhelming evidence to support them – the large numbers discovered. Collections of several thousand eoliths were quite common.

Whether the stones are or are not the work of man is a debate which continues to this day. Evans did not believe in eoliths but a great many other influential men did. Alfred Russel Wallace regularly visited Ightham to examine the rapidly expanding collection. Harrison also received encouragement from Joseph Prestwich. Many years later, in 1899, the grocer was invited to show his collection of eoliths to the Royal Society. It was greatly admired. The same year he was awarded a Civil List pension. Then the Royal Society purchased an annuity for him. All this was to the delight of the believers and the chagrin of their opponents.

There is little doubt that Harrison's discovery of the eoliths was welcomed as a relief from the realization that the gravel and sand pits of Britain failed to live up to the standard set across the Channel. If it could be believed that the marked pebbles were crude tools, then this was evidence that a race of primitive humans had once lived in Britain, compared with which the Neanderthalers and the ancients of the Somme were but of yesterday.

The palpable achievement of these years was the publishing in 1871 of Charles Darwin's *The Descent of Man*, in which he more than made up for his sins of omission in *The Origin* by predicting with uncanny accuracy the kind of fossil hominids which had yet to be discovered.

When Darwin died after a heart attack at Downe, Kent, on 18 April 1882, his achievement was magnificently recorded by J. W. Hulkes, president of the Geological Society. Hulkes saw Darwin as a man who had 'devoted his life to the development of those pregnant principles of evolution, the annunciation of which he had the happiness to see generally accepted'.

There was concrete evidence of this acceptance, for Darwin was laid to rest in Westminster Abbey. His pall-bearers included Huxley, Hooker and Wallace. Many of his old adversaries, or rather those of Huxley, such as Wilberforce and Buckland, had gone before him. One survivor was the seventy-eight-year-old Sir Richard Owen. Owen was buried at Oxford ten years later in 1892. It was a pity for Owen that he could not have held on another three years, for he undoubtedly would have derived great satisfaction from the fact that 'Darwin's bulldog', succumbing to influenza on 29 June 1895, did not 'make the Abbey'. The agnostic-in-chief was buried without ceremony at Finchley Cemetery.

8

The Netherlands East Indies (now Indonesia) lie in the great volcanic belt which curves south and westward from the North Pacific to the Indian Ocean. Nowhere in the islands are the volcanoes far distant; lofty truncated cones which radiate ridges to the sea. Brown ridges of recent eruptions stand out bold and barren. Others covered with dense forests hem in mountain torrents. Towards the coast the ridges open out to embrace wide fertile plains through which wind sluggish rivers. There is either jungle or cultivation. Even on the old volcanoes the patch-work of plantations stretches to the summits.

Towards the end of the nineteenth century, however, there were disturbances other than seismic ones. The riches born of the fertility tended to stay in certain hands. Very little perco-lated down to the lower orders. The East Indies were to Holland what Australia was to the United Kingdom and, apart from the planters, they were populated by industrious adventurers, the destitute striving for riches, and the indolent seeking peace. They were also the repository for the scapegraces of good families.

These factions blamed their continued lack of prosperity on a Dutch government policy which eschewed free trade and imposed import tariffs which stifled enterprise. The administra-tion, which represented the interests of the sugar and coffee plantation owners to the exclusion of all others, was unrepen-tant. It feared the intrusion of foreign interests. There was no guarantee that free trade would necessarily mean that the out-side finance thus unleashed into the islands would remain in the right hands.

But by far the most serious threat to peace came from the native population. Remembering the philanthropy of British administration under Sir Stamford Raffles[1] the natives attributed the generosity of a personality to a nation. They were at best discontented, at worst in open rebellion.

The ill-feeling had commenced when the British Crown surrendered its Batavia protectorate in exchange for that of the Gold Coast. By the end of the nineteenth century this had deteriorated into the Achinese War, the expense of which was threatening the whole economy of the Indies.

But the accompaniments of prosperity still survived. In Java there were railways, steam-tramways and an efficient telephone system. Important towns had splendid public buildings, pleasances and botanical gardens. But outside the towns travellers were warned not to pass beyond certain points or their safety was not guaranteed. The capital Batavia (now Djakarta) had become one vast military encampment, to the detriment of the last survivors of the British settlement who complained that their golf courses were being used by fat Dutch officers to exercise their ponies. This produced, they complained, an effect on the greens similar to artillery bombardment. It is an irrelevant but irresistible fact that one of these Dutch officers was Captain Rudolph MacCleod, whose wife many years later aggravated the French and the British military as the accomplished courtesan and vastly incompetent spy Mata Hari.

Another arrival in the steamy atmosphere of the East Indies summer of 1886 was a twenty-nine-year-old army lieutenant named Eugene Dubois. Dubois seems to have been quite unqualified mentally to be medical officer at the military fever hospital at Padang on the island of Sumatra, to which he was sent from Batavia. His many scientific biographers say as much but in a different way. They are more impressed by the fact that even as a lecturer in anatomy at the University of Amsterdam, Dubois had kept it no secret that he considered the 'missing link' could be found in the East Indies, that he had come expressly to seek him out.

But everything written about Dubois has been so highly charged with reverence that it gives rise to the suspicion that romance has been preferred to fact. Even the real reason for Dubois being in the East Indies – the Achinese War – is never mentioned. Certainly many authors, Darwin, Lyell and Wallace amongst them, had considered that a primitive forerunner of man might be found somewhere in the East. But they all specifically indicated Africa for the birth of humanity for the cogent reason that anthropoid apes – the most plausible early progenitors of man – were found in that continent to the almost complete exclusion of all others. The only exceptions were the islands of Borneo and Sumatra, the home of the orang-utan.

At first Dubois preferred Sumatra. He changed to Java only later when B. D. Van Rietschoten found a primitive Australoid skull in a marble quarry there. Java has no anthropoid apes at all.

Within weeks of arriving at the fever hospital, Dubois published his first paper, entitled *On the Desirability of an Investigation into the Pleistocene Fauna of the Netherlands East Indies, particularly Sumatra*. Dubois wrote that he found it odd that such a large, peculiar and advanced animal as the orang-utan should be confined to the islands of Sumatra and Borneo. He reasoned that this was significant. In other countries which had an animal stock confined to that territory, such as Australia with its kangaroos, the remains of primitive forerunners of these kinds of animals had been found. Surely a search of Sumatra would provide a similar early forerunner of the orang-utan. This might also be the forerunner of man himself.

Dubois then quoted R. von Virchow:[2]

All researches hitherto have only led to the presumption but not proof [of the existence of ape forerunners of man]. Is the question settled? Certainly not for the naturalist. Large regions of the world are still wholly unknown in respect of their fossil treasures. These belong precisely to the home region of the men-like apes; tropical Africa, Borneo, and the adjacent islands, are still entirely unexplored. One single new find can change the whole state of the problem.

Thus Dubois argued his case for a government-sponsored expedition to seek the forerunner of man. He was none too particular about his choice of authorities to support his argument. Von Virchow was still maintaining that the Neanderthal fossil was a microcephalic idiot. His 1870 paper was aimed at pushing the search out of Europe so as to exclude Neanderthal man from the running. When Dubois found his Java man, his glibbest opponent was von Virchow who said Java man was a form of chimpanzee.

Dubois negotiated a change from Padang to a small hospital for military convalescents at Pajokumbu in the interior. In the less demanding post of senior medical officer he had more time for exploration. He began his quest in the local limestone caves which provided a wealth of animal fossils. But these were of the Quaternary and thus too recent to provide the 'missing link' of his ambitions. By now the sympathetic government had considerably augmented the search party with two military mining engineers and fifty military convicts. But Van Rietschoten, though not so fortunate in assistance as Dubois, was having more success in Java. The fossils he sent to Dubois were of much older fauna, more reminiscent of the Tertiary deposits of the Siwalik Hills of India.

In 1890, after five years of what Dubois considered to be disappointment, he transferred the search to Java. In a volcanic tufa, mostly soft sandstone, Dubois found a hippopotamus jawbone with strong Siwalik affinities. This deposit, a few kilometres in width, extended east–west across the island, to the north of the 10,000-foot Lawu and Willis volcanoes. Dubois recognized this as an old river formation, resting on Tertiary marine marls, limestone, and volcanic breccia of indeterminate age. The adjacent Bengawen (now Solo) river had cut down through the deposit exposing a natural geological section. The bones recovered from this deposit, chiefly mammals and reptiles, had a distinct local character but a high degree of affinity with the Pliocene fauna of the Siwalik.

The first remains considered by Dubois to be those of early man were found in November 1890 at Kedung Brubus, forty kilometres east of the native village of Trinil. It was a fragment of a lower jaw which Dubois attributed to a human of hitherto unknown type, differing from any living or fossil man. In September 1891, at Trinil at the foot of the still-active Lawu volcano, on the left bank of the Bengawen, he found a right upper third molar tooth. He ascribed both finds to a very large and exceptionally man-like chimpanzee which he named accordingly *Anthropopithecus*. A month later, three metres from the tooth, a skull cap was excavated. The Bengawen site was flooded every 'wet' season, and Dubois had to wait until the next April before resuming his search. But in August 1892 he found another tooth, a left upper second molar, about a metre from the site of the first tooth, then a left femur ten metres from the skull cap.

Dubois published the results of his searches in 1894. He now attributed the remains to an extinct giant gibbon which he called *Pithecanthropus erectus*. Having discovered the first fossil man in the east, he became his own opponent. Dubois exhibited what was described as 'a grotesque reconstruction' of *Pithecanthropus* in Batavia in September 1895 and then left the East Indies for good. He now embarked with his fossil on a vigorous series of lectures, appearing at the Third International Zoological Conference at Leyden in Holland, Liège, Paris, London, Dublin, Edinburgh, Berlin and Jena, and the Fourth International Conference at Cambridge in 1898.

But although the discovery was a sensation, it was greeted with bared scientific teeth. Far from establishing any coherent scientific view, the Neanderthal man controversy merely seems to have served as a whetstone. Although the cranial capacity of the *Pithecanthropus* skull was so low that it prompted its discoverer to think it belonged to an ancient gibbon, the straight shaft of the femur had a close resemblance to that of modern man. This strongly suggested that *Pithecanthropus* was capable of standing and walking erect. This paradox of ape skull and human limb was seized on as clear evidence that the bones did not belong to the same individual; that Dubois had mixed the bones of an animal with those of a human being; that the distance between the discovery sites precluded all possibility that the bones belonged to the same creature.

By 1896, two years after the announcement of the find, five authorities were convinced that *Pithecanthropus* was a kind of anthropoid ape, seven asserted that he was human, and seven thought that he was intermediate between the two. Von Virchow was inclined towards the anthropoid ape theory but then reverted to his usual one of microcephalic idiot. Yet another authority disgusted his scientific colleagues by suggesting that the creature was the result of copulation between a native and an orang-utan.

More famous arguments took place over the size of the *Pithecanthropus* brain. Behind his heavy brow ridges, the frontal region of the skull recedes sharply, far deeper in fact than in Neanderthal man. Brain-room is further reduced by a sharp inward 'nip' at the base of the forehead. The lower portion of the skull was missing, so any estimate as to the cranial capacity of the skull was equivalent to sounding a bottomless pit, and therefore subject to the caprice of the measurer. Dubois estimated this capacity at 850 c.c. In 1939 this was enhanced by von Koenigswald and Weidenreich to 914 c.c., reduced to 850 c.c. again in 1957 by Boule and Vallois, but raised to 940 c.c. by Ashley Montagu in 1960.

It might be thought that it would have been wiser to arrive at a general concurrence of view on the brain capacity before the implications of brain size were debated. But it seems that the strong individualism of the many describing authorities made such concordance impossible. Brain size had more than an obvious importance. No pea-brained individual, it was argued, would ever have walked erect, so the small skull and straight limb bones belonged to two separate species of animal. Those that held that *Pithecanthropus* had a large brain considered that he had evolved to a point where erect walking was essential.

Dubois was deeply affected by the heated controversy. At length he withdrew from the debate entirely, retreating with *Pithecanthropus* to the privacy of a house at Haarlem. Only in 1920 was he at last persuaded to allow the fossil to be transferred to Leyden Museum. Over the years Dubois continued to debate with himself. He began to waver from his original view that *Pithecanthropus* was a gibbon, his writings describing the fossil as more human and less ape-like. He changed his mind again on at least three occasions, then finally reverted to his original opinion of fossil gibbon. In later years the old man kept his collection of bones in a cabinet protected from the view of his critics by sheets of newspaper pasted to the glass.

In 1907 the Berlin Academy of Science mounted a lavish expedition to Trinil under the leadership of Frau Selenka, the widow of a prominent German zoologist; but nothing further was found in the way of fossil man, in fact no remains other than those of a fossil antelope, which was named after Dubois. The expedition itself (at least according to von Koenigswald, a later and more successful searcher in another part of Java) left its own remains in the form of a litter of broken beer bottles.

Britain had to wait until 1898 for her first fossil man, although much later he was proved to be nothing of the kind. In fact the fossil had been discovered in 1888, or so the Geological Society was informed, the lack of immediate publicity being due to pressure of business on the part of the discoverer. For two years before the discovery, it had been the custom of Robert Elliot to visit at fortnightly intervals the gravel pits in the Northfleet area of Kent – Milton Street, Swanscombe and Galley Hill. During a visit to Galley Hill, Jack Allsop, an employee at the pit, who on Elliot's behest had looked out for and saved flint implements and curious stones while the ballast was screened, informed Elliot that a human skull had turned up. Elliot could hardly credit the information at first but the pieces of bone were duly produced.

Allsop conducted him to the spot of the discovery where more bones still embedded in the shingle could be seen. As they were dug out the remains were found to be so soft that they were placed aside to harden in the wind and sun. Indeed, it was explained later, Allsop had left the remains in the gravel only for fear of damaging them by unskilful removal.

The fragments were then taken to Elliot's private 'museum' where, after being dipped in a hardening solution, they rested for a decade until a Frank Cooper, of Poplar in East London, saw them and urged they be placed in the hands of someone qualified to describe them. The master of a local school, named Mathew Heys, appears to have been the first to see the skull after it was uncovered by the workmen excavating the gravel. He had hurried off, his intention being to obtain some indisputable evidence of the presence of the skull in the gravel either by photography or the testimony of two 'intelligent' witnesses. Heys did not consider that gravel pit workmen were qualified. Common workmen at the time were notorious for falsehood and drunkenness. But the schoolmaster's caution cost him the discovery. To his chagrin, when he returned the skull had been removed from the ground. It was retained by Allsop until handed to Elliot in exchange for a reward.

It fell to the lot of E. T. Newton, F.R.S., to present this exciting find to the Geological Society. The portions recovered were most of the skull but wanting the facial bones, the right half of the lower jaw with teeth, both femora, and parts of both tibiae and pelvis. When reassembled Galley Hill man resembled remarkably the Neanderthal man found at Spy. The skull possessed prominent superciliary ridges, and the femora were similarly curved, although the tibiae were less robust.

According to Newton, the flint implements found at Galley Hill in the past had been acknowledged as being of Palaeolithic type. Frank Corner possessed a hippopotamus tooth found at Milton Street. There also Elliot had found a deer antler. Lion bones had been found at Swanscombe. F. J. C. Spurrell had detected the remains of elephant, rhinoceros, horse and bison in a small patch of gravel near Northfleet railway station. Similar remains were found at Dartford Brent, west of the City Asylum. No one was better acquainted with the North Kent Pleistocene gravel deposits than Spurrell, said Newton, who agreed that the Galley Hill deposit was part of one original stretch extending from Dartford Heath to Gravesend. Spurrell had further informed Newton that human bones had been met with before in these gravels but had been mislaid, and no record kept of the conditions under which they occurred.[3]

The possibility that the human remains were the remnants of a comparatively modern burial, said Newton, must have occurred to every one of his audience but the peculiar character of the remains and the depth of eight feet of gravel at which they were found, pointed to considerable antiquity. Elliot and Heys were reliable witnesses as to the undisturbed state of the gravel above the remains; therefore there could be little doubt as to the Palaeolithic age of the human remains from Galley Hill.

In the discussion which followed Sir John Evans said that it was unfortunate that such a long interval had elapsed between the discovery of the bones and the attention of geologists being called to them. The nearly perfect skeleton strongly suggested a recent burial. On the whole he was doubtful and preferred to wait for more evidence before accepting absolutely that the remains were contemporaneous with the gravel in which they were found, however ancient the bones might appear. Professor W. Boyd Dawkins of Owens College, Manchester, said he would go further than Evans, for he was convinced that the skeleton was a recent burial.

A Dr Gason, however, was sure that Galley Hill man was of the same race as the specimens from Neanderthal, Spy and La Naulette. W. J. Lewis Abbot took leave to point out to Evans that the completeness of a skeleton was no guarantee of a recent burial. On one occasion he had discovered at West Thurrock the bones of a mammoth which were laid out as if the animal had been recently interred. Abbot said that he too had excavated the Galley Hill pit and had found numerous Palaeolithic implements.

J. Allan Brown thought the meeting was being over-cautious. In Brown's opinion, a more authenticated case of antiquity would be hard to find. He firmly believed in the continuity of mankind from the Palaeolithic through to the Neolithic. There had been no gap, said Brown, so why was it so surprising that a skeleton had been found which showed affinities with both periods?

Professor W. J. Sollas of Oxford regretted that the evidence presented to the meeting was not more perfect. Heys, said Sollas, had seen the skull *in situ* but only for a few minutes; on the other hand, Elliot's evidence was less open to question. On the whole, said Sollas, the anatomical characters showed that the Galley Hill skull was of the same type as those found at Neanderthal and Spy, so he thought it highly probable that the British specimen was not a recent burial.

So Professor Sollas, a leading geologist, was convinced that Neanderthal man had been found in Kent. Gason, Brown and Abbot supported him. Evans was not sure, and Boyd Dawkins, another leading palaeontologist, was strongly against the proposition.

In the event Galley Hill man passed to the British Museum as a rather late version of Neanderthal man. He was in fact a modern man, as suspected by Evans and Dawkins.

This debate provides an illustration of how enthusiasm can over-ride all other considerations, a not too infrequent occurrence in the case of fossil men. Animal remains and flint implements found over a wide area, and dubious pebbles claimed to be Palaeolithic, were all grist to the mill of the enthusiasts. We have also met W. J. Lewis Abbot, a curious, busy, dark-bearded little fellow, who was to play a minor role in the Piltdown controversy. In fact he claimed to have directed the attention of Charles Dawson to the antique gravel at Piltdown. As his kind was not untypical of the chronic enthusiast for 'antiquities' which throve about this time and into the 1930s, he deserves closer examination.

Abbot was a compulsive dabbler and in his own estimation an ignored scientific genius. At the time of the Galley Hill meeting he worked at Benson's, the London jewellers, but even as a young apprentice clockmaker he had been won over by T. H. Huxley's evolutionary biology as defined in *Evidences*. Self-educated, Abbot gave evening lectures on gem-stones at the Regent Street Polytechnic, London. He was one of a group of amateur antiquaries which formed about Benjamin Harrison. Like many others he had become infected with the cult of the eolith.

But in the 1890s Lewis forsook Benson's – and Harrison – and started a small shop on his own account at Hastings, Sussex. Possibly the grocer overshadowed him and he looked for fresh fields of undiminished authority. This move was rewarded. In the eastern Sussex coastal town he became the local fount of spurious geological information and general oracle on pre-historic archaeology. Indeed this esteem reached as far as the Geological Society in London. Everything was 'new' to him. He disinterred 'new' species of prehistoric mammals and reptiles, 'new' types of implements, which, if not immediately acceptable as such to Science, would be acknowledged – or so thought Abbot – in the fullness of time.

Abbot's great discovery was the 'Hastings Kitchen Midden men', a 'Neolithic' culture now known to be non-existent. His papers on scientific subjects multiplied, each one shamelessly plugging his discoveries, each a masterpiece in the art of the throw-away line which bolstered his scientific reputation. He demonstrated his method at the Galley Hill meeting by his carefree reference to the mammoth, while seeming to support Elliot and Newton. Lacking academic training, he gave the impression of such by peppering his writings with 'oids', 'isms' and 'iths'.

Some of Abbot's finds were genuine, however. For his work on Pleistocene fissures he was awarded 'the proceeds of the

Lyell fund' by the Geological Society. He opened a museum at his Hastings shop, which unfavourably affected his trade as clock and watch repairer without providing any pecuniary return, and unprofitably sold lantern slides illustrating his views on prehistoric anthropology. He got into financial difficulties, and out of them, with a frequency which dismayed his more staid contemporaries.

9

With the passing of such men as Darwin, Lyell, Falconer, Huxley, Prestwich and Evans, there was a perceptible dimming of the light of reasoned argument. In its place grew a predilection for the raspberry-flavoured wrangle. Alleged fossil human bones were found, described, disputed and ridiculed and rejected. Caves in Wales were discovered by one authority, only for it to be asserted that they had been explored years before by another. What a so-called 'discoverer' had mistakenly interpreted as the scratches of Ice-Age glaciers were in fact marks of the pickaxes of the real finder.

Popular Science Monthly (May 1903) was enlivened by a report of the find of a fossil man at Lansing, Kansas. The author said Lansing man was of very much the same stature as the Palaeolithic man of Europe, although he could be a woman. At roughly the same time Worthington G. Smith reported to the Geological Society the find of a human skeleton with Palaeolithic implements at Round Green, north of Luton, Bedfordshire. Unfortunately, said Smith, a temporary distraction had enabled the workmen to make off with the bones, causing them to fall to pieces during the rough usage. This news was received indifferently, as more likely to interest the police than a learned society.

Clearly British palaeontology was in the doldrums. The demand for news of discoveries, any kind of discovery, was insatiable. As a result all sorts of oddities were offered as evidence of Palaeolithic man in Britain. Pebbles alien to a district were claimed to have been brought there in antiquity by primitive hunters. Chalk bearing scratches, 'pot-boilers', stone 'loom-weights', played similar roles. Sticks with knotholes were revealed as 'arrow-straighteners', with knobs on one end as clubs, or with neither knob nor hole, as '*bâtons de commandement*'. The baton was supported by the intriguing reasoning that as primitive man wore no clothes he would need to carry some distinguishing stick as a badge of rank. A letter to *Nature*[1] said, however, that these sticks were in fact 'pomagans' or strikers. An example, said the writer, could be seen held in the hand of a North American Indian carved on 'Colonel' Townshend's tombstone on the south side of the nave of Westminster Abbey.

To the nudity of primitive man was also ascribed his evident frequent discarding of stone implements. In a paper advancing this view, he was referred to as a 'pocketless wanderer'.

But all this was very small beer compared with the happenings across the Channel. And the English knew and resented it, for in *Man*[2] appeared an article which was nothing more than a send-up of French enthusiasm. No reason other than pique could have prompted the editor of the magazine to consider that the tenor of the report on the first session of the *Congrès Préhistorique de France* held in September 1905 would be acceptable to his readers.

Although the report was anonymous, the touch is unmistakably that of Mark Twain. Certainly Samuel L. Clemens was in Europe at the time of the congress on a lecture tour. The writer found it impossible to enumerate all the scientific papers that were read but found them all of peculiar and rare interest. He described a visit paid by the congress to the nearby prehistoric sites of La Madeleine and Laugerie Haut, where 'everyone fell upon the debris with any instrument which was ready to his hand: lance-heads were extracted with walking-sticks and [flint] scrapers with umbrellas'. Clemens told how he descended into a deep and dark cave and of the terror which prompted him to think that no cave man could have painted the animal murals for fun. The low roof, according to the famous author, 'bristled with stalactites, impartially distributing wounds and contusions with unpleasant frequency'. The congress was concluded 'with the need for literary expression which stirs any large gathering of Frenchmen', being satisfied with two poems which 'pictured in verse of excellent quality the heroic struggle of primitive races with nature and fierce beasts.'

But diluvian man was now highly acceptable to the officers of the *Académie des Sciences*. He had gained entry by the sheer exuberance of his proponents. This acceptance was also possibly given impetus by a wave of militant atheism and anti-clericalism which seriously rivalled that of the First Republic.

After its sluggish start French prehistoric archaeology and palaeontology had overtaken and well outstripped their British counterparts. For example, at the second *Congrès Préhistorique* at Vannes, Brittany, in 1906, there were some thirty scientific communications producing a *Comptes rendus* of some seven hundred pages. At the third at Solutré in 1907, there were some forty papers producing a thousand pages; the fourth at Chambéry, Savoy, in 1908 produced one of nine hundred pages. This was after a strict attempt had been made to reduce the number of contributions, which now threatened to get out of hand.

These congresses, omitting the humour, were reported in envious tones in Britain's *Man* and *Nature*. Certainly the continentals had their controversies but these were conducted with an enthusiasm far removed from the parsimony of the English *chasseurs de cailloux* (pebble hunters), as the French disparagingly called them.

There was good reason for this sense of superiority. The French primitive man hunt had borne more fruit. Under the direction of the Prince of Monaco, excavations in the Principality in the caves of Baoussé-Roussé had produced two skeletons – adult and child – both of which presented very strong negroid features. But, as the describer Dr R. Verneau hastened to point out, the skeletons were not of true negroes but of a type somewhere between the Cro-Magnons and the Spy (Neanderthaloid) race, thus contributing a third ethnic element to the French fossil catalogue.

It might be noticed that the original Neanderthal man was now ignored in favour of the one found in Belgium. This did not intrude too much on Gallic priority.

Flint implements were being found in abundance, giving rise to the French names of the cultures which are still with us: Acheulean (St Acheul), Chellean (Chelles), Magdalenian (La Madelaine), Solutrean (Le Solutré), Aurignacian (Aurignac), Levalloisian (Levallois-Perret, Paris), Tayacian (Tayac, Les Eyzies), and Mousterian (Le Moustier). The last-named flint culture was found in such abundance with the bones of Neanderthal men that until comparatively recently the human fossil was referred to as Mousterian man or *Homo Mousteriensis*, a fact of which France was particularly proud.

There were many such finds of Neanderthal men in France. A portion of skull was found in a brickfield at Brechamps, Eure-et-Loire (1892), a complete skeleton at La Chapelle-aux-Saints, Dordogne (1908), the remains of possibly six skeletons in a rock shelter at La Ferrassie, Dordogne (1911–13). All the discoveries follow the same general pattern, first finds of 'Mousterian' implements and then the Neanderthaloid bones.

From Chapelle-aux-Saints emerged a rare glimpse of what today is called 'humanity'. The Neanderthal skeleton, although considered to be that of an individual not more than forty years of age, was toothless and deformed by osteo-arthritis to such a degree that he could not have hunted meat for many years before death. About the skeleton of 'The Old Man of Chapelle-aux-Saints' were many small mammal bones, Mousterian implements and fragments of ochre suggesting a ritual interment. No great stretch of the imagination was required to deduce that despite the individual's economic uselessness he was important enough to warrant formal burial in the cave, that there was solicitude for the incapacitated. Such, anyway, is the interpretation, despite the discovery of the fragmented bones of some eighty Neanderthalers at Krapina, Yugoslavia – putative evidence that Neanderthal man was a cannibal.

In 1904 trouble arose over some recently discovered Rivière cave paintings. The primitive painters – almost certainly the Cro-Magnons – had illustrated their human subjects with a fine disregard for propriety. Most of the early-twentieth-century illustrators who were employed to copy the paintings omitted the huge genitalia for fear of giving offence. Some, however, were not so particular. Unfortunately, both versions – the virile and the castrated – came into the same hands and their owners were quick to conclude that someone was having an extremely vulgar joke at the expense of science, and that this someone was getting at the cave paintings. This threw doubt on the authenticity of the whole picture gallery, both human and animal. But the problem was quickly resolved. Albert Jean Gaudry was able to reassure his fellow members of the *Académie* that the offensive drawings were covered with the same smears of clay as the inoffensive ones. This was positive proof of antiquity. Oddly enough similar disbelief sprang from an identical cause some thirty years later when more cave paintings were discovered at Lascaux.

There was more trouble some four or five years later. It was a case of archaeological body-snatching which particularly incensed French palaeontologists and acquired an exaggerated significance because the site concerned was Le Moustier, French heartland of flint implement discovery. The culprits, said Marcellin Boule darkly,[1] 'came from beyond the Rhine'. The names in the indictment sound like a *mitrailleuse* – 'Klaatsch, Virchow, von der Steine, Hahne, Wüst and others'. According to Boule, one Hauser, a Swiss dealer in antiquities 'who had only too long exploited for German profit the deposits of the Dordogne, that is to say the most valuable archives in France', had revealed how he was paid the enormous sum of 125,000 francs. He admitted that with his connivance a party of German scientists had exhumed a human skeleton at Le Moustier.

Boule continued that the scientific value of the relic was remarkably diminished by the 'poverty' of significant stratigraphical and palaeontological evidence and by the 'deplorable' manner in which the skull was restored by the anatomist Klaatsch. A second reconstruction in which Klaatsch was aided by several distinguished colleagues was slightly more faithful, the third was manifestly inadequate. Even the fourth reconstruction was still very imperfect, according to a countryman, H. Taeger. Klaatsch, however, was unrepentant. In his scientific description he said that the skeleton was that of a youth of sixteen years who had been found lying on his right side with legs slightly bent and head pillowed on a pile of flint flakes. Mousterian implements were deposited about the skull and 'the most beautifully worked of all the implements' lay within reach of the left hand. The skeleton was presented to the *Museum für Volkerkunde*, Berlin.

Germany made another contribution in 1907 – a jawbone from a sandpit at Mauer, near Heidelberg. This massive mandible with modest teeth excited little comment, apart from an initial quibble which likened it to the jaw of an orang-utan. From the accompanying animal fossil remains, Heidelberg man is now placed at the First Interglacial or Second Glaciation (Mindel).

Although the cult of the eolith was also detectable in France by the end of the first decade of the twentieth century, for Britain it seems to have acted as a kind of insulation against thoughts of Gallic supremacy, certainly if the number of articles, lectures and exhibitions on the subject is any guide. Of the amateurs, and it must be admitted the cult was fostered mainly by amateurs, S. Hazzledene Warren led the unbelievers. J. Reid Moir and our old friend J. Lewis Abbot were strong for the faith. But by far the most powerful supporter of eoliths was a professional, Sir Ray Lankester, a director of the British Museum.

Lankester, a former pupil of T. H. Huxley, was a large rumbullion of a man with an immense literary output ranging from the life of the tsetse fly to prehistoric archaeology. In addition to his scientific works Lankester was a regular contributor of 'science for the layman' articles to the *Daily Telegraph* and semi-scientific and popular journals. With this large outlet for his opinions he was a powerful ally of any view he favoured and an almost insuperable adversary to any he did not.

At the age of seventy years Lankester embraced the cause of the eolith with a Johnsonian gusto. After an illustrated lecture before the Royal Society, as a prelude to the discussion that normally followed, Lankester hoped 'that no one would venture to waste the time of the society by suggesting that sub-crag flints (a kind of eolith promoted by J. Reid Moir) had been flaked by natural causes, as by so doing it would be plain that they had a very scanty knowledge of such matters.' The president, Sir Archibald Geikie, although himself a believer in eoliths, saw that the cause of free opinion was being subverted and called on the meeting to ignore the outburst, urging the members 'in spite of what Sir Ray Lankester had said, to express their opinions freely'. One did, only to be told by Lankester that he had been listening with 'amazement to the sort of thing I would expect to hear from a savage'.

On another occasion, following a talk given to the Society by Lankester, Worthington Smith said that nothing would induce him to believe in the pebbles. He said: 'We have here choppers that do not chop and borers that do not bore.' 'You, sir,' said Lankester, 'are a bore who does bore.'

The old man did not confine his homilies to the lecture room. A friend's wife hoped that he would not take any notice of the foolish womanly things she had said, and was informed 'gravely' that 'they were nothing to the foolish things your husband said'.

The collector of these anecdotes of the scientist's irascibility was J. Reid Moir[4] and as they advanced the cause of the eoliths by making Lankester's victims seem ineffectual and stupid they are not beyond suspicion. To the contrary, Lankester's writings suggest a calm, reasoned, perceptive approach. It is possible, however, that advancing age and ill-health lent him an intolerant attitude regarding what had been a life study of flint implements. As a young man he had visited Abbeville and one of the favourites of his large collection of flint implements was an artificially stained implement which he said had been given him by Boucher de Perthes.

Flint implements of one kind or another were the main diet of the British palaeontologist. Finds were reported from India, Mombasa and Somaliland, in Chinese Turkestan and German East Africa, near the south end of the Victoria Nyanza, and in Egypt. The most important find was some Neanderthal teeth in Jersey, Channel Islands, during excavations conducted by the *Société Jersaise*, but this did not bring much solace, being too near the French mainland, and apart from lengthy reports in *The Antiquarian* was little noticed.

10

In 1903 Professor Johnson Symmington, titular head of the Royal College of Surgeons, in his presidential address apprised the British Association's anthropological section of the marked similarity between the skull of Neanderthal man and that of a chimpanzee. But, cautioned Symmington, as nothing would ever be known of the kind of brain the fossil skull had contained any conclusions arising from the similarity were a waste of time.

This sweeping observation went unchallenged by the meeting. No contradiction would ever be offered at the time as a matter of precedent, but no British anatomist seems to have objected.

The rock which disturbed this tranquil pool of acquiescence came from Egypt. It was thrown by one of those brilliant young men who from time to time take their branch of science by the coat-tails and pull them irreverently. One such man was T. H. Huxley. Another was the Australian-born Grafton Elliot Smith. In a letter to *Nature*[1] he said that Symmington's statement was nonsense. Had he not, asked Smith, heard of a brain cast? If not, this was strange as there were many in the collection in the Hunterian Museum of the Royal College of Surgeons. Although, said the writer, he had better ones in his collection at Cairo. He also thought it surprising to find that such an eminent professor of anatomy was repeating 'the time-worn fallacy' that the interior frontal convolution of the brain was known to be more highly developed in man than in the apes. Anyone aware of the true facts would advise him that in this region the ape was relatively much bigger than man. Symmington did not deign to reply.

It would be convenient to encapsulate Smith as the irreverent but brilliant young man of science, but it is perceptible that he possessed certain other disquieting attributes. He frequently sword-slashed at lesser lights with apparent conceit and superiority. He also thought himself, and was, a humorist. He reported his scientific repartee faithfully to his colleagues, with the inevitable outcome that the tail began to wag the dog.

Smith had arrived in England from New South Wales in 1896, with an H.B. and a gold medal for his M.D. thesis on the brain of non-placental mammals, and to his credit eleven well-received papers on the cerebrum, cerebellum and olfaction in primitive mammals. He continued anatomical research at St John's College, Cambridge, lodging with Mrs Worral, an aunt and Indian Army widow who, according to his friends, talked amusingly and smoked pungent cheroots. The nephew was a great favourite with the widow who was reported to be 'unconventional' although in what way this manifested itself is not known.

A Fellow of Smith's College was the renowned anatomist, Alexander Macalister. Macalister seems to have favourably impressed his other students. Smith wrote of the don[2] that he was a very busy man but implied that his extra-mural distractions kept him so. He continued that:

He seems to be intensely devoted to Anthropology of, I am sorry to say, the bone measuring variety and devotes all his time that is not absorbed in Early Christian History and Oriental Philology to the personal superintendence of the work in the Anatomical School.

Not a bad start for a new arrival, even such a well-qualified one. But two months later[3] he amplified the theme, writing:

I see a good deal of Macalister. His chief anatomical interest is anthropological. If anything delights him more than inventing a new craniometric index it is the manufacture of some cacophonous name to brand it. But he is equally interested in Egyptian history, in Irish and Gaelic literature and archaeology, in the Evolution of Ecclesiastical Vestments, in the Cambridge collegiate system, in the specific identity of the Egyptian cat, and the progress of the Cambridge Presbyterian Church, among more or less (principally less) kindred subjects.

From the first Smith seems to have been unimpressed by Macalister's impersonal teaching methods, divorced as they were from any contact with a live subject. This was then the customary method of teaching anatomy. The late T. H. Huxley had been of the same opinion as Smith. In fact, the Australian unashamedly confessed that he was a staunch admirer of the great man. He had been impressed in youth by Huxley's *Principles*. One wonders whether Smith fancied the Huxleian role himself.

In Smith's obituary in *The Times*[4] a colleague praised him for his 'child-like simplicity of approach to scientific trust' and said that 'his work was done in spasms, periods of idleness alternating with bursts of intense energy'. The first observation is too open to individual interpretation to be of much use and the second is certainly undetectable in his early career. Between 1896 and 1897 he published eight papers on cerebral morphology and began a descriptive catalogue of the brain collection at the Royal College of Surgeons. In 1899 he was elected Fellow of his college after three years' residence, five years' qualification being normal. Between 1900 and 1909, during which time he became the first professor of anatomy in the new government medical school at Cairo, he published fifty anatomical papers on the brain of extinct and modern mammals. While employed, with others, on the ambitious Archaeological Survey of Nubia, a part of which involved the examination of some twenty thousand prehistoric burials and the collection of 'sixty-four cases of remains', he also paid visits to the United Kingdom to take an active part in council meetings of the Anatomical Society, in Dublin in 1906, in Birmingham in 1907.

In the main, Smith's vacations were spent either in England or abroad taking part in archaeological digs, or as he termed it 'bone-grubbing'. At the Birmingham meeting he presented several communications. He recalled a month later that he:

... was talking on the pelvic fascia ... and no one raised a word of protest against my heresies. When I read a paper on the anatomical localization of the human cortex, Paterson got up and in a rather insolent tone asked: 'What was the use of it all?' I replied that: 'I did not think it was necessary to explain to the Anatomical Society my reasons for studying the anatomy of the human body.'

Although Smith was Boswell to his own Johnson the minutes of the meeting said the sally was 'greeted with tumultuous applause'.

In 1907 Smith was elected to the Fellowship of the Royal Society and in 1909 he was offered the chair of anatomy at the University of Manchester, which he accepted. He was thirty-eight years of age.

Grafton Elliot Smith's impact on the teaching of anatomy at Manchester University was swift and revolutionary. Smith believed that the teaching of anatomy, the most venerable subject in the medical curriculum, needed a drastic reappraisal. The traditional dissection of the cadaver, the *tour de force* of the medical student, seemed to him to be divorced from its objective. Smith did not pioneer the use of X-ray equipment, the living model, the introduction of a live patient to demonstrate the facts of the structure and function of the body, but in 1909 such teaching methods approached innovation. Certainly few had realized their value.

The dissecting room at Manchester assumed a new spirit. Through intimate contact with the students he was extremely popular although, according to his biographers, he rated the average student's intelligence too high, and many were unable to keep pace with his mental agility. Dr Davidson Black, a Canadian from the Western Reserve University, Ontario, who came to Manchester to do neurological work, fell under his spell. He became so interested in Smith's preoccupation with anthropology that he transferred to the study and making of human brain casts. It was reported that there was mutual understanding and affection and that this was the happiest period of Smith's life.

But Smith suffered from the kind of distractions he criticized in his mentor at Cambridge. Like Macalister, he interested himself in matters unconnected with anatomy. He investigated the origins of magic and religion, the early migrations of man and the diffusion of culture, and with ease found lively opposition to his views. That he enjoyed controversy for its own sake is illustrated by his delight in the rage which greeted his assertion that a carving at the Mayan city of Copan in the West Honduras was of an elephant. He recalled how a group of experts in Mayan archaeology afforded the spectacle of being united to prove him wrong while unable to agree amongst themselves whether the carving was of an extinct mammoth, macaw, tortoise, tapir or squid.

His enthusiasm for fun was not widely known; his brilliance was. And he used his ascendancy to belabour his adversaries. His big opportunity came at the British Association meeting at Aberdeen in 1912 where during his address as president of

Section H (Anthropology) he gave full rein to his intolerance of the attitudes of many of the assembled anthropologists and anatomists.

Concluding a lengthy harangue, he said that comparative anatomy could supply the evidence needed and its neglect was due in large measure to the singularly futile pretensions of some of the foremost anatomists who opposed Darwin's view at the British Association more than forty years before. Smith referred to Owen's contention about the *hippocampus minor* and described Charles Kingsley's ridicule as apt and justified. This, he said, served as an illustration of the nature of the discussions which distracted men's minds from the real problem.

Smith then gave his views on the evolution of man, that towards the close of the Cretaceous (some seventy million years ago) some small arboreal shrew-like creature had taken another step forward, that there was a reduction in the part of the brain occupied by the sense of smell in favour of that of vision. This enhanced sight and awakened curiosity to examine, supplied guidance for hands to perform more precise and skilled movement. Smith believed that the genius of man's intellectual pre-eminence was thus sown at the dawn of the Tertiary. The first primates were small, humble folk, leading unobtrusive and safe lives in trees, taking no part in the fierce competition waged below by their carnivorous and other brethren. Instead man's ancestor had cultivated equable development of senses and limbs and special development of the more intellectually useful faculties of the mind. In learning to execute with delicate precision movements to which no ape could attain, which the primitive ape-man could only attempt once his arms were completely emancipated, 'that cortical area [of the brain] which seemed to serve for the phenomenon of attention became enhanced in importance'.

He then said:

Hence the prefrontal region, where the activities of the cortex as a whole are focussed and regulated, began to grow until eventually it became the most distinctive characteristic of the human brain, gradually filling out the front of the cranium, producing the distinctly human forehead. However large the brain may be in *Homo primigenius* [Neanderthal man] his small prefrontal region is sufficient evidence of his lowly state of intelligence and the reason for his failure in the competition with the rest of mankind.

Smith leant heavily on Huxley for his hypothesis but ignored the biologist's plea for more inductive reasoning and less philosophizing. But the speaker's contribution was unique inasmuch as he rejected hypotheses which distinguished fossil men more by their differences from modern human beings than by their similarities. A number of those responsible were present.

His address was uncompromising. His allusion to twentieth-century anatomists with nineteenth-century attitudes was received with an angry growl. It must have appealed to Smith's sense of humour to be able to rib his colleagues in a formal presidential address, which by tradition was sacrosanct. But the opportunity for revenge did arise.

In the absence of a Mr Peet, Smith read the absentee's paper which proposed that megalithic monuments had originated in Egypt and had spread to Western Europe with the migration of their builders. The spread of culture by migration was a subject dear to the heart of Smith. In fact, it became an obsession. Smith incorrectly believed that all culture had a single place of origin; that no two races living in different parts of the earth could have duplicated inspiration. All culture, he argued, had to be transmitted by physical contact of one tribe with another, and on a larger scale, by one race with another. Indeed Smith could have written Peet's paper himself.

According to the report of the meeting in *Nature*[5] 'strong exception was taken to this theory which derived the round form of Western European megalithic monuments from the square Egyptian variety . . . the views of the paper were very strongly criticized'.

This description of the reception of the paper, read by Smith and reflecting his own views, was strong meat in the subdued parlance of such a journal and almost certainly meant shouting and thrown papers. Those mainly responsible, as must be suspected, were the stick-in-the-mud theorists scathingly referred to by Smith in his address. The objectors named by *Nature* were the professors Boyd Dawkins, Ridgeway, Myers and Bryce.

Amongst the other papers before the British Association that year was one by the forty-seven-year-old anatomist and palaeontologist Professor Arthur Keith, keeper of the Hunterian collection of the Royal College of Surgeons and lately president of the Anthropological Institute. He held the same progressive views on the teaching of anatomy as Smith, who was six years his junior, but they never quite hit it off. Certainly the future Piltdown controversy did not make for cordiality but it is possible that Keith considered the Australian to be a maverick and held himself aloof. They were dissimilar personalities. Smith was an elocutionist. Keith spoke slowly, with the suspicion of an Aberdeen accent, slightly hesitant. He was, however, a skilful writer, with a keen-edged style which must have made an adversary timorous of opening a scientific journal. But there seems to have been little malice in him, only a soft, good-humoured, occasionally testy, impatience. Smith would sneer where Keith would gently and convincingly show the offender the error of his ways.

His arguments, nevertheless, were sometimes highly controversial and challenging. Much later, in 1931, he enraged an entire pacifist England by referring to war as little other than 'Nature's pruning hook'.

At the Dublin meeting Keith said that recent discoveries in the Dordogne showed that Neanderthal man was confined to a late period in the Pleistocene, therefore we must go much further back in time to find man's ancestral form. By the middle of the Pleistocene at least, said Keith, long before 'Mousterian Neanderthal man' had appeared in France, modern man had appeared in England, as proved by datable human fossils found in this country. Keith said the most likely places where further proof of the fact might be obtained were the Pliocene and Pleistocene deposits of East Anglia. Particular care must be taken to watch every quarry and excavation so that no remains were discarded as lacking in scientific interest just because they resembled those of modern man. Keith illustrated his lecture with a plaster cast of the now long-forgotten Neanderthal man of Gibraltar.

This speech was delivered in Keith's usual style, without notes, but it was in fact a curious one. It is now accepted that Neanderthal man was a comparative latecomer compared with the earlier hominids such as *Pithecanthropus* and *Australopithecus*. But Keith's reference to English fossils which supported this view is inexplicable, unless he had heard a whisper of the developments at Piltdown. There was Galley Hill man, but this fossil was thought to belong to the Neanderthal race. And Keith had no faith in this specimen. He certainly was not referring to the Kent's Cavern fossil.

At the same meeting, W. L. Duckworth made an ambitious claim for the Kent's Cavern jaw, forgotten since its discovery in 1867. Now Duckworth claimed that undoubtedly the jaw belonged to a Neanderthal man and was the first example to be found in this country.

Keith remained silent as Duckworth's Neanderthal man was trotted out, but after the session he told a reporter from *The Times* that he considered the whole affair ridiculous and unscientific. He told the newspaper that nobody seemed to know anything about the jaw, for example the depth in the cave floor at which the bone was found.

The outcry was immediate and intense, giving the impression that the jaw's proponents had been waiting for fifty years or so for an excuse to stage a demonstration. A dozen or more letters to *Nature*[6] said that William Pengelly had been most particular to note in his diary all the relevant particulars about the discovery of the jaw.

Keith was astounded. He said in a footnote to the correspondence that he was being misjudged. His sole object had been to draw attention to the fact that a claim that Neanderthal man had been found in Britain was supported merely by a rough sketch of a jaw which looked nothing like it. Keith said that he fully believed that Neanderthal man might one day be discovered in this country – Duckworth might even be right in regarding the Kent's Cavern jaw as such – but no discovery could be accepted unless the evidence was produced.

Then where was the famous jaw? The remains had been presented to the British Museum in 1870 where they had lain ever since. Duckworth was allowed to sketch the fragment but that was all. The museum authorities feared the hacksaw and hydrochloric acid of the enthusiasts might deprive them of the fossil altogether. Many demands were made that the bone should be produced for testing, that it should be placed on display or be made more accessible for examination. The British Museum refused.

This impasse brought an outburst-cum-puff from Hastings. J. Lewis Abbot wrote:[7]

Will you kindly allow me, as one who has made considerable additions to our Pleistocene fauna, vertebrate and invertebrate, to support the appeal for the resurrection of that vast amount of material now stored away that was obtained at Kent's Cavern? Those of us who have paid close attention to the subject are aware that the recorded lists give us but a poor idea of what the cave could tell, that from the waste dumps [Abbot's spurious Kitchen Midden Men] have been obtained a large number of new species, and even from the lowest layers these bones include those of man himself. In these circumstances we feel that the time has come, not only for this material to be put into competent hands, but for the caves to be reworked on modern lines and in the light of recent research.

Keith later came out fully against the Kent's Cavern jaw, writing that the teeth it contained differed only from those of modern Englishmen in a high degree of wear and complete freedom from disease. Keith was right. Abbot's plea for further excavation of the cave was answered, but the search was un-successful. In 1925, however, a Mr Powe, extending his garden, dug into the face of the limestone cliff near the north entrance of the cave and recovered fragments of a human skull. When assembled at the Royal College of Surgeons by Keith the skull, which was 'of the same colour and consistency' as the Neander-thal jaw, was found to be that of a modern woman.

There were fears for attendance at Dundee, for the Associa-tion's annual meeting coincided with the 14th International Congress of Anthropology and Prehistoric Archaeology at Geneva. They were justified. The counter-attraction proved too much for the hoped-for guests. For French palaeontology the congress was as a Nuremberg rally for the Nazis.

French was the official language of the congress. It had for-merly been English. Of the two hundred papers presented, only five were not of French origin. Marcellin Boule rose to state that only twenty authenticated Neanderthal men had been discovered and none, he said pointedly, were English. Professor Emile Carthailac delighted the meeting with a lecture on Palaeolithic cave murals of France and Spain, which was illustrated with lantern slides in line and colour of paintings of bison, reindeer, elephant and horse, and even impressions of the cave-dwellers' hands. The Abbé H. Breuil, *the* expert on the Aurignacian flint culture, gave a lecture on it.

Also several references were made to a new *Institut de palaeon-tologie humaine*. It marked, it was said, 'a new era in research pertaining to fossil men', and was international in conception. In fact, the faculty was composed of three Frenchmen and one

Belgian. Delegates came from all parts of the world, including two from Australia and several from the United States, but there was no official British representative. There was, however, one Englishman present. Reginald Smith of the British Museum asked whether there was a resemblance between the flints found in the chalk of his native country and those of Aurignac.

There was yet another sensational Gallic find. *The Times*[8] gave an account of a remarkable discovery by Count Begouen and his son of clay animal figures, a bull and cow bison, in a cave at Ariège, where three months previously Palaeolithic murals had come to light. The floor of the gallery was found to be impressed with about fifty human heel-marks 'suggesting ritual dances and observances similar to those of the present-day natives of Australia and Africa'. A large number of engraved pieces of bone and ivory depicting animals were also recovered.

The one bright spot for English prehistorians was the result of a visit to England by 'the Professor Abbé Breuil, the greatest authority on Aurignacian remains', according to *Nature*. As a consequence, Professor W. J. Sollas and the abbé departed from Oxford for a tour of caves in the region of Gower, Wales. Both were hopeful of finding wall paintings. A halt was first made at Swansea to examine a collection of flints found at Paviland (Wales). These were identified by Breuil as Upper Aurignacian, some proto-Solutrean. Thus heartened the pair began their systematic search, beginning with the caves of Paviland in the west, working eastwards. As hope began to wane, said *Nature*, as cave after cave failed to yield any signs of paintings, as they entered Bacon's Hole at the extreme eastward end of the search, some colour was seen on the right-hand wall. Closer examination revealed ten bright red bands arranged in a vertical series, perhaps a foot in length. The stalagmite which tapestried the wall completely sealed the red pigment so that it could not be removed by rubbing. Breuil, an enthusiastic little man who closely resembled an advertisement for Gauloises, said that a similar arrangement of bands, but only eight, had been found at the end of the Great Gallery in the Font de Gaunna, Dordogne.

British human palaeontology had to be content with this superior wall decoration and a small rattle of disputed human fossils.[9] Eoliths, however, were being found in greater numbers.

At this point *Nature*,[10] after the obituaries, announced in *Item 8* of *Notes* that:

Remains of a human skull and mandible, considered to belong to the early Pleistocene period, have been discovered by Mr Charles Dawson in a gravel-deposit in the basin of the River Ouse, north of Lewes, Sussex. Much interest has been aroused in the specimen owing to the exactitude with which its geological age is said to have been fixed, and it will form the subject of a paper by Mr Dawson and Dr Smith Woodward to be read before the Geological Society on 18 December [1912].

One week later, on 12 December, *Nature* reported at greater length:

The fossil human skull and mandible to be described by Mr Charles Dawson and Dr Arthur Smith Woodward as we go to press is the most important discovery of its kind hitherto made in England. The specimen was found in circumstances which seem to leave no doubt of its geological age, and the characters it shows are themselves sufficient to denote its extreme antiquity. It [the remains] was met with in a gravel which was deposited by the River Ouse near Piltdown Common, Fletching, Sussex, at a time when the river level flowed at a level eighty feet above its present course. Although the basin of the stream is now within the Weald and far removed from the chalk, the gravel consists of iron-stained flints closely resembling those well-known in gravel deposits on the downs and among these are many waterworn eoliths identical with those found on the chalk plateau near Ightham, Kent. With the flints were discovered two fragments of the molar tooth of a Pliocene elephant and a waterworn cusp of the molar of a mastodon. The gravel therefore is partly made up of the remains of a Pliocene land-deposit. The teeth of hippopotamus, beaver and horse, and part of the antler of red deer were also found, with several unabraded early Palaeolithic implements. The latter seem to determine the gravel as Lower Pleistocene. The human remains, which are in the same mineralised condition as the associated fragments of the other mammals, comprise the greater part of the braincase and one mandibular ramus which lacks the upper portion of the symphysis ... the bones [of the skull] are nearly twice the normal thickness ... the brain capacity is about 1,700 c.c. ... The forehead is much steeper than in the Neanderthal type, with only a feeble brow ridge; and the back of the skull is remarkably low and broad, indicating an ape-shaped neck. The mandible ... is identical in form with that of a young chimpanzee, showing even the characteristically simian inwardly curved flange of bone at the lower border of the retaining symphysis. The two molars preserved are of the human pattern, but completely long and narrow. At least one very low type of man with a high forehead was therefore in existence in Western Europe long before the low-browed Neanderthal man became widely spread in this region. Dr Smith Woodward accordingly inclines to the theory that the Neanderthal race was a degenerate offshoot of early man while surviving modern man may have arisen directly from the primitive source of which the Piltdown skull provides the first discovered evidence.

As can be seen, not only was it asserted that Piltdown man was far older than Neanderthal man, it was immediately proposed that Neanderthal man was a freak, that the only real ancestor of modern man was represented by the remains found in Sussex. British palaeontology rubbed its hands with pleasure.

11

A fugitive from the surge of French anti-clericalism which aided fossil man's acceptance by the *Académie* was a novice of the Society of Jesus, Marie-Joseph Pierre Teilhard de Chardin. This enmity had driven the Society's scholars from France and Teilhard de Chardin had been dispatched first to Egypt, then to the Channel Islands, to continue his training.

In 1909, at the age of eighteen, Teilhard de Chardin was at the Society's scholasticate at Ore Place, an ugly, red-brick edifice on the hill above Hastings. The student's days were spent in the study of theology, a subject which he found boring. His extra-mural activities sustained him, however, and he seems to have been delighted by all he saw of Sussex.

Teilhard de Chardin wrote home to describe Hastings as the '*Cannes de l'Angleterre*'. His letters to the family home, three kilometres from the village of Orcines, near Clermont, in the Massif Central, bubbled with accounts of elegant Eastbourne, of Winchelsea, Wadhurst, Bodiam, Camber, Rye, Folkestone, Hythe, of snails and whisky at Battle Fair, of Selsey and Chichester. But Teilhard de Chardin's primary interest was the geology of the chalk of the Sussex Weald, which was notable for the fossil remains of iguanodons and other saurians.

Evidently geology was not a new interest. As a boy he had collected pebbles and geological curios. When a juvenile at the Jesuit college of Notre Dame de Mongré at Villefranche-sur-Saône, this preoccupation, coupled with the Society's claim to teach the sanctification of science by religion and the service of religion by science, led him to his vocation. At the college he was rated brilliant but distracted. He attained first place in examinations without exertion but as geology had no place in the curriculum distinction did not impress him. A tutor, Henri Bremond, wrote of Teilhard de Chardin[1] that:

Thirty years ago one of my classical pupils was a little fellow from Auvergne, very intelligent, first in every subject, but disconcertingly well-behaved. The most backward and thick-skulled members of the class occasionally came alive, their eyes would light up when they were given something more thrilling to read and something more exciting to do. But he, never; and it was only a long time afterwards that I learnt the secret of his seeming indifference. Transporting his mind far away from us was another, a jealous and absorbing passion – *Stones*.

This was written when Teilhard de Chardin had an international reputation as a discoverer of Peking man and Piltdown man, and so there is a strong possibility that the recollection has benefited from hindsight. It is certain, however, that the student won but one prize for religious knowledge. His tutor's memory is possibly defective in one particular: the priest seems never to have been 'little'. He had the stature of his father, indeed both his parents, for his mother was a tall woman. A local farmer once remarked: 'I just met one of the little Teilhards – eight years old and not more than six feet tall.'

Teilhard de Chardin and a fellow student at Ore Place, Felix Pelletier, embarked, as a relaxation from the austerity of the theological instruction, on a self-imposed archaeological survey of Sussex. No doubt not a small part of the appeal was the freedom to wander about the English countryside. The religious persecution in France meant that even the sight of clericals provoked animosity, and civilian clothes had to be worn for safety. On 31 May 1909 he wrote to his father of a new friendship:

... I have made the acquaintance of a local geologist, Mr Dawson, in amusing circumstances. Visiting a local quarry near here [Hastings], we were astonished to see the manager prick up his ears when we talked to him of fossils. He had just discovered a huge bone of the pelvis of an iguanodon, and had [received] a telegram from Mr Dawson announcing his intention to visit the quarry. I have learnt since that the iguanodon was found pretty well intact, bit by bit, and that the fragments are being packed in a case to be sent to the British Museum. Mr Dawson turned up while we were still on the spot, and immediately came up to us with a happy air, saying: 'Geologists?' He lives at Newhaven, but he may be able to help us. At least we shall have someone we can inform about anything which is too big to manage ourselves.[2]

There is evidence that this meeting was not accidental. Arthur Smith Woodward[3] recounted how Dawson had learned of the visits of the Frenchmen from the quarrymen. Dawson rewarded the quarrymen for fossils brought to his attention. If Dawson wished, wrote Woodward, they would be glad to prevent these 'poachers' from entering the quarry. Woodward concluded this anecdote with:

Mr Dawson, with characteristic generosity and scientific zeal, replied that the workmen should rather welcome his fellow collectors, and he himself would give them the 'tips' of which they felt deprived. At the same time he asked about the customary days and hours of the Frenchmen's visits and soon made an opportunity to meet them in the quarries.

Woodward's interpretation of Dawson's direction to the workmen is possibly too generous. The part-time scrabblings of the Frenchmen could in no way be as productive of fossils as full-time quarrying. His offer to reward the workmen for directing their attention to finds would also be too much open to abuse and fiction; the poverty, even starvation level, of the quarry employees being well known. It is also an inescapable conclusion that Woodward came to hear of this generosity from Dawson himself. But Woodward always spoke well of Dawson. Their friendship was of long standing.

Charles Dawson, one of two sons of a barrister-at-law, was born at Fulkeith Hall, Lancashire, but the family moved to St Leonards-on-Sea, Sussex, while he was still a boy. His life followed a typical pattern: a boyhood passion for archaeology, then geology. He was guided by a keen amateur, S. H. Beckles, F.R.S., his schoolmaster at the Royal Academy, Gosport. In 1885, at the very early age of twenty-one, Dawson was elected to the Fellowship of the Geological Society. The previous year at Society meetings he had met Woodward, his lifelong scientific mentor, then a recently entered second-class assistant in the Geological Department at the British Museum, South Kensington, London. Woodward wrote of Dawson in an obituary[4] that:

He [Dawson] had a restless mind, ever alert to note anything unusual; and he was never satisfied until he had exhausted all means to solve and understand any problem which presented itself. He was a delightful colleague in scientific research, always cheerful, hopeful and overflowing with enthusiasm.

The only thing to be said for death is that one cannot be spoiled by one's obituaries, but in this case the praise is genuine. Dawson appears to have been generally liked. Arthur Keith wrote in his journal:[5] 'Charles Dawson comes to see me. A clever, level-headed man.' In his autobiography Keith wrote also of this first meeting: 'We had a pleasant hour together. His open, honest nature and his wide knowledge endeared him to me . . .' Teilhard de Chardin wrote of Dawson as '. . . methodical and enthusiastic' and said he was 'big, genial and enthusiastic . . .' An obituary in the *Hastings and East Sussex Naturalist* said of Dawson that he was:

. . . always cheerful, hopeful and overflowing with enthusiasm. The premature loss of his inspiring and genial presence is indeed a great sorrow to his large circle of devoted friends.

The oft-quoted enthusiasm for his hobby is amply illustrated in the variety of Dawson's output. Keith described him as 'the lawyer-antiquarian' and 'the exemplar of the English country amateur'. Dawson discovered natural gas at Heathfield, Sussex. The gas was used to illuminate the Geological Society meeting[6] to which the paper was presented, and Heathfield railway station thereafter. He exhibited a 'Toad in the Hole' – a fossil toad in a flint nodule – to the Linnean Society.[7] His private collection, purchased by the Hastings Museum after his death, included flint implements, bone objects, antique glass bottles, a cast-iron statuette said to be Roman, a Norman 'prickspur', and an anvil dated 1515.

Dawson published *Dene Holes and their Makers*, *A List of Wealden and Purbeck Wealden Fossils*, both in 1898, *A Description of the Battle of Beachy Head* (1899), *The Services of the Barons of the Cinque Ports at the Coronation of the Kings and Queens of England* (1901), *Sussex Ironwork and Pottery* (1902), *The Restoration of the Bayeux Tapestry* (1907), and a two-volume work, *The History of Hastings Castle* (1909). Professionally Dawson had a legal practice at Uckfield. He was also clerk to the magistrates of the Uckfield Petty Sessions Division, and to the Uckfield Urban Council. He was Steward of the manors of Netherfield and Cauwes and from 1898 of Barkham, three miles from Uckfield. From 1905, however, the year of Dawson's marriage, there is a perceptible dimming of Dawson's interest in his legal affairs in favour of his hobby. The bride was Mrs Hélène Postlethwaite, an attractive widow with a son. The Dawsons took up residence at Castle Lodge, which nestled in the ruins of the Angevin castle at Lewes.

Dawson befriended Teilhard de Chardin, introduced him to the Geological Society, and assisted him to make his first big discovery.

Dawson had been an honorary collector – a somewhat nebulous title – for the British Museum for some thirty years. During this time he had contributed three new species of iguanodon – a large extinct reptile – and one species of *Plagiaulex*, a small fossil mammal. A species of iguanodon and the *Plagiaulex* had been named in his honour. At a meeting of the Geological Society on 22 March 1911, which was little less than a public testimonial to Dawson, Woodward played the declaimer. He described how Dawson, since learning of Professor O. C. Marsh's discovery of early mammal bones in the grit of Wyoming, Kansas, over twenty years before, had searched similar deposits in Sussex. This was a search, said Woodward, of painstaking persistence and self-sacrifice. There was prolonged applause.

Dawson rose and thanked the speaker for his kind encouragement and willing readiness to assist in the identification of specimens. He said that during the last two years he had been favoured with the skill and assistance of Teilhard de Chardin and Felix Pelletier, to both of whom the ultimate success of the search was due.

Later in that year, in November, the partnership was further rewarded when A. C. Seward, professor of botany at Cambridge, gave more news of the activities of Dawson, Teilhard de Chardin and Pelletier to the Society. Commenting on a collection of fossil plants submitted to him by Dawson for examination, he said that although several of the specimens had been previously recorded, two had not. The result was *Lycopidites teilhardi* and *Salaginella dawsoni*.

Teilhard de Chardin described Arthur Smith Woodward as 'a little man, with grizzled hair, very hale and hearty, but externally rather cold'. He had come to the British Museum at eighteen years of age highly recommended by Professor W. Boyd Dawkins, his principal at Owens College, Manchester, as 'the best student in Geology and Palaeontology of his year'.[8]

Like Dawson, Woodward came from the North of England but he was the son of a Macclesfield silk-dyer and therefore lower in the social order. Educated at a local grammar school, Woodward launched into scientific authorship at the age of eleven with an account of a holiday in North Wales which included an appendix on the natural history and geology of the area. Two years later he printed this on his own press, producing a small *octavo* volume of about thirty pages.

Woodward went to Owens College to read chemistry but under the influence of Boyd Dawkins he soon turned to palaeontology. His success in competing for the post at the British Museum was despite the wishes of the keeper, Dr Henry Woodward, who not only had another candidate in mind but for some obscure reason disliked the idea of another unrelated Woodward in his department. Woodward's rapid transfer to paid employment was for reasons of finance rather than aspiration. He continued to educate himself at evening classes at King's College, London.

As Teilhard de Chardin seemed never to have looked small, Woodward had neglected to look young. He is always recollected as an intensely busy man, completely without humour, a devoted researcher and describer in his chosen field of fossil fishes, a field in which he became an international authority and probably the greatest palaeoicthyologist of his time. He was elected to the Geological Society on the same day and at the same early age as Charles Dawson. Henceforth the Proceedings of the Society seldom fail to mention him in some particular.

In 1896 he was already being referred to as 'an accomplished palaeontologist of the vertebrates' and credited with more than a hundred papers on fossil fishes. In that year he was awarded the Royal Society's Lyell medal. In 1898 he was elected to the council of the Society, which he relentlessly papered; on a new species of *Aerolepsis*, and the jaw of *Ptychodus* in 1903, on the fossil fishes of New South Wales (1905), on a new species of Chimeroid fish (1905), on the Cretaceous of Bahia and on a new dinosaur from Lossiemouth, Scotland (1907).

As vice-president of the Society in 1908 Woodward read a paper by the recently deceased Sir John Evans on Palaeolithic flints and proposed an amendment which would admit ladies to the Geological Society. From 1914 to 1916 he was president.

At the museum he was promoted to assistant keeper in 1892. From 1898 to 1901 was spent preparing a catalogue of the fossil fishes in the collection. In the latter year he became keeper and remained in this position until his retirement in 1924.

On 24 February 1912, Woodward received a letter from his old friend about the find in a very old Pleistocene bed between Uckfield and Crowborough, at Barkham Manor. Dawson wrote that he had found part of a human skull 'which would rival Heidelberg man'. He invited Woodward down to Sussex, adding that a fellow antiquary, Edgar Willet, would drive them by motor car from Uckfield to the site. Woodward replied that he would come down to Sussex as soon as he could. In the meantime he counselled discretion. On 24 March Dawson wrote, however, that: 'The roads leading to it [Piltdown] are impassable and excavation is out of the question'. In the winter the mud roads about Piltdown were churned into deep, water-filled ruts. The pit itself, as a contemporary photograph shows,[9] was often completely submerged. On 26 March two Piltdown specimens arrived at the museum by post. One, Dawson thought, could be part of a hippopotamus tooth; the other was to him a mystery. Woodward replied that Dawson had correctly attributed the tooth. The other specimen was merely a fragment of ironstone. On 28 March Dawson wrote that he would take care 'that no one sees the piece of skull who has any knowledge of the subject and leave it to you. On second thought I have decided to wait until you and I can go over by ourselves to look at the bed of gravel. It is not very far to walk from Uckfield . . .'

Woodward does not seem to have considered that the developments at Piltdown warranted an urgent visit. In April he went to Germany to examine dinosaur bones. Dawson announced by letter on 23 May he was coming up to London, and would bring the Piltdown specimens to South Kensington on the following day, Friday, probably after lunch.

The meeting took place, as Woodward soberly wrote later,[10] 'to talk about them [the discoveries] and to learn whether his conclusions were justifiable'.

According to Dawson,[11] however, his entry into the office was scarcely commonplace. Dawson produced the piece of skull with a flourish, remarking: 'How's that for Heidelberg?' The lawyer did explain the reason for this remark. The recent discovery of the massive skull-less jaw in the sand-pit at Maur suggested to Dawson that the thick Piltdown skull bones might have common ownership. In this article Dawson told how he came to make the find. At the end of the last century, he thought, he had gone to Piltdown to preside at the Court Baron at Barkham Manor. While awaiting the customary dinner given to the tenants of the Manor, Dawson strolled outside. His attention was at once attracted by some iron-stained gravel unusual in the district. It reminded Dawson of some Tertiary gravel he had seen in Kent. He also remembered that in the view of geologists there were no flint-bearing gravels in the central area of the Weald; such gravels finished some three or four miles north of the South Downs in the Ouse valley. He was therefore surprised when on enquiry he was informed that the gravel had been dug on the nearby farm and had been used to repair roads for as long as anyone could remember.

Dawson said that he was glad when the dinner finished so that he could visit the pit, where he found two farm hands digging. On inquiry the men explained that they had never yet found any fossil bones. Dawson 'specially charged the workmen to keep a lookout'. Since then Dawson had made occasional visits to the pit but it was worked according to the requirements of road repair.

On one of these visits, however, a labourer handed Dawson a portion of human cranium of unusual thickness. At first this thickness was the only point of interest, according to Dawson, but he at once made a long and fruitless search. Soon afterwards he spent a whole day at the pit in the company of a friend, A. Woodhead, but the bed appeared to be 'unfossiliferous'. Many pieces of dark-brown ironstone raised false alarms and the wetness of the season hampered the search.

'It was not until several years later' that Dawson, when looking over the rain-washed spoil heaps, found a second and larger piece of the skull, and soon afterwards he found the portion of hippopotamus tooth.

Despite Woodward's quoted enthusiasm, Dawson had to write an ultimatum on 27 May. He said that the pit was now dried out and:

'Next Saturday (2 June) I am going to have a dig at the gravel bed and Fr Teilhard de Chardin[12] will be with me. He is quite safe. Will you be able to join us?' Teilhard de Chardin, who breakfasted that fateful morning with the Dawsons at their home 'perched among the ruins of the castle', wrote[13] that at 10 a.m. he and Dawson set out for Uckfield where they were joined by Professor Woodward.

We embarked [he wrote] in a motor car, with the elements of a picnic, which took us three miles across Uckfield Park and deposited us at the place where the hunt was on. This was a stretch of grass, four or five metres in width, beside a wooded glade leading to a farm. Under this grass there was a layer of pebbles, about fifty centimetres thick, which they are digging up, bit by bit, for road-mending. A man was there to shift the earth for us.[14] Armed with spades and sieves, etc., we worked away for hours and eventually with success. Dawson unearthed a fragment of the famous human skull – he had already found three other pieces – [according to Dawson's account, so far only two pieces of skull had been recovered, plus the piece of hippopotamus molar] – and I myself laid hands on the fragment of an elephant's [*Elephas planifrons*] molar. This find considerably enhanced my reputation with Woodward, who jumped on the piece with the eagerness of a boy and I could see all the fire which his apparent coldness conceals. I had to leave before the others in order to catch my train. This first tooth of an elephant impressed me in the way another man is impressed by bringing down his first snipe.

According to Woodward both he and Dawson were fully occupied with 'ordinary duties'. Weekends and occasional holidays only could be spared for the task. He said that this was probably an advantage because the detection of fossil bone and teeth stained brown in a dark-coloured gravel, full of bits of ironstone and brown flints, necessitated a close and slow examination of every fragment. Only one labourer could be employed on the heavy digging as each spadeful had to be passed through a sieve by the expert. The residue in the sieve was piled aside in 'spoil heaps' which were re-examined after the natural washing by rain made the task easier. The gravel was spread thinly over the ground so that mid-week rain prepared it for the weekend search.

Woodward said that Dawson obtained permission to explore the gravel pit from Robert Kenward of Barkham Manor without telling him what the search was about. The clandestine activities of that first weekend's dig excited much local curiosity. The Piltdown police constable appeared at Dawson's office on the following Monday and reported to him as clerk to the magistrates that 'three toffs, two of them from London, had been digging like mad in the gravel at Barkham, and nobody could make out what they were up to'. The embarrassed Dawson had 'calmly and quietly' explained that there were interesting flints in the neighbourhood and perhaps the men were merely harmless enthusiasts. The lawyer used the occasion to enrol the constable, explaining where flints might be found on his beat, and asking him to report any he might find. The digging then continued undisturbed until winter flooding of the pit prevented further work.

Woodward described the further finds thus:

In one heap of soft material rejected by the [farm] workmen we found three pieces of the right parietal bone of the human skull – one piece on three successive days. These fragments fitted together perfectly. After much inspection which prevented my discarding it as a piece of ironstone, I found in another heap an important fragment [of skull] which fitted the broken edge of the occipital bone and gave us the line of contact with the left parietal bone [found by Dawson]. Finally on a warm evening after an afternoon's vain search, Mr Dawson was exploring some untouched remnants of the original gravel at the bottom of the pit, when we both saw the human lower jaw fly out in front of the pick-shaped end of the [geological] hammer which he was using. Thus was recovered the most remarkable portion of the fossil which we were collecting. It had evidently been missed by the workmen because the little patch of gravel in which it occurred was covered with water at the time of year when they had reached it. On different days we also picked up three undoubted flint implements, besides several eoliths, and fragments of a tooth of an elephant, teeth of a beaver, and one much-rolled tooth of a mastodon – the first to be discovered in a river gravel in Europe. On the surface of an adjacent field we found a piece of antler of a red deer and a tooth of a horse, both fossilized, which we supposed to have been thrown over the hedge by the workmen.

As Woodward commented, 'we met with enough success to publish the first account of our discoveries in December'.

Woodward refers to the secrecy of the Piltdown dig as a matter of course. No specific worker at that time would have thought any explanation was necessary. Certainly any premature publicity would cause damaging public intrusion at such an excavation. But the discoverer feared the public far less than his professional colleagues. He feared carefully rehearsed evidence in rebuttal. Past experience would have shown him that any claims for such a find would be highly controversial. Therefore the fewer who knew about the discovery the better its chances of success in the debate which would inevitably follow.

How big then was this select band? Certainly A. Woodhead, Dawson's friend and an original searcher, was a member. Almost definitely another would have been Edgar Willet, the amateur chauffeur. Then, of course, there was Teilhard de Chardin, possibly Felix Pelletier, the priest's archaeological companion, and Woodward himself. As the dig progressed this number increased to include F. O. Barlow, an expert plaster-cast maker at the British Museum's anthropological section under Woodward, and another museum employee, W. P. Pycraft, an authority on dentition and head of the museum's anthropological section under Woodward. Then the help was enlisted of the Australian anatomist, Grafton Elliot Smith, who had made a special study of fossil men, and lastly Sir Ray Lankester.

Certainly Lankester's support had been sought either by Woodward or Dawson for he threw a heavy hint to J. Reid Moir, the leading amateur authority on eoliths, in an undated letter (according to Moir, Lankester never dated personal letters) which said:

... It seems possible that it [the Piltdown remains] is our Pliocene Man – the maker of rostro-carinate flints [eoliths]! At any rate if they [the anti-eolith cadre] say to us 'you say we call in vague, unknown agencies such as torrents and pressure to produce these flints by natural force, but you are in the same position of calling in a hypothetical man. You have no other evidence that such a man was there!' Now we can say 'Here he is.' It is wonderful that, after so many years, man's bones should turn up in a gravel. I do not despair now of you finding a sub-Crag human cranium and lower jaw. You must keep this dark for a month or so yet as the discoverers will not be ready to publish before that lapse of time and more will be found some day in the same place.

This letter, quoted by Moir *op. cit.*, has a certain interest as the recipient himself had just alleged that he had found such a fossil human near Ipswich, Suffolk. It had not stood a chance, however, as the remains were accompanied by Roman pottery.

The *Manchester Guardian*[15] was the first to break the news of the Piltdown discovery to the public at large. Under the headlines 'The Earliest Man? A skull "millions of years" old. One of the most important of our time' the newspaper reported:

In spite of the secrecy of the authorities who are in possession of the relics the news is leaking out and is causing great excitement among scientists, although there are very few even among geologists and anthropologists who have any first-hand information.

The report continued inaccurately that the skull belonged to the same age as the Heidelberg 'skull' and resembled the Neanderthal specimen 'but belongs to a much lower and more primitive type of mankind'. It commented that the experts would not venture an opinion but probably the man represented by the new skull lived millions of years ago, well before Galley Hill man, even before the recently discovered Ipswich skull (J. Reid Moir's find). The newspaper deliberated that as the human bones had been discovered with the remains of extinct animals it was possible that he had met his end 'while following his prey'. The report claimed that the search for the 'missing link' had been narrowed by the Sussex discovery although Eugene Dubois' *Pithecanthropus erectus* (Java man) might be mentioned in this respect. It concluded that 'other links are still missing'. *The Times*[16] carried the following note:

Excavations in Sussex by an anthropological student have brought to light the fragments of a human skull. The skull, said by the experts to be that of a Palaeolithic man, is the earliest undoubted evidence of man in this country. A detailed description of this and other discoveries will be presented at a meeting of the Geological Society to be held on 18 December. The skull would appear to carry anthropological knowledge back to a much more remote date than the human skeleton discovered by Mr J. Reid Moir in the Ipswich district last year.

By its restraint this report was more accurate apart from the error that Dawson was a student of anthropology. This incorrect association is unimportant other than as evidence that the source of the report was neither Dawson nor Woodward. J. Lewis Abbot claimed later that he had pointed out the antique gravel at Piltdown to Dawson and he would have been a likely suspect apart from the vaunting of the Ipswich find, which might indicate Reid Moir or Lankester. Many people later made claims that they knew of the Piltdown discovery, even that they knew of the fraud from the outset,[17] but as none of these thought it necessary to come forward before it was detected some forty years later one must doubt the veracity of such statements.

On 18 December 1912, at Burlington House, London, the offices of the Geological Society, Piltdown man made his public debut. It is traditional that no meeting before or since attracted such attention and attendance. Arthur Keith described the meeting that evening as 'crowded and excited'. *The Times*[18] said 'there was great interest and it was attended by geologists from many parts of the country'.

On a small raised dais at the end of the hall sat Dawson and Woodward. On a table between the discoveries was a plaster reconstruction of the skull; the 'missing link' between man and his ape ancestors. F. O. Barlow had given him a ferocious but cheerfully encouraging look, the patchwork of deep red of the fragments of the skull so far discovered shown up by the white of those absent but provided by Woodward and Barlow.

Dawson spoke first. It is alleged that within a few words he had talked himself into trouble; that he carefully avoided stating the year when he was handed the first piece of skull by the workman. On the discovery that Piltdown man was nothing more than a forgery the omission of this detail was interpreted as just one example of the cunning of Dawson, in this case an attempt to cover his nefarious activities with a veil of confusion.

The official paper,[19] as published in the Geological Society's quarterly journal,[20] is the usual source work for Dawson's alleged sin of omission. The paper merely quotes Dawson as saying that he was walking along the farm road close to Piltdown Common when he noticed that the road had been mended with some peculiar brown flints which he thought were unusual in the district. He then says:

Upon one of my subsequent visits [my italics] one of the workmen handed me a small portion of an unusually thick human parietal [side] bone . . . It was not until some years later, in the autumn of 1911, on a visit to the spot, that I picked up, among the rain-washed spoil heaps of the gravel pit, another and larger piece.

Writing of the discovery in 1945 the now totally blind Woodward merely quotes the official publication, adding the detail that on this *subsequent* occasion the workmen handed Dawson what they thought was 'a piece of coconut'. He also picked out from Dawson's account in the *Hastings and East Sussex Naturalist* the statement that the lawyer's attention had been drawn to the gravel at 'about the beginning of the present century'. In fact Dawson did supply the missing detail.

A reporter from *The Times* at the Geological Society meeting quotes Dawson as saying that 'four years ago' (that is 1908) he was walking near Piltdown when he observed some workmen digging gravel for farm roads. On this occasion one of the workmen gave him the fragment of skull. The report continues that during the last winter (which would be 1911) Dawson was fortunate enough to retrieve two more fragments.

It seems, therefore, that the missing detail was deleted from the official paper before publication the following March. The Geological Society talk was delivered from notes and not from the official paper, which was not published until the next year. Certainly Dawson, and Woodward for that matter, made a mistake, but surely it is not an incriminating one, as is normally suggested.

Dawson told the meeting that Woodward considered the human remains of such importance that as soon as the floods had subsided at the end of May attempts would be made to discover the remaining fragments. By September sufficient fragments of the skull had been recovered for a reconstruction to be made. Dawson said that the diggings had also produced bone fragments of two species of primitive elephant, a hippopotamus, red deer, horse and beaver, and numerous flint implements of a 'very primitive type'.

While the search was in progress Dawson had thoroughly examined the geology of the neighbourhood and the position of the gravel proved to be of great antiquity. The gravel rested on an old land surface over which the Ouse used to flow. Since the gravel was deposited the Ouse had deepened along its seaward valley by sixty to eighty feet. Dawson concluded that the human remains and some of the fossil mammals were of the early Ice Age. The other animal remains were probably older and belonged to the late Pliocene; they had somehow been washed naturally into the gravels.

The flint implements, said Dawson, were of two kinds. The most recent were Pre-Chellean; the others belonged to the class known as eoliths on which, he said, there was much debate as to whether they were of human authorship or not.

Woodward told the meeting that, with the aid of Barlow, he had been able to restore the skull. It had proved different from any class hitherto met with in France, Belgium or Germany. It had the steep forehead of modern man with scarcely any brow ridges. In fact the only external appearance of antiquity, it seemed to Woodward, was the position of the occiput, which showed that the attitude of the neck was like that of an ape. The most striking feature of the skull was the thickness of the bone, said Woodward. It was twice as thick as that of modern man, even thicker than that of the Negro and Australian 'black'. It was well known, said Woodward, that the skulls of Negroes and 'blacks' were far thicker than any ape's.[21]

Then Woodward turned to the most sensational part of Pilt-down man – the jaw. It differed markedly from that of man and, he said, 'agreed exactly' with that of a young chimpanzee. The jaw, however, still retained two molar teeth with crowns which displayed 'a marked regular flattening such as has never been observed among apes, though it is occasionally met with in low types of men'. 'If the molars were removed,' said Wood-ward, 'it would be impossible to detect the jaw was human at all.'

Woodward reached his main conclusion. All cavemen (the Neanderthals), he said, were characterized by low foreheads and very prominent brow ridges resembling those of a fully grown modern ape. But the Piltdown specimen was proved by the antique gravel to be much older than the cavemen. Woodward found it very interesting to note that the new skull was very similar in shape to that of a very young chimpanzee while the skull had the brows of a fully-grown animal.[22] He was inclined, therefore, to the theory that the caveman was an offshoot of early man that had probably become extinct. Modern man, said Woodward, might have derived directly from the primitive source represented by the Piltdown skull. Woodward was sure that Piltdown man was a hitherto undetected genus and proposed therefore that his discoverer should be honoured by naming the specimen *Eoanthropus dawsoni*, the Dawn man of Dawson.

The next speaker was Grafton Elliot Smith. From the context of the paper it is clear that he said something but its exact nature is not known. His main findings were in the form of an appendix to the printed paper published the following March. The appendix said that Smith's observations were upon a cranial cast submitted to him by Woodward.

To his first sight the brain seemed to resemble the well-known Palaeolithic brain-casts, especially those of Gibraltar (Neanderthal) and La Quina. Taking all the features into consideration, Smith regarded the Piltdown specimen 'as being the most primitive and most simian human brain so far recorded; one, moreover, such as might reasonably have been expected to have been associated with the mandible which so definitely indicates the zoological rank of its original possessor'.

Smith said the apparent paradox of the association of a simian jaw with a human brain was not surprising 'to anyone familiar with recent research upon the evolution of man'. In the process of evolving from ape to man 'the superficial area of the cerebral cortex must necessarily be tripled ... The growth of the brain preceded the refinement of the features and the somatic characters in general.'

In the discussion which followed Sir Ray Lankester seems to have done some verbal fencing. He said that the part of the jaw which connected it to the skull was quite unlike that of a human. The jaw certainly indicated something new in the remains of early man. He found it difficult to believe that the eolithic implements were of the same age as the skull, or even that the skull and jaw belonged to the same individual.

Arthur Keith, however, was more confident. Speaking from the body of the hall, he said that the discovery had fulfilled the prophecy of what the ancestor of man was likely to be. The skull was much earlier than Neanderthal man but showed modern characters not found in that specimen. He considered that Dawson and Woodward had made a much bigger discovery than they were actually aware – they had found Pliocene man, not Pleistocene man. He had turned out to be just as the speaker had expected. Maybe, said Keith, the later of the two kinds of flint implements had made the authors think that the skull was of a later date than it really was. He did not think so. The Heidelberg jaw was of Early Pleistocene date. The Piltdown jaw, being more primitive, must belong to an earlier age – to the Pliocene.

The next speaker, W. Boyd Dawkins, could not agree. That remains of Pliocene animals were found with the skull, he said, was a pure accident. Ignoring the eoliths, which were too open to individual interpretation, said Dawkins, the other flints clearly showed that the human remains were of a later date than the Pliocene animals. Call them Chellean or Aurignacian or whatever anyone chose, he personally attached no importance to such 'sub-divisions'. He said that there was no doubt that the skull was Pleistocene but he complimented Dawson, Woodward and Smith on their exposition. He concluded that the Piltdown skull was as complete a 'missing link' as that found in Java some years ago. To anyone who doubted whether the ape's jaw was capable of formulating speech he would reply that there was no connection between making flints and this faculty.

It seems that the enthusiasm for Piltdown man was such that Charles Dawson got near to being chaired from the hall. Even in 1912 the length of the Pleistocene Epoch still had an elastic quality. The estimates varied from 150,000 to 1,500,000 years (about 2,000,000 is correct). The consensus of opinion was for 500,000 years. But whatever the estimate, Piltdown man qualified by his primitive aspect for placement at the beginning of the Pleistocene if not earlier. His brain capacity, as estimated by Woodward, and the position of the occiput placed him neatly between man and ape. That he was capable of some sort of human reasoning was thus assured but his ape jaw postulated animal menace: the ability to defend himself with teeth if required.

The human remains were found with two groups of animal bones, which offered two datings. The earlier was the Pliocene (now termed Villafranchian) group, which consisted of primitive elephant, mastodon and rhinoceros. Then there was the later Lower-Middle Pleistocene group: beaver, red deer, hippopotamus and horse.

The flint implements were in two similar groups, the eoliths and the 'Pre-Chellean'.

Woodward was cautious. He regarded Piltdown man as of approximately the same antiquity as the Heidelberg jaw, that is Middle Pleistocene. Dawson thought that perhaps his friend erred on the side of caution. He was prepared to accept Early Pleistocene. E. T. Newton, F.R.S., who had made a special study of both the Pliocene and the Pleistocene, preferred the former, earlier period for Piltdown man. The Belgian authority Rutot did not hesitate to place the deposition of Piltdown gravel as early as the closing part of the Pliocene.

It seemed that the meeting had been amply forewarned that such a creature as *Eoanthropus* should figure somewhere in the evolution of man. T. H. Huxley had hinted as much in his lectures at the Royal Institute a half-century before and Charles Darwin had written of the progenitors of man[23] that 'the males had great canine teeth, which served them as formidable weapons'. W. L. Duckworth stood at the meeting to declare that 'the anatomy of the Piltdown skull realized largely the anticipation of students of evolution'. Arthur Keith had said as much.

At the outset, Lankester, Keith, even Woodward had reservations about the jaw. Woodward said that although the flat wear of the molars appeared to be human, only the missing eyetooth would provide irrefutable evidence that the jaw was human. He considered that the Piltdown jaw was too long to be filled by normal human teeth and from his reconstruction he concluded that the canine must have been much larger than in modern man and separated, as in the ape, from the next tooth to the rear with a space to facilitate an interlock with the opposing large tooth of the upper jaw. He noticed, however, that the worn surfaces of the molars were remarkably flat, proving that during mastication the jaw must have been as free as that of modern man and not restricted to the ape's slight side motion. He therefore mounted the chimpanzee canine substitute so that it projected but slightly above the molars. Keith was of the opinion that the canine would be completely human in character and in a separate reconstruction he modelled the jaw so as to accommodate typically human teeth.

The French were unfortunate in that they did not have a Mark Twain to visit Piltdown during the excavations of the summer of 1913 for the diggings were overcome by the boisterousness of the 1905 *Congrès Préhistorique de France*. It seems that most of the British luminaries of geology and kindred sciences, and not a few from the Continent and the United States, were as a matter of courtesy allowed a token dig, sieve or search. Dawson and Woodward were frequently interrupted by the arrival of motor coaches laden with natural history societies. On 12 July

1913, a visit was paid by some sixty members of the Geological Society, an excursion said to have been organized by Dawson. He could barely restrain most of this party from entering the pit. A few succeeded. Other visitors included Arthur Keith, Sir Ray Lankester, Grafton Elliot Smith, Davidson Black and Arthur Conan Doyle, the inventor of Sherlock Holmes.

Pecuniary interests became involved at Piltdown. A penny picture postcard of the diggings with the inset heads of Dawson and Woodward, entitled *Searching for the Piltdown Man*, a local confection, could be purchased at the Lamb Inn, about a mile from the site. The owner himself later succumbed, changing the name of the inn to *The Piltdown Man*. In increasing numbers the public found the pit, stared at what they knew not, and went away refreshed. Then such things impressed people to a degree which is unfashionable now.

In a contemporary photograph the diggers stare at the camera with the fixed expressions of an execution; Woodward stern, Dawson in a straw hat looking like a pork butcher. With the discoverers in the workings was a goose. According to a later commentary this bird was always present.

On Saturday, 30 August 1913, the long sought for and vital canine tooth was recovered. Teilhard de Chardin had written home of the Woodward–Keith controversy that: 'In my opinion all these reconstructions . . . add nothing definite to the interest of the fragments. The important thing is to look for more pieces.' At intervals throughout the summer he had dug with Dawson and Woodward, staying with the Dawsons at Lewes. Teilhard de Chardin's search had been interrupted by a retreat at Ore Place but he returned that day. Woodward described the momentous find thus:

We had washed and sieved much of the gravel, and had spread it for examination after washing by rain. We were then excavating a rather deep trench in which Father Teilhard, in black clothing, was especially energetic; and, as we thought he seemed a little exhausted, we suggested that he should leave us to do the hard labour for a time while he had comparative rest in searching the rain-washed gravel spread. Very soon he exclaimed that he had picked up the missing canine tooth, but we were incredulous, and told him we had already seen several bits of ironstone, which looked like teeth, on the spot where he stood . . . so we both left our digging to verify his discovery. There could be no doubt about it.

Woodward described how he and Dawson had spent until dusk crawling over the gravel in a vain quest for more fragments. Teilhard de Chardin after 'a few moments of excitement had returned lightheartedly to Hastings'. There was one more important discovery that season; two nasal (turbinal) bones were found by Dawson on a vertical section of gravel close to the spot where the workmen said they had found the braincase. Hoping to find the remainder of the facial bones, the lawyer dug round the bones with the blade of a pen-knife but there were no more.

The canine was all that Woodward had predicted, except that it was slightly smaller, more pointed and fitted more vertically into the Piltdown jaw. The enamel of the inner face of the tooth was completely worn away down to gum-level 'exactly as in apes'. Dawson wrote in 1915 that 'the tooth is almost identical in form to that shown in the restored cast'.[24]

All the teeth were now X-rayed. Dr A. S. Underwood, commenting on the remarkable resemblance of the canine to that of the ape used by Woodward in the text which accompanied the reproductions of the radiographs, said that the tooth was absolutely as modelled at the British Museum, that the wear, for all its unusual degree, was natural enough, and that the X-ray clearly showed a patch of secondary dentine such as was always deposited progressively with natural wear.[25] But another dental authority, C. W. Lyne, would not agree at all. He said that the canine was an immature tooth and so the degree of wear it displayed was quite out of keeping with its apparent youth.[26]

Woodward announced the discovery of the canine to the British Association meeting at Birmingham in September and then to the Geological Society. The general conclusion was that the tooth proved that Piltdown man's dentition was extremely ape-like and not similar to that of human beings as proposed by Keith. Confronted by this implacable evidence Keith climbed down, remarking rather tamely that the roots of the Piltdown teeth seemed human in type.

Having achieved partial victory Woodward strove to quiet Keith on the score of the capacity of the skull. Keith was now strongly insisting that the volume of Piltdown man's brain was as large as that of modern man. He based his argument on the premise that the fossil skull was too early in the evolutionary pattern to have developed a feature common to modern skulls – the left-hand side dominating the right in size. Keith stressed that in very primitive skulls both sides are symmetrical, thus he gave the left side of the Piltdown skull similar volume to that of the right. Woodward, the fish expert, advised the human anatomist Keith that he was wrong. Make the volume of the right side of the plaster reconstruction less than the left, he urged, then we will be in accord.

The famous Piltdown gravel according to Sir Arthur Smith Woodward. The parts of the layers that have been removed by weathering and washing away by rivers are indicated by dotted lines.

Key: a, Chalk, the upper part containing flints which fall on the surface below (as indicated by arrows) when the surrounding chalky material is washed away; b, Upper and Lower Greensand; c, Weald Clay, the upper part of the Wealden Formation; d, Hastings Sands, etc., forming the middle part of the Weald; p, Position of Piltdown; x, Region of the original chalk where the men who made the eoliths lived (according to the eolith supporters).

(From *The Earliest Englishman*. Watts & Co. London, 1948.)

Grafton Elliot Smith, however, attributed Keith's 'error' to ignorance of the original specimens. In a letter to *Nature*[27] he warned Keith not to place too much reliance on what could be deduced from inaccurate plaster casts. Woodward, he said, had free access to the original. Smith thought it was undesirable that misunderstanding which arose from this simple fact should be allowed to breed further confusion.

Despite its professed pacific intention, the letter naturally contributed nothing towards this end. Smith aggravated Keith further in another letter to the magazine[28] saying that he might have been inclined to go along with Keith in the matter of skull volume before he had seen the actual skull fragments, which he had done recently. Now, said Smith cheekily, he was convinced that Keith's reconstruction was impossible.

Keith was furious. He replied that Smith was doing grave injustice to both Woodward and Barlow, the plaster-cast maker.

Woodward was only too eager to allow anatomists to examine the Piltdown fragments. This facility had been freely extended to himself, who thought that the British Museum reconstruction was erroneous. And, said Keith, Barlow's skill had made the casts highly accurate. Keith admitted that he had given similar volumes to both sides of the skull. But by doing so, wrote Keith, he was only placing the discovered fragments in their correct anatomical position. He advised Woodward to ignore Smith and follow suit.

Smith replied[29] that Keith put a finger on his own problem when he mentioned similar volumes. Woodward had, he wrote, started off by giving the skull similar proportions but fortunately he had seen the error of his ways before the Geological Society meeting. Although the brain of Piltdown Man was a primitive form, instructed Smith, it had strong modern affinities. The skull therefore was non-symmetrical. Keith should change his views, not Woodward.

The debate on the brain volume of Piltdown man continued in this vein for the rest of the year and into the next. Keith maintained that his construction was the correct one; Smith calling him wrong and flicking out annoyances. Keith used his presidential address to the Royal Anthropological Society in January to insist that he was right, therefore the capacity of the skull was grossly underestimated. Smith argued eloquently before the Royal Society in February that the small brain of Piltdown man, although definitely human, was of a type from which had been derived those of primitive races, such as Neanderthal man, the Australian aborigine and the Negro. Dubois' *Pithecanthropus*, or Java man, he argued, represented an unprogressive branch which had died out in the Pleistocene. *Eoanthropus*, Dawson's fossil man, had progressed to modern man.

Unfortunately for Smith his adversary was also at the meeting. Keith rose to state that the small brain referred to by Smith was in fact being deprived of some three hundred cubic centimetres of volume by Woodward's faulty reconstruction. Of this collision Keith wrote:[30]

I did not mince my words in pointing out the glaring errors . . . It was a crowded meeting and he [Smith] and I filed out side by side. I shall never forget the angry look he gave me. He must have felt that I was right for he never published his Royal Society paper and when at a

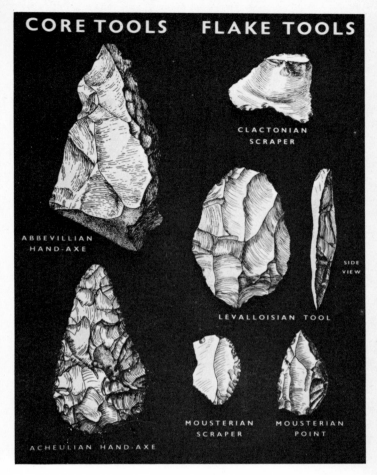

CORE TOOLS   FLAKE TOOLS

CLACTONIAN
SCRAPER

ABBEVILLIAN
HAND-AXE

SIDE
VIEW

LEVALLOISIAN TOOL

MOUSTERIAN
SCRAPER

MOUSTERIAN
POINT

ACHEULIAN HAND-AXE

Palaeolithic flint implements ranging from the Clactonian scraper
through the more sophisticated examples from St Acheul
(Archeulian), Le Moustier (Neanderthal) and La Vallois-Perret,
Paris (Lavalloisian). Neanderthal Man's flint scrapers show a refined
method of producing a sharp edge i.e. the 'pressure technique'
where the flint is splintered away by bearing down on it with a
pointed flint tool.

Forged flint implements from Moulin Quignon. Example on left bears label signed by the famous Abbeville amateur, J Boucher de Perthes. Example on right clearly shows the sharp dividing ridges and shallow facets indicating modern production with a metal hammer.

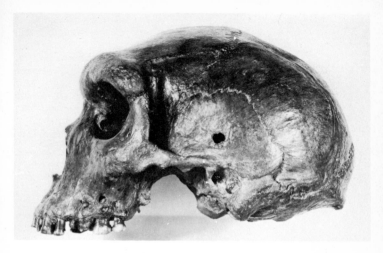

The skull of Rhodesian Man: 'Cyphanthropus' or Stooping Man according to the ornithologist W P Pycraft, head of the British Museum (Natural History) Anthropology section.

Heidelberg Man – a massive jaw discovered at Mauer, near Heidelberg, in 1907 which later prompted Charles Dawson to at first suspect an association with his thick-skulled 'Piltdown Man'. He entered Arthur Smith Woodward's office at South Kensington crying: 'How's that for Heidelberg?'

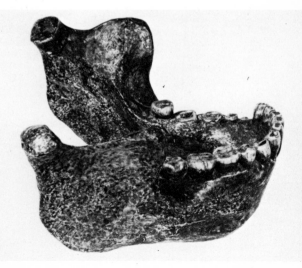

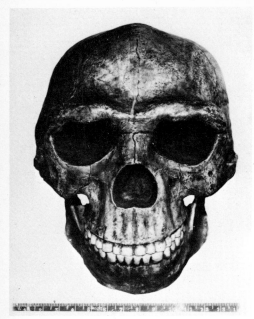

A reconstruction of Peking Man (female) – one of the skulls that vanished sometime in 1941 when the Japanese occupied Peking, China. The entire Choukoutien assemblage is said to hav been aboard the *SS President Harrison* sunk by enemy action.

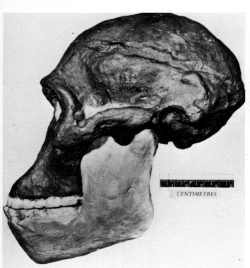

Australopithecus (africanus). The missing link which now occupies the place in evolution formerly occupied by Charles Dawson's 'Piltdown Man'.

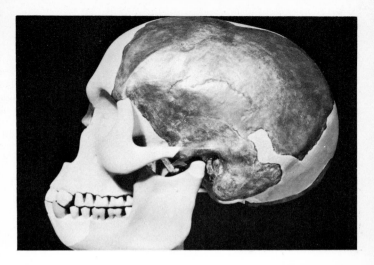

'Piltdown Man' (Eoanthropus dawsoni). The dark portions were bones found at Piltdown, Sussex. The white portions are of plaster and were contributed by the British Museum of Natural History, South Kensington, London.

A comparison of skulls in descending order of refinement from front to back: Modern Man (Caucasian); Neanderthal Man (Generalised); Peking Man (adult); Gorilla.

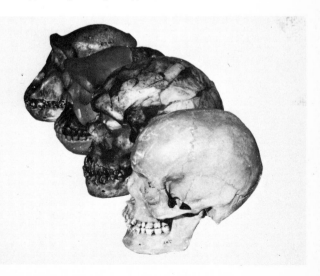

The Piltdown Men: (Left to right) Front Row: W P Pycraft, Arthur Keith, A S Underwood, Ray Lankester. Back Row: F O Barlow, Grafton Elliot Smith, Charles Dawson and Arthur Smith Woodward. John Cooke, R A, rather tactlessly shows Keith measuring the skull of 'Piltdown Man' under the direction of Smith. Teilhard de Chardin is absent on war service.

Piltdown Man's jaw now attributed to a 500-year-old orangutan. Modern opinion is strong for the proposition that the jaw 'hinge' (lymphoid process) was artificially broken away to remove evidence of its ape origin and its unsuitability for fitting into the Piltdown cranium.

The fossil elephant thigh-bone implement from Piltdown. Marks of a modern steel blade used to sharpen the point escaped notice until 1948, and their implication until 1953.

Far right: the Piltdown molars showing the non-alignment of the flat crowns. This unnatural placement cried out for notice in 1912 but oddly escaped attention for some forty years.

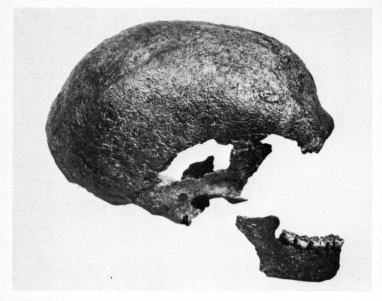

The skull and fragment of jaw of Galley Hill Man – Britain's 'Neanderthal Man' – now thought to be a recently-buried woman. The eyebrow ridges hailed as prominent and characteristic of Neanderthal Man are well within the range of modern man. The curvature of the limb bones was caused by posthumous deformation after deliberate inhumation.

An 'eolith' from Piltdown, Sussex. Whether human workmanship – ancient or modern – was employed is conjectural.

later date he made a reconstruction of the skull it did not differ greatly from mine.

Smith's impugnment of Keith's ability to reconstruct early human skulls resulted in a demonstration. Keith re-assembled a specimen Egyptian skull which had been carefully broken into

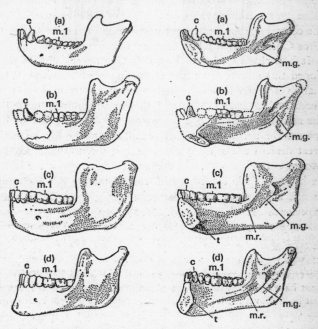

Sir Arthur Smith Woodward compares the Piltdown jaw with those of a chimpanzee, Heidelberg man and modern man.

Fig. (a) Young Chimpanzee; (b) Piltdown Man; (c) Heidelberg Man; (d) Modern Man; c. Canine tooth; m.l. First molar tooth.

(From *The Earliest Englishman*. Watts & Co. London, 1948.)

small pieces by an independent party. The reconstruction was found to be accurate to within a few cubic centimetres. This sensational feat was the talk of scientific circles for many a day.

It is hard to say who was right about the reconstruction. Keith was right inasmuch as the Piltdown skull was represented as that of an early kind of humanity. The Java skull and another found later in China showed no dissimilarities in the right and left sides of the crania. Woodward's ignorance of the subject caused him to reconstruct the Piltdown skull in line with the asymmetry of modern skulls.

In fact Woodward made another error which made the brain seem to him even smaller. As Sir Wilfrid Le Gros Clark said many years later [31] Woodward, not being a human anatomist, had mistaken a small side ridge on the roof of the Piltdown skull for the central (median) ridge not uncommon in ancient skulls. Le Gros Clark said that Keith detected this error immediately.

It is perhaps typical of Keith that he never publicly mentioned this glaring error, merely noting it in his diary. When many years later he was invited to write an introduction to the deceased Woodward's saga of Piltdown he confined himself to the admission that he had been wrong. Admitting that he had 'played the part of the stormy petrel' he said he had learned a great deal from the excavations he had recently conducted at Mount Carmel (now Israel). On his return in 1938, wrote Keith, he had 'yet again spread out in front of me the Piltdown fragments, and set out to reconstruct them in the light of recent experience'. Keith continued:

I soon found myself involved in all the puzzles which I had encountered a quarter of a century earlier. The mistake I had been making all along I found to be this: I shared the common idea that the earlier the type of man, then the more symmetrical would be the left and right halves of the hemispheres of his brain. It is not until I realized that in Piltdown the left hemisphere dominated the right both in size and complexity, that the discrepant parts fell into their appropriate place. The specialization of the left half of man's brain at so early a date took me by surprise. [32]

The Piltdown excavations proceeded into 1914, progress being reported to the Geological Society or the scientific journals by either Charles Dawson or Arthur Smith Woodward. So far, this season's yield had been confined to another piece of mastodon molar, and part of a rhinoceros molar which was picked up by Davidson Black on a visit to the site with Grafton Elliot Smith.

But Piltdown was by no means exhausted. Woodward was watching labourer Venus Hargreaves slashing away with a mattock under the nearby hedge when he saw splinters of bone scattered by a blow. Searching the spot with his hands Woodward pulled out 'a heavy blade of bone' covered with sticky yellow clay. When washed it was observed that one end of the bone was recently fractured. Dawson accordingly 'grubbed' with his fingers in the earth and retrieved the other half. One end had been trimmed by sharp cuts to a wedge-shaped point.

Woodward took the two pieces of bone to South Kensington where Frank Barlow 'hardened' and fitted them together. Further examination showed that although unstained the bone agreed with the high degree of mineralization of the bones from the Piltdown pit, and so must have come from there, being thrown out unnoticed by workmen seeking gravel.

The sharpened end suggested to Woodward the work of a primitive flint tool. The bone, some sixteen inches in length and four inches in diameter, was part of the thigh-bone of a fossil elephant.

Scientific speculation as to the use that Piltdown man could have made of the tool was rife but unproductive. One end seemed to have been rounded for comfortable handling and the other pointed for performing work. A groove, presumed by Woodward to be the remains of a hole of which part had broken away in antiquity, could have been threaded with a strip of skin for carrying. Woodward attached importance to this feature, concluding that as the point was sharp and showed little sign of wear, the breakage had rendered the tool useless. On the whole, the tool suggested a stick for grubbing up roots.

The inevitable opposition to Piltdown was gaining momentum. It was not, however, claimed that he was the product of disease or relic of Russian invasion but that he was two animals. Despite Charles Darwin's prediction, the jaw, as the chief British objector, Dr David Waterston of King's College put it, had too much of a striking resemblance to that of a chimpanzee. The teeth not only approached those of the ape in form, he said, they were in several instances identical. Associating the jaw with the skull, he said, was like articulating a chimpanzee's foot to a human leg.

The French palaeontologist Marcellin Boule was of like opinion and wrote that he 'saw no reason to regard the jaw as belonging to the man whose brain-case was deposited in the gravel where both were found'.

More robust attacks came in 1916 from the United States. Gerrit Miller, curator of mammals at the National Museum of the Smithsonian Institute, Washington D.C., sent a chimpanzee jaw to the Geological Society recommending that it be compared with the Piltdown example. Miller wrote that the Piltdown mandible had nothing to do with the skull. It belonged, he said, to a fossil chimpanzee which must have inhabited England during the Pleistocene. From the morphology of the teeth he suspected a hitherto undetected species and named it *Pan vetus*.

On the American's attack, *Nature*[1] unfavourably commented:

If mankind had been evolved from an anthropoid stock the occurrence of a combination of human and anthropoid characteristics in earlier or dawn human forms, such as occur in *Eoanthropus*, is just what we ought to find.

At the Manchester Literary and Philosophical Society, in February 1916 Smith conducted a one-man debate on what he described as 'the new phases of controversy regarding Piltdown man'. These were, he said, that the canine tooth belonged to the upper and not the lower jaw; that the mandible belonged to a chimpanzee; that the features which differentiated the mandible from that of modern man had been exaggerated;[2] that the canine could not have belonged to the skull and jaw because of the apparent difference in age, one authority believing it to be definitely older, another definitely younger.

Smith said he had examined all these arguments but had found no evidence to support any of them. He drew particular attention to the inference that the cranium was not sufficiently ape-like to be associated with the jaw. To this he replied that the skull revealed certain features of a more primitive nature than any known representative of the human family.

In *Man*,[3] T. E. Nuttal appealed for reason. Describing himself as a medical practitioner and student of anthropology, he said that even after a second reconstruction by Woodward there still existed a considerable discrepancy between his version and Keith's. Keith's demonstration on the Egyptian skull was impressive, his anatomical skill could not be denied but it must be admitted that his Piltdown skull erred on the large side. There could be, said Nuttal, a rational explanation for the dispute. Keith believed in the high antiquity of man, holding that he had originated in the Pliocene. If it could be proved, therefore, that such a large-skulled individual had existed in the Pleistocene Keith's views would be given strong support. Precisely the same reasoning could be applied to Woodward's view. He believed that man originated in the Pleistocene so if he could prove that at that time humans possessed but a meagre cranial capacity then his views would be upheld. Nuttal was sure that neither Keith nor Woodward would consciously allow his views to influence his reconstruction, still 'all of us, quite unconsciously, find what we desire and expect to find'. This sober reflection was somewhat spoilt by Nuttal's closing remark that he thought Keith's reconstruction was nearer reality than Woodward's.

Meanwhile, W. P. Pycraft, an ornithologist who was head of the museum's anthropology section, was countering a series of letters from Gerrit Miller. In 1917 he gave a final reply to this vexatious correspondence with the approval of Woodward, Smith, Keith, Underwood and Barlow, writing:

The jaw has peculiarities which make it human despite the fact that it presents many points of likeness to that of a chimpanzee. All supposed disharmony between the jaw and the skull is imaginary. The molar teeth are human, radiographs and the other evidence show that they differ conspicuously from the corresponding teeth of great apes.

Not one authority expressed any doubts concerning the age of the skull. Although neither hydrochloric acid nor tongue-test had been applied doubts on this score had already been stifled by scientific advance. The Geological Society's quarterly journal[4] carried the following impressive notice:

A small fragment of the skull has been weighed and tested by Mr S. A. Woodhead, M.Sc., F.I.C., Public Analyst for East Sussex and Hove, and Agricultural Analyst for East Sussex. He reports that the specific gravity of the bone (powdered) is 2.115 (water at 5 degrees C as standard). No gelatine or organic matter is present. There is a large proportion of phosphates (originally present in the bone) and a considerable proportion of iron. Silica is absent.

One wonders why the same test was not applied to the jaw bone, but it seems that such a test was never contemplated. As it was, Woodhead's criteria were worthless as later events proved.

Dawson wisely kept out of the anatomical controversy, leaving the field to Woodward, Keith and Smith. On 26 August 1916, he died. Those familiar with the lawyer's energy were greatly shocked by his sudden demise at the age of fifty-two years. Dawson had suffered from anaemia which had suddenly turned to septicaemia. The present author was considerably mystified by the sudden death of Charles Dawson while to all appearances at the height of his vigour. Could his anaemia in any way have affected his mental faculties either partially or to a degree which would diminish his sense of responsibility? Dr Stefan Varadi, a consultant haematologist of international standing, kindly informed him that certainly the manifestations of long protracted anaemia usually are fatigue and shortness of breath. Mental capacity, however, does not suffer, except in extreme cases where there is an unsatisfactory supply of oxygen to the brain. The only exception is perhaps the so-called *pernicious* anaemia where, even in its relatively mild form, psychiatric manifestations can occur. This form of anaemia is due to lack of vitamin B_{12}, which is also an essential vitamin for the normal function of the brain tissue. But if it is true that

Dawson 'was renowned for his remarkable energy which persisted until the time of his death' it is unlikely that he had pernicious anaemia. Especially as all Dawson's obituaries referred to 'a protracted illness'.

Dawson certainly showed no sign of the onset of mortal disease. After Piltdown he made another discovery which Keith, if he had heard about it, would not have received too warmly. It concerned the skeletons in his Hunterian Museum at the Royal College of Surgeons.

Dawson was struck by what he described as 'the persistence of a thirteenth dorsal vertebra in certain human races which had not attracted scientific notice'. He detected this extra vertebra in the skeletons of an Arawak Indian, a Niva-Fu whale-hunter, a male and female Eskimo, and an ancient Egyptian.

Dawson attributed this phenomenon to a common factor in the lives of these races: the canoe or kayak, and the constant manipulation of the hips to maintain equilibrium, necessitating an additional muscle attachment in this region. The lawyer's findings were never published but he certainly prepared a lengthy paper on the subject. It is possible that Woodward may have advised him against publication. The manuscript for the abandoned project is still in the Geological Department's collection.

On 24 March 1915 Dawson was at the Royal Anthropological Institute to give a remarkable demonstration aimed at the destruction of the argument for eoliths. Eoliths had been recovered from the Piltdown pit and why Dawson, if he were the forger, should wish to cast doubt on them is inexplicable. It must have been an honest attempt to be objective about Piltdown. The lawyer had shaken pieces of common starch stained to resemble the 'old brownies' of the Kent plateau and had produced, to the intense indignation of J. Reid Moir and J. Lewis Abbot, starch 'eoliths'. He repeated the experiment before the Geological Society.

Woodward, creating a precedent, asked the artist John Cooke, R.A., what he thought Piltdown man would have looked like in life. As he commented later with evident satisfaction, Cooke, 'could not avoid making the portrait altogether human'. Dawson had smiled at the drawing and observed that 'he could match it in Sussex today'. This desire to belittle the great difference between the appearance of fossil man and modern man is not an unusual feature of the period. Indeed W. L. Duckworth once exuberantly exclaimed that if Neanderthal man entered a bar in modern dress the majority would not notice him. One marvels at the sort of person Duckworth drank with.

A better-known portrait by Cooke is of the discoverers and those connected with Piltdown. Dramatically lit and seated in the centre of the group at a table littered with skulls is Keith. Standing to his left are Dawson and Woodward; to his right, Smith and Barlow. The others in the group are Lankester, Pycraft and Underwood.

Nature[5] commented that the likenesses were excellent and the composition of the group pleasing, but failed to detect a flaw. An outstanding absentee was Teilhard de Chardin. At the time of the painting he was a private soldier of France under heavy bombardment at Ypres on the Western Front.

As was the custom, Dawson's obituary was read by the president of the Geological Society and published in its quarterly journal.[6] In the circumstances it is curiously short, certainly not fulsome. J. Lewis Abbot fared far better later. Dawson had been a 'resident and contributing' member of the society for thirty years. He had given at least one financial donation to the society. The society had been preferred to others before which to announce his sensational find, the most important discovery of fossil man in Britain, indeed as far as the British were concerned, in the world. The Royal Society would have been overjoyed to have been thus favoured. Possibly the lawyer was unfortunate in his president. Alfred Harker was a 'pure' geologist, his particular interest being igneous rock and movement of the earth's crust, and he may not have cared a fig for fossil man.

The brief obituary mentioned Dawson's work in the Wealden formation and the valuable collection of reptilia deposited at the British Museum, that he was widely known in connection with his discovery of the Piltdown skull, that he had died at Lewes after a protracted illness, and that he had been a Fellow since 1885. Dawson fared much better in *Nature*[7] with a longer notice which listed all his contributions adding that 'his comparatively early death is a distinct loss to science'.

Woodward waited until 17 February 1917, two years after the event, to announce sensationally that his late friend had in fact discovered a second Piltdown man. The delay is strange and indeed unkind if the modern view that Dawson's lust for glory was the reason for the forgery is correct. Nothing would have pleased the lawyer more than to pass away to the sound of acclaim.

That Woodward was secretive is beyond doubt. Keith frankly admitted that no small part of his hostility to Woodward's reconstruction of the Piltdown skull had stemmed from a resentment that the exact nature of the first discovery had been kept from him until a bare fortnight before the Geological Society meeting in 1912. He could not quite understand why Dawson had taken the fragments to the British Museum instead of, in his opinion, more correctly to the Royal College of Surgeons.[8]

In his paper on Piltdown Man II[9] Woodward said that in the joint paper of 1913 Dawson had shown that the characteristic Piltdown brown flints could be traced in the ploughed fields of the district. One large field, about two miles from Piltdown, had especially attracted Dawson's attention. Both he and Dawson had examined this field several times during the spring and autumn of 1914 without success. But during the winter the farmworkers had raked the stones from the field and piled them in heaps, making the task easier. Woodward stated:

'Early in 1915 he [Dawson] was so fortunate to find here two well-fossilized pieces of human skull and a molar tooth, which he immediately recognized as belonging to at least one more individual of *Eoanthropus dawsoni*.' Shortly afterwards in the same ground, continued Woodward, 'a friend' found part of a lower molar of a species of fossil rhinoceros, as highly mineralized as the Piltdown specimen.

In this casual way did Woodward announce the second search, the discovery of the second Piltdown Man and the participation of an unnamed friend at the new site. The effect was tremendous. Most of the doubters of Piltdown I went over to the believers. The new human molar and skull fragments proved beyond doubt the correct association of skull and jaw at Piltdown. No coincidence of nature could have brought the bones of a man and an ape together at two separate sites.

Woodward's view was the correct one and David Waterston and Gerrit Miller were wrong.

After Dawson's death Woodward continued his search at Piltdown alone. In 1917 *Nature*[10] noted that:

During the past season Dr Smith Woodward has spent six weeks, partly in association with Professor Grafton Elliot Smith and Major C. Ashburnham, exploring the Piltdown gravel. Although a large amount of undisturbed material was sifted and carefully examined round the periphery of the pit in which the original discovery of *Eoanthropus* was made, nothing was found but one unimportant fragment of the tibia of a deer.

Surprisingly, there was no further mention of the Piltdown II site. Woodward wrote[11] that later he opened a series of pits along the other side of the hedge in the field adjacent to the original Piltdown site. At times he was helped by Grafton Elliot Smith, Professors W. T. Gordon and Barclay Smith, and others. The searchers began 'close to the spot where the skull was found, and worked in both directions from this place'. The work was slow because of the overlying loam being deeper here and the efforts 'were all in vain'. He mentioned that in later years (on retirement from the British Museum in 1924 Woodward went to live at Hill Place, Sussex, to be near his beloved Piltdown) the new owner of Barkham Manor, D. Kerr, dug some of the gravel at a spot near the farmyard, allowing him to watch the labourers. Only a 'pot-boiler' was recovered. As Woodward commented picturesquely, 'the search was now outside the eddy which brought the scientific treasure to its resting place'. Nothing more was found at Piltdown.

Sure evidence that minds were changed by Piltdown II came after the end of the war. In the second edition of Marcellin Boule's book[12] the former antagonist of the one-creature theory now accepted that the skull and jaw belonged to the same individual. Not so his countryman Ernest Robert Lenoir who wrote that '. . . This curious bone enjoyed a period of great notoriety but since the American mammalologist [Gerrit] Miller in two very serious papers of 1915 and 1918 showed that Smith Woodward's fossil was only the remnant of an anthropoid, silence has gradually descended on this find.'[13] Lenoir must have been hard of hearing.

In the United States Professors Fairfield Osborn and W. K. Gregory left Gerrit Miller to his opinion of duality. Osborn, according to his own account,[14] was converted on Sunday, 24 July 1921. Possibly he had been placed in the right frame of mind by a visit to Westminster Abbey. He described how on that day 'Smith Woodward produced from an old fire-proof safe these few precious fragments of one of the original Britons ... preserved in this manner from the bombs thrown by German aviators.' Osborn was reminded of the opening words of a prayer of college days by his professor of logic at Princeton: 'Paradoxical as it may appear O Lord, it is nevertheless true ...' He explained the relevance by adding:

We have to be reminded over and over again that nature is full of paradoxes and that the order of the Universe is not the human order; that we should expect the unexpected and prepare to discover new paradoxes.

Gerrit Miller watched his support dwindle. He ironically contrasted this conversion on sight of the holy relics with the effect on Professor Ales Hrdlička. Hrdlička said[15] that thanks to the courtesy of Woodward he was able to submit the original lower jaw to a detailed examination. He found there was 'a feeling of strong incongruity' and that to 'connect the shapely wholly normal Piltdown jaw with the gross, heavy Piltdown skull into the same individual seems very difficult'. He preempted scientific opinion by thirty years when he also said of the Piltdown II discovery that:

The additional molar tooth of the Piltdown remains is in every respect so much like the first molar of the Piltdown jaw that its procedure from the same jaw seems certain, and it would seem probable that the account of it being discovered at a considerable distance away might be mistaken. The tooth agrees with the jaw perfectly, not only in dimensions and every morphological character, but also in degree and kind of wear. A duplication of all this in two distinct individuals would be almost impossible.

Miller commented[16] that Hrdlička's suggestion that there had been a mistake met with no response. Miller too wondered whether some misunderstanding had arisen from the sudden death of Dawson. He wrote:

In thinking about it we must remember that Dawson personally described the circumstances of both the earlier finds [skull and jaw] but the last set of discoveries was announced after his death and unaccompanied by direct word from him.

Hrdlička found it impossible to believe that the skull and jaw had been supplied by the same creature. It is possible that his scepticism sprang from recent experience. Searching amongst the National Museum collection in 1913 he had encountered two human skulls discovered in 1857, both of supposed vast antiquity. The skulls, encrusted with lime stalagmite containing charcoal and shells, were attributed to a Pliocene deposit in Calavaras County, California. But after removing the incrustation Hrdlička found that the skulls were entirely modern, almost certainly North American Indian. Shortly afterwards he encountered a report of a third skull discovered in 1856 by a goldminer named Mattison at Table Mountain, Calavaras County, California. J. D. Whitney, State Geologist of California, had removed the incrustation and sent the skull to Harvard where this too was found to be typical of the North American Indian. Hrdlička quite rightly suspected all three skulls were a hoax at the expense of the goldminer Mattison.

Arthur Keith remarked of this discovery [17] that it 'made about as much sense as finding an aeroplane in a church crypt that had been bricked up since Elizabethan times'. In 1919 Hrdlička went further. Discussing the finds of supposed fossil man in North and South America [18] he discounted all of them completely as the remains of American Indians and intentional burials. He added the useful warning:

... those in whose work credulity and fancy have no part and who possess sufficiently hard-earned experience in these matters, can be convinced of geologically ancient man in America only by facts that will make all conscientious doubt on the subject impossible. As chances of peculiar associations of human bones and artefacts are infinite therefore anthropology must be called on again and again to pass judgement on claims of the antiquity of such objects. But burden of proof lies with those who urge such claims, they must show clear, conclusive evidence. Our colleagues in collateral branches of science will be sincerely thanked for every genuine help they can give anthropology but they should not clog our hands.

Piltdown man did not entirely absorb Charles Dawson or mono-
polize the time of the professionals Woodward, Keith and Smith.
Each continued to pursue his line of interest, indeed it might be
profitably speculated that the Piltdown discoveries were used as
a cart in which to push the individual's theories.

Woodward, when not at the British Museum, was either on
some scientific project overseas or in attendance at the Geological Society as contributor, officer or president. The Proceedings of the Society show his diversity of output: *On
Mammal Teeth* (with Dawson and Teilhard de Chardin) (1912);
Fish Remains of the Upper Devonian (1913); *On an Engraving
of a Horse on a Bone from Sherborne School* and *On the Lower
Jaw of Dryopithecus* (1914); *Presidential Address on Fossil Fishes*
(1915); and *On an Archaeopteryx* (1918).

Woodward had a further surprise for the Society in 1915
which dramatically supported the find at Piltdown. He showed
his audience lantern slides of a reconstruction of a human
skull brought to the notice of the British Association meeting at
Sydney, Australia, in 1914. According to Woodward the skull
had been recovered from a river deposit on a sheep station at
Talgai, Queensland, together with the remains of large extinct
Pleistocene marsupials. The skull was 'typically human' and 'of
primitive Australian type' but the strangest feature was its
large canine teeth which interlocked, like those of an ape, and
precisely like those of Piltdown man. The lantern slides had
been loaned by Grafton Elliot Smith who had visited his homeland.

This was not the first British appearance of the Talgai skull.
In February of that year (1915) Smith had shown the slides to
the Manchester Literary and Philosophical Society, asserting
that the important discovery proved that man had reached

Australia when the great fossil marsupials were still living. In *Nature*[1] Smith wrote that the fossil man was of sufficient antiquity to be placed in the last ice epoch of the northern hemisphere, commenting: 'The presence of the skull might seem to explain how Australia, with its marsupials, had invaders, like the dingo' which 'had no more right here than the Germans had in Belgium'. The skull, he said, 'was worth its weight in gold'.

In 1917 the Australian Professor Arthur Smith of Sydney University, one of the original describers at the Association meeting,[2] and elder brother of Grafton Elliot Smith, increased the size of the teeth. He said they were the largest so far discovered. He mentioned that the skull was more primitive than any hitherto described except Piltdown in the 'great squareness and enormous size of the palate and teeth'. The fact that the brain-cage had already reached the stage of the modern aborigine was, he said, further confirmation of the view that the brain had first acquired human status, the facial features coming afterwards.

Another describer of the Talgai skull had been Charles Dawson[3] who was in no doubt that the skull bore a close resemblance to Piltdown man. He said that:

A curious and somewhat swift confirmation has occurred with respect to this subject of interlocking canines from an unexpected source . . . Numerous skulls had been unearthed from various parts all over the colony and forwarded to [visiting British Association] scientists for examination. One from Darling Downs, Eastern Australia had cranial features typically those of the Australian aboriginal, but the upper canine tooth was very large and prominent and bearing traces in its wear that it must have interlocked with its lower canine tooth.

Dawson went on to explain that the lower jaw was missing but added the surprising details that Grafton Elliot Smith had informed him that the place nearest to where the skull was found was 'by curious coincidence called Pilton, so to avoid confusion it was decided to call it the Darling Downs skull'.

The confirmation of the Talgai skull was not only 'curious' and 'somewhat swift'; it was also timely. If such a fossil man had inhabited Australia in the Pleistocene then considerable support was lent to the Piltdown example. There is a curious lack of emphasis on the real facts surrounding the Australian Piltdown man. Nobody but Dawson mentioned that the lower jaw was missing in the Talgai specimen and so as supporting evidence it was not so impressive as it at first seemed. Moreover, Arthur Smith innocently announced in *Nature*[4] that the Talgai skull had in fact been found some thirty-one years before by a stock-man on Talgai station, and so its attribution to a Pleistocene deposit must be purely conjectural and the statement that it was found in the company of Pleistocene fauna is highly suspect. A later reconstruction of the skull revealed that it had been some-what misinterpreted, the teeth being nowhere near as large as had been originally suggested. The skull was found to be well within the type-range of the modern aboriginal. The Talgai skull is possibly of fair antiquity. It might even be Upper Pleistocene, although most authorities put it much later. But one may well question whether the original interpretations were entirely free from the desire to establish firmly evidence for Piltdown man at the expense of fact.

No doubt Woodward would have been only too glad to for-sake the contentious sphere of fossil man and return to his old love – fossil fishes. The trouble over his reconstruction of Pilt-down man must have revealed to him his shortcomings as a human anatomist. But his position at the British Museum made a withdrawal impossible. As luck would have it the next fossil man to be thrust under his nose was highly puzzling.

Although the remains, discovered in Rhodesia in 1921, possessed a Neanderthal skull, the limb bones lacked the curva-ture normally associated with the European specimens. But the foramen magnum (a kind of cable entry for the nervous system in the base of the skull) was so far back that a slouching atti-tude was certain. A baffled Woodward confined his involvement to a bald description in *Nature*[5] suggesting a new species – *Homo rhodesiensis* (Rhodesian man). He then passed the buck to the bird-man W. P. Pycraft. Pycraft was as perplexed as Wood-ward – but then came inspiration. He reconstructed the hip bone to give the fossil a forward lean. Thus was born *Cyphanthropus* ('Stooping Man').

Neither description was well received. There were loud asser-tions that Rhodesian man was in fact made up of two men – *Homo sapiens* (body bones) and Neanderthal man (skull).

Pycraft was hotly criticized over the hip reconstruction. Woodward must have cursed the day that Rhodesian man came to South Kensington. He left Pycraft to haggle and withdrew from the controversy – only to be dragged into another.

In 1922 A. Leslie Armstrong described two harpoon heads found by him and another, a Mr Morfield, in a pit in a peat bed at Hornsea, East Yorkshire. These, he said, showed definite features belonging to the Maglemosian culture. The Maglemosians were a Mesolithic hunting people, adapted to a river and shore life in the forestation of the full Boreal times about 8,000 to 10,000 B.P. (Before the Present). Their relics have been detected over an area extending from Northern Europe to the East Baltic. These include equipment for tree-felling, carpentry, fishing and fowling, and carved bone implements. Armstrong considered the harpoons to be evidence of the Maglemosians in eastern England. He offered the harpoons to the Hull Museum only to be told by the curator, T. Sheppard, that the find was impossible. He questioned the authenticity of the implements, implying that Armstrong had made them himself. Sheppard said that no other find of the kind had been recorded even though this culture had been closely watched for. It was unbelievable that the harpoons could have remained so sharp if they had weathered at least 7,000 years of geological and climatic onslaught.

Also there was, said Sheppard, a discrepancy in the account of the find. Morfield, the owner and finder of one harpoon, had said that he found his specimen at a depth of fourteen feet. Allowing for natural erosion of the bed since the time they were said to have been buried of, say, ten feet, this made the depth of the peat in which the harpoons were said to have been discovered to be some twenty-four feet. There was no peat bed on the coast of Yorkshire of even a quarter of this thickness.

In reply Armstrong had said his harpoon was not in fact found in the peat bed but in boulder clay at the base of the peat. Sheppard found his explanation highly unsatisfactory.

A. C. Haddon, Miles Burkitt and J. E. Marr, all of Cambridge University, had examined the Hornsea harpoons, comparing them with four authenticated examples from Kunda, Estonia. In type, mineralized condition, even workmanship of the harpoon barbs, they were identical. Sheppard would not have this, and the matter was referred to the Royal Anthropological Institute which formed a committee which included Woodward to look further into the matter.

Armstrong and Sheppard were called before the committee and questioned 'minutely' on the harpoons. Morfield had recently died. The committee reported that in general 'there was no evidence against their genuineness'. There was, however, one curious feature, the workmanship on the harpoon barbs suggested that they were the work of one individual though they were found some four miles apart. One wonders whether the bogus flints of Moulin Quignon came to mind for the committee added that there were no Maglemosian harpoons in the British museums from which they could have been copied. The committee said that Sheppard appeared to have strong grounds for doubting the authenticity of the specimens but 'the evidence on which his [Sheppard's] judgement was based was no longer available'.

With this intriguing innuendo the report ended. But the finds are now accepted as evidence that the Maglemosians lived on the Yorkshire coast. Miss D. A. E. Garrod wrote to *Man*[6] that she had been informed by Abbé H. Breuil that similar harpoons had recently been found at Béthune, Tuberguy, Pas de Calais and La Heine in north-western France and at Ninone, Belgium. Such a find in eastern England, she said, was therefore likely.

Grafton Elliot Smith had enlivened the British Association meeting in 1912 with his reading of the paper on the single origin of the megaliths of Egypt and Britain. He had neglected no opportunity to sound the migrational drum ever since.

Smith lectured the British Association in 1917 on the matter. He said that man's mental and moral attitudes were largely determined not only by primitive instincts which he shared with his simian ancestors but by the conscious and unconscious influence of the tradition amidst which he had grown up. At no stage in his career had he acquired the highly complex and specialized instincts which, for example, impelled him, unprompted, to build megalithic monuments, or invent the story of the Deluge, independently of others doing the same arbitrary things. Smith urged that these facts seemed to emphasize how confusing was the word 'age' and they revealed 'how devoid of foundation was the mis-named evolutionary theory that claimed that all phases of culture were just natural stages through which every people has passed in virtue of the operation of the blind forces of an arbitrary and inevitable process of evolution'.

At the British Association the following year[7] he regarded the changes from one flint culture to the next as definite breaks in continuity, the Aurignacian, Solutrean, and Magdalenian cultures, for example, representing successive waves of immigration by representatives of *Homo sapiens*.

He took the view that the idea of domesticating animals spread in this way from one source. Smith considered that the primeval source of humanity was North America.

In an essay[8] he traced the primates from an origin in America across the Eocene land-bridges, eastward to Europe and Africa and with somewhat less certainty westward to Asia. Each step towards modern man, he said, must have had a single local origin. Later, when psychological factors came into play, there may have been a transmission of culture with a minimum transmission of race, only those features being accepted for which the recipients were, in a sense, already prepared. As there was no sign that evolution had produced in different areas identical forms by different routes, so there was no reason to suppose that cultures could have arisen as spontaneous, sporadic creations of the human intellect independently and simultaneously in different parts of the world. He added that as the frontal region of the brain was the last to reach full development in the child, so the precursors of present-day man were also deficient in this region.

Smith's main contribution to the war effort was an investigation into the causes and treatment of shell-shock. Keith made strident statements on science in war.

Keith had found out about the Gibraltar skull affair for he wrote to the editor of *Nature* in 1914,[9] on the subject 'Soldiers as Anthropologists', that a certain Major Collins, whilst engaged in trenching operations in the Boer War, had collected enough material for a paper on the prehistoric stone implements of South Africa; that this soldier's interest in anthropology did not interfere with his duties was evident for he had won the D.S.O. Such a letter was pointless except as a direct warning to the incumbent at the War Office that Science would not tolerate a repetition of the situation which had led to Broome's expulsion from the army because of his interest in prehistory. No doubt all this was lost on Earl Kitchener of Khartoum who was involved in matters of greater concern than fossicking soldiery. He did not subscribe to the journal; his one hobby was the collection of china. He had once, however, received a sharp note from Queen Victoria for permitting his soldiers to play football with the skull of the Mahdi.

At the British Scientific Products Exhibition, London, in 1918, Keith pointed out that physicists and laboratory workers were of the greatest value in war, rather than medical men in hospitals, since they discovered scientific instruments, iodine for dressing wounds, X-ray, and so on. He remarked that it used to be said that wars were won on the playing fields of Eton, but in future they would be won in the country's laboratories. This platitude was no doubt highly acceptable to the manufacturers of scientific equipment but it could be faulted on humanitarian grounds as he was told in no uncertain terms by the Red Cross. It is as a writer and writer on writers that Arthur Keith was known. As the country's foremost anatomist with a special inclination towards anthropology he was in a good position to review articles written by human palaeontologists. He had no need, as Huxley had said of scientific reviewers, to imitate the Ethiopians and 'cut steaks from the ox that carries them'.

As officer and one-time president of the Royal Anthropological Institute, Keith had the run of that body's publication, *Man*. His lengthy reviews of scientific works must have made their authors grind their teeth. By way of footnotes he demolished any complaints. Of Fred G. Wright's *The Origin and Antiquity of Man*[10] he remarked that there was little that threw light on this 'origin', and that the writer refused to accept what had happened in the past as a clue to what happened in the present. The most outstanding example of this was his opinion that woman was the result of direct creation. Keith said that Wright seemed to have as much faith in miracles as he did in science.

The following year, however, Keith published the first edition of his *The Antiquity of Man* but Wright, on being given the chance of getting his own back, seems to have been too aware of Keith's authority and his attacks are qualified with flattery. Wright urged that Keith ought to have been more cautious than to apply dates obtained from the examination of human skulls to the reconstruction of the Piltdown jaw which the reviewer thought was that of an animal. He said that Keith rightly admitted the possibility that the cranium and the jaw could have belonged to different individuals, then he 'left the stable ground of biological experience for that treacherous country in which reign the co-efficients of chance and argued well and ingeniously for the mandible belonging to the cranium'. He said his reconstruction of the Piltdown cranium was nearer the mark than 'the first ill-fated construction [Woodward's]'.

Keith neglected to reply. He may have felt that to do so in the circumstances was improper. In any case the review brought a letter from Grafton Elliot Smith who did not at all care for the reference to the first construction. In a highly technical reply he pointed out that 'with all its admitted faults' it was a closer approximation than any of the reconstructions for which Keith had been responsible. Smith concluded that 'this was a fact, the truth of which any anatomist who carefully examines the specimens and the whole literature of the dispute can convince himself'.

The next anthropologist to feel the Keithian ruler was Professor Wood-Jones, a professional colleague of Smith at Manchester. Wood-Jones theorized that man could be the ancestor of the anthropoid ape.[11] The orthodox view held that the common ancestor of man and ape was the small tree-dwelling *tarsius*. Not a few authorities at this time had begun to question this and reason that man, because of his refinement, had branched out from the main stem of evolution first, that the branching of the *tarsius* had come later, hence the more primitive ape. In complete contradiction to man's usual lack of humility in these matters it was also held by some authorities that as the ape was highly specialized for arboreal life he was the progressive phylum. Man, the ground-ape, they argued, was non-progressive, even degenerate.

Commenting on the Wood-Jones hypothesis, Keith congratulated the author on clearing away minor evolutionary difficulties by substituting major ones.[12] He said that there could be no progress in anatomy, any more than in cultural anthropology,

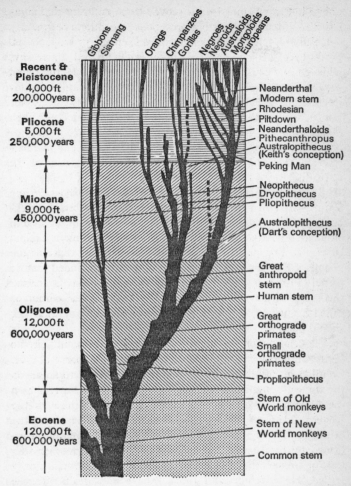

Sir Arthur Keith's placement of Piltdown man in 1931. He is shown as a branch which left the main stem of evolution in the Pliocene. Dart's *Australopithecus* was an anthropoid and a non-starter.

Another interesting point is that the Keithian 'tree' shows that he considers that Negroes left the main stem of evolution in rather the same way as the other variants of the human species. Note the alarming discrepancy in the length of the geological periods.

(From *New Discoveries Relating to the Antiquity of Man*. London, 1931.)

unless it was presumed until proved to be contrary that similarity and identity of custom presuppose a common origin.

Keith did, however, pick a formidable enemy in W. J. Sollas, professor of geology and palaeontology at Oxford University. This emnity was of long standing. Keith constantly railed against certain geologists who, he said, were completely uninterested in helping the anatomist to supply dates for human fossils. The leader of this faction, thought Keith, was Sollas.

Sollas argued [13] that Europe had once been inhabited by Eskimos and that this race had migrated north in the wake of the retreating ice of the last glaciation. He based his theory on a skull found at Chancelade which he considered displayed Eskimo features to a marked degree, particularly in its broad cheekbones. Keith said that he had seen the skull in question and although it possessed a few superficial resemblances to the Eskimo 'it was as European in its essential characters as those of the people of England and France today'. Keith concluded that he feared 'Professor Sollas' most cherished and most fascinating theories may have to be scrapped before another edition is called for, which, if truth is to be served and deserts rewarded, should be soon'.

Sollas did not suffer this attack in silence. [14] He could cite no better authority on the subject than the Professor Abbé H. Breuil 'who of all anatomists was best competent to speak on the subject'. Breuil had written: 'Dr Testut has clearly shown the resemblance of the Chancelade skeleton to those of the Eastern Eskimos . . . there is an array of facts in favour of the existence of an actual relationship, which is so admirably confirmed by the Chancelade skeleton'. By quoting another who was quoting another, Sollas considered the matter satisfactorily settled. He concluded: 'I think I have now dealt with the matter of the review; on its manner I cannot comment, for *le style c'est l'homme.*'

Sollas reiterated his view, to spite Keith further, in an article on the subject in *Man.* [15] He wrote that the ancestors of some at least of the Magdalenian people were to be found among the existing races of the arctic region, particularly those with large brains and Mongoloid features. Testut, he said, had unexpectedly arrived at this conclusion in 1889 when he said that the

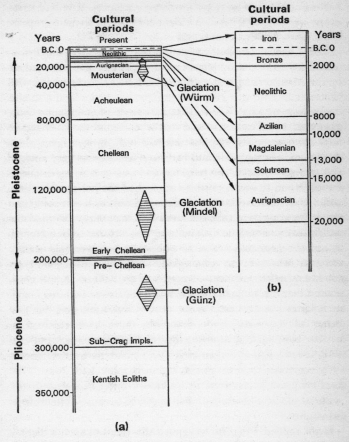

Sir Arthur Keith's view of the dates of flint cultures (a). (b) shows an amplification of scale (a). The scales show highly erroneous placement of the great glaciations and grossly underestimated durations for the Pleistocene and Pliocene. The Riss glaciation is undetected. Keith continually railed at geologists, particularly Professor W. J. Sollas, for their lack of enterprise in dating geological deposits.

(*New Discoveries Relating to the Antiquity of Man*. London, 1931.)

skulls that most resembled those of Chancelade were those of the Eskimos. The only doubter of this theory was Sir Arthur Keith (knighted in 1921 for services to science), who had written in his *Antiquity* that Chancelade man was of a true European racial kind. This was nonsense.

The Chancelade skull, wrote Sollas, represented the European during the closing phases of 'the Ice Age' and was marked by the Magdalenian flint culture. Keith had also stated that the Chancelade nose was long and straight but had added that the bridge was broken away so that its degree of prominence was unknown. But Testut had said that when found the Chancelade nose bone was complete but this had been broken later when the cast was being made and had been lost. It was very narrow and strongly bent to the left side and inflected so as to curve forwards and upwards until it approached the horizontal. This, said Sollas, fits the description of most Eskimos. Keith could not avoid the admission that the skull face was very wide and on this feature Chancelade man had the 'misfortune' to be assigned by him to a Mongoloid race. The question, however, said Sollas, was not whether the Chancelade skull was Mongoloid or not but whether Chancelade man was an Eskimo. Keith considered that the angle of the jaw was inconsistent with his being an Eskimo but any assessment of this was unreliable for the owner of the Chancelade mandible must have received a terrible blow on the head during his life which fractured the skull. Testut had cited the case of a similar blow experienced by a coachman whose horses had run away with him. The coachman had succumbed to his injury but Chancelade man, 'without medical assistance', had survived because of his splendid vitality.

Keith replied[16] that he welcomed the views of such a distinguished professor of geology on anatomical matters. He considered that brain size was not relevant to the issue, as people living in France before Chancelade were renowned for the size of the brain, for example, the Cro-Magnons. In fact Chancelade had more in common with the Cro-Magnons than with any known form of Eskimo. He regarded him as at one with the people of 'the so-called white races'. Sollas regarded him as a Mongol, the particular race he had chosen being the Eskimo. How could the matter be settled? 'By mere stroke of the eye.'

Keith said he had been familiar with this procedure for over half a century, and Sollas even longer.

We became anthropologists [he said] as soon as we could distinguish one race from another. As boys we had no need of callipers, nor indices, nor any mathematical procedure in identifying different breeds of dogs. The same method applied when out in the world and meeting diverse races of mankind. Some racial types were less well-marked than others but fortunately the Eskimo had a most sharply characterized form of human skull . . . Sollas seems to think that when a craniologist has a skull of unknown history in his hands, he sits down and measures its angles and calculates its indices and then sets out to search for a skull possessing similar angles and indices. Craniologists, I am glad to think, still have a trace of humour as well as common sense left to them; they do not stop strangers in the street to see if they are negro, Mongol or Caucasian. I do not believe that even Sollas does this . . . the cast of eye is sufficient for diagnosis of making racial identification of man or skull.

Keith said that it was ungallant of Sollas to throw the entire onus of mistaking Chancelade man for an Eskimo on the late Professor Testut. He said that it must be remembered that anthropologists of Testut's time believed races and cultures spread together (this is a heavy dig at Grafton Elliot Smith). Had it not been for the similarity of the cultures no one would have seen any resemblance between the races. Keith said that in racial diagnosis the nose bones were a more reliable guide than any other. The Chancelade nose bone had broken away but its roots were still in place and such a kind had never been seen in any Eskimo. Chancelade man had a large nose of a moderate width; such dimensions not only occurred in the Eskimo but in Europeans, especially in certain parts of France. Anatole France had such a nose but he bore no resemblance to an Eskimo. But Sollas would never be convinced. If Chancelade man was not an Eskimo then the whole pyramid that he had reared came tumbling down. In such circumstances it was too much to expect him to be impartial.

Professor Karl Pearson[17] tried to mediate. He thought the difference of opinion stemmed from the fact that Chancelade man had elements of modernity lacking in existing Eskimos, but he also had certain Eskimo features not present in modern man. Keith had said that 'a cast of eye' and an intimate knowledge of skulls of the races of mankind were essential qualifications of the craniologist. Pearson agreed with this view but the results of such a doctrine would seem to be that when two craniologists disagreed the only way to measure their authority would be by counting the number of skulls each had held in their hands. 'Is there not a touch of the mediaeval schoolman in this doctrine?' he asked.

Sollas replied[18] that ever since Testut's masterly description of the Chancelade skull was published in 1889, eminent anatomists had all agreed on his close relationship to the Eskimo. From what Keith had said he was beginning to fancy his Chancelade skull must be different from the one known to Sollas.

W. E. (later Sir) Le Gros Clark, a future execrator of Piltdown man, also interceded. He said that in 1920[19] he had published the result of a study of Eskimo skulls from old graves in Greenland. He had compared the contours with those of the Chancelade skull and there was no doubt that there were remarkable resemblances but there were also obvious differences, certainly enough to preclude a conclusive answer.

But Keith dropped the matter, possibly considering that Sollas' remarks about the different skulls might be taken as a capitulation or at least as a signal that he did not want to argue any more. This debate is an example of the kind which engaged the minds of two of the most distinguished scientists in Britain. Who was right? The present author can but quote an extract on Cro-Magnons from the authoritative *Guide to Fossil Man*[20] that:

... the Chancelade remains have been likened to the skeletons of modern Eskimos. . . . Whether or not these are valid distinctions it is apparent that the European Upper Palaeolithic men exhibited a wide range of variation.

Jacquetta Hawkes, writing in 1963[21] of the culture of southwestern France during the Upper Palaeolithic, said Chancelade man could be singled out as one of those responsible for:

... creating the last and most brilliant Upper Palaeolithic culture of south-western France . . . whose skull is universally admitted to have Eskimoid affinities in its vertical sides, pointed keel, and somewhat broad cheek bones. Although the old view that this race withdrew northwards in the wake of the ice after the last glaciation to form the ancestors of the modern Eskimo has now been much blown upon, it may have an element of truth in it. There seems no reason to deny that Chancelade man may have been involved in both the genetical and cultural inheritance of the Eskimo peoples.

A footnote is added:

The majority of anthropologists today reject the view that an affinity exists between the Chancelade type and the Eskimo . . . Nor is there any longer much support for the argument in favour of a connection between the late Upper Palaeolithic Magdalenian culture in western and central Europe and the Eskimo. All the available ethnographic and archaeological data testify to ties linking the forebears of the Eskimo with the Asiatic and American continents, not with western Europe.

Keith continued his disruptive reviews but he devoted more time to his *Antiquity*, which was published in 1925 as a two-volume work; a revised edition came out in 1929, and another, as *New Discoveries*, in 1931. It says much for the skill of Keith that he was able to write on his highly technical subject in a way that could be understood by the educated public without recourse to the 'Up jumped Baby Bunny' style thought fit for laymen by his professional colleagues. Another example of this rare talent was Sir Ray Lankester, and to a certain extent Grafton Elliot Smith, although the latter was also prone to unnecessary simplification.

Keith did, however, take time off to stamp on a claim for a South American anthropoid ape. The New World is completely devoid of this type of ape. The claim was made by a Dr Montandon on ten-year-old evidence. Writing in 1929[22] Keith said that he had heard about this so-called discovery. A Dr de Loys and a party were camping in jungle west of Venezuela when noises caused them to arm themselves with branches. Two animals, thought at first to be bears, 'behaving shamelessly by defecating into their hands as they advanced, had halted and threw their excrement at the invaders'. The company shot one, a female; the other, presumably a male, had made off. Keith wrote that de Loys had made no notes of the characteristics of the animals at the time and his recollections were somewhat vague. He simply mentioned that the animal had no tail. There was a photograph of the deceased animal seated on a box of unknown size which gave no indication of scale. The identification was further complicated by the abandonment of the animal's skin and skull when the party encountered hardship. Nonetheless Dr Montandon, ten years afterwards, was asserting that a new race of anthropoids had been discovered in South America and had named it *Ameranthropoides loysi*. Keith said the object on the box looked like a spider monkey. He concluded:

Thus we fear that the latest discovery which ascribes to South America a higher or lower kind of anthropoid ape, is doomed to go the way of so many others which have been announced from that continent. Since the beginning of this century there have been many alleged discoveries of such human ancestors but all have been proved to be other than this.

Keith had another interest which was as dear to his heart as his reviews or his writing. As president of the British Association in 1927 he had appealed for the preservation of Downe House, Kent, nineteen miles from London, where Charles Darwin had lived for forty years and had written his *The Origin* and *The Descent*. He had died there in 1882.

Keith was successful. The property was purchased by Sir Buckstone Brown, F.R.C.S., who transferred it to the Association with endowment funds for its maintenance and preservation 'for all time'. Later Brown endowed a building on an estate near Downe for use as an experimental surgical unit. On retirement Keith went to live there as Master of Buckstone Brown Institute where he continued surgical research. In his appeal Keith told the British Association of Downe's additional claim to fame. He said: 'We know now that as Darwin sat in his study at Downe, there lay hidden at Piltdown, in Sussex, not thirty miles distant . . .'

14

Dr K. A. Heberer was an example of that type of anthropologist which Arthur Keith said did not exist. He actually measured human skulls. In 1902 he had embarked on the task of measuring the skulls of live citizens of Peking, North China. He published a monograph on his findings.

Heberer also searched Chinese pharmacists' shops for fossil bones. Known locally as 'Dragon's bones' the fossils, when powdered and swallowed, were said to have remarkable medical qualities beside which today's penicillin seems pallid.

The results of Heberer's search were sent to Professor Max Schlosser at the University of Munich. He reported in 1903 that amongst the collection was the upper left molar of either a man or an anthropoid ape of a hitherto unknown genus. Schlosser recommended that anyone who might enjoy the privilege of carrying out palaeontological investigations in China should search for the remains of a new fossil ape or a Tertiary or Early Pleistocene human.

This advice seems to have been the starting point of what for the next twenty-four years became the preoccupation of any palaeontologist who visited the country. But it was an unrewarded task. The 'Dragon's bone' collectors, sensing competition, were non-committal about where in China they had been obtained. The pharmacists freely sold the fossils at a high price but said that as far as they were concerned the bones came from Heaven.

In 1916, however, the Chinese Department of Commerce invited Dr J. Gunnar Andersson, a former director of the Swedish Geological Survey, to administer similar work in China. The aim was an estimate of the country's mineral resources. Feeling that such a vast undertaking would deter the most zealous and ambitious geologist, the Chinese government added the inducement that part of the general activities of the survey would include the establishment of a museum of geology and palaeontology. Although the local authorities might have been aware of their country's palaeontological promise they must have been quite unprepared for its furtherance at the cost of the country's economic expansion.

The survey had not been in progress for more than a few months when Andersson decided that the programme could not be carried out without devoting some attention to the geology of the Western Hills, about twenty-five miles to the south-west of Peking. The Chinese were mystified by this attention. Here were the quarries of the 'white jade' and limestone, and the coalfields. The geology of this sector was well-known. But it was no coincidence that another feature of the Western Hills was a red clay, the soil of which had been found in the roots of the molar described by Schlosser.

Andersson began his hunt at Chikushan, some thirty miles south of Peking, but with no immediate success. Two years later, it is said that as the result of overhearing by chance workmen's conversation which informed him that 'Dragon's bones' could be found in plenty nearby, Andersson transferred operations to a limestone cliff near Choukoutien village. Within a short time he had found pieces of quartz quite foreign to the area. He is reported as saying (to whom is not known): 'This is primitive man'. Grafton Elliot Smith[1] reported the words in a less dramatic and more explicit form as: 'In this spot lies primitive man. All we have to do is find him.' The Nanking government thought otherwise and intimated that the survey was suffering in the interests of foreign palaeontology. Andersson was told to confine his attention to geology. An appeal was made to Stockholm and the industrialist Ivar Kreuger provided an endowment which enabled the importation of a young German geologist, Dr Otto Zdansky, to continue the search in place of Andersson.

The archaeology of parts of China was by no means a closed book, particularly to France. Père Emil Licent of the Society of Jesus had been at Tientsin since 1914 and was a regular correspondent of Marcellin Boule and the omnipresent Abbé Breuil. The fossils he sent Boule were in the main turned over for examination to Père Teilhard de Chardin.

In 1923 Teilhard de Chardin arrived in China. For two years past Emil Licent had been pressing him to come to the country to help with his collection and take part in an expedition to the interior. The priest disembarked at Shanghai and proceeded to Tientsin by train; two soldiers to each coach to ward off attacks by bandits.

The visitor wore several hats. His visit was sponsored by the Paris *Musée de Science*, which had the backing of the *Ministère de l'Instruction Publique*, the *Académie des Sciences* and the *Institut de paléontologie humaine*. By prior agreement any important discoveries were to go to the *Musée* in Paris, and duplicates to Licent's *Musée Hoang-ho-Pai-ho*, a wing of the *École des Hautes Études* in Tientsin.

Teilhard de Chardin was unimpressed by his archaeological colleague and fellow Jesuit Licent, who was touchy and quick-tempered and whose palaeontological work suffered from the distraction of a vast and chaotic collection of butterflies and moths. It is a mystery how the relationship of this ill-matched pair survived a 900-mile journey to Kansu province, which marches with Tibet to the west and Mongolia to the north. In addition to the threat of bandit attacks there was a plague of some deadly fever. Teilhard de Chardin reported dead bodies at numerous villages.

It seems, however, that safe passage was guaranteed by General Ma-Fou-Sian, mandarin and war lord, various lesser mandarins providing escorts *en route* for the caravan of six carts drawn by oxen. By the return to Tientsin in September 1924, after a journey worthy of Burton or Speke, the pair had collected fifteen packing cases of animal fossils and, according to Teilhard de Chardin, found traces of the ashes of two Palaeo-lithic hearths. Nevertheless, it appears, that the visitor was glad to return to Paris.

By 1926 Otto Zdansky had collected a large assemblage of fossil bones at Choukoutien but as there were no reference works in China which would enable an exact identification of the remains he returned to the University of Uppsala, where he devoted the summer of that year to the task.

Mingled with faunal fragments were two molars 'of human type'. But Zdansky was cautious, writing[2] that he was convinced that the evidence of the teeth was

wholly inadequate to venture any far reaching conclusion regarding the extremely meagre material described, and which, I think, cannot be more closely identified than *Homo sapiens*. I find I am credited in certain quarters with the discovery of 'Peking Man' (*vide* the daily newspapers); my purpose here is only to make it clear that my discovery of these teeth (which are of Quaternary age) should be regarded as decidedly interesting, but not of epoch-making importance.

But whether he liked it or not Zdansky was becoming the reluctant toast of palaeontology. On 22 October 1926 Grafton Elliot Smith's old associate at Manchester University, Dr Davidson Black, now professor of anatomy at the Peking Union Medical College, had made a 'confidential announcement' about the find of the human teeth to a scientific congress attended by Edwin Aintree, the then secretary to the Rockefeller Foundation.

It might be thought that an open secret would be as safe in Peking as anywhere but it appears that nothing was further from the case. The scientific congress was attended by delegates from Australia, New Zealand, the United States and France, with rounds of cocktail parties, intellectual conversation and 'rose-scented wine' which reminded Teilhard de Chardin of Paris. (The priest had returned to China for the conference.)

To this was added the pomp of a visit by the Crown Prince of Sweden. Indeed there was an element of Grand Guignol. There was political chaos and no central government. Although the Chinese Nationalists were in peaceful occupation of the city, the Chinese Communists were at its outskirts. There was even an 'interventionist' Russian armoured train in Peking Station. Feints at both sides were mounted by General Ma-Fou-Sian's private horde and bandits appeared like tumblers at a circus when the excitement seemed about to flag. Despite the unsettled state of the country and the military operations which for a time threatened Peking, two native representatives of the Chinese Geological Survey, Wong Wen-hao and V. K. Ting, appeared at Choukoutien to take over operations.

On 27 October 1927 Dr Birger Bohlin, another Swede, financed this time by the Rockefeller Foundation, found a third molar at Choukoutien. Arthur Keith adds the detail that the tooth was rushed to Peking by 'jinrikisha', a drive of some thirty-seven miles through country infested with 'soldier bandits'. It was on the strength of this discovery that Davidson Black astounded the scientific world in December by the announcement of the discovery of a new fossil man, naming him 'Peking Man' (*Sinanthropus pekinensis*).

This spectacular feat, based as it was on a single tooth, got a mixed reception. Grafton Elliot Smith commended Black for his courageous decision. Keith said it was audacious and ran the risk of egregious blunder. Boule said, however, that Black had been more or less obliged to make such a bold claim to support his previous one. Black in his description[3] seemed to have no doubts about Peking Man. He said the tooth could not be attributed to any race of known species of mankind, living or extinct. So much did it differ from other molar teeth, it represented not only a new species but a new genus. He believed the tooth belonged to a child of eight years old and that it was derived from the same jaw as the lower premolar discovered by Zdansky.

The following year Birger Bohlin, with two new arrivals at Choukoutien, C. C. Young and Pei Wen-Chung, found fragments of two jaws and braincases. In April 1929 a renewal of the Rockefeller Foundation grant enabled a section named the Cenozoic Research Laboratory to be set up; this was established in Lockhart Hall, a building formerly belonging to the London Missionary Society. Davidson Black became honorary director, C. C. Young his assistant and palaeontologist, and Pei Wen-Chung was placed in charge of field work. Teilhard de Chardin was appointed adviser and collaborator.

Teilhard de Chardin's continued presence in China with but short breaks from 1926 onwards, despite his chronic homesickness, was the result of conflict between his personal beliefs and those of his Church. In 1922 he had been invited by a fellow Jesuit, a professor of dogmatic theory, to prepare a paper indicating ways in which original sin might be represented to those unsatisfied with its official formulation. Teilhard de Chardin did no more than undertake a mental exercise by attempting an explanation of a doctrine he did not dispute. He wrote that original sin was a kind of necessary flaw in the universe.

But the paper found its way to Rome, and via Cardinal Merry de Val and the General of Jesuits, Father Ledochowski, back to the priest's Provincial at Lyons. The memory of the Modernist witch-hunt was still fresh in the mind of Père Costa de Beauregard[4] and Teilhard de Chardin was asked to promise neither to say nor to write anything against the traditional position of the Church in the matter of original sin.[5] A glimpse of Teilhard de Chardin's dissent was contained in a letter[6] to a Jesuit friend, Père August Valensin. He wrote:

In a kind of way I no longer have confidence in the exterior manifestations of the Church. I believe that through it the Divine influence will continue to reach me, but I no longer have much belief in the immediate and tangible nature of official directions and decisions. Some people feel happy in the visible Church, but for my own part I think I shall be happy to die in order to be free of it – and to find our Lord outside of it.

There is an account of Teilhard de Chardin's appearance at this time of exile. Henry de Montfried said:[7]

... his long face, forceful and finely drawn; the features emphasized by premature lines, looked as though carved out of tough wood. There was a lively twinkle in his eye; humour too, but no hint of irony; forbearing and kind.

That excellent narrator Leonard Cottrell, a historian who has done for Egyptology what the late Gavin Maxwell did for the otter, has so rightly commented[8] on the number of times archaeological searches have been rewarded just as the searcher was about to give up in despair. In 1873 Heinrich Schliemann was about to pay off his workers when he discovered at 'Homer's Troy' what he thought was the fair Helen's jewellery. Howard Carter's six-year quest in the Valley of Kings had reached the end of its last season when Tutankhamen's Tomb came to light in 1922. And it was so with Peking man.

The 1929 winter was fast approaching. W. C. Pei dismissed the labour force on 2 December. Late that afternoon he walked to the excavations at the foot of the Choukoutien escarpment and probed into the sand with his yard-stick, exposing the smooth dome of a skull embedded in cave travertine. According to George Barbour[9] he loosened the block containing the skull with a hammer and chisel and 'saw at once that the top of the cranium was larger than any ape so far unearthed'. A battery of candles from the village store gave just enough light for a time exposure of the skull *in situ*. He carried the skull back to his room with care. He got another photograph of his prize wrapped in burlap soaked with flour paste, and balanced above three braziers so that it could dry out during the night. By dawn he was able to set out for Peking without fear of shedding fragments on the road. Pei wrapped the treasure in his soiled linen, bargained with a rickshaw puller, and set out for the city, his precious bundle between his feet, hidden by the long skirt of his Chinese scholar's gown. Pei covered the thirty-five miles safely and delivered his trophy to Davidson Black at the Peking Union Medical College well before dusk.

Of this skull Grafton Elliot Smith wrote:

There can be no doubt that just as the finding of the jaws [*sic*] in 1928 suggested the possibility of the same kinship with the Piltdown man, the skull in 1929 caused opinion to swing in the other direction, and suggested a nearer kinship with *Pithecanthropus* [Java man].

Black published his scientific description of the find in 1930 but an earlier announcement was made to the Press. *The Times*' correspondent in Peking, under the headline 'Early Man in China: Pre-Neanderthal Skull Found', wrote:[10]

At an open meeting of the Geological Society of China on 28 December the closely guarded details of the finding in North China of the skull of a man hundreds of thousands of years old were officially revealed. The discovery was claimed to be the most important of its kind. The credit for the actual discovery goes to a young Chinese geologist, Mr W. C. Pei. The skull belongs to an entirely new genus, known to science as *Sinanthropus pekinensis* and is definitely placed above Java man in brain capacity but below Neanderthal man. The skull is considered to antedate that of Neanderthal and held to be nearer the genus *Homo* than either Piltdown or Java. Although not the 'missing link' in the popular sense, the Peking man has been described here as a cousin to the dawn ancestor of man [Piltdown], and estimates of the age of the skull vary greatly. Dr [A. W.] Grabau, adviser to the China Geological Society, states that the Peking man lived at the beginning of the Quaternary, and gives his age as 1,000,000 years, but Père Teilhard de Chardin, president of the Geological Society of France, and also adviser to the Chinese Survey, favours an estimate of 400,000 to 500,000 years ... [Modern estimates agree with Teilhard's.]

Arthur Keith wrote in *New Discoveries*, on the evidence of the teeth, that the owner must have been as distinctive as *Pithecanthropus erectus* and *Eoanthropus dawsoni*. In his next chapter, however, on the discovery of the skull, he amended this to say that it closely resembled *Pithecanthropus*. He left his original statement unaltered, he said, 'so that readers could see for themselves how the methods of anthropologists are fallible'.

Grafton Elliot Smith wrote that Black had hoped that by prompt publication of his find and wide circulation of manuscript reports he would avoid misunderstandings 'such as those that marred the discussion of previous fossil men but despite these precautions eminent palaeontologists in Germany [possibly Weidenreich – an expatriate] and France [Boule] are already claiming that *Sinanthropus* belongs to the genus *Pithecanthropus*. In America there is the suggestion that *Sinanthropus* is merely a Far Eastern example of Neanderthal man. Others believe the Chinese fossils are not human at all.'

An obviously angry Marcellin Boule had in fact put it more forcibly, writing that:

Black, who had felt justified in forging the term *Sinanthropus* to designate one tooth, was naturally concerned to legitimise this creation when he had to describe a skull-cap. It is now quite evident by studying Black's table of measurements, the differences between *Pithecanthropus* and *Sinanthropus*, far from possessing generic value, are less than variations recorded within the very natural specific groups of Neanderthal. Correctly the Choukoutien fossils should be called, until there is proof to the contrary, *Pithecanthropus pekinensis*.

Old Eugene Dubois, not seeing any resemblance at all, resented this allusion. He said that only his *Pithecanthropus* justified the name 'ape-man' and that *Sinanthropus* belonged to the Neanderthal race and was in fact a primitive type of *Homo sapiens*.

Smith wrote in 1931 that he could see an analogy, 'though it is not identical' to the Piltdown jaw. He regarded it as evidence in support of the claim that the Piltdown skull and jaw were part of the same individual. He said that features of the *Sinanthropus* jaw suggested the possibility that the fossil man of China 'might be more nearly akin to the Early Pleistocene man of Piltdown rather than Java man'. The *Sinanthropus* braincase had many features unknown to both *Eoanthropus* and *Pithecanthropus* and threw a great deal of light on their common ancestor. He continued:

In studying early man's remains it is always very important to search for tools and implements to mark a particular phase of industry. It was a very significant phenomenon that during the last three years there was no trace of implements.

The absence of tools, concluded Smith, was no coincidence. *Sinanthropus* was at too early a stage of development to have begun to shape stones. He added that 'it was impossible to state whether he had perishable tools such as wood, although it was probable with his type of brain he would have had sticks as means of defence and of obtaining food either by digging or killing animals'.

This statement was an amalgam of oversight and peculiar reasoning. Smith himself had quoted Andersson's remark on the discovery of the pieces of quartz. These certainly came into the eolith category. If *Sinanthropus* was akin to the tool-making Piltdown man, why was it significant that no tools had been discovered at Choukoutien?

Now the discoveries came quickly. Under the directorship of Pei more skulls and bones were brought to light. By 1935 the material attributed to Peking man was eight more or less complete braincases, a dozen fragments of lower jaws, two fragments of humeri and radius, one semi-lunar bone and four ungual phalanges. According to the German authority Franz Weidenreich, the discovered population of Choukoutien was represented by the remains of ten children, two adolescents and twelve adults, men and women. By 1939 this had risen to thirty-eight individuals, fifteen being either children or adolescents. There were ashes, implying the use of fire, and evidence of bone and stone tool industries.

The Abbé Breuil wrote that *Sinanthropus* must have been able to kindle fire and must have done so frequently; he used bone implements and he worked stone 'just as much as the palaeolithics of the West'. In spite of the skull, he said, which closely resembled that of *Pithecanthropus*, he was not merely an ape-man but a human, with an ingenious mind capable of inventing, and hands sufficiently adroit to fashion, tools and weapons.

But Boule condemned such conclusions, writing that 'in order to give *Sinanthropus* human status the anatomists leant on the

173

archaeologists and the archaeologists on the anatomists'. The palaeontologist, he urged, must consider the circumstances of the deposit and the unvarying nature of the *Sinanthropus* remains. How could an almost complete lack of 'long bones' be explained?

Franz Weidenreich had a sensational answer. The *Sinanthropus* skulls, he said, were brought to the cave by hunters who chiefly attacked women and children and chose heads as spoils or trophies. He proposed that these hunters were superior beings, probably the usurping *Homo sapiens*. He thought the stone tools were by no means primitive – many of their features were not present in the tools belonging to the Upper Palaeolithic discovered in France. This sophistication, however, was thought by Weidenreich to support his argument that there had been a superior race present at Choukoutien. Boule entirely agreed. He argued, remarkably, that no one could contest this theory by asking why no remains of the *Homo sapiens* oppressors had been found in the cave. Such were not necessary, said Boule, as in Western Europe there were grottoes and caves rich in Palaeolithic implements in which no *Homo sapiens* remains had been found. So the Choukoutien remains must be 'a mere hunter's prey' and *Sinanthropus* was no more than an animal exploited for food.

In the light of this reasoning it must be wondered how any implement could be attributed to any human fossil. A fractious authority could always introduce a higher cannibal which could despoil, leave his tools and then vanish without trace.

Sir Wilfrid Le Gros Clark,[11] however, wrote that there was no evidence to support the assumption of this superior being and that Peking man was well able to develop the Choukoutien culture. In spite of his low average cranial capacity, some individuals found in the cave came within the normal range of *Homo sapiens*. His findings were also based on the discoveries by Dr G. H. R. von Koenigswald from 1936 to 1939 of more Java men which were so closely akin to the Chinese fossils it is now presumed that the vast differences Black saw between *Sinanthropus* and *Pithecanthropus* were due in the main to his enthusiasm for a new genus. Even the title *Pithecanthropus* has now been rejected in favour of *Homo erectus* – a mere species of the genus *Homo* to which modern man belongs.

In his discussion of the Choukoutien fossils Le Gros Clark said carefully that the modern assumptions had to be based on the plaster casts and the reports made at the time. He had good reason. After the death of Davidson Black in 1936, according to one account from silicosis caused by dust from drilling the fragments from their mineral covering, the control of the Central Cenozoic Laboratory passed to Dr Franz Weidenreich. The excavations continued into the occupation until 1941 when increased interference by a far more tangible usurper than that erroneously postulated by Boule – the Japanese – made further work at the site impossible.

By this time, however, Weidenreich had already departed for the United States with a set of plaster casts. The original fossils remained at the Peking Union Medical College. What happened next is uncertain. Evidently Wong Wen-hao decided to send the bones to Weidenreich in America and obtained the co-operation of the American, Dr Henry Houghton, director of the Medical College. The bones were crated and taken to the United States Embassy which itself was in the throes of departure from China. The crates have never been heard of since. What is certain, however, is that today the Chinese People's Republic blames the United States for the loss.

Work at the site was resumed under the Chinese Republic in 1959. On 6 July of that year a fragment of another mandible was discovered. The close of the scientific description of the jaw [12] contains the following not too subtle indictment:

As the world famous *Sinanthropus* remains uncovered before the liberation were all disappeared during World War II while in American hands at Peking this new *Sinanthropus* discovery is of especial value.

Carleton S. Coon [13] stated that all the *Sinanthropus* material was lost in an accident as a result of military action while being transferred from Peking to the S. S. *President Harrison*. W. Howells [14] supplies the further information that the fossils were given to a Colonel Ashurst who commanded the U.S. Marine detachment at the embassy. The remains left Peking by train at 5 a.m. on 5 December 1941, and arrived at the port of Chingwangtao two days later. The crates passed from the control of the Marines when they were interned by the Japanese.

The second decade of the twentieth century had begun with four contenders for the title of ancestor to modern man. These were Neanderthal, Java, Heidelberg and Piltdown. The problem seemed insoluble and many and bitter were the debates between those who favoured one as the direct ancestor of modern man and those who would not have him in the family at any price.

The ape-jawed Piltdown man seems to have been the favourite. His ferocious jaw was overlooked because of his noble forehead. Indeed his intellectual prowess, it was thought, saved him from annihilation. As Neanderthal man and his kind had sat in caves scowling helplessly at the glaciers, the superior intellect of Piltdown man had caused him to take off southwards to warmer climes. Neanderthal man and his Java cousin had perished of cold and starvation. By his survival Piltdown man had become our ancestor.

But then had come Peking man, another silent witness to the uniqueness of the Sussex fossil. The debate which ensued was in its later stages coeval with another of greater implications. Indeed it cast a shadow over *Sinanthropus*. The real missing link, so its discoverer claimed, had been found at last.

In 1922 Dr Raymond Dart had arrived in South Africa to take up the chair of anatomy in the University of Witwatersrand. Dart was a former assistant in Sydney of Grafton Elliot Smith's brother, Arthur. World War I had brought him to England in the army medical corps. After the war Dart worked under the great Grafton Elliot Smith at University College, London. Dart fully admits[1] that this was the fulfilment of a student dream. He had never forgotten the lecture on fossil men delivered by Smith to the British Association in Sydney in 1914.

There can be no doubt that Dart was fascinated by his distinguished countryman. He wrote that Smith was tall, ruddy-complexioned with immaculate white hair ... the complete antithesis of the woolly-minded genius of fiction. Elliot Smith with all his brilliance, in every sense, was a man of the world, a great *raconteur* and popular with his colleagues and assistants who could usually rely on him to attend and enliven their daily tea parties.

Dart also recollects the comparatively sombre Sir Arthur Keith and the professor of anatomy at the Royal College of Surgeons remembered him. Keith recommended Dart for the Witwatersrand chair but with slight misgivings, writing in his autobiography in 1950 that he had done so with 'a certain degree of trepidation. Of his [Dart's] powers of intellect and imagination there could be no question; what rather frightened me was his flightiness, his scorn for accepted opinion, the unorthodoxy of his outlook.'

Dart stood in awe of these contemporary giants of anatomy and prehistory. He was also overshadowed by them. Not many years had elapsed before he sought escape from the Olympian aura. He found it at Witwatersrand.

Within three years of his arrival in South Africa Dart had fully justified Keith's fears. Miss Josephine Salmons, a student demonstrator in Dart's department, while on a social visit to the home of a mine-owner, E. G. Izard, was shown a skull of a fossil baboon which had been blasted out of fifty feet of limestone in a quarry at Taungs, some eighty miles north of Kimberley.

The skull was new to Dart and he asked a colleague, Dr R. B. Young, who coincidently was planning a study of the Taungs quarry, to keep an eye open for similar examples. Young returned with a box of samples amongst which Dart found a natural cast in limestone of the left side and mandible of some sort of anthropoid. Further chipping of the limestone revealed an almost complete skeletal face.

In Dart's view this was clearly no baboon, and no anthropoid, living or fossil, had ever been encountered in this area. The anthropoids were confined to forestation and jungle. But what impressed Dart most was the size of the brain suggested by the skull. Dart considered that this creature was immature, possibly of some six years of age, but the brain cast suggested a cranial capacity of some 300 c.c., certainly approaching that of an adult chimpanzee. Dart saw other striking features. The flat skull bore no eyebrow ridges and the teeth, Dart thought, were decidedly human in pattern.

The present writer has been unable to discover whether it was ever Dart's intention to inform the British Museum's Natural History department at South Kensington, London. A fellow discoverer of *Australopithecus* (Southern ape), as the fossil was named by Dart, Dr Robert Broom, felt that this neglect of a time-honoured custom was at the root of the initial anger at Dart's claim. The discoverer certainly played his cards badly but through no fault of his own. Dart prepared a scientific description of *Australopithecus* for *Nature*. Unfortunately the editor of the South African newspaper *Star*, B. G. Paver, had got wind of the story. In exchange for a promise not to publish before the description appeared in *Nature* Dart gave Paver full information on the find and photographs. But the editor of *Nature* tarried while he canvassed opinions about Dart's claims from expert anatomists such as Arthur Keith. The result was a cabled ultimatum from Paver to *Nature*. He said that he could not hold the story beyond the evening of 3 February. Pressure was once more put on Keith who told the editor of *Nature* to go ahead. But by the time it did, on 7 February, it was too late. The *Star* had beaten *Nature* to the punch by four days.

As is usual with popular treatment of scientific subjects lengthy reflection was sacrificed on the altar of impact and sensation. Dart's find was hailed in the *Star* as the one and only missing link, and only Dart knew what he was talking about. London journalism, indeed that of the entire Western world, took up the cry. The real missing link had been found at last. Scientific opinion, particularly that of Sir Arthur Smith Woodward (knighted in 1924) and his colleagues at South Kensington, was caught napping. Poor Woodward had officially retired but was still in attendance at the museum. He thought that Dart had stolen a march on him and was trying to sneak a fossil man in under his nose. Forgetting his own caution over Piltdown Woodward thought that this was carrying secrecy too far and told the besieging journalists so.

The news was first broken in England by *The Times*.[2] The report said that *Australopithecus* was a creature neither anthropoid nor human in form or brain power. Only two weeks before, said the newspaper, Sir Arthur Keith had said that Rhodesian man was in the direct line of human ascent but maybe the new discovery would cause this view to be modified. The following day the newspaper went further, saying that 'many times the unearthing of a primitive skull has been hailed as the missing link but Grafton Elliot Smith had told a reporter that if Dart's discovery lived up to his description then such a creature had now been discovered'. Smith had told *The Times*:

An interesting point which emerges is that the discovery [of *Australopithecus*] supports Darwin's theory that Africa was probably the home of the human family. That view has not been favourably regarded by many writers though I have always inclined to that view.

It is a pity that nobody asked Smith how he equated this inclination with his views on human migration from its source in the Near East or Asia. It will also be noted that Darwin was mercilessly used to support any proposition in hand. His *The Descent of Man*, being a comprehensive review of evidence both for and against a particular proposition, readily lent itself to such subversion. Like Dr Johnson, Darwin can be reliably quoted as saying almost anything about everything. In the case of Dubois he could be cited as preferring the East for the origin of man, now he was being quoted as being in favour of Africa. In fact he had mentioned both continents.

In the next report in *The Times*[3] Dart was announcing that thousands of fossil *Australopithecines* had probably been unearthed at Taungs and thrown away. Gone with the lime, he said, to destruction at the Natal sugar refineries or the carbide works at Germiston. Dart said he had been informed that 'a very good complete skeleton' had been blasted out of the limestone and thrown on the quarry dump. We must, urged Dart, watch every deposit in future.

But what claims had Dart actually made for *Australopithecus*? The long-awaited *Nature* article appeared at last on 7 February. It lived up to its promise. Dart wrote that in the past the search for the missing link had overlooked one thing – incentive. What had possessed the evolving ape to leave his four-footed mode of progression and walk erect?

'For the production of man,' Dart reasoned, 'something was needed to sharpen wits and quicken intellect – in fact a more open veldt country [rather than jungle] where competition was keenest between swiftness and stealth and where quickness of the mind and movement were so important for the preservation of the species.'

Dart continued that no country in the world more abounded with ferocious animals than South Africa, and he quoted Darwin as saying so. The great biologist, said Dart, had used the expression 'wild' but he meant to imply ferocity. In Dart's opinion these ferocious predators, when combined with the vast open veldt country around Taungs, where there was only occasional forested shelter, and a shortage of water, had heightened the 'bitter animal competition'. At Taungs, wrote Dart, a swift-moving, fast-thinking anthropoid had evolved. This was the birth of mankind. His name was *Australopithecus*.

Dart received many congratulatory telegrams. One was from General J. C. Smuts who at the time was being snubbed politically and had chosen natural history as a subject with which to kill time. Another came from his old mentor, Grafton Elliot Smith. Sir Arthur Keith did not oblige, merely writing in his journal (1925) that he thought the so-called *Australopithecus* seemed more akin to ape than to man. At first he was inclined to leave statements to the press to Smith, but a few days later he told the reporters that 'Dart was not likely to be led astray. If he has thoroughly examined the skull we are prepared to accept his decision.'

In fact 'they' were not. In a combined rejoinder to Dart's claim for *Australopithecus* which was published in the next issue of *Nature*[4] Keith set the tone. He wrote that he had found it easy to enlarge Dart's profile drawings of *Australopithecus* to adult size. The result seemed to him to belong to the same sub-family as the chimpanzee and the gorilla. It was, he wrote, nearly akin to both. Sir Arthur Smith Woodward, who had examined photographs of the fossil, found that he could see nothing in the orbits, nasal bones and canine teeth nearer to those of humans than those displayed by the skull of a modern young chimpanzee. Professor W. L. Duckworth thought that Dart's claims were entirely unjustified. Even Grafton Elliot Smith turned a shoulder on his disciple. He said he did not disagree with Dart but he required more proof than had been supplied so far.

He enlarged his theme in a lecture at University College in May which was fully reported in *The Times*. He said that although *Australopithecus* had been classed as the missing link it was not one of the 'significant' links for which science had been searching. It was unmistakably an ape, nearly akin to those still living in Africa. He added:

It is unfortunate that Dart had no access to skulls of infant chimpanzees, gorillas or orange-utans of an age corresponding to that of the Taungs skull for had such material been available he would have realized that the posture and poise of the head, the shape of the jaws, and many details of the nose, face and cranium on which he relied for proof of his contention that *Australopithecus* was nearly akin to man, were essentially identical with the conditions met in the infant gorilla and chimpanzee.

Professor R. von Virchow was now dead so his usual greeting of 'microcephalic idiot' was wanting in the case of *Australopithecus*. But Professor A. Robinson in a lecture in Edinburgh did dismiss the fossil as the distorted skull of a chimpanzee.

With scientific rejection of *Australopithecus* came world-wide derision for Dart. The music-hall comedians substituted *Australopithecus* jokes for mother-in-law anecdotes. In London the *Morning Post* ran witty commentaries about the South African find. Readers were invited to contribute 'epitaphs' to mark the demise of *Australopithecus* 'in not more than six lines of verse or sixty of prose'.

One ran:

> Here lies a man, who was an ape,
> Nature, grown weary of his shape,
> Conceived and carried out the plan
> By which the ape is now the man.

The winning contribution was:

> Speechless with half-human leer,
> Lies a monster hidden here,
> Yet here, read backwards, beauty lies,
> And here the wisdom of the wise.

Most newspapers carried a cable from New York which read:

Professor Dart's theory that the Taungs skull is a missing link has evidently not convinced the legislature of Tennessee, the governor of which state has signed an 'Anti-Evolution Bill' which forbids the teaching of any theory contrary to the Biblical story of the Creation, and that man has descended from the lower orders. Similar legislation which is at present before other state legislatures marks the growth of a strict Biblicist movement represented by so-called fundamentalist churches whose leading propagandist is the silver-tongued orator, William Jennings Bryan.

At Witwaterstrand Dart received threatening letters. One said that he was sitting on the brink of the eternal abyss of flame and would later 'roast in the general fires of Hell'. Another hoped his 'heresy would be punished by being unblessed with a family which looks like this hideous monster with the hideous name'. A letter to the editor of the *Sunday Times* under the heading 'Hammer and Taungs' from 'A Plain but Sane Woman' asked Dart 'how he could become a traitor to his Creator?' 'What,' asked the plain woman, 'does your Master [Satan] pay you for trying to undermine God's word? Or do you not know his wages?'

The South African government nonetheless invited Dart to exhibit *Australopithecus* at the country's pavilion at the British Empire Exhibition held at Wembley, near London, in the summer of 1925. Dart also prepared a chart to explain in simple terms the place of *Australopithecus* in the evolution of mankind. He placed his fossil as a direct ancestor of *Pithecanthropus* (Peking man) and related Rhodesian man to Heidelberg and Neanderthal. The caption read: 'AFRICA: THE CRADLE OF HUMANITY'.

When he saw it Keith was immensely upset. He issued a statement to the press saying: 'The famous Taungs skull is not that of the missing link between ape and man.' He followed this up with a lengthy letter to *Nature* which firmly rejected *Australopithecus*. He wrote:

Professor Dart has described it [*Australopithecus*] as representing an 'extinct race of apes intermediate between the living anthropoids and man' . . . The skull is that of a young anthropoid ape – one which was in its fourth year of growth, a child – and showing so many points of affinity with the two living African anthropoids, the gorilla and chimpanzee.

Keith found that the development of the jaw and face showed a certain refinement not met with in the modern anthropoids, indeed it showed human traits, but *Australopithecus* had occurred much too late in prehistory to have any place in man's ancestry.

But Dart had his supporters, one of whom was the American sceptic Dr Ales Hrdlička. In 1925 Hrdlička had set out on a world-wide palaeontological survey, visiting sites in India (Siwalik) where *Ramapithecus*, an early hominid with anthropoid affinities, had been discovered, Java, China and then Taungs. He examined the *Australopithecus* skull and declared for Dart. But later in London he seems to have fallen under the spell of Keith and Smith and said before the Royal Anthropological Society that the relationship of the Taungs fossil with mankind could only be determined 'when the specimen is well identified'.

In 1931 Dart realized that the only chance for *Australopithecus* was a direct confrontation with his adversaries in London. With the fossil in a wooden box carried by his wife Dora, who could be relied on not to lose it, Dart arrived in England and immediately got in touch with Smith, Keith and Woodward. All three gave him an enthusiastic reception but it was misleading. They only wanted to tell him about *Sinanthropus*.

Smith, however, gave Dart a chance. Smith had recently returned from Choukoutien and was engaged by the Zoological Society in London to speak on the Chinese fossil on the evening of 17 February. 'Will you come as my guest – and bring your Taungs baby with you?' Dart joyfully agreed.

The evening was a disaster. Woodward was in the chair and Smith was at his best. Playing the audience like a harp he gave a scintillating account of *Sinanthropus*. With lantern slides he showed how the Chinese fossil was confirmation of but different from Java Man. Eloquently Smith described how it was strongly suspected that *Sinanthropus* was a cannibal because of the numerous cracked skulls and split bones which had been encountered at Choukoutien – and how he was sufficiently advanced to know how to make fire. Smith sat down to resounding applause. After a brief introduction Dart was thrown to the lions.

At once Dart knew that this audience, after imbibing the heady wine of Smith's oratory, was not an ideal one before which to vindicate his claims for *Australopithecus*. He was no speaker. He described his own performance as 'pitiful' and 'fumbling'. The look of polite attention on the assembled fourscore faces became fixed. As Dart feared, it was an anti-climax. A feeble rattle of applause greeted him when he resumed his seat.

Smith who, according to Dart, sensed his guest's disappointment, invited Dart to dine the following evening at the Royal Society Club. He was placed on the left of the famous physicist Sir Charles Boys. Dart reported that he was well received but he decided to return to South Africa.

Dart left his fossil with Smith, who persuaded F. O. Barlow of the British Museum to make some plaster casts. Dora, who had collected the skull from Smith's Hampstead home, left it in a taxi. Smith spent until four the following morning on the telephone attempting vainly to trace the whereabouts of *Australopithecus*. The cabby, however, had handed the box in at Fulham police station.

It is traditional that poor Dart, defeated and dejected, followed the cue of Dubois and retired into obscurity with his fossil. Dart hotly denies this and with justification. The scepticism and anger which met his claims for *Australopithecus* in some strange way had brought distinction to his university. Dart detected a change in the attitude of his colleagues. In the year of the discovery he was elected Dean of the Faculty of Medicine. That same year he was invited to become president of the South African Association for the Advancement of Science and a Fellow of the Royal Society of South Africa.

Robert Broom was one of the most tireless palaeontologists of all time. His work on the extinct reptiles of the Karoo drew the attention of J. C. Smuts who by now had become premier. Broom was offered the post of curator of palaeontology at the Museum of the Transvaal; his real task, however, was to find another *Australopithecus* for though Dart had continued his search at Taungs he had had no further success. In 1936, within a few weeks of commencing operations at a limeworks at Sterkfontein, a few miles west of Johannesburg, Broom brought one to light. But because of differing anatomical features the new discovery was named *Australopithecus transvaalensis*. He later changed this to *Plesianthropus* (near ape-man).

Other discoveries followed rapidly. Some more *Australopithecines* came to light at Sterkfontein, others at the nearby quarries of Kromdraai and Swartkraans. But because of their size these later finds were attributed not only to a different species but a new genus. They became *Paranthropus robustus* (robust apeman) and *Paranthropus cressidens* (larger ape-man).

The search was interrupted by World War II but was resumed in 1947. In this year Dart's persistence was rewarded at Makapansgat, 120 miles north of Pretoria. The new fossil was thought to have used fire, as some charred sticks were found along with the bones in the newly-revealed limestone cave. Dart therefore gave him the title *Australopithecus prometheus*. In 1959 Professor L. S. Leakey found *Zinjanthropus* – Nutcracker man – so called because of a suspected but absent enormous jaw. This has not been found, however. Nutcracker man was found in Tanzania, 2,000 miles north of Taungs, but there is no doubt about his *Australopithecus* affinities. In this area *Australopithecines* are today being discovered in abundance.

The peculiarities that gave rise to the generic and specific names of these fossils are still the subject of much debate. But all the *Australopithecines* have in common features which justify to an amazing degree the claims made by Dart in 1925.

Australopithecus has a long face which protrudes in a snout, a steeply slanted forehead, ape-like lower jaw and human-type dentition. The brain of an adult varies with the individual from 450 c.c. to 650 c.c.[5] The foramen magnum, the cable entry by which the skull is articulated with the top of the spine, is distinctly further forward than that of the chimpanzee or gorilla. This suggests that *Australopithecus* held his head upright and could walk erect.

Adult individuals come in two sizes. At Taungs, Sterkfontein and Makapansgat, he is the size of a modern adult pygmy, about five feet tall, and weighs just less than a hundred pounds. At Kromdraai and Swartkraans, however, he is a much more imposing individual, both taller and heavier, well within the full-size human range in height and weighing about one hundred and fifty pounds; this of course is another species of *Australopithecus*.

There are three main views as to the place of *Australopithecus* in evolution. First, that he is a true anthropoid allied to the chimpanzee or gorilla with certain features curiously like those of man. Second, that he is a hominid, his resemblances to man being far too numerous to be explained other than by a direct relationship; in this view if he is not man's direct ancestor then he is very closely allied to the first men, a collateral branch to that of human stock, which died out without issue. Third, that he represents a group of anthropoids in the process of evolving towards humanity which, however, never actually crossed the threshold into humanity; the promise of his erect-walking and high brain capacity being unfulfilled.

That *Australopithecus* could walk erect is now generally accepted. But how erect and for how long is highly debatable. Sir Wilfrid Le Gros Clark suggests that his posture would be something less than human. S. L. Washburn feels that he only rose to two feet when running and reverted to all fours as soon as possible.

The degree of erectness is an important issue and has far-reaching implications. If the creature could stand, this would free his hands to use pebbles as tools or even to fashion them.

When Dart found *Australopithecus prometheus* in 1947, by naming him such he made an extravagant claim. He never actually found evidence of fire or ashes to support it. But he went further. He said that *Australopithecus prometheus* was a hunter of small mammals for food. His weapons, claimed Dart, were stones and chipped bones.

This claim was not made idly. The *Australopithecus* remains were found in the company of a large number of baboon skulls. Forty-eight out of fifty-two of these skulls show impact fracture. Le Gros Clark agrees that this kind of fracture is consistent with well-directed blows from an implement of some kind. He finds it difficult to offer a more likely explanation. If *Australopithecus* was in fact a missile-throwing hunter, this certainly suggests a skill not possessed by anthropoid apes. Killing by use of weapons is the prerogative of the human race.

The American Carleton S. Coon, however, has suggested that this evidence has been misinterpreted. As in the case of *Sinanthropus* he considers that *Australopithecus* was more likely to be the hunted than the hunter. Coon based his theory on the statistics revealed by the total animal remains found with the fossil at Makapansgat. Ninety-two per cent were antelope of various

Caption for diagram opposite.

The modern view of evolution agreed by the majority of authorities today. *Australopithecus* plays the part of Piltdown man. The specialized type of Neanderthal man occupies Piltdown man's later position before the Sussex fossil's final dismissal from the fossil catalogue in 1953. (From *History of the Primates*. 9th edition. Sir Wilfrid Le Gros Clark, British Museum, 1965.)

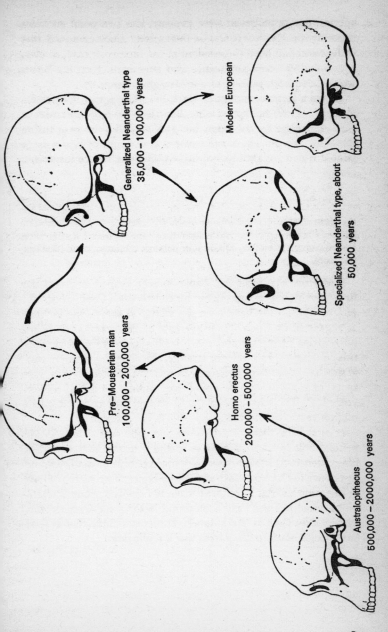

Generalized Neanderthal type
35,000 – 100,000 years

Modern European

Specialized Neanderthal type, about
50,000 years

Pre–Mousterian man
100,000 – 200,000 years

Homo erectus
200,000 – 500,000 years

Australopithecus
500,000 – 2000,000 years

species, one point seven were baboons and two point six were those of the *Australopithecines* themselves. Coon reasoned that if the fossil had been the resident of the limestone cave, or even a cannibal as some authorities had suggested, then his bones would have been present in a greater proportion.

It was a former student of Dart, his successor at Witwatersrand, G. W. H. Schepers, who claimed to have found evidence that *Australopithecus* hunted his own kind for the pot. Inside the skull of a *Paranthropus robustus* at Kromdraai was a large pebble which apparently had driven the bone before it into the cavity.

The presence of this rock is evidence suggestive that the claims that have been previously made that the *Homunculi* as represented by the *Australopithecoid* and *Plesianthropoid* [derived from *Plesianthropus*, Broom's later name for *Australopithecus transvaalensis*] fossils were skilled enough to employ missiles for defensive, offensive and predator purposes.

Unfortunately Schepers' paper merely heaped coals on the fire of the hunted versus the hunter controversy. Could *Australopithecus* then really have been the victim of some superior race as suggested by Coon? As in the case of *Sinanthropus* there are no remains of a later and more sophisticated race to support this contention, and modern stratigraphical dating strongly suggests that *Australopithecus* seems to have existed over a vast space of time, from two and a half million to a half-million years B.P. Tools have been found dating back two and a half million years, well in the range of *Australopithecus*.

It is certain that something or someone was flaking crude pebble tools in *Australopithecus* territory in the later period of his existence. At Makapansgat seventeen pebble tools were found just above the layer of *Australopithecus* bones. Two pieces of rock in the same layer at Kromdraai seem to have been shaped. Definite worked pebbles have been found in the same layer as *Australopithecus* teeth at Sterkfontein. It seems definite that at least one species of *Australopithecus* was a toolmaker.

16

In addition to more *Australopithecus*, and *Pithecanthropus* from both China and Java, the thirties offered a proliferation of Neanderthalers from Tabun and Magharet es-Skuhl on Mount Carmel, Palestine (now Israel). The remains were excavated from caves in the side of the mountain by a joint expedition of the British School of Archaeology, Jerusalem, and the American School of Prehistoric Research. These discoveries proved that the Neanderthalers were not the monopoly of Europe and demonstrated the truth of the archaeological saw that the number of discoveries of fossil men is directly proportional to the number of *Homo sapiens* in the area.

The Mount Carmel finds were a revelation. The Neanderthalers appeared in a range of forms from the slow-thinker of the Neander valley to a highly-evolved near-*Homo sapiens*. Here was strong evidence that early *Homo sapiens* had inter-bred with Neanderthal man. True *Homo sapiens* remains were in fact found on Mount Carmel.

To the present author at least Neanderthal man has a certain mordant appeal. Despite his cannibalism as displayed by the discovery of ten butchered adults and children at Krapina in 1904, he had many human attributes; the sustenance and ritual burial of the crippled Neanderthal man at La Chappelle-aux-Saints, for example. There is overwhelming evidence that Neanderthal man existed as a contemporary of *Homo sapiens* for about one hundred thousand years, and it comes as a shock therefore, when it is realized that Neanderthal man must have been hounded out of existence by *Homo sapiens*.

Neanderthal man divides into two main morphological groups. The earlier and what is called 'generalized' kind (35,000–100,000 B.P.) were gradually replaced by a different type of 'specialized' Neanderthaloid. It seems likely, therefore, that the later group were in fact reversions, the victims of a terrible kind of oppression which it is difficult for the modern mind to visualize. It might even be possible that early *Homo sapiens* were the cannibals of Krapina, although the present author takes full responsibility for this theory.

There was, however, an entirely different kind of find in July 1933 at Steinheim, Germany, which scientific opinion is having difficulty placing. The skull shows strong features of both Neanderthal and *Homo sapiens*. Sir Wilfrid Le Gros Clark proposed in 1955 that Steinheim man is ancestral to both. But more recently (1958) Dr J. S. Weiner has said that he represents a stage leading to *Homo sapiens* and that both Rhodesian man and the Neanderthalers arose from a different and more primitive source, this being represented by the owner of the Heidelberg jaw. Present authorities find this doubtful.

The year 1933 was also notable for a complaint from the president of the Geological Society that Europe had too long been the holy ground of geological terminology with serious consequences for the rest of the world. Sir Thomas Henry Holland said that no geological classification could have world-wide application and that we should have to be content to examine each area of the earth independently and wait for evidence which would establish conincidence between the records. It was becoming obvious to Holland that the practical effects of the ebb and flow of the Pleistocene varied from total to none at all and that the arbitrary naming of the world's geological periods by a European standard was leading to widespread chaos and misunderstanding. Too often journalism was making stock of 'paradoxical' stories of drowned fossil men being recovered from desert areas such as Timbuktu 300 miles from the nearest sea, when obviously this area had been flooded by the pluvials caused by the northern ice.

Two years later another fossil man was discovered in England. Fear of the tumult which normally followed such finds bore fruit in the dilemma which faced the finder. Dr Alvan T. Marston, a dentist, had for the past two years regularly visited a gravel pit at Swanscombe, Kent, not far from Galley Hill. He was alone on Sunday, 29 June 1935, when he noticed a piece of bone sticking out of the gravel. Knowing the ritual penalties for unwitnessed archaeology, Marston hesitated. If he left the bone in the gravel while he went to get an independent witness there was a likelihood that it would be reburied by the shifting gravel. If he removed it before it was witnessed or photographed then there was more than an even chance that the site would be disputed. Marston hit on a peculiar compromise. He removed the bone, a piece of skull, and marked the spot with a stone wrapped in a handkerchief. On his way out of the pit, however, Marston encountered a mechanic working on the crushing plant. He returned with the man and showed him the handkerchief. The witness must have thought Marston had lost his mind. Marston then made a sketch of the spot and posted a notice asking quarrymen to watch for further fragments, returning to the site the following day to take a photograph. As it happened the account of the find was not disputed but one wonders what would have been the fate of this evidence if it had.

Marston wrote to H. Dewey of the Geological Survey announcing the find of a human occipital bone 'in good condition' and that the remainder 'had a very good chance of turning up'. He spent the week-ends of the next few months searching the gravel until March the following year when he and his son John uncovered a second piece of skull. Leaving his son to mount guard Marston sought and returned with a local chemist with a camera.

Marston exhibited his fossil at the 1936 meeting of the British Association at Norwich. The implements found at the site in the past were identified by Abbé H. Breuil as Acheulean. The faunal remains, representing in all twenty-six species of extinct animals, including wolf, straight-tusked elephant, lion, rhinoceros, horse, red, fallow and giant deer, placed the deposit at the Middle Pleistocene (*Mindel-Riss* or Penultimate Interglacial), which corresponded perfectly with the flint culture. In his paper Marston said:

I might as well say here and now that both Sir Arthur Keith and Sir Arthur Smith Woodward have already made a cursory examination of the [human] bones and whereas Keith said it was *Homo sapiens* closely resembling Piltdown, Smith Woodward believed it Neanderthal and expressed the hope that when more was found that the bones would prove to be Heidelberg.

Marston himself believed that the Swanscombe skull was not much later than Piltdown; that it might even be earlier. It certainly wasn't Neanderthal, he said, although it might be Heidelberg.

In justice to its important contribution to palaeontology in 1936 a memorial was unveiled at Piltdown at the site of the famous gravel. This event was not unprecedented. Although the Neanderthal cave was no longer in existence, indeed the entire valley had been transformed by limestone quarrying, the area had been proclaimed a National Park. The Piltdown gravel presented similar difficulty for the original bed had been excavated away.

The memorial – a monolith of Yorkshire stone – was unveiled on 22 July by Sir Arthur Keith at the invitation of Sir Arthur Smith Woodward. The engraved words read 'Here in the old river gravel Mr Charles Dawson, F.S.A., found the fossil skull of Piltdown, 1912–1914'.

Teilhard de Chardin was still in China and could not be present. Keith and Woodward were the only English survivors of the Piltdown band. Sir Grafton Elliot Smith (knighted in 1934) had died on New Year's Day the previous year. He had spent the last four years of his life incapacitated by a stroke.

Keith made a brief oration to the small crowd of thirty. He said that Dawson had given them the

entrance to a long past world of humanity such as never had been dreamed of, and had assembled evidence which carried the history of Sussex back to a period to which geologists assigned a duration from half a million to a million years . . . Professional men took their hats off to the amateur, Mr Charles Dawson, solicitor and antiquarian. They did well to permanently link Mr Dawson's name with this picturesque corner of Sussex and the scene of the discovery.

He added that Dawson should be considered in the same light as the French 'lock-keeper', Boucher de Perthes.

The monument was erected by private subscription, which included a donation from the American convert, H. Fairfield Osborn. General E. G. Godfrey-Fausett, on behalf of the Sussex Archaeological Society, offered to take over the task of the up-keep of the monument. But this was considered unnecessary and the generosity was declined with thanks.

Possibly the unveiling at Piltdown prompted Keith to make amends to his dead adversary. That year he began a lengthy 'resurvey' of the Piltdown skull,[1] saying that after many trials over the last six months he wished to withdraw from the argument and that he was inclined to accept Smith's views on the dissimilar proportions of both sides of the skull.

On another matter, he said that geologists agreed that the Swanscombe skull belonged to the latter end of *Mindel-Riss* Interglacial and therefore the fossil was much older than all the Neanderthal remains found in Europe, excepting the Heidelberg jaw which he regarded as early Neanderthal stock attributable to the *Gunz-Mindel* Interglacial. Piltdown man was attributable, in his opinion, to an early phase of the same Interglacial. He said that if we hadn't discovered Piltdown man we should have been content to assign Swanscombe man to modern *Homo sapiens*, but it was probably more correct to regard Swanscombe as a later member of the Piltdown phylum but greatly changed by the immense interval of time between them. He thought that while *Pithecanthropus* was being evolved in the East, the totally different Piltdown man was in existence in the West. The Western type continued to survive and change until the Middle Pleistocene, resulting in Swanscombe man.

In 1941 a debate of a new kind took place at the Geological Society. In his address the president, P. G. H. Boswell, dealt with the Society's declining membership. His point was taken up in a general discussion on 'the Function and Practice' of the society. Professor Trueman thought that recruitment had definitely been affected by what Boswell had called 'a lack of public awareness'. He felt that the society's journal should contain subjects of a more general nature. He also raised the question of concessions to members of allied societies and institutes and a reduced subscription for overseas members.

In the light of this Sir Arthur Smith Woodward, as Foreign Secretary, might not have been the right man to seek overseas enthusiasm. Advanced in age he was now totally blind. Within two years he would be dead, having dictated from memory – which Keith assures us was as strong and active as ever – his last work and final tribute to Piltdown man, *The Earliest Englishman*, his preoccupation for over thirty years.

Dr A. J. Bull, however, assigned the decline to different reasons. He said the membership of kindred societies had increased in the last two years. What was needed was the framing of a more progressive policy, that the society should adjust itself to modern conditions. Professor Cox agreed. He thought that public interest might be stimulated by the more practical applications of geology such as ore deposits, oil geology and geophysical prospecting. Sir Lewis Fermor said that 'if geology really was in the dumps in Britain the best thing to do was to have an earthquake'. Fermor meant a seismic disturbance – but in a different sense his statement was prophetic.

Cox's proposal of a broader scope was adopted. In 1943 Dr A. H. Lewis of the Imperial Chemical Industry's research station at Jealott's Hole read a paper on the relationship between sub-soil and health.[2] On the geological side, said Lewis, much remained to be done, for example, on the fluorine content of soil. Talking of fluoresis, he said, nearly a hundred years ago Owen Rees had read a paper to the society which had drawn attention to the fact that whereas the fluorine content of recent bones is negligible, fossil bones long buried in the earth might contain up to ten or fifteen per cent. The work of Rees was followed in 1873 by the French chemist A. Carnot who showed that fossil bones acquire an increasing fluorine content with increasing age until they are almost transformed into fluorapatite. The average proportion of fluorapatite in modern bones was 0·058 per cent; in Pleistocene fossils 0·33; Tertiary 0·62; Mesozoic 0·91 and Palaeozoic 0·99.

Dr Kenneth Page Oakley of the British Museum, in a written contribution, agreed but said the progressive increase in the fluorine content of bones with increasing geological age was directly concerned with the amount of fluorine present in the deposit in which they were found. It was a statistical law, he said, and not applicable to individual specimens. The correct figure could, Oakley said, be arrived at by averaging the determinations made on specimens from a number of geological deposits. He thought, however, it would be an advantage for the fluorine content of fossil human bones to be determined as a routine measure. Although a negative result, he suggested, would not be proof that a bone was recent, a high fluorine content would be strong evidence of antiquity 'in case of doubt arising'.

The following year Sir Arthur Smith Woodward died, aged eighty, at his home at Hill Place, Sussex. It is just as well, for the results of the fluorination paper would have killed him. The presence of fluorine in fossil bones and its application to geological dating requires some further explanation.

194

The test developed by Oakley depends on the fact that a fossil buried in a porous deposit such as gravel absorbs fluoride ions present in the soil and part of its substance converts into a stable compound – fluorapatite. The longer the fossil remains in the deposit the greater the amount of fluorine it will contain. Chemical analysis of a bone sample will give an approximate indication of its antiquity. The test, however, has an inherent flaw. The amount of fluorine passed into the bone is directly proportional to the fluorine content of the soil water of the deposit. Nevertheless, the test can indicate a later intrusion of fossil bone by revealing a discrepancy between the fluorine content of the various bones in the deposit. There is another snag. A human fossil was a rare and highly valued commodity. He would definitely have to be strongly suspect before any museum would allow a sample to be taken from him for testing.

A. T. Marston, the discoverer of Swanscombe man, became a constant adversary of the Sussex fossil; not on the grounds of falsity but through conviction that priority in age should be given to his Swanscombe skull. In a discussion following a paper on the Swanscombe fossil presented to the Royal Anthropological Society in 1937[3] an unnamed contributor had deprecated the fact that Dawson had used a potassium bichromate solution to harden the Piltdown cranial fragments. Woodward noted in his account, *The Earliest Englishman*: 'The colour of the pieces which were first discovered was altered a little by Mr Dawson when he dipped them in a solution of bichromate of potash in the mistaken idea that this would harden them.'[4]

The implications of this hardening had been lost on Marston until he recovered a piece of ox pelvis during a visit to Piltdown and immersed it in a similar solution. The colour of the bone had been changed from grey to the dark-chocolate brown which characterized the Piltdown skull and mandible. Marston now complained that it was on the grounds of the chocolate colour that Dr A. T. Hopwood had concluded that the human fossil belonged to the older group of fauna. He argued that Piltdown man might have belonged to the later faunal group.

Marston was also impressed by an almost unnoticed report in 1925 by F. H. Edmonds of the Geological Survey. Edmonds wrote that the Piltdown gravel was not one hundred and twenty feet above sea level as Charles Dawson had told the meeting in

1912 but only one hundred and two feet. This sensibly reduced the antiquity of the gravel.

By July 1947 not only had Marston come to doubt the extreme antiquity of the Piltdown remains but he also embraced the earlier theory that the jaw was that of a fossil anthropoid ape, a view, it may be recalled, held by a number of anatomists at the time of the discovery and after. Marston was of the opinion that the mandible and canine tooth were much earlier than the skull. This was amply demonstrated, he said, by the survival of the delicate turbinal bones found by Dawson. The skull, he urged, must be considered to be comparatively modern.

Oakley was developing his fluorine test. The root of a sheep's molar from the top-soil of Barnfield gravel pit, Kent, possessed a fluorine content of 0·1 per cent; a modern human skull from Swanscombe, Kent, 0·1; a modern human skull from Northfleet, Kent, 0·2; a human skull from chalky soil said to contain Romano-British pottery at Northfleet, 0·3; a human tibia from a Saxon grave, Northfleet, 0·05.

Oakley now claimed his first victim. He tested the bones of Galley Hill man – skull 0·3; mandible 0·4; right tibia 0·4; fragment of limb bone 0·4; left femur 0·2. As a result Galley Hill man came off the Middle Pleistocene pedestal on which he had stood for fifty years. He was well below the 2·0 required for this age in Kent. He was even well below the 1·0 required for the Upper Pleistocene. He was in fact a comparatively recent interment.[5]

It well might be wondered how Galley Hill man came to possess 'prominent superciliary ridges' which qualified him in some people's eyes for the Neanderthal category. These are in fact quite faint and his supporters' enthusiasm for an early dating must have enhanced their size in their imagination. The curved limb bones owe their Neanderthal character to the rigours of burial. Galley Hill man was attributed to our present era – the Holocene; one authority says it is comparatively recent. He is certainly no fossil.

Next Oakley applied the test to Swanscombe man. The Swanscombe animal bones produced a high average of 2·0 per cent. It must not be thought that there was any doubt about the Middle Pleistocene date of these specimens but Oakley was ascertaining a standard against which to check the human

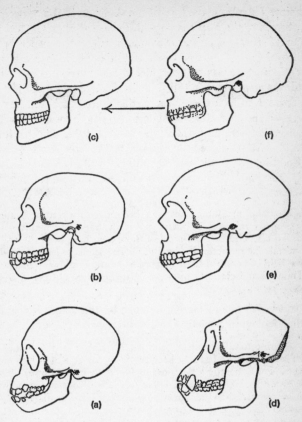

Sir Arthur Smith Woodward pushes Piltdown man out of the line of human evolution. He comments that he now considers Predmost man (Aurignacian) to be directly ancestral to man via Neanderthal man. He uses the skull of a young chimpanzee (a) to illustrate what our original ape ancestors were like, another reference to the spurious 'Peter Pan' theory of evolution. Peking man (*Homo erectus*) does not figure at all.

Key: (a) Young chimpanzee; (b) Piltdown man; (c) Modern man (Ainu of Japan); (d) Adult gorilla; (e) Neanderthal man; (f) Predmost man (Aurignacian).

(From *The Earliest Englishman*. Watts & Co. London, 1948.)

remains. Then came the turn of the skull: parietal 2·0; occipital 1·9. Swanscombe man passed with flying colours.

On 14 July 1949 there was another Marston paper before the Royal Anthropological Institute. Although Swanscombe man was genuine, he was still considered a late arrival compared to Piltdown man. Marston called for justice. He said that Piltdown man was even later than Neanderthal man. His brain, he said, possessed the characters of modern man and he was in no sense a Lower Palaeolithic fossil as was supposed. He said that it had been clearly established (by himself) that the ape jaw and canine had nothing to do with the skull. They had been found separately and any association was unclear and misleading. He passionately concluded:

It is clear that many mistakes have been made concerning Piltdown man – many mistakes by many highly qualified and highly placed men. To err is human and none of these men have been divine. Let the mistake be recognized. The fluorine test seems to have opened up a new field of enquiry; let it be applied to the Piltdown remains; let us know what light it throws as to whether they are pre-*Würm* or post-*Würm* in age.

Oakley did. On 14 December 1949 he announced his finding to the Geological Society:

The fluorine (and phosphate) content of every available bone and tooth from Piltdown has now been tested by Dr C. R. Hoskins of the Government Laboratory. All those undoubtedly of the Lower Pleistocene group (beaver, red deer, horse) proved to contain 2·3 per cent fluorine, whilst those of the post-Villafranchian fossils (primitive elephant, mastodon, rhinoceros) [almost certainly of several ages] the fluorine content ranged from 0·1 to 1·5 per cent. The *Eoanthropus* material, including all the scattered cranial fragments, the jaw and canine tooth, and the remains of the second skull found two miles away showed little fluorine (average 0·2 per cent).

In his conclusions Oakley made one other observation which later assumed great importance. He said that during the drilling of the teeth to win dentine for the chemical analysis, he noticed that below the ferruginous surface stain the dentine was pure white, apparently no more altered than 'new teeth from the soil'.

What then had the fluorine test proved? The oldest mammal bones contained less fluorine than the later ones, in fact suggesting that the Piltdown deposit was a hotchpotch of faunal remains. Of the supposed human remains Oakley wrote in 1950:[6]

The results of the fluorine test have considerably increased the probability that the [Piltdown] mandible and cranium represent the same creature. The relatively late date indicated by the summary of evidence suggests moreover that Piltdown man, far from being an early primitive type, may have been a late specialized hominid which evolved in comparative isolation. In this case the peculiarities of the mandible and the excessive thickness of the cranium might well be interpreted as secondary or gerontic developments.

This then was the final verdict. Piltdown man was too recent to be considered in the line of evolution that led to man. If he was Villafranchian or even Lower Pleistocene it was reasonable that his kind might have developed into modern man, but his low fluorine appeared to push him well up into the Pleistocene and such a great change in so short a period was impossible. But he was still thought to be a valid fossil man. Who could say what might happen to a tribe of hominids isolated by ice for hundreds of thousands of years? Darwin himself had suggested that under severe conditions over long periods such specializations were possible. But by far the greatest consideration was that a deliberate deception on such a grand scale was not to be contemplated. In fact Piltdown man's displacement, if given time, would have started a new round of debates on his place in nature. The jaw matched the skull in fluorine content admirably, thus confounding Marston with his own argument. This error is explainable inasmuch as the fluorine test still could not be employed with anything like high accuracy. That there was still no suspicion of fraud is demonstrated by a move that year to perpetuate the Piltdown gravel as a national monument.

A new thirty-two-foot-long section of the gravel was opened up in 1950 with the intention of providing a 'witness section'. The gravel recovered was carefully sifted by H. A. Toombs, Kenneth Oakley and a Mr Rixon but no bones, teeth or implements were found. The problem now confronting the Nature Conservancy was how to protect the section in a bed subject to flooding. It was solved according to Toombs[7] by bricking it in save for a couple of small glass doors through which the famous gravel could be seen. A concrete path led to the Yorkshire stone monument and the whole area of some sixty feet square was enclosed by a fence of chestnut paling. The report concluded that in the enclosure west of the hedge there was no sign that the gravel had been disturbed. This left about two hundred and thirty square yards for later excavation when time and money became available. As the gravel was an average eighteen inches deep this would yield over a hundred cubic yards of gravel – 'many months' work if proper care is taken'. The site was generously given to the nation to be a permanent geological monument by W. F. Lutyon of Barkham Manor.

There was another hair-raising insinuation about Piltdown man late that year.[8] F. H. Edmonds, the author of the 1925 paper on the height of the Piltdown gravel, confessed he was perplexed. The older group of Piltdown animals, he said, were alleged to have been washed from a Pliocene deposit somewhere in the Weald. Edmonds thought there must be some misunderstanding. There was no Pliocene land deposit in the entire Weald which could have produced them. The only local Pliocene beds were marine in origin and lay above the five-hundred-foot contour line.

Another attack on Piltdown man came from the United States in 1951. This quoted the arguments made twenty years before by Ales Hrdlička.[9] M. F. Ashley Montagu of the department of anthropology of Rutgers University said that he had examined the skull and mandible that year and he had noticed a striking disparity. The cranial bones of Piltdown I and II were extraordinarily thick when compared with the mandible. He knew of no skull which showed this disparity, not even the 'enormous' *Australopithecine* skulls or that of a gorilla. In both these instances the mandible was as thick as the skull.

Ashley Montagu said that to support Piltdown man's jaw it had been argued that no fossil ape had ever been found in England. This was untrue for the remains of two Pleistocene anthropoids had been described by Sir Richard Owen in 1845 and Dr Hunter in 1908. And so, concluded Montagu, 'the occurrence of an anthropoid mandible with the skull of a fossil man as late as the Middle Pleistocene is a possibility somewhat less remarkable than it has hitherto appeared'.

Alvan T. Marston did better. His argument was the same as Montagu's but he accompanied it with a demonstration which must have stirred at least a few anatomical minds in the right direction. But none has ever acknowledged it. In a massive article in the *British Medical Journal*[10] accompanied by illustrative photographs Marston explained how he had inserted a model of the Piltdown canine into the socket of a female orang-utan jaw. With figures and diagrams he demonstrated that the canine was an immature tooth 'belonging to a young adult ape'. He insisted that the Piltdown skull was modern, and repeated his theory of the modernity of the fragile turbinal bones. He said that even though the fluorine test had shown that the canine and jaw were the same age they were both incompatible with the skull. He had examined copies of the original Piltdown X-rays of the jaw. These had revealed a typical anthropoid bone structure. The skull, he said, was of a person who could not have been less than forty years of age. So he could not have been the owner of such an immature third molar and canine. Marston concluded:

The writer hopes his readers are fully convinced that a complete case has been made out for the final rejection of the Piltdown mandible and canine tooth as being human and as having belonged to the Pilt-down skull.

In July 1953 an international congress of palaeontologists, under the auspices of the Wenner-Gren Foundation, was held in London. The world's fossil men were put up, admired and set down again. But, according to Dr J. S. Weiner, Piltdown man got barely a mention. He did not fit in. He was a piece of jig-saw puzzle; the right colour but the wrong shape.

But at a dinner attended by, amongst others, Weiner, Dr Kenneth Oakley and Professor Wilfrid Le Gros Clark he was mentioned. Oakley remarked to the American Professor S. L. Washburn that because of the sudden death of Charles Dawson the British Museum had no exact record of the spot where Piltdown II had been found. The remark transported Weiner into a post-prandial review of the Piltdown discovery, which outlasted his return to Oxford. He wrote later[1] that the lack of precise information was distinctly puzzling. Piltdown II had convinced many doubters that Piltdown I was a valid fossil man; that he wasn't just a chance association of a human skull with an animal jaw. Such an association might conceivably occur once by chance, but twice was impossible. As a lawyer, Weiner thought, Dawson should not have been prone to slipshod archaeological methods. Weiner considered that maybe Sir Arthur Smith Woodward had been informed of the precise location of Piltdown II but somehow this important detail had gone unrecorded. It seems to have gone undetected that Woodward had visited Piltdown II (see page 145).

Nevertheless, it was Dawson's supposed neglect which led Weiner's thoughts to range over wider issues.

Weiner then realized with 'astonishment' that there were only two theories about Piltdown man. First, that he was one individual as proclaimed by Woodward. Second, that he was two creatures. Neither theory being satisfactory, he thought, the riddle might be reduced to simpler terms if he concentrated on the two-creature theory. Assuming two creatures, if both had not got together in the Sussex pit by some whim of nature, could they have got there by human agency? Could someone by mischance or error have dropped the ape jaw in a deposit occupied by a human fossil? But this accidental intrusion seemed impossible. It would have to have been repeated at Piltdown II. The inevitable outcome of Weiner's cogitation was an advance to the horrifying view of deliberate placement in the gravel.

It was possibly at this juncture that the whole kaleidoscope of inexplicable errors, slack reporting, half-innuendos, suggestions and downright disbelief of the past fifty years hardened into a coherent suspicion that a fraud of almost unbelievable pretensions and magnitude had been perpetrated on science: Dawson's error over the height of the Piltdown gravel corrected by Edmonds; Oakley's remarks on the whiteness of the dentine beneath the ferruginous stain of the teeth; C. W. Lyne's statement in 1916 that the canine was worn to a degree out of keeping with its youth; Woodward's misgivings about the staining solution which Dawson had used on the first skull fragments, and his statement in 1912 that it would have been difficult to attribute the ape's mandible to a human being but for the teeth. In fact the description 'ape' pulsed through the history of Piltdown man's jaw with the insistence of the counterpoint of a Bach fugue.

Weiner mentioned his suspicion to Le Gros Clark. This led to the examination of the Piltdown casts in Oxford University's department of anatomy. The claims for the human features of the jaw rested entirely on the flat wear of the molars. Inspection of the casts revealed features consistent with artificial abrasion of the crowns. Weiner's next step was to reproduce the Piltdown molars. He used specimens from a chimpanzee jaw, filing down the crowns to form flat biting surfaces. He stained them with potassium permanganate. According to Le Gros Clark[2] when Weiner showed him the result he 'looked at the teeth with amazement, for they reproduced so exactly the appearance of the unusual type of wear in the Piltdown molars'.

Weiner, Le Gros Clark and Oakley met at the Natural History Museum at South Kensington. Le Gros Clark said later that a study of human and ape teeth had shown the anatomists that there was a certain number of reliable features by which natural wear of teeth could be distinguished. Because the first molar erupts earlier than the second molar it is usually more worn; the outside edges of upper molars overlap and grind down the opposing edges of the lower teeth; when enamel is worn from the molar caps this produces shallow cavities in the unprotected and soft underlying dentine; the biting surfaces of adjacent teeth function as a unit in the backward and forward and side to side motion of chewing so they present a uniform surface.

The original Piltdown teeth were produced and examined by the three scientists. The evidence of fake could be seen immediately. The first and second molars were worn to the same degree; the inner margins of the lower teeth were more worn than the outer – the 'wear' was the wrong way round; the edges of the teeth were sharp and unbevelled; the exposed areas of dentine were free of shallow cavities and flush with the surrounding enamel; the biting surfaces of the two molars did not form a uniform surface, the planes were out of alignment. That the teeth might have been misplaced after the death of Piltdown man was considered but an X-ray showed the lower contact surfaces of the roots were correctly positioned. This X-ray also revealed that contrary to the 1916 radiograph the roots were unnaturally similar in length and disposition.

The molar surfaces were examined under a microscope. They were scarred by criss-cross scratches suggesting the use of an abrasive. 'The evidences of artificial abrasion immediately sprang to the eye,' wrote Le Gros Clark. 'Indeed so obvious did they [the scratches] seem it may well be asked – how was it that they had escaped notice before?' He answered his question with a beautiful simplicity. 'They had never been looked for . . . nobody previously had examined the Piltdown jaw with the idea of a possible forgery in mind, a deliberate fabrication.'

The wear of the canine was confined to the crown, in fact a considerable portion of the enamel was worn away. This conflicted with evidence that the tooth was a young one which had not yet, or only just, completed eruption. This fact was established by a later X-ray which showed that the pulp cavity possessed the youthful feature of being wide open at the apex of the root. Closer examination of this tooth revealed that the perpetrator of the hoax had made a mistake. A small patch stated by A. S. Underwood in 1916 to be secondary dentine, a normal development as a reaction to excessive wear, was nothing of the kind. It was an over-abrading which had been remedied by a plug of some plastic material, remarkably like chewing-gum.

The canine surfaces showed the same fine scratches. The pulp cavity was full of sand. This had always been taken to be the result of the tooth's being rolled about on the bed of the River Ouse in antiquity, the cavity being gradually infiltrated with fine grains through the root's open apex. But the X-rays revealed that the sand grains were loose and not cemented together with the ferruginous matrix of the Piltdown gravel. They were also the wrong size for Piltdown, being one to two millimetres in diameter; the local sand grains were much finer.

Le Gros Clark agreed that this alarming turn of events was enough to warrant a full-scale examination. A series of chemical and mechanical tests were conducted on the entire Piltdown illusion. These tests were quite rightly claimed to be the most complete and exhaustive of any carried out on a fossil and could not have taken place without strong representations to the British Museum. The British Museum's report of the investigation (issued 1953) said that since the discovery of Piltdown man some forty years ago he had been the source of continuous controversy but that it was probably true to say that most anthropologists had remained sceptical and frankly puzzled by the contradictions. There was, said the report, another explanation – the mandible and canine were actually those of a modern ape (chimpanzee or orang-utan) 'deliberately faked to resemble fossil specimens'. But it was not until J. S. Weiner had put forward this proposition 'fairly and squarely' as the only possible solution to the Piltdown puzzle that a critical restudy of all the Piltdown material was decided on.

The report, quite short considering its implications, calmly gave the evidence yielded by the Piltdown teeth, then gave the results of a new series of fluorine tests. It explained also that Oakley's previous test had served well enough to place the Piltdown cranium and mandible in the Upper Pleistocene but it had not distinguished, nor was it intended to, between this and a later date. Oakley's original tests, it was explained, were not accurate enough when applied to samples of less than ten milligrammes of sample with the consequences that no difference in the fluorine content of the skull and mandible had been observed. But improvements in technique had resulted in greater accuracy. The result was that the cranium might well belong to the Upper Pleistocene but the mandible, canine and isolated molar (from Piltdown II) were quite modern. These results were:[3]

	% Fluorine
Local Upper Pleistocene bones	0·1
Local Upper Pleistocene teeth	0·1
Piltdown I cranium	0·1
Piltdown II frontal	0·1
Piltdown II occipital	0·03
Piltdown mandible (bone)	0·03
Piltdown molar	0·04
Piltdown canine	0·03
Isolated molar (Piltdown II)	0·01
Molar of recent chimpanzee	0·06

The report continued that dating by organic content of fossil teeth and bones had long been regarded as fallacious and that no serious attempt had been made to date the Piltdown remains by these means. But work on bones from early occupation sites in North America conducted by G. S. F. Cook and R. F. Herzer had shown that nitrogen present in living bones was lost at a relatively slow and uniform rate and this could be used as an important supplement to the fluorine analysis. The results of these tests were:[4]

	% Nitrogen
Fresh bone	4·1
Piltdown mandible	3·9
Neolithic bone (Kent)	1·9
Piltdown cranium	1·4
Piltdown II frontal	1·1
Piltdown II occipital	0·6
Upper Pleistocene bone (London)	0·7

Nitrogen content of dentine samples

Chimpanzee molar	3·2
Piltdown canine	5·1
Piltdown I molar	4·3
Piltdown II molar	4·2
Piltdown Upper Pleistocene horse molar	1·2
Upper Pleistocene human molar (Surrey)	0·3

The report said that the black coating on the bones described by Dawson as 'ferruginous', or iron-stain, was in fact a tough flexible, paint-like substance (the National Gallery suspected Vandyke Brown paint). The cranium was deeply stained but the coating on the mandible was superficial. This discrepancy indicated that stain had been used to make one resemble the other and to make both appear aged.

The report now pointed a small finger at Dawson, so subtly it is not immediately apparent. It quoted Woodward on the potassium chromate dip and said that the analysis at the Clarendon Laboratory, Oxford, had confirmed that all the cranial fragments seen by Woodward in the spring of 1912 (before the commencement of systematic searches) did contain chromate; on the other hand there was no chromate in the fragments collected that summer – either in the right parietal or the small occipital fragment found *in situ* by Woodward himself. As Woodward was now himself conducting the excavations, said the report, it was not suspected that the mandible would be stained for he would have advised Dawson of his mistake. But in fact it was stained: unavoidable evidence that the faking of the mandible and canine is so extraordinarily skilful, and the perpetration of the hoax so entirely unscrupulous and inexplicable, as to find no parallel in the history of palaeontological discovery.

The report concluded:

Lastly, it may be pointed out that the elimination of the Piltdown jaw and teeth from any further consideration clarifies very considerably the problem of human evolution. For it has to be realized that 'Piltdown man' (*Eoanthropus*) was actually a most awkward and perplexing element in the fossil record of the Hominidae, being entirely out of conformity both in its strange mixture of morphological characters and its time sequence with all the palaeological evidence of human evolution available from other parts of the world.[5]

The report was signed by Dr J. S. Weiner, Department of Anatomy, University of Oxford, K. P. Oakley, Department of Geology, British Museum (Natural History), and W. E. Le Gros Clark, Department of Anatomy, University of Oxford.

When told of the deceit Sir Arthur Keith said: 'I think you are probably right, but it will take me some time to adjust myself to the new view.' Though not as deeply involved as Woodward the effect of this news on an eighty-six-year-old man who for over forty years had believed implicitly in the Sussex fossil can be imagined. He died eighteen months later on 7 January 1955, at his home at Downe. He had been pruning fruit trees the previous day.

The only other survivor was Père Teilhard de Chardin. According to his biographer Robert Speaight, the priest, who now belonged to the Wenner-Gren Foundation in New York, was invited to give his views on the forgery in an article. But he preferred not to make a public statement. In a reply to a letter from Oakley which told him of the exposure he said:[6]

No one would think of suspecting Woodward. I knew pretty well Dawson – a methodical and enthusiastic character. When we were in the field I never noticed any suspicion in his behaviour. The only thing which puzzled me, one day, was when I saw him picking up two large fragments of skull out of a sort of rubble in a corner of the pit (these fragments had probably been rejected by the workmen the year before). I was not in Piltdown when the jaw was found. But a year later when I found the canine, it was so inconspicuous among the gravels which had been spread on the ground for sifting that it seems to me quite unlikely that the tooth would have been planted. I can remember Sir Arthur [Smith Woodward] congratulating me on the sharpness of my eyesight. Don't forget; the pit at Piltdown was a perfect dumping place for the farm and cottages. It was flooded in winter, and water in the Wealden clay can stain at a remarkable speed. In 1912, in a stream near Hastings, I was unpleasantly surprised to see a fresh-sawed bone (from the butcher's) stained almost as deep brown as the human remains from Piltdown. Had a collector possessing some ape bones thrown his discarded specimens into the pit? The idea sounds fantastic; but, in my opinion, no more fantastic than to make Dawson the perpetrator of a hoax.

The idea of an ape-bone-bearing collector in such a little-inhabited part of Piltdown is fantastic. The other alternative was not so. On 23 November 1953 *The Times* broke the news. A two-column picture of the jaw and canine arrested attention and a full report of the revelations was carried under the headlines 'Piltdown Man Forgery: Jaw and Tooth of Modern Ape'. The story continued:

The authors of the [Bulletin] article do not identify the perpetrator of this fraud – but 'Who did it?' is a question many will ask. The discovery of the 'Piltdown Skull' was due to Charles Dawson, a solicitor who lived at Hastings and who was an amateur of fossils. He died, highly regarded by scientists, in 1916, aged sixty-two [sic] . . . These finds he took to Sir Arthur Smith Woodward, of the British Museum (Natural History), an authority of international reputation and unassailable integrity.

The story mentions Teilhard de Chardin and describes him as then a young priest studying for Holy Orders. Having placed these two latter participants beyond suspicion the correspondent concluded with the following accusation:

Thus two witnesses of the highest character either found, or helped to find, the bones now known to be spurious, and it is hard to resist the conclusion that the jaw and tooth had been put there by some third person in order that they might be unimpeachably discovered. If that third person were to prove to be Charles Dawson it would be but one more instance of fame (since money was certainly not the object here) leading a scholar into dishonesty. That the deception – whoever carried it out – has, though cunning and long successful, at last been revealed is a tribute to the skill of modern palaeontological research.

The *Manchester Guardian* gave the story similar prominence. In its fifth leader it said that the Piltdown skull had lost some of its importance but the revelations still caused a considerable flutter among scientists and laymen. The newspaper told how the discoverer of the Swanscombe skull, A. T. Marston, had steadfastly maintained that the skull and jaw could not possibly belong to the same individual, that he had been much criticized but was now vindicated. The leader continued:

. . . the report reads like a story of shrewd detection but what science cannot say – and what, after forty years, is probably left uninvestigated – is who the extraordinarily skilful and entirely unscrupulous hoaxer was. Piltdown Hoaxer is certainly a most successful specimen of Forging Man.

The newspaper chose as its precendents Thomas Wise, the 'discoverer' of first editions of poets and Van Meegeren and his 'Vermeers', but pointedly said that these forgers had been found out in their lifetimes. It concluded:

. . . but this one, we are probably justified in assuming, died in the knowledge that whoever had the last laugh he would not be there to hear it.

A reader objected to the view that the identity of the hoaxer was best left unrevealed. M. J. Lighthull of the University of Manchester said that such information would help reduce wasted effort by accelerating detection in future instances.[7]

The *Daily Telegraph* accompanied its story with the opinion of Dr A. E. Wilson of Brighton Technical College who knew the Piltdown site well. He said:

In Sussex we have always been a little doubtful about the jaw. We thought it was possibly of an ape of 50,000 years ago, contemporary with the cranium, but never suspected until now that it was that of a modern ape and had been faked. It was introduced into the pit after it was known that the cranium had been found and further researches would take place. This was done by someone who knew a good deal about fossilising bones. These were very heavily faked and seem to have been done by someone indulging in faking for its own sake. He could derive no financial satisfaction from it. I do not think that Mr Dawson had anything to do with this hoax. He was genuine, keen and anxious over such matters.

Marston told the newspaper that he was convinced that the mandible and the canine tooth were not faked but that he had never been convinced that they belonged to a human being. He mentioned Dawson's use of the hardening solution which had dyed the bones a chocolate brown. This, said Marston, was the extent of the supposed faking.

The *Daily Express* came to the defence of Dawson. Under the headline of 'That Man – The Great Whodunit. Did Charles Dawson give Mr Piltdown his fake jaw?', the newspaper said that no answer had been given in the British Museum bulletin. George Eade, a solicitor's clerk who had worked with Dawson in 1910–14, said that the lawyer would never have stooped to such a thing. Sixty-year-old Margaret Morse Boycott knew Dawson when she was a member of the Piltdown Golf Club and said:

He was an insignificant little fellow who wore spectacles and a bowler hat. Certainly not the sort who would put over a fast one.

Professor H. J. Fleure told the newspaper that it was most unlikely that Mr Dawson had anything to do with this. The TV personality and archaeologist Sir Mortimer Wheeler thought the 'new Piltdown discovery removes an awkward customer from the line of human evolution, and at the same time redounds greatly to the credit of the three scientists concerned . . .'

The *Daily Sketch* did not think so.

Anthropologists refer to the hoax as 'another instance of desire for fame leading a scholar into dishonesty' and boast that the unmasking of the deception is 'a tribute to the persistence and skill of modern research'. Persistence and skill indeed! When they have taken over forty years to discover the difference between an ancient fossil and a modern chimpanzee! A chimpanzee could have done it quicker.

The *Sydney Morning Herald* entirely missed the local-interest point that an Australian, the late Sir Grafton Elliot Smith, had been connected with the Piltdown discovery but thought that maybe it was the century's biggest scientific hoax. The following day the newspaper's third leader cited the precedent of Thomas Chatterton and added that an unnamed German archaeologist had detected Mithraic worship in the Roman army with the help of a bronze bull's head, which later revealed itself as part of a British army can-opener. The editorial concluded:

Such errors, no doubt, are very regrettable and very humiliating for the learner but they are a useful reminder of the need for caution. And they are very funny.

The *New York Times* said that Sir Arthur Keith and the late Franz Weidenreich had negative views about the jaw; the latter had stated bluntly that the jaw was that of an orang-utan. The story concluded that the writers of the bulletin were not prepared to say categorically that it was Mr Charles Dawson who had planted the jaw. The newspaper quoted the president of the Royal Society, Professor Edgar Adrian, as saying that 'the hoax ... was rather sad but exceedingly interesting', and reported that Fleure thought the hoax 'a very clever deception by someone with some scientific knowledge – perhaps a student who wanted to play a practical joke'.

The newspaper's editorial on 24 November said that some eminent comparative anatomists were the subject of 'considerable unearned ridicule' and that:

Apparently nothing pleases the mind of the multitude more than the spectacle of a learned professor fooled by some able forger. Who planted the bones? Someone who knew his bones and chemistry ... Perhaps an overpowering sense of humour, perhaps to prove that he knew as much as comparative anatomists and anthropologists.

In his column Meyer Berger told his readers that the Piltdown hoax hadn't caused as much astonishment at the American

Museum of Natural History as might have been expected. Berger continued:

Almost unanimously the men and women who work on the Oldest Races of Men series at the museum agreed twenty years or so ago that Old Piltdown was not one creature but two. They made no public issue of it for ethical reasons. There is, and always has been, a sly reference to the Piltdown exhibit in the museum as to the dual nature of the Old Boy from Sussex Downs. 'The brain case', says the card in the case, 'represents a very early and human type ... The lower jaw much resembles that of a chimpanzee'. The museum may have to change this label. It will say, in effect, 'This restoration, once thought to be a genuine reproduction, has since proved to be spurious'. Nothing sharper than that.

Two days after its first report[8] *The Times* revealed that the forger's depravity had not ended with the supposed human remains. Not only was it now discovered that the Piltdown flints had also been artificially stained, but Kenneth Oakley told the newspaper that the Piltdown II fragments were as phoney as Piltdown I. The report commented that it was hard to resist the inference that the forger 'whoever he was had the coolness and scholarly skill to try to outmanoeuvre expert doubts about the 1912 remains by making possible in 1915 the discovery of a corroborative kind'.

This facilitated the accusation:

Mr Charles Dawson makes his appearance in the second discovery as in the first. Sir Arthur Smith Woodward . . . is said never to have been shown the second site, and Dawson died before he fixed it on the map.

The story continued that Oakley had told the newspaper that the flint implements 'were not all they should be', that they had been artificially stained to look more than their age. The famous elephant thigh bone implement had also been worked in a way that would be impossible with a crude flint implement. In fact, said the newspaper, the implement was too perfect.

The reader was further informed that:

The Piltdown ape-man is not the first forgery to deceive scholars. In archaeology there has been a number of deceptions. One was the eighteenth-century case of Beringer, whose students carved objects and left them for their unsuspecting master to find. Another case, in zoology, involved the Austrian Kammerer, who sought to prove the so-called inheritance of acquired characteristics. In lay terms, it turned out that somebody had made the swellings in newts on which proof of the theory depended by injecting Indian ink.

The writer was obviously having a hard time finding precedents. It would have suited his purpose better if he had cited the almost parallel case of the Moulin Quignon jaw. But from the substance of the two examples quoted it will be noticed they were of the 'student japing the master' kind. They may even have been chosen with care.

On 24 November the Piltdown forgery was rated a *Times* first leader which gave a lengthy and informative exposition of the story of evolution and how Piltdown man had been the cuckoo in the palaeontological nest for too long. From this it was but a short step to the House of Commons.

In the House on 25 November a motion was tabled by W. R. D. Perkins and five other members 'That this House has no confidence in the Trustees of the British Museum (other than the Speaker of the House of Commons) because of the tardiness of their discovery that the skull of the Piltdown man is a fake.' The three principal trustees of the British Museum were the Archbishop of Canterbury, the Lord Chancellor and the Speaker. Two days later Brigadier Terrance Clark asked if time could be afforded for the motion on the Piltdown hoax (Cheers). Mr Bowells said he understood the caution of its sympathizers for it offended against the rules of the House that members should not attack the Lord Chancellor and the Archbishop of Canterbury who were both members of the House of Lords (laughter). The Speaker said: 'My attention has been drawn to the matter and I am not sure how serious the motion is (laughter). I shall have to consider it, but speaking for my co-statutory trustees . . . I am sure that they, like myself, have many other things to do besides examining the authenticity of a lot of old bones (loud laughter).' Mr Cruickshank, Lord Privy Seal, said that Brigadier Clark's question was awkward because his predecessor was also a Trustee and he was himself *ex-officio* (laughter). But as he had told the House two years ago, the (Conservative) Government had found so many skeletons to examine when they came into office that he had not found time to extend his researches into skulls (laughter). Mr Beswick cried: 'What has happened to the Dentist's Bill?' (laughter).

Cruickshank said he had no announcement to make on that, beyond that it was not a fake (laughter). Brigadier Clark asked to be allowed to withdraw his name from the motion in view of the excellent answer he had received (laughter). The Prime Minister, Sir Winston Churchill, said nothing. The parliamentary levity brought a furious letter to the *Manchester Guardian*. The correspondent said: 'By all means let the people laugh – and the Commons – but these matters are not fundamentally funny.'[9]

But another debate at the heartland of palaeontology, at the Geological Society on 25 November, did not pass off so gaily. Oakley had explained with the help of lantern slides why the team of experts had concluded that the ape mandible had been faked to match the Upper Pleistocene brain-case. The next scheduled speaker was the finder of Swanscombe man, Dr Alvan Marston. The meeting was clearly expecting his usual scientific views on the jaw but it did not get them. Instead Marston said he was there to protest against the attacks that had been made on Charles Dawson in *The Times* and in the BBC broadcast the previous Saturday. He said:

It has been very strongly hinted, if not definitely stated, that Mr Dawson took the canine tooth and lower jaw of an ape . . .

The chairman, Professor W. B. R. King, interrupted Marston. The meeting, he said, was not attempting to justify or condemn anything that had appeared in the newspapers or on the BBC, but it was hoped to get Marston's views on the jaw itself. But Marston persisted. He had received a letter from Barkham Manor confirming the integrity of Dawson. The chair again intervened but the speaker continued: 'They should not attack this man – it is so simple to prove that the canine tooth was not modern.' He then showed a number of lantern slides which in his opinion proved that the Piltdown canine and jaw were not modern but in fact those of a fossil which had not been artificially stained or abraded. He then returned to his theme. He asked how the British Museum could accuse a dead man's memory and besmirch his name? How could they account for the fact that a lawyer had such deep insight into anatomy and physiology that he could puzzle the greatest anatomists for years? The charge, he said, had been made to hide their own ineptitude and that the 'sycophantic humility' of the museum tradition had itself been playing a hoax on public opinion. Now they had made a scapegoat of the dead Dawson who could not answer back. He shouted: 'Let them try to tackle me.' He again asked the chairman to read the Barkham Manor letter which was 'from a person who knew that Dawson didn't fake anything'. But the chairman declined, saying that the revelations did not accuse Dawson in any way, and merely said that the skull was faked. Marston made further attempts to read the letter but was restrained by the chair. K. P. Oakley then rose and said he had taken part in the broadcast in question. He said that he had stated that they did not know who was responsible for the hoax. J. S. Weiner, another of the broadcasters, said that they had accused nobody. They did not know who had perpetrated the hoax. The hubbub at this meeting was wrongly reported in the United States to have developed into a series of fist-fights.

But someone must have been putting in some hatchet work. *The Times* surely had not exonerated Woodward and Teilhard de Chardin and left Dawson out on a limb on its own account. Dawson's stepston, F. J. M. Postlethwaite, wrote to the newspaper[10] that he had read with considerable indignation its Museum correspondent's insinuation and that he could not overlook 'this unnecessary sentence in an otherwise excellent statement of fact'. Postlethwaite said he had spent short periods at Dawson's home while on leave from the Sudan 'during 1911 and 1912 when the search for the fragments was in progress', and so had Sir Arthur Smith Woodward and Teilhard de Chardin. He then incorrectly said that as the pieces were found they were handed to Woodward for safe custody. He appears to have hoped that this statement would cause his stepfather to be removed from suspicion on the grounds that he could not have stained the fragments, but of course this did not follow. Dawson could have stained them before they were planted at Piltdown. On his stepfather's character Postlethwaite commented:

Charles Dawson was an unassuming, thoroughly honest man and very painstaking when he wrote *The History of Hastings Castle* entailing years of research. From an early age he was interested in flint implements and fossils, uncovering the bones of some saurians near Hastings and natural gas in Heathfield. His interests extended in many directions, but it is doubtful if he could be described as a great expert in any single subject. Until the discovery at Piltdown he did not display any particular interest in skulls, human or otherwise, and so far as I know had none in his possession. To suggest that he had the knowledge and skill to break an ape's jaw bone in exactly the right place, to pare his teeth to ensure a perfect fit to the upper skull and disguise the whole in such a manner to deceive his partner, a scientist of international repute, would surely be absurd and personally I am doubtful whether he had the opportunity of doing so. No – Charles Dawson was at all times far too honest and faithful to his research to have been accessory to any faking whatsoever. He was himself duped, and from statements appearing in the Press this is the opinion of those who knew him well, some of whom are scientific people.

Teilhard de Chardin in fact told *The Times*[11] that 'from his acquaintanceship with Dawson and Smith Woodward it was virtually impossible to believe that Dawson, still less Smith Woodward, could have been guilty of the hoax'. His qualification is unfortunate, though probably unintentional.

The British Museum, duped for forty years, was in a highly vulnerable position. The advertising tenet that there is no such thing as bad publicity certainly did not apply in this case. To its credit the museum decided to tell the whole story, albeit a qualified one, in the form of a 'special' exhibition at South Kensington, containing four sections. First, *The Problem of Piltdown man* with a display of the original finds with photographs of the excavations in progress and palaeontologists discussing the Piltdown skull in the Geological Society rooms in London (in fact the John Cooke portrait). The second section showed the fraud being detected, the revelation of the fluorine analysis and the evidence of the staining and artificial abrasion. The third dealt similarly with the Piltdown II skull. The fourth pointed out Piltdown man's position hitherto in the story of evolution. To this was added the following notice:

The removal of the 'ape-jawed Piltdown Man' from the fossil record considerably clarifies the problem of our ancestry. The Piltdown braincase is still regarded as a genuine fossil of Upper Pleistocene age. It is interesting on account of its unusual thickness, the absence of browridges, and the primitive characters of its endocranial cast. While not so old as the Swanscombe skull, it is nevertheless important as representing an early member of our own species.

It might have been more tactful if the British Museum had avoided the use of Woodward's original description of the skull and the exhibition did tend to give the impression that its purpose was to announce a triumph for British palaeontology rather than its deception for so many years.

Martin A. C. Hinton, former Keeper of Zoology at the British Museum, wrote to *The Times*[12] that in 1912 he was working as a volunteer in the Geology and Zoology departments and he had not seen the Piltdown material until the reading of the Dawson–Woodward paper. Hinton said that as soon as he saw the jaw and the tooth he knew that, had they come into his hands for description, 'they would have been referred without hesitation to the chimpanzee which was already known to occur in some of the Pleistocene deposits of Europe'. His future chief, Oldfield Thomas, had been of the same opinion. But Gerrit Miller had published the results of his interpretation of the Barlow casts, and Thomas and Hinton had been delighted for it relieved them of the necessity of expressing an opinion that would have aroused hostility at the museum at the time. Hinton said that 'Pycraft's feeble criticism of Miller was replied to with great skill and dignity and there the matter ended as far as Thomas and I were concerned'. That they were faked specimens had not entered either mind for they had been accepted by the Geological Department, and neither Thomas nor Hinton had access to the originals.

Later another letter to the newspaper also mentioned that lack of access to the real specimens had made the deception undetectable. This gives the impression that science had been deceived by plaster casts but, as shown earlier, this was not the case. Keith had remarked long ago (1913) on the ease of access to the specimens by anatomists.

Next July came further evidence of the pains taken by the perpetrator of the Piltdown fraud to achieve his end. A new method of dating bones had been applied to the Piltdown bones. Mineral phosphates contain uranium and this is infiltrated into fossil bones by soil water. The longer the bone remains in a deposit the more uranium it absorbs. There is a progressive build-up of the isotope with advancing geological age which can be measured by radiometric assays. The impregnation of the bone, like fluorine, is proportional to the uranium content of the deposit, so the test could give a fair idea as to where the specimens had originated geographically.

By this means it was ascertained that the elephant molar (*elephas planifrons*) could certainly not have been supplied by Britain. In fact the geological deposits in France, Italy and India where this type of fossil had been found in fair quantity must also be absolved from blame. The most likely place was Tunisia. In striking contrast, the low radioactivity of the hippopotamus tooth could indicate a site in Malta or Sicily. *The Times* said in its third leader that the Geological Society meeting at which the latest advent was announced had accomplished Piltdown man's complete destruction.

... not a single thing is thought to be genuine in the sense that it was actually found there [at Piltdown]. Never was a bogus goldmine so successfully 'salted' as were those Sussex gravels. It would be easy to say that the moral lies in the gullibility of scientists but that would be to miss the point, no injury could be risked from experimental methods of investigation. But once suspicion of fraud was aroused retribution came with sure steps. The striking thing is not that the scientists were gulled, even for a long time, but the extraordinary patience, thoroughness, scientific ingenuity and teamwork by which the exposure was finally brought about.

The leader listed the authorities to be commended as the Department of Geology and Minerals, British Museum; Department of Human Anatomy, Oxford University; Atomic Energy Department, Geological Survey; Physics Department, King's College, London; Government Chemist's Department; Micro-chemical Department, Oxford University; National Gallery; Soil Survey.

The leader commented finally:

What chance has a single malefactor against such an armoury? And yet perhaps he has the last laugh. His crime, indeed, is discovered, but he himself has eluded detection – at least, so far.

These winsome, yet sinister words were prophetic. Charles Dawson had slipped up. His conduct of the Piltdown hoax or fraud as it came to be called was impeccable but he had reckoned without J. Mainwaring Baines, curator of Hastings Museum, where Dawson's private collection of archaeological curios had rested since his death in 1916.

At Hastings was proof that Dawson was not only a forger but that he had plagiarized his *History of Hastings Castle*. Baines announced in his annual report to the museum trustees in November 1954 that enquiries had been proceeding since Piltdown man had been announced as a fake some twelve months before. The prickspur from Lewes that Dawson claimed to be Norman had not been recognized by the British Museum. Grave doubts had also been cast on a small axehead which he claimed he had found in a slag-heap at Beauport, near Hastings, a Roman iron-working site. From this site Dawson had also acquired a small statuette, a replica of a colossal statuary group at Rome. Said Baines: 'This statuette had been accepted by the Society of Antiquaries at the time (1893) but some doubt was cast on it and the story of its discovery seemed to be as enveloped in mystery as the Piltdown skull.' It had been submitted to a number of authorities and although it was undoubtedly of cast-iron it was almost certainly of recent date 'and might have been brought home from the Continent by Dawson'. Another suspicious item was the anvil marked 1515.

If this was not enough, said Baines, some months ago a local bookseller had brought to his notice a manuscript volume relating to Hastings Castle. He had immediately recognized the hand-writing as that of William Herbert, who carried out excavations at Hastings in 1824, for he had examined that author's notes in the London Guildhall library. The words of the manuscript and Dawson's *Hastings Castle* were almost identical, although rearranged and with a lot of extraneous matter added. Baines wrote:

It appears that his bound volume of manuscript was the actual one used by Dawson, for in a preface he makes reference to it in five lines saying that he had made full use of it. There can be little doubt in my mind that Dawson used Herbert's material and, saving his conscience in a few lines, had passed it off as his own work.

Baines himself qualifies his accusation by admitting that Dawson's preface refers to 'free use' of Herbert's manuscript but even so he fails to do justice to the dead lawyer. Dawson not only made full acknowledgement to William Herbert in his *History*. He explained how he had used the manuscript, considerably augmenting it with Herbert's further drafts in the Guildhall library. He said that on hearing that he was writing a history of the castle Lord Chichester (the fourth earl) had presented him with the Herbert record. The record, wrote Dawson enthusiastically, was 'noted and planned in almost every detail'. Dawson goes so far as to state that Herbert had made good use of an earlier historian's work, Moss's *History of Hastings*, without acknowledging his debt to that writer. Dawson said he was also indebted to nine other authorities whom he names. In fact the attribution amounts to eighty-four lines: thirty-two in the case of Herbert and fifty-two devoted to the other authors. Moreover the attribution is couched in fulsome terms and is a far cry from the niggardliness alleged by Baines.

Baines' attack did in fact bring about some sort of defence of Dawson. John Thorne of the Battle and District Historical Society wrote to *The Times* [13] to point out Baines' error over the attribution.

There was also objection to the reference to the cast-iron statuette from R. L. Downes of the Faculty of Commerce, University of Birmingham. He said that as he had originated the investigations referred to by Baines he wanted to make it clear that all that could be said with certainty about the statuette was that it was cast-iron and a miniature replica of a Roman statue. Downes said his suggestion of a recent and Continental origin was only one possible explanation – the possibility of its being genuine could not be ruled out. The other three objects were doubtful but if they were fraudulent there was no evidence to prove that any particular person was responsible and it would be unwise to draw any conclusions from such debatable evidence. He concluded:

We must wait for a complete review of the evidence of Mr Dawson's activities, ranging from his honest and talented work to his undoubted deceptions, before passing any judgement on him or on such debatable specimens.

The following year Dr J. S. Weiner's work *The Piltdown Forgery* [14] was published. His excellent account of the events that led to the discovery that a hoax had been perpetrated on science is marred by a strong bias against Dawson. This reveals itself in Weiner's choice of witnesses; in the main bandwagoners who had apparently known of Dawson's deception and had kept mum for forty years. I have no wish to doubt the motives of these witnesses but their revelations must be flavoured by a desire to get out from under, to remove themselves from the ranks of the gulled. In the book Woodward and Teilhard de Chardin are summarily dismissed as suspects and appear as lay figures manipulated by the puppeteer and arch-villain Dawson.

But singular would be the author capable of completely objective appraisal. Weiner obviously believed in Dawson's guilt from the outset, just as I was biased in favour of Dawson's innocence. But even Weiner, after skilfully implicating the deceased lawyer and completing his destruction, had to remark at the end of the narrative that the evidence of Dawson's guilt which he had assembled was insufficient to prove anything beyond all reasonable doubt and 'that our verdict must rest on suspicion and not proof'.

It would be difficult to envisage a more ideal situation for the passing off of a bogus fossil man than that which existed at the British Museum's Natural History Department in 1912. The department's keeper, Sir Arthur Smith Woodward, although pre-eminent as a palaeoicthyologist, was certainly no human anatomist. This shortcoming was amply demonstrated by the misreading and malconstruction of the Piltdown cranium. Sir Wilfrid Le Gros Clark drew my attention to another surprising example of what he describes as 'the odd custom of the Natural History Museum at that time'.[1] Woodward's subordinate in charge of the anthropology section – the section which dealt with fossil humanity – was W. P. Pycraft, an ornithologist. It is due to Pycraft's poor knowledge of human anatomy that *Cyphanthropus*, the 'Stooping man' of Rhodesia, was credited with a stoop and peculiar gait that he did not possess. He mistook one part of the pelvis for another and reconstructed 'an impossible kind of acetabulum' (the cavity which receives the thighbone). In fact the pelvis is quite like that of modern man. Rhodesian man had no stoop and walked normally. Le Gros Clark pointed out 'this remarkable error' to Pycraft in 1928.

It is not, then, unjust to claim that Woodward's Natural History department was incompetent to handle Piltdown man or for that matter any kind of human skeleton – antique or modern. Charles Dawson may have decided to take advantage of this astonishing state of affairs but surely it would take a skilful anatomist to recognize an incompetent one.

One of my main objections to the assumption that Dawson is inevitably the culprit is that as the discoverer he was wide open to suspicion. He is too obvious a culprit. Even a cursory study of the events which surrounded the discovery of fossil men would have warned Dawson clearly that such finds are highly controversial. If the bogus fossil escaped detection by his friends at the museum he surely could not have expected that it would withstand scientific inquiry for ever.

I find it impossible to believe that Dawson would pit his meagre knowledge of anatomy (if it is accepted that he had any at all) against that of any skilled human anatomist. The strain on the nerves would be too great. The threat of exposure would be perpetual. If the forgery had been detected any time in the next ten or twenty years (for Dawson had at least this expectancy of life) then he would have had to face the odium and full wrath of Science. Surely the destruction of the high esteem earned by his many other discoveries would be too high a price to pay? Even if he knew he was about to die, would he be prepared to sacrifice his posthumous esteem? It was most unlikely.

As it was Piltdown man had a charmed life. Because of the poor quality of the original X-ray photographs the bogus jaw remained undetected at the outset. Le Gros Clark has emphasized that the forger's crude workmanship on the teeth was there for all to see if only someone had looked for it. The same critical examinations in 1912 would have revealed as much. Although advanced microchemical techniques were used in 1953 to prove that Piltdown man was bogus, no more than Dr J. S. Weiner's suspicions and a visual examination started his decline. One point that seems to have passed unnoticed hitherto is that owing to the British Museum's incompetence the skull of Piltdown man was reassembled to a smaller size than it actually was. Surely the forger could not have foreseen this circumstance?

Another matter quickly dismissed was the high degree of specialist skill that went into the conception of Piltdown man. The forger supplied the correct clues in the form of 'remains' from which certain (and erroneous) deductions would be arrived at. Any evidence that the skull had possessed features found in modern man other than the noble brow were missing. The brow was needed to supply the paradox. The connecting mechanism on the jaw by which it is hinged into the skull (condylar process) was missing. If present this feature would have clearly shown that the jaw could not have belonged to the skull. The Piltdown teeth are masterpieces of ape plus human features.

I argue that a forgery of such subtlety is beyond the conception of a layman such as Dawson. Most anatomists, including Dr J. S. Weiner, think otherwise: that the anatomy of Piltdown man is well within the scope of a knowledgeable layman. One might wonder to what degree this knowledge might extend before it was classed as 'professional' or 'expert'. After all, what is an anatomist other than a knowledgeable layman?

I have, however, an unexpected ally in one of the detectors of the Piltdown forgery. Sir Wilfrid Le Gros Clark remarked to me in a letter that: 'The forgery is extremely skilful and the forger (possibly in collaboration with someone else) certainly knew the relevant details of palaeontology, archaeology and anatomy.'[2] As this reservation was made by a former professor of human anatomy in the University of Oxford one may be forgiven for wondering whether it might not be something of an understatement.

The cleverness of the forgery is also far underestimated. A high degree of knowledge was required to ensure that Science, although eager, would find such a fossil man plausible. One present view on the evolution of mankind, briefly, runs from the early primates (prosimians) of the Eocene, roughly fifty million years ago, such as the tarsoids, small tree-dwelling animals, through early apes such as *Dryopithecus* and *Proconsul*, then in order *Australopithecus*, *Pithecanthropus* (Peking and Java man), Neanderthal man, then Modern man through his earlier forms such as the Cro-Magnons. Piltdown man neatly played the part now filled by *Australopithecus*. In fact there is a striking resemblance. The American authority E. A. Hooton stated after the revelations of 1953 that if *Australopithecus* had not been brought to light by Raymond Dart then Science would still be looking for something very much like Piltdown man. He was a highly plausible 'missing link'.

But, as was revealed in 1953, if the conception of Piltdown man was knowledgeable and skilful, the workmanship was not. It is now known that some of the fragments missing from Piltdown man I can be supplied by Piltdown man II. It is impossible to accept that Dawson could have believed that such an obvious device would for long have remained undetected. It is far more likely that this was the forger's next step. He was presenting the British Museum with another chance to detect that the whole affair was an absurdity. Another manifestation of a desire to reveal all must have been the mysterious elephant thighbone tool.

The knife marks on this bone are only too clear. That this feature escaped notice is almost beyond belief.

It has been claimed[3] that Dawson was once accidentally interrupted while actually engaged in dark experiments with potassium bichromate stain and human bones. This was damning evidence. But in those times the 'hardening' of fossil bones by such methods was quite usual. The Galley Hill fragments were hardened in this way. Woodward himself innocently commented that the elephant thighbone was given similar treatment by the British Museum (see page 139). Dr Kenneth Oakley has informed me that 'staining' is a hopelessly inadequate way of describing what must have happened to the Piltdown fragments before they were planted. The skull, he said, must have been boiled in some acidulous solution. He suspects iron sulphate. So drastic was this treatment that the calcium phosphate normally present in bone was entirely changed to calcium sulphate. Potassium bichromate is not detectable at all.

Quite a lot was also made of suggestions that a number of people in Sussex, particularly members of the Sussex Archaeological Society, suspected, knew even, that Dawson had forged Piltdown man; that he was known as the 'Wizard of Sussex', a faintly bantering title which suggested that he discovered rare fossil bones or antiquities with suspicious ease. It is surprising, therefore, that his accusers were able to contain themselves for forty years. This has been explained as the result of the closely-knit comradeship of amateur archaeology: the exposure of Dawson would in some way have reflected on the honour of Sussex archaeology. I do not believe it for a moment. We have a strange parallel case in the bogus trimaran circumnavigation of Donald Crowhurst. The mere suspicion that something was not quite right was enough to launch a private letter to the *Sunday Times* adjudicators from Sir Francis Chichester. It is noticeable that single-handed circumnavigation has not gone into a decline as a consequence. Another sure indication that these 'suspicions' owe a lot to hindsight is that the headquarters of these doubters of Dawson, the Sussex Archaeological Society, offered to take over the upkeep costs of the Piltdown excavation site. A strange act indeed if the Society was suspicious.

Since the revelations of 1953 in which he played a prominent part, Kenneth Oakley has continued to examine the Piltdown specimens with a view to discovering the source. He stresses that his work is heavily supplemented by the work of others. Oakley has now proved that the Piltdown cranium is nowhere near as old as had been previously thought. It is not Pleistocene, and no more than a mere 620 ± 100 years B.P. This result was obtained by supplementing the fluorine, nitrogen and uranium estimates with the C-14 (carbon dating) technique.

This highly accurate dating method has also ascertained that Piltdown man's orang-utan jaw is not 'modern' in the true sense, nor could it have been easily come by. It is in fact attributable to 500 ± 10 years B.P. Like the skull the ape jaw is 'mediaeval'.

This result pushes the forgery even farther beyond the range of Dawson. It has been stated that Dawson could have obtained the jaw 'off the peg' from any dealer of zoological specimens. But mediaeval orang-utan jawbones are a rarity; even if available such a purchase would have attracted much attention. Oakley at last saw a breakthrough. A number of such specimens were brought to England in 1875 by the zoologist A. H. Everett. While on the island of Sarawak Everett discovered that the natives suspended the truncated heads of orang-utans from the rafters of their huts. Many of these 'fetishes' or 'trophy-heads' had hung there for centuries. In 1879, Oakley discovered, Everett's collection was presented to the British Museum. Oakley checked the collection against the fossil catalogue: they were all present. Oakley thinks it possible that Everett may have withheld a specimen or two, even selling them to a dealer. But the trail had ended. He had proved, however, that the Piltdown jaw was a rarity and by no means easily obtainable. If Dawson had come by one then the fact would have been well known.

It is a similar story with the 'Pre-Chellean' flint implements from Piltdown. I was at first inclined to suspect that these flints, like those of Moulin Quignon, were produced by the iron-struck method. Oakley assures me that this is not the case. He says that the Sussex specimens were manufactured by the true primitive method – by striking flint against flint; that they are genuine Neolithic 'wasters' – partially completed tools that were rejected by primitive man on discovery of some incipient flaw in the material.

Oakley's researches, and those of his collaborators, suggest that the Piltdown animal remains came from different sources of supply. The rhinoceros and mastodon teeth most likely are from the Tertiary Red Crag deposit in Suffolk. The elephant thigh-bone 'implement' may have come from the gravel in the region of Swanscombe, Kent. The strangest fragment, however, is the molar tooth found by Teilhard de Chardin. It is undoubtedly that of an *Elephas planifrons*. This highly radioactive molar could not have come from England. The only site where such highly radioactive remains have been discovered is at Ishkul, Tunisia. This tooth has another claim to attention. It was the first *planifrons* tooth ever discovered. Such a discovery was not repeated until well into the 1920s. Now that this information is to hand some idea of the true importance of the Piltdown assemblage can be appreciated.

The most convincing evidence against Charles Dawson is that Piltdown was his special province. Even now it is an isolated place. By his own admission Dawson had regularly visited the site 'since just before the end of the last century'. This adds up, for it was in 1898 that Dawson was appointed to the stewardship of Barkham Manor in the grounds of which the Piltdown pit was discovered. Indeed, the manor house overlooks it. At any time Dawson could have 'planted' the bones without attracting notice, that is if he did not introduce them as the search progressed.

But was Dawson the only person to know about Piltdown and the expectations of the gravel? Dawson said that such antique gravel had not been 'experienced' in Sussex by geologists. Where did he get this information? Having discovered what he suspected was antique gravel at Piltdown Dawson must have spoken or written of it to many. Woodward stated that Dawson frequently sought advice about his finds from experts. So it is not impossible that the lawyer's surveillance of Piltdown was an open secret. Woodward counselled discretion in 1912. But Dawson had discovered the pit in 1898. Ten years had elapsed before the first piece of bone appeared at Piltdown in 1908.

Unfortunately there is no evidence of such an interchange. It is believed that the lawyer's private correspondence was destroyed when Castle Lodge was vacated in 1931. But reticence does not seem to have been Dawson's strong point. In fact, he was gregarious and garrulous. Therefore it is by no means unreasonable to suppose that such a lengthy search would have become known. That the pit was under regular scrutiny by an amateur enthusiast such as Dawson would have been sufficient for the forger's purpose. Who then was the forger?

Sir Arthur Smith Woodward has hitherto entirely escaped suspicion. He seems to have gained even more from Piltdown in the way of fame than Dawson. His long friendship with Dawson would have assured that the 'planted' bones would be returned to him almost automatically. We have only his word that Dawson discovered Piltdown man II. He had ready access to human and animal fossils. He could have sneaked the orang-utan jaw from the museum collection. But Woodward can, I think, be dismissed on the grounds that he was too dedicated, too studious, for such an undertaking. He was a queer fish – almost the archetypal boffin. His ascetic approach to his chosen subject was a by-word. He scurried about the museum work-rooms, head down, oblivious of the living world. This resulted directly in two nasty accidents.

On the first occasion he collided with a glass exhibition case and fell to the floor snapping a leg. Woodward refused emphatically to go to hospital or to be attended by a surgeon. He set the limb himself with the result that henceforth he walked with a limp. Some human anatomist? A similar collision resulted in a broken arm. His younger assistants, with the expectation of being free of the Woodward thrall for a few weeks, were shocked from recumbent positions on benches by the conscientious professor's appearance for work the following day.

It is unlikely, therefore, that such a man would even dream of perpetrating such a fraud. Especially if one takes into account his nigh on a lifetime's search at Piltdown.

The other successful searcher at Piltdown was Père Teilhard de Chardin. The evidence against the priest is as black, if not blacker, than that against Dawson. One has merely to recall the incredulity of Dawson and Woodward when Teilhard de Chardin discovered the missing canine tooth in a stretch of gravel which had just been thoroughly searched. Oakley's discovery in connection with the *Elephas planifrons* molar is highly significant in this case. Before his arrival at Ore Place, Hastings, the student-priest had actually stayed near Ishkul, Tunisia.

Teilhard de Chardin is a hard man to place. His lifelong struggle with his religion made him deeply introspective. He was a prolific author but one can gather little of the quality of the man from the output. The books are for the most part quasi-scientific explanations of his conception of the place of evolution within religion. In this last task he sees no contradiction imposed by one on the other.

The priest has by no means escaped suspicion in some quarters. Sir Wilfrid Le Gros Clark told me that because of the Tunisian association he at one time strongly suspected Teilhard de Chardin. Oakley agreed, but like Le Gros Clark, he feels that not only lack of the requisite anatomical knowledge but the whole nature of the man must exonerate him.

The discovery that Piltdown man was a deception deeply hurt Teilhard de Chardin. According to Oakley he took the news far harder than Sir Arthur Keith. He miserably told Oakley that throughout the vicissitudes of his life the main consolation was that he had helped to discover the Piltdown man. Teilhard de Chardin might have been putting on an act but he did in fact arrive in England too late to have 'planted' the original find in 1908. It is just possible however, that he might have added the *Elephas planifrons* molar to gain some kudos. That he likewise planted the controversial canine is highly doubtful.

Sir Arthur Keith, as one of the world's paramount comparative anatomists, is possibly the only person who can escape suspicion purely on prestige. He is further exonerated by his misinterpretation of the skull, by treating it as that of a primitive hominid which had existed too early in time to have developed the more prominent left side. If anything, the joke was on him as much as on Woodward. But contrary to expectations he took the terrible news quite calmly. Oakley recalled the visit he paid with Dr J. S. Weiner to the old man's home at Downe. He had, Keith said, in any case heard the news on the radio. He said at the outset of the interview: 'I know why you have come to me . . .' The visitors gave Keith the full story. He said that they were probably right 'but it will take me a little time to adjust to the new view'. Poor Keith. How bitter that moment must have been for him. Someone had made a fool of him for forty years.

But now let us return to Woodward's ill-fated construction of the first Piltdown skull. Owing to an imperfect knowledge of human anatomy, shared by the bird man Pycraft, he made a grave error over the reconstruction. Another mistake was his failure to recognize that the cranial bones of Piltdown man II rightly belonged to Piltdown man I. By contrast the American Ales Hrdlička found himself able to suggest that the Piltdown II molar must have come from Piltdown I after an examination which cannot have been more than brief. The incompetence at South Kensington is understandable for clearly the department did not know what it was about. But the most surprising feature of the whole mess was the non-intervention of Grafton Elliot Smith.

Not only was Smith an accomplished human anatomist but he was also an expert on prehistoric and ancient human skulls. He had certainly examined enough of them not many years before during his archaeological survey of Nubia. Smith was called in to the affair well before the unveiling of Piltdown man in December 1912. That he stood by and watched the baffled Woodward and Pycraft wrestle with the reconstruction is therefore certain. By no stretch of the imagination can it be accepted that he too was incompetent. A word from him would have put Woodward on the right track; certainly so in the case of the side ridge of the skull which Woodward took for the median ridge. His complete failure to assist Woodward is, in my opinion, highly incriminatory.

What then was Smith's motive? Two immediately come to mind. First, if a sufficiently primitive man were to be discovered in England, this would lend support to Smith's almost obsessive views on migration. He argued that as the new waves of culture spread from 'somewhere in the Middle East' the exponents of the new learning, so to speak, drove the more primitive occupants further out. A near-animal Piltdown man as far west as Britain would lend admirable support to this view.

Alternatively, at the time of the 'planting' of the fossils, Smith was in what might be considered a backwater appointment in Cairo. It is therefore possible that he coveted the job at South Kensington. He must have known that neither Woodward nor Pycraft were human anatomists. His cataloguing of the Hunterian Collection had brought him into close contact with both.

I was at first inclined towards the second motive. I thought that as Smith grew in professional stature and the forgery refused to let itself be discovered, he allowed the matter to stagnate. He could not do otherwise, for a sudden revelation at this late stage would be highly suspicious. But as my research advanced, and I realized that Smith was a highly likely suspect, my view of the actual motive changed. In its place came the conviction that Smith would have loved a chuckle at the expense of what he thought, possibly correctly, was stick-in-the-mud palaeontology and anatomy. Somehow the whole affair reeks of Smith.

At the time of the Piltdown discoveries Smith was mostly in Egypt. But his tumultuous appearances in England coincide remarkably with the turn of events in Sussex. Smith had all the qualifications, both esoteric and professional, for what I believe is more accurately called the Piltdown hoax. Access to the remains of extinct fauna would have presented little difficulty to a professor of palaeontology. If Dawson had attempted such a remarkable aggregation then suspicion would have been drawn to him at once. Moreover, Smith's work in Nubia had made available a vast collection of human skulls. In his catalogue there are many thousands that are 'mediaeval'. Many have peculiarities caused by disease and whim of nature. Not a few are as thick in section as the Piltdown skull.

But what would have been Smith's excuse when the Piltdown forgery was detected, as he must have thought it inevitably would be? Would his pontifications about the value of the Piltdown skull bring him a share of the opprobrium heaped on Woodward? At first this seems an insurmountable objection to my hypothesis, but it is in fact not so. I have examined all Smith's writings on the subject with care and in not one instance does he fail to state carefully that his findings were based on the examination of a *plaster cast* of the skull. He even used his argument with Keith to imply that these plaster casts were inaccurate. If Keith had access to the actual skull, he said, like Woodward, then Keith would have to revise his opinion as to the morphology of the skull. He did not think plaster casts were inaccurate in 1903 when he wrote from Egypt to Symmington advising him to have a good look at them (see page 103). Another clue to his method is that even as late as November

1915 he wrote that he had actually seen the skull fragments for the first time. It seems highly unlikely that three years had passed without sight of the actual fragments, that his Geological Society paper was based on the examination of a mere plaster cast. In fact, would any anatomist wage war with an authority such as Keith on the basis of a plaster cast when Woodward would have been only too pleased to show him the original?

I asked Oakley if it were not possible that the Piltdown skull might have come from Egypt, from Nubia. He replied that there was as much for the proposition as against it. All that was known of the skull, he said, was that it was Caucasian in type and over a half-century old. Egyptians certainly have Caucasian skulls, he said. Oakley must have guessed the drift of the question for he asked me whether in the course of my research I had not come to some conclusion as to the identity of the Piltdown forger. At the time I did not know that Oakley had studied under Sir Grafton Elliot Smith. The naming of Smith did not bring an objection from him. He raised his eyebrows. Indeed, Oakley thought that I could be right. He recalled Smith's arrogant delivery of a lecture. Oakley was not impressed with this superiority or by the air of conceit that Smith exuded. It is only fair to mention, however, that Sir Wilfrid Le Gros Clark was most favourably impressed by the Australian, by Smith's kindness and assistance in the way of laboratory space at University College when Le Gros Clark returned from a tour of fossil men sites overseas. Le Gros Clark also considers that the evidence against Dawson is considerable but he does suspect a professional accomplice.

One might speculate endlessly on the permutations of layman and scientist. Could Dawson have been in league with Smith against Woodward? This is not at all likely. It will be recalled that Dawson and Arthur Smith Woodward had been friends for many years. Dawson was a regular house guest. Lady Woodward had a special tablecloth on which eminent scientific visitors were invited to scrawl their signatures. It was an honour that had been extended to Dawson. Any such treachery would have been entirely foreign to Dawson.

So Piltdown man can be summed up as a hoax that went sour. It was certainly not intended as a forgery that would stand the test of time. It was skilfully contrived but clumsily put together. Although the realization that Sir Grafton Elliot Smith might be the hoaxer dawned on me about halfway through the preliminary research for this book, try as I may I have not been able to come up with concrete evidence of the Australian's participation. In fact it is hard to visualize anything that would come into this category other than a straightforward confession. I do hope, however, that I have shown that Dawson does not fit the bill. And that Smith does.

One thing that certainly emerges is the extraordinary waste of time, the absorption of brilliant minds, that was the result of the Piltdown hoax. The blind Woodward dictating the results of a search which lasted over a quarter of a century creates a poignant picture. Or is it too unkind to suggest that all concerned would have wasted their time anyway?

Sir Wilfrid Le Gros Clark is inclined to take a brighter view. He anticipates with relish the discovery of yet another Piltdown man. 'What would Science think then?' he asked me. In a more serious vein, he said that the major outcome of the Piltdown episode was that Science was now on its guard; that it would be impossible for a similar fraud to be perpetrated. Maybe all budding palaeontologists should be taken down to Sussex to see the now derelict stone tribute to Charles Dawson at Piltdown just to make sure.

Many a hero has lost his glory posthumously because a historian has credited him with the peculiar gift of talking in italics. Others have been brought down by being quoted out of context. Grafton Elliot Smith was ill-advised enough to tell the 1912 Geological Society meeting that the association of the simian (ape) jaw with a human brain was not surprising to anyone familiar with recent research on the evolution of man. Now that the whole Piltdown edifice has crashed down, how strange this remark sounds. Could he have been laughing at his colleagues?

Grafton Elliot Smith also told poor Dawson that Piltdown man's brother or cousin from Talgai was found at a place called Pilton in Queensland. In fact, there is no such place in the whole of Australia. Could Smith's eyes have watered just a little as he watched the innocent dupe Dawson swallow this gobbet of false information?

Let us be even unkinder with a little test of absolutely no consequence. Turn to the picture of the Piltdown men in the illustrated section. One of this distinguished group almost definitely was the Piltdown forger – or hoaxer. *Nature* assures us that all are excellent likenesses. Pick the hoaxer out for yourself. I will not state the obvious.

Appendices

Appendix 1

Brief Glossary

Acromegaly   A disturbance of the pituitary gland causing accelerated growth, particularly of the nose, cheekbones and jaw. There are authenticated instances of the afflicted strongly resembling Neanderthal man. This disease was used to great effect to deny that this or that fossil man was indeed a fossil at all. Sir Arthur Smith Woodward similarly despaired of Rhodesian man and suspected the disease in this case.

Aurochs   An extinct species of wild ox; now erroneously applied to the modern European bison, *Bos bison*, still extant in Lithuania.

Autochthones   An early description of primitive man, implying that he had sprung from the soil. The ancient Athenians claimed to have done just this. The philosopher and writer Sir Thomas Browne (1605–82) observed in *Religio Medici* (*c.* 1635) that 'there was never any *autochthone* but Adam'.

B.P.   Before the Present. An estimate of the age of a fossil human being is now given in a number of years B.P.

Brachycephalic   If the width of a skull is 80 per cent or more of its length it is said to be *brachycephalic*, implying roundness. If the width is less than 75 per cent of the length it is *dolichocephalic*, implying length. Between 75 and 80 per cent the skull is said to be *mesocephalic*.

Coprolite   A round fossil resembling a stone supposed to be the petrified excrement of an animal. There are many early reports of *coprolites* being found in British caves and attributed to the hyena.

Cranial capacity   An estimate of the brain volume. Millet seed, even rice, was once commonly used to arrive at this measure.

Dentrites   The presence of these 'brilliants' on fossil bones or flint implements was said to indicate vast antiquity. Also *limnites de fer*. The theory is now discredited.

Devonian   A geological age. See Table I.

Drypopithecus   A fossil ape.

Endocranial cast   A plaster cast on the interior of a skull. Great anatomical sport was had with these casts, some authorities drawing mighty conclusions from what they considered were impressions of the brain on the bone. Modern thought tends to belittle the importance of such deductions but there are instances of some of the earlier findings being valid. Sir Wilfred Le Gros Clark told the present author that because of the crudity of the earlier plaster casts they were open to all sorts of false interpretations and conjecture. Modern endocranial casts are plastic, which has resulted in a greater degree of accuracy and reliability.

Flint implements Primitive stone tools worked by the hand of man. For culture types, see Appendix B.

Fossil As a rule fossils are formed by the least destructible part of the body, such as bones in the case of faunal fossils. Under favourable conditions these parts become impregnated with mineral salt derived from the deposit in which they are buried. Most resistant to decay in faunal skeletons are, strangely, the teeth.

Gisement The conference of French and British geologists and archaeologists used *gisement* – the finding of flint implements *in situ* at Moulin Quignon in 1863 – as valid evidence that the implements were authentic works of primitive man.

Glaciation or Glacial A major icing-up of the earth's surface during the Pleistocene. There were four European glaciations named *Würm*, *Riss*, *Mindel* and *Gunz*. The intervening 'warm' period is known by its preceding and following glaciations, e.g. Riss–Würm *Interglacial*. A temporary rise in temperature during a glaciation is termed an *Interstadial*.

Holocene The geological age in which we live. In fact Pleistocene conditions still apply, the condition of polar ice being unknown in 200,000,000 years. That another ice age with its glaciation will again be experienced by this planet is highly likely. The present author calculates that on previous form this should happen in about 15,000 years' time. See Table I.

Hominid A creature with strong affinities with man. Earlier workers used abilities such as firelighting and tool manufacturing as qualification for the title *hominid*. Modern thought, however, relies more on anatomical features of similarity but as has been observed more than once the qualification is not entirely anatomical. It seems much easier to define what isn't a hominid than what is.

Interglacial See Glaciation.

Interstadial See Glaciation.

Loess Wind-borne dust of immense use to stratigraphers, for such deposits mark 'warm' periods of the Pleistocene.

Marsupial An animal, such as the kangaroo and the opossum, which has an abdominal pouch for carrying its young.

Matrix A mineral or rocky mass surrounding a fossil bone.

Mesocephalic See Brachycephalic.

Moraine A stratigraphical term for an accumulation of debris marking the extent of an ice sheet.

Neolithic   New Stone Age. See Palaeolithic.

Pachyderm   Order of mammals invented by Cuvier which included ungulates or hoofed animals such as the elephant, rhinoceros, hippopotamus and horse. More recently, the term implies the thick-skinned quadruped the elephant.

Palaeolithic   The Old Stone Age. An expression of antiquity of indefinable pretensions. At first used to contrast with Neolithic or New Stone Age but later used generally for fossil men for which vast claims of antiquity were being made. Palaeolith was another and earlier term for 'eolith'.

Palaeontology   The study of fossils.

Phylum   A tribe or race of organisms related by descent from a common ancestor.

Pithecoid   Resembling or pertaining to the apes, especially the anthropoids. It is more common now to use *simian*.

Pleistocene   The age previous to the present (Holocene), first age of the Quaternary. Duration generally accepted to be in excess of 1,000,000 years but according to some authorities as much as 3,000,000. See Table II.

Pliocene   The age immediately preceding the Pleistocene and the final age of the Tertiary, duration about 9,000,000 years.

Quadrumana   Order of mammals which includes monkeys, apes, baboons and lemurs, whose hind- as well as fore-feet have an opposable digit or thumb so giving the animal, as it were, four hands. The expression Bimana is used for the two-handed variety such as man.

Quaternary   Successor to the Tertiary, including the Pleistocene and Holocene.

Rock-shelter   An overhang of rock forming a shelter thought to be a usual habitat for human beings during the mild weather of an Interglacial.

Secondary   Now usually called the Mesozoic. See Table I.

Simian   See Pithecoid.

Sulci   A fissure or depression between two convolutions of the brain.

Tertiary   The age preceding the Quaternary, from the Palaeocene to the Pliocene, duration about 60,000,000 years.

Travertine   Limestone deposited by water in which it was held in suspension.

Tuffa   Or *tuff*. A consolidation of volcanic ash.

Villefranchian   In recent terminology Villefranchian refers to the pre-glacial part of the Pleistocene.

Appendix 2

Possible correlation of archaeological and geological terminology for sub-divisions of the Pleistocene.

Upper Pleistocene	Würm Glaciation
	Riss–Würm Interglacial
	Riss Glaciation
Middle Pleistocene	Mindel–Riss Interglacial
	Mindel Glaciation
	Gunz–Mindel Glaciation
Lower Pleistocene	Gunz Glaciation
	Pre-Gunz (pre-glaciation)

Possible correlation between flint cultures and geological terminology in the Pleistocene.

Magdalenian	Würm III Glacial
Solutrean Gravettian	Würm II/III Interstadial
Aurignacean	Würm II Glacial
Chatelperronian replacing Mousterian	Würm I/II Interstadial
Main Mousterian and Upper Levalloisian	Würm I Glacial
Early Mousterian, also Middle Levalloisian	
Tayacian and Micoquian (Acheulian VI, VII)	Riss–Würm Interglacia
Acheulian V, Tayacian High Lodge, Clactonian and Lower Levalloisian	Riss II Glacial Riss I/II Interstadial Riss I Glacial

Acheulian III/IV and Proto-Levalloisian	Pre-Riss 'Cold Phase'
Acheulian III also Clactonian	
	Mindel–Riss Interglacial
Aucheulian I–II facies	
'Abbevillian' i.e. facies of Early Clactonian	Mindel II Glacial
	Mindel I/II Interstadial

Table I

Geological Time Table (from *The History of the Primates*, British Museum, Sir Wilfrid Le Gros Clark).

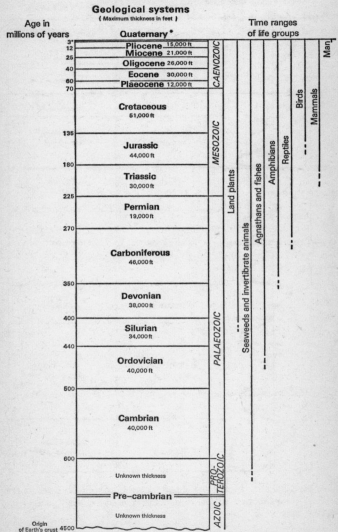

Table II

Approximate datings for the four great glaciations and interglacials of the Pleistocene.

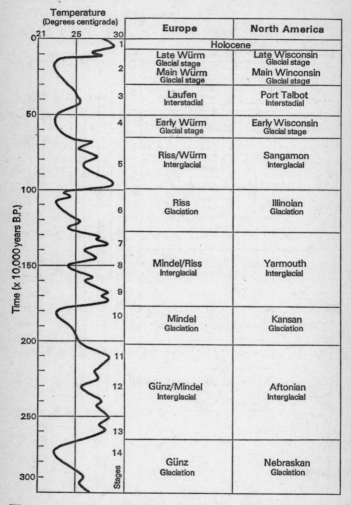

Temperature (Degrees centigrade) / Time (x 10,000 years B.P.)	Stages	Europe	North America
	1	Holocene	
	2	Late Würm Glacial stage / Main Würm Glacial stage	Late Wisconsin Glacial stage / Main Winconsin Glacial stage
	3	Laufen Interstadial	Port Talbot Interstadial
	4	Early Würm Glacial stage	Early Wisconsin Glacial stage
	5	Riss/Würm Interglacial	Sangamon Interglacial
	6	Riss Glaciation	Illinoian Glaciation
	7, 8, 9	Mindel/Riss Interglacial	Yarmouth Interglacial
	10	Mindel Glaciation	Kansan Glaciation
	11, 12, 13	Günz/Mindel Interglacial	Aftonian Interglacial
	14	Günz Glaciation	Nebraskan Glaciation

The temperatures in the left-hand column, obtained from cores drilled from the bed of the Caribbean Ocean, reflect changes in surface water.

Select Bibliography

Anters, E. 1947. 'Dating the Past' (review), *J. Geol.*, vol. 55.

Barbour, G. 1965. *In the Field with Teilhard de Chardin*, Herder and Herder, New York.

Black, D. 1925. 'The Human Skeletal Remains from Shakuot'un', *Palaeontologia Sinica*, 1925, vol. i, fascide 3.

——. 1927. 'Lower Molar Tooth from Choukoutien Deposit', *Palaentologia Sinica*, 1927, vol. ii.

——, Teilhard de Chardin, P., Young, C. C., and Pei, C. C. 1933. 'The Choukoutien Cave Deposits with a synopsis of our present knowledge of the Late Cenozoic of China', *Mem. Geol. Surv. China*, Ser. A., no. 11.

Blake, C. C. 1864. 'On the Alleged Peculiar Character and Assumed Antiquity of the Human Cranium from Neanderthal', *Proc. Anthrop. Soc.*, 16 February 1864.

Bordes, F. 1957. 'Some Observations on the Pleistocene Succession in the Somme Valley', *Proc. Prehist. Soc. Lond.*, vol. 22 (1956).

Boule, M. 1911–13. 'L'Homme fossile de la Chapelle-aux-Saints', *Annls. de Paléont.*, 6, 7 and 8.

——. 1921. *Les Hommes Fossiles*, 2nd edn, Masson et cie, Paris.

——, Vallois, H. V. 1946. *Les Hommes Fossiles*, 3rd edn, Masson et cie, Paris.

——, Breuil, H., Licent, E., Teilhard de Chardin, P. 1928. 'Le Paléolithique de la Chine', *Arch. de l'Institut de Paléontologie humaine*, memoir iv, 1928.

——. 1929. 'Le Sinanthropus', *Anthropologie*, 39, pp. 455–60.

Bovyesonie, A. and Bardon, L. 1908. 'Découverte d'un squelette humain moustérien à La Chapelle-aux-Saints, Corrèze', *C.R. Acad. Sci. Paris*, 147: 1414, 1415.

Breuil, H. 1912. 'Les Subdivisions du Paléolithique supérieur et leur signification', *C.R. Congr. Internat. d'Anthrop. et d'Arch. Préhist.*, 14th sess.

——, Koslowski, L. 1931–2. 'Etudes de Stratigraphie paléolithique dans le nord de la France, la Belgique et l'Angleterre', *L'Anthropologie*, vol. 41.

Broca, P. 1865–75. 'On the Human Bones found in the cave of Cro-Magnon, nr. Les Eyzies', in *Reliquae aquitanicae*. Lartet, E., and Christy, H., Williams and Norgate, London.

Broom, R. 1938. 'The Pleistocene Anthropoid Apes of South Africa', *Nature*, 142: 377–9.

——, Schepers, G. W. 1946. 'The South African fossil ape-men, the Australopithecinae', *Trans. Mus. Mem.*, 2: 1–272.

Buxton, L. H. Dudley. 1928. 'Excavations in Beluchistan', *Arch. Surv. India Report*, 1929.

Cambell, B. 1964. *Classification and Human Evolution*, Methuen & Co. Ltd., London.

Capitan, L. and Peyrony, D. 1909. 'Deux squelettes humaines au milieu de foyers de l'époque moustérienne', *Rev. anthrop.*, 21: 148–50.

du Chaillu, Paul. 1861. *Explorations and Adventures in Equatorial Africa*, London.

Chang, K. C. 1960. 'New Light on Early Man in China', *Asian Perspec.*, vol. 2 (1958), no. 2.

Clark, W. Le Gros. 1950. 'Evolution of the Hominidae', *Quart. J. Geol. Soc. Lond.*, 150, part 2.

——. 1955. *The Fossil Evidence for Human Evolution*, Chicago University Press, Chicago.

——. 1955. 'The Exposure of the Piltdown Forgery', *Royal Institution paper*, 10 May 1955.

——. 1955. 'Further Contributions to the Solution of the Piltdown Problem', *Bull. Brit. Mus. (Natural History)*, vol. 2, no. 6, 1958.

——. 1965. *History of the Primates*, 9th edn, British Museum.

Coon, C. S. 1963. *The Origin of Races*, London.

Cuénot, C. 1958. *Pierre Teilhard de Chardin, les Grands Etapes de son Evolution*, Plon, Paris.

Dart, A. 1925. 'Australopithecus africanus: The Man-Ape of South Africa', *Nature*, 115: 195–9.

Dart, A. 1926. 'Taungs and its significance', *Nat. Hist.*, 3: 315–27.

——. 1948. 'The Makapansgat Proto-Human, Australopithecus prometheus', *Am. J. Phys. Anthrop.*, 6: 259–84.

Darwin, C. 1859. *The Origin of Species by means of Natural Selection*, John Murray, London. Also 1902 edn, Grant Richards, London.

——. 1871. *The Descent of Man*, John Murray, London.

Darwin, F. 1887. *The Life and Letters of Charles Darwin*, London.

Dawson, C. 1909. *The History of Hastings Castle*, 2 vols, London.

——. 1913. 'On the Discovery of a Human Skull and Mandible at Piltdown, Sussex', *The Hastings and E. Sussex Naturalist*, vol. 2, no. 2, 25 March 1913.

—— and Woodward, A. S. 1913. 'On the Discovery of a Paleolithic Human Skull and Mandible in a Flint-bearing Gravel . . . at Piltdown (Fletching) Sussex', *Quart. J. Geol. Soc. Lond.*, 69: 117–51.

—— and Woodward, A. S. 1914. 'Supplementary Note on the Discovery of a Paleolithic Human Skull and Mandible in a Flint-bearing Gravel . . . at Piltdown (Fletching) Sussex', *Quart. J. Geol. Soc. Lond.*, 70: 82–90.

Day, M. H. 1965. *Guide to Fossil Man*, Cassell, London.

Dubois, E. 1894. 'Pithecanthropus erectus, eine menschenaehnliche übergangsform aus Java', *Landesdruckerie*, Batavia.

——. 1922. 'The Proto-Australian Fossil Man of Wadjak, Java', *Proc. Acad. Sci. Amst.*, 23: 1013–51.

Emiliani, C. 1955. 'Pleistocene Temperatures', *J. Geol.*, vol. 63.

Flint, R. F. and Brandtrer, F. 1961. 'Climatic Changes since the Last Interglacial', *Amer. J. Sci.*, vol. 159.

von Fuhlrott, C. 1859. 'Menschlicke Uebereste aus einer Felsengrotte des Dusselthals', *Verh. naturh. Ver. der preuss. Rheinl.*, 16: 131–3.

Garrod, D. A. E. and Bate, D. M. A. 1937. *The Stone Age of Mount Carmel*, vol. I, *Excavations at the Wady el-Mughara*, The Clarendon Press, Oxford.

Geikie, A. 1885. *Text-book of Geology*, 2nd edn, London.

Geikie, J. 1877. *The Great Ice Age*, 2nd edn, London.

Gorjanoric-Kramberger, K. 1906. *Der diluviale Mensch von Krapina im Kroatia*, C. W. Kradels Verlag, Weisbaden.

Grabau, A. W. 1927. 'Summary of the Cenozoic and Psychozoic deposits with special reference to Asia', *Bull. Geol. Surv. China*, 1927, vol. vi.

Gregory, W. K. 1922. *The Origin and Evolution of the Human Dentition*, Williams and Wilkins, Baltimore.

Grenet, P. 1965. *Teilhard de Chardin*, trans. Rudorff, R. A., Souvenir Press Ltd., London.

Hawkes, J. 1963. *Prehistory and the Beginnings of Civilization*, vol. I, George Allen and Unwin, London.

Henri-Martin, G. 1947. 'L'Homme fossile tayacian de la grotte de Fontéchevade', *C.R. Acad. Sci. Paris*, 288: 598–600.

Holmes, A. 1944. *Principles of Physical Geography*, London.

Howells, W. 1960. *Mankind in the Making*, London.

Hoyle, F. 1950. *The Nature of the Universe*, Oxford University Press, London.

Hrdlička, A. 1922. 'The Piltdown Jaw', *Amer. J. Phys. Anthrop.*, Ser. 5.

Huxley, T. H. 1863. *Evidence as to Man's Place in Nature*, Williams and Norgate, London.

Jones, F. D. 1929. *Man's Place among the Mammals*, Edward Arnold, London.

——. 1948. *Hallmarks of Mankind*, Baillière, Tindall and Cox, London.

Jones, N. 1926. *The Stone Age in Rhodesia*, Oxford University Press, London.

Keith, A. 1915. *The Antiquity of Man*, Williams and Norgate, London. Also 2nd edn, 2 vols, 1925.

——. 1928. 'The Evolution of the Human Races', *J. Roy. Anthrop. Inst.*, vol. 58.

——. 1931. *New Discoveries: The Antiquity of Man*, Williams and Norgate, London.

——. 1948. *A New Theory of Human Evolution*, Watts and Co., London.

——. 1950. *An Autobiography*, Watts and Co., London.

King, W. 1864. 'The Reputed Fossil Man of the Neanderthal', *Quart. J. Sci.*, 1: 88–97.

King, W. B. R. 1955. 'The Pleistocene Period in England', *Quart. J. Geol. Soc.*, vol. iii.

Lawrence, J. W. P. 1935. *Stone Age Races of Kenya*, Oxford University Press, London.

Leakey, L. S. B. *et al.* 1933. 'The Olduvai Human Skeleton', *Nature*, vol. 131.

———. 1959. 'A New Fossil Skull from Olduvai', *Nature*, 184: 491–3.

———, Leakey, M. D. 1964. 'Recent Discoveries of Fossil Hominids in Tanganyika; at Olduvai and near Lake Natron', *Nature*, 202: 5–7.

———. 1965. *Olduvai Gorge, 1951–1961*, Cambridge University Press, Cambridge.

Lubac, M. 1967. *L'Obéisance du Père Teilhard de Chardin*, Paris.

Lyell, C. 1830–33. *The Principles of Geology*, London.

Lyne, C. W. 1916. 'The Significance of the Radiographs of the Piltdown Teeth', *Proc. Roy. Soc. Med.*, 9 (3 Odont Sect.): 33–62.

Marston, A. T. 1936. 'Preliminary Note on a New Fossil Human Skull from Swanscombe, Kent', *Nature* 138: 200–1.

———. 1950. 'The Relative Ages of the Swanscombe and Piltdown skulls with special reference to the results of the fluorine estimation test', *Brit. Dent. J. London*, 88: 292–9.

Miller, G. S. 1915. 'The Jaw of Piltdown Man', *Smiths. Miscell. Coll.*, Washington, 65: 1–31.

———. 1918. 'The Piltdown Jaw', *Amer. J. Phys. Anthrop.*, Washington (N.S.), 1: 25–52.

———. 1920. 'The Piltdown Problem', *Amer. J. Phys. Anthrop.*, Washington, 3: 585–6.

———. 1928. *Smiths. Rep. for 1928*, Washington, 1929.

Moir, J. R. 1911. 'The Flint Implements of Sub-Crag Man', *Proc. Prehist. Soc. E. Anglia*, 1: 17–24.

———. 1927. 'On Deposits at Hoxne, Suffolk', *Proc. Prehist. Soc. E. Anglia*, vol. 5.

———. 1935. *Prehistoric Archaeology and Sir Ray Lankester*, Adlard & Co., Ipswich.

Morant, G. M. 1925. 'Study of Egyptian Craniology from Prehistoric to Roman Times', *Biometrika*, vol. xvi.

de Mortillet, G. and A. 1900. *Le Préhistorique: Origine et Antiquité de l'Homme*, 3rd edn, Paris.

Oakley, K. P. 1948. 'Fluorine and the Relative Dating of Bones', *Advanc. Sci.*, London, 16: 336–7.

———. 1949. 'A Reconstruction of the Galley Hill Skeleton', *Bull. Brit. Mus. (Natural History) Geol.*, vol. 1, no. 2.

Oakley, K. P. 1950. 'New Evidence on the Dating of Piltdown Man', *Nature*, 165.

——. 1951. 'A Definition of Man', *Science News*, Harmondsworth, London.

——. 1953. 'Dating Fossil Human Remains', in *Anthropology Today* (edit. Kroeber, A. L.), Chicago University Press, Chicago.

——. 1957. 'Stratigraphical Age of the Swanscombe Skull', *Am. J. Phys. Anthrop.*, Washington, 15: 253–60.

——. 1958. 'The Dating of Broken Hill (Rhodesian) Man', in *Hundert Jahre Neanderthaler* (ed. von Koenigswald, G. H. R.) Kemunk en Zoon, Utrecht.

——. 1961. *Man the Toolmaker*, 5th edn, British Museum (Natural History) Geol., London.

——. 1964. *The Problem of Man's Antiquity: an Historical Survey*, Bull. Brit. Mus. (*Nat. Hist*). Geol., vol. 9, no. 5.

——. 1969. *Framework for Dating Fossil Man*, 3rd edn, Weidenfeld and Nicolson, London.

Owen, R. 1840–45. *Odontography*, Hippotyte, Baillière, London.

Pei, W. C. 1929. 'The Discovery of an Adult Sinanthropus Skull', *Bull. Geolog. Soc. China.*, vol. 8.

de Perthes, C. B. 1846. *Antiquités celtiques et antédiluviennes: de l'industrie primitive ou des arts à leur origine*, Abbeville.

——. 1863. 'Moulin Quignon', *L'Abbevillois*, 9 April 1863, Abbeville.

Pycraft, W. P. *et al.* 1928. *Rhodesian Man and Associated Remains*, ed. Bather, F. A., Brit. Mus. (Nat. Hist.) Geol.

Ramstrom, M. 1919. 'Der Piltdown-fund', *Bull. Geol. Inst. Uppsala.*

Raven, C. E. 1962. *Teilhard de Chardin*, Collins, London.

Selenka, M. L. and Blankenhorn, M. 1911. *Die Pithecanthropus-Schichten auf Java*, Verlag von Wilhelm Engelmann, Leipzig.

Schaafhausen, H. 1858. 'Zur Kenntnis de Eillensten Rasseuschädel', *Archiv. Anat. Phys. Wiss. Medicin*: 453–478.

Schoelensach, O. 1908. *Der Unterkiefer des Homo heidelbergensis aus den Sanden von Mauer bei Heidelberg*, Verlag von Wilhelm Engelmann, Leipzig.

Smith, A. 1917. 'A Pleistocene Skull from Talgai, Queensland', *Proc. Roy. Soc. Queensland*, 4 October 1917.

Smith, G. E. 1918. *The Evolution of Man*, Oxford University Press, London.

——. 1931. *The Search for Man's Ancestors*, Oxford University Press, London.

Speaight, R. 1967. *Teilhard de Chardin*, Collins, London.

Teilhard de Chardin, P., and Licent, E. 1924. 'On the Discovery of a Palaeolithic Industry in Northern China', *Bull. Geol. Soc. China*, vol. 3.

Teilhard de Chardin, P. 1956. *Lettres du Voyage*, Grasset, Paris.

——. 1957. *Nouvelles Lettres du Voyage*, Grasset, Paris.

——. 1959. *The Phenomenon of Man*, Collins, London.

——. 1960. *Le Milieu Divin*, Collins, London.

True, H. L. 1902. *The Cause of the Ice Age*, Cincinnati.

Underwood, A. S. 1913. 'The Piltdown Skull', *Brit. Dent. J.*, London, 56: 650–2.

Vallois, H. V. 1954. 'Neanderthals and Praesapiens', *J.R. Anthrop. Inst.*, London, 84: 113–30.

von Virchow, R. 1872. 'Untersuchung des Neanderthal-Schädele', 2 *Ethn.*, 4: 157–65.

de Vries, H. and Oakley, K. P. 1959. 'Radiocarbon Dating of the Piltdown Skull and Jaw', *Nature*, vol. 184: 224–6.

Wallace, A. R. 1866. *The Malay Archipelago*, London.

——. 1903. 'My Relations with Charles Darwin', *Black and White*, 17 January 1903.

Warren, S. H. 1948. 'The Crag Platform, its Geology and Archaeological Problem', *S. E. Nat. and Antiq.*, vol. 53.

Waterston, D. 1913. 'The Piltdown Mandible', *Nature*, 92: 319.

——. 1913. 'Discussion on Piltdown', *Quart. J. Geol. Soc. Lond.*, 69: 150.

Weidenreich, F. 1945. 'Giant Early Man from Java and South China. Anthrop'. *Pap. Amer. Mus.*, 40: 1–135.

Weiner, J. S., Oakley, K. P. and Clark, W. Le Gros. 'The Solution of the Piltdown Problem', *Bull. Brit. Mus. (Nat. Hist.) Geol.*, vol. 2, no. 3.

Weiner, J. S. 1955. *The Piltdown Forgery*, Oxford University Press, London.

Woo, J. K. and Chao, T. K. 1959. 'New Discovery of a Sinanthropus mandible from Choukoutien', *Vertebrata Palasiatica*, 3: 169–72.

Woodward, A. S. 1917. 'Fourth Note on the Piltdown Gravel with evidence of a second skull of Eoanthropus Dawsoni', *Quart. J. Geol. Soc. Lond.*, 73, part I: 1–10.

——. 1921. 'A new cave-man from Rhodesia, South Africa', *Nature*, 108: 371–2.

——. 1948. *The Earliest Englishman*, Watts and Co., London.

Wymer, J. 1955. 'A further fragment of the Swanscombe skull', *Nature*, 176: 426–7.

Zdansky, O. 1923. 'Ueber ein Saugerknochenlager in Choukou-tien', *Bull. Geol. Surv. China*, vol. I, No. 5.

——. 1927. 'Preliminary Notice on two teeth of a hominid from a cave in Chehli (China)', *Bull. Geol. Soc. China*, 5: 281–4.

Zeuner, F. E. 1946. *Dating the Past*, 1st edn, London. Also 4th edn, 1959.

——. 1959. *The Pleistocene Period*, 2nd edn, London.

Notes

CHAPTER 1

1. Published 1793.
2. *Annals of the Ancient and New Testament.* 1650.
3. *Tour in Ireland.* 1807.
4. *History of Warwickshire.* 1650.
5. *Archaeologia.* 1800.
6. For explanation of geological periods, see Table I.
7. *Theory of the Earth.* 1785.
8. 1743–1805.
9. 1784–1856.
10. 1787–1857.
11. 1788–1868.

CHAPTER 2

1. The antiquity of bones was long thought to be established by adherence to the tongue, lack of gelatine and black specks sometimes identified as iron pyrites. Later these criteria were discarded as useless but in modern times the hydrochloric test was resurrected in another form and found to be valid.
2. 1817–1911.
3. 1804–92.
4. *Letter from Huxley to E. Forbes.* 27 November 1852.
5. 1798–1874.

CHAPTER 3

1. 1809–82.
2. 1766–1834.
3. 1823–1913.
4. 1757–1817.
5. *Black and White.* 17 January 1903.
6. Letter from Huxley to Darwin. 23 November 1859.

7. This attitude was demonstrated in 1860 when Lartet submitted a paper on the probable antiquity of man. The *Académie* printed the title in its *Comptes rendus* but it did not publish it. This was strictly against custom.

CHAPTER 4

1. *The Life and Letters of Charles Darwin*, Vol. 2, p. 109. London, 1888.
2. Ibid., p. 263.
3. 1805–73.
4. April 1860.
5. 3 January 1861.
6. *Punch*, XLIII, p. 164. 18 October 1861.
7. Letter from Huxley to Hooker, August 1860.
8. 8 July 1861.

CHAPTER 5

1. *Man:* 56.
2. Ibid. 5:1862.
3. 26 June 1862.

CHAPTER 8

1. 1811–1816.
2. 1870.
3. This neglect may seem to be surprising, but at the time the misplacement of bones seems to have been so usual as not to give rise to comment. Footnotes in the Geological Society's quarterly journal frequently mention bones being mislaid on the way to lectures, even lost altogether. Often, it seems, parcels of elephant bones trundled across country by railway until they found rest at the Lost Property Office or were lost beyond recall.

CHAPTER 9

1. 25 December 1902.
2. 6:1906.
3. *Les Hommes Fossiles.* 2nd Edition. 1921.
4. *Prehistoric Archaeology and Sir Ray Lankester.* Ipswich, 1935.

CHAPTER 10

1. 5 November 1903.
2. 7 September 1896.
3. 18 November 1896.
4. 2 January 1937.
5. 6 September 1912.
6. 3 October 1912.
7. *Nature.* 5 December 1912.
8. 31 October 1912.
9. Strangely enough these marks have since vanished.
10. 5 December 1912.

CHAPTER 11

1. Les Nouvelles Littéraires. 11 January 1951.
2. Robert Speaight. *Teilhard de Chardin: A Biography,* 1967.
3. *The Earliest Englishman.* Watts & Co. London, 1948.
4. *Geological Magazine,* 3. 1916.
5. 28 January 1913.
6. 18 June 1898.
7. 18 April 1901.
8. Letter to British Museum. 21 April 1882.
9. At British Museum of Natural History, South Kensington.
10. *The Earliest Englishman,* op. cit.
11. *The Hastings and East Sussex Naturalist,* 2:2. 25 March 1913.
12. He was ordained on 24 August 1911.
13. 3 June 1912.
14. Probably Venus Hargreaves, a labourer.
15. 21 November 1912.
16. 23 November 1912.
17. See J. S. Weiner. *The Piltdown Forgery.* Oxford, 1955.
18. 19 December 1912.
19. C. Dawson and A. S. Woodward. 1913. 'On the Discovery of a Palaeolithic Human Skull and Mandible in a Flint-bearing Gravel overlying the Wealden at Piltdown (Fletching), Sussex.'
20. 69:1913, pp. 117–51.
21. In his book Woodward mused that this thickness could have been the result of exposure to sun and air. He quoted Herodotus (Book III, Thalia) that Egyptians have shaved heads from childhood but Persians wear hats to such effect that battlefield skulls of the latter could be fractured with a single pebble while those of the former could scarcely be fractured by striking them with a stone. Woodward enlarged this view to include the 'spongy texture' of the Piltdown skull which would give resistance to heavy blows. He consulted Dr. R. S. Shattock, Royal College of Surgeons, who 'repeatedly' examined the fragments to assure himself the skull was not diseased.

22. This is a reference to the then widely held opinion that the embryo of a descendant resembled the adult of its evolutionary ancestor. This theory of recapitulation is now known to be false. Embryonic stages of descendants are generally the repetition of corresponding embryonic stages of the ancestor. There are, however, instances in insects, vertebrates and man where the adult descendant resembles the ancestor in youth. This type of descent is known as paedomorphosis, or 'Peter Pan' evolution, because the youthful characters of the ancestor are present in the descendant which appears not to have grown up.

23. *The Descent of Man*, London, 1871, p. 248.

24. *The Hastings and East Sussex Naturalist*, 2, p. 182.

25. *British Journal of Dental Science*, 56, pp. 650–2.

26. *Proc. Roy. Soc. Med.* 9, pp. 33–62.

27. 2 October 1913.

28. 13 November 1913.

29. *Nature*, 30 October 1913.

30. *An Autobiography*. London, 1950.

31. *The Exposure of the Piltdown Forgery*, Royal Institution, 20 May 1955.

32. Sir Arthur Keith's Foreword to *The Earliest Englishman*, op. cit.

CHAPTER 12

1. 8 June 1916.

2. In addition to the views of Arthur Keith, Professor A. F. Dixon had told the Royal Dublin Society that the ape-like peculiarities had been over-emphasized, that the assumption of absence of chin and prognathism were not necessary.

3. 17: 1917.

4. 69:1913.

5. 13 March 1915.

6. 73, p. vii.

7. 17 August 1916.

8. *An Autobiography*, op. cit., pp. 324–5, 1950.

9. *Q.J.G.S.* lxxiii, part i. 1917.

10. 13 September.

11. *The Earliest Englishman*, op. cit., p. 13.

12. *Les Hommes Fossiles*. Paris, 1921.

13. *Quid de l'homme?* p. 77. Paris, 1934.

14. *Natural History*, 21, pp. 581–82, 590. February 1922.

15. *Am. Journ. of Phys. Anthrop.* 5: pp. 337–47. December 1922.

16. *Smithsonian Report for 1928*. Washington, 1929.

17. *Antiquity of Man*, 2nd ed, 1925, Vol. 2: xxiv.

18. *Bureau of American Ethnology, Bulletin 66*.

CHAPTER 13

1. 196, 1915.
2. *Proc. Royal Soc. of Queensland.* 4 October 1917.
3. *Proceedings of Hastings and Sussex Natural History Society.* 1915.
4. 9 September 1915.
5. 108. 1921.
6. 24, p. 48.
7. *Proc. B.A.* vii. 1918.
8. *The Evolution of Man.* Oxford, 1918.
9. 10 December.
10. *Man,* 13:58, p. 116.
11. *The Problem of Man's Ancestry.* London, 1918.
12. *Nature,* 101. 1918.
13. *Ancient Hunters and their Modern Representatives,* 3rd Edition. London, 1924.
14. *Man,* 14, 1924, p. 189.
15. 25:90, p. 157.
16. *Man,* 25:98, p. 186.
17. *Man,* 26:27, 1926, p. 46.
18. *Man,* 26:40, p. 168.
19. *Roy. Anthrop. Inst. Jour.* 50. 1920.
20. Michael H. Day. Cassell 1965.
21. *Prehistory and the Beginnings of Civilization, Vol I.* George Allen & Unwin, 1963.
22. *Man,* 29, p. 135.

CHAPTER 14

1. *The Search for Man's Ancestors.* London, 1931.
2. *Bull. Geol. Surv. China* 1927, Vol. 5, Nos. 3–4.
3. *Palae. Sinica,* 1927, Vol. II.
4. Modernism was the tendency to diminish the stature of Christ. Père George Tyrell S.J., its advocate, was excommunicated and a number of books on the subject, including Henri Bergson's *L'Evolution Créatrice,* were placed on the *Index Librorum Prohibitorum.*
5. Père Henri Lubac, S. J. *L'Obéisance du Père Teilhard de Chardin.* Paris, 1967.
6. 10 January 1926.
7. Robert Speaight. *Teilhard de Chardin: A Biography.* London, 1967.
8. *The Bull of Minos,* 2nd Edition. Evans, 1962.
9. *In the Field with Teilhard de Chardin.* Herder and Herder. New York, 1965.
10. 30 December 1929.
11. *Fossil Evidence for Human Evolution.* Chicago, 1955.

12. *Vertebrata Palasiatica*. Peking, 1959, p. 169.
13. *Origin of Races*. London, 1963.
14. *Mankind in the Making*. London, 1960.

CHAPTER 15

1. *Adventures with the Missing Link*. Hamish Hamilton, 1959.
2. 4 February 1925.
3. 6 February 1925.
4. 14 February 1925.
5. For brain size comparison: apes, such as gibbon, orang-utan, chimpanzee, gorilla – 100–700 c.c.; ape-men, Java and Peking – 750–1,250 c.c.; Neanderthal Man or Neanderthaloids – 1,050–1,750 c.c.; modern man (normal) – 1,750–2,350 c.c.

CHAPTER 16

1. *Journ. Anat.*, Vol. LXXIII. Oct. 1938, Jan. 1939.
2. *Q.J.G.S.* 99–100, p. xii.
3. *Journ. of Royal Anthrop. Inst.* Vol. xvii.
4. The statement appears also in *Recent Progress in the Study of Early Man. Rep. Brit. Assoc.* London, 100, pp. 129–42.
5. 'A Reconsideration of the Galley Hill Skeleton. *Bull. of B.M. (Natural History) Geology*, vol. 1, no. 2 (1949).
6. 'New Evidence on the Antiquity of Piltdown Man.' *Nature* 165.
7. *The South-Eastern Naturalist and Antiquary*, Vol. LVII, 1952.
8. *Q.J.G.S.* 106.
9. *Journ. Phy. Anthrop.* Vol. 6, No. 4. NS, 1951.
10. Vol. XCII, No. 1. 1 July 1952.

CHAPTER 17

1. *The Piltdown Forgery*. Oxford, 1955.
2. *The Exposure of the Piltdown Forgery*. Paper delivered to the Royal Institution 20 May 1955. Reprint.
3. 'The Solution of the Piltdown Problem'. *Bull. Brit. Mus. (Nat. Hist.) Geol.*, vol. 2, no. 3.
4. Ibid.
5. Ibid.
6. Robert Speaight. *Teilhard de Chardin: A Biography*, London, 1967.
7. 26 November 1953.
8. 23 November 1953.

9. 3 December 1953. C. D. Orey. St John's College, Cambridge.
10. 25 November 1953.
11. 26 November 1953.
12. 22 December 1953.
13. 19 November 1954.
14. Oxford, 1955.

CHAPTER 18

1. Letter to the author. 18 September 1970.
2. Letter to the author. 22 July 1970.
3. See The *Piltdown Forgery*. J. S. Weiner, Oxford, 1955.

Index